Ex-National Hunt Champion Jockey John Francome has been voted TV's most popular racing commentator for his broadcasting for Channel 4. His electrifying racing thrillers have also won him legions of fans. He lives in Berkshire.

Praise for John Francome's other novels:

'Francome provides a vivid panorama of the racing world . . . and handles the story's twist deftly' *The Times*

'Thrills to the final furlong . . . Francome knows how to write a good racing thriller' *Daily Express*

'Francome brings authenticity to tales of the horse-racing circuit and, like Dick Francis, goes beyond the thunder of the turf to the skulduggery of the trading ring . . . the twists and turns of the last few hundred yards prove Francome to be a winner on the home stretch' *Mail on Sunday*

Also by John Francome

Stone Cold
Stud Poker
Rough Ride
Outsider
False Start
High Flyer
Safe Bet
Tip Off
Lifeline
Dead Weight
Inside Track
Stalking Horse

Also by John Francome and James MacGregor

Eavesdropper
Riding High
Declared Dead
Blood Stock

Break Neck

and

Dead Ringer

John Francome

headline

BREAK NECK first published in Great Britain in 1994
by HEADLINE BOOK PUBLISHING

DEAD RINGER first published in Great Britain in 1995
by HEADLINE BOOK PUBLISHING

First published in this omnibus edition in 2004
by HEADLINE BOOK PUBLISHING

A HEADLINE paperback

10 9 8 7 6 5 4 3 2

ISBN 0 7553 2251 7

Typeset in Times by Avon DataSet Ltd,
Bidford on Avon, Warwickshire

Printed and bound in Great Britain by
Mackays of Chatham plc, Chatham, Kent

Papers and cover board used by Headline are natural,
recyclable products made from wood grown in sustainable
forests. The manufacturing processes conform to the
environmental regulations of the country of origin.

HEADLINE BOOK PUBLISHING
A division of Hodder Headline
338 Euston Road
London NW1 3BH

www.headline.co.uk
www.hodderheadline.com

Break Neck

Prologue

'Don't bother searching the cupboard for skeletons, because there aren't any.' Eland's visitor sounded completely sure of himself. 'So you'll have to provide one – a totally convincing one.' The word 'totally' was emphasised.

On the day after St Valentine's Day, two weeks before the Thames Land Trophy, England's most valuable amateur chase, was due to be run at Kempton, two men talked in a house near Slough.

Beneath a dismal February sky sat the unexceptional house, built in the early sixties, like hundreds of others on drab estates all over England. Externally, it had little to say about its occupier. Inside, however, among the discordant smells of rich Havana tobacco and stale frying fat, among the cheap modern furniture and the banana-leaf-patterned carpet of the front room, the occupant's interests were more apparent.

Pornographic video tapes stacked from floor to ceiling, lurid covers of magazines strewn across a teak coffee table and purple sofa, framed, signed photographs on the walls of unforgiving women wearing few clothes and hard smiles while they brandished whips and leather straps were evidence of the owner's preoccupation.

There wasn't anything particular about the man himself to suggest it. He was a little shorter than average. His colourless hair, moist with sweat, was thin across his scalp. A few red spots glowed livid on his pasty face. His pale blue shirt was dull with infrequent washing and strained across a waist six inches wider than it should be.

Arthur Eland sat nervously picking at a scab on the back of his hand as he listened to his visitor and watched him suck the last few moments of pleasure from a Bolivar corona.

He had dealt with hard men before, but the man sitting opposite him was more than hard. From the calm, icy smile that spread across his thick lips, Eland recognised that here was a man who could be completely unpredictable and very dangerous.

The foundation of this man's fortune had been the international trading of human lives; acquiring them, despatching them, smuggling them: African maids, Filipino prostitutes, Indian houseboys; even well-bred English girls for demanding Middle East clients.

And he had found through long experience that the best way to manipulate such stock in trade was to hold something of theirs that was dear to them – their passport, their identity, their family, their reputation.

It was to talk about a reputation – at least the destruction of one – that had led him to Slough.

Eland made a living by his skill with a camera and an

ability to pose his subjects in unlikely but convincing attitudes and circumstances. Taking photographs of people engaged in unusual sexual congress was his job, as well as his hobby. And it paid him enough to indulge his own particular and expensive sexual tastes.

'So, your job is to provide a skeleton.' Eland's visitor's deep voice was just perceptibly foreign, though too well disguised to place. 'I want pictures that would disgust a King's Cross pimp.'

'But,' Eland whined, 'how the hell am I supposed to get someone like that into the studio? I'm a photographer, not a kidnapper.'

His visitor's eyes narrowed as he took a last long drag on his cigar until the end glowed like a furnace between the tips of his thumb and forefinger. He glanced down at a large ashtray on the coffee table between them, leaned forward to stub out the cigar then paused for a moment. Staring deep into Eland's moist blue eyes, he moved his hand to one side and crushed the glowing butt straight on to the table top.

Eland blinked and his face twitched with unease.

His visitor smiled again, satisfied. Sometimes he had had to hurt people's children to gain their cooperation; with Eland it had taken no more than a cheap, nasty coffee table.

'Say it's a vicar's tea party,' he said. 'I don't care; that's your problem, if you want to earn enough to keep you wallowing in little boys for a month.'

'It . . . it'll be expensive,' Eland stammered, '. . . and risky.'

'If it was easy, I'd ask my secretary to do it, wouldn't

I?' The big man reached inside his jacket and pulled out an envelope which he put on the table. 'Here's a name and address, and a photograph taken last week. Get on with it. I need the job done by the end of the month and I need this person so tight in my fist they won't want to take a shit without asking me first.'

'It all depends how sensitive . . .' Eland said.

'Don't you worry about that. You just take the dirtiest pictures your nasty little mind can think of.'

Eland shrugged. 'Okay. But . . . the money?'

'Two grand for the shots, when I get all the prints and the negatives. I don't want you looking for bonuses elsewhere.'

He gazed with distaste at Eland's sweaty face. He wrinkled his nose at the smell that seemed to hang around the photographer, but he knew that men with unwholesome passions and no family or friends could be pushed much further than most. 'Then there'll be more money,' he said. 'I want no one else involved – understand?'

Eland understood; more money was more interesting. He nodded.

The other man stood up and started towards the door. 'Get those shots by the end of the month. Then I'll tell you what to do with them.' He walked out into the narrow hall, taking a closer look at the stained carpet. 'Why do you live in this hovel?'

Eland followed him towards the front door. 'No one bothers me here.'

His visitor shook his head in disgust, let himself out and banged the front door shut behind him.

Eland muttered a few obscenities as he heard the Mercedes start up and drive away. Why the hell did everyone think they could push him around? They always had – his parents, his brothers, the kids at school. He still hated it, and loathed himself even more for not having the courage to stand up for himself.

Then he thought of all the young boys he would be able to buy and bully with the money he would earn for a few hours work, and he sighed.

He went back into the living room. Ignoring the cigar butt on the table, he picked up the envelope and carried it across his narrow hall, through a door which led to what had been built as an integral garage. Now it was a well-equipped studio.

His neighbours didn't know about the studio; they thought he always left his car outside because he was too lazy to open the garage doors. But this was where he most liked to be alone, immersed in the sickly-sweet smell of developing fluids and his own stale sweat.

He sat down on a cantilever chair in front of his light box and switched on the bulb beneath the opaque surface which he used to view transparencies. He noticed that, through lack of recent use, a large spider's web had been spun between the box and the wall.

A fat, evidently replete spider crouched in the middle of the filigree pattern. Gleefully, Eland felt in his pocket for a box of matches. He struck one and held the flame to the bottom of the web. He watched in delight as the silk threads flared and disintegrated. The dozing spider sensed the conflagration too late. Eland let out a strange cackle of childish laughter. The creature was frazzled to a small black ball and fell to the ground.

Satisfied, Eland opened the envelope which had been left for him.

The kind, compassionate face which stared up at him from the first photograph also displayed a strong sense of purpose.

This wasn't going to be an easy job.

But a smile crossed Eland's pale grey face as he pondered his prey, a trap and an approach which he had found from experience worked well for both male and female victims.

Chapter One

That same February morning, Laura Mundy drove half a mile down an avenue of lofty, waving limes from the noble Tudor manor house in which she lived to the stable yard where she worked.

When Laura had first suggested to her husband, Luke, that she knew enough about training racehorses to take out a public licence, he had responded by ordering the construction of a set of racing stables that would surpass every other jump-racing establishment in the country in both elegance and technical facilities. He didn't care how much he spent, as long as Laura got the best. Then, if she failed – he told his friends – she could blame no one but herself. Those who knew him well knew that he wasn't joking; so did Laura. At first that had been her greatest incentive.

Now she wasn't thinking about Luke; she had trained herself to ignore the discomfort that he had once caused. The pain had become no more than a dull ache, easily displaced by concentrating her mind on her horses.

As the Land Rover rumbled along the smooth black Tarmac on their private road, she threw a quick glance at the small, weathered face of the man beside her – a glance which showed affection and respect.

'If you're happy about Jimmy, that's good enough for me,' she said.

'He's sound as a church.' Patrick Hoolihan spoke with the cadence of an Irish jig. 'That sore heel has cleared up quicker than I thought it would; he pulled Tony's arms out when he went for a canter yesterday.'

Laura never suffered from overconfidence in her horses. 'He's got to give Fancyman nearly two stone this afternoon. Those couple of days without exercise might just swing the balance against him.'

'Fancyman'll not trouble him; so long as Dai gets our horse settled,' her head lad reassured her.

'Who's riding Fancyman?'

Patrick consulted the *Sporting Life* on his lap. 'Rory Gillespie.' He gave a respectful sideways nod of his small head. 'But he'll have trouble doing ten stone.'

Laura didn't answer at once.

Rory Gillespie.

It seemed strange now, and absurd, how the very syllables had once made her tingle. And yet, despite more than ten years of avoiding him – tricky in the small world of jump racing – she still couldn't suppress a slight tremor.

It had been easier at first, after she and Rory had split up and Luke Mundy had swept into her life. Luke's was a presence which allowed no room for competition. But, she remembered, she had felt physically sick the day Rory had married Pam Fanshaw – sick and bewildered.

Rory had been the star apprentice then in old Mick Fanshaw's yard; his boss's daughter had been the stable tart. When Laura heard eight months later that Pam had given birth to a baby boy, it was no surprise, but no more comprehensible.

She had asked Dai Price's opinion when he'd joined her yard as stable jockey. He and Rory had been apprentices together at Mick Fanshaw's, but Dai didn't offer an explanation. 'Can't think what he saw in the old slapper,' he had declared in his grating Valleys accent. 'Wham-bam-thank-you-Pam we used to call her. Wouldn't touch her myself.'

Laura had recently recalled Dai's opinion of Pam. She had seen the little Welshman talking and laughing with her in the bar at Ascot sales, and not behaving as if he found her at all repulsive. There was no denying, Pam was a desirable woman. She'd had no more children, had kept her figure by race-riding herself – quite successfully – and had become a bit of a personality.

Laura wondered how much Rory suffered from his wife's overt flirtations and the rumours they provoked. She knew how it felt, after ten years of marriage to Luke. All her instincts were to sympathise with Rory, despite the misery he had once caused her.

'It'll be a good race,' she said to Patrick, 'if they jump the last upsides. Dai always rides better when he's against Rory.'

'What is it between them two?' Patrick shook his head, not really needing an answer.

Laura swung the Land Rover beneath the clock tower arch into the yard, and didn't offer one.

The lorry was parked with its ramp down, ready to take their three runners to Newbury. The first wasn't due to run until two forty-five, and it was only half an hour's journey. Patrick got out and gave the order to load. He always liked the horses to arrive at least three hours before a race, so that they had time to settle.

Laura watched the horses being led from their handsome brick stables, gleaming with condition, carrying a little more flesh than was fashionable, all three of them alert but unruffled. She looked closely at Flamenco Dancer, her star six-year-old chaser, known in the yard as Jimmy. He walked out with long strides from his well-muscled back end, with no hint of soreness.

'Just trot him up for me, please, Tony,' she called to his lad.

The lad proudly geed the horse into a leisurely bouncing gait. Patrick stopped to watch, too.

'What did I tell you?' He turned to his guv'nor with a grin.

Laura nodded. 'You've done a good job, Pat. Look, as we've got no late runners, why don't you come to the races with me – get away from the yard for a change?'

Patrick took a moment to consider what horses had to be looked at, what jobs had to be done, then nodded. 'Good idea.'

Laura drove to Newbury in her new Mercedes Sports, with Patrick nestling in the bucket seat beside her. As head lad, Patrick rarely had a chance to go racing; his job was to look after the horses at home. But when he did have an afternoon away, he always went with Laura. It gave them a chance to have a really good talk about what was happening in the yard. Over the years Patrick, though he didn't know it, had come the closest to being her confidant.

Laura knew she could rely on Patrick's discretion without reservation; it had been implicit in their relationship since the day she had taken him on when she had started her yard. At that time, no other racing stables in the country would touch him – none of them would believe he had finally given up the booze, which had been responsible for him losing every post he'd ever held. He'd come to Laura, frankly pleading for the chance, vowing in the name of the many things that were sacred to him that he had beaten the bottle. His skills and knowledge weren't in question: he'd been the main man behind two Champion trainers. Laura wasn't normally interested in gambling, but she'd taken a punt, despite everyone else's advice, and she had won. In the eight years he had been at Langlands, Patrick had once again become the most respected head lad in the business.

When he had asked Laura if she would also take on his son, Declan, as an apprentice jockey, and she had agreed, Patrick's gratitude was such that he would willingly have killed for her.

As they drove to Newbury, Laura talked to him about their runners that day and some of the other seventy horses back in the yard.

'How are the six that came from Mick Fanshaw's yard settling in?' she asked.

Patrick laughed. 'They're a lot happier than Mick Fanshaw. He drove them over himself yesterday and was trying to have a good snoop around. He's sore as a fox in a trap now we've had ten away from him. I thought he'd never leave. But the horses are fine – just carrying a little too much fat. We'll have them right in a week or two. I don't know if any of them are any good but they certainly look the part.'

Laura nodded, but she felt a pinch of guilt at being the principal beneficiary of Fanshaw's bad luck. She'd always liked the old scoundrel.

Like every other National Hunt yard in the country at that time of year, their ambitions were focused on the festival meeting at Cheltenham. With over three weeks to go, Laura still had six runners entered. One of her first intake of ex-Fanshaw horses was heavily fancied for the Ritz, and her husband's horse, Midnight Express, was widely considered the form horse for the Two Mile Champion Chase. Patrick was concerned about a possible hiccup in his preparation.

'Will Mr Mundy still want to ride him in these two hunter chases before Cheltenham?' he asked in a way that made it clear that was the last thing that should happen.

Laura made a face. 'I hope I've convinced him there'd be more glory in being a winning owner at Cheltenham than the winning jockey of an amateur chase. But I'm afraid he may insist on riding in the race he's sponsored – the Thames Land Trophy, I ask you! He thinks it'll be the biggest hunter chase in the calendar and he's set on winning it himself. But I should be able to talk him out of running the horse in the Grand Military.'

'He shouldn't run him in either.' Patrick replied with more authority than he had intended. 'The horse takes a long time to recover; if he gives him a hard race over three miles, even as much as two weeks before, it'll spoil him for the Champion.'

But, as they talked, Laura found her thoughts returning to Rory Gillespie, Mick Fanshaw's son-in-law, riding the danger in Flamenco Dancer's race that day.

With a feeling of confusion, she realised she preferred the idea of Rory winning rather than her own jockey, Dai. But she quickly pushed the sentimental thought from her head.

It was Patrick who brought it back as they drove into the trainers' and jockeys' car park.

'There's yer man,' he said and nodded in the direction of Rory Gillespie climbing out of a fast-back Rover with his name and that of the sponsoring garage plastered along the side of it. 'He's wearin' well for a jump jockey.'

Rory Gillespie was feeling well. He had worked hard to do the weight for that day's race without losing any strength. He hadn't sweated it off, just cut the booze for a week and taken a lot of light exercise – nothing that would put heavy muscle on as any surplus fat came off.

It wasn't a big race, but it was an important one in Fancyman's campaign, and he was glad of the work. Although the horse's trainer, Jack Suter, had wanted to use his own stable jockey, the owner had insisted that Rory take the ride.

Since Rory had taken the risky decision to go freelance two seasons before, it was usually owners who were responsible for booking him. Experienced, knowledgeable owners liked Rory's honest opinion of their animals' abilities; this sometimes resulted in a horse being taken out of training. Trainers were less enthusiastic about frank assessments which contradicted their own stated views – 'he needs a little more time'; 'he'll win a race for you'; 'he needed the run' – anything to keep the owner in promise land and the horse in the yard.

Rory had already spotted Laura's Mercedes glide into the car park. He gave her a quick glance as he walked briskly past, heading for the jockeys' changing room with a leather grip over his shoulder. It was a month since he had ridden Fancyman, but Jack Suter had told him on the phone the night before that the horse was as fit as he had ever been. Flamenco Dancer was a better horse – Rory knew that – but he was sure he wasn't two stone better over three miles; and that Dai Price was riding the favourite was in itself a strong incentive to win.

The other jockeys welcomed the sandy-haired Scot. At five feet nine, he was taller than most of them but managed to avoid that half-starved look even when he was doing his bottom weight. His good looks were enhanced by the self-confidence he had developed through the knowledge that, given the right horse, he was more than a match for anyone.

Rory Gillespie had upset few of his colleagues in his fifteen-year career. He never crowed when he won and seldom blamed anyone else when he lost. If a younger jockey asked his advice, he gave it willingly. If he didn't think he got on with a particular horse, he was never too big to say so. 'Best to get someone else to ride it,' he would honestly advise.

He was almost universally liked and had the kind of smiling face and blue eyes that made it hard not to smile back.

Only Dai Price, sitting under his peg at the far end of the room, let his mean features curl with hostility.

Rory deliberately didn't look at him, and sat down to pull out his tobacco tin and create a tidy roll-up.

'How's the weight?' a young jockey next to him said with a grin. 'I see you've got ten stone to do.'

'Is that all?' Rory widened his eyes with surprise.

'You'll never do that, will you?'

'I'll tell you when I'm sat on the scales,' Rory said.

'Won't make any bloody difference whether you do or not,' Dai Price called across the room.

Rory looked at him briefly and nodded. 'You could be right.'

Laura Mundy stood in the parade ring with Flamenco Dancer's owner, George Rutherford. They inspected their horse, then Fancyman.

'He looks well,' Laura admitted.

'Ours is in a different class,' Rutherford drawled, giving an impression of experience he didn't possess. 'Why do they use this chap Gillespie? He's a bit long in the tooth now, isn't he?'

'Not at all. He's still one of the best.'

'He doesn't win that many races.'

'He doesn't get the rides. He's too independent. Too honest.'

Rory passed the scales at ten stone one pound and walked into the ring relaxed and animated as he joked with one of the other jockeys.

As she half listened to her owner rumbling on about Flamenco Dancer's chances, Laura thought that Rory wasn't showing much sign of suffering from his wife's infidelities. She wondered just how much was concealed by his famously incorrigible sense of humour.

'Is your husband here today?' she heard Rutherford ask.

'No. He usually only comes when he's riding himself,' she answered without emphasis.

'I wonder how much longer he'll be doing that,' her owner mused.

'As long as he thinks he stands a chance of winning.'

'Hmm,' Rutherford grunted, as the bright-coloured pack of jockeys split and mingled with small groups of drab brown- and khaki-clad connections around the ring.

Dai Price strutted across to get his instructions from Laura.

'Afternoon, ma'am, sir.' He held out a hand to Rutherford who shook it perfunctorily. The jockey turned back to Laura. 'There's a couple that want to be up there, so they're sure to go a good gallop. He ought to settle all right.'

Laura looked hard at her jockey. Recently she had found that she was trusting him less. She'd been getting the impression that he was losing his nerve. There was nothing she could seriously reprimand him over, but enough to worry her.

'Good,' she said. 'Get him switched off at the back and try not to hit the front too soon.'

The bell rang to mount up.

'You shouldn't have any trouble,' Rutherford boomed at the jockey.

'That's what the man who built the *Titanic* said to the captain,' Dai muttered just loud enough for Laura to hear.

Laura smiled, but thought Dai would need to come up with more than a few old jokes if he was going to keep his job.

Connections bustled around the paddock to their horses. Jockeys got mounted and their lads led the horses out along the path to the course. The ten steeplechasers, all experienced, knew what was coming and got on their toes as they stepped on to the grass. They jig-jogged their way across the track to the centre of the course, before cantering down in front of the huge number board towards the start.

Jumping is always the name of the game, but the adage is never more apt than at a Grade One course like Newbury where the fences are that much stiffer. It was on just this type of course that a big rangy horse like Fancyman excelled. He was one of those rare equine athletes blessed with the ability to stand off a long way from a fence then somehow stretch again in mid-air.

As the starting tapes flew up, Rory eased the horse ahead of the pack to take full advantage of his jumping and the light weight he was carrying.

Two horses took him on at the first fence but Fancyman pricked his ears and took it like a greyhound over a hurdle, while the other two fluffed their takeoffs and jumped awkwardly.

That first fence set the pattern. From then on, Rory was able to dictate the race at Fancyman's cruising speed. This was plenty fast enough and, with his jumping, much too good for the others.

At the big open ditch on the far side and at the downhill

cross-fences, Fancyman put in jumps that had everyone gasping, including the jockeys sitting in the changing room watching the race on closed circuit television.

As they raced round the bend into the straight for the second time, it was obvious that only Flamenco Dancer was travelling well enough to make a race of it with the leader. Dai was closing the gap slowly but surely. Flamenco Dancer's jumping wasn't as quick or flamboyant as Fancyman's but he had class. At each of the four fences in the straight, Fancyman gained at least a length, only for Flamenco Dancer to claw it back with interest on the flat until the run from the last became a desperate battle.

Rory could feel how tired his horse was. He could sense a challenger, too, but dared not look back. He clenched his jaw; if only there were another fence to jump. Up ahead, he could hear the crowd roaring. He urged Fancyman on with everything he had, trying to keep his tired legs from rolling. The winning post appeared like a mirage as the brown head of his challenger came up by his right boot. But that was as close as it got.

Fancyman dug to a depth in his reserves that only the bravest horses reach for. There was no way he was going to let anything pass him now. Rory grinned at the animal's sheer bloody-mindedness while Fancyman held on to win by half a length.

Rory leaned forward and gave the gelding a grateful pat down his sweaty neck. As he gently reined back to a trot, Dai Price cantered past.

'You're a lucky bastard!' he shouted.

Rory didn't answer and turned the weary Fancyman back towards the stands.

Jack Suter, with no owner to bother him, came up and took Fancyman's head at the side of the track and led them back towards the winner's enclosure. Laura and a rock-faced Rutherford were already waiting there for Flamenco Dancer.

To Rory's surprise, there was genuine sincerity in Laura's voice as she called, 'Well done, Rory' – the first words he could remember her addressing to him in nearly ten years. He did a double take before he could stop himself. Though he would never admit it, there was still something about Laura that tugged at him.

Rory didn't have a ride the next day, so there was nothing to stop him having a couple of drinks. As he walked through to the bar, he met George Rutherford.

'That was a very good ride you gave Fancyman,' he boomed with pompous affability, while blocking Rory's path.

'Thanks,' Rory acknowledged with a modest nod. He didn't even know this man's name. He wondered if he would introduce himself. Rutherford didn't; he knew who Rory was and he expected the same in return.

'Come up to my box and have a drink. It's quieter up there.' When he saw that Rory was going to turn him down, he went on quickly, 'I own Flamenco Dancer. I wanted to talk to you about riding him in future.'

'Thanks for the offer, but the horse would have to change yards before I'd ride him. And I'm okay for a drink.'

Beyond Rutherford, Rory could see his father-in-law Mick Fanshaw, trying to catch his eye and toting an

imaginary glass in invitation. Mick could be dangerous if
he'd had more than a couple of drinks, but anything was
better than the self-important, oversized Jack-the-lad he
now faced.

Rutherford didn't take rejection well. His eyes blackened as if someone had flicked a switch.

'When I make an offer, I only make it once. You'll be
sorry you turned it down.'

Rory felt the full force of the man's personality, and it
shook him more than he would have liked; but he wasn't
going to let it show. He raised his eyebrows a fraction,
muttered an excuse and brushed past Rutherford
towards Fanshaw.

'Rory!'

He had nearly reached his car. He stopped walking.
She had always had an unmistakable way of saying his
name. He didn't turn.

'What do you want?'

She caught up with him and had to walk round in front
to face him.

'I wanted to talk to you.' She was slightly out of breath
and there was a warm flush on her face despite the damp
chill of the winter evening.

Rory was both shamed and elated by the sense of
triumph this gave him. He showed nothing; just raised
an eyebrow.

'Your owner's already asked me if I'll ride Flamenco
Dancer for him,' he said. 'I said No, and I haven't changed
my mind.'

A flash of regret crossed her face. 'Okay, but there are
a few other rides you might like. I mean – you're not

getting as many as you should.'

'What makes you think I'd ride for you?'

'Why shouldn't you? You're not under an obligation to anyone else, are you?'

'No one, except myself.'

'What does *that* mean?'

Rory shook his head and stepped sideways to carry on towards his car.

'Rory! Hang on.' She turned and caught up with him. 'What's the point in being like this? You're a professional jockey; I'm a trainer with some good horses – some very good horses – to ride, and from what I've heard you could do with a few.'

'I get all the rides I want on horses I like from yards I like. Thanks for thinking of me, though,' Rory added with a forced smile.

He felt her hand suddenly grip his upper arm with surprising strength. He stopped walking and looked at her.

There was nothing in her eyes or her attitude to tell him what she was really thinking. She had always had a lot of self-control.

'Why are you being like this?' she asked quite calmly.

Rory stared back at her. 'Why the hell do you think?'

'For goodness sake, Rory, what happened between us was years ago. Don't you think it's time we forgot all that? And anyway, it was you who cheated on me, remember?'

'I don't want to talk about it.'

'Rory, please, I *need* to talk to you.' Her big brown eyes were soft as velvet now. 'Come on,' she grinned. 'It's not a lot to ask.'

Rory shrugged. 'Okay. I'm listening.'

'Not here. Could you come to Langlands? This evening?'

Rory hesitated for a moment. 'I suppose so. What about your husband, though? He won't be too pleased to see me.'

'Luke won't be there. He hardly ever is. He's rather busy at the moment. Come at about eight. I'll give you some dinner.'

Rory thought about his wife; she'd be quite happy if he rang to say he'd be late getting home. But he'd promised his son Tommy they would put the finishing touches to the station on his Hornby track that evening.

'I won't be able to get to you until nine,' he said, and was surprised by the look of relief in her eyes.

'Great!' she said, leaned forward, put warm lips on his cold cheek and was gone.

He climbed into his car and watched her for a few seconds, picking her way through the puddles towards her Mercedes.

Luke Mundy signed the bill for lunch at Le Gavroche. For the first time in years, he looked at the amount and privately winced. He shouldn't have ordered the Dom Perignon and Petrus '66. But then the bill would probably never be paid, so he might as well enjoy these things while he could.

Of course, he didn't let his thoughts show. To the man sitting opposite him – a still impressionable investment banker – Luke was as confident and optimistic as ever. This was not the first time Luke Mundy had wallowed in a business trough before hauling himself back to the crest of the wave with uncanny foresight, and a lot of luck – luck which he gave the impression of having created for himself.

Johnathan Martin's bank had made considerable profits in joint ventures with Thames Land, Luke Mundy's development company, and Luke had been Johnathan's find. The banker had a proprietorial pride in his client which muddied the waters of his normally clear thinking.

What he saw facing him now were the familiar male-model, chunky good looks and dark eyes which creased and sparkled with amused cynicism. In the ten years Johnathan had known Luke, it seemed to him that his client hadn't changed at all. At forty-five, Luke's hair was as thick and black as ever, and his waist as trim. Ten years of indulgent living seemed to have preserved rather than ravaged him. And he still approached each new deal and each new crisis with the same detached air of knowing all the moves long before it was his turn to make them.

'I'm glad it was your turn to pay,' Johnathan thanked Luke. 'We've all been encouraged to cut our peripheral expenses by half, or pay them ourselves.'

'That bad, is it?' Luke said with a smile that dissociated him from the prevailing gloom in the City.

'If you knew how many people have had to restructure,' Johnathan said confidentially. 'You're one of my few clients who hasn't come crawling back to ask for a little kindness and understanding. If it weren't for the profits our foreign exchange boys are making, we wouldn't be too comfortable ourselves; though it's rather degrading having to rely on barrow boys and Greek spivs – and they don't let us forget it.'

'As long as you're not going to want your money back from me in a hurry,' Luke grinned.

'Lord, no. You'll be all right, provided the repayments keep coming.'

'No problem,' Luke said with confidence.

Johnathan was satisfied that he'd made his point and turned the conversation to a less sensitive topic.

'I read in the *Mail* yesterday that you're riding Midnight Express in this race you've sponsored.'

Luke nodded. 'As we've put up twenty grand in prize money, I thought I ought to try and win some of it back,' he grinned. 'And I'll be surprised if I don't. Either way, it's turned out to be a great stunt. It's worth twice as much as any other hunter chase and it's getting tremendous coverage which won't do our public image any harm. In fact, I'd go so far as to say that if I win, it'll probably give our price a bit of a boost. And we can do with all the help we can get in this bloody awful climate.'

Johnathan thought privately that it would need more than the chairman winning a horse race to boost the stock of any property company at the moment, but he agreed that any positive media coverage would help.

'Should I have a bet on you, then?' he asked.

'Put a few of your best shirts on it.'

Luke kept a smile on his face until he had clambered into the back of his Bentley and settled where his chauffeur couldn't see him.

He wondered how Johnathan would have said goodbye if he had known that he'd already had his last repayment. It would be three weeks before the bank would find out, but then, unless Luke was the beneficiary of a miracle he didn't deserve, he had no moves left.

He had sold every last acre of undeveloped land – dog land, some of it, without even the inkling of planning permission – at prices it hurt him to think about, just to keep the money coming in. And his Thames Valley Business Park was as resolutely unlet and unsold as it had been a year before. For the bank's benefit, he had managed to put flesh on to the vaguely expressed interest of the multinational companies he had approached with suicidally discounted terms. It surprised him a little that Johnathan still hadn't smelt a rat, but then, he had spent many years, and many thousands of pounds developing Johnathan's trust.

Why the hell, he thought, was the man so gullible? If Johnathan hadn't been so convinced that he, Luke, was infallible, he wouldn't have lent the money in the first place – at a time when every indicator said he shouldn't.

Luke cursed the performance he'd put up then. 'There's no question,' he had predicted with a flourish, 'that when this Gulf War's over, public consumption and business confidence will surge, and land prices with it.'

If only Johnathan and his colleagues hadn't believed him; had told him to wait, like every other experienced developer. If only they had said No, he wouldn't be wallowing, not just in a trough, but beneath the surface of a turbulent sea with no shore in sight.

It was their bloody fault, their own tough shit if they lost their money. He had never claimed to be a prophet . . . or had he?

He wanted to bury his head in his hands and weep, but

it was unthinkable, so contrary to the public image that had become his private self, that he was incapable of it.

And he thought of the women who would laugh and sneer at him, however bold a face he put on the catastrophe of being broke. How they would titter at the stark announcements in the broadsheets, and the snide crowing of the tabloids, who so liked to kick a man fallen from a great height.

Just thinking about the women made him sick, more even than his grand racing friends, or the MPs and television faces he liked to entertain at Langlands and who were only too happy to drink his champagne, laugh at his jokes and make him feel like a prince.

Sod them!

He didn't care. He'd started with twenty quid, thirty years before. He'd do it again, much quicker this time, with all the knowledge and wisdom he had gained first time round.

What knowledge?

What wisdom?

After thirty years, he had still managed to go out and dig himself such a deep hole in such a mountain of shit that his crowning achievement would be to break a few records for personal bankruptcy.

And he thought about Laura.

Guilt was a sensation unfamiliar to Luke Mundy. Yet now, when he thought of the one person who would care about him and offer gentle, tentative sympathy when he fell, he knew that she, of all people, owed him nothing.

True, he had given her a beautiful home in which to feel miserable and lonely; true, he had funded the racing yard which had enabled Laura to build considerable self-respect and recognition in her own right.

But while he had regarded the state of marriage as no more than a mildly restricting social category and had been as free with his attention to women as he had ever been, she had never stopped loving him and longing for him to be the kind-hearted, eager twenty-six-year-old he had been when she, just sixteen, had first met him. She hadn't told him that for several years now; he had discouraged her, cruelly and with none of his famous charm. But he still knew she felt it, and he really didn't want to let her down.

At first, Laura Mundy had treated her horses and the business of training them as an anaesthetic – something to deaden the bitter realisation that she ranked in her husband's scale of priorities somewhere below his newest Bugatti and his latest property deal.

She had not even the compensation of children to rear. At considerable cost to her own self-esteem and Luke's personal bank balance, she had submitted to many and various fertility clinics in London, Zürich and Houston. No clear reason had been found to explain her lack of conception. Although she had pleaded with Luke to have his own functions scrutinised, he had absolutely rejected any possibility that the trouble might lie with him. At first she had been heartbroken; now, she was relieved.

Without children or the demands of a sensitive husband to distract her, she had chosen to throw herself into the job of training horses to the exclusion of everything else, and that very single-mindedness had been the key to her success.

But it was Luke who arranged the weekend parties,

and told their cook what to serve. It was Luke who was the host and decided who would sit beside whom. Laura, the leading lady jump trainer, was paraded with the same easy pride as were the horses in the yard.

Because he didn't like awkwardness, Luke always made sure that Laura had an owner or two at the dinner table beside her, while he concentrated on the wives or daughters of the influential men he asked to stay in his vast, labyrinthine Tudor manor house.

During the week, of course, he was never there. He lived in Cheyne Walk by the Thames in London, in a house lavishly decorated by a woman who had been a lover until there was no more decorating to do. Laura hated it and rarely stayed there. Nowadays the only time she saw her husband during the week was at the races, where, with great flamboyance, he liked to ride his best horses in the big amateur races, as he fully intended to do on Midnight Express in those critical weeks before the Cheltenham Festival.

Chapter Two

'But, Dad,' Tommy said, with tears in his voice, 'you promised we'd finish it tonight.'

Rory knew it didn't matter to Tommy whether his model railway station was finished tonight or next month. That wasn't the point – the boy just didn't want him to go. His mother was out. The babysitter, a bulky girl with a face like lard, was glued to a can of Coke and *The Bill* downstairs – about as stimulating as a dead cod to a boy of ten. Kids thrived on stimulation, Rory thought, and this one got none from his mother.

Rory looked down at his son and smiled. The boy wasn't yet ten years old but was already just like his father; same golden hair and blue eyes, and just as devious at getting his own way. 'All right. I'm supposed to be down at a trainer's house in half an hour to fix up a few rides but she can wait. Only I don't want to do all the work on this station myself. You start doing the roof while I do the walls, okay?'

Rory disguised his impatience and was rewarded with

a spell of strong, silent communion between father and son as each concentrated on his share of the job.

When the small wooden building was constructed, Tommy knew that he'd had a generous helping of his father's time, and he didn't object when Rory got to his feet.

'Right, Tommy, I've got to go and see this trainer now. And it's time you were thinking about bath and bed. Tell you what, if I sort out some good rides, I'll take you for a couple of days' fishing up the Wye, like I said I might, okay?'

Tommy's eyes lit up. 'Brill! You won't forget, will you?'

'Of course not. I'm looking forward to a bit of fishing myself. You'd better check that all the lines and rods are working. I'll see you in the morning.'

In the car, Rory told himself he wouldn't let Tommy down. God knew, he spent enough time with the boy, but somehow he had to make up for Pam's constant lack of interest. He felt, unjustly to himself, that he should have stayed this evening until Tommy was tucked up in bed.

Pam hadn't told him where she was going. He hadn't asked and he found that he no longer cared. She was a selfish woman; she always had been, though for the first few years of their marriage Rory pretended she wasn't. It was when Tommy had been diagnosed as a diabetic at the age of two that she had made it plain that she had no time for a boy who was dependent on a daily shot of insulin. Now she was a lousy mother and a worse wife. Rory had thought about divorce, but he knew the statistics: over ninety-five percent of cases ended with the mother gaining custody of the children. Rory couldn't expose Tommy to that.

But what the hell was he doing, he asked himself, almost allowing himself to jeopardise his own relationship with Tommy so that he could see Laura?

Laura – who had been the *raison d'être* of his early adult life and had filled it with overwhelming sensations of pleasure and tenderness, pain and guilt.

Rory had told her at the races that he didn't want to talk about it. Now he didn't even want to think about it. Abruptly, he leaned forward and switched on the radio to listen to whatever Radio 4 offered to block further thoughts from his mind.

Laura, with a docile and devoted yellow labrador in her wake, opened the front door of the huge house. She looked small and young against a background of a massive carved oak staircase and gallery, panelled walls and hanging tapestries.

There was a short moment of awkwardness. It seemed too unreal that after years of animosity and slander they should be meeting without hostility.

'Hello.' Rory felt a shy boyish smile on his face.

'Come in,' she invited, with a hint of apology for the grandness of the place.

They didn't speak as she led him across the hall into a small panelled sitting room where logs blazed in a broad inglenook, and the flames sparkled off a battery of Waterford glasses and decanters on a Jacobean table. The only lights in the room shone on a pair of classic eighteenth-century equestrian paintings. Midas, the dog, flopped down in front of the fire and gazed at his mistress.

'Glenmorangie?' she offered, going to the drinks table.

'Yes, please.' Rory nodded. 'I haven't changed that much.'

'I hope your taste in food hasn't changed either. There's a truck-load of Chinese on its way up from the takeaway in Andover. The cook nearly walked out when I told her. Sit down if you want to.'

Rory thought about asking if she'd ordered a 69er but decided now was not the time for smutty jokes. Instead he smiled. Pam hated Chinese food. He was glad that Laura hadn't forgotten the takeaways they'd shared in the cosy fug of his little room at Mick Fanshaw's. He sat in a deep, tapestry-clad armchair and reached into his jacket pocket for his tobacco tin.

'Still smoking those nasty little roll-ups, then?' Laura asked.

'Sure. I'm quite good at it now. D'you want one?'

'Why not.' She put a full tumbler of pale whisky on a table beside him. 'I'll swap it for a Monte Cristo after dinner.'

Rory meticulously rolled two thin cigarettes, passed one to Laura and lit it for her.

She sat opposite him in a high winged chair.

'So,' he asked, 'what makes you suddenly want to talk to me?'

She gave him a smile, not the self-conscious, seductive look of her early twenties, but a wide, generous grin. 'There wasn't anything sudden about it.'

Rory looked at her, the firelight on her long, rich black hair and the shadows cast by her large, well-formed breasts in a cream silk blouse. He tried to remember her naked body, and wondered if it had changed.

'No,' she went on with a short laugh, 'I've been thinking about talking to you for a long time. Rutherford going mad and blaming me because you won't ride his horse just gave me an excuse – that and the fact that Dai isn't riding too well.'

'It's not business, then?'

'No. I mean – I *do* want you to ride for me – but that's not the main reason I wanted to see you.' She paused, she seemed to be having difficulty getting to the point.

Rory picked up his glass and sucked in some of the single malt whisky. He waited; he couldn't help her.

She leaned forward in her chair and waved a hand round the room. 'What do you think of the house?'

Rory shrugged. 'It's magnificent, like something in a movie. Way beyond what I'm used to.'

'You're right. It's very beautiful. I suppose it's one of the best Tudor houses in England.' She gave a tight little smile. 'My gilded cage.'

Rory frowned. 'You, in a cage? It doesn't sound too likely. You're a successful woman, you could leave any time you pleased.'

'Maybe, now. You've never met Luke, have you?'

'You didn't ask me to the wedding.'

'But you've seen him at the races, when he's been riding?'

'Sure.'

'One of the boys; all macho charm and healthy ambition. When the mask's down, he's a different beast. He's got an almost manic need for power and control over the people around him, and he uses any weapon he can lay his hands on to achieve it.'

'He beats you?'

'Only mentally.'

'But you can handle that.'

'For God's sake, I was twenty-three, and feeling incredibly unsure of myself after you'd gone off with Pam, when he reappeared in my life. Luke's got a very forceful personality and if he can't dominate someone head-on, he undermines them, knows all their weak points and how to exploit them. When he married me, I was a pushover.'

'Our splitting up wasn't entirely one-sided,' Rory said quietly.

'Okay,' Laura came back more gently. 'There's not much point going over that now. As you say, I'm a successful woman, in my own right. And I think I probably am strong enough to walk out. I just need someone to convince me. Unfortunately, though I've got all this,' she waved her hand around the room, to take in the whole house, the pictures and tapestries, the park outside, the stable yard, the seventy-five thousand pound Mercedes in the garage, 'I haven't got a single close friend.'

'You must have been scraping the barrel if you had to resort to me,' Rory chuckled.

'Yeah,' she said with a grin, 'but I'm glad I have, aren't you?'

Rory picked up his glass and tilted it towards her before taking a drink. 'Sure,' he smiled.

They looked at each other, bridging a gap of ten years in their lives. In the gentle silence there was a tap on the door and a tiny Filipino woman came in.

'Mrs Mundy, your dinner ready.'

Laura glanced up at her. 'Thanks, Maria. We'll come straight in.' She turned back to Rory. 'I've ordered masses, so we're eating in the dining room. I hope you're not riding tomorrow.'

'I'm not, and I haven't had a proper meal for three days.'

An hour and two bottles of Burgundy later, Rory laughed at the remains of their Chinese feast.

'I already feel like a Sumo wrestler, and there's enough left to feed a football team.'

While they had eaten, by the light of two silver candelabra and another log fire, they had taken themselves back to the time when they had first met at Mick Fanshaw's mucky yard on the Sussex downs.

Rory, just nineteen, had arrived a month before from his home village beneath the mountains in the upper Esk valley. It was his first visit to England, undertaken despite the anxiety and disapproval of his strict Presbyterian parents. He had never sat on the back of a horse before leaving Scotland, but Mick Fanshaw had taken him on without any hesitation; one glance into the good-looking boy's bright blue eyes had told him all he needed to know. Before the end of that first month, Rory was riding work, and Mick had already decided that he was his best discovery in a decade. But he didn't tell Rory that.

Rory knew even less about girls than he did about horses. There had been little scope for experimentation in his village and his parents' small house beside their post office. Girls were something admired and desired from afar, mostly on a television screen.

When one of Mick Fanshaw's owners, Edward Brickhill, had come to visit the yard, he'd brought his daughter Laura with him. One glimpse had sent the blood rushing around Rory's body and struck him dumb when Laura and her father reached the horses he looked after for them.

After that, Laura always came with her father whenever he visited the yard. It wasn't until her fourth visit that Rory spoke to her.

In some ways, Laura Brickhill could not have been a more unlikely candidate for his first love. While he was from a poor Scottish Presbyterian family, her parents were rich English Catholics. He had been to the village school in Eskdale and a comprehensive in Dumfries; she had been to Lady Eden's in London and St Mary's Convent, Ascot.

But, in common, they had both possessed streaks of rebelliousness against their respective backgrounds. Laura loathed her mother's small-minded snobbishness, which gave more weight to a person's accent than their intelligence and Rory was reacting to the unforgiving narrow-mindedness of his parents' faith.

Nevertheless, these influences had left on both of them indelible and conflicting attitudes which they had never been able to reconcile and which became the last resort in any arguments between them. It was her scathing personal criticisms, issued with the complacent confidence of her class, which stung hardest; Rory was too naive then to deflect and discredit them, in a way he could easily have done now.

But their rapport was sustained by a fierce physical attraction which always overcame the differences between them. They revelled in newly discovered mutual pleasures and tacitly acknowledged the equal strength of each other's personality.

They had known one another for nearly three years, while Rory's career as a jockey was beginning to take off, when a trivial argument about his attitude to her father so stung him that he cancelled a date with her and went instead to a party at Fanshaw's stable.

He arrived a little drunk and was foolish enough to tell his junior colleague, Dai Price, the reason. Dai, malicious and more worldly than Rory, had plied him with double strength vodka before challenging him to 'score' with Pam Fanshaw, the guv'nor's daughter.

It wasn't much of a challenge.

Rory, though he hadn't learned to appreciate it, was by then a very good-looking man, already fancied by most of the girls in the yard and village. If Pam had any thoughts about resisting, she kept them well under control. And, either by instinct or experience, she knew what men liked and how to provide it.

Still smarting from Laura's criticism, Rory didn't find it hard to go along with what Pam was offering. Next morning – a Sunday – the thought of how Laura would react if she found out quickly replaced his sense of euphoria with a vicious, guilty hangover.

He left Pam sleeping in his narrow bed in the loft above the stables and went to find Dai Price to beg him not to tell Laura what had happened.

Before he had even finished asking the sharp little Welshman, he knew he had been betrayed already.

Rory tried to ring Laura throughout the day. Her mother answered each time with the implausible statement that she didn't have the slightest idea where Laura was.

That evening, Laura appeared at the yard in her twenty-third birthday present, a Golf GTi. She drove right into the yard and skidded to a halt. Some of the lads were giving their horses the last feed of the day. They told her Rory wasn't about. With a sour smile, she spotted Pam emerging from a stable with an empty feed rubber in her hand.

'I was looking for your little Scottish lover boy,' Laura said loudly. 'But you'll do.'

Pam confronted her rival with a hand on her hip and a big grin on her face.

'That's what he said,' she jeered.

Laura shook her long black hair and angrily tugged off the small gold earrings that had been Rory's one, modest present to her in all the time they had been going out together.

'You can give these back to him. If you're lucky, he'll give them to you – they're worth at least a fiver.' She hurled the earrings on to the ground at Pam's feet. She couldn't avoid a convulsive heave of her shoulders as her voice broke. 'And tell him I never want to see him again.'

'I don't suppose he'll want to see you again after last night,' Pam said triumphantly, to the laughing cheers of the two or three lads who had stopped working to watch.

Their ridicule gave Laura strength. She stiffened herself, glared at them haughtily and walked as calmly as she could back to her car. She climbed in, started it and drove quietly away from the yard.

When Rory got back to the stables late that evening, still hung over and slightly drunk, he listened with a tightening of the guts to the story of Laura's visit and public rejection of him. He lay in bed that night, half sleeping, torn between anger and remorse. When he woke next morning, he knew that if she came, he would beg her to come back. He sat down at the rickety table in his room and spent a pen-chewing hour composing a letter to her. He posted it early next morning but never received a reply.

A month of silence from Laura passed before Rory finally accepted that it was all over between them.

Pam Fanshaw watched and bided her time. She didn't hurry him or tease him over his loss like Dai and the other lads in the yard. She just told him quietly that if he wanted someone to talk to, she was around. She knew that sooner or later, Rory's sexual urges would bring him to her.

Losing Laura was more than just a blow to Rory's pride. He knew that he had really loved her. And he had made it clear to her that as soon as he was on his feet as a jockey, he would marry her. Despite the difference between them, she had been just as keen, and Rory had scarcely been able to believe his luck.

Now he was baffled and hurt by her rejection, because he was sure there was still something between them. Until he heard that Luke Mundy, a rising star of the gossip columns and the burgeoning property market, was taking an interest in her.

It was Dai Price who first showed him the picture in the *Daily Mail* of Laura at a party in Berkeley Square, hanging on to Luke's arm, grinning happily.

It never occurred to Rory that he was the one person in the world who Laura hoped would see the picture.

Pam Fanshaw skilfully took her cue.

Rory was the jockey on the up in her father's in-form yard, and a good catch. Mick Fanshaw made it clear that he thoroughly approved of the idea of Rory as a son-in-law. To have a jockey of Rory's calibre in the family could only have advantages, which he made sure to spell out.

From Rory's point of view, to marry Pam would be to marry guaranteed employment, with the pick of the rides. Besides, he had no complaints about their physical affinity, and Pam had made it her business to nurse and revitalise his battered ego. Any pangs of guilt that troubled him he quelled with the thought that it was, after all, Laura who had taken the initiative in terminating their affair.

Rory had tried to make the most of his new marriage, and to be fair to Pam, she hadn't been a bad wife to begin with.

She was certainly decorative, in an obvious way. She had big eyes, full lips and large breasts, and knew how to make the most of them. She cooked surprisingly well and was never too tired for sex. She worked hard, keeping spotless the tiny cottage Fanshaw had given them. When, after eight months, Tommy appeared, she dutifully performed her maternal tasks. She even gave up her own race riding career and helped Rory with his, hustling for rides when her father didn't have one for him.

She was ambitious for Rory, always a few steps in front of him. She spotted corners he could cut, deals he could do which would increase his income and advance his career, and which caused him agonies of self-disgust, until, after two or three years, he refused to go along with them any more. That was when he and Pam had ceased to communicate beyond the practical.

She was already bored by her toddler son and the extra care his diabetes required. But she stayed with Rory for his status as a leading jockey and for the income he brought in, which was steadily increasing in spite of his refusal to respond to her urging to ring up trainers for other jockeys' rides.

Rory stayed with Pam for Tommy's sake.

Over the years that followed, his father-in-law's yard suffered from an intermittent virus and the winners began to dry up. Rory took the unilateral decision to move on and ride as a freelance jockey. He worked hard and with the money he had carefully saved he bought Camp Farm, a sixty-acre property near Lambourn, with a brick and flint house.

Philosophically, he had resigned himself to his deteriorating relationship with his wife by devoting his energy to his son, his brood mares and more recently the building of his new barns and stables – until today, when Laura had asked him to Langlands.

Now, looking across the broad oak table and the debris of the Chinese dinner, she smiled at him.

'I think I've talked to you more tonight than in all the time I knew you before.'

'I hope it's been some use to you.'

'You know it has, and more than just useful. Apart

from the men in the yard I never have a good discussion with anyone, and I can't really ask them whether or not I should leave this place, even if I can find somewhere else to take them all.'

'It's none of my business, but if you left Luke, would you be sure of having the money to start elsewhere?'

Rory sensed an evasiveness in her reply. 'Well, if the worst came to the worst, my father would always back me.'

'You mean, you think Luke might not cough up?'

'There could be problems.'

'Nothing that a good lawyer couldn't deal with, surely?'

'The way I'm feeling now, that's a secondary factor. I've just come to the absolute end of my tether, being the chattel of an arrogant, pig-headed megalomaniac who still thinks he's a god. I just can't stand any more fighting. I should have gone years ago.'

'Despite all the fringe benefits?'

'Give me some credit, Rory. I've never been that mercenary. After all, I was prepared to marry you when you had nothing.'

'But you're older and wiser now.'

'Older, certainly.' Laura made a face.

'And twice as beautiful,' Rory added.

Rory nodded to himself as he drove through the blustery night and the narrow lane that led away from Langlands. She was more beautiful, all right. And somehow, there was more depth to her, too.

Thirteen years ago, he felt the beauty had only been on the surface, which was all that had mattered to a healthy young man finding his first real taste of sexual adventure.

He gazed through his busy, swishing windscreen wipers and was glad nothing serious had happened between them tonight. Just the warm moistness of her lips on his had been enough. Besides, with Luke still on the scene, however sporadically, it would be a mistake to get involved. He wasn't convinced that she really would leave Luke. If and when she did – that would be the time to think about it.

He smiled to himself again.

He would take Tommy on the fishing trip, even though, as far as his racing career was concerned, the evening had yielded nothing. Apart from the few words when he had first arrived, they hadn't talked about his riding for her. He thought now that he didn't mind; he didn't really want to ride for Laura, until Luke was out of her life.

If he was going to stray from Pam, he wasn't going to do it lightly.

Rory's farm lay in a valley in the southern slopes of the White Horse Hills below the ragged double rings of an Iron Age hill fort. The wind was less fierce here, but the rain still fell in large drops as he ran from his car towards the back door. He saw that Pam's car was already back and slowed to a walk. He wasn't in the mood for a fight.

He let himself in and looked at the messages on the pad by the phone. There wasn't anything important – no one had rung up in a panic needing his services the next day. He poured himself a small whisky and sat down to look through the plans which had been drawn for the new barns and stable-block he was building.

It had long been his aim, his long-term career strategy, to make himself a toehold in the bloodstock breeding business so that he had something to go on to when his body had taken enough of a hammering from jump riding. He had seen too many other National Hunt riders carry on longer than they should have done simply because they hadn't organised any other way of making a living.

Since he had moved to Lambourn, Rory had used his spare time in the summer to track down good quality mares at bargain prices. He had developed an excellent eye for a horse and had intensively studied the history and many arcane theories of bloodstock breeding. Now he had five brood mares and had sold a dozen home-bred foals. This season he had had the intense pleasure of seeing the first of these, a four-year-old gelding called Camp Follower, winning his first two races over hurdles.

This success had encouraged him to look for a good-quality jumping stallion to stand at his yard. It was to accommodate Long Run, the stallion, and mares who would be coming to visit him that he had planned new brick buildings to replace the old existing timber-clad stables.

Long Run was a big, rangy, rather unfashionable sort of horse. His only wins had been in two-and-a-half mile Cup races. No one breeding flat horses would have looked at him. But Rory judged him ideal to put a bit of bone and muscle into the offspring of slighter, quicker fillies.

Long Run had had two crops when Rory bought him and those of his yearlings which had come to market had fetched depressingly less than his stud fee. The stallion's owner hadn't needed much persuasion to part with him.

But Rory had made a particular study of Long Run's progeny, and he was convinced that the potential would be realised as they grew.

Another reason for Long Run's cheapness was that he took a lot of handling. He was well behaved in the field but in the stable he could be a savage. Rory attributed this to an incident in the horse's youth which had made him associate people in his box with imminent pain. With patience and gentleness, though, Rory was slowly convincing the animal that the connection wasn't inevitable and he was pleased that the first few coverings that season had gone as well as they had. When the new covering shed was ready for the next season, it would be even easier.

But looking at his plans now failed to absorb him as it usually did. His mind kept straying back to the soft brown eyes of the woman alone in her bed in the grand Tudor manor house.

'Rory, what the hell are you doing?'

Pam was wearing a short nightie, too flimsy for warmth or modesty.

'Just studying my plans.'

'If you spent as much time hustling for rides as you do looking at the plans for those bloody barns, you might make enough money to build them.'

'I've already bought most of the materials, and I'm going to do the bulk of the work myself,' he said, not for the first time.

'And I see you're drinking again; you know what that does to you and I might want a bit of action tonight.'

'You mean you haven't had any?' Rory raised an eyebrow.

'I don't know how you've got the nerve to say that! I

know bloody well where you've been.'

'Do you? How?'

'Just putting two and two together. You're spotted in the car park being kissed by Laura Bloody Mundy when you say you haven't spoken to her for over ten years, and Sharon says you've gone off to see someone about some rides.'

'You just said I should be hustling for more rides.'

Pam looked at him speculatively for a moment. 'Did you get any?'

'No, as a matter of fact, I didn't.'

'Well what the hell did you get?'

'A couple of drinks, and some Chinese takeaway.'

'Christ, is that all she can run to? I expect she's as useless at cooking as she is at training. She didn't want you to ride her, by any chance?'

'She didn't say so.'

'Everyone says what a frigid bitch she is. Come on, are you coming up?'

'I don't think so; not until you're asleep.'

'Bastard! I bet you screwed her.'

She turned her head angrily and spun out of the room, banging the door behind her.

Rory put his head in his hands, prayed for patience and wondered for the hundredth time how he had ever come to marry Pam.

The rain had blown off in the night, so Rory took advantage of the fine, crisp morning to get out early and begin lining up the footings for his new stable-block. It was a job that really needed two people, but he had plenty of time and just wanted to be out of Pam's way. The site was a hundred yards up the valley from the house, in front of the old stable block. In the paddock beyond, his five precious brood mares, bulging with imminent birth, grazed quietly in the sunshine. In the stand of beeches beside him, a pair of jays clattered through the budding branches. It was a peaceful scene in which Rory found refuge from his marriage and the duplicitous world of racing.

'Rory!' Pam's voice fanfared up the valley.

Philosophically, he stopped what he was doing and turned to walk back down to the house. If he didn't, he knew, she would only pursue him up here.

She was waiting at the back door as he neared the house.

'Telephone!'

'Couldn't you take a message?'

'I thought you'd want to take this one now. It's your new favourite trainer.'

Rory walked past his wife into the kitchen to pick up the phone.

'Hello?'

'Rory, it's Laura. I meant to talk to you about this last night, but there was so much else to say, I never got round to it. We never discussed your riding for me.'

'You know me, never known to hustle.'

'You should, you know.'

'So my wife says.'

'I expect she does. But what I wanted to say was that I'm not happy with Dai at the moment.'

'Isn't he obeying orders, or should I say, isn't he obeying *your* orders?'

'No, it's nothing like that – no more than usual. I think he's got a bottle problem.'

'He's always boozed a bit.'

'No, I don't mean that. I mean I think he's losing his nerve. He won't have a real cut at a fence any more, and he's getting windy about riding the novice chasers.'

'It's funny you should say that; a couple of jockeys have mentioned the same thing to me.'

'He'd have beaten you yesterday if he'd really committed himself at the last two fences.'

'What can I do for you then?'

'I want you to ride Midnight Express in the Two Mile Champion Chase at Cheltenham.'

Rory didn't answer for a moment. He was booked for eight rides at the festival, so far, with a strong chance in the Ritz, a modest chance in the Champion Hurdle but nothing in the Champion Chase. Laura was offering the possibility of a very lucrative double – just what he needed with the building work beginning.

'What would your husband have to say about me riding? It's his horse, isn't it?'

'That's my problem; I'll face Luke.'

'You mean, he'll object?'

'I mean I'll deal with it. Will you take the ride?'

Rory took a deep breath. 'Yes. Of course.'

'Great! And there could be some others.'

'Let me know.'

'I will. I'd like you to come and work on Express, just to get the feel of him. He's a really smashing horse – the best I've ever trained – but he takes a bit of getting used to.' Rory could hear the pride in Laura's voice as she spoke about a horse that promised to be a true champion. 'He takes a hell of a hold when he wants to,' she went on, 'and he can get himself worked up if he's worried about anything. Once you've ridden him at home, you'll know what I mean.'

'Okay. When do you want me to come?'

'Next week, Monday or Tuesday. Can I let you know?'

'It'd have to be Tuesday. I'm working at Richardson's Monday.'

'I'll ring you to confirm. Thanks very much, Rory, and thanks for last night.'

'No problem.'

She laughed. 'No problem? Oh well, 'bye.'

'Cheers.'

Rory put the phone down to find, as he had expected, his wife looking at him.

'Well?' she asked.

'I've got a nice ride in the Champion Chase.'

'What? Midnight Express?'

Rory nodded and walked out of the door to get back to his new barn.

Chapter Three

'Would you stop the car please, Taylor.'

Luke Mundy's chauffeur half turned in surprise. They were still a mile from Langlands, but surely, if Mr Mundy wanted a pee, he could wait. He decelerated in the narrow lane, and pulled into the side of the road.

'I'll walk down to the yard from here,' Luke said. 'You go on to the house and get the bags up. Then I'd like you to help out with drinks and things when the guests arrive.'

'Right you are, sir.' The chauffeur showed no surprise at his employer's desire to walk across the fields on a drizzling February afternoon. It would be dark and a lot damper before he reached the stables. But Mr Mundy didn't pay him to give advice on health matters.

Luke climbed out of the back of the Bentley and set off along the lane towards a stile which marked a path down to the valley bottom where he had sensibly placed his wife's stable yard, screened as it was by a horseshoe of old oaks.

In the fading light, he gazed down at the avenue which

51

led his eye up to a riot of roofs and the irregular chimneys of the great house which showed above the tops of the limes.

He half smiled. There was a tidy irony in knowing that he had bought Langlands and its thousand acres in a forced sale – a result of Black Monday in 1987. All his friends had congratulated him on his bargain, at the time. It didn't look such a bargain now, especially if, once again, it was to be the object of a forced sale.

Indifferent to the wet grass that heightened the gleam on his spotless Lobb shoes, he struck off down the hill, and thought about how he would break it to Laura.

The lads in the yard had to look twice before they recognised the bedraggled, wet-haired figure as their guv'nor's husband. Luke walked into the floodlit quadrangle where the final jobs of the day were being finished off before their two runners got back from Worcester.

'Is Patrick here?' he asked.

'Yes, sir, he's in the tack room.'

Luke walked across the yard and found Laura's head lad staring at the exercise board on the wall watched silently by four or five lads. Down the left-hand side of the board was a column of white magnetic name tags for everyone who ever rode work at Langlands – lads, jockeys and owners. Besides these, mostly arranged in columns for each lot, were yellow tags with the names of all the horses in the yard.

Patrick was clutching one of the yellow tags, trying to decide which lad would get on best with a nervous grey filly which had just arrived. He looked round, ready to issue some instruction or reprimand to his visitor. When he saw who it was, he fumbled for something to say, unable to hide his astonishment.

'You're looking a little damp, sir, if I may say so. Can I get you a towel?'

'No. I'll dry off when I get to the house. I walked down from the road but it was raining rather harder than I thought. Anyway, it doesn't matter,' he dismissed the problem. 'I wanted to ask your opinion before I talk to my wife about running Midnight Express in the Thames Land and the Grand Military.'

'You want my honest opinion?'

'If possible.'

'He has a tremendous chance in the Champion Chase, but he'll have none at all if he's had a hard race over three miles a week or even two weeks before, let alone both.'

'Irrespective of that, what I want to know is how good you think his chances are of winning the Thames Land?'

'I'd say he'd walk it, even, if you'll not take offence, with you on board.'

Luke laughed. 'Fortunately, there won't be any great jockeys on board any of the opposition either.'

'I had taken that into consideration.' Patrick nodded.

'Thank you for your honesty, Patrick. I'll definitely declare him, then. I'll give Sandown some more thought.'

Patrick didn't hide his disapproval. 'It would be much better for the horse's career if he were to win the Champion Chase. It seems a terrible shame to deprive him of that for the sake of an amateur race. He's the best horse I've ever had anything to do with.'

'You're too pessimistic, Patrick. You'll have him back

on top form in time for Cheltenham, I've no doubt, and then we'll all be happy.'

The head lad shrugged his narrow shoulders. 'He's your horse, sir. Was there anything else?'

'No. Just get the horse right for Kempton.' He paused. 'I've a feeling this might be my last ride for some time, and I'd rather like to go out on a winner.'

He turned and walked out into the wet evening.

Patrick looked at the lads, who had all been listening to the conversation. 'That's the first time I've ever heard him talk like that. Something must be up.'

'If 'e's that keen, it's got to be worth a tenner,' one of them said.

'Nah,' another disagreed. 'I wouldn't back anything he was riding. Any case, I don't think the horse will stay three miles.'

This comment provoked a loud argument among the lads. Each had his own view to put. The one point they all agreed on was that they only wanted the best for Midnight Express; he was everyone's favourite.

This prompted Patrick to go outside and check that their star performer had eaten his supper.

Midnight Express was stabled in the biggest box in the yard, next door to the feed house. Here he received a lot of attention from anyone while the feeds were being mixed. If he didn't get his own meal first, he stood and kicked the door with his front foot until something appeared.

Patrick pulled back the top door and looked in at the magnificent bay chaser, who had his ears back as he licked the remains of his evening feed from his manger. Putting on an angry face was just a show. A couple of quiet words from Patrick brought him over eagerly to take a sugar lump that the head lad always had ready for him.

Patrick let himself into the stable and felt inside the gelding's thick, striped under-rug to make sure he was warm enough, while Midnight Express nuzzled his pocket for more sugar. Patrick stroked the big bay head with real affection; there was something about this horse that he had never felt with any other. And he certainly didn't want to see his chances spoiled by the vanity of a rich amateur jockey.

Pride, vanity, inflated ego. Luke Mundy thought of these failings as he walked in the dark beneath the scanty cover of the towering, leafless limes, and for the first time in many years he was inclined to feel humble.

When his débâcle became public knowledge, which couldn't be avoided beyond another fortnight, he would blame other people and cite a dozen causes beyond his control – from Lawson's budget to the collapse of the Berlin Wall.

He had always taken the credit for his achievements, but he didn't have the stomach to admit the blame for this failure. Though privately he knew he was the only culprit, he would tell no one. Except Laura.

The lights of the ancient house glowed warmly, and now that he was on the point of losing it, he saw qualities in it he had never appreciated before.

He didn't walk up to the front door, as he had planned. He went round to the rear of the house and let himself in by a back door that opened into a warren of gun rooms and fishing tackle stores. In the luxury of a deeply carpeted cloakroom, he dried his hair and discarded his sopping jacket. He opened the door and checked that no one was about, then slipped up a service staircase to the main landing and hurried along a broad corridor to his dressing room. In the quiet and rich colours of the large, low-ceilinged room, he shook off the rest of his wet clothes, wrapped a towel around his waist and walked through to the adjoining bathroom to run a hot bath.

When he came back into his room, Laura was waiting for him with a look of nervous triumph in her eyes.

'You must have crept in.'

'I did. I walked down to the yard and got caught in the rain.'

'That seems very unlike you.'

'Nonsense. I often walk.'

'I meant getting caught in the rain.'

Luke shrugged his bare shoulders. 'A bit of rain never hurt anyone. Anyway, I'm glad I've seen you before anyone else. I wanted to talk to you.'

'Goodness, I am honoured! I suppose it's about your riding Midnight Express?'

'There was that too . . .'

Laura's eyes flared. 'It's out of the question. He's my best Cheltenham horse and if he has to do either of these bloody hunter chases, he won't stand a chance.'

Luke's new humility retreated fast. 'May I remind you that he's my horse; I paid a hundred thousand guineas for him, despite your advice to the contrary, so that I could win races on him myself.'

'He'll be worth a lot more than a hundred thousand if

he wins the Champion Chase; and I gather that, right now, you might find that useful.'

Luke looked at her with the arrogance and disdain she knew so well. 'He's already worth double that; and who the hell told you I might need the money?'

'I'm not telling you. If it's not true, that's fine.'

'Was it George Rutherford?'

Laura didn't answer.

'You can take no notice of anything he says. He's still sore about the deal I did with him on the Chelsea Gaming Club. He knows he sold it too cheap. That's his problem, not mine.'

'I don't know anything about that,' Laura said. 'Anyway, you can ask him yourself. He's invited himself for dinner tonight.'

Luke's eyes blazed and his fists knotted. For a moment, Laura thought he was going to hit her. 'What the hell do you mean?' He forced himself to be calm. 'It'll mess up all the numbers and he'll have nothing in common with the other guests. Why didn't you tell him he couldn't come?'

'Because, in case you've forgotten, he's my biggest owner.'

And because – she added to herself – he'll come up with the money for a new yard if I decide to move out of here.

Luke, becoming at once furtive and remorseful, took a deep breath and a couple of paces towards her. He put a bare arm around her shoulder. 'Look, I'm sorry. I didn't want to be angry with you this weekend, but I'm really determined to ride in the race I've sponsored, and the

Grand Military – I don't spend fourteen days a year messing around in the TA for nothing. And frankly, yes, I do have a cash-flow problem. I'm telling you, because you should know, but it would make matters a lot worse if anyone else did.'

Laura quivered at his touch. Luke, misinterpreting, smiled. 'We've got a bit of time and there's something going on beneath this towel that needs attention,' he murmured.

'Well I'm sorry. I can't do anything about that now. I've got to get down to the yard. One of the horses has got a temperature.'

She didn't look back at him as she left the room.

His surly voice followed her. 'Just try and be back before my guests arrive.'

An hour later, Laura had transformed herself into the perfect hostess. She wanted Rutherford to see how well she could cope. There was nothing about him that she liked, but she recognised several useful characteristics in him. He was rich – so rich that nobody quite knew the extent of his wealth; he was the only man she'd ever met who frightened Luke; and he made it very obvious that he fancied her.

She loathed his unsubtle leering and innuendo; but she was, by now, a thoroughly pragmatic woman.

Rutherford was the last guest to arrive. As he walked into the room, Laura saw Luke stiffen but carry on talking as if he hadn't noticed.

'Luke,' Laura said loudly, 'here's George.'

Luke turned unwillingly, flashing his irritation at Laura.

'Oh hello, George. I'm so glad you could come.'

'I'm glad to have been invited. I wanted a word with you – in private.'

Luke shrugged easily at his other guests, suggesting that a small but essential bit of business had to be dealt with. 'Sure.' He led Rutherford from the hammer-beamed hall into the small sitting room where Rory and Laura had sat and talked before dinner two evenings before.

Luke carefully closed the door behind them.

Twenty minutes later, Laura sensed that the other guests were beginning to get restless and huffy that their host had abandoned them. She walked over to the sitting room door and let herself in.

To her surprise, Rutherford and her husband looked as though they were about to shake each other by the hand. But they didn't complete the gesture. Rutherford tucked a folded piece of paper into his breast pocket, which he patted. 'Right,' he nodded.

'Come on, you two,' Laura chided them. 'You're rather conspicuous by your absence. If you stay out much longer, people might start spreading rumours about you.'

Both men gave her an indulgent smile.

As they walked back into the hall, Laura wondered what they'd been discussing. A loan, perhaps, or – more likely – some kind of settlement over the Chelsea Gaming Club. Certainly, if Luke had somehow acquired the club from Rutherford at less than its real value, Rutherford would have had his reasons. At least, he would want redress.

For the rest of dinner, Luke was quieter than usual, answering his neighbours mechanically and without any of his normal dazzling, skilfully wielded charm. Laura almost felt sorry for him but she didn't let him into her bed later without protest.

That night, though, he didn't persist as he would normally have done and after ten minutes climbed out and went to sleep in his dressing room.

He had never done that before; Laura guessed his problems must be bigger than she thought.

Pam Gillespie shook her implausibly blonde and curly head across the table at Rory.

'You know you said you were riding Midnight Express in the Champion Chase?'

Rory glanced up from the paper he was reading, chewing on a piece of lean, tender sirloin steak his wife had cooked for his supper. He nodded. 'Yes.'

'It's still declared to run in this ridiculous Thames Land race.'

'So?'

'I saw Dai at Ascot on Saturday and he told me if it runs at Kempton, you can forget it winning at Cheltenham.'

'Why's that?'

'He didn't say. I suppose he takes time to get over his races.'

'Did Dai know I was booked to ride him at Cheltenham?'

'No, but I told him.' She giggled. 'He wasn't too happy.'

'You really have an incredible taste for stirring things up, don't you?'

'Well, he would have found out sooner or later,

wouldn't he? Anyway, he says the horse hasn't got a chance if he's run the week before.'

'I'm going down to ride work on him tomorrow morning. I'll ask Laura about it then.'

'Lucky bitch had two winners at Fontwell today.'

'That makes her a lucky bitch, does it?'

'She is a lucky bitch.' Pam didn't conceal her loathing. 'She'd be nothing if her husband wasn't a millionaire.'

'She works hard at it; she's always had a good eye for a horse,' Rory said quietly, knowing it would annoy Pam.

'And a jockey.'

'Has Dai been obliging her, then?'

'God, no! He says he wouldn't touch her with a barge pole.'

Rory laughed. 'He'd be lucky to get that near.'

'You fancy her again, don't you? There was a time when you used to call her a snotty bitch.'

'I never said she was a snotty bitch, but anyway, people change; or, at least, some people do.'

'What's that supposed to mean?'

Rory shook his head. 'It means whatever you want it to mean.' He turned his attention to the Welsh collie lying on his feet. 'Come on, Taffy, let's go and take a look at the horses.'

Arthur Eland knew from the dossier he had been given where his victim would be at about twelve on that Monday morning. He decided to set his trap for half past ten.

He had arranged over the phone to take a stable in a scruffy livery yard. He had sent the rent, two weeks in advance, using a post office money order.

To bait the trap, he needed a horse.

'Good home wanted for much-loved old family friend,' the advertisement said.

Eland grinned. They'd rather give it away than let the knacker have it.

'15.2hh dun cob; 18 y-o, but sound, ideal quiet lady's hack or suit teenage beginner.'

He took a boy with him. 'Try and look like my son,' he said.

'That's a bloody joke,' the boy said with a hoarse, coarse laugh. He was just twelve, but hardened by exposure to Arthur Eland and clients like him.

'What d'you think of him, then?' Eland had inspected the horse; he'd run his hands nervously down one of its hairy legs and asked the sad-faced woman who was selling the cob to trot it up for him.

''E's lovely, Dad,' the boy said. Eland had rehearsed him in the car coming over. 'Can we get 'im?'

'I dunno. He *is* nice, but I don't think I can afford him.'

'Oh, Dad!' the boy whined.

Eland turned to the woman who was holding the horse's head and looking with compassion at the slight, pretty child who didn't look as though there was much joy in his life. 'Would you take four hundred?' he asked. The broad-backed horse was worth more than that in meat.

'Well, my husband did really think we should get six hundred for him.'

'That's a real shame,' Eland said, shaking his head. 'The

boy really likes him, and he'd have done him very well.'

'Yes, he'd be a lovely first horse; even though he's a little big, he's very kind.'

'I can see that.' Eland allowed his voice to quiver with disappointment. 'But I just couldn't go higher than four hundred.'

The woman smiled, pleased at the decision she was making. 'To be quite honest, the money's not all that important. I think he would have a very happy home with your boy, so you can have him for four hundred pounds.'

Eland and the boy bubbled with gratitude.

'That's great, Dad! Can we take him now?'

Eland smiled indulgently at him. 'If the lady will let us. I've got the cash and I've got the trailer,' he addressed the woman, who nodded with a soft smile.

'What do you want the bloody thing for anyway?' the boy asked as they drove between the silver birches that lined the drive from the cob's old home.

'That's none of your business. I'm taking you back now.'

'What about my money?'

'Here's twenty.' Eland produced a note and passed it to the boy, who disdainfully tucked it in his shirt pocket.

Eland dropped the boy outside an arcade in Slough. A few minutes later he was unhitching the trailer from his Jaguar and hitching it back on to a nondescript, untraceable Japanese pick-up.

Twenty minutes after that, he arrived at the livery yard. He didn't drive straight in. He wanted to be sure there was no one around to see him; it had been enough of a risk to use the boy, and Eland wanted no more – no chance of a finger being pointed at him once the photos were taken and put to work.

After the last time, he'd vowed never to spend another day in prison. It had only been an eighteen-month stretch, but eighteen nasty months of persistent and painful sexual harassment by the harder inmates. Just thinking about it made him gag.

When he was sure there was no one around, he backed the trailer into the yard. Quickly, he grabbed a leading rope and a whippy plastic crop he had brought with him and went round to lower the trailer ramp. He clipped the rope on to the head collar which he had bought with the horse and unloaded it to lead it into the box he had identified over the phone.

But the horse had another plan. There was a paddock full of fairly fresh grass on the far side of the railings beside the trailer. He quickly slipped his head through and stretched down to chomp. Eland tugged hard but fruitlessly to bring the horse's head up. The horse moved its back end around, squeezing Eland against the fence.

''Ere, what're you doing?' Eland squealed in panic. He had experience of dominating only very small creatures. Letting out the rope, he began nervously to sidle past the horse's hefty quarters. Transferring the rope to his left hand, he raised the thin crop with his right and brought it down as hard as he could across the animal's back.

The cob was taken by surprise. He lashed out his rear offside leg. The freshly shod hoof caught Eland a glancing blow on the thigh.

'You fuckin' bastard,' Eland yelled and cut viciously

with the crop at the cob's flanks.

The horse had never known this kind of treatment. He tried to tug his head back through the railings, caught it for a moment before getting free, then jerked it up to loosen the rope from the man's grasp.

Eland, despite his terror, hung on. If he let the animal escape now, all his efforts at anonymity would be wasted. But the cob was several times stronger than he. It headed for the open space in front of the stables, dragging Eland behind. Eland stumbled, fell to the ground but hung on as the cob reached a concrete forecourt in the 'L' of the stable block. Here it checked and gave Eland time to get painfully to his feet, still clutching the rope and the whip in both hands. He rushed at the animal, snarling, with the crop raised.

When he was near enough, he laid about the animal's face and head with a manic, unrestrained force until the beast was backed into a corner, terrified. Then he stopped. The sudden outburst had left them both blowing heavily, Eland's eyes bulged and he began to sweat as he stood regaining control of himself.

The cob was frightened but submissively it consented to being led in through the open stable door of Eland's box. Eland secured the end of the rope to a ring on the wall, and stood back, well out of range of the horse's rear end.

'Right, you bastard. Don't you do that to me again,' he said, still panting slightly.

He stayed for a moment in the stable, listening for sounds of anyone outside. The house to which the stable block belonged was a hundred yards away. With luck, the fracas hadn't been noticed. When he was satisfied that no one had been alerted, he let himself out and walked swiftly back to the trailer. He heaved a bale of straw from the front of the box and dumped it outside the stable door, under cover of the overhanging roof. He filled a hay net and took it in. The cob snorted his appreciation and Eland surveyed his new purchase with wary satisfaction. It would serve its purpose next day, then he'd collect it and drive it straight to the knacker. He judged he should even make a profit out of it.

Next morning, clad in the khaki uniform of a countryman, he left the pick-up and trailer in a public parking place, and walked a mile to the yard. This time, he made very certain there was no one to see him before he slipped into the yard and let himself into the cob's box with the crop in his hand.

The horse, still tethered, sidled away from him and set back his ears. Eland swished his crop through the air. 'That's right, my son, you know who's boss now, don't you?'

He walked across, plucked the hay net from its hook on the wall, went out to refill it and brought it back in.

Once the horse was busy munching in the corner, Eland settled down beside the door, like a spider waiting for a fly.

From the pocket of his khaki jacket he pulled a single black nylon stocking.

From his other pocket, he took a large wad of cotton wool and a small bottle of chloroform.

Prepared, he clambered up between the wooden roof trusses of the stable.

Eland heard the car pull off the road into the top of the

track. His face twitched and he lifted the stocking to his head and pulled it over, stretching it down to his neck. He unscrewed the top of the bottle and tipped most of the contents on to the wad of cotton wool.

Instinctively, all his muscles tensed to spring.

The car's engine was turned off. A door slammed with an expensive-sounding clunk. Firm footsteps crossed the concrete apron of the yard, hesitated a moment as the box was identified.

A moment later, the light from the open upper door was obscured. The bolt was drawn back.

Eland held his breath as the door opened and he saw his victim in the flesh for the first time.

Laura had phoned Rory at the weekend and asked him to come to Langlands at ten on Tuesday morning, in time to go out with the second lot.

A morning mist was beginning to lift to reveal a pale, low sun as Rory drove south to the Hampshire hills. He had heard about the spectacular private gallops at Langlands, and he looked forward to seeing them. And each mile closer he came, the more he realised how much he was looking forward to seeing Laura.

Rory arrived early. He took the back drive to the yard and parked his own car among the lads' old Capris and rusting pick-ups behind the main block. He spent a moment admiring the architecture of the place and the details – the corbelling and old roof tiles – which might have been specified for a high-grade private house.

The first lot was coming back to the yard as he walked in. He was impressed with the quality and condition of the horses as they walked past him into the yard. He also noticed how unusually clean and tidy the lads looked – each in matching dark blue cap and jacket.

Following the horses in a long Land Rover was Patrick, the head lad. He jumped down from the vehicle and walked across to Rory with his hand stretched out and a broad smile on his face.

''Morning, Rory. And it's a pleasure to see you here.'

Rory took the Irishman's hand and shook it. He knew who Patrick was, of course, but he didn't know him. His instinct was to like him, but he had been disappointed too often by Irishmen with more charm than scruples.

'Lovely yard you keep here,' Rory said.

'Thanks. I helped Mrs Mundy with the planning of it, so she always blames me if something doesn't work,' he laughed. 'But it's worth it. Now, I was to tell you that you're riding Midnight Express up to the gallops. You're to go with Declan on Jimmy – that's Flamenco Dancer. Hack up the shavings gallop and then let him stride along for five furlongs on the grass. Declan will look after you, and you look after the horse; he's the best we've got.'

Rory smiled at the Irishman's enthusiasm.

'Isn't Mrs Mundy coming down herself?'

'She will be on the gallops and she said you're to have breakfast with her after, up at the house.'

'I see. Is Dai Price here this morning?'

Patrick gave half a smile. 'He is not.'

Feeling a discontent at not seeing Laura which he didn't want to admit, Rory was legged up by Midnight Express's lad and followed the first two horses out of the yard and on to the green lane that zigzagged through the oak woods up the steep hanger.

Declan was Patrick Hoolihan's twenty-three-year-old son. He had started at Langlands five years before, with a little persuasion from his father. At first, as an apprentice, he had become a competent horseman, but seemed to lack the competitive edge that would turn him into an effective jockey. He still held a licence and Laura gave him the occasional ride in a race, though it was two seasons since he'd had a win. Philosophically, and without rancour, he had accepted that he was never likely to make the grade, and now put all his energy into getting to know and schooling the horses of which he had particular charge.

Now racing was Declan's life. He had happily settled for a job in a good yard with a lovely cottage which he could never have bought himself. It was also a yard where he felt appreciated. Although his race riding ambitions had come to nothing, he took a lot of pride in the ability he had developed to judge at an early stage which horses had any real talent. Using this knowledge, he liked to bet, and he was one of the few who made it pay.

As they approached the bottom of the all-weather gallop, he turned to Rory.

'That's the best horse you'll ever sit on,' he said with complete conviction. 'He'll try to run off for the first twenty yards, but if you just ride him on a long rein and sit quietly, he'll settle; then you can do what you want with him.'

Rory nodded, confident of Declan's advice.

'Just sit ten lengths behind me,' Declan went on. 'We'll pull up after the bend.'

Laura's gallop man stood at the bottom of the all-weather track, leaning on a long-handled divot fork. Midnight Express used his presence as an excuse to whip round to his right, and almost drop Rory in the mud. Declan, seeing it, grinned at Rory, now back in the saddle.

'I forgot to tell you,' he said. 'He can drop his shoulder when he's feeling well.'

There was nothing lads liked more than to see jockeys fall off.

Rory smiled back. 'Funny with kids, I expect.'

Midnight Express behaved just as Declan had said he would. Once he had settled into his stride, Rory began to appreciate that he was sitting on something special. The horse was cantering as effortlessly as if he were out for a walk.

Rory pulled up quietly behind Flamenco Dancer. His horse squealed with well-being as he patted him on the neck.

'What a tool this is!' he shouted to Declan.

'Wait until you let his head go on the grass; then you'll know what he's all about.'

In the ten minutes it took to walk back to the bottom of the gallop, Declan filled Rory in with everything he knew about Midnight Express's likes and dislikes. It seemed, as the stable favourite, there wasn't much the horse wasn't allowed. He liked, for instance, to be let loose during evening stables to graze on the lawn in front of the yard – a privilege granted to none of the other inmates at Langlands.

When they reached the bottom of the slope, Declan's conversation reverted to the job in hand.

'I won't be able to lay up with you for long when we turn in, so just let him run along on the bridle in his own time. Then pull up just after you've passed the boss.'

It occurred to Rory that Laura must have immense confidence in her staff; although he had seen her in the distance at the top of the gallop, she still hadn't spoken to him.

He wheeled his horse around on to the grass gallop.

For the next fifty seconds, he experienced a feeling he hadn't had for so long that he'd almost forgotten it.

Power, balance, comfort, control – Midnight Express had everything, even brakes.

They flew past Laura and the small group with her at the top, before Rory slowly eased back to a walk. He headed for home as he'd been instructed and let his thoughts dwell exuberantly on the prospect of his ride at Cheltenham.

Half a mile from home, Rory loosened his girth, ran his irons up the leathers and hopped lightly to the ground. He led Midnight Express the last part of the journey, allowing some air under the horse's saddle to cool him off.

Back in the yard, he let him pick grass for a minute or so until a lad came to take over.

'How'd he go?' the lad asked.

'Incredible, once he settled. Do you do him?'

'No, Declan does. I just help when he's busy.'

'He looks great,' Rory encouraged him.

Patrick had walked over to join them.

'Everything okay, Rory?' The two enthused over the horse for a while until Patrick told the lad to put him back in the box. 'D'you know your way up to the house? It's straight out of the yard and up the avenue. You can't miss it,' he laughed. 'And use the front door.'

Rory thanked him and walked out of the yard to collect his car. He felt a vague uneasiness that he hadn't spoken to Laura yet. He had expected her to have come down from the gallops by the time he'd ridden back. Still, she'd asked him to breakfast. He hoped – though it was a lot to expect – that there wouldn't be anyone else there.

At the house, the Filipino maid who had served the Chinese dinner the week before showed him into an empty room with a big round table laid for breakfast for an indeterminate number. It was a large, softly decorated room, lit by a pair of French windows which gave on to a broad flagged terrace and semi-formal gardens beyond. Even with only clusters of snowdrops and a few early roses to brighten it, it was still an exceptionally lovely view.

Rory walked across to a sideboard where a coffee percolator gave off a seductive aroma. He filled a big French cup and walked across to look out of the window.

He didn't hear Laura come in.

He was lifting the cup to his lips when she spoke.

'Hi, Rory.'

An involuntary jerk of his hand spilt a little coffee down his chin. He turned and smiled ruefully, reaching for a napkin from the middle of the table.

'Sorry, you gave me a start.'

Laura was looking as fresh as she had the last time he'd seen her, wearing a large Arran sweater and a loose-fitting pair of Levis. Her long black hair was gathered up in a grip at the back of her head and the pile of folders and papers she carried made her look incongruously businesslike.

'I hope Express didn't,' she said.

'No. Declan told me how to ride him and he was fine.'

'He settles better for you than Dai.'

'Who doesn't?' Rory grinned.

'Who indeed?' Laura said meaningfully.

Rory didn't answer.

There was, he had already noticed, something slightly reserved about Laura's manner compared with the way she had said goodbye to him five days before.

'Sorry,' she said. 'That was meant to be funny. Have I put you off your food?'

'I only want coffee and a wee slice of toast anyway.'

'Help yourself. Patrick and Henry Straker will be here soon.'

She poured herself some coffee and sat in the nearest chair. Rory followed her lead and placed himself opposite her.

'So, what do you think about the Champion?' she asked.

'Provided the ground doesn't come up like a bog, he must have a great chance. But what about these hunter chases – are you going to run in them too?'

'No way,' Laura laughed. 'If we have to, we'll induce a temporary condition that will convince the vet he can't go. He's had corns on his feet before.'

'That's a bit risky, isn't it? Wouldn't the vet just veto him if you asked?'

'Not Henry Straker. He's as straight as a die, and Luke

knows that, so he won't quibble.'

'The only problem I've got,' Rory said, 'is that I've just been asked to ride one of the Irish horses – a bit long in the tooth, but he might have a squeak. It's not a great race this year, you know.' Laura was going to interject, but Rory went on, 'But provided your horse doesn't go to Kempton or Sandown, of course I want to ride him – who wouldn't? How did Dai take it when you told him?'

'Someone else had already told him. He's not too happy, but I said Luke had insisted, and even Dai wouldn't argue with Luke.' She laughed. 'Luke actually talked about riding him himself at Cheltenham. If he wasn't so bloody vain, he would, but even he realises he'd just make a fool of himself if he did.'

The big panelled oak door to the room swung open. Midas the yellow labrador trotted in, followed by a tall man in his mid-forties with an air of great dependability and strong blue eyes of amiable directness. He wore a pair of slightly furry cavalry twill trousers, a houndstooth tweed jacket and a BFSS tie. Rory recognised the Jockey Club's Chief Veterinary Officer, Henry Straker, well respected and universally liked by the racing community – a rare distinction. He had a boyish sense of humour but he had won the Jockey Club's utter confidence in the High Court recently. He had appeared for them in a case against an owner who had contested the validity of their blood analysis. If Henry Straker had failed, racing's rulers would have lost not only a vast sum of money, but also, more importantly, their credibility, then under serious scrutiny.

''Morning, Laura, Rory,' he greeted them warmly

'Gosh, that bacon smells good.'

"Morning, Henry. Help yourself,' Laura invited.

'I wish I could, but I haven't got time. If you could just let me have a list of the horses you want tested, I'll go and get on with it.'

Laura handed him a sheet of paper from the pile beside her. 'Here you are. Sorry you can't stay.'

'I've got the results of the last tests in my car. They're all normal. Shall I leave them in your office?'

'Yes, if you would. Not that they'd mean anything to anyone besides a vet.'

'You're right. Anyway, nice to see you, Rory. I hope Laura's going to give you plenty of rides. 'Bye.'

He left the room with his long, busy stride.

When the door had closed behind him, Laura said, 'He doesn't think much of my stable jockey.'

'I wonder why,' Rory laughed.

Laura didn't. 'Henry thinks he's bent, but I don't agree. He hasn't stopped any horses I've wanted or expected to win.'

'Maybe he's more of a craftsman than you realise. There are all sorts of strokes you can pull.'

Laura glanced at him. For a moment in her eyes there was a hint of the old haughtiness. 'I have learned by now to recognise when a jockey isn't trying.'

'Maybe, but it's a lot easier than you think.'

'How do you know? Have you done it?'

'What do you think?' Rory was indignant.

Laura looked at him for a second or two, then smiled. 'Probably not.'

'And I won't, ever.'

'All right, I admit, I am worried about Dai. But I can't give him the elbow without a plausible reason, and he's still giving some of the horses a good ride.'

'Why does Henry think he's crooked?'

'I don't know. He's never mentioned any particular horse or race. You know what he's like – he's a good man and unbelievably honest. He adores horses and racing and just hates the idea of anyone cheating.'

'You've got to admire him for it,' Rory said.

'And the way he's handled his own personal disasters.'

'What disasters?'

'You know. His two little boys were killed in that car crash – three and five, I think they were – a couple of years ago.' Rory suddenly remembered, their mother was driving, and was so badly injured she was unable to have any more children. Henry had been absolutely devastated. Laura continued, 'I spoke to him about it a while ago; he said he still thinks about them every single day. His wife hasn't really got over it – Henry says she's still racked with guilt – but he's determined to pull them through it. He's really thrown himself into running the boys' club in Reading and has done brilliantly with it. Their soccer team's been winning everything. They're his pride and joy now.'

Rory nodded, and thought of Tommy. 'Yes, of course; I had heard about it.'

The door swung open again, and Patrick walked in.

'Hello, Patrick,' Laura greeted him. 'Grab a chair.'

'I will,' he said but walked over to the sideboard first.

'Now,' Laura said, 'Rory's worried about Luke riding Midnight Express in this hunter chase, so we'll have to make sure he's off games for the day, and somehow we'll have to get Henry to confirm it.'

Patrick grinned. 'I was hoping you'd say that. Leave it to me. There's a lot of stable money on him already for the Champion Chase, and I'd hate to see the lads miss their spring bonus.'

The Irishman poured himself a large cup of coffee and sat down next to Rory.

'I suppose you want your usual fry-up, Pat?' Laura asked.

Patrick nodded. 'I do. Thank you. This is the best part of my job.' The Irishman winked at Rory then turned to tell Laura that her assistant trainer had gone to oversee the blood tests.

Laura stood up and pressed a buzzer above the side-board. When the maid had taken her instructions, Laura sat once more, looking across the table at the jockey.

'Patrick and I,' she said to Rory, 'would really like you to ride every horse in the yard. That's not possible yet, but there are quite a few where I can say the owner wants you. If we run through their entries for the next few weeks, you can tell me which you can do.'

Rory drove away from Langlands with the fullest diary he'd had for a long time, and a feeling of emptiness.

That morning there had been none of the intimacy of the previous week's Chinese dinner. But after all, they had been talking business. Rory had to console himself with the knowledge that he had deprived Dai Price of a few good rides. He also felt that he had gone some way to justifying his decision at the beginning of that season to do without the services of an agent to fix his rides. At least when he fixed his own, he always knew exactly what he was taking on.

He picked up the A303 at Andover and headed for Wincanton thinking of the time when he and Laura had been together.

As he drove his Rover into the westerly wind towards the Somerset racecourse, he knew with certainty and misgiving that everything he had ever felt for Laura, and more, had been revived; it was already too late to reverse the process if it turned out that all she wanted was a replacement for a stable jockey who had lost her trust and his nerve.

In a haze of anger at this lack of control over his emotions, Rory produced two winners from three moderate horses. On both he was brave to the point of foolishness at the tricky downhill fence before the straight. But the risk paid off; it was always hard to peg horses back once you had them running from there.

Later that evening at home, he grudgingly told Pam about the improvement in his prospects for the rest of the season, knowing that the irony that Laura should be the provider of this bounty had eluded neither of them.

Chapter Four

At twelve thirty on the day that Luke Mundy was due to ride Midnight Express in the Thames Land Trophy, Laura turned her Mercedes into the owners' and trainers' car park at Kempton. She was feeling guilty and irritable. She hadn't told Rory that the horse was still running and she hadn't worked out exactly what she was going to do.

Patrick hadn't been happy either when she'd announced that the horse was going to run. She knew as well as he did that they were throwing away their chances in the Champion Chase by asking Midnight Express to do two races so soon before it at a distance he didn't like.

Irresolute and uncertain, she parked her car. She was jerked out of her thoughts by a loud blast on the horn of the car that had pulled up beside her. She looked across to see George Rutherford grinning at her with his thick lips. By the time she had got out, he was beside her, offering her a camel-hair-clad arm.

'I hear you didn't want your husband to ride today,'

Rutherford said blandly. 'Don't you think he'll win?'

'Frankly, he should piss it,' Laura said with deliberate coarseness. 'But that's not the point. He joined the TA and kept up his fourteen-days-a-year service just so he could ride in the Grand Military next week, but he has to enter this one as well – and why the hell ride this horse? He's got four others he could have gone round on. He just wants to be absolutely certain of winning. I think he loathes the idea of having to give all that prize money to somebody else.'

'So you think I ought to have a bit on him?'

'That's up to you. You won't get much of a price, though. I think he's had a big one on himself.'

'Has he indeed?' Rutherford seemed interested. 'Then I think I'll back his judgement, though I must say, there are a few malicious rumours going around about his lack of judgement in other areas,' he added softly, without any particular rancour.

Laura glanced at him. 'So you said the other day, but I don't think he's suffering any more than anyone else in this recession.'

'I sincerely hope not, for your sake.' Rutherford paused to look at her meaningfully. 'But I must tell you, if you ever did find that Luke was forced to sell up, I'd be more than willing to help you out. I'm delighted with the results you've given me so far.'

He had made this suggestion before. Laura had been hoping he might have been able to flesh out the rumours he had hinted at, but she suspected they only related to whatever bad experience Rutherford had had in his dealings with her husband over the Chelsea casino. His desire to take Luke's place as her backer was probably motivated by bruised macho pride as much as anything else. But she was sure the offer would stand, and that was comforting to know.

Laura was still, reluctantly, on Rutherford's arm as they walked towards the weighing room. She extracted herself as subtly as she could when she saw Henry Straker striding briskly towards her.

''Morning, Laura; 'morning, Mr Rutherford,' he said with a professional politeness which showed no distinction between those he liked and those he did not. 'I need to have a word with you, Laura.'

Rutherford gave no sign of leaving their company.

'Would you mind awfully if I had a chat with Mrs Mundy alone?' Henry asked.

'No, of course not,' Rutherford said smoothly with a smile. 'I'll leave you to it.' He walked off, parting the crowd before him, towards the stand.

The vet was looking worried.

'What's the matter, Henry?' Laura asked.

'I'm not sure. Something rather odd has come up. I received a call in the office a few moments ago telling me that your horse had been got at.'

'What!' Laura couldn't contain the shock in her voice. She wanted to ask a question, but the vet continued.

'It's probably just a hoax. I've spoken to the stewards and we've agreed it's most likely that somebody's trying to get him withdrawn. They don't want a big fuss. I mean, it could set a terrible precedent. So they've asked me to take a blood sample, then let the horse run provided we're both happy that he looks all right. Of course we

81

won't have the results of the test for a week or two, though I dare say they'll rush it through faster if anything sinister happens. Either way, you're perfectly in the clear.'

'I'm glad to hear it. But I don't see how anyone could have got at him. There should have been a lad with him all the time since early morning and surely he'd be showing signs if he'd been doped before then.'

'Well, I'm sure you're right, it's almost certainly nothing but I've still got to take this test. The Jockey Club security man has to be present, of course; I'm meeting him over at the stables in a few minutes.'

'Okay.' Laura spoke in a way that implied she was more than a little concerned about the news she'd just received. 'I'm just going to check he's been declared, then I'll come down to make sure he's all right.'

'I'll need to examine him thoroughly,' Henry said. 'I must give the Stewards my honest opinion. After all, you do see what could happen if we don't let him run? The next time these people want to stop a favourite, they know they only have to make a phone call.'

'Yes,' Laura sighed, 'I do see that.'

Ron Rowland, the Jockey Club security officer, had left the Met. ten years before, but he had retained the speech habits and mannerisms of a policeman. Outwardly, it was only his checked tweed suit that now set him apart from his former colleagues.

Henry Straker found him standing outside Midnight Express's box chatting to Declan Hoolihan.

Straker and Rowland nodded at one another in recognition of their official positions.

'So how does he seem?' Henry asked as Declan pulled back the stable door.

'Pretty normal; a bit on edge maybe, but then he knows where he is.'

'Stick a head collar on him and trot him up for me, would you?'

The lad had to take off the muzzle which Midnight Express was wearing to stop him eating his bed. He took him outside and jogged the horse twenty-five yards up the tarmac and back again.

Henry Straker stroked his chin. 'He looks bright enough to me. Let's have him back inside.'

Ron Rowland followed Straker into the stable and stood with his back to the door.

The short burst of exercise had made Midnight Express come to life. He fidgeted while the vet looked into the corners of his eyes.

'They look normal,' Straker declared as he went to get his bag from the doorway. 'I'll just take his temperature and some blood, and that'll do.'

Midnight Express resented having a thermometer pushed into his rear end. He rushed his hind quarters over to the other side of the stable.

Once he and Declan had managed to settle the horse enough to get the job done, the vet had difficulty in reading the result. 'Bloody thermometers! Why don't they colour the mercury so you can see it properly?' After a few moments' scrutinising it at different angles, he announced, 'A hundred and one – normal.'

Extracting a blood sample from the horse seemed to be more difficult than taking his temperature.

'It's no good; we'll have to put a twitch on him,' Straker said testily.

While Declan kept a cord twisted tightly around the horse's top lip, Straker disappeared the other side of his head, where there was more room to work, to jab a needle into a vein in his neck.

He soon reappeared with two plastic tubes full of thick crimson fluid. 'Right, that'll do, lad.' He patted Midnight Express on the neck. To Declan, he said, 'Okay, you can let him down now. If you're at all worried about him, come and find me.'

Laura arrived as the vet was closing his bag.

'What's the verdict?' she asked.

'He looks perfectly all right to me,' Straker answered. 'Here's your phial of the blood sample; I'm sending this other one off straight away for analysis; I'm sure it'll be clean.'

Luke Mundy sat in the jockeys' changing room, quivering nervously. He'd had no trouble doing the weight this time; the mounting pressure on his business had made sure of that. The flesh had been falling off him and his face was drawn and dull. For the first time in his career, matters were beyond his control and the influence of his bullying charm.

The other jockeys, all amateurs, were for the most part too nervous themselves to notice the absence of Luke's normal boastful ebullience. When they were called into the parade ring, Luke went with the rest of them as if he were in a trance. He saw Laura's stony face in the centre of the circle and tried to put a spring in his stride as he crossed to her.

The closer they were to the race, the more Laura resented having her hand forced.

'I don't know why the hell you're doing this,' she hissed when he reached her. 'The horse is too good and you're not good enough.'

'I'm doing it for you, actually,' he replied.

'The day you do anything for anyone besides yourself will be the day the world stops turning.' Laura made no attempt to disguise her bitterness.

Luke ignored it. 'I heard the stewards asked for a dope test?'

'Yes. Henry had a phone call with a tip-off that he had been got at.'

'And it was negative?'

'I presume it will be. At least, Henry said he couldn't see anything wrong with him, otherwise the horse wouldn't be here, would he?'

Luke didn't need a lot of convincing. 'Thank God. I thought maybe . . .' He gazed around at the other owners and trainers.

'You thought maybe what?'

'Nothing. It's okay. Henry would never have let him run if he had any doubt.'

'No, you're right. He wouldn't. Frankly, I wish to God the horse *couldn't* run, so make sure you pull him up immediately if he's not feeling all right,' Laura pleaded.

'Look, Laura, winning this race means more than you'll ever know, so I just hope to hell you've done your job properly.' There was naked desperation in Luke's voice. Laura softened; she almost wanted to encourage him.

'I've done everything I can, despite the fact that I never wanted him to run. Whether he lasts three miles or not . . .

Well, you'll know sooner than me.'

Luke Mundy clenched his jaw and whispered, 'He'd fucking better.'

Rory Gillespie was looking down from the back of the members' stand.

He saw the horse and, numb with anger, glanced at his race card again. Of course it was on the card; Laura and Patrick had said they were only going to get it pulled out that morning. But they hadn't. What the hell was going on?

He glanced at the paddock again, looking for the jockey. He spotted the colours of red with orange disc and watched Luke walk into the parade ring with the other amateurs, and his blood seethed.

Rory shook his head, perplexed. Laura had been so adamant, when he'd talked to her about it, that Midnight Express wouldn't run; but there she was, legging up her arrogant pig of a husband to flog round in a race of little value to anyone except himself. The horse would never recover in time for the Champion Chase. Why the hell was she doing it?

It wasn't just the fact that Midnight Express was running that was hurting; it was the duplicity of the woman who had promised to keep the horse fresh for Cheltenham.

The jockeys were called to mount up and Rory watched in final disillusionment as Luke and Midnight Express were led on to the course. He saw Laura heading back towards the stands. Almost at a run, he hurried to catch her on the way to Luke's box.

He reached her at the top of the stairs. Still hoping for a logical explanation, he kept his voice calm.

'Hi. I thought you were going to miss this race?'

Laura looked embarrassed. 'I was. Come with me to the box and I'll tell you about it.'

'I haven't got time,' Rory lied. 'Tell me now.'

Laura glanced round to see if they were being listened to. Satisfied that they weren't, she said quietly, 'Look, don't worry. I'm still going to run him in the Champion, and he'll be all right. Luke won't give him a hard race.'

'What the hell's he running him for, then?'

'I'll explain it all to you afterwards, I promise, but I can't now, Rory.'

Rory shook his head and pretended to make light of what she was saying. 'Okay, but I don't like being told one thing, then seeing exactly the opposite going on.'

Laura touched his arm, seeking his trust and patience. 'You'll understand. But look, I've got to go and watch the race.' She gave his arm a quick squeeze, released it and turned to take the last flight of stairs to the top of the stand.

Rory looked after her for a moment, and tried to work out what he was feeling. Sighing, he decided to trust her, but angry doubts still crowded his mind. He walked back through the stand to the box of the owner for whom he had won the previous race and, against all his professional instincts, accepted another large tumbler of Scotch.

A gambler knows – or ought to know – that he has become an addict when, with only ten pounds in the world to his name, he is prepared to stake fifteen on the turn of a card, the spin of a ball or the result of a race.

Luke Mundy was in just that position, only playing for vastly greater stakes.

The confidence he had felt when he had struck the bet was deserting him, being replaced by an insistent doubt that perhaps he'd got it wrong. The effect of this doubt is one of the reasons why so many people like to bet – the sweaty palms, the tightening of the colon, the constant licking of the lips; gambling to lose all is a very efficient stimulator of adrenaline. But never does the gambler quite allow himself to consider what might happen if he loses; that would be sanity, and sane people wouldn't put themselves through this self-inflicted torture.

Luke wouldn't admit even to himself that, for him, this race was a matter of shit or bust.

'Fuck it! I *can't* get beaten! Think positive!' he urged himself as Declan led Midnight Express out on to the course. The lad grudgingly winked at him and wished him luck. Luke didn't reply.

Luke had ridden Midnight Express often enough. He knew how the horse liked to be treated. He knew about his idiosyncrasy when it came to being settled. He gave him a long rein and let him hack past the stands before pulling up and turning back to the three mile start, round the bend behind the water jump.

He tried but failed to push to the back of his mind the nagging thought that the horse might have been got at.

Maybe he was on a horse which couldn't win, no matter what he did.

But then, he reasoned, Henry Straker wouldn't have let the animal run if he hadn't been a hundred percent certain about it.

And Laura, he knew, would have withdrawn the horse at the slightest excuse.

He thought of the party with whom he'd struck the bet. Would they cheat? There was more than enough money at stake for most people to have considered it; but few people had any idea how to go about doping a racehorse in the conditions of security that now prevailed on British race courses. It was a lot more difficult than the general public realised.

Down at the start, a handler tightened Midnight Express's girth and surcingle before he slowly walked round with the five other runners, waiting for the starter to call them into line.

Up until that moment, Midnight Express had behaved quite normally, getting a little warm on his neck. But as Luke pulled down his goggles and jogged across towards the inside of the track, he knew something was wrong.

The horse would usually have been tugging his arms out in eagerness to get on with the race, and Luke should have been struggling in his amateurish way to get it settled. But Midnight Express felt alarmingly as if he didn't want to go anywhere.

They were under orders.

Would he lose the bet if he shouted 'No' to the starter and didn't race?

He didn't have time to decide. The sight and sound of the tapes jerking up suddenly brought the horse back to life. Luke's confidence returned with a surge as he felt his horse spring forward with the rest of the field.

Within five strides, he found himself in the lead and being run away with – just what he did not need.

Though he would never have accepted it, Luke's riding

ability was, at best, basic. He should have given the horse his head and let him settle in front; instead he tried to fight with him. He was still struggling to pull him back to the others when the first fence loomed.

Midnight Express got in close to it, going too fast to give himself time to tuck his front legs up beneath him. Luke braced himself as the horse hammered the fence. But, such was the animal's momentum, he parted the birch two feet from the top and carried on through. The unusually steep drop behind the fence caught him out and he pecked slightly as he landed.

Luke, still desperately trying to hold him up, had such a tight grip on the reins that when Midnight Express stretched his neck to recover his balance, the jockey was yanked forward and almost out of the saddle.

There was a split second when Luke thought he'd gone beyond the point of no return before his horse bobbed his head back and caught him full in the face.

Luke's terror momentarily subsided when he felt his feet in contact with the stirrup irons. In the next instant, his body balance was violently overcorrected by the speed of the horse galloping on. Midnight Express took a vicious tug in the mouth and Luke would have turned a backward somersault if he hadn't still had a limpet grip on the reins.

By the time he was balanced again, he'd lost all control of the horse. Midnight Express wasn't just running freely towards the next fence, he was bolting. Luke had never experienced this before; it was like careering downhill in a loaded lorry with no brakes or steering. Worse, the horse seemed unaware that it had anyone on its back. For the first time in his life, Luke knew raw fear.

He knew that something terrible was going to happen at any moment. But even in his terror, he knew what he should do and forced himself to do it. He sat as quietly as a nun and prayed to an unfamiliar God.

But Midnight Express galloped on as if he'd gone mad and would have run blindly into a brick wall if he'd met one.

Luke was too petrified even to think about bailing out, or the outcome of his bet.

Three strides before the next fence, he prepared himself for the inevitable shattering fall.

Miraculously, as if someone had tripped a switch, the horse suddenly regained his senses. He popped over the fence accurately as if that had always been the plan.

Luke heaved out the lungful of air he'd been holding in.

There were approximately three hundred yards before the next fence: an open ditch. It was just enough to get the horse settled.

Now the danger was past, Luke's thoughts quickly reverted to his bet. He was alive, his horse was running; there was still a good chance he could win.

He was almost back in control as they jumped easily over the ditch and began the long turn into the back straight. The ground here was well worn and rough on the inside from months of racing. Midnight Express faltered slightly as his feet adjusted to the new conditions. Luke grasped the chance to get him properly anchored. If the horse's erratic behaviour hadn't taken too much out of him, he could still win. The elation at having him settled lasted as long as it took to gallop the hundred yards to the apex of the bend.

When he reached it, Luke knew without any doubt that Midnight Express wouldn't be winning anything.

The absurd sickening sensation that only gamblers know surged through his body – a sensation of complete and utter hopelessness, failure and despair. And bubbling up beneath was a violent anger.

It was obvious even to Luke's limited experience that the horse had been drugged.

His tongue was hanging from the right-hand side of his mouth; his legs seemed to be made of rubber. Common sense and an instinct for self-preservation were screaming at Luke to pull up, but they were outvoted by a desperation to claw back the disastrous bet.

Reckless, vain hopes filled his head.

Just let him jump one more fence; maybe he's swallowed some mud, Luke pleaded.

Midnight Express stumbled in a patch of soft ground. With instinctive bravery, he tried to save himself, but he'd already lost control of his limbs. As his nose crashed into the soft turf, his big frame carried on rolling. His neck snapped.

Luke, still clutching at implausible hopes, felt the horse's legs buckle beneath him. The big, honest head dropped from his sight and the ground rushed up to meet him as he was catapulted from the saddle. His instincts bade him put out an arm to save himself, an instant too late. His helmet hit the ground like a cannon ball as the dead horse took its last, almost gentle turn on to him. The scissor action – the dread of all jockeys – snapped Luke's neck an inch below the base of his skull.

The release of death was longer coming to Luke than

it had been to his horse – several pain-racked seconds in which every nerve end in his body was rubbed raw. As he lay in paralysed agony, his only thoughts were of bitter hatred for the person he knew had been responsible for his fall.

He opened his eyes. An ambulanceman was leaning over him, telling him not to move. Luke struggled to open his mouth to speak.

The ambulanceman saw the jockey straining and tried to calm him. A soft, voiceless gasp escaped the white lips of the suffering man before he gave up and his head lolled to one side. No more breath came; eyes stared blankly across the damp turf.

Rory Gillespie, seeing it all from the nearby stands, couldn't stifle an outraged gasp at the sight of one of the nastiest falls he'd ever seen. Accidents on the flat, when one was least expecting them, were always the worst. If the jockey survived at all, he wouldn't be on the back of a horse for a very long time, unless he was owed a miracle.

Beside Luke, the horse, once a beautiful, highly tuned athlete of an animal, a personality in his own right, was now a motionless mount of so much skin and flesh. The rest of the field thundered past the stricken horse and jockey and on round the bend towards the next fence; they had a race to win.

Laura, not many yards from Rory in her husband's private box, uttered a horrified scream as Midnight Express crunched down on to Luke. She gripped the rail of the balcony to hold herself up as the blood drained from her face.

When it was obvious to all his guests that Luke Mundy was not going to get up, they looked at Laura with appalled embarrassment, guiltily putting down their drinks, uncertain now about accepting Luke's hospitality. A few moved towards her tentatively, offering comfort.

George Rutherford was the first to take control. 'Come on, Laura, I'll take you down to see what's happened. Let's hope they're both just winded.' He sounded genuinely concerned.

She stared at him for a moment, numb with horror, shaking her head. Wordlessly, she fled from the box and along the corridor to the stairs. Reaching the ground floor, she ran blindly through the bar at the west end of the stand, down the track where the horses walked to the course, and out on to the soft turf.

Her view of the prone horse and the smaller red and orange bundle beside it shook and juddered as she ran. She accepted a lift from the course doctor, who was already in radio contact with the St John's ambulancemen at the scene.

Laura felt tears streaming down her cheeks as the doctor solemnly said, 'All right,' into the handset, his eyes confirming what Laura had been dreading. 'I'm sorry but your husband's dead.' The doctor slowed the car and firmly clasped Laura's hand.

Henry Straker was climbing out of the duty Range Rover as they pulled up. They stood quietly as the field came round on the second circuit and were flagged around the bodies on the ground. Then Straker walked straight across to the horse and knelt beside it. He looked up at Laura and shook his head, tears of regret in his eyes. He stood and turned to the knacker who had arrived to remove the carcass.

'They'll want him up at Hawkshead,' he said quietly, 'for an autopsy. He's obviously died from a broken neck. Just tell them to check his heart. I'll get on to them later.'

Fred Willis, the knacker, nodded and started to sort out the winch in his trailer to get the horse out of sight and off the course as fast as possible. 'And treat him with some respect,' Straker added solemnly.

Laura stared, still not wanting to believe it, as the big bay body was dragged across the grass. Reluctantly she turned away and walked the few yards to her husband. Two St John's ambulancemen were lifting him on to a stretcher. They began to lay a blanket over him. When they dropped it gently over his face, she felt as if her stomach had been wrenched from her. And she was struck by the bizarre fact that she cared more about the man dead than she had when he was alive.

Before they picked up the stretcher, she knelt beside it and lifted back the blanket. She gazed at the familiar face, softened in death, and prayed that now he would be at peace in a way he never had been in life. She let the blanket fall back and stood up to find Patrick Hoolihan beside her.

'Is there anything I can do, ma'am?'

She looked at his weathered, dependable face.

'Yes. I'm going to go with Luke. Can you get my car and bring it to the hospital?'

'Of course.'

'The keys are in my Puffa, up in the box.'

Patrick nodded, then reached out and squeezed her

hand before taking a last look at Midnight Express in the trailer for his final journey and turning to go back to the stands.

'Would you like me to come with you?' Henry Straker asked.

She shook her head. 'Thanks, Henry, but I'll be all right. I know there's nothing I can do; I just want to be there and hear it confirmed.'

Midnight Express had started even-money favourite. The punters who had backed him, deprived of any further involvement in the race, carried on gazing at the flurry of activity around the dead horse.

Some – the regular racegoers and professionals – had a feeling that something just wasn't quite right about the way Midnight Express had performed. But then maybe the amateur jockey had simply got the horse upset. Most accepted it as one of those horrible, tragic accidents that happen from time to time in racing.

For Rory, there were too many questions that couldn't be ignored.

He was shocked by Luke Mundy's death, even though he hadn't known the man. It brought home to him bluntly the risks which he and every other jump jockey took each time they rode. But he had two more rides that afternoon.

By the time he had weighed in and changed after winning the last race of the day, he wasn't surprised to hear that Laura had gone.

He considered, then rejected the idea of driving straight to Langlands. Instead, he went home, confused and apprehensive. Luke Mundy was dead; so was Rory's best prospect for the Cheltenham Festival.

As a matter of course, Luke Mundy's crushed body was taken to the hospital in Esher which had seen a hundred broken jockeys pass through its doors. Laura listened in silence as a registrar told her that her husband had died of a broken neck. He would – the doctor said – have died very quickly. The hospital staff were justly proud that few left the way Luke Mundy did, in an undertaker's van.

With rather less ceremony, the body of Luke's horse was driven off the course. Unlike most of the equine victims of the race-track, Midnight Express's last journey was not to the abattoir. Fred Willis had to fulfil a contract with the Royal Veterinary College's pathology lab at Hawkshead in Potters Bar, and this horse would require an autopsy.

His order was for a fresh carcass of a horse killed while racing. The consultant pathologist and his students were studying the effects of trauma on an animal's organs.

At the service doors of the college labs, two porters and the knacker expertly winched the half-ton carcass into a cavernous cold store, and Professor Douglas, the head of the pathology department, was phoned with the good news.

The morning after Midnight Express fell and killed Luke Mundy, the back pages of the papers gave the event full coverage.

The Jockey Club had confirmed the rumour that before the race the stewards had received a tip-off that Midnight Express might have been doped. They had ordered a pre-race sample to be taken and tested. In the light of the fatal accident, that test had been processed without the normal delay of ten to fourteen days and the results were expected to be announced shortly. It was also reported that the duty vet who had inspected the horse before the race had given his view that there was nothing wrong with the horse before it raced.

For many people, the reason for Midnight Express's unusual behaviour became obvious; towards the front of the papers, other aspects of the event were being considered.

The flamboyant 'Lucky' Luke Mundy, it was reported, had timed his demise well. It had just been revealed that Thames Land, the development company he controlled, had substantially defaulted on major loans. A mole at a crisis meeting of the remainder of the board the previous evening had supplied the information that their assets, conservatively valued, fell short of their liabilities by several hundred million pounds. After Canary Wharf and other spectacular failures of large property companies, it wasn't an uncommon sort of story, but Luke's picture, with his famous, macho grin as he held high yet another racing trophy, added an extra dimension to it.

Rory drove down to Lambourn to buy the papers as soon as the shop in the High Street opened at six-thirty. He tried to eat his breakfast, but his system wasn't taking in food. He wanted to believe what he was reading, that what had happened the day before was a simple, though tragic matter of a tired horse stumbling. But every line of thought led him back to the probability that there was more to it than that.

He went out to ride work in the last lot for one of the local trainers. As he rode out, and that afternoon, driving to Worcester, he couldn't rid himself of his doubts about Laura. He scarcely noticed he'd ridden a winner and two thirds.

Driving home, twice he picked up his mobile phone and dialled the number at Langlands. Both times, he failed to push the 'send' button.

Three days later, after a weekend that seemed to have stretched itself into a fortnight, Laura received a telephone call from the Jockey Club.

She was alone in her study at Langlands, staring out at the wet afternoon.

'Could I speak to Mrs Mundy, please?'

'Speaking.'

'This is Major Caswall from Portman Square.'

Laura tried to disguise her anxiety. 'Oh good,' she said. 'Have you got the results?'

'Yes, I'm glad to say we have. We've had the sample taken from Midnight Express analysed and there are no irregularities.'

Laura let out a gasp of relief. 'You mean it was clean?'

'Yes. No problem there at all. I thought I'd let you know right away, what with all the ghastly speculation there's been in the gutter press.'

Laura composed herself. 'Thank you very much indeed. That's great news.'

'I thought it might be. I'm posting you a copy of the lab report; you'll have it in the morning.'

With a brisk, though not unfriendly, 'goodbye' Major Caswall rang off.

Laura held the phone to her ear for a few moments, listening to the hum on the open line. After a moment, she pressed the plunger to get a dialling tone. Slowly, she punched out Rory's number. She reached the last digit, allowed her finger to hover over it, and, with a shrug of regret, cleared the line and dialled Patrick Hoolihan at the yard.

Professor Ewan Douglas tried not to gloat over his unexpectedly fine carcass. He was not interested in the sport of horse racing, but he was passionately interested in the physiology of the animals which took part. Very often, when he came into contact with them, they had died carrying little fat, at the peak of their fitness; they were fine specimens to handle.

The blood in the vessels of this animal – killed on course, not in an abattoir – was coagulated and of no autoptical value. But there were plenty of other fluids and secretions to examine.

Carefully he oversaw the dissection, removal and isolation of the animal's internal organs. He instructed a group of three of his students to carry out a detailed analysis of the contents of the animal's bladder.

'As you know, we can tell a lot about the condition of a mammal from the state of its urine. That's why the first thing you're asked to do in a medical is to pee in a jar,' Professor Douglas announced as he inspected the bottle of thick yellow fluid before handing it over to his students.

The professor walked back into the lab after lunch. The

two students – a man and a girl – detailed to analyse the horse's urine looked up excitedly.

'How are you getting on, then?' he asked.

'Well,' the girl said, 'the specific gravity seems low.'

Their professor nodded. 'Within reason, that's what you'd expect – a direct result of a high level of exercise. Nothing odd there. What else have we found?'

'Well, sir,' the young man ventured eagerly, 'it seems rather odd in a horse that's just come off the racecourse, so maybe I've got it wrong, but I thought I found traces of a pre-med.'

'That sounds more than odd; it sounds bloody impossible. But what exactly do you think you've found?'

'Well, er, I *think* it's xylazine.'

'Do you now? I don't think it can be. You'd better run your tests again in the morning.'

After they had gone, Professor Douglas carried out a series of his own tests.

Jim Knight, the official whose job it was to arrange the acquisition of appropriate animals, dead and alive for the lab, had gone home. Professor Douglas badgered the college switchboard into giving him the man's home telephone number, wrote it carefully in his diary and drove home to Barnet. On the way, as was his habit, he bought an *Evening Standard* from a paperboy at the lights on the Great North Road.

By the time he had settled down in his small tobacco-smelling study, he reckoned Jim Knight would have arrived at his home in Richmond and telephoned him.

'Hello, Mr Knight. It's Professor Douglas here. I'm sorry to trouble you at home, but I've rather a particular enquiry about the horse that was delivered at the weekend.'

'Yes?'

'Yes. I wondered if you could tell me the horse's name, and where it died?'

'Good heavens, I'm afraid that's not the sort of thing I normally carry in my head. I've got all the details in the office. As you know, we're required to do a partial autopsy on the animal. All I can tell you off the top of my head is that it fell while racing and broke its neck. I can tell you the rest tomorrow.'

'I need to know tonight, please.'

He could almost hear the resigned shrug at the other end of the line. 'I suppose I could ring Willis from here. I've got his number.'

'Who's Willis?'

'The knacker who usually supplies us with equine carcasses.'

'I'd be most grateful if you would, and let me know right away, as much as you can.'

The professor gave the man his telephone number and wished him a polite goodbye. He walked to the gramophone in the corner of his study, put on a record of Bruckner's Third Symphony, and sat in a large armchair to light his pipe and open the *Evening Standard*.

After he had read the front page, he started to leaf on to the arts section when his eye was caught by a small half-column.

The piece was following up the speculation that had been provoked about the plight of Thames Land Plc in the wake of Luke Mundy's death. And Luke Mundy, he read, had been killed after a fall on his horse at Kempton in an amateur race the previous week.

It was the final edition of the paper, published late enough to include the news that the blood sample taken from the horse before the race had now been analysed and found free of any introduced substances.

Professor Douglas read the piece again, then got up to fetch his battered briefcase from the hall where he'd left it.

In his chair once more, he pulled out the notes he had made of his readings and conclusions on the analysis of the horse's urine and shook his head with pleasurable excitement.

The telephone beside him rang. He picked it up unhurriedly.

'Professor Douglas?'

'Speaking.'

'Knight here. I got hold of Willis. He knew right away what the animal was called. Apparently it died in a fairly dramatic fall.'

The professor broke in. 'And it was called Midnight Express.'

'You knew anyway?' Knight sounded tetchy.

'Not when I last spoke to you, but I've been reading the evening paper since. Thank you for confirming it. I'm most grateful.'

He replaced the receiver, then stood and turned down the strident brass chords of the third movement before consulting the directory and picking up the phone again to dial.

'Hello. Is that racecourse security? . . . My name is Professor Douglas, from the Royal Veterinary College,

Hawkshead. I'd like to speak to whoever's in charge, please ... Good evening. I've just read a report in the paper about the horse, Midnight Express, which fell and died last week ... I see that a blood sample that was taken before the race has been declared by the Jockey Club to be free from any introduced substances. Is that right? ... I see. Well, the carcass of this animal was delivered to our labs, and we started work on it today. Our preliminary analysis of the urine shows clearly that the horse died with significant traces of the drug xylazine in its system. This is not what actually caused death, but there is no question that it would have affected the horse's performance very radically ... Yes, I'd say that whoever introduced it could be held responsible for its fall, and therefore its rider's death.'

Two men called at Langlands that evening. Ron Rowland, the head of security at Kempton, and Detective Inspector Stuart Wood announced themselves soberly to the small Filipino woman who opened the door to them.

'Is Mrs Laura Mundy at home?' the policeman asked.

'Sure. I get her for you.'

The maid ushered them into the sixteenth-century hall and scuttled up the stairs to find her mistress.

Laura came down looking tired but resigned. She had been to the stables that day, but hadn't been able to face going racing – not to anyone's great surprise.

She recognised Ron Rowland from Kempton.

'Hello. What can I do for you?' she asked.

'Good evening, Mrs Mundy.' Ron Rowland knew her

face well. 'We're sorry to have to trouble you at a time like this, but I'm afraid it's come to light that there are circumstances surrounding your husband's death that lead us to suspect foul play.'

Laura looked blank for a moment. 'I'm sorry? You mean you think it was planned in some way?'

'We've got new information that makes it look that way.'

'I don't see how. It was just Luke and the horse out there. And we know the horse went off all right. Portman Square have already phoned me to say the blood test had shown up negative.'

'I'm afraid subsequent tests on the carcass of the horse have shown otherwise,' the policeman said.

'What do you mean?' Laura asked indignantly. 'You were there when the sample was taken.' She looked at Rowland.

'Please, don't get upset, Mrs Mundy,' the security officer said. 'But the lab which carried out the autopsy found traces of a drug in the animal's urine.'

'What drug?'

'Xylazine.'

'That shows in the urine?' Laura asked with surprise. 'But it's used as a pre-med; it would knock a horse out completely.'

'That would depend on the size of the dose, of course,' the policeman said. 'So you can see that we do need to ask you a few questions. Is there somewhere convenient?'

Laura glanced at him with annoyance. She had always disliked pompous officials. 'What's wrong with here?' She waved the two men to a large Knole sofa in front of the great empty fireplace.

Ron Rowland smiled gratefully. 'After you,' he said, gesturing at a chair opposite.

Laura walked across and flopped into it under sufferance. Rowland and the detective inspector perched themselves on the front edge of the deep sofa.

The detective was a tall, lean man with lank brown hair falling over his forehead. He wore a thick patterned pullover beneath a drab grey anorak. He looked more like a schoolmaster than a policeman. But there was a restlessness in his eyes that gave him a furtive, faintly hostile look to anyone whom he was questioning, however innocent he thought them.

Having got this far in the proceedings, he evidently considered that Rowland had served his purpose and took no further notice of him.

'Can you tell me who was with the horse from the time Mr Rowland and the official vet . . .' he glanced at the notebook he had pulled from his pocket '. . . Mr Straker left?' The policeman subjected Laura to an intense scrutiny as he asked the question.

Laura glared back at him. 'Am I right in thinking that you think *I* might have had something to do with this?'

'You're right in thinking that I think somebody must have got at the horse between the time the blood test was taken and when it reached the course. Unless, of course, it was trained to inject itself.'

Rowland winced.

Laura stood up. 'I'm sorry, I have absolutely no intention of answering questions on the basis that I am a suspect. I will tell you this, though. The whole time, from the moment Henry Straker left the stable, there were at least two people with the horse. Either myself, Declan Hoolihan, his lad, Terry, the travelling head lad, or Pat Hoolihan, my head lad who had come to the races for the day . . . to watch Midnight Express run. He was a bit of a favourite in the yard, and the best horse I've ever bloody trained.' Rowland turned his eyes away from the sight of tears in her eyes. The policeman continued to gaze at her superciliously. 'And you come here suggesting that I might have given him the drug which killed him!'

Detective Inspector Wood didn't blink. 'It wasn't the drug that killed it, Mrs Mundy. That just slowed it down, anaesthetised it a little. It died by breaking its neck when it fell.'

Laura glared at him with irritation. 'I know that! I was there when he was winched on to the trailer. You know perfectly well what I mean! Now, if you want to talk to me again, you can make an appointment and my solicitor will be present. I've heard about what you people can do when you've made up your mind you've got a culprit.'

The detective shrugged his shoulders to imply that Laura was being very foolish, and stood up. 'If that's the way you want it, Mrs Mundy. I take it you've no objection if I question some of your staff?'

'I don't suppose I could stop you if I wanted to, but just don't give them a hard time. They've taken it extremely badly. When you've lavished a lot of care and time on a horse like Midnight Express, you feel it when they go. It's like losing a close friend.' She turned and walked back towards the stairs. 'You can see yourselves out.'

'We'll just have a brief word with your maid before we

go,' the policeman said and nodded his colleague towards
the nether regions of the house where he guessed the
little Filipino was to be found.

Maria was reading a Spanish magazine when they
walked into the kitchen. She put it down and leaped up
on her short legs.

'It's all right. No need to stand up. Mind if we join
you?'

The maid sat down. 'What you want?'

'Just to ask you a few questions about Mr Mundy, and
Mrs Mundy?'

'I don't know nothing.'

The two men smiled and sat down at the table
opposite her.

'Don't worry. All we want to know is how they got on.'

Maria looked blank.

'What I mean,' the policeman pressed, 'is whether you
ever heard them arguing.'

The maid looked back at them both for a moment
before she spoke. 'They argue,' she nodded. 'Some time,
he shout, *very* loud. And she too. He make her very
unhappy, I think.'

'Did he ever hit her or anything like that?'

Maria shook her head. 'I don't know. I never see.'

'But they used to argue a lot?'

She nodded. 'Very much.'

'What about?'

The little woman shook her head again. 'I no listen.'

The policeman smiled at her. 'Never mind. You've been
very helpful. If we have to come and see you again, try
to remember if you can recall anything you ever heard
them say, okay?'

The maid nodded glumly, aware that she had somehow betrayed her employer's trust, but more scared of this gimlet-eyed policeman.

The two men left silently. Laura heard the great oak front door clunk home behind them, and sighed. She'd handled them very badly, she knew, but she never had been able to control her temper.

The security officer and the policeman drove down to the stable yard. They were told by a small, tight-lipped Irishman that the horse's lad had been with him from the moment he left the yard that morning to go to the races until he had let him off on to the course to canter down to the start. The lad in question was Declan Hoolihan, the Irishman's son, and he could be found at the Axe and Cleaver.

There were half a dozen lads in the pub, sitting around a pool table. They had been there a few hours. One of the novice hurdlers in the yard had won earlier in the afternoon. It had come as no surprise to the lads, and the small bookmaker in Andover was cursing his lack of prudence in not laying off some of their bets.

But the celebration that would normally have followed a win like this was dampened by the death of the most popular horse in the yard. There wasn't one among them who didn't feel upset by what had happened; Declan, in particular, trying to drink away his depression, had become loud and maudlin.

He had just lost a game of pool when the two men walked in, looked around and came straight across to the bench where he sat banging the end of his cue on the wooden floor.

'You're not going to feel too good getting up for first lot tomorrow,' the racecourse security man remarked.

'What's it got to do with you?' Declan challenged, recognising him.

'Is this him?' the policeman asked.

'Yes. Declan, this is Detective Inspector Wood from Surrey CID. He'd like to talk to you about what happened at Kempton.'

Declan looked up sulkily. 'What for?'

'Because your father told us you were with the horse the whole time until he raced and we need to clear up a few details. The horse had been doped,' the policeman said. 'Do you want to talk here in front of your mates, or shall we go back to the station where it's a bit more private?'

Although Declan was drunk he could detect the hard edge behind the man's friendly manner. He shuffled to his feet and hitched up his faded denims. 'How long will it take?'

'I doubt you'll be back here by closing time. You come in our car; we'll drop you back at the stables.'

The detective sat opposite Declan at the tubular-framed table in a small room in Andover police station. He checked that there were two cassettes in the tape recorder that he'd placed in front of him, and switched it on. He cleared his throat.

'DI Stuart Wood interviewing Declan Hoolihan, twenty-one forty-five, Monday, March fifth. Now, Declan, I want you to tell me everything you did from the time you woke up that morning until the moment you led Midnight Express out on to the course for his race.'

'What's the cassette for?'

'So that we've got an accurate record of what you tell me. You'll have one of the copies to take away with you. Now, tell me exactly what happened yesterday.'

Declan looked at him. Although he spoke with the rural accent of the Berkshire Downs where he had been reared, his Irishness gave him a natural enthusiasm for talking. All right, he thought, you want to know what happened; I'll tell you.

'I got up the usual time, just after six. I was down in the yard by six thirty. I looked on the board to see if any of the horses I look after were going out with the first or second lot. I knew Midnight Express was running, so I mucked him out first, gave him half a bucket of water then let him down to relax. I left a clean bale of straw outside his box so that once we'd left for the races someone else could shake it up – otherwise he'd have been stuffing his face with it.

'The other two horses I do were both going out first lot, so when I'd mucked them out, I left them tied up. Then I went off to tack up the horse I was going to ride, but when I went to pick his feet out, I found he'd got a loose shoe, so I had to see Dad – he's head lad – and put my tack on something else. I got a bollocking for not picking his feet before I'd tacked him up. I just had time to get his hay and a bucket of warm water to wash him down before we pulled out at seven thirty.

'I was going racing at nine thirty, so I had to get my skates on, we didn't get back in from first lot until ten to.

I had to wash and change then get Midnight Express
ready – you know – the usual things; grease his feet, put
his travelling sheet on. Terry – he's travelling head lad –
he'd already plaited his mane and picked up his passport
and my stable badge, and he'd got my tenner – day's
expenses. Then we loaded and went off to Sandown.'

The policeman raised his hand to stem Declan's flow.
'Hang on. Let's just go back a bit. When you got back
from riding out, were you with the horse until you
loaded it?'

'Not in his box, like, but around the yard.'

'Did you see anyone else go into his box – another of
the lads?'

Declan shook his head vehemently. 'No one at the yard
would have touched him.'

'But did you see anyone besides yourself go into the
horse's box?'

The lad thought for a moment then shook his head
again. 'No. Just Mrs Mundy.'

'Why did she go in?'

'She's the bloody trainer, that's why. She nearly always
has a look at the horses that are racing that day, before
we load 'em.'

'Okay, so you put the horse in the box, then what?'

'Checked we had everything – there was three of them
went to Sandown Tuesday.'

'And who went with them in the lorry?'

'Me, Terry and Lofty.'

'Another lad?'

Declan nodded.

'What did you do when you got to Sandown?'

'Us lads unloaded the horses while Terry went off and found which stables we were in.'

'What then?'

'Terry said for me to stay with the horse.' Declan shrugged. 'He usually does – so me and Lofty hung around outside the boxes sorting the tack.'

'Did you have to do anything to the horse?'

'Yeah. I put a muzzle on him and gave him a quarter of a bucket of water, then I put his stable rug on and let him loose. I locked his top door and went to the lads' canteen with the others. I hadn't been there five minutes when Dad came in – he'd driven up – and told me to get back to the horse.'

'Was there anyone around your box when you got back?'

'No. Dai Price was chatting to the lad who looked after the horse in the box next door – he was riding him later.'

'Dai Price is Mrs Mundy's stable jockey,' Rowland interjected.

'Yes, but he was outside the wire security fence; he didn't have a stable pass.'

'Right. Did Mrs Mundy come to see the horse?'

'Not then.'

'Not at all?'

'Oh yeah, but not till the vet came with the security bloke.'

'Right. What time did the vet come?'

'I dunno – about one, I should think. He and that bloke,' Declan nodded at Rowland, 'came up and said they had to take a sample. I didn't know what was going on – I mean, the horse hadn't even run. Anyway, they checked that the horse had been locked up all the time and been behaving normally.'

'What did they do?'

'The vet asked me to put a head collar on the horse and trot him up. Then I put him back and Mr Straker came in and tried to take his temperature. The horse played up a bit, but I settled him. Mr Straker said he'd take the blood sample, but Express wasn't too keen, so he told me to put a twitch on him.' Declan shrugged. 'Normally he's all right, but he was getting a bit excited. Anyway, I put the twitch on and held him, while Mr Straker took the sample.'

'That's correct,' Rowland nodded. 'I was present throughout. It's all in my report.'

'Thanks, Ron,' the policeman said. 'I'd like to hear the lad's version, though.' He turned back to Declan. 'Have you seen the vet take a sample before?'

'Yeah, 'course I have. They're always testing their blood these days; everybody does it.'

'And do they often need this twitch?'

'Not often, but sometimes, and the horse was a bit on his toes, knowing he was going racing.'

'Okay. Then what happened?' The detective had become more tense.

'Mr Straker told me to take Express out and trot him again, so he could check him. I led him out and trotted him up and down a few times. He seemed all right and Mr Straker said to put him back in the box and not to take my eyes off him. Mrs Mundy came up and said, "What's the story?" Straker said he couldn't find nothing wrong with him. So I put the horse back in the box.' Declan shrugged.

'What did Mrs Mundy do?'

'She had a chat with Mr Straker and the other bloke, then they went off and she came up to me and said, "How does he look?" I said, "Fine." She gave a funny sort of laugh and said, "That's a pity, I'd rather he didn't run today." '

The detective's eyes narrowed fractionally. 'Do you know why she said that?'

Declan laughed. 'Yeah. None of us wanted him to run; he had a bloody good chance in the Champion Chase – two miles, better distance for him – and quite a lot of us had money on him for it. But this bloody hunter chase would knacker him . . .' Declan faltered at the thought that it had indeed knackered the horse. 'He was a horse that didn't want too much work; he lost a load of condition after a hard race and took two or three weeks to put it back on. But Mr Mundy didn't want to know. Even Dad told him straight he shouldn't waste the horse in a race like that.'

'And Mrs Mundy didn't want him to run either?'

'No, 'course not. It's much better to win at Cheltenham than some poxy amateur chase.'

'I see. Then what did she do?'

'She went in the box to have a look at the horse.'

'Did you go in with her?'

'No. While she was with him, I went off to get my grooming kit.'

'Were you gone long?'

'I dunno. A couple of minutes.'

'Was Mrs Mundy carrying anything when she went in?'

Declan thought a moment. 'I can't remember. 'Ere, you don't think she gave it something then, do you?'

'I don't think anything yet. I'm just getting all the facts together.'

'But we heard the blood test showed up clean anyway.'

'Yes, but Mr Straker had already taken the sample by then, hadn't he?'

Declan's jaw dropped. 'No. She wouldn't have. Not to Express. She's not like that; besides, Express was one of our best horses.'

'You may be right, but I just want to ask you a few questions about Mrs Mundy. Now, you've said she didn't really want the horse to run that day, but her husband who was riding it, insisted?'

'That's right.'

'Do you know if there was much disagreement between them about it?'

'I dunno. I should think so. I mean, it was common knowledge they weren't getting on too well.'

'Common knowledge?'

'Well, some of the lads had heard them arguing; he could be a helluva sod when he wanted. Dad reckoned there was something up between them and he's often up at the house with Mrs M. We didn't like him down the yard. He was always throwing his weight around. Whenever he got beaten on a horse, it was always someone else's fault. He wasn't much of a jockey – hands like a fork-lift truck.'

'Interview terminated at twenty-two-o-three.' The detective switched off the tape recorder and leaned back in his chair. 'Right, Declan. That'll do for now. But I'll need to speak to you again. Here's your copy of your interview. And I don't want you talking about it or playing it to anyone else – understand? Right. I'll get one of the local bobbies to take you home.'

Next morning, with no arrangements to ride out, Rory slipped out of the house before his wife came down. He got into his car and headed for Langlands. He hadn't rung Laura to tell her he was coming. He knew she wouldn't be surprised but he wondered if she was ready to see him yet.

He spotted Laura's second lot walking in single file from the trees below the ridge, up on to the wide bend of pale and dark green stripes that curved and rose gently towards the horizon. He squinted into the bright sun in an attempt to see if Laura was among the three figures standing beside the Land Rover at the top of the gallop, but he couldn't identify her without binoculars.

He decided, anyway, that he didn't want to talk to her in front of anyone else. He carried on towards the back entrance to the yard.

Rory sensed a subdued air about the place as he walked in. There was none of the normal banter and laughter as the few lads who weren't riding out went about their chores. Patrick came out of his office with no hint of his famous grin.

''Morning, Rory. I didn't know we were expecting you this morning.'

'You weren't.'

'Well, you're not the first unexpected visitor, by any means. I've already sent a few up to the house.'

'Journalists?'

Patrick nodded. 'And police. They were here last night

too. They went and got Declan out of the pub and took him to Andover. He was gone an hour or more. Of course, they had to let him go. They'd already been up to the house but I heard Mrs Mundy sent them packing with a flea in their ear.'

'That doesn't sound too clever,' Rory said.

Patrick shrugged. 'She's nothing to hide. I suppose it's their job to be suspicious, but, God knows, the poor woman has just lost her husband.'

'Is she at the house or on the gallops?'

'She's at home. Michael's in charge today,' he said with a measure of sarcasm.

Rory nodded. Michael Thynne was Laura's young assistant, the son of one of her owners, and a lot more keen than knowledgeable.

'Right, well, I'd better go and join the queue.'

'I'm sure she'll give you priority,' Patrick said. 'She'll want to see you. It's a terrible shame about the horse,' he added gloomily.

Rory drove up the long avenue, queasy with foreboding. The police wouldn't have come without a reason. And yet, no one could have deliberately planned an accident like Luke's.

As he turned on to the large gravel forecourt of the house, a Daimler swept up to the front entrance and stopped alongside four other cars. A tall man in a pinstriped suit leaped out of the car and almost ran round to the front door. His noisy bell-ringing was answered at once and he was let in, with the door closing behind him before Rory had left his car.

Rory hadn't seen the man before, but he guessed he was Laura's solicitor. If a highly paid professional man was running around, Rory thought, there was already trouble. The churning in his guts quickened as he walked across and rang the bell himself.

The maid recognised him with a half-smile and showed him into the small sitting room where he and Laura had talked so intimately two weeks before.

There were already three other men waiting – the journalists Patrick had spoken of, Rory guessed.

They looked up, and knew at once who Rory was.

One of them, the youngest and fittest, was on his feet in an instant. 'Rory Gillespie, right?' He had a quick, London delivery – streetwise and free of glottal stops.

Rory nodded.

'What are you doing here?'

'I came to ride work.'

'But you're not dressed for it.'

'My gear's in the car. I usually have a chat with Mrs Mundy first, but she's not up on the gallops this morning.'

'You thought it would be business as usual, did you, despite her old man getting killed and all the fracas that's going on?'

Rory shrugged. 'Horses have to be exercised. Owners pay a lot of money for it.'

'What d'you know about her relationship with Luke? People say they weren't getting along too well.'

'If you know people who are saying that, ask them. I don't know anything about it. I've only just started riding for her. I don't think I ever spoke to him.'

An older man, more conventionally dressed, whom Rory recognised from one of the racing papers, reckoned he had better questions to ask.

'You must be disappointed about Midnight Express. He

had a good chance in the Champion Chase.'

'Sure, I'm disappointed, but a man's been killed. That's a bit more important than winning a bloody race.'

The younger man didn't like being outmanoeuvred. 'Never mind the philosophy, what we want is the story. I mean, did it look like a regular racing accident to you?'

'I don't know what you're trying to say. A horse came down in a race; it happens twenty times a day during the jumping season. Once in a while, the jockey gets hurt bad. This accident was a lot worse than usual, that's all.'

'But it came down on the flat, and that hardly ever happens. And why are the police here?' the young hack challenged.

'Ah, there you have me. I was as surprised as you when I heard.'

'And some heavyweight-looking brief just ran in. He wouldn't have got himself in a sweat without a good reason.'

'Look, I don't know anything about it. I don't want to talk to you people. I'll wait somewhere else.'

Rory turned and walked out of the room, shutting the door firmly behind him. Out in the great panelled hall, he didn't know where he was going to go. He thought he'd find out from the maid where Laura was and simply butt in. He was looking around for the way to the kitchens when a procession appeared from across the hall.

Laura, white and damp-eyed, was being escorted without being touched by two casually dressed men. The pin-striped lawyer was walking quickly, close behind them, like a tall, thin, worried hen.

Laura glanced at Rory, with a twitch of her tight lips.

The policemen ignored him until he spoke.

'Laura, for God's sake; what's going on?'

'Mrs Mundy's coming in to help us with our enquiries,' one of her escorts answered. 'That's all I can tell you at this point in time.' He evidently thought Rory was a journalist.

Laura, halfway across the hall, turned back to him. 'Don't worry, Rory, I won't be there long. Do you think you could just hang on to Midas until I'm out of the house – I think he's rather worried.' She gave a faint smile. 'I'll ring you as soon as I get back.'

The faces of her escorts didn't show what they thought of her view. Rory watched in glum silence as the party went out through the front door and two of the cars were driven away.

The journalists, seeing this from the window of the sitting-room, burst out and ran through the hall to their own cars.

Rory waited until the sounds of their departure had faded completely before leaving the house and walking down the lime avenue to the stables.

He found Declan just back from the gallops, but the lad couldn't tell him much more than he already knew, beyond the fact that Luke had been unusually nervous before his last, fatal ride. He hadn't expected much but he had to try and find out what was going on. He wanted desperately to believe that Laura's arrest was a case of overzealous police bungling. But he couldn't entirely rid himself of a niggling doubt about Laura's attitude and motives.

He drove away from Langlands bewildered and resenting these uncertainties, knowing that his judgement was being subverted by the revival of his old feelings for Laura.

He hadn't brought his racing gear with him; he hadn't even thought about it when he'd left the house that morning. Now he had to make a detour home on his way to ride at Stratford. He was in a hurry when he arrived at Camp Farm, but he took the time to go up and chat to Tommy, who was home from school with a touch of flu. He wished he could have stayed longer. But Pam came up too, wanting to know what was going on at Langlands. Reluctantly, Rory went downstairs with her. He didn't want to talk about it in front of his son.

'I told you there was something dodgy about that woman,' Pam declared triumphantly when Rory told her about Laura's compulsory visit to Andover police station. 'She probably knew her old man was in trouble and she's going for the insurance.'

'Don't be ridiculous!' Rory snapped. 'Nobody could have planned an accident like that.'

'Not to the jockey, maybe, but she'll get the money for the horse, won't she?'

'She never planned it; it's out of the question,' Rory said, suppressing his own uncertainty.

'You're still taken in, aren't you? Just because she's got a posh accent and lives in a bloody great mansion, you think she's above all that. But she pulls strokes, same as anybody else; Dai's told me.'

'Dai seems to be telling you a lot these days. Are you having some kind of scene with him?'

'He's just a friend,' Pam replied indignantly, but then couldn't control her spite. 'At least he's got bollocks.'

Rory forced himself to stay calm.

'Dai Price is a second-rate little shite and if it took any bollocks to pull horses to order, he wouldn't be doing it,' he said, barely keeping the anger from his voice.

'He's still managed to get more winners than you this season.'

'The season's not over yet.'

'That's why you're so keen on Laura Bloody Mundy, isn't it, because she's giving you some of Dai's rides. She won't be able to if she gets locked up.'

'Of course she's not going to get locked up. Now, I'm late; I'm not going to stand here arguing with you. I'll be back about seven.'

'Well, I'm going out to play squash at seven, so you'll have to look after Tommy.'

'Fine.' Rory picked up his kit and walked out of the house.

The gossip in the changing room at Stratford was dominated by Luke Mundy's death. Dozens of different versions of the event were circulating, most of them based on hearsay or the shoddy reporting of the tabloid papers. Rory was more worried by another rumour beginning to take shape – that the dead horse had been the subject of a formal autopsy, despite the negative results of the pre-race blood sample.

After riding a no-hoper in the novice hurdle for his father-in-law, Mick Fanshaw, Rory slipped into the press box to find the one journalist he trusted. Arthur Brian, wedged comfortably in his seat, was battling with his mobile phone and his lap-top PC. He greeted Rory warmly and beckoned him to sit down in the next chair.

'Hello, Arthur,' Rory said, pulling out his tobacco and papers. 'I didn't think you'd be here today.'

'I wanted to see Moon Chariot run once more before the Triumph.'

'Is she your big nap for Cheltenham?'

'That depends on how she runs today.'

'She'll beat my horse,' Rory said.

'Yes, she will. I'm sorry you've lost your ride in the Champion Chase. Though I see Laura's definitely running Flamenco Dancer now. Maybe you could jock Dai off that one too?'

'Maybe.' Rory lowered his voice. 'I think I'll still be able to ride the Irish horse in the Champion, but I wanted to talk to you about Midnight Express. There's a story going round that someone's already done an autopsy on the horse.'

Arthur nodded. 'There's been a little leak from Portman Square.' It wasn't the first time Arthur had been the recipient of information from the Jockey Club – they trusted him to stick to the facts they gave him and not to speculate. 'In a manner of speaking. There wasn't a complete autopsy. After all, the horse had only been tested an hour before he appeared in the parade ring. And that test was clean. But the poor animal was delivered to the veterinary college in Hawkshead and a professor and his students carried out some standard tests on it, researching the effects of trauma, and found traces of xylazine, which, as you may know, is a fairly common pre-med. Even a very small, discreet dose would have made it pretty dozy and certainly slowed it. I've already done my piece on it for the *Standard*, you can read all about it this evening.'

'So the horse was got at, after the sample had been taken?'

'So it would appear.'

Rory looked at the journalist; he couldn't quell the churning in his guts.

In those circumstances, it was hardly surprising that the police had felt Laura might be able to tell them something.

Rory rode two more races that afternoon, but he rode without conviction, while Dai Price barged his way through to win the handicap hurdle for his absent trainer.

Rory arrived home as Pam left to play squash, with a 'girlfriend'. 'We'll probably have a drink after, so don't expect me back too early.'

Rory shrugged, and thought of Dai Price. The Welsh-man hadn't been able to look him in the eye that after-noon but Rory couldn't have felt jealous if he'd tried. He cajoled Tommy back to bed and read him a Roald Dahl story without taking in a single word of it; his mind was full of Laura's predicament. But he didn't let his preoccupation show. When he reached the end of the story he left the boy to read a couple more himself while he went downstairs to feed his dog and do what he had been wanting to do all day.

Laura answered the phone herself. Rory felt absurdly relieved at the sound of her voice.

'The police let you go, then?' he said.

'Yes, thank God. I think they eventually believed that I had nothing to do with what's been going on. But what I can't understand is how anyone managed to get at him. At least, they've accepted that nobody would plan to kill someone that way.'

'How are you feeling about it?'

'Pretty miserable.'

'I'll come over.'

'No . . . no, Rory, don't, not now. I don't think that's a good idea. But come and ride work tomorrow. I'm really sorry about Midnight Express, but I still want you to ride the others.'

'All right,' Rory said flatly. 'But if you want me to come before then, just ring, okay?'

'Thanks, I might do that.'

Rory put the phone down, shaking his head with frustration. He wished he could understand what was going on and why the hell Laura had let the horse run. Of course, she was very shaken by what had happened – anyone would have been – being questioned about Luke's death. But a gap seemed to have opened up between them since the intimacy of their evening two weeks before.

He went back up to Tommy's room and settled down to talk about the kind of flies they should take with them to tackle the Wye salmon. Tommy wanted to tie some himself, so they wrote a list of what he would need, which Rory promised to get for him.

As he talked with his son, Rory resigned himself to the fact that Laura wouldn't ring him that night and stayed with Tommy until he went to bed two hours before his wife came home.

There was a palpable tension at the yard when he

arrived at Langlands next morning. Everyone knew, of course, that Laura had been to 'help the police with their enquiries'; the journalists had obligingly come straight down to tell them and to try, unsuccessfully, to get their reactions. The mood in the yard now was one of confused outrage.

Laura hadn't been down to the yard yet and Michael Thynne gave Rory his instructions. On the way up to the gallops, the lads and work riders relaxed a little, joking clumsily about Declan being taken in by the police. None of them believed he had anything to do with what had happened. Although they didn't say so, Rory sensed that they were less sure about their guv'nor's involvement.

Rory rode work on Rear Gunner, an ex-flat horse entered for the Triumph Hurdle at Cheltenham. At the top of the gallop he was almost surprised to see Laura standing by the Land Rover with Michael. She beckoned him over. Rory wheeled his horse round and walked back to her.

'Rory, that was great. If you get down, Mike can ride Gunner back.'

Rory swung out of the saddle and legged Michael into it.

As Michael and the horse walked away to join the rest of the string circling beneath a cloud of steam in the crisp morning sun, Laura turned to Rory.

'I'm sorry I've been so cagey,' she said with a sincerity that made Rory's head sing with relief. 'I think there's a tap on my phone, and I don't want to give anyone any grounds for suspicion.'

'Do you really think so?' Rory said, alarmed. 'What kind of suspicion?'

'That I might be involved with you, again.' She gave him a crooked smile.

Rory nodded. 'Okay, but I still want to know what's happening.'

'Let me deal with this lot, then I'll drive you back to the yard.'

When she had had another look at the horses and a quick word with some of their riders, she and Rory climbed into the Land Rover with Midas and bounced across the soft turf to the green lane that led down to the valley.

Laura, concentrating on the rutted route, didn't look at Rory as she spoke.

'I know you think I had something to do with what happened at Kempton,' she said bluntly.

'Not at all,' Rory said, a little too quickly. 'But after the conversations we'd had about your withdrawing the horse, I couldn't understand why you were still running him.'

'Listen, Luke promised me that if he won, he'd transfer the horse into my name. Now I realise what he was doing. He knew he was in trouble and he wanted to be sure I'd go on training the horse. In fact, I discovered afterwards that he'd already transferred him. Midnight Express was officially mine that morning. Luke shouldn't really have ridden him in his own colours.' She shrugged. 'His only condition had been that he rode in that race. Besides, he was threatening that if he didn't, he'd ride him in the Grand Military *and* the Champion Chase, and I wouldn't get the horse. In the circumstances, I didn't have much choice.'

'But you'll get the insurance money, I presume?'

'I may not. I knew Luke had problems, but I had no idea that they were as bad as they are. When the whole mess is cleared up, if there's not enough money in the kitty, his creditors could come after me for the money.'

'It seems like an unusually generous gesture for him,' Rory said.

'Not very characteristic, I admit.'

'But somebody killed the horse, Laura!'

'And Luke.'

'Do the police think Luke was murdered?'

'No, not now. They realise that it would be far too chancy a way of trying to kill someone. I mean, how many falls end in fatality? They've ruled out suicide for the same reason.'

'Do *you* think he might have tried to kill himself?'

'No. To give him his due, he wasn't a coward.' There was the hint of a break in Laura's voice. 'It's funny, I still can't quite accept he's dead, even though I'd been dreaming of leaving him, getting free of him for the last few years. Now, suddenly, the problem's gone and I haven't really got used it it.'

'I can understand that,' Rory said quietly. 'There must have been *some* good in him; I mean, he must have meant something to you once, or you wouldn't have married him, and when people die, at first we block out the negative things about them.'

'I suppose so. I suppose he must have meant something, as you say, but I couldn't tell you what. I just feel as if a chunk of me has been removed, because he was part of my life for such a long time.'

'Yeah, I can see that, but you'll get used to it.'

Laura gave a short, bitter laugh. 'I hope it doesn't take too long.'

They had arrived at the yard. Laura stopped the Land Rover and looked at Rory. 'Do you mind if we don't look *too* friendly? I just don't think it's sensible for the moment.'

Rory nodded. 'Sure.'

'So, I'll see you at the races tomorrow afternoon – your first ride for Langlands!'

Chapter Five

George Rutherford drove into Langlands by the South Lodge as Rory was leaving. Rory gave him a surly nod. Laura hadn't told him that Rutherford was coming to see her.

He felt a quick jab of jealousy. He was sure Laura didn't have any physical feelings towards the other man, but he resented the influence Rutherford seemed to wield over her yard. And Laura had already told him of the businessman's offer to finance a move to another stables if the crisis Luke had left behind made that necessary.

The sight of Rory leaving Langlands was a source of irritation to George Rutherford, but he wasn't going to let Laura see that. He burst into the house as if he were family, ready to commiserate and offer advice.

'Things aren't looking good for you, Laura,' he said when he had poured them both a glass of the champagne he had brought with him. 'As far as I can tell, Luke didn't have a single asset that wasn't hocked up to the eyeballs, including this place and most of his horses. And whatever wasn't formerly charged will have to be sold to clear the personal guarantees he's left all over the City. His creditors will see to that. As it happens, I'm one of them. He owed me a final tranche for the Chelsea Gaming Club. Mind you, under the terms of the contract of sale, if there's a default on any of the payments, I get the club back and he loses the payments he's already made.' He couldn't resist boasting a little in front of Luke's widow. 'I must admit, I had rather foreseen that might happen, but Luke was so insistent. I'm afraid he thought he'd got a bit of a bargain out of me. He thought the gaming board would automatically renew the licence. I knew for a fact that there would be a doubt. He's sailed too close to the wind in the past, and you need to be whiter than snow to hold a gaming-club licence. But his estate is going to be so in the red, it wouldn't have made any difference to the final outcome,' he added quickly.

'I'm glad you're going to do so well out of it, George,' Laura said with sarcasm.

'Don't worry, we'll both do well, I'll make sure of that, even if he didn't have the good sense to provide for you.'

'Surprisingly enough,' Laura said, 'he did do me one good turn the day he died. He transferred Midnight Express into my name. At least I should get the insurance for that.'

Rutherford didn't speak for a moment. His lips tightened and he turned sharply to look out of the window. 'Did he indeed?' he said quietly. 'That was very generous of him.' He turned back to face Laura, wearing the avuncular smile with which he had entered the house. 'But very unlike him, and rather extravagant, given his circumstances. I'm afraid, my dear, that his creditors may judge it to have been an evasive tactic and claim any proceeds from you. But don't worry, I'm here to help.' He placed a fleshy hand on her shoulder with a light squeeze.

Laura tried not to flinch.

Eland stared, white-faced, at the front page of the *Sporting Life*. It contained a speculative rehash of Arthur Brian's piece about the autopsy on Midnight Express which had appeared in the *Evening Standard* the day before.

There was no mention of it, but it was clear to him that if the police weren't already looking for a murderer, they soon would be. And if they found a culprit, they'd find a motive.

He picked up the telephone on the coffee table, then hesitated. He had been told – ordered – not to make contact under any circumstances. But that was before anyone had been killed.

He dialled.

'Well?' His client didn't sound pleased to hear from him.

'I've got to see you.'

'Why?'

'You know fucking well why!' Eland shouted, bold with fear.

There was a silence at the other end of the line. Eland trembled. He could almost feel the other man's fury.

'Listen,' the deep voice growled at him, 'Get yourself up here, right now, and I'll tell you just what you can and can't do.'

Then the line went dead.

Eland was let into the top-floor apartment by a secretary who looked as though she normally worked in the Raymond Revue Bar. He stood nervously in a large reception room, furnished without taste or regard to expense. Monstrous white leather sofas sat either side of glass and brass coffee tables. Full-length orange slubbed silk curtains were drawn across a window which stretched the whole height and breadth of the far wall.

'Some drum,' Eland tittered fatuously.

The woman looked at him disdainfully. 'Haven't you ever been in a place like this before, then?'

'Yeh, 'course I have.'

'He only has the best,' the woman said proudly, smoothing her skirt over her hips.

While he waited, Eland began walking around, in an attempt to take his mind off the quaking in his guts.

He glanced through a door into the next room, a crude replica of a Victorian library, and beyond that a bedroom containing a round bed, more brass and glass tables and heavy, Victorian mahogany chests and wardrobes.

'Is there a toilet?' Eland called back to the secretary. She barely looked up as she pointed towards the other side of the bedroom. 'Yeh, over there.'

Eland started to walk towards one of two doors on the opposite wall.

'Not that one,' she said impatiently. 'That's the sauna; the other one.'

'What, a sauna with no window,' Eland quibbled to justify his mistake.

'That's because the boss doesn't like people peeking, 'specially if he's got a crowd in there,' she added with a titter.

Eland went through the second door in the far wall of the bedroom and entered a warm, humming, deep-carpeted palace of a bathroom. He used the black lavatory bowl and flushed it with a gold-plated handle.

'Feeling better?' the woman asked with a grin, when he returned. 'Don't worry, he won't eat you.'

She was waving him to one of the vast sofas when the door opened and his client walked in.

'Okay, Samantha, you can go now.' The big man nodded towards the door behind him.

She didn't question him and walked out with a provocative swinging of her hips.

Eland looked at him nervously, wishing he'd followed his instincts and turned this man's business away. His client wore a pair of navy blue mohair trousers, held up by a pair of broad bright red braces over a cream silk shirt open at the collar.

'This, my friend,' the man growled, 'is the last time you come here – understand?'

Eland nodded. 'Yeah, yeah. But I had to talk to you, didn't I? I mean, now the filth's involved. Of course, I knew the bloke would fall off, but I didn't think he'd bloody die. And they've found the dope in the horse. They're going to get on to us. We've got to point them in another direction before they turn up on my doorstep.'

'Stop panicking. They're concentrating on the trainer. They've already had her in for a day. What you've got to do is give them a reason for getting her back to the nick.

Use your head, give them a bit of help. That shouldn't be beyond your nasty imagination. And there's nothing she can tell them that'll put them on to you.'

'There might be. She might work it out for herself, 'specially if they charge her with something.'

'Not if you've done your job properly. And don't forget, even if they do come sniffing round you – God help them—' he wrinkled his nose, 'it's got fuck all to do with me, remember? That's why you got paid so much.'

'Look,' Eland said with a burst of courage, 'the thing's got out of hand now; it wasn't my fault. The horse must have had too much of that stuff to make it pack up like that.'

'I paid you to make sure it went right. If you want any more money and you want to keep the skin on your back, you deal with it. I'm sure you'll think of something. Just don't get caught, and remember, if you point the finger at me you'll be in terminal trouble.' Eland quivered before the unequivocal message in the black eyes. 'I don't want to hear from you again. Understand?'

Eland twitched and nodded.

But his client's faith was justified; he had already thought of something.

He made the first of two calls from a public phone in the street outside.

Rory's first two rides for Laura Mundy were at Hereford. On a Saturday with half a dozen meetings around the country, the big races were at Kempton, where Laura had three more runners, to be ridden by Dai Price.

Rory had managed to fix a couple of other rides for

himself at the West Midlands course, and he would be the most experienced jockey there. That would shorten the bookies' prices and heighten the punters' expectations for his mounts, Rory thought ruefully as he drove between the dripping apple orchards and red-brick hop kilns of Herefordshire towards the small cathedral city.

Before he crossed town to the race course, he stopped in a small medieval side street outside a fishing tackle shop which he knew from past trips. He had remembered to bring a list of what was needed to make the flies he and Tommy had decided to use when they came back this way for their fishing.

A few minutes later, he drove off the old Roman road on to a grass car park. Despite Laura's parting words this morning, he didn't expect her to choose to come to this unfashionable little course rather than Kempton.

But he was wrong. One of the horses he was due to ride that afternoon was owned by a local farming baronet, an old friend of Laura's father and her longest-standing owner. She gave this as her reason for being there. That was just about plausible, but Rory suspected she had chosen to keep away from the crush of journalists who would be looking for her at Kempton. She greeted Rory with a formality that he hoped was put on for the sake of anyone who might be watching.

In the parade ring before the three-mile chase, she gave him his riding instructions as she would have done any other jockey. 'All he does is gallop, so keep him as close as you can. I don't mind if you make the running. He only cost ten grand, so Sir Ralph isn't expecting miracles, but you should be able to get him in the frame.'

Rory looked with approval at the big, old-fashioned Irish-bred horse striding easily around the ring. The animal was fit and he had a good jumping record. 'If he's halfway willing, he should give me a good ride,' he said to the owner who came up to join them. 'And the opposition doesn't look much.'

The baronet looked pleased. 'He needs someone like you on him, just to give him some confidence. I was delighted when Laura said she was booking you instead of Price.'

'She needed Dai for her Kempton runners, but I'm sure he would have given it just as much of a chance,' Rory said with a generosity he didn't feel.

A few minutes later, he was mounted and jogging down towards the track. When the lad released them to canter round to the start, Rory found the horse keen but well mannered – just the sort of horse he liked, with big wide shoulders and plenty of neck in front of him.

It was always a problem, trying to find suitable races for slow horses. The big galloping tracks, like Newbury and Ascot, were perfect for them but the horses they would have to compete against would be far too good. Therefore one had to run them in their class at the gaff tracks and just hope that they didn't get out-paced.

From the feel that he got on the canter to the start, Rory knew that Commoner – as his mount was intuitively named – wasn't going to do anything in a hurry. The chances were that if he wasn't careful he'd lose not only valuable lengths at the start, but also his position against the inside rails. Once all of the runners were ready, Rory used his experience over the younger jockeys, gave Commoner a crack with his whip and hit the tapes running.

The sudden flourish took the horse by surprise, sparking him into life to such an extent that Rory found himself almost going too quickly. The fences at Hereford came quite fast, and Rory felt as though he was almost constantly on the turn, with Commoner gaining ground at every one. His long, powerful stride lengthened to measure each fence precisely, before neatly flicking through the top couple of inches of birch.

The horse was as close to being a perfect jumper as one could get and for a circuit and a half Rory sat on board and enjoyed himself; Commoner needed barely any assistance at all. Then, as the race began to hot up halfway down the back straight on the last circuit, the other runners started to close in. Rory felt certain that nothing would be able to pass him quickly but Commoner's jumping was now more important than ever as he struggled to keep in front. One horse briefly came upsides as they raced flat-out to the downhill fence, the second from home, and Rory, by this stage, trusting Commoner with his life, rode towards the fence as if it wasn't there. He knew that if he couldn't trust the horse he was on now, he would never be able to trust any other. Rory saw Commoner's big, noble head lower slightly as the horse prepared itself and then it put in a mighty leap that landed him far from the back of the fence while the other horse bottled out and threw away any chance of winning. Another spectacular jump at the last had the race completely sewn up, allowing Rory to coast home as he liked.

'What a perfect piece of riding!' The horse's owner

beamed in delight. 'I thought you were cooked at the top of the hill.'

'The horse deserves most of the credit,' Rory said as he jumped down after steering the animal to the winner's spot in front of the changing rooms. He removed the saddle, pulled the breastplate over the horse's head and patted it on the neck.

Inside, the other jockeys were generous too, though their congratulations were tinged with doubts about Langlands' future.

By now, it was common knowledge that Luke Mundy had died in a state of spectacular insolvency. His every personal asset was reported to have been pledged – several times over – against the various loans he had raised to keep his companies alive through the recession. There wasn't much doubt that Langlands would have to be sold.

Rory pondered the irony of renewing his friendship with Laura and getting some good rides just as it was all about to come to an end. Or was it coincidence?

Sitting on the changing-room bench, taking in the gossip, he realised just how much it mattered to him that Laura should carry on training, whatever happened to Langlands.

Laura, in contrast to the hot debate going on behind her back, was calm and cool, ignoring any references to the sensational events earlier in the week. Rory was impressed, and determined to add his support.

He made another contribution to her record by winning the seventh race – a well-subscribed handicap hurdle – on an unfancied outsider carrying bottom weight. Laura smiled her thanks once again in the winner's enclosure, but by the time Rory had weighed in, showered the mud off and changed, she had left.

Sir Ralph Devereux, the owner of his earlier winner, invited him back for a drink at his house. Rory thought for a moment; one of the Lambourn trainers was holding a big party to celebrate his fiftieth birthday. Laura's problems would certainly be the central topic of conversation and he didn't want to miss any useful snippets of information, but it was possible that Sir Ralph might know a little, too, so Rory accepted his invitation and twenty minutes later followed the baronet up his long drive to an ungainly red-brick mansion surrounded by untidy parkland.

Sir Ralph Devereux wasn't as out of touch as his red face and thirty-year-old tweed suit suggested. After he had introduced Rory to the dozen friends he had also invited to celebrate his win, he led him away from the main group and took him to a quiet corner where they could talk privately.

'I can't tell you how glad I am that you're going to ride some more for Laura,' he said. 'Of course, I know that you and she haven't seen eye to eye for quite some time but I'm delighted that you have buried the hatchet now.' He was looking out of the window at the dying sun. Suddenly he turned round and fixed Rory with a stern eye. 'But don't do the dirty on her again.'

It was the first time anyone had articulated the guilt which had nagged Rory for over ten years. He shook his head with embarrassment.

Sir Ralph looked back at the setting sun. 'Frankly, if

you ask me, Laura's going to need all the friends she can get over the next few months.'

Rory nodded. 'It looks as though she's got problems.'

'That bastard Luke Mundy!' Sir Ralph exclaimed with unexpected venom. 'The man had a strange sort of hold over her, you know. I don't think so much recently, but earlier on, she was terrified of him.'

'Terrified? Sounds a bit strong.'

'I've known Laura since she was wearing nappies and I know just how independent she was, believe me. I had to sit and listen often enough to her father worrying about his lack of control over her. Her affair with you wasn't the first he hadn't approved of – though I don't suppose he'd disapprove at all now. But Luke Mundy was a very domineering sort of a man. Oh, he was fine at a party – charming and quite amusing, provided he was the centre of attention and everyone deferred to him – but he was an absolutely ruthless shit if he didn't get his own way. I never had any dealings with him, except once when I had a horse he wanted. I sold it to someone else for less money than Luke had offered, and I told him so.' Sir Ralph laughed. 'Taught him a lesson.'

'Why do you think he transferred Midnight Express into Laura's name on the morning of that race?'

'I've no idea, but, whatever the reason, I can tell you that it wouldn't have been out of the goodness of his heart. It's my guess that she was supposed to do something for him.'

'But who the hell had the horse doped, and why?'

'That's what everyone wants to know, isn't it? Especially the police and the Jockey Club. And frankly, I think Laura's still on a pretty sticky wicket until they can pin it on someone else. I had her father on the phone for an hour last night and he's worried as hell about it. I must say, I was very impressed by how calm she was today, as if nothing had happened; it seemed almost unnatural. Anyway, what I wanted to say was that Eddie Brickhill would be very grateful for anything you can tell him now that you're seeing something of her, even if it is only in a professional capacity – which I suspect it isn't.'

'I don't think anything I could do would please her father.'

'Nonsense. He forgave you a long time ago for what happened. I don't think he blames you at all, particularly when you consider the bastard she did marry. Give him a ring; he wants to hear from you.'

Rory thought about Laura's father as he drove away from Sir Ralph's mansion, twenty minutes later. When he'd first started seeing Laura, Edward Brickhill hadn't been keen. On the half-dozen subsequent occasions they had met, Rory got the impression that Brickhill hadn't changed his mind. But he felt inclined to trust Ralph Devereux's view.

Pam was waiting impatiently for him when he reached home. She was dressed to make the most of her more obvious physical attributes, and Rory wondered if this effort was aimed at anyone in particular, or the Lambourn racing crowd in general. He went upstairs to change and to show Tommy all the kit and feathers he had bought to tie their flies. As he talked, he thought again that if it weren't for his son, he'd end his farcical marriage tomorrow.

Rory and Pam walked into the large barn which was

normally their host's indoor school. The interior had been decked out in pink cloth, like a vast marquee, and the sand floor had been covered with carpet and a dance floor. The tables scattered around the barn were already packed and the sound of noisy, drunken laughter echoed up to the roof. It looked as though anyone who was anyone in Lambourn was there, but the first person Rory spotted was one of the last he had expected to see.

His father-in-law, Mick Fanshaw, had been one of jump racing's heroes when Rory had first arrived at his yard, but a long run of bad luck and worse management, combined with ever heavier drinking, had changed all that. Pam's mother, no martyr, decided she'd had enough and ran off with an amateur jockey, putting in her alimony bid while there was still something left to claim. Mick had been forced to sell the freehold of his land in Sussex and now rented a small, run-down yard outside Lambourn where he trained the dozen or so second-rate animals which a few loyal friends had left with him. He still knew as much about training as anyone else in the business, but his will to win seemed to have faded, and he spent most of his time pottering around the racetracks, living on his past glories and trying to earn a living from his betting.

As far as Rory could tell, Fanshaw had never completely forgiven him for leaving his yard but still rated him the best jockey in jumping. He also, Rory thought, gave him credit for having stayed married to his daughter.

'Hello, Rory, you Judas,' Fanshaw greeted him with his customary sourness.

Rory, rolling a cigarette, watched Pam dive off into the

crowd towards a gang of similarly clad women before he answered.

'What have I done now, Mick?'

'First you ride two bloody horses for Laura Mundy, and then you go and win on the bastards without telling me. What kind of son-in-law do you call yourself?'

'If I'd had any idea they were going to win, I'd have told you, you know that; and if I get offered rides, who am I to turn them down?'

Fanshaw scowled. 'Bollocks! You've never ridden for her before. Why start now? The only reason the bitch has got the horses she has is because her old man bought lots of them for silly money, and her other owners are only there because they think they can get her into bed. I've lost ten horses to her this season, and a couple of those were just coming right when they left me; of course she's gone on and got all the glory. I mean, look at Flamenco Dancer!'

'It's a pity they weren't winning when they were in your yard, Mick, but what can I say? I've got an expensive wife to keep, I can't turn business away.'

'I wish you'd keep her on a rein as short as her skirt,' her father growled. 'Look at her, looks like a French floozy, waggling her tits all over the place. I don't know how you stand for it. She's turned into a right tart; she's been egging on her mother to try and get more money out of me – as if I had anything left, for God's sake! And I know she's been giving you the runaround. But look, it's not helping you, or me, you riding for Mrs Mundy. Anyway, things are going to happen there, I can tell you. She'll get her comeuppance. 'Specially after the mess that bastard Luke left behind.'

'I don't suppose she'll have any trouble finding the money if she has to set up a new yard,' Rory said lightly.

'No chance. This business at Kempton is going to leave her with mud over her face. I mean, the police are going to have to charge somebody with Luke's murder, aren't they?'

Rory stiffened, then tried to remind himself of Fanshaw's vindictiveness and colourful imagination.

'Don't be crazy, Mick. They're not going to blame anyone for a jockey getting killed in a steeplechase.'

'Oh, no? The horse didn't fall at a fence, did it, like they usually do. It came down on the flat, because someone had a go at it. And that someone had to be Laura Mundy. I heard back from one of her lads that she's even getting the insurance for it – that'll be a few hundred grand.' The old man's eyes were shining. 'They'll have her,' he nodded. 'And if they don't get her for that, they'll find something else.'

Rory was startled by Fanshaw's certainty and spite, which did nothing to quell his own doubts.

'I think you're going a bit over the top, Mick.'

'Just don't reckon on getting too many more rides out of her,' Fanshaw growled before turning abruptly and heading back to the bar.

Rory stared after him for a moment, half wanting to press him for a few facts, though he knew it would be a pointless exercise.

After an hour, he decided he was wasting his time at the party if he expected to hear any more plausible theories about Laura and the future of Langlands. He'd picked up nothing but a lot of wild speculation – too much of it along the same lines as Mick's. Philosophically, he assumed a brightness he didn't feel, and threw himself into the event with enough of his usual good nature to disguise his anxiety over Laura. He saw Pam across the room a few times, laughing loudly at other men's jokes and making it clear to anyone who was interested that she was her own woman. Rory found that this time he didn't care and quietly left the party without telling her.

Rory woke next morning to find his wife in bed next to him. He didn't feel like a confrontation about his leaving the party, so he slipped out and was tiptoeing silently out of the room when he heard Pam's voice.

'What are you getting up so early for?' she said softly.

Rory turned. She had propped herself on one elbow and there was a seductive smile on her sleepy, sensuous features.

'I heard Tommy wandering about downstairs. I thought I'd take him with me to get the papers.'

'Well,' she said, with uncharacteristic winsomeness, 'if I'm not going to get a cuddle, the least you could do is make me a cup of tea.'

'Okay.' Rory nodded willingly, wondering if her attitude was a perverse reaction to his having left her at the party – something he had never done before.

By the time he arrived back with the Sunday papers, Pam was asleep again. He settled down to read the new revelations that had been dug up about Luke Mundy. A liquidator had already been named to wind up Thames Land, and not a stone would be left unturned in his efforts to recover the vast debts to the banks who had appointed him. Every corner of the late Luke Mundy's empire would be subject to scrutiny, 'including his considerable dealings in international bloodstock'. Rory winced. That had to be bad news for Laura.

He thought about ringing Laura, but his instinct now was not to press her. He was sure she had only told him part of the story. He would probably learn more if he waited until she contacted him in her own time.

When Pam appeared at midday, he told her that he and Tommy were going to the pub to play pool. There was a warm, welcoming crowd at The Harrow. Rory and his son stayed for some roast beef, then settled down in front of the television with everyone else to watch the British Lions trounce the French.

Driving back through a blustery, sunlit late afternoon, he thought that, although he'd achieved nothing tangible that day, he'd felt closer to his son than he ever had before. As he walked in through the back door, the phone was ringing.

Pam picked it up before he reached it.

She listened for a moment with a supercilious expression, then said, 'He's here.'

She looked at Rory. 'Your friend's in a bit of trouble,' she mocked with hint of triumph.

Rory grabbed the phone.

'Laura? What's happened?'

There was a moment's silence during which Rory sensed that Laura was trying to get a grip on herself. 'I'm sorry to ring, Rory, but I can't get hold of my father and I can't tell my mother what's happened. I've been ...

arrested. They've charged me with manslaughter.'

Rory heard a quick intake of breath, almost a sob.

'I'll come now. Where are you?'

'Andover. Rory, I'll be so glad if you come. I've got to appear in front of the magistrates tomorrow. They should give me bail, but I don't know how much for. Could you try and get hold of my father, and get him to come?'

'Leave it to me. Have you spoken to your solicitor?'

'Yes. He's on his way.'

'So am I. Don't worry; we'll get it sorted out.'

'God, I hope so. Thanks, Rory.'

'That's okay,' he answered awkwardly. 'I'll get there as fast as I can. 'Bye for now.'

Rory put the phone down and turned to Pam. 'You heard?'

'She's got what she was asking for.'

'Oh, for Christ's sake! She's been charged with killing her husband. There's no way she did it! I don't know what went on with that bloody horse, but I just don't believe she was responsible.'

'I told you, it's obvious; she was after the insurance money.'

'I'm not going to discuss it with you. I'm getting down there to sort things out.'

'Why the hell should you? And what do you think you can do?'

'Laura and I may have fallen out over you a long time ago, but she needs help, and she's asked me for it. I made the mistake of letting her down once before; I'm not going to do it again. Anyway, I'm not arguing about it. I'm off. I'll ring you later.'

'Rory,' Pam was pleading now, 'don't get involved.'

He looked at her and spoke without emphasis. 'I'm already involved.'

The rain that had been promising all day had arrived with a fury. The wind howled up the valley as Rory set off. Driving fast, he tried to concentrate on the road as he stabbed numbers on his car phone.

First he got the number of Edward Brickhill's home in East Sussex. When Laura's mother answered, it was the first time he had heard her voice in over ten years. It still had exactly the same uncompromising superiority to it. But it didn't daunt Rory in the way it had years before.

'Good evening. Could I speak to Mr Brickhill, please?'

'Who is that?'

'This is Rory Gillespie.'

There was a pause. 'Oh. I'm afraid he's not here.'

'Can you tell me where I can contact him? It's very urgent.'

'What's it about?'

'I'm afraid I can't say. Can you tell me where he is?'

'No, I can't. But I'll be talking to him later and I'll tell him you rang.'

'I'll give you the number of my mobile; I'll keep the line open.'

'Oh, all right.' Mrs Brickhill made some play of her exasperation at being bothered by anyone as unimportant as Rory. 'What is it?'

Rory gave her the number and rang off with a scowl. With a mother like that, it was surprising that Laura wasn't more difficult.

He dialled the police station at Andover and asked if

he would be allowed to see Mrs Mundy. He was told that he would. He put the phone back and made no more calls so that Edward Brickhill could get through to him if he tried.

The black, wet night slid by with Rory's eyes fixed on the end of his headlight beam. He was surprised that he felt as calm as he did. He thought that his brain should be in turmoil, but the gravity of Laura's position seemed to have focused his mind. The first thing to be done was to make certain that she got bail. No doubt her lawyer was already working on that. It would be harder to do the next job – finding proof that she hadn't doped Midnight Express. That would mean finding out who had.

A few miles before he reached Andover, his phone bleeped at him in the dark. He picked it up.

'Hello?'

'Is that Rory Gillespie?'

'Yes.'

'This is Edward Brickhill. I gather you wanted to speak to me urgently?' There was none of his wife's reticence in his voice.

'I do. Thanks for calling back. I can't give you details over the phone. It's about Laura. She's been arrested. Can you get to Andover this evening?'

'Andover? In Hampshire?'

'Yes.'

'Where shall I meet you?'

Rory named a pub two miles out of the town on the main road. 'How long will it take you?'

'Make it an hour and a half. I'm on my boat.'

'Right. I'll see you later.'

Rory was on the outskirts of Andover now. He headed towards the centre where he guessed the police station would be. Ten minutes later a policeman was showing him into an interview room. Shortly afterwards, Laura came in.

She stood for a moment just inside the door. Her face was pale and there were worry lines on it which Rory hadn't seen before. Her expression was embarrassed and nervous.

'Hello, Rory. Thanks for coming.'

'No problem,' he said as he walked over to her.

The policeman who had ushered her in left the room and closed the door.

Rory had never seen her so helpless. He wanted to wrap his arms around her and stroke her hair, but he didn't.

'At least they're letting us talk in private. Are you being treated all right?' he asked.

She gave a faint smile. 'Yes, they couldn't be more polite. The man who arrested me was almost apologetic. And my little cell is reasonably civilised. Not much of a view, though. Simon Agnew's been.'

'Your solicitor?'

She nodded. 'He says he'll get me out in the morning. There'll be bail, of course, and they may take my passport away, but I wasn't going anywhere anyway.'

Rory sensed she was showing more bravery than she felt. 'Here, let's sit down. I'll make you a roll-up.'

She gave a weak laugh as they sat on two tubular steel chairs at a plain square table. The top was covered with scratches and a few barely eradicated obscenities. There was a half-full ashtray on it. 'I suppose I'll have to get used to roll-ups again.'

'Don't be stupid,' Rory said, more sharply than he'd intended. 'They can't make this charge stick.'

'Rory, they found an empty xylazine phial in my car. I don't know how the hell it got there, but the police say it was the stuff that was found in the postmortem. Unless somebody comes in and confesses, everything's in their favour. I had the opportunity to dope the horse, and I had several possible motives. Declan told them he'd left me alone with the horse for a few minutes after Henry had gone.'

'Did he?'

'Yes, but only for a moment, and for God's sake, Rory, whose side are you on?'

'I need to know as much as possible if I'm going to help you.'

'I don't see there's much you can do. I think they're going to charge me with conspiring to defraud the insurers as well. I'm afraid they're convinced I did it, and they're not looking too hard anywhere else.'

'Where else should they be looking?'

Laura looked away for a moment without speaking. She sighed. 'Look, when I get out tomorrow, I'll tell you what I think. I've already told the police, but they just think I'm lying.'

'If there's anything that needs doing, I'll do it.'

'Oh, Rory, why should you? You don't owe me a thing. I felt bad enough asking you to come here this evening.'

'I want you back training. You promised me a few good rides, remember?'

'Sure.' She looked at him. The slight smile on her lips showed confidence in him, guilt in herself. 'God, I'm sorry to drag you into this. Did you get hold of my father?'

'Yes. He should be on his way up from the Hamble now. He was on his boat.'

'Is he coming here?'

'No. It'll be too late. He's meeting me at a pub. I'll break the details to him gently there. If we want to, he and I can stay the night there and come in tomorrow to sort out your bail.'

'Thanks.' She shook her head. 'The other thing is to try and keep the press off the scent. Of course, they might pick up something at the hearing tomorrow, but with luck we'll get away before they're on to it.'

'They'll only come and pester you up at the house.'

'I'll worry about that then. Would you mind talking to them for me?'

'I think it would be better if your solicitor was your spokesman.'

'He's not a great communicator, but I suppose you're right.'

'What does he think?'

'I think he thinks I did it. In so far as Luke had any friends, he was one of them.'

'Try not to worry. If the police aren't going to follow any other lines, then I'll have to and maybe you'd better think about getting another lawyer.'

'That wouldn't look too good, would it?'

'No, I suppose not,' Rory shrugged. 'We'll see what he's like tomorrow.'

They were interrupted by the shirtsleeved constable who had shown Laura in.

'I'm sorry, Mr Gillespie, sir. That's your lot, I'm afraid. She's already had one more visitor than she should have.'

Rory didn't quibble. 'That's okay. She should be out of here tomorrow.'

'I couldn't say, sir.'

Rory turned to Laura. 'I'll see you in the morning. And don't worry, you'll be all right.'

Laura suddenly looked defeated again, but she wanted to believe him. 'Thanks,' she said in a small, tight voice. 'Thanks for coming.'

Rory nodded, and turned away quickly to leave the room. He couldn't let her see what he was really feeling.

Chapter Six

Rory arrived at the Dog and Badger half an hour before Edward Brickhill. It was a large pub, still crowded with drinkers and diners at eight o'clock on a Sunday evening. Rory hadn't eaten since lunch with Tommy, but the smells of hot food didn't tempt him.

He ordered a Scotch, then borrowed a *News of the World* from the barman and tried to read it while he waited for Laura's father. But the only item that held his attention was half a page of sensational revelations about the life and loves of the late Luke Mundy. The paper's indefatigable hacks had dug deep to unearth the identities of half a dozen women who claimed to have had affairs with Mundy. There was in the delivery of the piece a thinly disguised admiration for the scale of the dead tycoon's philandering. Rory wondered what Laura's reaction would be to see his activities so exposed. He hadn't forgotten Ralph Devereux's words – 'He had a strange sort of hold over her.'

Edward Brickhill made his commanding presence felt

the moment he walked into the pub. He stood for a moment in the doorway, looking around for Rory, and strode straight over when he spotted him.

'Hello, Rory. How are you?' He held out a hand, as if they were old friends who hadn't seen each other for a few weeks.

Rory bought drinks for them both – a Glenmorangie for himself, a large Hine for Brickhill. They settled down either side of a small round table, and satisfied themselves that they wouldn't be overheard.

'Okay, what's happened to Laura?' Brickhill asked.

'They've arrested her and charged her with manslaughter,' Rory told him bluntly. 'Maximum sentence, ten years.'

The older man didn't react or speak at once. Rory waited.

After a moment, Brickhill asked, almost as if gossiping about a stranger, 'Did she do it?'

Rory wasn't taken in. With surprise, he realised that Brickhill was prepared to accept his answer whatever it may be, and that that would affect his whole attitude to Laura's position.

Rory shook his head firmly. 'No. No way. Luke's death was a pure accident; no one could have planned it, and Laura certainly didn't want that horse to die.'

Brickhill took a pipe from his pocket, and filled it slowly. 'But the police think she did. And they must have some pretty strong evidence to charge her. And I dare say, as far as they're concerned, she had a strong motive. Laura is the beneficiary of a very substantial insurance policy on Luke's life.'

Rory paled. Why hadn't she told *him* that? But he stuck to his conviction. 'That may be so, but like I said, no one could have planned to kill Luke in that way.'

'No,' Edward Brickhill agreed, 'but they could have taken a chance on it. And Laura told me that she could benefit from a disability policy as well. A hundred thousand a year. It's a lot of money.'

'Do you really think she could do a thing like that?' Rory asked incredulously.

'No, of course I don't. Unfortunately, what you'd have to do to convince anyone else she didn't is to find hard proof – in other words another culprit.' He lit his pipe and raised an eyebrow. 'And you're going to do that, aren't you?'

Rory met Brickhill's steady eyes and knew that Laura's father wasn't ordering him, nor was he pleading with him; he was simply stating a fact. Rory nodded slowly.

'Are you still in love with her?' Brickhill's question took Rory by surprise. He gulped a mouthful of whisky before answering.

'I don't know. I honestly don't. I'd be lying if I said I had a happy marriage myself, but I've tried to stick it out, for my boy's sake. I really don't want to put my son through a divorce.'

'Frankly, though I was delighted at the time, I can't think why you married Fanshaw's daughter.'

'Well, I did.'

'And did Fanshaw keep all the promises he made you?'

Rory smiled at Brickhill's shrewdness. 'After a few years he wasn't in a position to, was he? But I did well enough while I was at his yard. What you've got to remember is that I was an uneducated, working-class boy; I wanted to get on. I'd have done anything for the chance of a good ride. If Laura had only let me talk to her, it might have been different, but she wouldn't even get in touch. I tried hard enough, and after a while Pam seemed like the answer to a lonely man's prayers. I guess I've grown up a lot since then. Anyway, you and your wife didn't do much to encourage me.'

'I've had cause to regret that since. I might say, I was no keener on Luke Mundy than I was on you, but Luke offered my daughter a glamorous alternative, and he had a very overpowering charm, if you could call it that. Still, he's had his just deserts, and I don't suppose anyone is mourning much.' Brickhill took a sip of brandy. 'That's not our concern, though. What we've got to do is get Laura off the hook.'

Rory nodded. 'Sure, but what do you mean by "we"?'

Brickhill ignored the question. 'If the police have arrested Laura, they aren't going to spend too much time looking for another culprit. You're going to have to find the leads to tempt them. Circumstantially, the evidence is stacked against her, I can see that. I spoke to her two days ago, and she told me then that she thought she was in trouble. What made the police charge her today?'

'They found a phial of the drug that was used on Midnight Express in her car. She told me it was planted there; she told the police too but they didn't believe her. It's ridiculous; I mean, for God's sake, if she had done it, the last thing she would do is leave the stuff lying around in her car.'

'I wouldn't say that. I wouldn't have thought anyone

was trying to kill the horse, just stop it. The way it was planned was quite ingenious, but either by bad luck or the wrong dose, the animal died, which prompted an autopsy. So it was pure chance that anyone discovered that it had actually been doped. The subsequent revelation – that the Jockey Club had had a tip-off, had the horse tested and found it clean – I'm afraid only compounds Laura's apparent guilt.'

Rory nodded. 'I realise that, of course. I'll do everything I can. I let her down once before, I won't do it again.

'Luckily, I'm not getting that many rides at the moment, which is why I was prepared to go and see Laura when I did. I've got a few this week, and then half a dozen at Cheltenham, but I'll do everything I can.'

'It might be a good idea to start with the professor from the vet college.'

'I will; then there's Declan, the lad, to talk to, and, of course, Henry Straker. He might be able to tell me more about the tip-off.'

'Any help you need from me,' Brickhill said, 'let me know. I'll give you a number where you can always contact me. Now, let's see if we can stay the night here. Then we'll go to court in the morning and get my daughter out of prison.'

Laura Mundy was formally charged with the manslaughter of her husband, and remanded to appear before a sitting of a high court judge at Winchester at the next sessions. The police did not object to her being bailed on her father's surety of £50,000, though they stipulated that she should yield up her passport.

To Laura's relief, only the regular duty journalist from the local paper was in court. They didn't doubt that he would be quick to earn a healthy bonus by selling the story to the agencies, but at least there were no photographers waiting outside. Laura, her father, her lawyer and Rory drove out of town to talk the situation over in the Monday morning quietness of the Dog and Badger.

Edward Brickhill behaved as if nothing worse had happened to Laura than her being expelled from school, which had happened twenty years before. His attitude was that it was an embarrassing misunderstanding which should be cleared up as quickly as possible. Simon Agnew, the solicitor, was less happy, but did his inadequate best to disguise it. Edward Brickhill proposed that Rory should take on the job of looking for evidence for the defence, until he had something concrete to offer the police. They would not at this stage instruct another investigator.

The solicitor noisily sucked air between his teeth. 'With respect to Mr Gillespie,' he said, turning to Brickhill, 'I think I'd be inclined to hire an investigator right away.'

'Under normal circumstances, I would leave everything to the police, but I've lost faith in them during the course of the past few years. We're talking about the possibility of my daughter going to prison for a very long time.' Brickhill stared hard at the solicitor and paused for a moment. 'I don't want her to spend one more minute behind bars. I want someone who is as keen on her acquittal as I am.' The tone of his voice indicated that this was the last word on the matter.

After half an hour of discreet conversation, it was

agreed that Rory would start his enquiries as soon as he'd driven Laura back to Langlands.

The cloud cover that had started the day was breaking up, letting in shafts of sun to light patches of the Hampshire Downs. For the first few miles of their drive, Rory and Laura didn't speak. Laura sat in the passenger seat gazing straight ahead, wincing every so often as they drove into a patch of sun. At last, she broke the silence.

'It's a terrible thing to admit, but I'm more upset about losing Midnight Express than losing Luke. I hope you're not too upset about losing your ride in the Champion Chase,' she said.

Rory turned his head quickly and glanced at her, to see if she was being serious, but he couldn't be sure.

'It's a pity you ran the horse at all. Even if he'd survived, he'd never have got back in shape for Cheltenham. You were going to have him withdrawn; it wouldn't have been hard to fake something.'

'That was the plan, until Luke threatened to ride him in the Grand Military as well, and even the Champion Chase. I told you, I had no choice.'

'Couldn't you have talked him out of it?'

'I tried. I told him I didn't think Express would get the trip, but he's won over three miles in modest company several times before, and frankly, in a field like that, it wasn't asking much. Anyway, it didn't make any difference what I said. Luke didn't actually tell me, but I think he'd had a monster bet; thank God they can't pursue a dead man for his gambling debts.'

'What sort of a monster bet?'

'I don't know; I'm only guessing he had, but I've never seen him so nervous, and considering the mess he's left behind, it seems likely, doesn't it?'

It did, Rory nodded. It also gave someone a reason for stopping the horse.

'Who did he bet with?'

'I haven't the slightest idea. I don't think he bet much. He certainly never referred to it. But he had his back to the wall in a way he never had before, so I suppose he was desperate.'

'Do you know what's going to happen to Langlands yet?'

'Not precisely, but I can't imagine I'll be able to stay there long. I mean, there are people howling for money, especially now they realise there isn't much left.'

'But you'll get the pay-out on his life insurance.'

Laura didn't answer for a moment. 'Only if I'm cleared of manslaughter.'

'How much is it?'

'Quite a lot.'

'Why didn't you tell me about it last night?'

Laura glanced at him, guiltily. 'I don't know. I suppose because it might be considered a motive.'

'People have been accused of killing their husbands without any financial incentive. And the rubbish papers were making quite a thing about Luke's affairs. Some people might think that was enough of a motive.'

'I haven't been charged with murdering Luke, for the simple reason that if I had wanted to murder him, there would have been less chancy ways of doing it. The police don't think I murdered him, they think I doped the horse and that he died as a result.'

'You could,' Rory echoed her father's proposition, 'have been taking a gamble on it, though.'

'Yes, I could have been – a million to one chance – but I wasn't,' she snapped.

Rory raised a hand from the steering wheel in a calming gesture. 'Look, I'm only trying to see it from the police's point of view. If I'm going to help you, I've got to know how they're thinking. I know you didn't do it.'

'Do you, really?' she asked, subdued.

'Yes. I do. And you've got to believe me and tell me *everything*.'

'Why are you doing this, Rory?' Laura held his gaze, already sure of his answer.

'Hmm,' Rory grunted. 'I'll tell you another time.'

'So, you're a *jockey*, then?' Professor Douglas asked as he poured Rory a whisky.

'Aye. Do you mind if I smoke?'

'No. I'll join you.' The professor carried the drinks over to a table placed between two chairs. He waved Rory into one of the chairs and sat in the other himself. 'As a matter of curiosity, do you have any authority to come here asking me questions?'

Rory had pulled his tobacco and papers from his jacket pocket. He began nimbly to roll a twig of a cigarette. 'Only the authority of natural justice. I'm here for Laura Mundy. Her father has asked me to help.'

'I see. What do you want to know that you haven't already read in the newspapers?'

'I wanted to be sure of what you found, and your opinion of how it would have affected the horse.'

'That's simple enough. What we found in the animal's

urine was a trace of a drug called xylazine which is commonly used as a pre-med before operations. Obviously, a smallish dose was used here, enough to make the horse drowsy, and from the report of the race, it didn't take long to work its way through. It shouldn't have had any damaging effect whatsoever. Unfortunately the horse died as a result of a fracture to the neck sustained in the fall.'

'So, I'd be right in saying that whoever gave it the stuff was intending to tire it, not kill it?'

'In principle, yes, though from the films I have watched of steeplechasing, it would be a pretty fair assumption that it would be in the act of jumping that the horse was most likely to come to grief, which has been known to result in death.'

'Usually, when a horse shows signs of becoming that tired, a good jockey would pull it up,' Rory said.

'But I gather this man, Luke Mundy, was an amateur?'

'There are amateurs who know what they're doing, but he wasn't one of them. Besides, it was a bit of time before the drug seemed to take effect. Before it tired the horse was going like a runaway train, and apparently Luke was desperate to win the race.'

'It's extraordinary the lengths to which vanity will drive some men.'

'In this case, it wasn't only vanity. Could you say how long it would have taken to administer the xylazine?'

'A dose of a few millilitres? No time at all – a few seconds perhaps, from a small syringe.'

'And where would it be injected?'

'Any convenient artery.'

'Right, that's very helpful.' Rory got to his feet. 'Thank

you very much, Professor, for the drink and the information.'

'Before you go, Mr Gillespie. There's something about this case that puzzles me, and I've already mentioned it to the police. The horse had been given far more xylazine than was necessary just to stop it from winning.'

'What are you saying, exactly?'

'I doubt very much that the drug was administered by a professional.'

Rory's heart sank.

No wonder the police were reluctant to spend time looking for another suspect.

The scientist showed the jockey to the door and they shook hands warmly. An open invitation to further scientific questions was swapped with an invitation to the races. Rory climbed into his car knowing that though it had been time well spent, he'd learned nothing that would help Laura.

He had called in at Douglas's house on his way back from Towcester races. It was now half past eight on Monday evening. Rory reckoned he just had time to get to Henry Straker's house in the Kennett Valley in Berkshire.

As the ten o'clock news started on his radio, he turned into the neat gravel drive that led up to the Strakers' handsome Georgian rectory.

A light still showed in a ground-floor window, so he climbed out of his car and crunched up to a large front door with a fine fanlight above. He pressed the discreet brass button and waited.

It was a while before the door was opened.

Susan Straker, a strong, good-looking but disappointed

woman, greeted Rory warmly enough. They didn't know each other well but had met and chatted at a few drinks parties.

'Sorry to call so late, Susan. I was hoping I might catch Henry in.'

'I thought it would be Henry you wanted to see,' she said with mock disappointment. 'But I'm afraid he's in bed. He came back from a session of five-a-side soccer with the boys' club feeling pretty knackered and he's got a very early start tomorrow.'

Rory judged it unproductive to press, and quelled his impatience. 'That's a shame; I did want to talk to him quite urgently. Look, do you think I could arrange to see him tomorrow night, after the races, say seven o'clock?'

'I don't see why not. I'll tell him. Just check first to make sure he hasn't got held up anywhere.'

'Right. Thanks. I'll see you tomorrow then.'

At seven the next morning, Rory was walking back from his stables with his dog, Taffy. He was surprised to see Pam leaning out of their bedroom window. It was early for her to be awake.

'Phone!' she yelled hoarsely.

Rory quickened his pace. He guessed it was Laura.

'Who is it?' he shouted back.

'It's my bloody father. He wants to know if you can do ten-two this afternoon. Micky Fortune can't ride because he's hurt his back.'

Rory slowed down. 'Tell him I'll ring him back in quarter of an hour.'

Pam's head disappeared. Rory thought about his father-in-law. Fanshaw had mentioned he might want Rory to ride a moderate mare in the handicap hurdle at Warwick that afternoon. Without giving it too much thought, Rory had looked up the form. Carrying almost bottom weight over three miles, it was in with a very slim chance – no more. If Mick was planning to have a punt on it, he must be feeling bloody desperate. Rory had forgotten all about it.

Inside, Rory checked his weight on the scales in his bathroom. To get down to ten stone two pounds he'd have to be in a sauna for an hour or so – time for which he had much better uses.

Downstairs he said to Pam, 'I don't think I can ride your father's horse. I won't be able to do the weight.'

'I don't care one way or the other. Anyway, he must be mad if he thinks he can win with her.'

Rory picked up the *Sporting Life* that the postman always brought up for him. 'The betting forecast's got her at thirty-threes; maybe he's going for a place. There are nineteen runners – she only needs to come in the first four. At eight to one, that's not such a bad bet.'

'I'm all for him winning something, then he might be able to pay Mum some of the money he owes her.'

Rory shook his head in despair and picked up the phone.

'Hello, Mick?'

'Rory! Can you do it?' Fanshaw didn't believe in preamble.

'No, I won't make the weight.'

'That won't matter. All you have to do is get her in the frame.'

'That's what I thought.'

'Look, you'll have no problem. She's not a bad horse and there's fuck all to beat.'

'Having a big one, are you?'

'I've got to, Rory. There isn't a feed merchant left that'll deliver here. Your mother-in-law's lawyers are getting heavy and I haven't paid the rent for four months.'

Rory sighed. 'I might put up a pound or two overweight.'

'So long as it's only a pound or two.' There was real relief in Fanshaw's gravelly voice.

'See you there then,' Rory said and put the phone down, not sure whether he'd agreed in order to please his father-in-law or annoy his wife.

He poured himself half a cup of black coffee, which in the circumstances would count as breakfast, and glanced at the other paper.

There was a photograph of Laura on the front page of the *Daily Mail*, standing at her husband's graveside at his funeral the day before. She looked good in black and though she wasn't smiling, she didn't look particularly heartbroken. Rory wondered why she hadn't made more of an effort.

He thought of her, and Professor Douglas and Henry Straker, as he drove up to Warwick at midday.

He hadn't expected to see any of them at the races, but Henry Straker was there, talking to Laura and George Rutherford by the paddock before the first race.

Rory clenched his jaw. Rutherford seemed to be moving in fast. He hoped Laura knew what she was doing.

Although the news of Laura's arrest and subsequent

charging with the manslaughter of her husband had been on the front pages of every national newspaper for the last two days, with pictures of the funeral getting star billing in most of them, it was clear she planned to carry on as though nothing had happened. The Jockey Club helped by holding back from making any comment or ruling on Laura's position, on the advice of their lawyers, as her case was now *sub judice*.

Rory couldn't help admiring her courage as she went about the job of saddling five runners, dealing with their owners, and ignoring the rubbernecking of the crowd and the occasional harassment by journalists. She showed no sign of the doubts he had seen when he had driven her home the day before.

Rory had one ride for her, on her second string in the second race, a handicap chase, where Dai was on the favourite for her, with the weights against him.

She didn't disguise her pleasure when, in the face of the Welshman's open hostility, Rory returned to the winner's enclosure.

Rory was riding his father-in-law's horse in the last race, the handicap hurdle. Fanshaw was waiting for him on the way to the jockeys' changing room. Rory reflected that he seemed to have aged ten years in the last six months. He looked drained and his thick hair, once a rich brown, was almost white now.

'Everything okay, Mick,' he said in an effort to get a spark out of the old man.

Fanshaw tried to put a smile on his worried face. 'Not so bad. Nice win you had there. Hope you make it a double on mine. She's come on terrific since her last run, the top weight's giving her two stone and the rest are all beatable. I got a monkey on her each way at thirty-threes. She'll be lucky to win, but she can't be out of the first four,' he said with a hint of desperation in his voice.

'I'll do my best.' Rory tried to sound confident and took the colours Fanshaw was holding for him. 'I'll see you in the ring.'

Fanshaw's owner, one of the few still loyal to him, was standing with the trainer when Rory marched out into the parade ring.

Fanshaw turned to Rory. 'I was just telling Mr Vickers here that if anyone can get his mare to win, it's my son-in-law, eh, Rory?'

Mr Vickers didn't look convinced. 'As long as she gets in the frame in this company, she can stay with you and I'll be happy, Mick. But I must have some kind of result or the missus'll just carry on moaning until I get rid of her – the 'orse, that is, not the missus.' He laughed. 'Though, Gawd knows, the mare's cheaper to run.'

'Look, Mr Vickers, if you can still get her at twenties, you have a good each way. There's nineteen runners – they'll pay to the fourth. That'd be good value.'

'She certainly looks well,' Rory said, watching the horse being led around the ring. 'And the ground will suit her, if I remember from last time.'

'It will,' Fanshaw said eagerly.

Jogging down to the start, Rory was thinking more about Laura Mundy and his date that evening with Henry Straker than Fanshaw's bottom-weight hurdler. But as they approached the start, his mind automatically applied itself to the job in hand. Despite everything Mick Fanshaw had ever done, from talking him into marrying his daughter to systematically welshing on almost every verbal agreement they had ever made, Rory still liked him. Mick had always been a real racing character, and there were few enough of them around now. He also had a natural affinity with horses. A few seasons with a virus in the yard and not many winners didn't suddenly make him a bad trainer. And, perversely, they had become closer as a result of Pam's behaviour.

Rory had almost subconsciously been assessing the opposition in the ring and on the way down. He guessed he had a reasonable chance of getting home among the first four. To help Fanshaw keep one of the few horses left in his yard and take £4,000 from the bookies, he'd make sure of it.

That the mare was going to struggle began to show as she landed just behind the leader at the second-last flight. Rory felt her begin to tie up. He had brought her over to the better ground on the stand side and had the rail to help her, but she was tired and her legs felt heavy. The winning post was still two furlongs away. Rory sensed another horse waiting to pounce. It came past him quickly, followed by another. Whatever happened, he couldn't let one more by.

At the last flight, the mare, with a heart bigger than her small frame, tried to stand off, landed in a heap and lost all momentum.

Rory did everything legal he could think of to keep her going, to make her stretch out and quicken, but with a sense of failure out of proportion to the event, he watched helplessly as another horse moved up into fourth

173

place twenty yards from the line.

Pulling the mare up past the post, Rory turned and walked her back towards the stands. He caught up with the horse which had passed him into fourth place. With relief, he recognised its jockey as a hungry young hustler who had just lost his allowance and already fancied himself hard and worldly-wise. He hadn't been racing long enough to appreciate Rory's reputation for honest riding.

'Hey, Bruce,' Rory whispered hurriedly, wanting to talk before the lads took hold of their horses, 'do you want to earn five hundred quid?'

The young jockey swivelled quickly in his saddle with a greedy grin on his face.

'S'long as it's easy.'

'It is. Just forget to weigh in.'

A big, knowing smile crossed the other jockey's face. 'No problem.'

'Good lad,' Rory said, feeling sick. 'Are you at Folkestone tomorrow?'

The young jockey nodded.

'Fine, I'll pay you there, okay?'

Bruce nodded briefly and turned to talk to the lad who had come out to greet him.

Rory reined back his horse and let the other get ahead. Once in the unsaddling enclosure, he headed back to the weighing room, not wanting to show any presumption about the imminent announcement that the fourth horse had been disqualified on account of his jockey failing to weigh in, with the fifth horse being promoted.

Mick Fanshaw was too old a hand to show any open

appreciation for what Rory had done for him. He wouldn't have placed the bet in his own name, had probably anyway placed it in half a dozen shops. No one would notice a connection. The only reference Mick made to the outcome later on was in a quick whisper out of the side of his mouth. 'Tell me how much it cost you, and I'll see you about it.'

'I'll tell you another time, Mick,' Rory said quickly.

At the same time, he saw Laura walking towards him, and he didn't relish a confrontation between her and his father-in-law. Mick gave him a nod and walked off to deal with his horse.

There was quite a crowd outside the weighing room. Laura conveyed with a look that she knew exactly what Rory had done, and that he'd made nothing from it.

Aloud, she said, 'Can you come and work Flamenco Dancer tomorrow?'

'Yes, of course. What time?'

'First lot. Be in the yard by seven thirty.'

'I'll be there.'

Chapter Seven

When he had showered, Rory went to the big steamy bar under the main stand to look for his wife.

Pam had wanted to come to the races that day, and they usually met in this bar afterwards. Rory's search was held up by friends and complete strangers wanting to congratulate him on his win earlier in the afternoon. He answered them all with his usual good nature. He gave no sign of impatience as he evaded an interview with a journalist anxious to know what he thought about Dayglow, the horse which it had just been announced he would ride in the Champion Hurdle the following week.

But he didn't find Pam and he had no intention of scouring the other bars. He left briskly, clutching his bag and wearing a purposeful expression to deter more conversation.

Pam had arranged for Tommy to have tea with a school friend in Lambourn, but their son would be waiting to be picked up at six and Rory knew that Tommy fretted if he thought he had been forgotten – a result, Rory guessed, of having a father who was away a lot of the time and a mother who didn't give a damn.

Tommy was pleased Rory had come to pick him up. Though he was used to his father being a jockey, he had become acutely conscious that, in a town dominated by racing, to be the son of a leading jockey meant a lot to his peers. As they drove the few miles up the valley to Camp Farm, Tommy took advantage of his father's undivided attention.

'Dad, can we do that fishing trip this weekend? You did promise we'd do it soon.'

Rory felt guilt tugging at his guts. He wanted to devote every available moment to uncovering the truth about Midnight Express and Luke Mundy's death.

He sighed to himself as he spoke. 'Sure, Tommy. I'll fix it. We'll drive up Saturday night and spend all of Sunday fishing. Okay?'

The boy's eyes gleamed. 'That'd be brill, Dad. Thanks.'

Taffy wandered out of the house to greet them, wagging his tail, but there was no sign of Pam. Rory phoned Henry Straker's house to confirm that Henry would be back by seven. He dialled the farm in the next valley and spoke to the bovine babysitter, who agreed to come down and take charge of Tommy while he was out.

He arrived at Henry Straker's house a little before seven. Susan showed him into their old-fashioned drawing room, spotless through lack of children.

'Can I offer you a drink?' she asked.

'A wee Scotch, please.'

She poured a large one and a matching gin and tonic

for herself. They sat down in large chintz armchairs either side of an empty fireplace.

'Do you mind my asking why you're so anxious to talk to Henry?' Susan asked.

Rory made a sucking sound through his lips. He looked at a framed photograph on the small round table beside him – Henry with twenty or so of the boys from the youth club to which he devoted most of his spare time. He turned back to look at Susan. 'I'm sure you can guess.'

'Midnight Express?'

Rory nodded and took a sip of whisky.

Susan looked a little distraught. 'Poor Henry. It seems to have upset him no end. He had the police here for hours last Friday. The whole thing has really shaken him. He's always hated that side of racing.'

'I know,' Rory said. 'He's a very decent man, and I'm sorry to have to go on about it, but now the police have charged Laura . . .' He shrugged.

'You're doing this for her, then?'

'Aye.'

'But I thought you and she didn't really get on.'

'We didn't.'

Susan looked surprised. 'Oh, I see,' she said knowingly.

'Anyway, I wouldn't want to see her locked up for something she didn't do, would you?'

'But how can you be so sure she didn't? After all, I gather from Henry she stands to get nearly two and half million from the insurance company.'

Rory was startled to hear the sum. 'As much as that? Well, she certainly wouldn't get it if they found she had a hand in what happened. Anyway,' Rory continued, trying to build his confidence, 'I'm bloody sure she didn't do it and I intend to find out who did.'

'But Henry's told everything he knows to the police. If he'd given them any other leads, they'd have followed them up, surely?'

'I guess so, but I just wanted to see if there was anything else; I might be able to jog his memory a bit. I mean – I was riding that day.'

They both looked up at the sound of the front door being unlocked.

'Here he is,' Susan whispered. 'Try not to go on too long.'

Rory nodded.

As he walked in, Henry assumed his normal, cheerful manner, but couldn't entirely hide from Rory the strain he was feeling.

'Hello, Rory. Nice to see you. Ah, good, you've got a drink. Susan, ready for another?'

'No, thanks,' she answered, rising to her feet. 'I've got a few things to get on with, if you'll excuse me.'

She left and shut the door behind her.

Henry poured himself a small glass of amontillado, and remained standing in front of the fireplace.

'Well, Rory, I gather you dropped in last night after I'd gone to bed; sorry about that. Anyway, what can I do for you?'

Rory started hesitantly. 'I'm afraid I want to ask you about Midnight Express.'

A fleeting look of consternation flashed across Henry's face.

'Oh,' he said, and sat down where Susan had been.

'What a ghastly business. It's been hell being caught up in it. And to think I wasn't even supposed to be on duty that day; Charters cried off – flu or something.'

'Laura and her father asked me to find out more about what happened. I mean, though the circumstantial case against her looks pretty bad, I know she didn't do it.' Rory made the statement vehemently, as much to convince himself as Straker. The vet winced slightly.

'I admit, I was rather surprised. I wish I knew who else it could have been, or why.'

'Okay, but you know her well enough. She's a tough woman, I'll grant you, and Luke Mundy was a bastard, but there's no way any sane person would try to murder someone like that – on the off-chance they might be killed in a fall.'

'Well, no, that's not what the police think, but they found a phial of xylazine in her car. Why on earth would she have it otherwise?' Henry looked puzzled.

'It could easily have been planted. Even if she left her car locked, any experienced car thief could have opened it, put the stuff in and locked it again – no problem. Even easier at the yard.'

'I suppose so, but as the police said, why should anyone want to pin it on her?'

'Can you think of anyone who might?' Rory asked sharply.

Straker looked taken aback by Rory's tone, but didn't protest.

'Er, well. No, I'm afraid I can't.'

'Someone who might be jealous of her, maybe?'

Straker wrinkled his brow. 'Well, it's rather embarrassing to say it, but there's always your father-in-law or, for that matter, your wife.'

Rory laughed. 'It certainly wasn't Pam. Nothing's happened between Laura and me since I married Pam, and even if it had, I don't think Pam would care much.'

'All right, I'm sorry to suggest it, but what about Mick Fanshaw? He's lost a lot of horses to Laura's yard over the last season.'

'And to a few other yards,' Rory added.

'But most to Langlands. I think he's probably quite a bitter man now.'

Rory thought of Fanshaw's face after he had squeezed his mare into the frame in the last race. He had to admit that Fanshaw was quite capable of harbouring a grudge. 'He's bound to be feeling sore about it, but he wouldn't bother to do anything like that, not if he wasn't going to make any money out of it.'

'I'm not so sure. Anyway, he's the only person I can think of. Maybe he thought if Laura's horse was found doped, she'd lose her licence and he might get some of his horses back.'

Rory considered this for a moment. 'I don't know. Of course, Mick's an old rogue, but I really don't think he's that vindictive. Now, are you absolutely certain that you sent the right blood sample to the lab for testing?'

Henry, looking gloomily into the fire, jerked his head up to give Rory a sharp look. 'What are you implying?'

'I'm not implying anything. I'm just wondering if it was possible you got the sample mixed up with another.'

'Of course I didn't,' Straker said, indignant now. 'I label each phial as soon as I've filled it, and anyway, I didn't do any other tests that day. There's absolutely no question that the horse was completely clean when I tested it – no question at all. The xylazine shots must have been administered during the hour or so between my taking the test and the horse being led to the pre-parade ring.'

'Did you happen to see anyone who looked out of place hanging round his box?'

'Well, there are always people milling around – lads, trainers, transport. Obviously, I don't *know* them all, but I don't recall seeing anyone who looked particularly alien. Anyway, the horse's lad – Declan, I think – told the police that he had been with the horse or near its box all the time, and no one besides Mrs Mundy went near it.'

'Yes, I know he said that, but he could have been lying, couldn't he? I mean someone might have paid him to lie, and he's quite a sharp little guy.'

'Well, I suppose if Fanshaw had done it – and he was around; he had a runner that day – he might have got at the lad, yes.'

Rory put his empty whisky glass down and stood up. 'Well, thanks very much for your time, Henry. You've given me a few ideas. Would you mind if I got back to you if I think of anything else?'

'No, not at all, but I don't really think you're going to find much. As you say, the circumstantial case against Laura is very strong.'

'But only circumstantial. I can tell you, I don't intend to give up until I've found out and proved who's done this.'

Henry Straker nodded slowly. 'Well, I quite understand. I just hope you can prove she *is* innocent. But I don't think you'll get any further than the police.'

'We'll see. Thanks for the drink. I'll see myself out.'

Rory was intending to drive into Langlands by the front entrance next morning, but the gates at the lodge were shut, and two cars were parked outside. Their drivers were leaning on one of them, smoking. It didn't need the camera with a 600mm lens hanging round the neck of one of them to tell Rory that they were reporters. He drove on and in by the more discreet entrance to the stable yard.

Up on the downs, with Flamenco Dancer stretching out under him, he was able to forget for a while what had now become almost an obsession with tracking down the truth about Luke's death. Laura was waiting at the end of the gallop; the few brief words they exchanged were limited to the gelding's performance and Rory's opinion of him.

But later, driving from the yard up to the house on the internal road, all the conflicting information he had gathered so far crowded back into his head.

Laura, still displaying the same calm she had shown at Warwick the day before, was concluding a deep discussion with Patrick Hoolihan over the breakfast table.

She looked up from the *Sporting Life* and smiled as Rory walked in.

'I see you've already got yourself another ride in the Champion Chase,' she said.

Rory nodded. He'd fixed it with the Irish trainer en route to Warwick the day before. If the ground came up soft, it would definitely have an each-way chance.

'Do you want to get off it and on to Flamenco Dancer?' Laura went on.

'Yes,' Rory said. 'But I won't.'

'Why not? There's no need to worry about Dai. I'm going to announce that we're parting company as soon as Cheltenham's over.'

Rory walked to the sideboard to pour himself some coffee. 'It's not that. It's loyalty: I've arranged to ride another horse, and I don't want to let people down.'

Laura raised her eyebrows with a rueful smile. 'For God's sake, Rory, no one would blame you.'

'Except me.' He sat down at the table and helped himself to some lukewarm toast.

Laura shrugged. 'Well, if anything goes wrong with your mount, the offer stands. I feel I owe you, and George Rutherford's very keen for you to ride. It's not as though you've got much else with a chance.'

Rory grinned. 'The bookmakers don't agree with you. Have you seen how Dayglow's been backed?'

Patrick Hoolihan laughed. 'That's a red herring.'

'We'll see.'

'I see you're riding against us this afternoon,' Patrick went on. 'You should beat us as easily as a nun gets to heaven.'

'Do all nuns get to heaven?'

'My mother used to tell my sisters they did,' Patrick shrugged. 'Anyway, our chap's not ready yet; he needs a couple more runs, for experience, does he not, Mrs Mundy?'

Laura nodded. 'But we'll win the first, as long as Dai does as he'd told. He's riding Pan Piper, another of George's that came up from Mick Fanshaw's yard.'

'And we don't want to give Mick the chance to bad-mouth Langlands in the bar afterwards,' Patrick added. 'I see, by the way, that you're riding Camp Follower. You bred him, didn't you?'

Rory nodded. 'Yes. And he'll be the very first winner I've ridden that I've bred myself,' he added confidently.

Rory's first ride at Folkestone that day wasn't until four o'clock. Edward Brickhill had rung the evening before to ask if they could meet on the way.

'I don't suppose you'll want any lunch, but we can talk while I eat mine.'

They met at a small restaurant on the river at Windsor. Once there, Rory couldn't resist the smell of cooking, and ordered a small, lightly grilled sole. He was, he excused himself, riding top weights in both of his only booked races and he had a good stone in hand.

'How was Laura this morning?' Edward asked when they had disposed of the formalities.

Rory answered him against the background murmur of people enjoying expensive food. 'I can't believe how calm she is. Yesterday at Warwick, she behaved as if nothing had happened. Of course, everyone's talking about it, but she just paid no attention.'

'She's a girl with a lot of guts, my daughter. I also think it's the right way for her to play it. These days, when a case like this gets so much publicity, it's as important to convince the media you're innocent as it is the judge and jury.'

'I know, but . . .' Rory paused, 'she's almost *too* calm.'

'That worries you?'

'It's just that I don't know what she's thinking. I haven't had a chance to talk to her alone for a few days; it's as if she doesn't want me to. And there are things she never told me, like the amount she stands to gain on Luke's life insurance.'

'That's a side issue, Rory. After all, the police haven't charged her with murder, which they would have done if they thought she'd planned it.'

'Aye, but they still could.'

'Look, don't get negative about it. You've known Laura for long enough to know that she's always been rather secretive. Some people are; they feel they're giving too much of themselves away if they let others know what's inside. I understand that; I'm the same.'

'Yes, I know what you mean, but I'm doing this for her, for Christ's sake. She's got to trust me.'

'Fair enough. I'll talk to her about it, but in the mean-time, how have you got on?'

'I saw Henry Straker last night and Professor Douglas on Monday. The professor confirmed that the horse hadn't been given anything like enough xylazine to kill him, but more than enough just to slow him down. His opinion was that it wasn't done by a professional. It looks as if it was a simple case of stopping it winning. Nothing particularly unusual about that. Laura told me she thought that Luke had had a bet on it, but she didn't know how much, or who with.'

'That's odd,' Edward Brickhill said. 'I was never aware of Luke gambling on the horses, not seriously, anyway. The odd tenner for interest's sake. I've a strong suspicion that he gambled on the stock market, or at least on the movement of share prices with one of these outfits that makes books on that kind of thing.'

'Are there many who do?'

'I think that anyone with a bookmaker's licence can do it, but I don't know which do. I could find out easily enough. So, since we're agreed that Laura didn't do it, it seems obvious that the horse *must* have been doped to stop it winning, and the police ought to be talking to the bookmakers.'

'I agree.'

'And what did Straker have to say?'

'Poor old Henry, he's well shaken up by the whole thing. He's absolutely certain there was nothing wrong with the animal when he took his sample, which leaves about an hour for someone to have got at him. He said he didn't see anyone around the stables who shouldn't have been there. He suggested it might have been Mick Fanshaw; he had a horse a few boxes away.'

'Why the hell did he think Mick would do it?'

Rory shrugged. 'To get at Laura maybe. If she loses her licence the horses will have to go somewhere. Mick probably thinks he would get them back in his yard. He's lost almost a dozen to her already.'

'I suppose that's just possible, but I had horses with Mick for a long time, and I knew him well. He certainly never used to be someone to harbour that kind of a grudge. But then, that was a few years ago when he was having a good run.'

'There's no question he's turned pretty sour over the last year. I mean, everything's gone wrong for him. I don't see him that much, though. He and Pam haven't got on for years, and I think he embarrasses her now.'

'And how are you getting on with Pam, if that's not too personal a question?'

'Like I told you the other day, it hasn't been much of a marriage for a long time now, but I won't leave her, not till Tommy's older and able to look after himself. He's insecure enough as it is.'

'Should one believe the rumours that occasionally do the rounds?'

'About her flirtations? I've tried not to notice, especially recently. To be quite honest with you, I don't really mind any more. She didn't leave with me after a party the other night, and didn't get back till about four in the morning. I pretended not to wake up, so I never asked her what she'd been doing.'

'Have you any idea who she might have been with?'

Rory made a face. 'I've got a nasty suspicion it was Dai Price, but then, they're two of a kind.'

'You don't think Mick's annoyed with you for letting that happen, and the fact that you're riding for Laura again?'

'No.' Rory shook his head. 'I really don't think so.'

'Okay, but we have to consider every possibility. Human nature can lead people to do the most unexpected things.'

As they ate their lunch, they went over the same ground. Rory agreed to follow up the Mick Fanshaw line by talking to Declan Hoolihan and one of Mick's lads with whom he was still on good terms.

He arrived at Folkstone to be greeted by the news that Dai had won the previous race on George Rutherford's ex-Fanshaw horse. The favourite had unexpectedly weakened and fallen three from home.

Rory saw Dai in the changing room. He made sure nobody saw him passing an envelope to Bruce for forgetting to weigh in the day before. From the embarrassed way in which Dai was behaving, he knew that what had once been a flirtation between Dai and Pam had developed into something more. Despite the indifference he had declared to Edward Brickhill at lunch, he couldn't avoid a spasm of jealousy. He gritted his teeth and tried to remind himself that this was a simple case of slighted male pride, but he felt a violent surging in his guts, and had to quell an urge to walk over and confront the flashy Welshman.

But he fought back the feeling, pushed it out of his consciousness, tried to enforce complete emotional dissociation from a wife for whom he had long ago lost what little respect he'd ever had.

Rory's mount, Camp Follower, a young gelding that Rory himself had bred and named, was the first foal he'd had from his first mare. Like most breeders, he retained a proprietorial affection for horses he had bred long after they had left his farm, especially the first one, and the closer it got to the race, the more Rory realised how much he wanted to win.

In the parade ring, the affable Lambourn trainer who legged him up into the saddle had no inkling of what had been going through the jockey's mind. He saw only the usual chirpy smile and uncomplicated attitude to the job for which Rory was famous.

'How do you want him ridden?' Rory asked.

'You know the horse, you bred him; he likes a late run. In this small field, hold him up until the last fence, then let him go. He'll have no trouble with the weight over this trip.'

Rory nodded. He hadn't identified any serious dangers and this was reflected in the price that was being offered about his mount. He was never complacent these days, but he cantered down to the start reluctantly confident that he was about to ride his forty-eighth, and most memorable, winner of the season.

Rory joined the other six in the field to inspect the first fence. Dai Price still hadn't looked at him, and Rory behaved as if he hadn't seen him either – it was easier for them both that way. This became more difficult as the horses circled behind the start, waiting for the starter to call them up.

When Rory did meet Dai's eyes, there was a look of such shifty guilt in them that he almost felt sorry for him.

He thought about it again as he cruised along at the back of the field, a couple of horses behind Dai's. Camp Follower was a well-balanced, experienced jumper who could see his own stride and needed little help from his pilot. Rory had schooled him regularly from the age of two.

Rory found his mind wandering, going back over the conversation he had had at lunch with Edward Brickhill.

Was there any possibility that Mick Fanshaw would feel so vindictive about Laura's success that he would want to remove her from the game? That certainly wouldn't help Mick or, as Rory had pointed out to Straker, make him any money. Still, he thought, he may as well talk to a couple of the lads, sound them out on Mick's movements that day at Kempton.

Rory's thoughts were interrupted by the need to concentrate on the big open ditch they were approaching, where horses always found it harder to judge their stride. In front of him, Dai's horse hit the guard rail with a massive crack and parted the birch on the way over. The mistake shot Dai up the horse's neck. Camp Follower momentarily lost concentration, took off a pace early and launched himself into a massive leap, just clearing the fence.

They landed to the right of Dai Price, who was scrambling to regain his balance. Dai was on the point of getting back into the saddle, when the horse picked itself up and galloped on towards the next fence. As Dai teetered on the horse's back, Rory noticed immediately that Dai's right boot had been forced through the narrow aluminium stirrup. In the next instant, he'd dropped over the side and his inverted body was being bounced viciously on his head and shoulders, caught every few strides by a galloping hoof.

Even if he survived to the next fence, he'd be seriously injured when the horse tried to jump it.

Rory took a quick look round and cursed; Camp Follower was going easily but he was the only one in a position to help. He had no option. His conscience wouldn't let him race on, even though this was the last man in the world he wanted to help.

He drew alongside and a little ahead of Dai's mount. To the confusion of Camp Follower, he started to pull him to the left, off the steeplechase course, away from the leaders.

Dai's horse had to come with them. They carried on turning in a wide arc within the confines of the running rails of the flat course, still deep and lush before mowing for the coming season. Rory was careful not to take too tight a curve, to avoid Dai's horse kicking the jockey any more than it had already done. As they turned, the horses lost momentum and the urge to follow. Rory was able to reach over and grab the bridle and pull up both horses to a trot, then a standstill.

He glanced back down the course and saw an ambulance already on its way. He leaped off his horse, hanging on to the reins, and walked round to unhook Dai's foot from the stirrup. Dai was conscious, and groaning as Rory lowered his legs to the ground. His eyes were closed, but he opened one for a moment, saw Rory, and groaned again. 'Thanks.'

Rory ignored him and led Camp Follower away. He'd chucked the race, and all for the man who was trying to take his wife from him.

Chapter Eight

The racing press next day reported that Dai Price hadn't been badly injured – bruised and cut by his horse's flying hoofs, half concussed, but with no bones broken. He hoped to be back in action in a couple of days.

One thing was certain, Rory thought as he drove once more across the Berkshire Downs in the grey morning light, Dai Price wouldn't be at Langlands today.

Patrick Hoolihan was the first to see him walk into the yard.

'Good morning, Rory. Bit of a hero yesterday, I hear?'

Rory laughed. 'A moment of madness, Pat.'

'So we imagined, though I don't think the public quite appreciated the irony of it.'

'No,' Rory agreed. 'But Dai did.'

'Still, he rode a winner for us on Pan Piper which took the wind out of Fanshaw's sails. It used to be with him and he'd been telling everyone it wouldn't win from our yard. Did you hear the stewards ordered a pre-race dope test on the favourite?'

'No, I hadn't heard that,' replied Rory, now much more alert.

Patrick shrugged his narrow shoulders. 'Mrs Mundy said he looked fine in the paddock, but later he was running with his tongue hanging out – a bit like Express did at Kempton.'

Rory's head jerked up and he slapped his whip against the side of his boot. 'I wonder if there's a link?'

The head lad looked at him sharply. 'That's what she thought.'

Rory rode up to the gallops on a horse that was new to him. Mrs Mundy, Patrick had said, wanted to hear what he thought of it.

Back at the house later with Patrick, he delivered his views, and hoped to find a few moments with Laura alone. This time the interruption was provided by Henry Straker.

Laura looked up at him with a smile. 'How have you got on?'

Henry sat down wearily and nodded his head. 'She'll be all right.'

'What's this?' Rory asked.

'One of the new fillies arrived from Newmarket with a lump on her ear like a football,' Laura said. 'Wouldn't let anyone near her with a bridle and nothing seemed to reduce it.'

'Well, it will now,' Henry said. 'We had to give her a shot, then I lanced it and drained it. Give her a week and she'll be fine.'

The vet discussed other horses that needed looking at and the blood tests he was to take and analyse that day, anxious, Rory guessed, to avoid any more discussion about the events at Kempton.

Rory, anyway, didn't want to talk about it in front of Laura and he thought that Straker wouldn't have anything new to offer.

Patrick and Henry left together to see the horses out for the next lot, leaving Rory and Laura alone at last.

'How are you feeling?' Rory asked as soon as the door had closed.

Laura pushed Midas's golden head from where it nestled in her lap and stood up. She walked across the room to stare out of the window at the garden where daffodils were beginning to flourish their yellow trumpets. She turned back to look at Rory and her face abruptly crumpled. He felt a guilty tingle of excitement as he watched her struggling to fight back her tears. He knew she wouldn't drop her defences like this for anyone else.

'It's hell. I don't know how much longer I can take the strain of pretending that everything's fine.' Her voice began to tremble. 'But that's the only way I can handle it.'

The moment of weakness passed and Laura took a deep breath. 'How are you getting on?'

'I know more than I did,' Rory said. 'There are a few lines for me to follow.'

'Like what?' Laura didn't sound hopeful.

'I'll tell you if and when I find anything worthwhile. But can you tell me something?'

'What?'

'Has my father-in-law ever expressed any kind of vindictiveness about the horses that you've had from his yard?'

Laura thought for a moment. 'Yes, I suppose he has, in the same way that you'd expect anyone to react.'

'With threats of any sort?'

'A bit of loud-mouthed slagging off, but not threats exactly, no. You don't really think he could have had anything to do with it?'

'It's possible. I'm fairly sure that whoever got at the horse only wanted to stop it, not kill it. The fact that some of the stuff was planted in your car would have been for one of two reasons. Either someone was simply laying a red herring to cover their own tracks, or they were deliberately trying to frame you, to get your licence taken away. I've been trying to think who might want that badly enough to go to all that trouble. Can you think of anyone who might?'

Laura gazed bleakly at Rory. 'Right now, I feel the whole world's against me, though I know they're not. Of course there are people who resent the success I've had, especially because I'm a woman. But I really can't think of anyone who'd go to such lengths, not even Mick Fanshaw.'

'Well, think about it, and if you come up with anyone, let me know. I'm going to meet one of Mick's lads at the races today, and I'll see if he can tell me anything. Like I say, it may not be likely, but it is possible.'

Laura nodded half-heartedly. 'Okay. And I'll let you know if I think of anyone.'

Rory wanted to talk to her about the insurance money as well, but he judged she'd had enough for now. He left her to get herself together for visitors – owners, she said – who they heard arriving at the house.

'Keep your chin up,' Rory said, giving her arm an affectionate squeeze. 'We'll get there.'

Olly Mullens had worked for Mick Fanshaw for twenty years. Like a lot of lads, he had started out with dreams of jockey stardom, soon dashed by two fruitless apprentice years. Olly had taken Rory under his wing when he had arrived at Mick's and had hero-worshipped him since he had ridden his first winner for the yard. Since then, Olly had been rewarded for his loyalty to Mick by being made travelling head lad and box driver and he and Rory usually found time for a quick word whenever they met at the races.

That afternoon, Rory found him about to unload a runner in the lorry park at Wincanton racecourse.

'Have you got a minute, Olly?'

'Sure,' the lad answered, dropping the side ramp at his feet.

'This may sound like a crazy question, but it's about Luke Mundy's fall. You know the horse was doped?'

'Of course, it was all over the papers, and Laura Mundy being charged with it and all.'

'Do you think she did it?'

Olly shrugged. 'How would I know? I don't have a clue. But they found the stuff in her car, didn't they?'

'Sure, but someone else could have put it there,' Rory said patiently. 'Look, what I wanted to know was how badly Mick's taken it, losing all those horses to Mrs Mundy, I mean.'

'No worse than anything else. He's sort of resigned now. I'm looking for another job meself.'

'What, you? After all this time?'

'The man's run clean out of money. I don't want to go, but if I'm to have a wage . . .'

Rory shook his head. 'I suppose I knew it was as bad as that.'

'That's why you helped him out Tuesday, isn't it?'

Rory had no intention of admitting to anyone what he'd done. 'I was just lucky Bruce forgot to weigh in.'

''Tis only you would do a thing like that for him now.'

Rory abruptly changed the subject. 'Look, can I ask you a straight question about this horse-doping. Do you think Mick had anything to do with framing Laura Mundy?'

The small man spread his hands. 'I don't know. He wouldn't have done, in the old days, but there's no knowing what he'll do now. The man's as down as he's ever been.'

'But fixing Laura wouldn't help him, would it? He wouldn't get the horses back if she lost her licence, would he?'

'I don't know, Rory, and that's the truth.'

Olly Mullens had given him no help, either in confirming or ruling out the possibility of Mick Fanshaw being involved. Rory had been relying more than he realised on some kind of pointer from the lad. He walked back towards the changing room feeling frustrated and ineffectual. He was passing the Clerk of the Course's office as Matt Charters came out.

Matt was sometimes Henry Straker's understudy at the courses where Straker officiated. On an impulse, Rory hailed him.

'Hello, Mr Charters.'

'Oh, hello, Rory. How are you?'

'Fine, thanks. Look, could I have a quick word?'

Charters looked surprised. It was seldom that jockeys needed his services at the races. 'Sure. Now?'

'Yes, if you've got time.'

'Certainly.'

They automatically began to stroll back towards the paddock. None of the people rushing around, getting ready to run their horses or back their selections, took any notice of them.

'What can I do for you?' Charters asked.

'It's just something I'm trying to clear up about Midnight Express.'

'The horse that fell at Kempton?'

'Yes. Weren't you meant to be on duty instead of Straker that day?'

'Yes, I was. I'd mentioned to him the day before that I had a bit of a cold, nothing serious, though, but he insisted that he'd do the duty himself; said I wasn't looking up to it. You know what he's like. He's a very considerate chap, old Henry.'

'Yes, he is. But you'd have been quite happy to go if he hadn't insisted?'

'Certainly. It was only a touch of flu. I don't know why I even mentioned it to him.'

'So you didn't actually ask to be relieved of your duty?'

'No, not at all. As I said, I wasn't that ill, and I enjoy Kempton, but he said we couldn't have the vet going round spreading a cold to all and sundry. Frankly, I had plenty to get on with at my surgery, so I didn't protest too much. Why do you ask?'

Rory looked at him for a moment. 'Oh, no reason

really but thanks all the same. Nice to see you again.'

'And you. Glad to be of assistance!'

Rory left him inspecting the runners parading around the paddock and walked back to get ready for the next race.

He didn't have a ride in the third race that afternoon. He used the time on his mobile phone to catch up on his racing schedule for the rest of the week. Then he phoned Henry Straker's house. Susan answered.

'Hello. It's Rory Gillespie again.'

'Yes?' Susan said flatly.

'I wanted to speak to Henry. Will he be in this evening?'

'No. We're going to Arthur Harris's presentation.'

As Rory had thought, and hoped; knowing that most of the local racing community would be going to see the venerable old trainer honoured.

'Oh. That's a shame. Will you be back late, then?'

'I can't see us getting home much before ten.'

'Oh well, never mind. It wasn't important. I'll try another time.'

'Fine,' Susan said politely.

They said goodbye and hung up.

Rory parked his car in a lane on the other side of the shallow valley where Straker's house stood. Thick, heavy cloud blotted out the moon and deepened the darkness of the night with a relentless drizzle. Rory pulled the green 1:25,000 map of the area from his glove compartment. There were two fields between the lane where he was and the brook – a tributary of the Kennett – which scuttled down the valley floor. The map marked a footbridge into a narrow belt of woodland on the other side, beyond which was a small paddock, and the back of Henry Straker's house, maybe half a mile from where Rory was parked.

He pulled on a pair of waxed leggings and a hooded Barbour, then swapped his shoes for rubber stable boots and slipped out of his car into the damp blackness.

There were no house lights visible anywhere, but he planned to restrict to a minimum the use of the torch he had brought with him.

He found a gate into the field that edged the brook, clambered over, and thanked his luck that it was grass and not corn on the other side.

Without the aid of the light, he headed down the gentle slope to the brook. There wasn't a lot left of the footbridge when he found it, but enough to pick his way across the broken boards with intermittent flashes of his torch.

The woodland on the other side was dense, uncared-for beech and hazel coppice. The map had marked a path which had long since disappeared through lack of use, but he knew that if he headed up the slope away from the brook, he was going more or less the right way.

Five minutes of struggling in the dark through the damp, overgrown woodland brought him to a barbed-wire fence and the small field marked on the map. With his eyes now sensitive to the subtle shades of black that surrounded him, he could just make out the unlighted bulk of the rectory on the far side of the paddock.

He set out across the long wet grass and began to think

about how he was going to get into the empty house.

Halfway across, he heard a muffled bark from inside the house, followed by a clapping noise as a dog came out through a cat-flap to investigate.

He shook his head in admiration at that extra canine sense which could tell a dog of an alien presence without the aid of sight, sound or smell.

The dog – it sounded like a terrier of some sort – barked once or twice. Rory, fifty yards from the house now, stood and waited for it to come to him.

It barked again, more insistently, as it came near.

'Come here,' Rory called in a hushed tone, still not moving. The dog understood that it wasn't being challenged. Its bark became more of a friendly yip as it trotted through the long grass.

Rory offered it the back of his hand. 'Hello, boy,' he muttered.

The dog sniffed the hand, and liked what it smelled.

Rory crouched to stroke the small head, then the damp, wiry body. The dog jumped up and licked his face, as Rory flashed his torch on the name engraved on the metal tag around the dog's neck.

'Okay, Jimmy. Show me the way home.'

Another barbed-wire fence and a small shrubbery separated them from the back of the large house.

Once through, Jimmy trotted ahead to the door by which it had exited and jumped back through the cat-flap.

Rory called softly until Jimmy came back out again. He crouched down and stroked it until he thought it was safe to pick up.

With the friendly terrier nestling against his chest, he turned the handle on the door.

It was locked, as he'd assumed.

He knelt down in front of the cat-flap and inserted an arm through it to see if he could find a key on the inside. He felt around, but couldn't even make contact with the handle.

He put the dog gently on the ground beside him, then lay down so that he could insert his shoulder in through the flap, giving him the use of the full length of his arm. His fingers found first the handle and then, with excitement, a key in the lock. He turned it and felt it click open.

He pulled his arm out, and stood up. If there was no alarm, he was in.

Again, he turned the handle slowly, and this time opened the door. He slipped in with his new canine friend and closed the door behind him before switching on his torch and flashing it around. He was in a room full of dog baskets, boots and washing machines. He shone his light into the upper corners for any signs of an alarm and around the door jamb for wires and connections, but found nothing.

He walked across the room to a door opposite and opened it into a back hall where rows of hooks were cluttered with mackintoshes and all the other wet-weather paraphernalia that outdoor English people keep.

He closed the door, shutting the dog behind him, and went on to make a quick appraisal of the other rooms on the ground floor of the house.

There was a formal dining room, sparkling clean and unused, he judged; next to it was the drawing room where he had sat with Susan and Henry three nights before.

Behind the drawing room was a study with two walls

shelved from top to bottom with rows of veterinary text-
books. In front of the window stood a large flat-topped
desk and a small chair. To one side of this was a Victorian
armchair with a reading lamp beside it.

Henry's surgery was five miles away in the Lambourn
valley, but Rory guessed he must bring work home with
him. He walked across to the desk and closed the curtains
behind it.

On the top, there was a telephone, a small calendar, a
leather-edged blotter and a pen stand – nothing else.

Rory pulled open the central drawer between the ped-
estals. Inside was an A4 diary. He took it out, put it on
the desk and began to leaf through it.

In Henry's neat, italic hand were noted various appointments, not, on the whole, professional ones. Rory guessed
those were looked after by the surgery staff. There were
times and places for dinners, parties, receptions, and fix-
tures for the Reading boys' football team, sometimes with
the results scribbled beside them.

Henry had also entered the names of the racecourses
where he officiated on the days when he was, presumably,
on duty.

Rory carried on chronologically until he reached the
last week of February. On Tuesday, the 27th, was written 'Kempton'.

The word was heavily circled in black, as if someone
had been absently using a biro while thinking of something else.

Rory's heart quickened. Fumbling now, he leafed
through the next few pages until, on Wednesday 7th
March, his eyes picked out the word 'Folkestone', circled

again, and beside it, '12.30', the time of the first race that day.

Rory told himself that Straker might have written that to remind himself when he had to be there, but he went right back through the diary. Those were the only two race meetings that were circled.

Convinced that he had a lead now, Rory looked through the whole diary again, then at all the other papers in the top drawer of the desk. But he found nothing that told him any more.

He shut the drawer with frustration, wondering where to look next. His eyes fell on the blotter in front of him. It was liberally covered with doodles – the sort of stylised notes and hieroglyphics that people write when they are talking on the telephone. He held his torch to see what he could decipher.

There were figures, dates, names of drugs – though not xylazine – and, in the top right-hand corner, with the letters heavily traced over several times, the words 'Midnight Express'.

Rory let out an audible grunt of triumph as he stared at it.

He couldn't think how or why Henry Straker – notoriously one of the most honourable men in racing – could be involved in stopping horses, but there had to be more than coincidence in his insistence on giving Charters the day off at Kempton, the two entries in the diary, two pre-race tests – both clean – and the subsequent underperformance of two animals. It had only been Midnight Express's final resting place in the path. lab of the Veterinary College that had revealed the true cause of his demise.

Rory reflected that, without doubt, Henry Straker was the best-placed man in the industry to tamper with a horse. He also realised that he could be leaping to a conclusion very wide of the mark. Two isolated diary entries and a doodle on a jotter – which could have been done after the police had been to see him, or while discussing the test results on the phone – didn't prove anything; nor were they likely to convince the police that they had another potential suspect.

Grimly, he set about searching for more evidence. He didn't know what he was looking for, or where it might be. He glanced at his watch. It was eight thirty. Susan had said they would be back about ten. He'd give them half an hour's grace, which left him only an hour.

During that hour he opened every book, every drawer in the study. He found the Strakers' large, elegant bedroom and searched through every drawer and cupboard.

He found nothing that wasn't entirely explicable by Henry's job as a veterinary surgeon.

Disappointed and frustrated, he went back downstairs and looked for a second time through the drawers of the desk in the study.

It was in a folder of assorted notes and receipts that he found a consignment docket for six fifty-millilitre phials of xylazine, dated 22 February. He picked it up and stared at it by the light of his torch. Then he froze.

The headlights of a car momentarily lit up the bushes outside the study window and he heard the crunch of wheels on gravel.

He held his watch under the light. It was already a quarter to ten. He could hardly believe that he had been in the house so long. The dog barked from the back of the house at the sound of the front door being unlocked. He would have to cross the hall to get back to the scullery by which he'd come in. That wasn't an option now.

Frantically, he looked around the study with a last flash of his torch. The big armchair was angled across the corner of the room. Rory hoped there was enough space behind it to accommodate him in his Barbour and leggings. Footsteps echoed on the flagstones in the hall. In the dark, he clambered silently over the chair. He settled behind it and listened to the vet and his wife making their way through to the back of the house.

'Shut up, Jimmy,' Susan ordered the dog who had started barking again. 'What's the matter with you?'

Rory prayed that neither of them would try the back door, which he hadn't locked behind him. He thought back over the search he had made of the various rooms of the house and tried to remember if there was anything he hadn't replaced as he had found it. With a sudden sagging in his guts, he realised that he hadn't shut the drawer of the desk and that Henry was a tidy, methodical sort of man.

The footsteps came back from the scullery and into the hall.

'I'll be up in a minute, Sue.' Henry's voice was nearer the half-open door of the study.

Rory stopped breathing. He heard the door swing open, and a click as the high, central light came on. With relief, he saw that he was still in shadow.

Henry's footsteps, halfway across the room, faltered.

'What the hell . . .?' he gasped loudly.

'What is it, dear?' Susan's voice floated in.

'Er, nothing. Something I'd forgotten about, that's all. I'll be up in a mo,' he said again.

Rory heard him cross over to the desk and rummage through the contents of the top drawer. He recalled that he had replaced the folder where he had found it, under the diary. After a moment, the drawer was pushed back. Henry gave a grunt of self-censure, evidently believing he had left the drawer open himself, and walked out of the room.

The light was switched off and the door closed. Rory breathed more easily and, clutching the incriminating slip of paper in his hand, listened to Henry slowly climbing up the stairs.

He waited where he was for ten minutes. The Strakers' bedroom was on the far side of the house; he could hear no sounds from where he was, but he was confident they had gone to bed.

Cautiously, he raised himself until he could look over the back of the chair. There was no light to be seen under the door. Silently, he climbed out and crept towards where he judged the door to be. Feeling the well-polished panels, he found a large wooden knob and turned it slowly. He swung the door back twelve inches and slipped through.

On the flagstones of the hall, his rubber shoes made a faint squeak. He stopped and listened – no reaction. He reached the door on the far side and managed to open it without a sound, until the dog barked. He slipped in quickly and closed it behind him, muttering to the dog. 'It's okay, boy; it's okay.' He stretched out a hand in the darkness until the animal came to sniff it and recognised it. He crouched down and gathered Jimmy up into his arms, stroking it and tickling it under the chin.

'You can come with me,' he whispered.

In the gloom, his eyes could just make out the glass panels in the back door. Silently, on some kind of coconut matting, he felt his way towards it, still fondling the dog.

He heard Susan's voice from beyond the hall door.

'What *is* it, Jimmy?'

He opened the door, slid through and closed it as light flooded through the glass panes behind him. He reached down, set the cat-flap swinging and tiptoed across the shrubbery towards the paddock fence.

He scrambled over, catching a barb just below his groin, and dropped into the lush, wet grass on the other side. He tucked Jimmy under one arm and sprinted for the woodland on the lower side of the field. More cautiously, he negotiated the next fence, and turned to look back at the house.

Lights still shone from a first-floor window and the glazed back door. But there was no obvious sound of pursuit. A few seconds later, the light downstairs went out, and he guessed that Susan Straker had been ready to believe that the dog had heard a fox or some other four-legged intruder and had slipped out to investigate.

Ten minutes later, the light in the upper room was turned out. Rory gave the dog a last quick stroke and tickle, and dropped him back over the fence into the paddock. With luck, Susan wouldn't check the back door until next morning.

'Home, boy,' he urged. He watched the small dog trot

back towards the house before he turned into the wood-land to find his way back to the footbridge across the brook.

Rory's car was undisturbed where he had left it. He pulled off his wet outer garments, got in and rolled a cigarette with shaking hands. He had not really wanted to believe his suspicions that Henry Straker had been responsible for the test on the favourite in yesterday's first race.

Even Matt Charters' information that Henry had insisted on taking his place at Kempton the day Luke Mundy was killed had only made Rory keener to elimin-ate Henry's name from his list of suspects.

But what he had seen that evening left him convinced that Straker warranted further investigation.

He also knew that that was only part of the answer.

Now he had to find out why. And, possibly, for whom.

Right then, most of all, he wanted to talk to someone about his discovery.

He picked up his phone and dialled Langlands. He hadn't seen Laura since that morning; it felt like a month ago. Her voice, when she answered, sounded unfamiliar.

'Hello?'

'Laura, it's me, Rory.'

'Hi, how's it going?' she asked lightly.

Rory sensed she was doing it deliberately, to stop him from talking openly. He followed her lead.

'Not so bad. I just wanted to confirm the ride on Star-gazer tomorrow.'

'He goes, and you're declared.'

'Good. Are you sure he's ready?'

'Are you sure you are?' She even managed a laugh.

'Yeah, I'm fine. I've been checking the form of another horse you might like to hear about.'

'Save it till I see you tomorrow,' Laura said quickly.

'Okay.'

He rang off, quickly picked the phone up again and dialled Edward Brickhill's mobile number.

Brickhill answered himself.

'It's Rory Gillespie here.'

'Hello, Rory. Any news on that sick horse?'

'Yes, I think so, though nothing confirmed.'

'Do you want to talk about it?'

'Aye.'

'Can you come here?'

'Where are you, in Sussex?'

'No, London. Do you know where I live?'

'Yes. I'll be there in an hour or so.'

Rory remembered the way and found a parking space in Eaton Place outside the high stucco building whose top two floors comprised the Brickhills' London residence. He hadn't been inside the place for twelve years, but it didn't look as though it had changed at all. The same portraits of great horses and ill-humoured ancestors hung in the same places. The quiet Georgian sideboards and plump sofas looked as though they hadn't been used in the twelve years.

So did the whisky in the decanter from which Edward Brickhill poured him a drink.

Laura's father didn't ask any questions until Rory was settled on one of the sofas in front of an elaborately fake log fire that burned in a classical fireplace.

'So,' he said when he was sure his guest had all he needed, 'what have you found out?'

'I think Midnight Express was got at by the Jockey Club vet,' Rory said hesitantly.

Brickhill's eyes, already sharply focused on Rory, widened very slightly, registering disbelief. 'Henry Straker? I don't believe it. I've known him for years.'

Rory nodded. 'So have I. But I'm sure of it. Have you read yesterday's race report?'

Brickhill shook his head. 'No, why?'

'Laura ran a horse called Pan Piper. He's a good horse and improving, but the form book said that the favourite should have walked all over him. It didn't, though; I watched the race on SIS last night. It started out giving Jimmy McShea a real handful, pinged round the first mile, then started jumping terribly and came home with its tongue hanging out. Pan Piper won easily. But guess what? The stewards had a tip-off that the favourite was got at, and the test was taken by Henry Straker.'

Edward Brickhill looked disappointed but relieved. 'Rory, I don't think that proves anything more than pure coincidence. There's absolutely no reason why that horse shouldn't have been tampered with between Henry taking the test and the start of the race – if indeed he was doped at all.'

'He was; I'm sure of it. Anyway, there's more.'

Rory told him about his visit to the Strakers' house that evening, the entries in the diary, the doodle on the blotter and the delivery slip for the xylazine.

When he had finished, Edward Brickhill didn't say anything. He looked at Rory, then into the fire.

'Look, Mr Brickhill, I know that's not enough to convict him, but it's more than enough to convince me.'

'I don't like coincidences . . . But for God's sake . . . *Henry? Why?*'

'Whatever the reason, it's got to be something serious.'

'Henry Straker's one of the most honest men I know. He would no more take a bribe than jump over the moon.'

'I heard them talking a bit when they got back this evening.'

'You were still there?'

'Aye, behind an armchair, but that's another story.'

'Do you think Susan knows anything about it.'

'I'm not sure,' Rory sounded doubtful. 'She may do. They're very close, especially since they lost their boys. If I can find out why, I can probably find out who's behind it . . . if there is anyone else behind it.'

'Is there anything I can do?'

'I don't think so. I've tried to come up with some connection between the horses that won the races on both occasions, but there's none. In fact, I'm afraid the only common denominator I can find is Laura. Her horse was the first to be doped, and another of her horses won when the second was doped.'

Edward Brickhill looked at him sharply. 'You're not trying to tell me that you think Laura might have had something to do with it after all?'

'Not that she did it; but I think there might be some connection that she doesn't know about. I'm seeing her at the races tomorrow, maybe when I tell her about Straker, she might be able to come up with something. I don't know . . .'

Brickhill walked away from the fire and put his glass

on a table behind the sofa. 'Just tread extremely carefully, because you might find you're barking up the wrong tree, and that would be very awkward. Now, I've had some enquiries made among Luke Mundy's staff at Thames Land. His secretary said that the receivers have discovered that he had been gambling on the price of his shares – in a bogus name, of course – and using his inside information, totally illegally. Apparently he had been making substantial profits on it. Just before he died, it looks as though he started on the horses. She didn't know if he'd backed himself on Midnight Express, but she said she wouldn't be at all surprised. He had given her the impression that he was very confident of winning his own race.'

'He had cause to be,' Rory said. 'Even though the horse wouldn't have liked the trip much, he should have walked it in that company.'

'Quite,' Brickhill nodded. 'Anyway, his secretary – Jennifer something – is going to see if she can find out who his bookmaker was. Unfortunately, a lot of the paperwork has already been removed from the office by the receiver, and the Serious Fraud Office have been sniffing around too.' Brickhill picked up his glass and took a long slug of whisky. 'It's typical of Luke. I was always fairly sure there was something wrong with his set-up, but he was an ace juggler, and he had a lot of bottle. It's just his luck that the fraud squad didn't catch up with him until he was well beyond their reach. It seems to me that the vital thing to find out is who he was betting with. I've got someone making enquiries into the firms that make books on share prices to identify any who took significant losses on the Thames Land price. I'll let you know how I get on.' He drained his glass and put it down. 'Now,' he said, making it clear that the interview was over, 'can I offer you a bed for the night?'

Rory declined. In the lift going down he smiled to himself. Until very recently, he had never expected to be asked to stay the night by either of Laura's parents.

Outside, he found his car in the quiet square and with some satisfaction headed back towards the M4.

Chapter Nine

'Where the hell have you been?' Pam asked.

Rory had left the Brickhills' flat after midnight. Pam was waiting for him when he let himself into the house an hour and a half later.

'Do you care?' he asked mildly.

'Of course I bloody care – I am married to you, aren't I?'

'That depends what you mean by "married".'

'You've been with Laura Mundy, haven't you?'

'No. I've been with her father.'

'What the hell are you doing with that pompous fool?'

'Not having sex, which is probably all that worries you.' Rory sighed. He got no pleasure from these confrontations with Pam, but sometimes they were unavoidable. 'Look, if you want to argue all night, I think I'll sleep in the spare room. I've had a long day.'

He walked past her to the stairs and went up to the little room which Pam had overdecorated for visitors who never came.

Despite the schemes and theories filling his head, Rory slept almost as soon as he had slipped between the sheets of the guest bed. He was woken by his own internal alarm clock at six-thirty next morning, and washed and shaved in Tommy's bathroom. He looked into the boy's room. 'Don't forget, we're going fishing on Saturday,' he said.

''Course I won't forget, Dad. Are you going already?'

'Aye. I've got some horses to work.'

'Okay, 'bye.'

Rory listened for a moment at Pam's door and heard nothing. Relieved, he went quietly downstairs and out to his car.

Five minutes later, he was heading down the Lambourn Valley towards Straker's house.

This time he neither drove up to the house, nor parked across the valley. He left his car on the grass verge outside the high stone wall that fronted the old-fashioned garden and walked through the gate. There were no obvious signs of life in the house. When he reached the front door, he pressed the big brass bell for a couple of seconds.

Henry Straker, dressed and shaved, opened the door a few moments later.

Rory thought he spotted a momentary twitch of apprehension in the vet's eyes before he assumed his customary affability.

Rory was suddenly discouraged. He hadn't credited Straker with any acting ability. He had been relying on the man's innate honesty to prevent him from disguising the truth for long.

'Good Lord, Rory, it's rather early for a social call.'

'It's important, Henry. Can I come in?'

A cloud of worry crossed Straker's forehead.

'Well, I am due out now. I'm calling in at Langlands, as a matter of fact.'

'It was partly about Langlands that I wanted to see you. I won't keep you long.'

Straker struggled for a moment, weighing up the position. In the end, he said, 'All right. You'd better come in.'

He opened the door wider and Rory followed him into the hall. Susan's voice came from the back of the house. 'Who is it, dear?'

'It's just Rory Gillespie.' He turned to Rory. 'We'll go into my study. Do you mind if I don't offer you coffee – I don't want to disturb Susan.'

'No, that's fine.' Rory looked around the room where he had hidden the night before. It was far less sinister in the daylight and he was finding it hard to believe what he had found there.

Straker closed the door behind them and waved Rory into the large chair behind which he had crouched less than twelve hours before.

Rory sat. Straker remained standing. 'Well, what can I do for you?'

Rory looked straight into Straker's eyes. 'I want to know why you gave Midnight Express a shot of xylazine before Luke Mundy rode him at Kempton.'

Henry Straker stared back at Rory. He seemed for a moment completely immobile, rigid, unbreathing. The normal healthy glow on his face had turned to a pale grey.

'You want to know *what*?' he asked, his voice conveying indignation and disbelief.

Rory faltered. Suddenly, he wasn't so sure. What, he

thought, if he had made a terrible misjudgement and all the pointers he had found were simply coincidence? It was an appalling thing to charge anyone with, especially someone of Henry's reputation.

Rory cleared his throat. 'I said, why did you inject Midnight Express with xylazine before he ran?'

Straker turned his back on Rory and paced across the room towards the bookshelves on the other side. After a moment, he turned and looked at him with a steady, penetrating eye.

'Rory, we've known each other quite a long time. I considered I knew you well. I've no wish to have a quarrel with you. I think the best thing would be for us to forget that you ever made such an outrageous accusation.'

Rory felt himself quail before Straker's steely directness. Doubts flooded in to wipe out the certainty he had felt about the vet's guilt.

And yet, what about the times in the diary, the delivery note for the xylazine, Midnight Express's name on the blotter, the arrangement to take Charters' place that day at Kempton?

But he couldn't admit that he had broken into the house the evening before and searched the place – not now.

He stood up. 'Okay. I'm sorry. I simply don't see who else it could have been,' he said lamely.

Straker put a hand on Rory's shoulder. 'I understand why you're so keen to find another suspect, but I'm not your man.'

'Who the hell planted that phial in her car, then?' Rory blurted. 'I'm sorry.' He shook his head. 'I just know Laura didn't do it and I don't want to see her go to prison for it.'

'None of us do, Rory. Why do you think I've stuck by her? Like you, I hope very much that she wasn't responsible.'

'I didn't say I hoped she wasn't responsible, I said I know she isn't. I'm sorry to have disturbed you. I'll see myself out.'

Rory climbed back into his car, weary with doubt and remorse. He started the engine and drove back on to the road towards the village to buy some tobacco before going to Laura's. Off the verge, Rory realised that his car was behaving oddly, trying to pull to the left. He turned the radio off to hear the depressing rumble of a flat front tyre.

The lane was too narrow to pull up and let other traffic by, but twenty yards on Rory spotted an opening in the hedge into a small farm track.

He nursed the hobbling vehicle up the road, and turned it a few yards up the muddy track.

Cursing the mud, the car and whoever had left a two-inch tack lying around on the verge, he changed the wheel.

He had the boot open, and was on the point of picking up the punctured wheel to stow it, when he heard a car turn out of Straker's gate.

He stood unnoticed and watched as the vet's Daimler drove past towards the village – the wrong way for Langlands. Maybe he'd had an emergency call?

Rory took a punt. He picked up the damaged wheel, hurled it into the boot without securing it and leapt into the driver's seat. He put the motor into reverse and spun furiously back through the mud and into the lane, just in time to see Straker's Daimler curve out of sight.

He kept his distance until they reached the main road. He let a couple of cars pull in between him and the Daimler and prayed that the vet wouldn't spot him. Unless Straker saw the sign on the side of the vehicle, he probably wouldn't pay much attention to a white Rover, even if he knew what kind of car Rory drove.

Straker carried on, driving quickly down the old Bath Road towards Marlborough. As Rory followed, he tried to sort out what he was doing. Straker's display of indignation in the study had been very convincing. The dignity with which he had dealt with Rory's accusation was exactly what Rory would have expected if he were innocent.

But Rory couldn't ignore what he had seen last night.

A few miles short of Marlborough, Straker turned off the road into the car park of a Little Chef. It seemed an unlikely place for him to have his breakfast. Rory carried on past and pulled into the forecourt of the garage just beyond the eating house.

Parking his car to one side, he got out and walked quickly round the back of the Little Chef. He reached the end of the wall from where he would be able to see Straker's car, and cautiously put his head round the corner.

Straker was still sitting in the Daimler showing no sign of leaving it.

Rory ducked back. Straker hadn't seen him, but sooner or later he would look up. Rory reckoned he would hear if Henry got out of his car. He walked about, out of sight of the car park, as if he were stretching his legs. As he walked, he pulled the last of his tobacco and papers from the pocket of his leather jacket and rolled himself a cigarette.

Several more cars pulled off the main road. Each time, Rory poked his head round the corner to see Straker still sitting in his car, reading a paper.

Impatiently, he wondered what the hell the vet was doing. Of course, it could be something completely innocent – a convenient rendezvous with a client to hand over some prescription or some X-rays – anything.

Rory was beginning to doubt the wisdom of following Straker and considered slipping away and getting to Laura's before the vet when he heard the bubbling rumble of a big bike pull into the car park.

A bike didn't seem a very likely conveyance for anyone meeting Straker, but Rory went back to the corner of the building to sneak a look.

A 1200cc BMW headed straight for the Daimler and pulled up in a space beside it. The rider turned off the engine and propped the bike on its stand. Without removing his full-face helmet, he got off, opened the saddle box behind his seat and pulled out a large brown envelope. He walked round the front of the Daimler and opened the passenger door.

Rory couldn't tell much from the full set of plain black leathers the rider wore. He couldn't even be sure it was a man – slightly built and, without a helmet, maybe five feet eight or nine. Either way, the biker got into Straker's car with confidence and no display of deference to the distinguished vet.

Rory saw them talking, Straker looking straight ahead,

speaking in short bursts, nodding his head, then shaking it. The conversation lasted little more than three minutes, after which the biker got out of the Daimler, without the envelope, walked quickly back to the BMW, swung a leg over and took off. A few seconds later, Straker went too. Although he took the same direction – back towards Hungerford – Rory didn't get the impression that he was following the bike.

Rory went back to his Rover and drove out on to the main road. He soon caught up with Straker, though there was no sign of the bike ahead. The vet was evidently not in a hurry. Rory followed at the same leisurely rate and guessed that Henry was now heading for Langlands. He switched on his phone and prodded Laura's number.

''Morning,' he said when she answered. 'I'm running a bit late, but I'll be down in time for your second lot. Is that okay?'

'Sure,' she replied. 'Don't be late.'

Rory knew a back route that cut off the right angle made by the main roads. Provided there were no tractors on it, he could get ahead of Straker and arrive at Laura's before him.

He was lucky. The only farm vehicle he came across immediately pulled over to let him pass. The tractor driver looked pleased with himself when he saw, from Rory's name blazoned on the car, who he'd pulled over for.

At Langlands, Rory was put on a four-year-old gelding which had shown moderate talent on the flat and which he was due to ride in its first hurdle race next day at Uttoxeter. When he could, he liked to sit on a young horse once or twice before riding it in a race.

He settled the animal on the way up and tried to join in the other lads' gossip. Predictably, this centred on the continuing drama of Laura's arrest and doubts about their own future. The tension in the yard had been heightened, Rory gathered, by a confrontation between Mrs Mundy and the stable jockey. Dai Price had been complaining about the increasing number of rides Rory was being given. The Welshman should have been there that morning, but hadn't turned up. In the circumstances, Rory was grateful for that. Generally, though, the lads seemed reluctant to say too much in front of Rory. His relationship with Laura was apparently common knowledge by now.

Laura was up on the gallops. When Rory pulled up near her after giving the gelding a quick four-furlong gallop, she beckoned him over and he gave up his saddle to a lad who had driven up with her.

'What do you think of him?' Laura asked first.

'He gave me a nice feel. If he stays two miles, he could be useful. How does he jump?'

'He's a natural; sees them and he's off.'

There was a kind of strained normality to their conversation, unnecessary because there was no one else within earshot now that the lad had ridden off, back towards the yard.

'I broke into Henry Straker's place last night,' Rory said with an abrupt change of tone.

Laura, closely watching the next pair of horses drumming up the all-weather gallop towards them, turned to look at him sharply.

'You did what?' she asked with disbelief.

'I had a hunch it was Henry, then I was certain, now I'm not sure.'

'But it couldn't possibly be Henry; that's crazy,' she almost shouted.

'Maybe it is; I don't know, but there've been two horses now tested by Henry as a result of tip-offs, and both went on to run bloody oddly. Okay, one we know about because of Professor Douglas's analysis, but the other they assume was clean because Henry had tested it and no one's insisted on a second test.'

'The one at Folkestone, you mean?'

'Yes.'

'No, that favourite ran badly, but not particularly badly. It didn't look much in the paddock. I noticed its tongue was hanging out – like Midnight Express's, but some horses just run like that. I hardly gave it another thought. Anyway, who on earth would Henry be helping?'

'Himself, maybe?'

'Don't be ridiculous. He never has a bet. I'm sorry, Rory, but I think you're barking up completely the wrong tree.'

'Have you got any other trees to suggest then?' Rory asked with a sharpness he immediately regretted. 'And by the way, it would help if you'd told me everything there is to know about the whole business.'

'I have, for God's sake!'

'What about that life insurance, then? Your father mentioned it and Susan Straker told me it was worth two and a half million.'

Laura burst out laughing. 'I don't know who told her that, but she's way out. I can show you the policy – if it ever gets paid – it's worth about four hundred thousand. Quite a lot of money, but peanuts, relatively speaking, if I'm going to lose Langlands and everything else to Luke's creditors – and it looks as though I am. Look, if I'd thought it was relevant I would have told you.'

'Okay,' Rory capitulated. 'But if Henry's got nothing to do with this, I'm getting nowhere fast. I can't tie the thing together at all. I followed him to a meet on the way here this morning. Some guy – at least I presume it was a man – turned up on a big bike, got into Henry's car with an envelope, talked to him for a few minutes, got out and roared off. I thought maybe Henry was just going to hand over some medicine or X-rays or something, but the biker wasn't carrying anything when he got out.'

'That doesn't tell us anything,' Laura said. 'Maybe the biker was delivering X-rays. As you say, he may have been discussing a case or something.'

'Sure, it's possible. Look, after Henry's reaction when I confronted him with it, I felt terrible, but last night I found he'd written the name Midnight Express on his blotter and marked the time of one of the races in his diary. And among a batch of delivery notes, I found he'd had a consignment of xylazine just before the first doping. I thought that was too much of a coincidence.'

'But it could have been just that. I mean, he may have written the horse's name after he'd tested it to remind himself or something.'

Rory sighed. If it was such hard work trying to convince the person he was aiming to help, it would be a lot harder convincing the police – if he ever had enough of a case to put to them. 'I also went to see your father last night. He's looking into Luke's gambling activities. He's discovered that he had been having some very large bets on the share price of Thames Land.'

'How do you mean?'

'Well, some people can't be bothered to go to all the trouble and expense of buying shares to speculate on their movement; they simply gamble on the price changes with a handful of bookies who run that kind of book.'

'My father thinks Luke might have been doing that?'

'He spoke to Luke's secretary; she said the receivers had discovered it. If he was, he was breaking the law, using his inside information. If somebody got to know, they could have used that against him, maybe to blackmail him. And it's possible he had a very large bet on Midnight Express. This secretary seemed to think he had been losing heavily just before he died.'

'I've never seen him so nervous as he was before that race,' Laura said. 'I told you that. I may not have shown it, but I was feeling terrible about the whole thing – having promised the ride to you in the Champion Chase. But I've no idea who he'd have had a bet with.'

'Listen, if we can find that out, we'll know who wanted him stopped. In any normal race, you'd have to look at the horse that eventually won, but in a field like that, there was no certainty that any of them would get round, let alone win. Nobody would bother to nobble the favourite in a hunter chase to make way for another horse.'

'No. You're right. It had to be whoever Luke was betting with.'

'And that could have been anyone. The bet wouldn't have been placed in his own name, I shouldn't think, if it was recorded at all.'

The last lot of horses had galloped past them as they spoke. Laura started to walk back towards the Land Rover.

On the far side of the valley, Rory spotted Henry Straker's Daimler snaking slowly down the lane towards the yard. He glanced at his watch. 'I wonder what he's been doing. He should have been here about half an hour ago.'

'He could have been doing anything,' Laura said. 'He probably made another call on the way. I really think you're wrong about him.'

When they were both in the car, she sat back in the seat and sighed. 'Rory, you've got to find something, somebody. Every day that goes by, more people are thinking it must have been me; I can tell by the way they look away when they see me. I don't know how long I can stand the pressure.'

Rory stretched out a hand and put it on her denim-clad thigh. Gently he squeezed it. 'Don't worry. I've got no intention of letting anyone lock you up. Not after it's taken me twelve years to come to my senses.'

Laura gave him a quick, rueful smile and switched the engine on.

They reached the car park behind the yard at the same time as the vet.

Straker climbed out and nodded at Rory as if it were the first time he'd seen him that morning. Rory saw that he wasn't carrying anything. All the equipment needed to test the horses' blood was kept in Patrick's small office.

Rory waited until the vet had walked round into the yard, talking to Laura, who glanced over her shoulder and made a face of disbelief.

When they were out of sight, he quickly slipped into the Daimler. There was a brown envelope, unmarked, and torn open, on the back seat. He reached back for it and looked inside; it was empty. He searched all the possible places in the car where Straker could have put the contents – in the map and glove compartments, under the seats – but found nothing likely. It was always possible, though unlikely, that Straker had put it in the boot, but Rory felt sure that whatever it was, it was connected with the doping of the horses, and the vet had disposed of it somewhere between the Little Chef and Langlands.

He had been in the car for less than a minute. He got out and walked quickly round into the yard. There was no sign of Laura or Straker. But Declan was just letting himself out of one of the stables.

Rory nodded at him with a smile. 'How's it going then?'

'All right.' The lad strolled across to him and added quietly, 'I got somethin' to tell you.'

Rory, with a look, stopped him from going on. 'Are you bringing a horse up to Uttoxeter this afternoon?'

'Just getting 'im ready now.'

'See me when I get there, before the first.'

The lad nodded co-operatively. 'Okay. See you there.'

The terror of another term at Her Majesty's pleasure gave Arthur Eland the courage to disobey his client once again. He dialled a City number.

His client wasn't pleased.

'I told you I didn't want you to ring me again,' he said.

'Someone's on to us. We're in trouble.'

'Stop worrying. Nothing's going to lead anyone back to you.'

'There's one person who can.'

'Well that won't happen, will it, after your splendid photographic session.'

'I'm not so sure. It's the one link. I think we should get rid of it.'

'Now you're being ridiculous. I have an investment which will yield a few more returns yet. And you'd do yourself more harm than good by doing anything stupid, I can assure you. I'll put you on a bonus when we've made more use of our asset. It's a big week next week and I'm not going to waste it. So, do nothing. I'll ring you with instructions Sunday night.'

The line went dead and Eland stared at the crackling phone for a moment before pressing the plunger to get a fresh line.

With his other hand, he thumbed through a grimy address book.

One of the few benefits of his time in jail was the access it gave him to a national network of practitioners of every conceivable type of illegal service. The serious discouragement of a man's inquisitiveness was easily bought.

A wet westerly swept across the soft green undulations of Uttoxeter racecourse. The sparse Friday crowd – Staffordshire farmers and town people from Derby and the

Potteries – looked dispirited and uninspired as mud-caked jockeys on slithery saddles did their disgruntled best to provide an afternoon's entertainment.

Declan was waiting at the door of the jockeys' changing room when Rory arrived.

'Let's walk down to the stables,' Rory said. 'What have you got?'

'Well, I was thinking of strangers who had been to the yard when the xylazine was found. There were a few, there usually are. But there was this one bloke, looked like he could've been a lad once, come round selling minerals and that. He asked me where Dad was, and I go, "You're out of luck, he's not here," and he goes, "Oh well, I'll call again." I knew I'd seen him before somewhere, but I couldn't think where. I asked Micky Parish, one of the other lads, if he knew him, and he says, "No, but he was at Kempton the day Express got done." And I remembered then, he was poking around the stables that morning. I didn't take no notice then, like I say, he looked like he could've been a lad – you know, not too big, right clothes and everything. But Mick was right, it was definitely the same bloke.'

'What did he look like, then?'

''Ard to say, really. Sort of mousy hair, thinning a bit. Little bum-freezer jacket, brown cords, I think. About forty, maybe. Not the sort of bloke you take much notice of.'

'How did he talk?'

'London, like.'

'I don't suppose he gave you a name?'

'Nah.'

'Can you remember if Mrs Mundy's car was down at the yard then?'

Declan thought for a moment, then nodded. 'Yeh. You was there that morning; Skinny rode your horse back, didn't he, and she came back down with you from the gallops in the Land Rover, dumped you and drove on straight back to the house. She'll often do that, leave her car at the yard if she knows she's coming back down again after.'

Rory nodded. 'Yes, you're right. I was parked next to her car. So when did this bloke turn up?'

'Just after you'd gone.'

'And would he have had time to put something in Laura's car?'

'Easy.'

'Would it have been locked?'

'No, 'course not, not down the yard. I mean, no one would nick it from there, would they?'

Rory nodded, thanked Declan and turned to walk back towards the changing room.

'D'you want me to tell the police about him?'

'Just keep a look out for him, for now. And if you see him again, find out who he is, okay?'

In the absence of most of the southern jockeys, who were at Newton Abbot, Rory had fixed himself a full card for the day. After two unspectacular losing rides, he walked out to the ring to mount up for the third – the novice hurdle – on Stargazer, the young horse Declan had brought up.

He had been through the opposition with Patrick

Hoolihan before setting out from Langlands that morning. If the horse settled, it should provide him with a winner. Viewing the other runners in the flesh now, he didn't change his mind.

The wind had dropped a little, and allowed a steady, misty drizzle to fall and soak into the already spongy turf. But, Rory thought, this ought to suit Stargazer's high action.

And it did.

The horse pulled straight to the front and then relaxed. Rory decided to leave him alone, to see if he would keep going without any opposition in his sights. Stargazer it seemed was perfectly content. He galloped on, seeing the small obstacles and bounding long and low over them.

Passing the stands before the last nine-furlong circuit, Rory turned to find out how far ahead he was. He could barely see the rest of the field through the grey drizzle. He relaxed. He didn't doubt that the rest of them would start to come back to him, but from where he was sitting, there could be only one outcome. Keeping a tight hold, he let Stargazer carry on steadily into the turn. The hurdle on the far side came up to meet them.

The horse saw it but was trying to pull up as it realised it was racing away from the stables. Rory gave it two good cracks down the left shoulder, pulled his whip through and hit it twice more on the other side. He felt that he'd got the horse on an even keel when, without warning, it swerved violently to the left and crashed through the wing of the jump.

The speed with which it changed direction took Rory completely by surprise. He was catapulted sideways out of the saddle and slammed into the wooden stake supporting the white plastic running rail.

. Before he had time to feel the pain, he rolled, instinctively, as any experienced, conscious jockey does, and got himself off the track.

As he moved, an excruciating pain pulsed through his left shoulder. With a groan he looked down and recognised the dreaded sight of dislocation.

He saw the bulge of his shoulder bone protruding between his armpit and his chest.

Rory curled his toes tightly, kept his breathing as shallow as possible and tried unsuccessfully to find a position to relieve his agony.

The rest of the field was passing him now, the jockeys showing the businesslike air of people who knew they were now back in with a chance. One of them called, 'You all right?' and sounded as though he meant it.

As Rory was stretchered gently into the ambulance, Terry poked his face through the back door.

'They're going to take you straight to the local knackers,' he said. It was traditional to make light of injuries which were an inescapable part of a jump jockey's life. 'I'll drive your car back and fix a local taxi to take you home. Sorry I won't be able to bring you any flowers.'

Rory met with more sympathy at the hospital. The painkillers given to him by the ambulancemen were beginning to wear off, but he was reluctant to ask for more.

An X-ray confirmed that his shoulder was dislocated. Two white-knuckle minutes with a doctor corrected the problem and the pain disappeared as if by magic. Rory was then given an instruction from the specialist not to ride for at least a fortnight.

Rory nodded even as he told himself there was no way he was going to miss Cheltenham.

Terry had remembered to put Rory's clothes into the ambulance that had brought him from the racecourse. Rory changed back into them, stuffed the muddy breeches and silks into his bag, and told the receptionist on casualty that he was expecting a taxi.

'It's already here, Mr Gillespie,' she told him. 'Came half an hour ago.'

Rory was impressed with Terry's efficiency. He had only been at the hospital for an hour and a half. The last race of the day wouldn't even have started yet. He considered going back to the race-course, but he didn't really feel like driving himself home.

Thanking the smiling nurses, he walked slowly, carrying his bag with his good arm, down to the front lobby of the hospital.

'Mr Gillespie?' A large man was waiting to take his bag. 'How's the arm?' he asked, glancing at the sling.

Rory smiled. 'Better than it looks.'

He followed the man out of the door to a waiting Ford Sierra. The driver opened the back door for him and put his bag on the front passenger seat. Rory climbed in, trying not to shift his shoulder, and settled back into the rear seat. He closed his eyes and hoped he wouldn't be expected to keep up a conversation.

The driver let himself in and they pulled away from the hospital.

Soon they left the small town behind them, heading along the road to Stafford and the M6. To Rory's relief, his driver didn't seem inclined to conversation. Once he was confident they were on the way, he closed his eyes again and tried to sleep.

He had almost succeeded when a change in the car's speed and progress made him jerk his eyelids up to let in the gloom of the late afternoon.

'What's this?' he asked. 'A short cut or what?'

They were travelling along a narrow lane, high-hedged with occasional oaks. Through gaps at gateways, Rory saw small flat fields of empty pasture.

'There's some roadworks ahead on the Stafford road. We'll miss them this way.'

Rory approved and relaxed.

The lane entered a tunnel of mixed woodland. The driver switched on the car's headlights. After a few hundred yards, the lights picked out a Forestry Commission sign announcing a parking area and access to a 'nature trail'.

Abruptly, the car swung off the road on to a patch of muddy gravel. Rory jerked forward and winced at the stab of pain in his shoulder. 'What the hell are we stopping for?' he asked with sudden foreboding. He saw with relief that there was another car in the clearing.

'Thought we'd have a chat,' the driver growled.

Rory froze. A hollow, tingling fear shuddered through his body. There was a fraction of a second when he couldn't move a single muscle as he tried frantically to work out what was happening. Then instinct took over.

He grabbed the handle of the door, yanked it back to

open it. He got his legs out of the car, stood up to look for somewhere to run.

A bulk of human body was blocking his path.

'Oh no, Mr Gillespie. You're not going anywhere yet,' the bulk growled in a flat Black Country voice. 'We need to talk to you . . .'

He provided a full stop to his sentence with a hard fist, deep beneath Rory's rib cage, hitting his sling and sending a wave of nauseating pain through his injured shoulder.

Rory jackknifed and gulped for air. The big fist caught him again on the side of his jaw and sent him sprawling. He lay for a moment, aching, gasping, trying to think.

'You've been poking your nose where it's not wanted. Know what I mean?' The driver's voice this time.

Rory didn't answer the question; he guessed it was rhetorical.

He raised his torso from the ground.

A heavy shoe caught him in the ribs. He collapsed again.

A booted foot exploded into his other side; a kick to his head, to his ribs again, his testicles, his throbbing shoulder.

He stopped thinking. He hadn't even started to fight back, but his job had taught him to deal with pain by blocking out communication from his sensory nerves.

He felt the blows as if detached from his own body. Some instinct, not cowardice, told him that the less he moved, the sooner it would be over.

He lost count of the kicks and any sense of time. When it was over, he couldn't have said if it had taken one minute or ten. But a period of blissful calm followed the final blow. He could hear the wind swishing through the tops of the conifers and budding broadleafs. Even the blood that seeped from his battered gums tasted sweet.

His reverie was broken by the harsh Brummy accent of the man who had been waiting for him.

'D'you understand now? Leave things alone and stop asking questions and we won't need to do this again.'

Rory understood. He didn't think it worth saying.

A boot caught him once more on his bruised ribs.

'Answer me! I want to hear you say you understand.'

Rory groaned. 'I understand.'

'Right, and if you go to the police, next time we won't be so gentle.'

The man underlined his point with a last kick to Rory's torn and bleeding ear.

Through pulsing pain, he heard the feet that had ravaged him crunch across the car park, the slamming of two car doors, motors starting, wheels spinning then finding a grip on the metalled road, engine sounds muffled by the dank woodland and fading to nothing until the only sounds were the wind in the trees and the pattering of raindrops in the puddles.

The drizzle which had been falling most of the day had turned gradually to serious rain. The trees provided some shelter, but Rory became aware that his clothes were sodden through and beginning to chill him.

Throbbing with pain in almost every part of his body, he began to raise himself from the ground, still half expecting to be kicked back down again. On his feet, he staggered to the side of the clearing where there was more shelter. He leaned against a tree and fumbled in his wet leather jacket for tobacco and papers. They were dry enough, but with his damp hands he could only produce a soggy sliver of a cigarette. He sucked at it gratefully, though, gathering the strength and will to walk out of these woods, back to civilisation.

The nurses who had bandaged him up a few hours earlier had been replaced by others, just as gentle and clucking with sympathy.

What terrible bad luck to have a nasty fall, and then be mugged like that – all on the same day!

The nurse at reception said she'd thought there was something funny going on when another taxi had turned up to fetch him. She could certainly give the police a description of the man who had driven him away.

Rory didn't take much persuading that he had to stay in hospital for the night. He phoned Pam and told her he wouldn't be back that night, or riding tomorrow. She sounded indifferent to the news, and said that she was going out and Tommy was staying with a friend in the village.

Laura, when Rory rang her, showed her sympathy by offering to drive up and collect him next morning. She understood what he had meant by 'mugged'. He was grateful, more than he could express over the phone, but told her not to be absurd. She had horses to run, and he could get a taxi.

Laura chose to be absurd.

Rory saw her through a mist of gratitude as she walked

into the small room the hospital had allocated to him for the night.

She watched while he ate some breakfast; left while he dressed, then carried his bag down to her two-door Mercedes.

Rory shivered as they passed the turning up to the woods where he had lain the evening before. He had walked the half-mile down to the turning, and another half-mile along the Stafford–Uttoxeter road before anyone had dared to stop for a battered, wet and bedraggled tramp. A busload of grimy New Age travellers, mistaking him for one of their own, had finally pulled up and driven him back to the hospital.

'That's where it happened,' he said to Laura, nodding towards the turning.

They hadn't spoken about it yet, wanting to get away from it first.

'Do you know who they were?' she asked.

'No. Local contractors, I should think.'

'Are you going to tell the police?'

'I have already, but they'll never find them. They were up from Birmingham and the car was probably stolen.'

'But if they did find them, that would lead straight to whoever's behind Henry.'

'Not a chance. These things are all done at arm's length. Anyway, like I say, they'll never find them.'

'Are you going to go on looking?' Laura asked nervously.

'Of course I am, now I know I'm getting somewhere.'

'I've arranged for Dad to meet us at your house. He phoned last night looking for you. I told him roughly

what had happened. He thinks he's found something.'
'Good; I need all the help I can get.'

Chapter Ten

They saw the police car outside Camp Farm as soon as Laura turned the Mercedes into the valley.

Rory groaned. 'What the hell do they want? I guess the hospital must have told them you were driving me home.'

'It may not be you they want to see,' Laura said.

She drove on to the forecourt in front of Rory's house. She sprang out; Rory limped. Taffy came bounding out of the house with his tail waving followed by a policeman in uniform and a second in anorak and jeans. They weren't smiling.

The detective spoke first. ''Morning, Mr Gillespie. We tried to contact you at the hospital in Uttoxeter but you'd already left.' He turned to Laura. 'And you're Mrs Laura Mundy, I take it.' His manner showed that he was well aware of who she was and her own current relationship with his colleagues in Surrey and Hampshire.

Laura nodded.

'Why did you want me?' Rory asked.

'I'm afraid your house was broken into last night.'

'Good God! But my wife was here.'

'She wasn't, sir,' the policeman stated baldly. 'She returned to the house this morning and found the back door forced and the place turned over.'

'What about the alarm?'

'Apparently it slipped her mind to set it when she went out.'

Rory shook his head. 'Okay. I'd better have a look.'

'If you don't mind my saying so, are you all right, sir?' The policeman looked at the bandages across Rory's ears and the bruises on his face. 'We heard you had a fall yesterday but I didn't know it was so bad.'

'I was mugged after leaving the hospital,' Rory said. 'The local police have got all the details, but there's no real harm done. I didn't have any cash on me.' He walked towards the house disguising his injuries as best he could.

Inside, starting with the kitchen, he found that every drawer in the house had been pulled out and tipped up.

The detective followed him around, making sure he didn't touch anything until the forensic people had been. 'They seem to have left most of the usual things, videos and such like,' he said. 'I'd say they were looking for something particular. Have you any idea what that might have been?'

'Cash, probably,' Rory said quickly. 'I sold a mare for cash the day before yesterday and hadn't had a chance to bank it yet.'

'Was it in a safe, sir?'

'No. I don't have a safe. I don't usually have a lot of cash about the place, not in my business.'

The detective gave a cynical, disbelieving grin. 'Is that so, sir?'

'Yes, it bloody well is so. All my earnings are handled by Weatherby's who pay it straight into my account. But the fellow I sold the horse to was a shady sort of individual.' Rory shrugged. 'Maybe he decided to come and get his money back.'

'We'll check him out if you let us have his name and address.'

'I haven't got a clue. He was a traveller of some sort.'

'Buying horses from you?'

'It wasn't a blood horse – just a nice old coloured pony we had for my son.'

They were in a small room that Rory used as a study. Pam came in as they talked. It was the first Rory had seen of her since he and Laura had arrived at the house. She had evidently been listening outside; she looked as though she was on the point of asking Rory what he was talking about. He managed to stop her with a look which didn't escape the detective. But then, the detective assumed, a jockey would have plenty of dealings in cash; as long as it hadn't been obtained by theft or fraud, it wasn't his affair until the Inland Revenue asked him to bring the jockey in.

'Where was the money, sir?'

'In an envelope. In this drawer.'

Rory pointed at one of the top drawers of the small desk. There was no sign of an envelope among its contents.

'Maybe it's still under the other stuff. We can have a better look after the fellows have dusted it. Now can you tell me if any ornaments or trophies or such like are missing?'

They walked around the house again. All the bronze

statuettes, equine figures and lead crystal bowls that Rory had collected as his share of the big prizes over the years were where they always stood, with their normal coating of dust undisturbed.

When he had assessed as much as he could without touching anything, the policeman took a brief statement from Rory; he had already taken one from Pam. 'That'll do for now. We'll leave you in peace, but don't touch anything until the forensic boys have been.'

'Can't we make a cup of coffee or something?' Pam asked.

'Oh yes. That'll be okay. They should be here soon anyway.'

The police car drove off down the valley, leaving Rory, Pam and Laura standing awkwardly in the kitchen.

'I don't know about you, but I need a bloody drink,' Pam said, reaching a bottle of vodka down from a shelf.

'Me too,' Laura said.

Rory helped himself to a whisky, and the three of them sat down around the table.

'D'you know what the hell's going on?' Pam asked.

Rory nodded. 'I think so.'

'It's to do with her, isn't it?' Pam said, nodding angrily at Laura.

'It's to do with Luke's death,' Rory corrected her.

'Same thing.'

'Pam,' Laura said, and Rory wondered if it was the first time she had spoken to Pam since she had thrown his earrings at her in her father's yard, twelve years before, 'I'm not getting involved in a slanging match with you. Rory's been helping me because he chose to. And it's because he's getting somewhere that he's in trouble.'

'Why? What's he found out?'

'I can't tell you, Pam,' Rory said. 'It wouldn't be fair on you.'

'Don't be so bloody pompous! You can't keep secrets from me. I'm your wife, for God's sake!'

'Talking of secrets,' Rory said, 'are you going to tell me where you were last night?'

Pam made a face and took another swig of vodka. 'I went over to Sheila's when you said you weren't coming home. There wasn't any point hanging around here – Tommy was staying with the Jones's. We had a few drinks, I admit it, and I reckoned I was too pissed to drive home. So I stayed at her house. I wasn't planning to, that's why I never turned on the alarm,' she added as an afterthought. She looked at Rory, then Laura, challenging them to question her version.

Rory didn't believe her, but he let it go.

'It doesn't matter. They didn't find anything to interest them.'

'Why did you give the police all that bullshit about cash from selling a horse, then?'

'I don't know why the hell we were raided last night, but I'm bloody sure it had something to do with whoever doped Midnight Express.'

'And what's all this about you being mugged?'

Before Rory could answer, they were interrupted by the sound of another car pulling into the forecourt.

'This must be the fingerprint blokes,' Pam said. 'They'll find bugger all. People who do this kind of thing don't leave their dabs all over the place.'

'Good morning.' Edward Brickhill walked through the open back door. 'I see someone didn't wait to be invited in,' he added, seeing the jemmy marks on the door frame.

''Morning, Dad,' Laura said, rising to greet him. 'Do you know Rory's wife, Pam?'

'Yes, of course I know Pam. I had horses with her father for about twenty years. Hello, Pam.'

Rory had also got to his feet. 'Let's go in the other room, Edward.'

'Don't bother,' Pam said. 'I suppose I'll have to go and pick up Tommy. You can have your little secret meeting without me.'

'I don't mind getting him,' Laura said quickly. 'He can spend the afternoon at the races with me. Perhaps he'd like to come back in the lorry.'

Rory looked at her gratefully. 'If he's not in the way, he'd enjoy that; I've got a lot to do before we go to Wales.' He turned to his wife. 'Pam, if you haven't already done them, can you deal with the horses. I'm just not going to have time.'

'And I have, I suppose? I'll go and get Sally to do them.'

She drained her glass, got up and walked sulkily from the room. No one spoke until they heard her car starting up.

'I take it you haven't told your wife what you've been doing?' Edward Brickhill said.

'You take it right,' Rory said. 'Laura says you've got something about Luke's gambling.'

'Yes. I think I have. One of my people made the rounds yesterday of every bookie who deals in City prices.'

Rory waved him to a chair and they all sat down. 'Drink?' he asked.

'No thanks. Anyway, one of the settling clerks in a firm called Square Mile Sporting said that they'd lost a fairly large amount on the Thames Land price, up till about two months before Luke died. I guess by then he thought things might get less predictable and backed off. Of course, we don't know that it was definitely Luke, but knowing that he was gambling on his price with someone, I think we can assume it was. Then it seems that the same individual, having been paid out somewhere in the region of three hundred thousand, began to back horses, right up until the time Luke was killed, at which point he was about a hundred and fifty thousand down.'

Rory felt himself shiver with excitement. 'What about Midnight Express? Did he have a bet on him?'

Brickhill shook his head. 'There's no record of it, I'm afraid. But he could have had it on with any other book-maker – possibly several; that'll be a lot harder to track down, but I've got someone working on it.'

'But if he was chasing a hundred and fifty grand,' Rory said, 'he'd have had fifty on it. Even if it was spread about, that should show up easily enough. Though I'd have thought he'd have put it on with the firm he owed it to.'

'Not necessarily. After all, he knew they couldn't sue him for the money he already owed them.'

'That's where you're wrong: bets with index makers are fully recoverable, and he'd have hated being warned off.'

'Yes,' Laura agreed. 'He'd have hated that. He would definitely have wanted to settle his account somehow. And now we know what his position was when he died,' she said with a sour grin, 'pulling off a big gamble was the only way. And I've told Rory how desperate he was to win that day.'

'I agree with Laura,' Rory said. 'He'd have had his bet with the same firm, this Square Mile set-up. Maybe he had a private arrangement with the owner of the firm. Do you know who that is?'

'I'd already thought of that, but I'm afraid so far I've drawn a blank. The chief executive of the firm which holds the licence isn't the owner. He's a bright young man who went there from another bookmaking firm about a year ago. But Square Mile Sporting is a private company owned by an investment trust based in Panama. The registered trustees are a pair of Panamanian lawyers.' Brickhill shrugged. 'It's almost impossible to get through that kind of smokescreen, though I wouldn't be surprised if it ultimately belonged to an English operator. It must be set up like that primarily as a cover, because there aren't any real tax advantages.'

'For Christ's sake!' Rory burst out in frustration. 'I'm bloody sure that's all we need to know, and we've found our man.'

Brickhill lifted a shoulder philosophically. 'You may be right, but I'm afraid even if he is we're going to have to find him some other way. And how on earth are we going to prove anything? If it had been an ordinary bookmaker, maybe we'd have had a chance, but this seems just too much of a professional operation.'

Their discussion was interrupted by a series of telephone callers checking on the state of Rory's health, since he had cancelled all his rides that day and the story of his 'mugging' was in some late editions of the papers. He promised all of them that he'd be riding again by the following Tuesday. Laura looked doubtful as she listened, but didn't question it when he finally put the phone down.

Any more discussion was prevented by the arrival of a scene-of-crime officer. Laura went to pick up Tommy on her way back to Langlands. She had left Patrick and her assistant in charge of sending six horses to Sandown that day, but she was anxious to get there to see them run.

The policeman took an hour to find nothing. Rory and Edward Brickhill walked up to the barns, going over and over the possibilities. When they returned to the forecourt in front of the house, Pam had reappeared with Sally, their part-time groom.

'I hope Laura doesn't get back too late with Tommy. He's really excited about your fishing trip and as you're not riding today, I told him you'd be able to set off nice and early.'

Rory groaned to himself, but wouldn't let his wife see his frustration. 'I can't go till this evening anyway. I may not be riding, but I've got a lot of other things to do. We'll leave about seven which means we'll be in Builth by nine thirty, ready to start early on the river tomorrow. Can you pack him a bag for the night?'

'I suppose so. It'll be great for him to have a day out with his dad for a change. A father should spend time with his son, don't you think, Mr Brickhill?'

'Yes, of course. Tommy's a lucky boy.' He opened his car door. 'Rory, we'll talk again later. Try to ring me before you leave for Wales.'

Eland's answer-phone was flashing at him when he arrived back at his house that morning.

He played the tape, not paying much attention to the messages until he heard the deep drawl which he had been waiting for.

'I've got some instructions for you. I'll ring again at twelve. Make sure you're there.'

It was only eleven. Eland didn't even consider ringing back. He'd sweat it out for an hour. When the call came, he would tell him he wasn't doing any more; it was getting too hot.

He sat down and absently picked at the inflamed scab on his hand. It seemed to have got worse in the last few days. His skin was always inclined to erupt when he was under pressure. He mopped his forehead with a grimy handkerchief and, with a shaking hand, poured himself a large tot of rum from a bottle on the coffee table in front of him.

He wished for the hundredth time that he had restricted himself to taking the photographs; that was what he was good at, not all this skulduggery. He could never forget what it was like in prison, and he knew that made him nervous and inept.

He'd had enough. Whatever the man said, he was going to knock this scam on the head; wipe out the elements that could link it all to him.

He'd sent the last batch of pictures yesterday, as he'd been told. They were good shots, as good as he'd ever done, but he was dealing with an unusual sort of victim, and he now had serious doubts that they would be as effective as they should have been.

Besides, he had a horrible suspicion that some of the first ones had gone astray. Even if there was the slightest chance that they had, he had to find them. He'd thought he was going to find them last night; he'd found nothing, but the warning had been delivered. They'd rung him to tell him, and the morning papers had confirmed it.

He let the telephone – two feet in front of him – ring five or six times before he picked it up.

'Hello?' He couldn't disguise the shake in his voice.

'Fancyman. Tuesday.'

'I . . . I don't think he'll do it.'

'Did you send the last photographs?'

'Yes, like you said, yesterday.'

'Then he'll do it. They were brilliant shots.'

'I don't know . . .'

'Listen, just do it. Understand?'

Eland sighed. 'Okay.'

'There's another thing. Did you have anything to do with that mugging yesterday?'

'What are you talking about?' Eland tried his hardest to feign ignorance.

'You know what I'm talking about.'

'Oh, that. No, 'course not. Why should I have anything to do with that?'

'It doesn't matter. I'll know soon enough. God help you if I get the wrong answer.'

The line was abruptly cut.

Eland held the receiver in his clenched fist and tried to stop himself shaking.

How the hell had he let himself get into this mess?

He hadn't got any choice now. This job was finishing. Too bad about the money.

He prodded the plunger on the phone to get a clear line and jabbed a number.

His call was answered after a few rings.

'I need you tonight,' he said.

He listened for a moment. 'Okay, five hundred, and bring a fresh motor.'

He put the phone down, pleased with himself. At least he'd made a decision. And he'd kept a spare set of contact shots for himself, as insurance.

Rory followed Brickhill down the drive. He told Pam he was going to the physiotherapist, but not where he was going after that.

A good long session with an experienced physio eased the aches and pains from the fall and the beating he'd had. Before he left, he pulled the conspicuous dressings from his head and found that the bleeding had stopped. He still wasn't looking well, but a lot better than he had done earlier that morning.

Once in his car, he applied himself to the one sure lead he had – Henry Straker. Somehow, he had to persuade Straker to tell him what the hell was going on.

He checked round the courses and found that Henry wasn't on duty that day. He rang his house, and was greeted by an answering machine.

He rang the surgery. Mr Straker wasn't in. He had taken his football team to play in Reading. The receptionist didn't know exactly where.

Two o'clock on a Saturday afternoon wasn't a good time to be tracking down a boys' club soccer team. But after half a dozen calls, someone at the library in Reading was able to give Rory the home phone number of the secretary of the club.

The secretary's wife was in. Her husband had gone

with the team to the match on the public playing fields in Reading.

Rory drove to the M4 and pointed his car east.

There were several sets of public playing fields in Reading. By half past three, Rory had found a maroon Daimler in a pitted and puddled parking area off a rough, muddy track lined by overgrown hazel and hawthorn. He had been told that this track led to a dilapidated set of changing rooms which served the playing fields in a public park on the outskirts of the sprawling town.

When he was sure it was Straker's car, Rory backed out and left his car in a side road a hundred yards from the entrance to the track.

He made his way back on foot, down the dripping dark lane – a remnant of the countryside that had been there before the town had swallowed it up. He passed the patch that had been carved out of the hedgerow to accommodate the cars of visitors to the playing fields. Besides Straker's car, there were two minibuses and a couple of cheap old saloons.

A hundred yards further on, he reached the back of the changing rooms. As inconspicuously as he could, he stepped from behind the dilapidated weatherboard building. He found himself looking at a couple of bald soccer pitches. On one of them, two teams of small boys, supported by a dozen or so spectators, were slugging it out in the mud.

Straker was in the middle of the field, looking quite out of character in a navy tracksuit and trainers. Even from a distance, his efforts at refereeing looked half-hearted.

Rory stared at the tall, thin figure and wondered what the hell he was going to do.

He couldn't talk to Straker now – not in the middle of this game, not among the kids he did so much for.

He hadn't come looking for Straker with any firm plan, just the idea that it was only through the vet that he could make any headway. Despite Laura's certainty that Straker wasn't involved, and her father's serious doubts, Rory felt in his guts that what he had found in Straker's house was more than coincidence. But he knew that he couldn't begin to prove it and he had nothing to offer the police.

As he stood there, undecided, the sound of someone coming down the muddy lane impinged on his consciousness. He turned and looked up the track.

Instantly, he sank further back between the changing rooms and the bushes behind them. Picking his way through the puddles and ruts was someone clad entirely in black biking leathers, wearing a full-face helmet, in every respect identical to the person who had met with Straker the previous morning to give him the envelope. This time, though, there was no sign of the big BMW bike. Rory guessed it had been left out on the main road, or more likely, a nearby side road.

Certainly, the biker was moving cautiously, but evidently hadn't spotted Rory. Rory held his breath until the black-clad figure turned into the parking area.

When the biker was out of sight, Rory crossed the track and walked as fast and silently as he could up the same side as the car park.

Fifteen feet from the gap, he stopped and inserted himself into the hedge. Through the budding hawthorn, he could see the black figure crouching beside the Daimler.

Within seconds the biker had picked the lock and opened the door. Still crouching, he pulled something from a pocket and inserted an arm underneath the driver's seat.

The whole operation took no more than twenty seconds before the car door was quietly closed and locked again, and the biker set off quickly down the lane.

Rory had to make a snap decision.

Either he went straight after the biker and followed him, or her, until he found where he came from.

Or he waited to tell Straker that someone had been tampering with his car.

But he knew that by the time he reached his own car, the big bike would be well on its way and uncatchable.

And he didn't want Straker killed.

He waited until the leather-clad figure had turned out of the top of the track before he stepped from his cover in the hedge and ran round to Straker's car. Of course, he couldn't open it – he didn't possess the skill or the tools. He peered into it, at the driver's seat and in front of it, but he couldn't see anything unusual from outside.

He tried wildly to guess what might have been put there – a bomb of some sort, timed, maybe, or triggered by remote control. Whatever it was, he was certain it was intended to do away with the Jockey Club vet.

'Come on, ref,' a boy's voice shrilled hoarsely across the misty pitch. 'How much longer?'

The sound of the young goalie jerked Henry Straker back from the maelstrom of his thoughts. He looked at his watch.

They were a good seven minutes over time. Agitated, he stuck a whistle between his lips and blew it. He tried to remember the score; he'd scarcely noticed the game.

One of his forwards came to the rescue. 'Three-two. Bit close, but at least we won, eh, Mr Straker?'

'Yes, well done. Good game.'

'It's lucky you didn't do anything about Darren's foul.'

'Darren's foul? Oh Lord,' Straker muttered, hoping that the other side's coach hadn't spotted the incident, whatever it was.

Rory ran back down the muddy lane to the football pitch where the game had just come to an end. He carried on towards Henry Straker, who was walking back towards the changing rooms with a group of his boys.

When he saw Rory coming towards him, Straker's step faltered a moment and a look of worried irritation flashed across his face. Rory was close enough by then to see the look, and its quick replacement by a bland, friendly smile.

'Good heavens, Rory, what are you doing here? If you came along to support the team, you'll be glad to hear they managed without your help,' he said, louder than was necessary. 'We won three-two.'

For Straker's sake, Rory went along with the charade.

'A good scoring game, pity I missed it. Took me a while to find the ground. Anyway, now I'm here, I wanted a quick word with you, if that's okay?'

Straker couldn't refuse him without sounding very churlish.

'Well, it'll have to be quick. I've got to get these boys changed and fed. Just let me get my coat from the changing room.'

He disappeared into the old shingle-built pavilion and came out a moment later with a waxed jacket over his tracksuit.

He gave his opposite number an apologetic smile and walked across to Rory, who had moved to a place where they could talk without being overheard.

'For God's sake,' Straker said. 'What do you mean by following me here? I hope it's got nothing to do with your ridiculous allegations yesterday.'

'It might have. I've just been watching someone tampering with your car.' He paused. 'Someone dressed in black bike leathers. They still had their helmet on so I couldn't get a look at their face.'

He saw Straker stiffen. 'What are you saying?'

'You heard. Someone's just planted something in your car – to do you damage. I think you ought to call the police.'

'You must be mistaken. Maybe they were just trying to steal it and couldn't get it started.'

'No, they weren't. Look, are you going to call the police or not?'

'I'm not going to waste their time. Presumably he's gone?'

'Yes, if it was a he. Must have left the bike back on the road. But look, you should have it checked out by a pro. I mean, if it's a bomb or something, you may trigger it.'

'I don't know how you've conceived the idea that anyone should want to kill me. Unless it's the other side's coach.' Straker forced a laugh.

'Look, if you're not going to do anything about it, *I'll* call the police.'

Straker shook his head irritably. 'For God's sake, I'll come and have a look then, but I'm sure you're wrong.'

He called over to one of the men in the party, evidently another supporter of his boys' club. 'Just got to fetch something from my car. I'll be back in a mo.'

He followed Rory silently up the dark track. He pulled out his key to open the door, then hesitated. 'You don't think this device is triggered to the lock?'

'No. He didn't do anything to connect it. He was here barely fifteen seconds. Just put something under your seat.'

Straker unlocked the door and opened it with relief. But he sighed as if it were all a futile waste of time. He leaned down and looked under the seat.

'Can you see anything?' Rory asked. 'If you can, don't touch it.'

Straker straightened his back. 'There's nothing there.'

'Let me have a look.' Rory almost pushed Straker aside and knelt down in the mud next to the car. After a moment of peering into the dark beneath the thick seat, he asked, 'Have you got a torch?'

'Yes, there's one in the glove compartment.'

Taking care not to put any weight on the leather upholstery, Rory leaned across to open the locker in front of the passenger seat. He took out a torch and crouched again to shine it under the driver's seat.

'There is something here,' he announced after a moment. 'It looks like a syringe.'

He lifted his head and placed both hands slightly apart on the soft, well-padded leather of the seat. Gently, he applied some pressure. Between his hands, the almost invisible sharp point of a hypodermic needle protruded up through the leather. He pushed a little harder and liquid spouted from the invisible aperture in the tiny needle's head.

He released the pressure, and the needle retracted from sight. He turned to Straker.

The vet, white-faced, was gaping at the seat. 'Christ! Why the hell should anyone want to do that?'

Rory nodded. 'I'd say that whatever was in that syringe wasn't going to do your health a lot of good. It's the latest joyriders' trick, after they've pinched a car and driven the hell out of it. But I don't think they usually bother to put anything into the syringe.'

He stretched his hand under the seat once more and extracted the weapon. He straightened his back. 'Are you still so sure you don't want to call the police?' he asked.

Straker took the syringe and gazed at it. 'There doesn't seem much point now, really, does there?' he said. 'If a kid's done it for some malicious kind of a lark, how the hell are the police going to find him?'

'But it wasn't a kid; it was an adult, someone who came on a bike, I'd say, not looking for a joy-ride. Come on, Henry, I think it's time you told me what's going on.'

For a moment, Straker looked as though he was going to give in and start talking. Rory held his breath.

But the vet suddenly pulled himself together.

'Listen, Rory, I told you yesterday, I don't know what you're referring to. How do I know you didn't just put the syringe there? I mean, it's very convenient you were just passing when it happened. Why should I believe all this cock-and-bull story about a chap on a motorbike? I don't know what your game is, but kindly stop pestering me.'

The tall man slammed shut the door of his car, stuffed the syringe into a pocket of his Barbour and strode off angrily across the mud and puddles towards the playing fields.

Rory stared after him, shaking his head in frustration. So much for Straker opening up. There was nothing he could do as long as Straker refused to admit what he knew. And he couldn't force him to come clean here. Rory turned and walked back up the track, trying to figure out what to do next. He had to do something.

By the time he'd reached his car, he'd made up his mind to go and see Laura. He didn't ring her. She'd just about be back from Sandown by the time he got to Langlands.

Henry Straker had done his best to oversee the return of his boys to their clubhouse on the other side of town. He tried gracefully to accept their thanks for his indefatigable coaching and support, as well as the tea he'd bought for them all on the way back. It was a fine performance and betrayed nothing of the turmoil in his head.

But when he reached home, the performance had to continue. Susan had just made tea, and produced toast and cake to go with it.

'Come on, Henry, sit down for a minute and relax,' she said considerately.

Disguising his reluctance, he joined her at the kitchen table.

'There are a few letters for you, by the way. The post came after you left this morning,' she went on, to keep the conversation going. She picked up a pile of mail from the dresser behind her and passed it across the table to her husband. He was glad of the excuse not to talk, and began mechanically to open the various envelopes. There were a few bills and confirmations of appointments. On the bottom of the pile was a stiff A4-size envelope. He hesitated a second, then quickly tore open the top. A small piece of paper fell out first. On it were typed the words 'INSTRUCTIONS TO FOLLOW'. He picked it up quickly and glanced across to see if his wife had noticed. But she was busy filling the teapot with more water.

'I'm just going to take this lot into the study,' Straker said with a quaver in his voice.

He stood up and walked across the hall. In his study he sat down at his desk and with trembling fingers began to extract the photograph from the envelope.

Before the black-and-white print was halfway out, a rush of nausea swept through him. Loathing even to touch the repellent photograph, he extracted it, absorbed the full, obscene horror of it and slammed it face down on the desk.

The previous two shots he had received, one through the post, like this, and one delivered by the biker, had been disgustingly graphic – enough to make him turn over every principle he had ever held. But this latest version was much worse.

He didn't know how they had done it, but to prove to anyone else seeing it that he hadn't been a willing participant just didn't seem possible.

With a sob, he buried his face in his hands and let his shoulders heave.

'Are you all right, dear?' Susan's voice was full of concern.

Henry stiffened. Fortunately, he had his back to her. He sniffed loudly. 'Nothing to worry about, just a bit of a cough coming on; running round a wet football pitch all afternoon, I expect.' It took a supreme effort to turn and face her with a rueful smile. 'I'll just put this lot away and come and finish that delicious cake.'

He turned back to the desk, certain that if Susan ever saw the photograph that lay there, she would never be able to spend a minute in the same room with him again, and that the grief it would cause would kill her.

He quickly dropped the envelope and photograph into a drawer of his desk and locked it. He would burn it, like the others, after tea.

Sitting at the kitchen table once more, he said, 'It's going to be a nasty, blustery old sort of night. I think I'll light a fire for you in the drawing room.'

'Oh, yes, Henry. That would be very cosy.'

Laura hadn't arrived back when Rory reached Langlands. But the Filipino cook let him into the small front drawing room and offered to bring him tea.

When she had left the room, he paced around, unable to sit, unable even to think clearly about what he should do next. Someone had tried to kill Henry Straker that day, he was certain of it. Someone who thought that the vet might very soon start talking and provide a link to whoever was pulling the strings.

But Rory couldn't get away from the one major flaw in his supposition – why someone of Henry Straker's unimpeachable good character should be involved in doping horses, especially when that had already led to one man's death and seemed likely to lead to his own. What was he set to gain?

His heart leapt when he heard a car draw up outside. He looked out and saw Laura, on her own, get out of her Mercedes. He walked into the hall to greet her.

She had already seen his car outside. She let herself in through the huge front door, pushed it to with her back and leaned against the ancient oak panels.

'Hi.' She gave him a wan, defeated smile.

'What's happened?' he asked.

'Nothing in particular. I'm just exhausted.'

'And how's Tommy?'

'I think he really enjoyed himself. He's a smashing boy.' Laura smiled. 'I drove him there, and Terry and Declan looked after him. He was adamant about being driven back in the lorry. He shouldn't be too long.'

'But something's bothering you,' he said.

'It's just the strain of it all. What if I go to prison?'

'I'll make sure you don't. You'll get off; I promise you we're going to find who did it.'

She shook her head, not taken in by Rory's false confidence.

'I know you're doing your best; you've been wonderful, but if the police haven't got any further, how the hell are you going to?'

'Come on. Don't be so defeatist,' he rallied. 'I want to tell you where I've got to.'

'I need a drink first,' she said.

'Your maid's gone to get some tea.'

'I'll go and cancel it. Pour me a large vodka and something for yourself.'

Taking her coat off as she went, she disappeared into the maze of corridors that led to the kitchens.

Rory went back into the warm comfort of the small drawing room and poured drinks for them both. Laura came in and closed the door behind her.

'I've told them we're not to be disturbed,' she said. She carried on walking towards Rory. When she reached him, she put her arms around his neck and her lips on his. Their tongues met and hungrily twined around each other, and she hugged him against her warm, tense body.

Rory couldn't remember a kiss so deep or so full of passion. Her flesh became softer as he absorbed her anxiety. When at last their lips reluctantly parted, he still held her in his arms and looked into her chocolate-brown eyes.

'Oh, God!' she whispered. 'I've been wanting to do that for such a long time.'

Rory grinned; he couldn't help himself. Until then, he hadn't been certain.

'Laura,' he breathed, 'you're so wound up.'

'Not now,' she said. 'Not with you. You're strong enough to take it.'

She turned in his arms and he let her go. She picked up her drink and sat on a small sofa. 'Come and sit next to me.'

Rory put himself beside her. For a while they didn't talk as he stroked her long black hair.

'I'm sorry if I seem so ungrateful,' she said after a

while, 'so negative about what you've been doing for me. It's just that I don't want to get my hopes up, and then get nowhere. Anyway, Agnew thinks they might have some trouble proving beyond doubt that I did it.'

'But that's not good enough,' Rory said indignantly. 'You didn't do it and we've got to prove that you didn't. Else the thing'll hang over you for the rest of your life.'

'Well, maybe I deserve it. I mean, I used Luke, didn't I? To get my own back on you, and to satisfy my own ambitions. Do you know, under all that bullying bullshit, I think he was a very insecure man. That's why he was so obsessed with making money and spending it. He used it as a kind of shield from the rest of the world. He would have had absolutely no idea how to cope without money. He'd have hated it, probably rather have died as he did.'

Rory considered this. 'No,' he said after a moment. 'He was a megalomaniac bastard, and don't you forget it. He probably still thought he'd crawl out of the shit and come up smelling of roses.'

'You may be right. I don't know. Anyway, I don't really want to talk about him.' Laura sighed and put an arm up to draw Rory's mouth to hers.

They talked and kissed and caressed, but no more than that. They both knew, without saying it, that that would have to come later. There was no hurry, and when it did come, it would be something much more special than the last time.

They talked a little about what Rory had discovered so far, but Laura was pessimistic. She didn't really believe that he would find out any more than he already had, and she wouldn't be convinced that Henry Straker was involved, or had had an attempt made on his life that afternoon, or that there was any Mr Big lurking behind the whole affair, pulling strings.

Rory didn't press her. He didn't want to spoil the moment. He was enjoying her complete trust and relaxation for once, sure that she wasn't holding anything back from him now.

He had been there with her for an hour when the maid came in to tell them that Tommy was now back at the yard.

Rory got slowly to his feet. 'I'm sorry, I'd better go. I promised we'd set off on our fishing trip tonight.'

'I understand,' Laura said softly. 'I'm just so glad you were able to stay as long as you have. I feel a hell of a lot better than I did.'

Rory knew that she didn't want to let him go, and it took all his paternal instincts to get him out of the house and into his car. Even then, he was reluctant to start the motor. Later, driving home with his son, he felt like a teenage boy who had just discovered love.

They arrived home to a barrage of complaints from Pam, who had been waiting for them.

'What the hell have you been doing?' she asked. 'I was due at Barry Short's drinks party an hour ago.'

'Have you packed all Tommy's stuff?'

'Yes, of course I have. There it is.' She nodded at a pink and yellow nylon bag on the floor.

'Okay,' Rory said, with as much good humour as he could muster. 'Let's go, boy.'

Through the drawing room window, Pam watched the

lights of the Rover bounce down the valley and dialled a number on the mobile phone.

'Hello, they've gone at last. You can come over now,' she giggled, absently pushing up one of her large breasts. There was a brief pause as she listened to a question from the other end. Then, 'No,' she answered, 'not till tomorrow night.'

Tommy, excited to be going at last on the long-promised trip, talked happily for the first half-hour of their journey. Rory let him rattle on, without answering more than he had to.

Gradually, the gaps between Tommy's questions became longer, until, as they crossed the Severn Bridge, they ceased altogether. Rory glanced down at his son, he was fast asleep now. Maybe in the morning, when they got out by the river, he'd be able to push the whole business of Luke Mundy's death and Laura's trouble to the back of his mind and they could concentrate on catching a few salmon.

They carried on quickly up the empty valleys of the Wye and Usk. At Brecon, Rory telephoned the hotel to tell them they would be arriving shortly. Tommy woke from his doze.

'We'll be there soon,' Rory said. 'I bet you'll be glad to get to bed.'

Tommy nodded sleepily.

'Have you had your injection yet?' Rory asked, feeling certain that he must have done.

Struggling to get the words out, Tommy didn't answer for a moment. 'No,' he replied slowly, 'I think Mum forgot to pack it.' Tears began to well in his eyes.

'Oh God!' Rory couldn't hide his exasperation. 'Are you sure?'

'I think so. She asked me to get it out and put it on my chest of drawers, but I don't think she ever went back to get it.'

'The useless . . .' Rory cut himself short. 'Okay let's check before we panic.'

He stopped the car at the side of the quiet road, got out and went round to the boot. He pulled Tommy's bag out and brought it back into the car. There he carefully took everything out, until it was empty. There was no sign of the small bottle of insulin and the syringe with which Tommy fought off the effects of his diabetes.

'We'll have to go back,' he said simply.

'Oh *no*. Dad, do we have to? Can't we get some here?'

'I'm not risking it at this time of night. Look, we'll go back home and get it, then turn right round and drive back, okay? I'm not going to let you miss anything. You'll sleep anyway, won't you?'

'Yeah,' Tommy looked at his father. 'Sorry, Dad.'

Chapter Eleven

A dark red Vauxhall Cavalier, stolen that afternoon from Ealing Broadway Station car park, drove down the valley from Camp Farm. A hundred yards from the main road, the lane became wide enough for two cars to pass.

The driver of the Cavalier saw a pair of headlights turn off the Hungerford road into the lane.

'Who the fuck's this?' Eland said to the man beside him.

'There's another farm up there, ain't there – must be one of them. Relax.' Like Eland, he spoke with the staccato delivery of inner London, which disguised the nervousness they both felt. 'For fuck's sake, this is meant to be your scam! If you don't do nuffin' stupid now, we won't have no trouble. Just take it easy back up to London and we'll dump the motor in Hammersmith. There's no one to tell the filth nothing.'

Eland wasn't so sure, but he hadn't a better plan. The other car was creeping up the lane towards them. He slowed and pulled over until his nearside wheels were on the narrow grass verge. Instinctively, he turned his head away from the oncoming lights until they passed.

'Shit!' his companion hissed. 'Rory Gillespie!'

Eland turned to him, eyes wide, more than nervous now. 'What the fuck are you talking about? How do you know it was him?'

'Didn't you see? His name was plastered all over the side of the car.'

'But was it him driving?'

'Yeah, it was him all right.'

'Then who the fuck was that other geezer?'

'I don't fuckin' know, do I? This is your bloody job, remember? And we never found nuffin'! A right fuckin' bollocks-up!'

'What the hell are we going to do? He'll start yellin' for the filth, and he's seen this car.' Eland's voice had risen in pitch. What had started out as a simple piece of evidence retrieval, well within his scope, had turned into something way out of his depth.

'Stop fuckin' screaming, you berk. We'll have to go back up there and deal with him.'

'No! That's crazy. We'll be walking straight back into it. Let's find a phone, call the nick and tell them we've heard something up there – a few bangs. If they get up there before 'e calls them, they'll think 'e's done it.'

'Are you mad? Do you think we've got time to go driving round looking for a phone box? Come on. Turn this motor round and get back up there. And don't piss about.'

Eland felt his bowels trying to empty themselves.

Everything had gone wrong. Straker had told him Gillespie had some of the photographs, but they'd found nothing, except that the house wasn't empty when it should have been.

Now he'd dug himself into a pit of shit he was never going to get out of. Straker and the jockey were both still alive.

If he went down, he vowed, he wasn't going down alone.

Rory parked beside Pam's Discovery. Leaving Tommy asleep on the passenger seat, he got out quietly and walked towards the back door.

He glanced down the valley. The car he had passed at the bottom had turned round and was coming back up. A flush of fear prickled his skin. It was half past midnight, and he hadn't recognised the car.

He quickened his pace until he reached the door, found it unlocked and let himself in.

'Pam! Pam!' he yelled. There was no answer from Pam, nor any sign of Taffy. He switched on the lights.

The kitchen was a shambles. Every cupboard door had been opened and every jar, tin, packet and bottle swept out on to the floor. He went on through to his study; the mess he had left it in that morning had been added to by every book having been pulled from the shelves, opened and flung in a heap on the floor. His desk had been dismantled, the carpets torn up and pictures taken from their frames.

What the hell were they looking for?

Somebody knew he was on to Straker. He knew that –

275

it had already earned him the beating in the Staffordshire woods. But they must have thought he knew a lot more than he did – and that somewhere he had the evidence to back it up.

He wished to God he had.

Now they were coming back.

And Tommy was still in the car!

Rory ran out, dimly conscious that Pam should have been around. Her car was here. Maybe someone had picked her up to take her to the party – Dai Price, probably.

The Vauxhall was rattling over the cattle grid across his gateway. He ran to his own car, opened Tommy's door and lifted him out. Tommy groaned and wriggled in his half-sleep. Rory heaved him over his shoulder and began to run towards the house.

But the car had almost reached the forecourt. Changing direction, he headed up towards the barns.

He staggered on under his son's weight. Now the boy was stirring. 'Dad! What are we doing?'

Rory set him down on his feet.

'Sshh!' he hissed. 'Can you run?'

'Why? What's happening?'

'Look, see that car? The men in it want something from me and they're after us. We'll have to go up and hide in the barns until they've gone.'

The idea appealed to Tommy. 'Great! We could hide next to Long Run,' he panted as he trotted along beside Rory.

'That's a bloody good idea.'

They passed the footings of Rory's new barns and carried on to the timber-clad stable yard which they were to replace. Once they'd reached the small three-sided complex they turned to look down the valley. The lights from the house glowed cosily in the black night. There were no sounds of pursuit.

The stallion was housed in a stable which also gave access to a further one beyond, in the corner of the block. More often than not, like now, it was unoccupied.

'Go and get a couple of carrots from the feed shed, and an armful of hay,' Rory told Tommy as he walked quietly to the stallion's stable door.

Long Run stirred and came to put his big handsome head over the door.

'Hello, boy.' Rory put out a hand to stroke the horse's nose. Long Run sniffed and blew in recognition, and expectation. Tommy arrived with the carrots and held one up to the big horse, who sniffed and recognised again and gratefully sucked up the offering.

All the time, Rory kept his eye on the farmhouse below them, where more lights had been turned on as the men searched through the house for him.

He caught a flash of a torch as one of them hunted round the garages and outhouses that clustered at the back.

The wind had dropped to a few occasional gusts, but the quiet up at the yard was shattered by a bang as a squall caught the food-store door which Tommy had left open.

The torch beam swung up the valley, too short to illuminate them, but the faint sound of shouting reached them and the flashlight began to jerk up towards them.

Rory quickly opened the stable door. He and Tommy

slipped in. With a gentle shove from Rory, the stallion obligingly shifted to let them pass. They stuffed the hay into the empty manger and squeezed past the horse to the door of the adjoining stable. Closing the lower door, Rory took the second carrot from Tommy and gave it to Long Run who grasped it between his teeth and stepped back to eat it. Rory closed the upper door and whispered to Tommy, 'Get down and keep quiet.'

From a grille at the back of the box, Rory had a clear view down the valley. The torch was fifty yards from them now, and coming fast.

Tommy was on tiptoes beside him. 'Is that them, Dad?' he asked.

'Yes,' Rory said. 'Now for God's sake, get down and don't say a word, or do anything to upset Long Run.'

He and the boy nestled below the grille, where no torch beam could reach them.

Eventually, on the concrete of the stable yard, they heard steps approach, stop, come on and stop again at each stable.

They heard the mares stirring at the disturbance as the men shone their light into the boxes.

The footsteps stopped outside Long Run. Rory and Tommy could see the flash of the torch above the partition between the two boxes.

A voice reached them clearly. 'Look, there's a door in there, must lead into the corner. Let's take a look.'

'That 'orse looks dangerous.'

'Don't be daft.'

'No, look at him.'

They heard Long Run cross to the stable door, snorting. The men backed off.

'All right,' the first said. 'Let's see if we can get in there round the back.'

A few moments later, the torch beam was shining over Rory and Tommy's heads.

'There's nuffin' in there.'

'I want to make sure.'

The footsteps sounded from the yard again, and stopped at the stable door.

'I'm going in.'

The stable door was unbolted and squeaked as it was opened an inch or two.

There was a shattering, splintering crash as the stallion's hooves lashed out at the inch-thick ply panels that lined his box, and the harsh scuff of his hooves on the ribbed concrete beneath the thick straw bed.

The stable door was slammed shut.

'Christ! It looks bloody wild! I'm not going in there. Gillespie could be anywhere in this fucking valley, for Christ's sake! We'll never find him. Let's get out of here.'

'All right then. We'll do what you said and hope it fuckin' works.'

Rory found he had been holding his breath for the half-minute they had been there. As their footsteps faded, he let it out in a long sigh of relief.

'Okay, Tommy,' he whispered. 'Don't move or make a sound until we've heard their car leaving.'

He felt beside him for the boy and found him trembling. The reality of the danger had evidently got through to him.

When they were certain the car was on its way down the drive, Rory opened the door to Long Run's box and talked to him as they let themselves out. They could see the car turning into the main road, and setting off fast down towards Lambourn. Out of habit, Rory quickly checked all the horses, closed up the feed store and led Tommy back down the track to the house.

They had just reached the back door when they saw a blue flashing light racing along the main road.

Rory waited to see where it was headed. He wasn't surprised when it turned off and came up towards them.

He and Tommy went into the kitchen. He made Tommy sit while he went up the back stairs from the kitchen to the boy's little room and found the insulin and needle on the chest of drawers.

Two policemen walked in as he came back down.

'Are you Rory Gillespie?' the first asked.

'Sure. How did you know what had happened up here?'

'We don't know what happened up here. We just got a call that there was some kind of disturbance going on. Someone reported gunshots.'

'What!' Rory said. 'I didn't hear any gunshots. I got back and found the place like this, and it was only raided last night. The two guys came back and chased after us. We hid in one of the stables until they gave up and drove off.'

'So there wasn't any shooting?'

'Not that I heard.'

'They've made a right mess of this place. We'd better have a quick look around.'

'Sure. I haven't had a chance to myself yet.'

He let them go, and organised Tommy's injection. He was preparing some warm milk for him when the police appeared. There was a tenseness about them which hadn't been there before.

'Are you telling us you didn't hear any shots?'

'That's what I said.'

The other policeman drew in his breath. 'There are two dead people upstairs – both shot.'

'*What!*' Rory stared at the man who had spoken. 'Who?'

'Don't you know?'

The milk on the hob started to froth noisily over the side of the pan. Rory ignored it. He glanced at Tommy, asleep with his head on the table; at least he wasn't hearing this.

Rory himself was finding it hard to absorb the information. All his instincts were to reject it. He didn't answer the question. In a state of dazed shock, he turned and switched the heat off under the bubbling milk, picked up the pan and poured some into a mug which he placed on the table in front of the sleeping Tommy.

'Are you going to tell us what we're dealing with here or not?'

'I don't know what you're talking about! There's no one else here.'

'Just come and see for yourself.'

'All right,' Rory said, still trying to block the idea from his head. 'I'm coming.'

Leaving Tommy fast asleep at the table, he led the way up the main stairs from the hall. At the top he turned into the corridor towards his bedroom, and stopped, frozen in mid-step.

Halfway along the passage, lying on her back with her

arms flung above her head, was Pam.

Her eyes were open and she was naked.

'Jesus Christ!' he whispered hoarsely. 'Don't let Tommy come upstairs.'

'Can you identify her?'

'Of course I can,' Rory said weakly. 'She's my wife.'

'That's what we thought. Now, can you tell us who the other body is?'

'Where . . . where is it?'

'In the bedroom.'

Rory turned his eyes away from Pam's once soft, warm body and sidled past her to their bedroom.

There was a lump beneath a rumpled top sheet, where a bloodstain, twelve inches across, had spread through the white linen.

The victim's head lay on one side, face towards the door. The familiar sharp features, for once immobile, came as no surprise to Rory.

'Who's that then?' a voice behind him asked.

'He's . . . was Dai Price – a jockey,' he added fatuously.

'Knew him, did you?'

'Oh aye. I knew him. I saved his life on Wednesday.'

The police in Newbury were quite polite when they took him in. They had let him carry Tommy, still sleeping, out to their car and dropped him at his friend's house in the village to spend the rest of the night there.

The two detectives, freshened with cups of strong coffee, questioned Rory rigorously but calmly for two more hours.

He didn't blame them.

They hadn't found him with a smoking gun, but he'd had the opportunity, and a hell of a motive to commit murder, and they had to start somewhere.

But Rory had the advantage that to the experienced eye, the state of the victims and of the house had all the signs of an interrupted burglary, rather than a *crime passionnel*.

In the end, two hours of questioning and the circumstances of Rory's discovery led the detectives to the conclusion that they hadn't sufficient grounds for detaining him.

A police car dropped him at the Joneses' house where Tommy was spending the night, so that he would be there in the morning when his son woke. The forensic investigation would be finished and the bodies removed to the police morgue before he got back home, and they'd need to talk to him again in the morning.

He sensed that he wasn't completely off the hook, though. He sat in a chair in the living room of the small house, with a glass of whisky in front of him, deciding whether to ring Laura or her father.

Though it was half past three in the morning, Edward Brickhill sounded wide awake when Rory got through to him and gave no audible signs of shock when he told him what had happened.

'Don't go into detail now,' he said calmly. 'I'll come down and see you first thing in the morning.'

The numbness he had felt the night before returned to Rory in the morning, followed by physical nausea. Now he was finding it harder to cope with the death of his partner of the last twelve years, despite the almost total erosion of affection between them. Regardless of all her shortcomings in the role, she had still been Tommy's mother. With his thoughts on Tommy, Rory rang his parents in Scotland to tell them what had happened.

The events had taken place too late to make the Sunday papers, and the radio stations were only just beginning to pick up the story. Old Mrs Gillespie had heard nothing about it and seemed to find it almost impossible to believe. Nevertheless, she agreed that her grandson should come and stay with them, as far away as possible from the scene and the local gossip.

Tommy's friend's parents, whom Rory knew only slightly, offered to drive Tommy to Scotland themselves. Rory's gratitude was increased when they also said they would see if they could fix the boy up with some fishing when he got there.

He went up to the small bedroom where Tommy had slept, and sat on his bed.

'Mummy's had a terrible accident,' he started. The boy's top lip began to quiver. Rory took a small hand in his and squeezed it. '. . . and she's died . . . We won't ever see her again.'

He let out a long breath. He had been dreading this job, and had decided the only way to handle it was as honestly as possible.

Tears seeped from the boy's eyes. For a while he looked away and stared at the ceiling, then, calmly, he said, 'I suppose that means we won't be going to Wales now.'

Rory shook his head. 'I'm afraid it does. But we will another time – a real long trip, I promise.'

'Mummy bought me some new Nikes the other day,' Tommy said, finding reasons for missing his mother.

'Did she?' Rory said gently. 'That was nice of her.'

'Will you look after me all the time now?'

'Of course I will.'

It was a damp, cold March morning, but Rory felt insulated from it by the warm, leather-scented interior of Brickhill's Bentley in which he was being driven back to Camp Farm.

'You didn't tell them what you think about Straker, did you?' Edward was asking.

'No, though I would have done if they'd looked like holding me there.'

Brickhill looked relieved. 'Thank God for that. I really want that kept from them until we know for certain that Henry was involved.'

'You still don't believe me, after what I told you.'

'I don't know. But I do know that if Henry *is* involved, it's because somebody's applying some very heavy pressure. We can't risk him being investigated until we really know what's happening.'

Rory shook his head vigorously. 'But, Edward, for God's sake, these people have killed three times now, and your daughter is on the line for one of those deaths.'

'Believe me,' Brickhill said quietly, 'I haven't stopped thinking about that since she was arrested.'

He went on to say that he was making full use of his contacts and his money in looking for connections between Luke's death and his gambling, and he was sure they would soon start to see results.

But Rory wasn't encouraged. 'For Christ's sake, Edward, I think we've got to hand over what we know to the police. If this thing started out as a simple plan to stop Midnight Express from winning, it's got way out of hand now and people are going to be more determined than ever to cover their tracks. I mean, Henry Straker's reputation won't matter much to him if he gets killed, too.'

Rory stood outside his house, thinking that he was getting nowhere fast. He was frustrated and uneasy about Edward Brickhill's anxiety to keep the police away from Straker. For a few minutes, he considered going straight back to the police station, but in the end, something Brickhill had said, 'You could be destroying the man's reputation for ever', echoed in his head.

Still feeling disoriented, he walked round the back of his garage with the vague idea of going to check on the horses before he confronted the police and the mess in his house.

It was then that he discovered the reason for his dog's absence. He found Taffy's wiry black and white body lying stiff and cold behind the garage. From the damage done to the animal's skull, it was impossible to guess what kind of weapon had been used, only that it had been wielded with strength, and unrestrained commitment.

Tears that hadn't come before flowed now from Rory's eyes as he gazed at his lifeless friend.

In a haze of grief, he fetched a spade and buried the guiltless dog.

There were still half a dozen policemen crawling around

the house. They told Rory that Pam and Dai had been removed.

Rory made himself some coffee and sat staring out of the window, up the valley towards his stable block. He ought to have been up there, dealing with his horses, but they seemed completely irrelevant at the moment. He was trying to come to terms with life without Pam; he didn't dare think about Laura.

Exhausted, confused, he sank into a vacuous trance in which all coherent thought was forced from his mind.

He was jerked out of it by the arrival of the two policemen who had interviewed him late into the night.

They wanted to talk to him about the burglary.

Slowly, unwillingly, Rory offered them the same story he had given the previous morning, after the first break-in – someone looking for the cash he had received for the sale of the coloured pony. They were still unconvinced about the source, but seemed prepared to believe in the cash.

'But it won't have been the same people, not after they found nothing the night before.'

Rory shrugged wearily. 'There's nothing else missing.'

'I'm afraid we can't rule out the possibility that the intention was to kill your wife and, er, the jockey. We know you had two visitors last night. Fresh footprints outside confirm that, and that they chased you and the boy up to the barns. And we've had confirmatory sightings of the red Cavalier you described.' The detective paused for a moment, before continuing abruptly, 'Why do you think anyone would want to kill your wife?'

'I don't know,' Rory mumbled.

'I know it's difficult, and I don't like asking this, but did she have other . . . boyfriends – someone who might have been jealous of her affair with Dai Price?'

'For Christ's sake,' Rory blurted, finally embarrassed, 'I don't know. Maybe. I didn't even know she was definitely having an affair with Dai.'

'Everyone else did, Mr Gillespie,' the policeman said with unexpected gentleness.

'Well, I suppose I knew there was something going on. To be quite honest, I tried to ignore it. Pam and I hadn't got on well for a long time. I mean, I only stayed with her for the boy's sake; I'm afraid she wasn't much of a mum to him.' Rory was surprised how disloyal to his dead wife he felt, talking to an outsider like this.

'Okay, I'm just asking. Do you think it's possible that happened?'

'I guess it is, but I can't think of anyone in particular.'

'That brings us to the other possible scenario, which is that they didn't realise that the man in the bed wasn't you. In the dark they wouldn't have been able to see and might have made the assumption that it had to be you.'

Rory didn't answer at once, now that the detective had hit the jackpot. He screwed up his face in an effort to look puzzled and startled. 'You mean, do I know of anyone who would want to kill me?'

The policeman nodded.

Rory sighed. 'It's possible. You know I was beaten up after the races at Uttoxeter on Friday; that wasn't a straightforward mugging. I was being warned to leave off asking questions about Luke Mundy's death.'

'What sort of questions had you been asking?'

'Listen, I know damn well Laura didn't dope that horse – it's just not possible – and you guys had stopped looking elsewhere, so I thought I'd bloody well find out what happened.'

'And what have you found out so far?'

'Not a lot.'

'Mr Gillespie, you must have got on to something if these people came to kill you.'

'I haven't. But maybe they think I have,' Rory said, voicing what he'd been thinking for some time.

The detective wasn't convinced. 'Listen, if you know anything and you're holding out on us, you could be charged with obstructing enquiries. My advice is tell us all you know, then leave it to us.'

'I haven't got anything to tell you. All I've done is draw blanks. D'you think I wouldn't tell you if I could give you a name? I mean, if they did want to hit me and didn't get me this time, they'll more than likely try again. Right?'

'Yes, you are right. So it would help us and you if you told us why anyone should want to.'

'I've told you, I don't know.'

The detective shrugged his shoulders. 'If they're after you, it's going to make our job a lot easier when you can tell us why.' He nodded his colleague towards the door. 'We've got to get back. You know where to get in touch with us. In the meantime, you'd better be careful.'

Rory watched them drive back down the lane. All their colleagues had gone now and, knowing that he would never hear Pam's voice about the place again, he found it strangely quiet. He wandered through the house, irresolute and unwilling to start putting right the mayhem caused by the killers.

They'd be back, he was sure of it, and he was crazy not to tell the police about Straker. Luke's death, partly self-inflicted, was one thing, but now double murder. There had to be more of a motive than just a bet. Rory toyed with the idea of letting Straker's reputation take its chance, then thought better of it.

He walked back into the chaos of the kitchen and poured himself a generous slug of Glenmorangie. He sat down at the table and tried to organise his thoughts.

Twice he reached out to pick up the phone and call Laura. Both times he held back. He didn't have anything good to tell her; he didn't want to end up crying on her shoulder, needing her support; it was meant to be the other way round.

The telephone trilled sharply, catching him by surprise. Laura, he thought. She'd have heard by now. He picked it up to talk to her.

'Hello.'

'Rory?' A man's voice; quiet, deep, well bred. He couldn't place it at once.

'Yes. Who's this?'

'It's Henry Straker.' There was an odd timbre to the voice, which somehow disguised it.

'Henry! My God,' Rory blurted.

'I've just heard what happened. I need to speak to you.'

'Okay,' Rory said, quickly recovering himself. 'Where?'

'Do you mind coming here?'

Henry Straker's face seemed to have withered. There was

a coating of sweat on the pallid wrinkles of his forehead.

He didn't speak when he opened the door to Rory and beckoned him in with a gloomy smile. He led him into his study and closed the door behind them.

He offered Rory the large chair and sat at his desk.

'I'm desperately sorry this has happened.' It wasn't just sympathy, it was an apology. Rory acknowledged it with a silent nod.

'You see,' Straker went on, 'I'm partly to blame. I'm afraid you've been right all along.' His face seemed to collapse; his large, normally firm grey eyes gave the impression of melting, until he could look at Rory no longer. He turned his bleak gaze to the dripping rhododendrons outside the window. 'I can't tell you what hell it's been. I've handled the whole thing utterly wrong, but . . .' his voice dropped almost to a whisper, 'I had to, for Susan. She just couldn't have . . .' The words faded on his trembling lips.

Rory could feel Straker's pain, but he didn't speak.

'So, I had to do it; nothing could have been further from my instincts.'

Rory held his breath.

'But, those photos!' Straker shook his head hopelessly. 'If she'd seen them, she could never have looked me in the face again.'

He turned his gaze back on Rory.

'Photos?' Rory prompted.

'I don't know how they did it. I remember nothing, nothing about it.'

'About what?'

'The photos they took; they were horrible, despicable;

291

they made it look as if I were enjoying it.' Straker shook his head in despair. 'The bastards!' he whispered.

'Are you trying to tell me that you've been blackmailed, and you did stop Midnight Express?'

'Yes, yes,' Straker said impatiently. 'Except it wasn't blackmail.'

'How do you mean?'

'I mean, what they had against me was something I didn't do – couldn't possibly have done. I was set up, very cleverly. The bastards had done their homework too; they knew just what would hurt most.'

'What exactly?'

Henry looked at him, pleading for his sympathy. 'I haven't told anyone else about this. In a way it's a hell of a relief, and now I don't think there's any way of avoiding the whole thing coming out. You see, they said if I went to the police and the police believed me and sat on it, they'd send copies of the photos to my wife, the Jockey Club, all the papers and the boys' club. Whatever the truth, my reputation will be shredded; I'll have to resign from every office I hold. I think I could handle that, on my own, but it would destroy Susan. She's had to cope with losing our boys, then bear the fact of her own subsequent barrenness, and she's found that terribly difficult. I'm not even sure that she'd accept my explanation for the photos and what they show.'

'Henry, it may not need to come out. If we can get to whoever's behind it first.'

Henry glanced up at him, surprised by his vehemence.

'But we haven't got a lot of time,' Rory went on, 'and Laura's in trouble.'

'I know,' Straker said guiltily. 'I felt terrible when I heard she'd been charged with Luke's manslaughter. I've tried to show as much loyalty as possible, but . . .'

'But what?'

Straker gave an agonised sigh. 'Oh God! Please don't hold this against me, but it did cross my mind that Laura might have been involved in some way. I mean, you know that she and Luke were at loggerheads most of the time, and Luke was in serious difficulties . . .'

After what he had felt with Laura the day before, Rory didn't want even to consider this again, but he made Straker go on. 'Why do you think she could possibly be involved, though?' he asked.

'It's not fair, really, to mention it – it was almost certainly sheer coincidence – but a couple of weeks before Midnight Express ran, she jokingly asked me what I would give a horse if I wanted to slow it down. It's the sort of question people often ask me, you know, in fun. Well, in the same spirit, I said a ten milligram dose of xylazine would do the trick, and not arouse much suspicion. Then she asked me, seriously, if the same drug would be suitable for tranquillising a tricky horse when it was being clipped – apparently she'd been having trouble with a new mare. I told her it would do, with the right dosage. She asked me to get her a phial of it and I dropped one off the next day.

'The horrible irony is that that's exactly what I was ordered to use by the blackmailer. I'm afraid it occurred to me that she might have tried it out on the horse at home, to see what effect it would have on its performance.

I knew that she wasn't keen on the horse running at Kempton.'

'No,' Rory agreed. 'She wanted to save it for the Champion Chase.'

'But, honestly, Rory, I really don't think she had anything to do with it, and if they got her as far as the dock, I'd have stood up and told them it was me who administered it.'

Rory stared at him, not knowing what to believe. 'Who planted the empty phial in her car, then? That's why the police arrested her.'

Straker sighed. 'It must have been the man on the bike, or someone working for him. He made me give him an empty phial.'

'This guy, this blackmailer, you seem to have seen him a few times. Surely you could have found out something about him?'

Straker shook his head. 'Of course, I tried. But he was always completely covered, with his helmet on and a scarf wrapped across his mouth under the visor. I couldn't even tell you the colour of his eyes. I persuaded a friend of mine in the police to check the number of the bike – I said it had hit my car and driven off, but he came back and told me it was a bogus number – the real vehicle had been written off three months ago. He spoke very little, and of course his voice was muffled by the helmet and the scarf; I certainly wouldn't be able to swear to it if I heard it again. He had a sort of Cockney accent, but that doesn't narrow it down much.'

Rory nodded. It made sense. The blackmailer evidently knew what he was doing, and he'd already shown the lengths to which he would go. If he and Henry were going to stay alive, they were going to have to get to him first, and very soon.

'What I don't really see,' Straker went on, 'is why anyone particularly wanted to stop that horse in that race.'

'That's simple,' Rory said. 'Whoever took the bet Luke had on it.'

'Did he have a bet?'

'We think so. Edward Brickhill's people are pretty sure. The only trouble is, they don't know who with. If we knew that, we'd know everything. There's got to be a bent bookie behind all this somewhere. The problem is, he might be an illegal bookmaker who can't be traced.'

Straker nodded. 'I suppose so.'

But Rory couldn't rid himself of the sickening, disloyal thought that perhaps Laura was still holding back from him, despite the complete trust he had felt yesterday. 'If it wasn't done to win a bet, then it was done simply to stop the horse running the race. Anyone other than Luke would have pulled it up after a few furlongs. What would have been the long-term effect on Midnight Express being doped? I mean, how long would it have taken for the horse to recover?' Rory asked.

'It depends entirely on the horse, and how much of the drug was administered,' Straker replied thoughtfully. 'It could take anything from a couple of days to a couple of months. Laura would have been taking one hell of a risk if she'd done the job herself with the Champion Chase in mind.' Straker shook his head. 'I'm sure Laura had nothing to do with it,' he said with conviction now. 'I'm sorry even to have suggested it, when I consider what

295

I've done myself and everything that's led to.'

'It's okay, I understand. Just tell me what happened, from the beginning.'

The vet looked relieved to confide in someone at last.

'It was about a month ago. I got a call from a man to go and look at a horse in a small livery yard near Sunningdale. Obviously, he gave a false name but he said Mick Fanshaw had recommended me to him. Despite everything, Mick's an old friend of mine, so I agreed; I never thought of checking with Mick. I was due to pick up the Daimler from servicing in Cobham, so it wasn't much out of my way. I found the place – I'd never been there before. I wandered about for a few minutes, called out, but there was no one around, though there were half a dozen horses in the boxes. This chap had told me which stable his horse was in. He'd said he might get there a bit late. Anyway, I thought I'd identified the right box and went in. I was pretty surprised to find that there was just an old cob in there. I'd assumed, as the recommendation had come through Mick, that it would be a blood horse, but I wasn't particularly suspicious or anything – I mean, if the old horse was precious to someone ... Anyway I thought I might as well get on with examining it and picked up one of his feet. Then suddenly somebody jumped on me and stuffed a rag of chloroform over my face, and that was that – everything went blank.'

'What time of day was it?' Rory asked.

'Just after ten in the morning.'

'What happened after that?'

'They must have given me a jab. I came round about two hours later, feeling like death, being driven along in the back of my own car. I was slumped on the rear seat, so I couldn't see much of where I was going and I didn't want whoever it was to know I'd come round yet – I was still feeling very groggy and not up to any kind of fight. So I kept my eyes shut for most of the journey. The only thing I saw which I could identify was Windsor Castle high on the skyline, so we must have crossed the Thames on the road that links Windsor and Slough. Anyway, ten or fifteen minutes later, the car stopped and the driver got out. I thought he was going to come round to the back, but I heard another car start up and realised he must have gone. I didn't dare look up, in case it wasn't him leaving; it was, though, so I never even saw what kind of car he was in or its number. When I did get up to look around, of course there was no sign of him. I was in one of those parking places in Windsor Great Park. There were a couple of other cars there, but nobody around. I didn't feel up to driving straight away, so I sat there for a bit trying to pull myself together. I couldn't think what had happened, or why I should have been abducted, and apart from being rather dishevelled, I didn't appear to be damaged in any way. My shoes were unlaced and my tie was in my pocket, but nothing had been taken or anything. I was absolutely mystified. I realised I must have been driven somewhere, and I knew we'd come back over the river. As I told you, I'd picked up the car from being serviced that morning, and the garage had marked the mileage on the service sheet which was in the glove compartment. Another thirty-four miles had been added. I reckoned it was about ten miles from Cobham to the yard in Sunningdale, so my round trip must have been twenty-four. I'm afraid that leaves a pretty vast area. I thought about trying to find where I'd been taken, but I didn't know where to begin, and at that stage, I didn't know what the hell was going on. I thought of going back to the yard, but frankly, it occurred to me that whoever it was might have gone back there.'

'Did you go to the police?'

'Yes, of course. But it was all rather embarrassing because I couldn't tell them much. I wasn't injured and nothing had been stolen.'

'Have you been back to the yard since?'

'No, nor to the police, because two days later I got an envelope through the post with the first of the photographs. A few minutes after the post had been, I got a phone call; a man's voice, London accent. He just said that if I contacted the police or tried to do anything to trace where the shots had been taken, they'd be sent to my wife and everyone else.' He placed his hands flat on the desk in front of him, then lifted them in a gesture of helplessness. 'I couldn't take that risk, and when the next call came, telling me to stop Midnight Express, I had to do it.' He shook his head with shame. 'If I'd even thought it could end up with anyone being killed, of course, I'd have taken the risk of them sending the photos. Now two more people are dead. I'll have to give myself up and simply hope for the best.'

Rory ignored this. 'Did they ask you to stop others? That favourite at Folkestone last week?'

Straker nodded. 'But I said I wouldn't do any more. I told the blackmailer I thought you'd guessed what was going on and it wouldn't work again. I'm afraid I told him I thought you'd stolen some of the photos.' Straker turned his eyes from Rory's. 'I'm sorry, I was desperate, and you'd been round asking questions. Yours was the most obvious name and it was plausible to suggest you were doing it for Laura. If I'd dreamt it would lead to all this . . .' He covered his face with his hands once more. 'I realised you suspected I was involved when Charters told me you'd been asking him why he hadn't been on duty at Kempton that day. Then on Friday morning, this man phoned again, just after you'd left, and told me to meet him. That time I was given another photo and instructions in person, by the man on the bike you saw yesterday. From his voice, it was the same person who had phoned me. He wanted me to dope a horse the next day. I said it was impossible because I wasn't on duty and it would look very suspicious if I tried to change that again at short notice.'

'As you did with Charters at Kempton,' Rory added.

Straker nodded. 'I'm afraid so. Anyway, the chap was bloody angry. He said that when I'd seen the photograph, I'd change my mind, and got out of my car. I'd already decided that I wasn't going to dope another horse, whatever happened, but I didn't open the envelope he had given me right away. I was due down at Langlands, but on the way there, I thought I'd better get rid of the photo. I stopped and took it out. It was horrible.' Straker faltered.

'What was it of?' Rory prompted.

'I'm sorry, I just can't tell you. It makes me sick to even think about it. And it was worse than the previous one. I thought about what everyone would say if they saw it – the papers, Susan – it was unthinkable. But I nearly decided there and then to have done with it. I drove to the police station in Newbury and sat outside in my car for about a quarter of an hour. Then I forced myself to get out and walk across to the front entrance. I'm afraid I dithered on the steps for a couple of minutes, and two constables came out and I thought, these people will never believe me, and I went back to the car. I decided I'd have to do this horse after all. But I chucked the photo into a litter bin by the lay-by where I'd stopped and set fire to the whole thing.'

'But you didn't go to the races yesterday?' Rory asked.

'No. I didn't have to. The horse was withdrawn. The man phoned me and told me, but he said there'd be another one, a big one, the following week. I said I wasn't going to do it, and I meant it. I said send the photos to whoever you like. Oddly enough, that seemed to panic him and he started getting very abusive. It occurred to me that maybe the thing was a huge bluff and I put the phone down feeling better, but that didn't last long when I thought how repellent and convincing the photographs had been. I slept terribly and next morning I was at my wits' end again, but I tried to carry on as normal. I'd arranged to go with my soccer team to the game in Reading, which is where you found me. I'm sorry I was so offensive to you again,' the vet said with true contrition, 'particularly as you saved my life . . .'

'What?' Rory asked.

'The syringe under my car seat contained neat strychnine.' The knowledge of how close he'd come to an agonising death showed on the vet's face. 'I analysed it at the surgery. With a small dose straight into the bloodstream, I'd have lasted only a few minutes, no more. I drove back home shaking, and when I got there I found a third photograph that had been posted the day before, I guess before the chap had phoned me. And it was even more horrible than the first two...' Straker shook his head. 'They picked the most damaging shot you can imagine. I could hardly cope any more, but I had to. I thought it was better that I should be killed than that Susan should ever see it.'

Rory was beginning to understand the agony that Straker must have been going through. He was suddenly intensely grateful that Edward Brickhill had persuaded him not to tell the police about what he'd found at the vet's house or about the attempt on Straker's life the day before.

Rory gazed at him, relieved but appalled now that Straker had confirmed the extent of his involvement. But he found he didn't want to blame the man, not at all.

'Look, Henry. Try and stall them for the next couple of days. Tell them you'll do another next week. A few more days may get us closer to whoever's doing this.'

Straker nodded bleakly. He didn't believe they could achieve anything.

'They may not phone again and I've got no way of contacting them. When they realise they haven't killed me, which they will have done by now, I imagine they'll try again.'

Rory nodded. 'That makes two of us. The people who came to my place last night must have thought I knew a lot more than I did.'

Straker bowed his head in remorse.

Rory stood up decisively. 'Right, this is what we do. Somehow you're going to have to persuade Susan that both of you have to go and stay somewhere else tonight. If you don't, you could both end up dead. These people aren't just trying to cover their tracks from blackmail and horse-doping, they've got two murder raps chasing them, and they're not going to be worried about a couple more if that'll kill the trail. I'm not going back home; I'm going to stay in a pub tonight. I want you to meet me in Ascot at the racecourse car park, tomorrow morning at eight. We've got to get to where those photos were taken before they get to us. Here's my mobile number if you get held up, but for God's sake, try and be there.'

Straker nodded. 'I'll come,' he said, not disguising the futility he felt.

Chapter Twelve

In the car outside, Rory dialled Laura's number.

After a couple of rings, she answered herself.

'Rory, where are you? I've been trying to get hold of you all afternoon. I've heard the news about Pam and . . . Dai. I can't believe what's happened.'

'I'm coming to see you now. I'll tell you when I get there. And make sure you're on your own.'

Rory drove in through the lodge gates as George Rutherford drove out.

Laura opened the front door of the house to him, greeting him with a warm hug. 'Rory, I'm so sorry.'

'I know. I can't believe what's happened . . . Is there anyone else here?' he asked.

'No. I've just got rid of Rutherford, thank God.' She closed the door behind him and led the way into the small drawing room.

'What did he want?'

'He's been coming on very strong since Luke died. He's

talking about buying the yard for me and getting involved in it himself. He says that now that he's my biggest owner, he feels he has some rights, and, even though Luke tucked him up over a deal, he won't make a claim on the estate if I go into partnership with him.'

'Would he get anywhere claiming?'

'No. The fact of the matter is he could claim on the estate until he's blue in the face but there's not going to be anything left anyway, so I haven't been showing the gratitude that he seems to think I should.' She shrugged. 'Of course, I don't want him taking his horses away but I'm not going to be bullied. Fortunately, the horses are running well so I doubt he'll do anything drastic. But, for God's sake,' she said, abruptly changing her tone, 'what happened last night?'

Rory told her everything that had occurred from the moment he and Tommy had arrived back at the farm. When he began to describe finding Pam's naked body on the landing, she stopped him.

'Rory, for God's sake, I don't think I can take it. How can you be so calm?'

Rory lowered his eyes. 'To be honest, I don't think it's quite hit me. But finding my wife with Dai wasn't too conducive to sympathy.'

'No,' Laura nodded. Then she gave a short cynical laugh. 'George Rutherford asked me if I'd done it.'

'Did you?'

Laura had been looking into the fire. She glanced at him now.

'Of course not. I knew it wasn't necessary.'

'I don't know. I wouldn't have left her, I don't think.

Not while Tommy was still so young.'

'I'm sorry,' Laura said gently. 'That was selfish and insensitive of me.'

'We're both in the same boat. What we are expected to feel and what we actually feel are two different things. Even so, I'll admit, I do feel a sense of emptiness. Numbness, really.'

'What about Tommy?' Laura asked.

'He's bound to miss her, isn't he? But I think he'll get over it in the end. He'll need me a lot more than he already does. But that's okay by me.'

'He's such a good kid. I hope he's okay.'

'Aye,' Rory nodded. 'But if we don't find out what the hell's going on, he's not going to have a dad, either. There's something else I wanted to ask you. Who do you think is Flamenco Dancer's biggest threat in the Champion Chase?'

'I don't think there is a danger, but if I were writing for the *Sporting Life*, I'd say Fancyman, even though he'll be level weights with our horse this time. But what's that got to do with all this?'

'I'm not sure. But let me ask you something else.' He was gazing at her intently now, knowing that he'd have to rely on his judgement of what Laura was thinking over the next few seconds. 'Who told you about the photos of Henry Straker?'

Laura stared back at him blankly.

Desperately, Rory tried to see if there was any discernible subtext to her apparent reaction. He held his breath, and expelled it with a sigh. 'I'm sorry but I needed to know how much you knew.'

'Rory, what the hell are you talking about? What photos of Straker?'

'I thought your father might have told you,' Rory bluffed.

'What photos?'

'I'll tell you another time.' He stood up.

'You still thought I had something to do with it – like the police?'

'I needed to be sure that you didn't. There's so much that points in your direction.' He sighed. 'I'm sorry. It's because I so badly want it not to be you that I have to be really certain. And time's running out.'

'You're not kidding,' Laura said. 'Agnew says the police are no closer to dropping the charges against me. It's not surprising really, is it, when even you don't believe I didn't do it.'

'I do, I promise,' Rory replied in earnest. 'We're doing as much as we can, but we haven't got anything solid to take to the police yet. Tomorrow I may have. I'll let you know.'

Laura stood too and put her arms around Rory's neck. She touched his lips with hers. 'Would you be doing this for me even if you thought I had done it?'

'Probably.'

'That's nice to know. Before you go, I'm sorry to bring things back to the mundanities of life, but without Dai I need a jockey. How long before you're back riding again?'

'I don't know. I haven't used my arm at all; except for doing isometrics.'

Laura looked puzzled.

'You know, exercising the muscles, but not the bones.

I think it should be okay, though.'

'Will you be able to ride Flamenco Dancer or are you going to stick with the Irish horse?'

Rory had a short struggle with his conscience. 'I'll ride yours, if I'm fit. Just this once, I'll let down another trainer. For you.' He grinned. 'Has George backed it?'

'No; he never punts. He says he'd rather rely on prize money – less risky. Actually, it's the glory he's after.'

At eight next morning, Rory waited for Straker in Pam's Discovery. He was outside the empty racecourse car park at Ascot.

When he arrived, the vet looked as though he hadn't slept all night, paler and more haggard than he had been the day before.

He climbed into Rory's car silently, not speaking until they were moving.

'Where are we going?'

'To the yard where you were first picked up.'

The half-dozen horses of various types appeared to be fed, watered and clean bedded, but there was no one around.

Leaving Straker in the car, Rory walked across a small paddock to the nearest house and knocked on the back door.

A young mother in jeans and sweatshirt opened the door with a baby dangling from her hip.

'What is it?'

'I wanted to enquire about the yard.'

'It's my husband you want to see, then. He'll be back

down the yard in about fifteen minutes. You can wait for him there.'

Waiting with Straker made Rory nervous. The strength Straker had shown when issuing his denial to Rory just a few days before had left him. He was a defeated man, ready to give in to forces beyond his control.

Rory knew he would have to get Straker committed to their search if he was going to be any help.

'If you look in front of you on the shelf there, I've got the local Ordnance Survey map. While we're waiting for this guy to turn up, we can narrow the field a bit.'

Straker reached forward for the map and passed it to Rory, who unfolded it and spread it out between them. Rory had already marked the position of the yard where they were.

'Can you show me exactly where you were left in your car?'

The vet looked listlessly at the map and put his finger on a point beside the main road that ran through Windsor Great Park.

'Right,' Rory said, and marked the spot with a pencil. 'I've cut a piece of string twenty-four miles long on this scale.' He produced the string from his pocket and put each end at the two points he'd marked. 'This'll only give us an approximate idea of where you were taken, but it'll narrow down the field a bit. Right, you know from seeing the castle that you were brought back by this road across the river, and presumably along this main road round the south of Windsor. And it looks likely that you were taken from Sunningdale by the same route'.

As accurately as he could, Rory laid the string along the bends and twists of both routes until they converged and ran side by side, under the M4 to a large roundabout on the west side of Slough. A small loop of string was left. Rory measured the loop against the scale chart on the bottom of the map. 'About two miles. Okay, that tells us you were taken no more than a mile by road from that roundabout.'

Straker nodded with a little more enthusiasm. 'But that still leaves a hell of a large populated area.'

'Sure, but it's a start. And the owner of this yard may be able to tell us something about whoever took you. This may be him now.'

An old blue Land Rover was bouncing down the dirt track from the road.

'You stay here. I'll deal with him.'

Rory climbed out of the Discovery and walked towards the approaching vehicle.

The Land Rover pulled up beside him and a heavy-faced man in his late thirties slid the window back.

'Yes, mate?'

'I'm trying to track down a horse. I think it was here for a bit about a month ago.'

The man, alerted by Rory's Scottish accent, looked at him more keenly. 'Aren't you Rory Gillespie?'

Rory nodded. ''Fraid so.'

The man opened his door and jumped down enthusiastically, holding out a hand. 'It's good to meet you, Rory. I'm Roger Williams – always been a fan.'

'Glad to hear it, Roger,' Rory smiled.

'Well, what was it you wanted to know?'

'Did someone take a stable, just for a week or two, about a month ago?'

Roger looked thoughtful for a moment. 'Yeah, there

was a geezer, funny bloke he sounded, never saw him. He paid for two weeks by post and only used the stable for a couple of days, and he certainly didn't have the kind of animal you'd be interested in – some old knackered cob, just come out the field.'

'Still, can you tell me where I can get hold of him?'

'Haven't a clue. He never gave me an address or nothing. He dropped this horse off when I wasn't here and phoned me to ask me to feed and bed it, and picked it up a couple of days later.'

'Well, what was he called?'

Roger laughed. 'Smith, Michael Smith.' He shrugged. 'When people tell you they're called Smith these days, you believe them, don't you?'

Rory grunted. 'So you never saw what kind of a car he came in?'

'Nope. Didn't see him at all.'

'When he talked to you on the phone, could you tell where he came from, by the way he spoke or anything?'

'No, not really. You know, same as me, sort of south-east.'

'Is there anything else you could tell me about him?'

The man shrugged regretfully. 'Sorry, Rory. Anyway what's it all about?'

'Oh, it's nothing. It doesn't sound like the right man, or horse. I think I've been sent on a wild-goose chase. Sorry to have wasted your time.'

'No problem, Rory. 'Ere, you haven't got a good horse you can give me for this week, have you?'

'Sure. Flamenco Dancer in the Champion Chase. He's still good value, and he'll win.'

'Thanks, Rory,' the man burbled enthusiastically as Rory walked back to the Discovery and climbed in.

'That's okay. Thanks for your help.'

'What now?' Straker asked as they drove out of the yard.

'Christ knows.' Rory didn't try to hide his frustration. 'We've got an area to search which may be where the BMW bike comes from. It's not a lot. I was counting on the people at the yard telling us something about the man who rented the stable, but they didn't see him at all. I thought we might have that or his vehicle to go on.'

'I've got an idea,' Straker suddenly blurted with enthusiasm. 'I've just remembered. That old cob I came to see – when I looked at its feet, I noticed they'd been shod with leather.'

Rory turned and looked at the vet, encouraged but not hopeful. 'What was that?'

'His front feet were shod with leather pads between the hoof and the shoe. A blacksmith will sometimes do that if a horse suffers from sore feet.'

'Yeah, sure, but not often.'

'That's what I mean. Hardly ever. So it shouldn't be that difficult to find a dun cob, shod with leather.'

'Great! We need to talk to every blacksmith in the area.' He began turning the Discovery back towards the yard they had just left. 'My new friend Roger will know some and the Yellow Pages will give us a few more.'

Roger Williams seemed pleased to see Rory back again so soon and happily produced his own address book and a recent Yellow Pages. He also offered the use of the phone. Rory set Henry Straker the task of going through the blacksmiths in the directory on Roger's phone, while he went out and tried the other list on his mobile.

There were the names of five farriers in the address book. Three were in, and had no recollection of shoeing a dun cob with leather pads within recent memory, if ever. The other two were out on calls; in both cases, their wives were vague about their exact itinerary. Rory told them both what he wanted and gave them his mobile number, in case their husbands came home sooner than they expected. He put the phone down and cursed. It could be hours before either of them got back.

He went back into Roger Williams' house to hear Straker's voice. 'Well, thanks very much. Sorry to have troubled you.'

'Any luck?' Rory asked.

Straker shook his head. 'No. But I've got a few more to go.'

He dialled another, and drew another blank.

He shrugged and dialled again.

Rory rummaged in his pocket with his good arm, and brought out his tobacco and papers. Roger looked at him nervously. 'Rory, if you don't mind, the wife can't stand smoke in the house.'

Rory nodded. He was used to being treated like a leper for smoking in some households. He let himself out of the front door and lit up. At first, he barely heard the trilling of his car phone, blending as it did with the bird-song from the woodlands all around. But then he became abruptly conscious of its regularity. He turned his ear to listen, and within seconds was pulling open the door of the Discovery and grabbing the handset.

'Hello?'

'Hello. Somebody phoned up wanting to know if I'd put pads on a cob.'

'Yes, yes. That's me. Have you had something in to shoe like that recently?'

'Yeh. That'd be Mrs Morrison-Phillips's. She always wants him padded. Doesn't need it, of course, but she thinks he does.'

'Is he a dun, quite old, about fifteen-two?'

'Yeah. That's him.'

'Great! Can you tell me where his owners live?'

'Morrison-Phillips? Yeah. Silver Birches, Belvedere Lane, round the back of Wentworth Golf Course.'

'That's great. Thanks.'

Rory put the phone down wishing he had been able to show his appreciation more, then ran back to the house to get Straker.

They thanked Roger Williams, who refused anything for the use of his phone, and two minutes later were heading at eighty miles an hour towards the famous golf course.

It didn't take long to find Silver Birches; the trees down the drive told them before they had even seen the sign.

From the road, Rory noticed two well-bred horses grazing in a paddock beside the drive. They drove on past.

'What do you think?' Straker asked. 'If this was our man, surely he'd have used one of those thoroughbreds?'

'Not necessarily.'

'But it's in quite the wrong direction. I'm absolutely certain about seeing the castle.'

'Okay. But if it is where you were taken, they'll know

313

both of us. We can't risk just walking up there.'

'Look,' Straker said, peering back over his shoulder as they passed the property. 'There's some kind of gardener pottering about. I'll go and sound him out.'

Rory stopped and watched Straker, suddenly more buoyant, jump down and walk back to where an old man in dungarees was clearing winter dead wood from a small patch of trees.

Two minutes later, the vet was back.

'No problem,' he said as he climbed back in. 'The dun cob used to live here, but the people, the Morrison-Phillipses, sold it a few weeks ago and it's gone.'

'Did he know who bought it?'

'No. We'll have to go and ask at the house. Apparently the wife's in and she's the one who deals with the horses.'

'You're sure it's not where you were taken?'

'I just don't see how it could be, and the old boy was absolutely genuine.'

'Okay. I hope you're bloody right.'

Mrs Morrison-Phillips looked and sounded like her name. She was well groomed, expensively dressed, about fifty. Rory, on the evidence of the horses in the paddock, wasn't surprised when she recognised him. Fluttering a little at the excitement of having a jockey in her spotless house, she invited them in before they had time to suggest it themselves.

They had told her vaguely that they wanted to talk about one of her horses. She looked very disappointed when she gathered it was the old cob they were interested in.

314

'I'll be quite honest with you, Mrs Morrison-Phillips . . .'

'Veronica, please,' she interrupted him.

'Veronica. It's the fellow who bought it that we want to talk to.'

'Why, what's happened?'

'Mr Straker here is a top vet – I'm sure you know his name. He and I do a lot of work for the RSPCA, and this animal's turned up in one of their shelters.'

It was an implausible reason for their coming, but Mrs Morrison-Phillips wasn't going to question it. She looked upset. 'Oh no. Is he all right?'

'The horse? Oh yes, he's fine now. Don't worry about that. But we do need to trace the present owner.'

'Well, he was rather an odd little individual. He said he wanted it for his son. He'd brought the boy with him, a very good-looking child, who seemed absolutely smitten by old Samuel. I let them have him for rather less than I'd planned, but I was most concerned about his going to a loving home. I'll certainly have him back straightaway, if he's been abandoned.'

'Oh no, I don't think that's a problem. I think the owner must have been away. Anyway, could you tell me his name?'

'Mr Smith, I think. He paid in cash, you see.'

'You don't have his address, I suppose?' Rory asked, holding out little hope.

'No. I'm afraid not. He simply rang up in answer to my advert and came round. He took the horse away with him there and then.'

'So you don't have a phone number or anything?'

'I'm terribly sorry, no,' Mrs Morrison-Phillips said,

embarrassed at not being able to help the famous jockey.

'Not to worry,' Rory said, controlling his frustration. 'Can you remember what kind of vehicle he came in?'

'Ah, yes, that I can tell you. He had a blue trailer – you know, a Rice or something like that – towed by a dark red Jaguar.'

'Dark red? Metallic or not?'

'Metallic, but quite faded. It was an oldish car; I think one of the old registrations with the letter at the end – a Y.'

'That's a help. He didn't happen to mention how far he had to go, did he?'

'I'm afraid not.'

'Okay, well we think we have an idea of that.' Rory and Straker stood up together.

'Thanks so much for talking to us,' Straker said. 'It's been very helpful indeed. And I'll make sure we let you know what's happened to your old horse, don't worry.'

'You bloody liar,' Rory laughed as they set off back towards Windsor in the Discovery.

'I'm not,' Straker replied with dignity. 'I'll make damn sure I find out what's happened to the animal and write to her.'

'What a gent you are, Henry. Anyway, at least we know our man has an old Jag. That'd need a bit of servicing, and if he lives where we think he does, there's a chance someone round there does it for him.'

'But how do you know he lives there?'

'I don't, but I can't think of any reason why he'd take you there if he didn't. At least it gives us a starting point, that and the BMW bike.'

Twenty minutes later they drove north across the River Thames by the road which bypasses the ancient town of Eton, and under the Slough intersection of the M4.

'If you're right,' Straker said, studying the map, 'this roundabout is within a mile of our target.'

Rory nodded. 'We've got to find a phone book and check the names of the local Jaguar dealers. We may as well start with them.'

Rows of shining cars and a landscaped forecourt suggested unashamedly high rates at the Jaguar and Daimler main dealers.

'I don't think I'd bring a Y-reg Jag here,' Straker observed. 'It wouldn't really be worth it.'

Rory agreed. 'But I'll go in and see the service manager anyway.'

He parked his muddy vehicle in front of the gleaming showroom and jumped out.

A few minutes later, he was back.

'You were right,' he said. 'They very seldom have older models in, but he's given me the names of two other garages who purport to specialise in Jags – both near here.'

Ten minutes later, Rory was talking to the owner of the first of the addresses he'd been given. His well-known face was once again sufficient to persuade the owner to look back through his records to see if he could identify a Y-registered metallic maroon car. No such vehicle had been in over the last year.

The visit to the second garage seemed just as fruitless until the service manager remembered a small one-man-band of a garage, which claimed to specialise in Jaguars, underneath the railway arches of the Windsor–Slough railway viaduct.

Straker was map-reading for Rory. 'That's well within our search area,' he remarked eagerly.

'Sure, but don't get too excited.'

Rory drove gingerly along the rough track beside the viaduct, past a range of various small, scruffy industrial workshops that still flourished beneath the substantial structure of the Victorian engineers of the Great Western Railway.

At the end of the track, announcing itself with several carcasses of deceased Jaguars in the muddy yard outside, were the premises they were looking for.

Rory parked his vehicle among a scattering of scrap iron, got out and picked his way towards the elliptical cavern.

The hiss of a welder from inside the arch encouraged him.

He went in. A pair of legs clad in oil-grimed denim protruded from beneath an old XJS. Blue flashes sprayed from the far side. Rory waited for a pause between bursts before he spoke.

'Hello.'

The legs wriggled away from the car; a torso and a head covered in a welding mask appeared. The oily figure sprang nimbly to its feet, dropped the welder on a workbench and removed the mask.

'Mornin', mate. What can I do you for?'

He was a youngish man, sharp-eyed and sure of himself.

'I'm looking for someone. I think you might service his car for him.'

'Who's that?'

'I don't know his name. But he lives somewhere round here and drives a maroon XJ6.'

'What's it worth?'

'Not much.'

'A pony?'

Rory nodded and plucked twenty-five pounds from his pocket.

'Bloke's called Eland – Arthur Eland.'

'Have you only got one customer with a car that colour and age?'

'Yeah.'

'What does he look like, then?'

'Average sort of height. Nothing special, about forty-five.'

'What does he do for a living?'

'I don't know. Some sort of photography, I think. There's always loads of empty film boxes and that in the back of the car.' The man gave a conspiratorial snort of laughter. 'And porn. He's into porn. He left some lovely stuff in the boot last time.'

'That sounds like him. Where does he live?'

'I can look up his address, but it'll cost you another pony.'

'No it bloody won't.'

The mechanic made a face and grinned. 'You never get if you don't ask, do you?'

He walked to the back of the arch, to an old desk covered in grimy papers, and found an old-fashioned hard-covered accounts book. He thumbed through it for a moment. 'Here we are. I'll even write it down for you.'

He tore a scrap from the bottom of one of the pages and with a pencil scribbled an address on it. 'There it is.' He passed it to Rory, evidently still pleased with the deal they had done.

Rory glanced at it and felt himself quiver with the excitement of a hound on the scent of a fox. 'Thanks. Here's another twenty,' he offered impulsively.

'Any time.'

'We'll have to get a street plan,' he told Henry Straker as he manoeuvred the Discovery off the muddy forecourt.

'Have you got an address, then?' Straker said, with a tremor in his voice.

'Yes. We've found him.'

They bought a street map of Slough from a corner shop. Straker identified the road they wanted and guided Rory there.

It was a long, quiet cul-de-sac in an uninspired estate of red-brick houses, backing on to open land and, beyond, the motorway.

They drove slowly down the road, past the number Rory had been given. On two strips of concrete in front of a garage stood the Jaguar.

'Bingo!' Rory almost whispered.

They drove on without stopping. The road curved away to the left and ended in a wide, circular turning area. Rory swung the Discovery round and stopped where they could see the Jaguar, but not the house. He turned off the engine and looked across at Straker.

'Okay, Henry. Are you ready for this?'

Straker, pale and nervous, nodded.

'Right. Let's go, then.'

Rory took one of the narrow alleyways that led between the houses to a path that ran all the way along the back of their gardens. He identified the back of Eland's house and waited until he reckoned Straker had reached the front door and rung the bell. Opening the back gate by a simple latch, he walked confidently down an overgrown path to the half-glazed back door of the house. Behind him, the scrubland was empty of humans, and the high hedges of Eland's privacy-conscious neighbours hid him from sight of any of the ground-floor rooms. He'd just have to take a punt that no one was watching from an upper room.

He listened.

He heard a door bell sound at the front of the house.

He waited for three more rings, ten seconds between each ring. Unless Eland was lying low in there, the house was empty. It was as good a chance as they were ever going to get.

Rory looked around for a suitable instrument, picked up a brick which was propping up a sagging water butt and gritted his teeth.

He struck the glass with the end of the brick in a short jab. With a tinkle of broken glass, this produced a small jagged hole above the door handle. He listened for reaction from the neighbours. There was no immediate outcry or sound of new activity. He inserted a hand through the hole, found the key inside the door and let himself in.

He closed the door quickly behind him and walked through a small, smelly kitchen to a narrow front hall.

He could see Straker's silhouette on the reeded glass.

He opened the front door. 'Come in, quick!'

Straker stepped through and closed the door behind him.

'We'd better make sure he's not here first,' Rory whispered.

Henry nodded and they headed up the stairs.

Two minutes later they were back in the hall. 'If he's here, he doesn't want to see anyone,' Straker said.

'He's out. Everything's cold. Right, I'll search. You stand behind the curtain and keep watch. If he comes, we'll scarper.'

Rory, from his preliminary search, had already decided where he was going to look first. He opened the door opposite the living room into what had been built as an integral garage but was now kitted out as a photographic studio.

There was only one piece of furniture – an old metal filing cabinet – suitable for storing prints and negatives.

He walked across to it and tried the top drawer. It was locked. So were the two below it.

He went back to the kitchen and searched around for the largest knife he could find – a heavy, old-fashioned carving knife.

Back in the studio, he inserted the blade between the top of the first drawer and the frame of the cabinet. With a quick surge of strength, he jerked the knife forward. The blade snapped three inches from the handle, creating a much more useful tool.

He jammed it back into the slit, next to the lock, and slowly forced it up again.

With a sharp crack, the blade of the lock slipped free from the frame and Rory pulled the drawer out towards him, right out of its runners so that he could lift it to the ground. The other two came out with even less trouble.

It took him fifteen tense, fumbling minutes to find what he was looking for, a set of monochrome contact sheets at the back of the bottom drawer. He pulled an Anglepoise lamp out from the wall and switched it on. He put the sheet of small prints on a large Perspex light box, and picked up a square magnifying glass lying on it.

A moment later, he saw in clear-cut, well-lit detail just why Henry Straker had been so unwilling to describe the photographs to him.

Eland had shot three rolls of film. Like any experienced photographer, he knew that the more you took, the higher were your chances of the right shot. Shaking his head in disbelief, Rory studied each of the three sheets.

Every single shot was grotesquely compromising, but in the worst of them, the vet was lying naked on a bare mattress; his eyes were closed but there was a sleepy smile on his face, while two equally naked boys, nine or ten years old, manipulated his erect penis.

Rory was more shocked than he would have believed possible. He had heard about paedophilia, read odd pieces in the more sensational Sunday papers, but he had never really believed that this sort of thing actually went on, and he had certainly never seen such graphic illustrations of it.

Even more horrifying was the apparently obvious enjoyment the distinguished veterinary surgeon was deriving from the activity.

It made Henry Straker's otherwise inexplicable behaviour suddenly completely understandable. Even the vet's closest friends would have taken a great deal of convincing that the pictures, or the poses, had been faked.

And outside his job, what Henry Straker was best known for was his charity work with young boys.

Quickly, Rory checked through all the drawers and folders of photographs, containing lurid scenes of every conceivable type of sexual activity, to make certain he had all those which featured Henry Straker. When he was satisfied that there weren't any more there, he scooped up the three sheets and folded them into an inside pocket of his jacket. He also took a photograph of a small, insignificant-looking man being hugged by a tall, naked woman. The picture was inscribed with the words 'To Arthur. Best Wishes, Lucy Leather.'

He checked the rest of the studio and the ground-floor rooms of the house for any clue to who Eland's client might be.

Twenty minutes searching yielded no leads. He suspected that this sort of information, if it existed in any kind of written form, would be on Eland's person, or kept very close to it.

In the living room, on a teak coffee table marked with a circular black burn, he found a small racing diary. He wasn't surprised to see the names of the two horses which Straker had doped written against the dates they had run. On the following day, Tuesday, the name 'Fancyman' had been scrawled.

He slipped the diary into his pocket with the contact

sheets and went to search the upper rooms. He had a foot on the bottom step of the stairs when he heard Henry hiss a warning.

He didn't stop to make sure it was a genuine alarm. In a matter of seconds he was through the kitchen and out of the back door with Henry in time to hear a big-engined bike rev up and cut out on the street at the front of the house. They walked briskly up the path to the back gate and along the rear track to the alley, four houses away, and climbed back inside the Discovery.

'Back it up, quick, so if he comes out he won't see us,' Straker urged.

Rory started the engine and put the car into reverse. He turned and steered back round the curve of the road until the bike and the Jaguar were both out of sight.

Straker lowered his window. 'Turn the engine off so we can hear him if he leaves.'

Rory did as he was asked.

'How do you know he's going anywhere?'

'I don't, but did you make much of a mess in there?'

'Aye, a bit of minor destruction.'

'And did you take anything?'

Rory nodded. He found he didn't want to admit to Straker that he had even seen the photos.

'Then he's going to panic, isn't he? He's not going to ring the police, he's going to go out and look for what's missing. What else would he do?'

'What if he's seen the Discovery?'

'I don't think he registered it; anyway, that's a risk we'll have to take. He won't see it when he comes out, and he won't come this way because it's a dead end. If he did see it just now, he'll assume it was you and probably head off after you.'

Rory nodded. It wasn't a bad bet. 'We'll just have to play it by ear,' he said. 'Anyway, I've got the evidence.'

Straker glanced at him sharply. 'The photos?' he asked with a tremor of shame in his voice.

'Aye. You were right to be worried people would think they were genuine. This bastard Eland certainly knows what he's doing. Judging by what he was keeping in there, this isn't the first time. Trouble is, there's probably another set of prints or negatives somewhere else.'

'At least we've got this far, though,' Straker said. 'I can tell you, I didn't think we had a hope.'

'Sure. We'll just have to see where Eland leads us now. If he goes back to my place, we'll corner him there, then we'll have to let the police take over.'

Straker nodded slowly. 'Yes, you're right.'

As he spoke, they heard the metallic click of a Jaguar starter motor, and the shriek of a loose fan belt.

'He's off,' Straker said. 'Thank God, he hasn't taken the bike.'

Rory started his own engine, and the Discovery inched forward. They caught a glimpse of the Jaguar's tail reversing into the road, then spinning off towards the junction.

Rory waited another thirty seconds before he pulled out. 'Thank God I didn't bring the Rover.'

They pulled away and round the bend in the road just in time to see Eland's car turn left at the junction.

Cautiously, Rory followed, trying to remember everything he'd ever read or seen about tailing cars without being spotted.

He followed the Jaguar up the slip road on to the M4 towards London and let out a sigh of relief as they joined a solid three-lane stream of steadily moving traffic.

Chapter Thirteen

'Hell!' Rory hissed. 'He must have driven like shit off a shovel.'

They were dropping down from the Hammersmith fly-over into west London and they hadn't see a sign of Eland's car in the last ten minutes.

'He couldn't have got off anywhere since we last saw him, could he?' Straker said.

'Yes, he could have turned off at the North Circular.'

The traffic had slowed to three crawling queues. Rory clenched his fists on the steering wheel, trying to contain his frustration at having got so close to his quarry, only to lose the scent.

They had concluded that Eland, panicking, was on his way to see his paymaster.

Now, Rory fought to calm himself, to make a new plan. He picked up his phone and stabbed Edward Brickhill's number.

The financier wasn't answering and Rory was switched through to a secretary at his City office.

'I'm sorry, Mr Brickhill is unavailable at the moment,' a bright, efficient voice fluted back at him. 'If you'd like to leave a message, I'll make sure it reaches him as soon as possible.'

Rory gave her his name, stressed the urgency and gave her the number of his mobile phone. He was putting it angrily back in its cradle when Henry Straker gasped triumphantly, 'Look! That's him, isn't it?'

They were in the left-hand lane, moving faster than the others as cars filtered off. Rory looked where Straker pointed. From the commanding height of the Discovery, he saw the Jaguar. It was in the middle lane, six or seven cars ahead, spewing a faint cloud of black smoke from its exhaust pipes.

'Our mechanic chummy doesn't seem to have made too good a job of servicing it,' Rory laughed with relief. 'I hope the old heap doesn't break down before he gets to his man.'

'How are we going to handle it when we get there?' Straker asked, more positive now.

'We'll just have to play it by ear, but if we can identify whoever Eland goes to see, Edward Brickhill should be able to help.'

'Edward? What has he got to do with all this?'

'He's not so keen on his daughter being convicted of manslaughter. He's also a big fan of yours; he wouldn't hear of you being remotely involved and he organised a lot of the investigation we've done so far.'

'Thank God for that. I wish I'd known before. Edward's a powerful man to have on our side.'

They were heading down the Earl's Court Road, always

keeping in sight of the maroon XJ6, though Rory took no chances by getting too close.

On the Embankment, Eland lost them at two sets of lights. Each time they caught him up, but Straker was getting nervous.

'You'll have to get nearer to him, Rory.'

'But if he susses us, we've blown it.'

'If we lose him we've totally blown it. He's not going to be thinking about being followed now.'

Rory nodded. 'Okay. I'll try to keep one car between us.'

They played Grandmother's Footsteps with the Jaguar the length of the Embankment until they reached the City and turned up by the Mermaid Theatre.

'It looks like we might be getting there,' Rory said, his pulse beginning to race. 'We think our man is connected with a bookie called Square Mile Sporting – runs books on the Footsie index, share prices and that.'

'What's the connection? Do they take bets on horses, too?'

'Oh yes. We think Luke had been having a gamble on the price of his own shares, and taking a lot of money off them. When that all started to fall apart, he carried on with horses and began losing – big money. I mean, like a hundred and fifty grand. What Edward's people haven't found is anyone having a big bet on Midnight Express. But my gut feeling tells me Luke did – a very big one.'

Straker didn't answer.

Rory glanced across at him. The vet had resumed the guilty, haggard look of a few hours before.

'How did I let myself do it?' he said quietly. 'No man's

reputation is worth three lives. And now, the part I played in the interference with two horses will have to come out. I imagine that whatever happens, I'll be struck off.'

'Not necessarily,' Rory said, without believing it. 'Not if the police don't bring charges.' His eyes were fixed on the XJ6, two cars ahead and creeping up Queen Victoria Street.

Abruptly, Eland turned off into a narrow road where there was a small, rare cluster of parking meters, one of which was free. The Jaguar pounced into the space, while Rory cursed and drove on twenty yards. Pulling up, he looked in his mirror.

'He's got out and is heading back up to Queen Victoria Street. You're going to have to follow him – but for God's sake, don't let him see you. Just watch where he goes and follow him as far as you can without letting it show.'

Straker's muscles seemed suddenly to fill out and take on a new alertness. He nodded. 'Right.'

He climbed out of the Discovery and walked slowly up the street behind Eland's disappearing back.

Rory settled down to wait. The misgivings he'd had about sending Straker had dissipated when he saw the man's natural strength and resolve returning.

He tried to stay calm but kept his eyes fixed on his mirror, watching for Straker to come back.

Six minutes later, he was rewarded by the sight of the vet walking briskly and confidently towards him.

Straker opened the door and climbed in.

'Well?' Rory asked.

'I can't tell you his name, but the offices are occupied by the Anglo-Maltese Beef Company. It's on the fifth

floor of the block just round the corner. Eland went up
to the reception and came out a moment later. He walked
across and buzzed the intercom on a private lift to the
floor above and was let in. I came back down by the stairs.
You're not going to believe what I found.' He looked at
Rory jubilantly. 'On the floor below are the offices of
Square Mile Sporting. It looks as though you were right.'

Rory grinned.

The phone bleeped.

'Hello,' Rory blurted into it.

'You rang.' Brickhill's voice.

'Thank God. We need some information.'

'What's that?'

'The name of whoever's behind something called the
Anglo-Maltese Beef Company. There's a good chance
he's connected with Square Mile Sporting – and if he is,
that's our man.'

'The Anglo-Maltese Beef Company?'

'Aye. Offices in Queen Victoria Street.'

'Leave it with me.'

Eland fought to control the trembling in his knees as the
private lift took him up to the second floor.

The small grey box reached its destination and the door
hissed open. Eland stepped out into the soundless, sealed
atmosphere. There was no sign of the secretary who had
received him before; the place looked deserted.

He faced a large panelled door and felt himself scrutinised by a camera mounted discreetly above the deep
architrave. He had been told that he should wait there
when he arrived. He tried to stand still and felt a flush of

sweat break out across every surface of his body.

The door was opened by the man who had been to visit Eland in Slough a month before. He wasn't wearing a Savile Row suit this time. He was naked from the waist up. Large globules of perspiration glittered through the thick black hair that covered his torso. His bare feet protruded from a soft black towel that was wrapped around his lower half.

His dark eyes burned up and down Eland's slight frame, then beckoned him in. He closed the door. Eland vaguely registered the large room where he had had his last encounter with his client. A slight haze of blue cigar smoke hung like cirrus cloud around the ceiling.

Facing him was a vast window with a southerly view over the tops of the office buildings that dropped away to the river. There was a dead unrealness to the view without its sounds and damp air.

'What do you want?' the large man growled.

There was nothing vulnerable about his semi-nudity.

'We've got to talk,' Eland stuttered.

'Is that so?'

'Yes. Someone raided my place this morning. We're in trouble.'

A rumble of humourless laughter rose from the hairy barrel of the other man's chest.

'We? Oh no.' A large index finger stabbed Eland between his ribs. 'You're in trouble. You fucked it up. Killing those people was very stupid.'

'But it was nothing to do with me,' Eland lied, hoping for inspiration.

'Gillespie's found his way to you. Let me tell you, that's

the end of the trail. If you should think of pointing the finger at me, there is absolutely nothing to implicate me.' He turned and started to walk across the room towards a door on the far side. Eland followed, as if drawn by a magnet. 'And what I can also tell you,' his client continued, 'is that if you try to involve me, you will be killed.' He was through the library and halfway across the bedroom. He turned and looked at Eland with a calm smile. 'You interrupted my sauna. Now leave. I don't want to hear from you again until Fancyman has run tomorrow.'

Eland stood, mid-step, irresolute. Of course, he'd known it would be a waste of time coming here, but he'd had to go to someone.

His client turned and carried on towards a narrow door between two chests of drawers. Before he opened it, he looked back over his shoulder. 'Goodbye. See yourself out.' He watched as Eland turned and walked back into the other room.

Eland padded across the deep carpet and opened the main door to the apartment. He opened it, and closed it.

Silently he turned and gazed, without seeing, through the picture window at the top of Tower Bridge. He waited until he had heard the click of the sauna door closing before he walked back across the footprints he had just left in the pile of the deep velvet Wilton carpet.

He paused at the entrance to the bedroom. He could hear no sounds from beyond the sauna door, sealed and insulated as it was. He saw with satisfaction, from the back of the hinges, that it opened out into the room. And he thanked his luck for the man's penchant for privacy and the lack of a window in the door.

He quickly glanced round to see what tools were at his disposal.

Beside the door to the sauna stood a massive Victorian mahogany chest of eight drawers. He walked across to it quickly and, putting his shoulder to one end, tried to slide it over the deep carpet. Despite the extra strength which the crisis had given him, it wouldn't move.

But he was calm now, and set on his plan. Without any fumbling or clumsiness, he removed the solidly made and heavily loaded drawers one by one and placed them behind him. Although the remaining empty carcass was a substantial piece, he found this time when he put his shoulder to it that after a moment's reluctance it moved slowly over the carpet and across the door of the sauna.

When he was satisfied that it was wedged under the wooden handle as tightly as possible, he efficiently and accurately replaced the eight heavy drawers. The whole operation had taken ninety seconds.

The temperature controls for the sauna were set to the side of the door, just above the top of the chest. He switched the small black dial to its maximum.

To test his barrier, he put his shoulder against the side of the chest and tried to shove it with every ounce of strength he could summon. It didn't budge a centimetre. He stood back, satisfied that even the substantial bulk of the man trapped behind it would not be able to move the door and the chest together.

Finally, he picked up a comb from the top of the chest and wedged the sliding panel of timber over the air slot so that it couldn't be opened from the inside.

He allowed a sulky grin to cross his face. 'Time you

lost some weight, you fat bastard!' he muttered as he padded back through the bedroom, the library and the flashy drawing room to the front door of the apartment.

Out in the lobby, the lift waited with the door open.

A minute later, he stepped out of the warm office building into the soggy, blustering March wind and the noise of the traffic swishing and roaring along Queen Victoria Street.

He turned the corner. The street was empty apart from three cars in the spaces either side of his. He walked quickly down to the Jaguar and got into it. He noticed with automatic relief that he hadn't been awarded a parking ticket, and started the engine.

He was driving west along the Embankment with the Temple on his right when he felt a cold, hard circle press into the thin flesh on the side of his neck.

'You've gone the wrong way, Arthur.'

Eland's hands jerked on the wheel. The courage temporarily granted him in the penthouse had left him. He opened his mouth to speak, but it was too dry for words to come.

'We're going to Bermondsey,' the voice behind went on. 'Cross over Westminster Bridge when you get there.'

It was a man's voice – the voice of a pro.

'Do we wait for Eland to come back out?' Straker asked when Rory had finished talking to Brickhill.

'No. No point. We've done all we can do here for the moment. And while he's in there, he's out of his house. We'll get back there and see what else we can find.'

'Break in again, you mean?' Despite everything he had

done over the last few weeks, Straker's strong regard for the rule of law was still intact.

'Yes. I didn't have time to search upstairs.'

'Okay,' Straker agreed.

They were crawling along the Fulham Road when Rory's phone bleeped.

'Rory?'

'Hello, Edward. What have you got?'

'Nothing yet. This Anglo-Maltese Beef Company, whatever it is, isn't registered at Companies House, or anywhere else, so we're having to go through other channels, using the address – rates, landlords and so on.'

'What will that tell you?'

'It might throw up the name we're looking for. I'll send a snooper round to his office, too, but this character's well skilled in keeping a low profile. What are you doing now?'

'Henry Straker's with me. We're on our way back to the house in Slough where the photos were taken. I've already got one set of prints from there, but we think we could find more leads as to who's employed this guy Eland, the photographer.'

'Well, be careful. The man's already killed twice, so he's got nothing to lose.'

On the way out of London, Rory stopped in the North End Road outside a baker's. Henry went in and bought a bagful of rolls. Neither of them had eaten since the evening before.

Half an hour later, the Discovery nosed into the drab cul-de-sac where Eland's house had stood; where what was left of it now stood.

They couldn't get within fifty yards of it. The road was cordoned off with police tape, and three fire engines revved loudly to pump between them a thousand gallons of water a minute at the blazing, blackened brick box.

Rory gazed at the annihilation of Eland's seedy dwelling and felt his guts quake.

Henry Straker was appalled. 'For God's sake, Rory. This is out of our league. Don't worry about my problems. We're going to have to go to the police now.'

Rory was thinking fast.

'Not yet. If Eland's client is having the place burnt, it's because he doesn't want any trace of the shots or the blackmail to be found – anything that might lead back to him. It's possible the only copies of the shots left are the ones in my pocket. And these people might just come to the conclusion that I've got them.'

'But how are we going to explain what was done to those two horses? How Luke Mundy was killed? Unless we do, Laura's still going to take the rap.'

'As far as the police are concerned there's only Midnight Express to explain. Over to you, Chief Veterinary Officer. Meanwhile,' Rory said, three-point-turning his vehicle, 'I think we'll get out of here.'

Three-quarters of an hour later, a Japanese jeep turned off the road on to a dirt track which marked the course of the ancient Neolithic route along the ridge behind Camp Farm.

The track was hedged with overgrown, straggling hawthorn. It gave little protection from the insistent southwesterly that had been blowing all day, but it was enough to stop the vehicle being seen from the valley to the south, where Rory Gillespie's house and barns nestled.

The two men in the car clad themselves in waxed jackets and rainproof hats and climbed out. Despite the rain, they both wore trainers on their feet. They walked back a hundred yards to a point where a stand of small beeches struggled up to the ridge from a steep, scrub-grown gully. Thirty feet below the ridge, a spring welled from a boggy patch in the thin-soiled sheep pasture. A brook appeared in the gully, where alders and sycamore had been encouraged to grow.

The older of the two men, about forty, with no spare fat and still, grey eyes, consulted the map he held.

'This'll be the best way down,' he said over his shoulder. 'We should be in the trees right down to the yard.'

Ten minutes of slipping down the chalky bed of the busy brook brought them to a point thirty feet from the back of Rory's range of timber-clad stables.

Dennis, the leader of the operation, raised his head over the shallow bank and peered through the spindly tree trunks. He was just able to see the back of the house.

He heard a horse in one of the stables stamp on a bare patch of concrete in his box. Others, wrapped in green canvas rugs, were grazing in the paddock beyond.

There was no sign of any other living being around the yard. Dennis beckoned Mac, his back-up, to follow.

Keeping low, they ran across to the stable block. When they reached it, they worked their way round the back until they could look round the edge with a clear view of the house and the forecourt.

Rory's sign-written Rover and the Discovery stood on the gravel.

Dennis allowed a thin smile to cross his lips. Two targets meant two fees. The contact sheets were worth another grand, and he guessed Gillespie still had them. He'd had the Discovery in sight most of the way from Queen Victoria Street after he'd left Bernie there to deal with Eland. It hadn't stopped anywhere long enough for anyone to dispose of anything and Eland had told Bernie that the photos he'd kept for himself were definitely gone. Dennis wondered what Bernie was doing to the little runt now. He turned to his back-up.

'They're home.'

Mac nodded and felt the adrenaline squirting into his system. He was half his leader's age, and five stone heavier. He'd lost count of how many men he had stalked and, frequently, despatched, but the excitement of it had never diminished. He'd left Glasgow only a month before to work for Dennis. It had been a great move; the quality of the work was so much higher, and much better paid.

He nodded with a smile and felt for the army-issue Browning in his pocket.

Dennis looked at his watch. 'It'll be dark in an hour. We'll wait.'

'What if they go again?'

'We'll have to follow – take whichever car they don't. But there's no way we can get to the house now without showing ourselves. If we're seen, we've got no chance. I'll see what I can do to make sure they stay put.'

He crouched back into the shelter of the stable wall, pulled a small mobile phone from his pocket and dialled a London number.

'Hello. It's Den. How's it goin'?' Dennis laughed at the

reply. 'Good. I'll ring you in about an hour to find out if there's more. Meantime, I want you to do something. Ring our friend down here and tell him you're from Thames Valley CID and you want to see him. Tell him you're coming over and you'll be there in about an hour, and he's not to leave until you get there . . . Yes, that'll do fine. Cheers.'

Dennis switched off and put the instrument in his pocket with a satisfied nod. 'That should keep 'em there till it's dark. Christ, I wish that fuckin' horse would give it a break!' he added as Long Run in the box behind them carried on stamping and snorting and whinnying.

'Are you sure you want to stay here?' Rory asked Henry. 'I wouldn't blame you if you didn't.'

'I'm not going to run out now. If they come here, you're going to need help.'

'They'll come,' Rory said with certainty. The grey Toyota had joined the M4 behind them, and left it with them. And Henry had spotted it again, a mile back, as they dropped down into Lambourn.

'But I still think we should call the police,' Henry said.

'We will, once we're sure there aren't any more of those photos anywhere. If you do decide to admit to doping Midnight Express and the other horse, people are bound to think the shots were genuine, aren't they?'

Straker nodded glumly.

Rory went on, 'But if we can get the blame pinned on this Anglo-Maltese Beef bloke, we should be able to get both you and Laura off the hook.'

As he spoke, the telephone rang. He picked it up.

'Yeah, speaking . . . Okay, I'll be here.'

He put the phone down and looked at Straker with a shrug. 'That was a man from CID, wants to come and see me here in about an hour. If nothing's happened by then, we'll tell him, okay?'

Straker nodded. 'I haven't much choice, Rory.'

Rory couldn't disguise his relief. 'Right, we'd better get ready.'

Upstairs they switched on a bedroom light and covered the windows of rooms on each side of the house. Rory opened some of them as listening posts, though the wind didn't help. On the ground floor, they turned on the television in the drawing room, lit a fire to give an illusion of normality and drew the curtains.

From a toolshed outside the back door, they selected weapons – an iron wrecking bar and a five-pound club hammer – to supplement Rory's one shotgun.

In the drawing room, the dry chestnut logs were burning well. Rory pulled the sheets of small black-and-white photographs from his pocket and dropped them in the flames.

Both men sensed a symbolic release as they watched the paper curl and disintegrate beneath a violet-blue flame.

Rory turned down the volume on the television and they went back upstairs to survey the landscape on all sides of the house.

The wind had dropped a little as Rory stared up the darkening valley behind the house. Between gusts, he caught the sound of Long Run snorting and whinnying in his stable. After a moment, he went to find Henry on the other side of the house.

'Long Run's making a hell of a fuss about something.

He may just be hungry, but it doesn't sound like it. I think there may be somebody up there.'

Straker came and listened. 'I think you're right, but it could be anything disturbing him. Assuming they don't just drive up, which way will they come?'

'I don't know, it depends what they know about the place, but the best way would be down that gully from the top of the ridge.'

'One of them's come out, look,' Mac hissed with disgust.

They watched a figure in a long coat cross the forecourt and climb into the Discovery.

'Not tall enough for the vet,' Dennis murmured. 'Must be the jockey. We can't do nothing about it. We'll have to deal with him later.'

They saw the car disappear down the lane to the main road and turn towards Hungerford.

Ten minutes later, they came out from behind the stable block.

It was dark now, but the cloud was breaking up and a three-quarter moon shed intermittent pale cream light.

Henry Straker peered out from a black upper room with his eyes tuned to the dark. He had been there twenty minutes, since Rory had left, and he caught the movement clearly.

God, don't let me mess this up, he breathed to himself.

They wouldn't try to come in by the front porch – that would mean opening two doors. This left them a choice of two back doors. Straker had to commit himself to one of them. He reduced the odds in his favour by locking one. The other which he left unlocked gave into a small utility room more suitable for his purposes.

He went through to the drawing room and turned up the volume on the television, which was showing an early-evening game show, with a lot of shrieking laughter and screams of encouragement from the studio audience.

Outside, the two men circled the house like a pair of hunting dogs.

They rejected the front entrance. Close up to the wall, they sidled towards the one lighted, but heavily curtained window on the ground floor.

They listened and caught the sound of laughter and screams of delight, and backed away.

'There's two doors round the back,' Dennis said. 'We'll take one each. If you get to him before me, don't kill him. I need to talk to him first.'

'Right.'

They worked their way round to the back of the house again.

'You take that door,' the Londoner whispered.

Mac slipped across to the small collection of sheds and outhouses that clustered at the back of the house and melted into the dark.

More slowly, his leader circled his way to a door which he guessed from the layout of the windows opened into the kitchen.

Henry Straker stood on a small stool behind the door into the scullery.

He heard the handle turn. His throat dried. With a

shaking arm, he raised the club hammer seven feet from the ground.

When it made contact, it made surprisingly little noise – less than the thud and clatter as the man fell to the quarry-tiled floor.

Surprised and oddly alarmed by his success, Straker stepped off the stool and crouched, shaking, beside his victim. The man seemed to be unconscious but he was still breathing. Straker put down the hammer and felt around the floor until he found the man's gun. He stood up and listened to the sound of the television show, his heart thumping against his chest. Harming anyone, even when they were prepared to do serious damage, was totally alien to Straker.

He waited for a full minute, nervous and unsure.

For God's sake, he told himself, you've got to do something.

The back door was still open, letting in sharp gusts of wind. If anyone was coming that way, they'd have come by now.

Straker walked towards the door that gave into the large central hall of the house. He poked his head through. The light from the drawing room left the corners of the hall in darkness. He took a step forward, holding the Browning in front of him with a shaking hand.

'Drop it or I'll blow your fuckin' head off.'

Straker felt an involuntary wetness dribble between his legs. He dropped the gun and turned his head towards the voice in the kitchen doorway.

'Now kick it across the floor to me.'

Straker kicked it, disgusted at his own cowardice.

The man emerged from the shadows. He had a short-nosed automatic trained on Straker's head and he was smiling.

'Good boy,' he said. 'Now, if you don't want me to hurt you, you can do something else for me. Tell me where the photos are.'

Straker tried to speak. He produced a croaking cough.

'Oh no, you'll have to do better than . . .'

The explosion deafened Straker for a moment.

He watched as the man with the gun dropped it, clutched his stomach and crumpled slowly to the floor. A thin cloud of smoke drifted into the hall, accompanied by the acrid smell of cordite.

Rory, with a finger on the second trigger of his shotgun, stepped over the khaki heap that the man had become.

'Where's the other one?' he asked quickly.

Straker opened his mouth in a startled shout. 'Behind you!'

Rory turned too late. The hammer caught him a hard, glancing blow on the side of the face. His legs sagged and he collapsed to the ground beside his own victim. Through the pain, at a distance from himself somehow, he heard a sharp report, and he was crushed beneath the limp weight of the other man's huge frame.

Unexpectedly, the weight was removed, dragged across him, and Henry was talking to him. 'Rory? Rory? Are you all right?'

Rory's mouth was full of blood and his nose full of mucus. He wanted to tell Henry, but he couldn't.

He felt the vet's arms wriggle beneath him and lift him, carry him, then lower him gently on to a soft surface.

347

'Okay, don't move,' Straker breathed. 'I'll be back.'

Rory didn't want to move. It hurt too much. He didn't want to open his eyes. He ordered himself to sleep.

Lights from a crystal chandelier which Rory had won in Ireland were shining brightly into his eyes when he flickered them open.

Henry had called the police. The detective inspector who had been at Camp Farm two days before was looking down at him.

'You have been in the wars, haven't you, Mr Gillespie?'

Rory coughed to clear his throat. 'For God's sake, can't you think of anything more original than that?'

The policeman laughed. 'That's good. There's no brain damage then.'

Rory, with his wounds bathed and deftly dressed by the vet, was sore and swollen, but soon able to sit up on his bloodstained sofa.

The man who had hit him was already in hospital, having a bullet from his own gun removed from his left lung.

The second intruder, hit in the back with Eley No. 4 shot from Rory's shotgun at a distance of six feet, was in worse shape, the policeman told Rory. There was a chance he would be paralysed, but he would live.

'Mr Straker's told us what happened, but of course we'll need to hear your version, Mr Gillespie,' the detective said.

Rory glanced at Straker, standing behind the policeman. He shook his head. 'Not yet.'

'That's okay. I've got to get back and talk to your two

visitors. We've done all we need to here. Maybe Mr Straker would bring you down to the nick in an hour or so, or I'll come back up. You let me know. But I'll need to see you this evening.'

'Sure.'

To Rory's relief, they went, leaving the house bright and silent.

'What did you tell them?' Rory asked as soon as the police car drove away.

'I told them that someone was trying to blackmail me,' Straker said simply. 'And that you'd found out who.'

Rory sighed. 'Did you tell them *how* you were being blackmailed?'

'No. I just said they'd faked some photographs.'

'What about stopping the horses?'

Straker shook his head with shame.

'Thank God for that!' Rory grinned.

'It just means that when they do find out, I'll be in even more serious trouble.'

'Then we've got to make sure they don't.' Rory smiled. 'Who would they get to run the boys' club football team? It would be really selfish to admit to the whole thing and deprive them of a manager.'

'I'd like to believe that, Rory, but the truth's bound to come out sooner or later. And for God's sake, I did it!'

'You didn't instigate the crime. You did what anyone else would have done in your position.'

'But, Rory, what about Luke? Your wife, for heaven's sake?'

'You didn't kill them.'

'Look, I just don't think I can live the lie. And anyway,

when they pick up Eland, he's bound to tell them about me.'

'You told them about Eland?'

'Yes, of course. I had to.'

Rory grunted. 'I suppose you did. Though God knows what they'll deduce from the fact that Eland's house has been burnt to the ground.'

'I said that we guessed he was being paid by someone else.'

'What about Eland's visit to Queen Victoria Street?'

'I thought it might be wiser to wait until we had a name from Edward Brickhill. Of course, when we do, if we pass it on to the police, he's going to tell them about my involvement, if Eland hasn't.'

Rory sank back on to the sofa with a sigh. 'I wish to God you'd left it to me, Henry. We're just going to have to rely on your word against theirs. I thought we'd have heard from Edward by now,' he added. As he spoke, the phone rang. 'That'll be him now.'

Rory stood for the first time since he had been hammered to the ground. He staggered a little, found his balance and limped out to the kitchen to pick up the phone.

'Hello?'

'Hello, it's me.'

'Laura!'

'You sound surprised.'

'I was expecting to hear from your father.'

'What's been going on then?'

'A lot. I can't tell you now. Can you get up here, now?'

'Okay,' she said, picking up the urgency in his voice.

'But just tell me, are you going to be all right to ride Flamenco Dancer tomorrow? I've declared you to ride, but you still haven't passed the doctor.'

With an effort, Rory jerked his mind back to his job. 'I don't know. I've had a bit more damage inflicted.'

'Oh no! Who by?'

'I'll tell you when you come. But look, I'll probably be okay. Will Rutherford mind if I'm not one hundred percent fit?'

Laura gave a hint of a laugh. 'Haven't you heard?'

'Heard what?'

'About George. It's been on all the news on telly. He was found asphyxiated in his own sauna.'

'Bloody hell! When was this?'

'They found him this afternoon in a penthouse in Queen Victoria Street.'

'It wasn't above the Anglo-Maltese Beef Company, was it?' Rory blurted.

'Yes, why?'

'Shit!' Rory hissed breathily.

'Why? What about it?'

'Get yourself round here and I'll tell you.'

'Tell me now.'

'No.'

'I'll be there in twenty minutes.'

'No. Don't kill yourself!'

She laughed and put the phone down.

Straker had followed Rory into the kitchen. He looked at him, eyes wide for information.

'Rutherford!' Rory shouted. 'George Rutherford! He's the man at Anglo-Maltese!'

'Are you sure?'

'Almost positive.'

'I *knew* there was something fishy about him. I never trusted him.' Straker paled. 'He's never going to take the rap for what I did.'

Rory laughed. 'Oh yes he is. He already has. He's dead.'

Straker's jaw sagged. 'Dead?'

'Aye. It must have been Eland. Banged him into his sauna and boiled him.' Rory laughed as he opened a bottle of Glenmorangie and poured an inch into two glasses. 'Eland must have been desperate; I guess Rutherford was going to drop him right into the shit on his own without a life belt.'

'My God! Then Eland will really be on the run now. He'll probably try to use those bloody photographs again.'

Rory handed him a glass. 'Just relax. He may not have any and he knows we're on to him. The police are looking for him. He's not going to do anything with those shots now.'

'But he could. He could threaten to send them to the papers; the awful Sunday tabloids would love it!'

Rory understood Straker's panic, but he wasn't going to share it. 'Henry, like I said, if it comes to it, it'll be your word against his as far as the doping goes. What we've got to do now is make sure Rutherford gets the blame.' Rory spoke with a conviction he didn't feel. It would be even harder for the police to extract anything from a dead George Rutherford than a live one. 'And I'm supposed to be riding two horses tomorrow. Where the hell am I going to find a doctor to pass me fit?'

Henry Straker hated lying, and he particularly hated lying to the police.

No, he told them, he had not been asked to pay anything or do anything since the first photos had arrived in
the post.

He told them that he'd already reported how he had
been drugged and then, with stumbling embarrassment,
how the shots had been posed.

The ashes of Eland's house had revealed nothing useful
beyond confirming that there had been a photographic
studio in the garage. The police accepted Straker's statement that the three photos he had received had been destroyed. They made a note of the descriptions of the boys.

It was Rory who told them about following Eland to
Queen Victoria Street, and the offices of the Anglo-Maltese Beef Company.

The Met. were called in. The hunt for Eland was given
priority status.

The most senior detective in the Thames Valley police
arrived at Newbury police station to talk to Rory.

'We're dealing with three murders here,' he stated
baldly. 'To cover up a crime which hadn't been
committed.'

'You're wrong there, Chief Superintendent. Luke
Mundy's death started all this. I guess he had a lot of
money on Midnight Express, and I think you'll find it was
with George Rutherford. The horse was doped, lost its
footing and killed Mundy, which Mrs Mundy has been
charged with. You've got that all wrong. I can tell you
Luke was betting heavily, and losing with Square Mile
Sporting. If you dig deep enough, you'll find that Square
Mile Sporting belonged to Rutherford.'

'And where do you think blackmailing Henry Straker
comes into this?'

Rory took a deep breath. 'I think he was set up so that Rutherford could take advantage of his position as Jockey Club Chief Veterinary Officer. Henry Straker has a very high profile both in racing and in his work with children. He's always been outspoken on public and private morals, particularly in racing, which makes his reputation much more vulnerable than most people's. Though the shots were so convincing they could have been very damning, I guess Rutherford didn't bargain for Henry's absolute sense of duty and honour.'

Rory paused, to underline his words, and to see how the detective was taking them. But the policeman's eyes were issuing no messages. Rory shrugged his shoulders.

'Anyway, Henry hadn't done anything, but Luke was dead, and Laura was the main suspect. I began snooping around and I'm afraid that's why my house was raided twice last week when my wife ... and Dai Price were killed. And again tonight. What started as a simple plan to stop a horse from winning had got totally out of hand. From thinking he'd covered his tracks, Eland suddenly realised he was liable for manslaughter. I guess that when Rutherford knew Eland was on his way up to see him, he ordered all traces of the scam to be destroyed, especially now there were two murders involved. And he thought I had some copies of the photos.'

'Why did you get yourself mixed up in it?'

'Because I knew Laura Mundy wasn't responsible for her husband's death, and she asked me to help her prove it.'

'Don't you think that might have been better left to us?'

Rory grinned. 'No, and apparently I was right. I *knew*

Laura hadn't done it, but as far as your people were concerned, it was bloody obvious she had. As it's turned out, I think I did the right thing.'

'And I'm told it was touch and go for a while that you might have been charged with shooting your wife and Price.'

'Aye, well, I accept it didn't look too good for me when your boys arrived. And I had to lie to them about the reason for the break-in. It's lucky I did, isn't it, because if I'd put you on to Eland, he'd never have led you to Rutherford.'

'And Rutherford would never have been killed,' the detective added drily.

'George Rutherford is no great loss to society.'

'It's not our job to make judgements about victims, merely to prevent and prosecute crime.' The policeman paused. 'But I take your point. Right,' he went on, switching off the tape recorder that had been running, 'I'll have this transcribed, and then you can sign it. Is there anything else you want to add?'

Rory shook his head, and prayed that Henry hadn't had a fit of remorseful honesty in the adjacent room where he was being questioned.

Chapter Fourteen

Rory let himself back into Camp Farm just after ten. He was carrying a bag of hot silver-foil containers from a Chinese takeaway in Newbury. He dumped them on the kitchen table and walked through the hall into the drawing room.

Edward Brickhill stood up. 'As someone's bust your back door again, I let myself in.'

Rory nodded. 'I saw your car. Have you poured yourself a drink?'

'No, but you look as though you need one.'

'You're darn right,' Rory replied and walked across to a drinks cabinet. 'Will you have one now?'

Brickhill nodded. 'I've been trying to get you all evening on the phone. Eventually I tried the police station on the off chance and they told me you were on your way back here. I suppose you've already heard what happened at the Anglo-Maltese Beef Company?'

Rory laughed. 'I heard. Laura told me, but of course she didn't know anything about the connection.'

'Does she now?'

'Sure. I've just seen her. She brought me back from Newbury nick.'

'What the hell were you doing there?'

'It's a long story.'

Rory told him as clearly as he could what had happened that evening. Brickhill didn't interrupt him until he'd described his interrogation by the senior detective.

'Where does this leave Laura?' he asked.

'Still on remand, I'm afraid. They believe that Rutherford was trying to set Straker up, but until they've got something that specifically ties him in with the doping, Laura's their prime target.' Rory shrugged. 'If Henry confesses to it, she'll be off the hook, but Henry would certainly go down. As it stands, they've only really got a circumstantial case against Laura. Unless they can come up with some strong forensic evidence, I don't think they'll stand it up. At the moment, she's prepared to take the risk. Henry says if it looks as though it's going against her, he'll own up.'

Brickhill nodded slowly. 'So we're balanced between a rock and a hard place.'

'Laura's been bloody brave about it, though. She's been under terrible pressure these last few weeks.'

'Is she going to Cheltenham tomorrow?'

Rory grinned. 'Oh aye. She thinks Flamenco Dancer will win. Mind you, it's not certain to run, now its owner is dead.'

'Are you riding it, if it does?' Brickhill looked doubtfully at Rory's bandages.

'Aye, Flamenco Dancer and Shebeen for Laura, and

Dayglow in the Champion Hurdle. I had a good session with the physio on Saturday and she's coming round here tomorrow morning. I think I'll be able to get past the quack.'

'But can you really ride?'

'Sure I can.'

'I hope so, for Laura's sake. Right, I'd better be going. I'll be in touch tomorrow.'

When he could see the Bentley's tail lights travelling down the lane, Rory remembered his Chinese food. He found that it was now only lukewarm. He put it in the oven and while it was heating, picked up the phone to call Tommy in Scotland.

'How's it going, Tommy?' Rory asked gently.

'Oh, okay. But I miss you . . .' There were a few moments of silence before he continued. 'At least I've still got you.'

'Listen, your mum wouldn't have wanted us to be miserable, would she?'

'No.'

'Of course not. So are you all right otherwise?'

'Yeah. I've been fishing and Grandad's been tying more flies with me.' The boy sounded brighter.

'That's great. Make a few for me; we'll use them when we get up to Wales.'

'If we ever get there,' Tommy laughed.

'We'll get there, don't you worry.'

When Rory put the phone down, he couldn't help feeling guilty at the great weight that seemed to have been lifted from him. He looked round at all the things in his house that reminded him of the unhappy life he had been leading and, guilty again, wondered how the hell he had put up with it.

He also tried hard to remember the good things about Pam, in a way he wouldn't have done if she had still been alive.

Whatever her faults, she had always been ready to enjoy life and have a good time. There was absolutely no way she had deserved to be killed.

And he wondered what Tommy would think about a new mum.

After the physiotherapist had been next morning, Laura called for Rory on her way to Cheltenham.

'Hell,' she said as he got into the car, 'you can't go looking like that. Let's go back inside and tidy you up a bit.'

Grumbling, Rory climbed out of the car and let Laura into his house.

'God, what a mess,' she said looking round. 'Where's Taffy?'

Rory gave her a bleak glance. 'They killed him too, the bastards!'

'Oh, no! Oh, Rory, I'm so sorry. I know what it must feel like. I suppose he was trying to guard the house for you.'

Rory nodded. 'Aye.' Then, pulling himself together, 'I'm sorry. I haven't had a chance to clear up after the first break-in, let alone the second and third.'

'And you look a bloody mess yourself. Have you seen the bruises round your eyes?'

Rory laughed. 'I've tried not to look in the mirror.'

'If you go to the races looking like that, someone's going to stop you riding. Are you sure you're up to it anyway?'

'I wouldn't have said I'd do it if I weren't.'

'If you'd got up from a fall looking like that, the quack would have banned you for a few days.'

'Yes, well, I didn't,' Rory said with a grin.

'How's the shoulder?'

For a reply, Rory slowly swung his arm up until it was vertical. He managed it without a wince.

'Very impressive. Are you sure you can do it, though?'

'I'm sure. Stop fussing.'

'Of course I'm fussing. Both the horses you're riding for me today could win.'

The Honorary Medical Officer looked sceptical as Rory stood in front of him in the medical room at Cheltenham racecourse.

'What about those bruises around your eyes?'

'That's nothing, honest, Doc. Just knocked myself on the wing when I came down last week. It's giving me no trouble.'

'All right. Just stand back and lean forward on to the desk with your left arm, and slowly push yourself back up.'

Rory did as he was asked.

'Okay, now raise your arm to the horizontal ... Okay, now the vertical.'

Rory hoped the doctor couldn't see how tight his jaw was clamped. He managed the manoeuvre without twitching a muscle on his face.

'Okay, let it down slowly,' the doctor ordered.

Rory held his breath and lowered the arm.

'Well,' the doctor said, 'I suppose you're old enough to know better than to go out with a dicky shoulder. Here you are.'

He scribbled a medical certificate and pushed it across the desk to Rory.

'Thanks, Doctor.'

Outside, Rory gave a grunt and circled his shoulder in its socket, thinking that he wasn't quite as old as the doctor supposed.

Declan Hoolihan knew he was going to be on television. He was wearing a new petrol-green fleece jacket he had bought himself for the occasion as he led Flamenco Dancer into the parade ring. He looked after both the horses that Langlands had sent to Cheltenham that day. Over the last six months, he'd done a lot of work on Jimmy – Flamenco Dancer – and even more on Shebeen, who was running in the fourth. As far as he was concerned this was the most important day of the year.

Flamenco Dancer was running in the name of the Executors of the Late Mr George Rutherford. Laura watched with quiet confidence as the gelding walked round the ring with his long, deceptively languid stride.

She just hoped the horse would have the stamina to do most of the work himself; his jockey wasn't going to give him a lot of help. It was the first time in her career she had allowed her emotions to interfere with her choice of jockey. Common sense told her she should have booked someone else.

Laura legged Rory up into the saddle and the tension

rose among the bulging band of spectators round the ring as the race drew nearer.

Rory sensed the atmosphere and wished he could respond to it in the way he usually did, but his adrenal glands had been overworked in the last two weeks. He'd thought several times that morning – at home, in Laura's car on the way – about getting off the ride, but he didn't want to let her down, didn't want her to see him weaken, so to speak, in the final furlong. Rutherford may have been dead, but she still wasn't off the hook.

Flamenco Dancer bounced him down the walkway that led on to the course, aggravating his shoulder as he went. The punters were ten deep on either side, straining for a closer look at their fancies.

Declan unclipped the leading rein from Flamenco Dancer's bit. The gelding gave a couple of steps of showy piaffe before getting back on his quarters and cantering happily away in front of the stands.

Laura and Patrick between them had trained the horse to the peak of its form. It looked in a different league to the other eight runners as they headed back down to the two mile start below the last line of marquees. Apart from standing a couple of inches taller, it had a massive frame that rippled with muscle under its conker-coloured coat. Here was a horse built for jumping at speed and, thankfully for Rory, it was a professional. It didn't pull at all, just took a firm hold of the bit, did what was asked and got on with the job in hand. Now that Rory's body had warmed up, the stiffness began to fade from his muscles. Apart from the worry of his shoulder, he felt fine. The few moments spent circling at the start, waiting for the race to get underway, discussing tactics with the other jockeys, had got the adrenaline flowing quickly around his body. The muscles in his stomach began to contract, his mouth become dry. As the starter called them into line, Rory took several deep breaths, coaxing his body back into working order, letting it take in the oxygen he needed.

Flamenco Dancer had no such problems. As they were coming under orders Rory could sense that the horse was keen to get away. He deliberately let it miss the break, settling it in fifth on the inside.

The going was just on the soft side of good, which Flamenco Dancer liked. As they flew the first three fences, Rory kept glued to the running rail. The horse in front was setting a good, even gallop; all Rory had to do was keep Flamenco Dancer balanced, ensuring that he didn't make any serious mistakes at the fences as the race developed. He didn't mind when he went to the front, as long as he was still there at the winning post.

At the second and final open ditch, the horse in front misjudged his stride and clattered the heavy wooden guard rail. It didn't fall, but for a half-dozen strides it lost its rhythm and Rory eased round, letting Flamenco Dancer move to within six lengths of the leaders.

On the top of the hill on the far side, with three fences still to jump, Rory was breathing right down their necks. He could hardly believe how easily he was travelling. The next couple of tricky downhill fences were always much simpler to negotiate when you weren't under pressure. Rory bided his time, his main concern being that one of the three horses in front might fall and bring him down. With that in mind, he eased Flamenco Dancer to the outside. Four of them in a line flew the third last and raced on towards the next fence. Rory looked across quickly at the trio on his inner; he had each of them cracked. He'd wait until he'd landed safely over the second last and then go for home.

All four horses were travelling at top speed but Rory knew he had won the race; that knowledge made him indecisive and Flamenco Dancer, not getting any particular signals as to where to take off, guessed at the last moment. Only a superb sense of balance kept the horse on its feet as it launched itself much too soon and came down through the stiff birch. The horse's nose almost touched the ground as it struggled to stay upright. Moving its feet quickly it bounced back to catch Rory's body as he came forward. Rory screamed as a vicious stab of pain ripped into his shoulder.

Despite all the massage, the stretched and weakened ligaments hadn't recovered from the damage they'd suffered. The ball had slipped from its socket and every nerve in his shoulder was screaming.

Rory was now nothing more than a passenger. He gripped as tightly as he could with his knees in a desperate attempt to keep the movement of his arm to a minimum. He held both reins in his other hand, crouching over Flamenco Dancer like a drunk as the horse galloped around the long turn towards the last fence. Rory braced himself for the inevitable surge of pain that would come from the jolt of jumping. He tensed his body as Flamenco Dancer ran on gamely. As the horse's feet thudded soundly on to the turf, Rory cried out and fought to stay conscious, but his vision was blurring fast. Winning the race didn't matter any more. His whole body was begging him to stop the pain. Flamenco Dancer stretched his legs to stay with the other horses but carrying a dead weight on his back was too much for him.

Laura knew immediately what had happened and ran down to the course, pushing her way through the crowds.

Now back to the relative comfort of a walk, Rory began to recover. He was being helped by one of the other jockeys when Declan and Laura came running towards him.

'Are you all right?' Laura asked breathlessly, as she reached up to put her hand on Rory's knee, while Declan clipped the lead rein on to the bridle.

'My shoulder,' muttered Rory through his clenched jaw.

'I thought so. You'd better stay on board. It'll be easier than walking back. We'd better get you straight to a doctor.'

'I'm sorry, Laura.' Rory's blue eyes were watering from the pain.

'It doesn't matter. Dad'll be able to buy Flamenco Dancer for twenty grand less than he'd planned!' Laura tried to make light of her disappointment.

Rory forced a laugh through his aching chest. 'What about Shebeen?'

'I'll find someone else to ride him. Don't worry about it.'

'Declan's still got his licence hasn't he, and his allowance?'

'Yes, but he's only had a couple of rides this season.'

'Give him the ride on Shebeen; he'll ride it as well as

anyone else you could get now, and he knows the horse better than anyone.'

Declan held his breath waiting for his boss's reply. Laura looked at him and gave a short laugh. 'Why not?'

From the stands, Rory watched Declan Hoolihan win his first ever race at Cheltenham.

The lad had put his heart and soul into it, and his knowledge of the horse had paid off. The result more than made up for Rory's own failure in the Champion Chase.

A few minutes later in the winner's enclosure, Patrick Hoolihan was red-faced and almost bursting with pride as he led his son in.

When the prize-giving formalities were over Laura and Patrick led the horse back to the stables.

'It was very good of you to give the boy the chance,' Patrick said as he and Laura walked away from the paddock.

'It was Rory's idea, actually. As Declan's done so much work with the horse I thought he'd do as well as anyone else. In fact he did rather better than that.'

'He did, and he's over the moon – all thanks to you.' The little man's blue eyes were shining. 'We've a lot to be grateful to you for, Declan and I, but you can be sure we'll find a way to repay you.'

'He won the race,' Laura said, smiling. 'What more could I ask?'

Patrick looked at her with real admiration. 'Jaysus, you're a strong woman, Mrs M, to be laughing and saddling winners with all that's been going on.'

'Not as strong as I seem, Pat,' Laura said soberly. 'If

you really want to know, I've hardly slept a wink in the last fortnight.'

Pat's face clouded. 'I'd not have known, unless you'd told me. Pray God, it'll come to an end soon.'

'I wish I had your faith, Pat.'

Edward Brickhill's green Bentley was parked in front of Langlands when Laura drove in with Rory.

They found him sitting in a large tapestry wing chair in front of a fire of blazing apple logs in the main hall.

'I'm glad you've made yourself at home, Dad.'

'Just getting used to the idea,' Brickhill said.

'What are you talking about?'

'Your late husband's receivers in bankruptcy have accepted my offer for the house and estate. Not a particularly generous offer, but they recognised the dearth of buyers for this type of property in current conditions.'

Laura was astounded. 'But you never said anything about it!'

'Like you, I never see the point of giving away my movements until I have to.'

His daughter leaned down and kissed him. 'You're fantastic. I was dreading having to move out, well, not so much out of here, but out of my yard.'

'You may still have to, if you can't come up with the rent I shall be asking for it,' Brickhill said, deadpan. 'Anyway, we've still got to clear up this other mess. I've been on to Agnew and I'm afraid he says that the police still haven't dropped the charges, though things are looking a bit more promising.'

'How?' Laura asked. 'Unless Henry gives himself up.

And none of us want him to have to do that, do we?'

'No, of course not,' Brickhill agreed. 'Look, it's clear that George Rutherford was behind the doping of Midnight Express. The police took everything away from Rutherford's penthouse in Queen Victoria Street and found an undertaking from Luke to the effect that if Midnight Express didn't win the race, the horse would become the property of George Rutherford. If he did win, all Luke's outstanding debts with Square Mile Sporting would be written off and not pursued.'

'That must have been what I saw them doing here the night George invited himself to dinner!' Laura exclaimed. 'I knew there was something going on. And that's why Luke transferred Midnight Express to my name.'

'But surely,' Rory said, 'if the police know about this bet, it takes the pressure off Laura?'

'Not entirely.' Brickhill shook his head. 'They know that Rutherford was prepared to buy this place and let Laura stay here, and they've been told by the staff here and some of the lads that Luke and Laura weren't getting on at all well. And that still leaves Laura with a motive as strong as Rutherford's. As it happens, it's Agnew's view that the agreement between Luke and Rutherford wouldn't have been a legally binding document. Possibly Rutherford saw it as the only way he was going to get his money. He knew damn well what Luke's position was. I don't know if you know this, but he was able to take back the Chelsea Gaming Club for nothing, though he'd already had seventy percent of the payment for it from Luke.'

'Yes,' Laura said. 'He couldn't help himself gloating

about it to me the other day. Luke must have flipped to have done a deal like that.'

'They also found details of all Luke's punting on the share price of Thames Land,' her father said. 'I suspect Rutherford was holding that over Luke as well. I mean, Luke could have been seriously run in for insider dealing. The SFO are desperate to get their teeth into a clear-cut case like that.' Edward shrugged. 'Poor old Luke. I almost feel sorry for him now. Transferring the horse to Laura's name at the last minute wouldn't have worked at all, I'm afraid. Even if you ever get the insurance money, his receivers will have a very solid claim to it.'

Rory, with his arm in a sling, listening to the gloomy tale, tried to guess what Laura was feeling. Despite their closeness of the last few days, he still couldn't repress a lingering doubt that he had completely got through to her. As she and Edward talked, he wandered round the great oak table that occupied the centre of the hall. At first unconsciously, his eyes fell on a copy of the *Evening Standard*, folded with only the front-page headline showing, and beside it, a photograph of Arthur Eland.

Suddenly focusing, he grabbed it, unfolded it and stared at the story below the picture.

Edward was watching him. 'I thought that might interest you. That's why I came down.'

'What is it?' Laura asked.

'They've just fished Eland out of the Thames with a hundredweight of chain wrapped round his legs,' Rory said as he read the piece. 'They say they'd been searching for him in connection with Rutherford's murder. They found him at low tide early this morning. He'd been in the water between twelve and eighteen hours.' Rory looked up. 'They're right there. I saw him go into Rutherford's office about three o'clock. Rutherford must have given the order to kill him before Eland banged him into the sauna.' Rory gave a grunt of a laugh. 'There's a sort of nice poetic irony to it, and at least it means that there aren't any more of those photos of Straker in circulation.'

'Maybe, but that doesn't help Laura much.'

Rory looked at him, then at Laura. 'I think I'll go down and see if Declan's back from Cheltenham with the horses.'

He walked across the hall and out of the huge oak door with Laura and her father staring after him.

'Hello, son. What do you want?' Detective Inspector Stuart Wood asked as he walked into the room where the duty sergeant had left Declan Hoolihan. The policeman had taken an hour to drive from his station in Surrey. They'd been friendly enough to Declan while he waited, brought him two cups of tea and offered him a few cigarettes. But he'd thought about walking out several times.

Now the detective, the same one who had come with the Kempton security man to the Axe and Cleaver, looked quite pleased to see him.

Wood was getting a lot of stick for not holding this case together. Apart from the empty xylazine phial, the case against Laura Mundy was looking too circumstantial. If only, he'd been thinking, they'd found something at Rutherford's to tie her in.

The lad had come into the local nick, claiming he had more to say. It had to be worth the trip. And he could take a drink off his brother in Hartley Wintney on the way home.

'There was something I didn't tell you last time,' the lad mumbled.

'Something you forgot?'

'No.' Declan spoke nervously. 'The man said he'd give me a monkey, cash, and said he'd kill me if I talked.' Declan shrugged.

'What bloke?'

'Eland. The one they pulled out of the river in London.'

The detective perked up. It looked as though it was going to be worth the trip. His chief would owe him a drink if he came back with something hard. He nodded encouragement.

'When did you talk to him, then?'

'At Kempton, that day. After Mrs Mundy had been and looked at the horse. I'd seen him around earlier, but he came up and said he wanted to take a look at the horse. I said, no way; he pulled out one of those long thin knives and prodded me in the gut with it. He said, "You're taking me in there, sunshine." He was only a small bloke, but hard, like.'

'Go on,' the policeman encouraged him. 'Did you let him in?'

Declan nodded, shamefaced. 'When he gave me the money.'

'What did he do?'

'He told me to hold the horse's head while he gave it a jab in the neck. Can't have taken more than ten or fifteen seconds. Then he said, "You tell anyone, and I'll cut your tongue out." That's why I didn't say last time, that and I'd've lost my job at Langlands.'

'Did you actually see Eland inject the horse?'

Declan nodded vigorously.

The detective looked at the lad for a moment, his eyes narrowing. 'Did you ever see him again?'

'Yeh, but he didn't see me, and he never gave me the money. He turned up at the yard, the Friday after. He told Micky he wanted to see Mr Hoolihan, said he was selling minerals. Mr Hoolihan wasn't around, so he went off back to his car.'

The policeman's eyes lit up. 'Where'd he leave his car then?'

'Round the back with the others.'

'Was Mrs Mundy's car there then?'

Declan allowed his brow to pucker as he thought about it. 'Yeh,' he said after a moment, 'yeh, I think it was. Mrs Mundy'd gone back up to the house in the Land Rover.'

The policeman stood up, walked to the door and opened it. 'Sarge,' he shouted, 'I'm going to have to do a formal interview in here. Can you sort me out a couple of tapes?'

Laura watched the first lot pull out of the yard next morning. She felt almost light-hearted. For the first time in weeks, the cloud that had been looming over her life seemed to be breaking up. Agnew had phoned her after her father and Rory had left the night before. He couldn't tell her much, just that the police had confirmed they were pursuing another line of enquiry.

She just hoped it wasn't Henry.

Pat Hoolihan came up quietly behind her in the deserted yard.

'Mrs Mundy, there's something I've been meaning to

give back to you these last couple of weeks.' He felt in the pocket of his tweed jacket and pulled out a small plastic phial, three-quarters full of liquid. He handed it to her.

Laura took it and her heart nearly stopped.

'What . . . what is it?'

'That'd be the stuff you wanted to use to quieten that tricky mare we couldn't clip.'

Laura felt her face redden.

'But where on earth did you find this?' she asked awkwardly.

'That day at Kempton, when I'd to get your keys from your Puffa jacket so's I could drive your car to the hospital, remember?'

Laura didn't need reminding.

'Susan's been staying with her sister in Salcombe since Sunday night,' Henry said when Laura asked after his wife. 'I thought it very likely these people would have another go at me – rightly as it turned out – and didn't want her staying in the house.'

Laura had asked Henry to come to Langlands for dinner with her and Rory that evening, the final day of the Cheltenham Festival. Several things merited celebration.

Langlands had sent out another winner that day. And the police had formally announced that they had dropped their charges against her.

For Rory, the gilt was taken from the first of these events by the fact that he had not been able to play any part in it.

For Henry, the second cause for celebration still left

him with a feeling of dishonour.

On the strength of Declan's new evidence, and the circumstances surrounding the deaths of George Rutherford and Arthur Eland, the police and the Jockey Club were satisfied that they had found the culprits, albeit posthumously. In the circumstances, they weren't charging Declan as an accessory.

Privately, Rory was very glad that there would be no trial where Declan would have to present his evidence in open court. He guessed that was beyond the lad's acting skills.

Rory nodded in reply to Henry. 'There's no question about it, but with Rutherford and Eland dead, there's no danger now.'

'Eland definitely had someone with him when he came to your house – when Pam was killed. The police found two sets of footprints.'

'A contract worker, like the ones Rutherford sent after me on Monday. The police are looking for him. They're doing the two who came after us for attempted murder and they've got a linc on whoever put Eland in the Thames. I should think they're quite pleased with themselves.'

The three of them were eating a simple dinner at the round table in Laura's breakfast room. She and Rory wanted to help Henry expunge his crushing sense of guilt. It should have been easier now that Laura was released from suspicion, and Rory had not told him about his conversation with Declan the evening before.

Henry was ready to believe that his life and his reputation were out of danger, but it was clear that no amount of well-reasoned pragmatism would exonerate him in his own eyes. He was more prepared, though, to share the blame.

'I must say,' he conceded, 'now that it's emerged that Eland also doped the horse, I don't feel quite so bad. The dose of xylazine I gave him would never have caused him to come down the way he did. I suppose Eland thought I just wasn't going to do it and was making sure to cover his own back from Rutherford.'

'Exactly,' Rory said. 'We know you'd never have done anything that might possibly have hurt the horse or led to it dumping Luke like that. You must stop blaming yourself, man. I was pretty surprised when Professor Douglas told me the horse had been given too much of the stuff just to slow it down. I was bloody worried when he told me he didn't think it could have been administered by a professional. But now we know what happened.'

'And Eland planted the empty phial in Laura's car. I must admit, Laura, for a while I thought it was the one I'd given you, and I'm afraid it occurred to me . . .' Henry looked at her, embarrassed. 'What *did* you do with the one I gave you?'

Laura stood up and walked out of the room without a word. A few moments later, she reappeared holding a phial, three-quarters full.

'Here it is,' she said. 'As you can see, I only gave the mare a small dose.'

Henry looked puzzled. 'That's funny. You see, the mare's lad told me they'd managed to clip her without it.'

Laura laughed. 'That's what he thinks.'

When Henry left to drive himself home, Laura and Rory went back into her small sitting room. She put her arms around him and gave him a long, tender kiss, careful not to put pressure on his shoulder.

At last she released him and stood back. She put her two hands either side of his sandy, stubbly chin.

'That was delicious,' he said.

She took her hands away and walked towards the drinks table.

She poured a long Glenmorangie for Rory and turned to give it to him. He took it with a wide grin on his battered face.

'That was a brilliant idea,' she went on, 'getting Declan to go to the police with that story. I'd no idea that's what you were doing yesterday evening.'

'It was the only way I could see of getting you off without Henry taking the rap,' Rory said lightly. 'And Declan was very obliging. I told him it was what you wanted and he was so chuffed about winning that race, I think he'd have done anything for you.'

Laura tugged him down on to the sofa beside her and looked into the fire without speaking.

'Rory,' she said after a moment. 'There's something I should tell you.'

'What about?'

'Midnight Express.'

It was Rory's turn to take her chin in his hands. He turned it slowly towards him until they were looking into each others' eyes.

'There's no need,' he whispered. 'I know.'

Dead Ringer

Chapter One

Fontwell, England: late October

'Do you think he's really who he says he is?'

The disbelief in Joe Peters's voice was mixed with more than a little envy. His pride wouldn't let him believe that David Tredington, supposedly so inexperienced, could be such a good jockey. Since he had arrived from Ireland less than two months before, David Tredington's name was one that had crept into racing conversations with increasing regularity as his tally of winners had mounted. As far as many of the professionals like Joe Peters were concerned, he looked too tidy, was too sure of himself, and knew too many moves for the amateur he claimed to be. As if that weren't enough to stir the bubbling cauldron of jealousy which was the jockeys' changing-room, David Tredington was also disarmingly good-looking and potentially very rich.

Joe shot a glance at the young man who sat beside him watching the race. 'Come on, Jason, you should know. What do you think?'

Jason Dolton pondered the question as if giving it thought for the first time – which Joe knew couldn't be the case.

1

Keeping his eyes fixed on the small closed-circuit TV screen in the corner of Fontwell Park weighing-room, Jason watched as the six runners in the Handicap Chase splashed over the water jump.

David Tredington had only one horse behind him. He'd been pushing hard for a circuit and a half of the tiny Sussex course, and although victory seemed, at best, unlikely, it was obvious to anyone watching that defeat was never going to be accepted until certain.

'I don't know, Joey.' Jason Dolton spoke slowly. His expression betrayed none of his feelings. 'But whoever he is, he can certainly ride.'

As the remaining half-dozen runners turned for home through the lashing rain, David Tredington felt he must be blowing harder than his horse. The ache in his legs from pushing it, together with his annoyance at its lack of effort, produced a sudden but not uncommon desire to pick up his whip and deal the lazy grey a couple of telling cracks across its generous quarters; but instinct, the rarest and most important quality in a racing brain, told him to wait. If Groats, his recalcitrant mount, was going to be beaten into any effort at all, it would only be for a short distance. Better to ask for it after the last fence than before the final open ditch which they were approaching.

David could barely see through goggles smeared with mud kicked up by the horses in front. He was contemplating whether or not he should quickly pull the back of his mittened hand across them and face the risk of making visibility even worse, when a lump of wet Sussex earth made the decision for him.

Smoothly, he slipped his whip into his left hand as it rocked with the motion of Groats's big head, and wiped away enough of the mud to restore his vision. His hand was barely back on the rein when, through the sound of sloshing hoofs and jockeys' urgings, came the familiar clatter of horn against wood as the horse directly in front galloped into the guard-rail. The animal hadn't got its back end high enough to fall but, as it crashed through the birch, it was turned sideways by the impact.

For an instant David felt sure he would slam straight into it but, even as the thought was being transmitted to his hands, Groats bobbed his head and moved his feet nimbly to the right, aiming for a narrow gap between the wing of the fence and the awkwardly angled head of the horse in front. David jerked both knees up into the relative safety of the slope of Groats's shoulders a split second before they barged into the other horse's head, shoving it back on course. Its jockey was still recovering from the first collision when the second almost fired him into David's lap. He made a desperate attempt to save himself from falling beneath the trampling feet of both horses, but David pushed him sharply away as he grabbed hopelessly at his slippery breeches. David hated doing it, but there was never a real choice in that situation; your own welfare always came first.

The excitement caused by the collision had somehow affected Groats with a rush of adrenaline. He showed a sudden willingness to take an interest in what was going on. By the time he had jumped one more fence and was approaching the last, he'd recovered the earlier lost ground and was less than two lengths from the leader.

With his horse running at last, David didn't risk the chance of Groats losing his enthusiasm. The prospect of a long uphill slog to the winning post had sullened braver horses than this one. He drew his whip and slapped his horse hard down the flanks to drive him at the final obstacle. For the first time, David sensed that the plodding grey was on his side.

Groats launched himself over and beyond the fence. He landed running, head down and ears laid flat against his neck. David was still pushing hard, squeezing with his legs, urging Groats through the sticky mud. As they rounded the left-hand curve to the post, the horse seemed to sense that it could win. He made one more effort. Twenty yards from the post, he strained his head into the lead, and stayed there, until victory was theirs.

Groats had eased his big frame back to a walk within ten strides of passing the line. His muddied head hung low from this rare exertion. David patted him gratefully on the neck while his own breath came in hard gasps. As they turned back towards the winners' enclosure, David pulled his goggles from his face. He stared down the course and felt some relief as he spotted the colours of the fallen jockey, now walking towards a Land Rover. He had done what any other jockey would have; he knew that. He also knew, because of his success, it would be resented.

David wished his father had been there to see them win. Sir Mark Tredington had bred Groats at his own Great Barford stud, and nothing gave him more pleasure than seeing home-bred horses win, especially now, with his son on board.

To David, Sir Mark's enjoyment from winning was as important as his own. To provide it was a way of repaying the kindness and affection with which his father had welcomed him back to the fold. He had arrived at Barford Manor eight weeks before, like the Prodigal Son returning, unannounced and totally unexpected, after having been away for more than fifteen years.

As Sir Mark hadn't come to the races that day, Sam Hunter, one of his two trainers, came out on to the course to lead Groats to the winner's slot in front of the weighing-room. David's slightly rotund, older cousin George was waiting there, grinning beneath his soggy brown trilby, and waving a bookies' ticket.

'Bloody well done!' he bellowed, slapping David on the back as he dismounted.

Pulling off the saddle, David smiled, still grateful for his cousin's genial reaction to his arrival in England and subsequent success on the race-course. He doubted that he would have reacted in such a gentlemanly way if the roles had been reversed. But then, he wasn't a gentleman, yet.

After he had weighed in and changed, David walked outside and stood under the veranda. The winter dusk was descending fast. The rain had eased to a drizzle that played a diminishing pattern against the light from the building opposite.

George appeared by his side and took him by the elbow. 'Come on, cousin. Time for a drink.'

The pair ran across the saturated lawn under the cover of George's umbrella to the timber-framed members' bar. George pushed his way through a damp, huddled mêlée of racegoers and effusively ordered a bottle of champagne.

David guessed that George had good reason to be grateful on this occasion. It had been Groats's first run for some time and, although everyone at Sam Hunter's yard and Great Barford knew he ran better when fresh, nobody had told the bookies, and he'd started at the generous odds of twelve-to-one.

On the other hand, since David had arrived at Great Barford, George had seen wiped out at a stroke his chances of inheriting most of the Great Barford estate – the baronetcy, the beautiful Queen Anne house, the four thousand acres that surrounded it, the historic stud, and who-knew-what investments in property, industry and international trade – an inheritance worth, it was rumoured, at least ten million.

You'd have to be a saint, David had thought, not to feel a little peeved at having all that snatched from under your nose.

And yet George had welcomed him with as much warmth as Sir Mark. The reception given to David by one of his sisters had been altogether cooler.

'David, that was a brilliant piece of riding!' George was saying. His big red face beamed with admiration. 'I thought you'd had it when that horse almost fell across you at the last ditch, but then you got the old sod going again. Where do you get your energy from?'

David shrugged modestly. 'Well, you'd get fit if you'd ridden some of the nags I have in the little races round Mayo,' he said with the West of Ireland lilt he'd brought with him to Barford Manor.

A few more people – some complete strangers, some

who had befriended him since he had started winning races in England – came over to congratulate him on his modest victory. He accepted their praise with diffident charm, a smile and a nod.

George stood by, sharing his cousin's glory. 'Do you need a lift home?' he asked when they had been left alone for a moment.

'It's OK. I've got the Range Rover.'

George nodded absently. 'It's a pity I had to come from London or we could all have come together. Are you going back home along the M27, then up through Salisbury?'

David nodded.

'Let's meet up for a half-way pint, then,' George said. 'There's a decent pub in Mere.'

'Sure. I'll see you there, but I'll be a while. I want a word with Sam before he leaves.'

George gestured his willing acceptance of this. 'No problem.'

David found Sam Hunter checking his two runners before they started their long journey home.

Sam was driving the lorry himself, and wouldn't reach his yard until an hour or so after David. For a while they discussed a mare David was going to look at there. As David left, Sam asked, 'How are you getting back?'

'In the Range Rover. I brought Mickey with me.'

'Mickey?' Sam asked. 'Who's he?'

'He's that lad who works in the stud; comes up with me sometimes when I ride work. He was that keen to come to the races, I asked Dad . . .' he hesitated, '. . . if he could come. He's just seventeen, a slip of a man and racing mad. It won't be long before he starts getting a few rides himself. He has a talent, that's for sure. I'll be sending him along to you when he's ready. Anyway, I'd better have a look for him before he gets into bad company.'

Mickey was outside the jockeys' changing-room, gazing with fascination at the familiar faces of the better-known riders as if they were film-stars. He turned to David with a mischievous grin across his boyish face. 'You ought to pick on jockeys your own standard. Then let's see how good you are.'

David laughed at his cheek and squeezed the young lad's left earlobe between his thumb and forefinger. 'I was just thinking what a nice easy ride he'd be for you to start your career on. He'd make you give up smoking soon enough.' David gave the ear a sharp twist.

'Well done!' Mickey squealed in submission.

'Come on. Let's get going.'

David collected his gear from the weighing-room and they walked together to the jockeys' car-park. They climbed into a brand-new metallic maroon Range Rover, and set off towards Chichester and the M27.

Sir Mark had asked David to stop off in Somerset to make a judgement on a well-bred mare that one of Sam Hunter's owners wanted to sell. It wasn't much of a detour on the long drive back to Devon, and David had only had the one ride; it was a small favour. Besides, he was pleased that his own judgement should be trusted.

Mickey subjected him, as he always did, to a barrage

of eager questions. 'Tell me when you thought you were going to win. Why didn't you hit him earlier?' the boy urged.

David responded with equal enthusiasm. He liked Mickey – he was totally uncomplicated, judged people on what he saw, not what he heard from others. He had been brought up to make the most of life by parents who doted on him and yet as an only child he hadn't been spoiled. He and David had spent hours chatting as they got on with the jobs around the yard.

'If I have to get blisters to get rides, then that's fine,' Mickey had once said. 'Of course, if I had a rich dad like yours, I'd have been champion jockey twice by now.'

The banter continued as they headed for the motorway; as they talked, David enjoyed the experience of driving the Range Rover, the smell of the leather upholstery, the four-speaker CD system, the phone and all the other gadgets which were new to him. In Mayo, his only motor had been a rusty Toyota pick-up which didn't even have a radio.

He was feeling thoroughly contented, savouring his eighth win since he'd taken out his English jockey's licence. Judging from what he'd seen of the other half-dozen horses his father had put at his disposal, there'd be plenty more to come before the season closed.

He thought, too, about the profound changes in his life that his decision to come to England had brought about.

When his son had turned up at Barford Manor in early September, Sir Mark Tredington, a life-long agnostic, had almost been prepared to believe in a good and merciful God.

David had disappeared when he was twelve, shortly after Sir Mark's wife, Henrietta, had died from a vicious fall whilst out hunting. The boy had been desperately fond of his mother, and the letter which had arrived, post-marked Bristol, had spelt out his deep unhappiness: he was finding it too hard to cope with his mother's death and his father's constant absences. It seemed he had simply decided to run away from home, for good.

Despite the intensive search that had been mounted, no trace of the boy had been found. Police had combed every inch of the estate, dragged every river-bed and lake, and searched every cave along the coast, but they had come back with not so much as a single sighting.

It had taken Sir Mark a long time to come to terms with the loss of his wife and his only son. Those few who knew him well agreed that he had never really accepted either; the dull ache of loneliness had never disappeared. It had just become more bearable as time passed.

For the past seven generations, the Tredington family had handed down their inheritance on a strict basis of primogeniture. That was what had kept the estate intact, and Sir Mark, though no rabid traditionalist, didn't want to break with this particular custom. Without David, his next natural heir was George, the son of his younger brother, Peregrine – a soldier, and one of the most senior officers killed by the Argentinians in the South Atlantic War.

George was a few years older than David, a podgy, awkward sixteen-year-old when his cousin had run away. Although his features bore a discernible likeness to David's, he lacked his lissomeness and precocious self-confidence.

But as hopes of David's return faded, George had grown increasingly aware of his new status, and he had taken the role seriously. He'd left his public school with results as good as his moderate ability allowed, and joined a merchant bank in the City where he had found his métier. He had an instinctive eye for a risk, and now, at the age of thirty-two, was well on the way to a directorship. The slightly disgruntled boy had become a secure and self-confident man, prospering and preparing for his eventual ownership of the Great Barford estate.

Sir Mark also had two daughters, Lucy and Victoria, who were fond of each other, but different in both character and looks.

Lucy, the elder by two years, was twenty-six, a committed artist with three years at the RCA behind her and two solo shows to her credit. She had had the good fortune to take after her mother; almost five feet ten tall, with a taut, well-kept body. Her dark curly hair, cut loosely around her oval face, fell to below her shoulders. Her brown eyes were perhaps a shade too close together, suggesting a sharpness of character, but overall she was a beauty. She still loved spending time at Barford, but now lived and worked in a small mews house in Chelsea.

Victoria loved horses and the country, which was as well. The glitz of London life could never have been a happy setting for her. Where Lucy's looks were guaranteed to attract attention, Victoria's plainness brought only the occasional curious stare. She was four inches shorter than her sister, stoutly made, with biceps that bulged from heaving feed-buckets. She had a square jaw and straight brown hair cut short. She refused to wear make-up, or a dress or a skirt on any but the most special occasions, normally, it was jeans, jumper and jodhpur boots.

To her family's thinly disguised disappointment, she had got married young, two years before, to a professional jockey a few years older than her. Jason Dolton was the son of an underpaid Somerset farm-worker. With no justification, he had grown up thinking that life owed him a living. He was a bad loser, and ungrateful on the rare occasions that success came his way. His short ginger hair, and a mouth that was little more than a red pencil line across his face, alerted observant strangers to the chippy character they were about to encounter. He was never going to ride more than a few dozen winners a season, and had a reputation for being easily persuaded to change his tactics for a race.

Everyone except Victoria assumed that he had married her for the four-hundred-acre farm which her father was rumoured to have settled on her. In fact, Sir Mark had always intimated that his daughters would receive a farm each; when George inherited he could incorporate Braycombe into the whole estate to make up for them. Now that David had come back, though, it looked as if this wouldn't happen.

The sisters took this change of fortune in their stride; Jason Dolton was less accepting. He viewed David not only as an unwelcome and privileged rival on the racecourse, but also as the cause of his being deprived of a farm he'd long considered as a dowry. Ingenuously, Victoria couldn't see why her husband resented David so vehemently, and tried to make up for it by being extra kind to her brother, which only increased Jason's resentment.

Although, since his return, the sisters had warmed to his charm and uncanny skill on a horse, their brother's return had not provided for them the life-line that it had for their father.

There remained between the girls and David a void, an emotional gap stretching back more than fifteen important years that could never be retrieved. Their brother, likable and charming as he was, had once betrayed them and lost their trust. He wouldn't recover it lightly; certainly not from the more self-sufficient Lucy.

The rain was driving harder as the Range Rover swept smoothly towards the motorway.

David glanced at Mickey, asleep now in the passenger seat, and grinned through the windscreen and hard-working wipers as his headlamps pierced the gloomy night. He had a vision of the reception waiting for him back at Barford – exuberance from Sir Mark and Victoria; quiet approval from Lucy; and grudging, ungenerous congratulations from Susan Butley, Sir Mark's secretary, who, while not exactly part of the family, was a resident influence in their lives.

Although she had started life from the other end of the social scale from the Tredingtons, Susan Butley possessed an aloofness and self-confidence normally associated with girls from privileged backgrounds. David had been

instantly attracted by the strength of her personality
and good looks. Her father, Ivor, had been a respected
head-groom at Barford, although he had left under a
cloud soon after his wife and child walked out on him
fourteen years before. But it wasn't out of guilt or pity
that the Tredingtons had absorbed Susan into their
lives as a necessary counter-balance to their own
mildness. Her intelligence and organisational skills
were obvious, and she was fiercely committed to
Barford. Perhaps that was why she had been the only
person besides Jason Dolton who had been unwilling to
accept David.

'A bloody cuckoo – that's what you are,' she had said to
him privately, soon after he had arrived. When he had
asked her to explain, she'd turned her back on him and
walked away. The hostility he had encountered in her
during those first days at Barford hadn't diminished in
the weeks since. She made it plain that she didn't trust
him or his motives in turning up in the way he had.

It was a not uncommon irony that, of all the people
who had come into David's life recently, she interested
him most; that for a very brief interlude, before she
knew who he was, there was no doubt that she had not
found him altogether unattractive.

The M27 motorway on the edge of Portsmouth was
bathed in orange light. David relaxed a little as he
pulled out into the fast lane to pass a pair of trucks
lumbering abreast of each other.

The Range Rover swished under the first exit at a
steady ninety, as if it were sucking up the road beneath.
David held the wheel lightly, tapping his fingers to the

beat of the music. He leaned across to turn up the stereo against the noise of the wind. As his eyes came back to the road, he almost dismissed as imaginary the solid object which seemed to part company from the overhead bridge at the Fareham junction.

A survival reaction less than a microsecond from his brain had both hands yanking the steering wheel to the left before he was even conscious that it was no illusion. In the same instant, he jammed his right foot on to the brake pedal. The tyres screeched as they strained at the wheel-rims; their rubber burned through the surface water into the tarmac.

David yelled, staring with wide-eyed horror as whatever it was crashed down and bounced straight across his path. The Range Rover's front off-side wheel smashed into the bulky object and sent the vehicle into a violent whirligig spin, pirouetting across the carriageway in front of the lorries they had just passed, heading uncontrollably towards the inner concrete piers of the bridge.

David froze with fear. On a bolting horse he'd have thought of a dozen different ways to deal with the crisis; in a careering Range Rover, he had fewer options.

The vast slab of a wall spun into view a matter of yards away now. The car was hurtling crazily towards it. And David knew there was nothing, absolutely *nothing* he could do.

He had only one trick left up his sleeve. 'Please Lord,' he begged instinctively, 'forgive me and save us.'

He didn't have time to specify if it was his body or his soul he wanted saved.

The Range Rover hit the wall at a forty-degree angle, smashing the near-side front wing on the unforgiving concrete, the car shrieking and scraping thirty feet until it met a substantial protruding buttress.

The left-hand side of the vehicle buckled savagely.

The front near-side pillar became a jagged spear – and a weapon which lanced the chest of his terrified passenger.

Beside him, David heard an anguished howl as the bucking vehicle rocketed out from under the bridge, slewed across the hard shoulder, mounted the shallow banking, tipped over on to its roof, slithered along the shingle at the edge of the road, mounted the bank again, rolled back on to its wheels and, mercifully, came to a juddering halt on the hard shoulder.

The engine had cut out and petrol vapour filled the crunched and shrunken metal box where David still sat, momentarily blacked out and still strapped in.

The silence which followed was broken by the hiss of steam from a ruptured radiator and the clatter of smashed, dislodged parts falling to the ground.

David blinked his eyes open, listening, disoriented, disbelieving.

After a moment, he raised his head until it touched the caved-in roof, moved his neck, his torso, his legs and knew that, if nothing else, he was alive.

In the eerie orange glow of the motorway lights he looked at the 'slip of a man' beside him.

Mickey sat rigid-still on a nest of shattered glass; pale, open-eyed, red-breasted, impaled to the back of his seat.

For several moments more, David couldn't move as he

tried to absorb the blunt, horrifying fact of the boy's death.

There was no sleep for David that night in the accident and emergency wing of Portsmouth hospital, only a few snatched moments of unconsciousness between conversations with ambulance-men, doctors and policemen – conversations in which he was restricted to monosyllables and gestures of the head, because he could barely hear or understand what was being said; everything was blocked out by the constantly recurring picture of Mickey's mutilated body. But he did manage to ask a policeman to phone Sir Mark and tell him what had happened to Mickey, so that the boy's parents could be told as gently as possible.

When his eyes flickered open in Tuesday morning's grim, grey-brown light, David's temples throbbed as if he'd spent the night drinking bad poteen with a Galway tinker. And the picture of the boy was still in his head.

He kept his eyes open to hold the vision at bay; took in the stark, functional furnishings of a hospital room. He moved and remembered there was nothing wrong with him, no more than a bruise or two, but – he had a vague memory – they were worried about delayed concussion, shock, trauma; he hadn't needed much persuading to stay.

He shed the hospital pyjamas. Slowly and mechanically he pulled on the beige cord jeans and checked shirt he had been wearing the night before. A nurse came in to chide him for getting up before he'd been looked at. He submitted himself to a simple examination, assured her that, physically, he was in no discomfort, and declined any breakfast. He wanted to ask about Mickey, but he didn't: there was no point; he knew the answer.

He asked for a telephone and dialled Barford. Victoria answered. He could tell from her voice that her relief that David was still alive was too great to admit the full impact of Mickey's death. Sir Mark and George, she said with a hint of resentment, were already separately on their way to Portsmouth to see him.

While David waited gratefully for his father, a policeman arrived to take a more coherent statement than he had been able to extract the night before.

There was, it seemed, no blame to be attached to David. The object that had fallen from the bridge had been one of a stack of old railway sleepers which had slipped from the back of a lorry as it swung through the roundabout above the motorway.

Half a dozen more sleepers had been found on the bridge; the lorry which had been carrying them had not. It was a minor junction, not much used; no witnesses had come forward so far.

Sir Mark could barely speak when he and George arrived, so great was his gratitude that David had survived. George was full of blustering sympathy.

'I've just seen the Range Rover. I can't believe you're still alive,' he said, shaking his head.

'I wish I wasn't.'

George ignored this. 'I thought something must have gone wrong when you didn't turn up at the pub in Mere, or at Sam's. I'm afraid it was only when I got home that I realised how bad it was, otherwise I'd have come back down last night. Now, you relax and I'll look after everything. Mickey's mother and father are already here. I don't think they can cope at all. I ought to go and see what I can do for them.'

He bustled out, leaving Sir Mark gazing at David with worried eyes in a face made haggard by a sleepless night.

'I can't tell you how thankful I am that you didn't die, David,' he said huskily.

David didn't answer for a moment. 'I'm sorry,' he said at last.

'Good God! What have you got to apologise for?'

'I'm not apologising. I'm just terribly sorry Mickey had to die.'

Sir Mark didn't react. He stood. 'Look, I'm afraid I can't stand hospitals. I gather you'll be here for a while so that they can check you out before you go. Now I've seen you're OK, I'm going back home. George can bring you back.'

Though he wanted to, David didn't try to stop his father. He watched Sir Mark leave the small room with his characteristic ambling gait, grateful for the concern.

On behalf of the boy's parents, George handled details of the transfer of Mickey's body back to Devon, and the parents left for their home without seeing David.

Later in the morning, the hospital let David go. Once he was installed comfortably in the passenger seat of George's car, they drove to the recovery yard to which the mangled Range Rover had been taken.

They inspected it in silence, neither able to refer to the

blood which was still visible on the buckled pillar. Walking away, George said again, quietly, 'It looks as though you were very, very lucky to get out of there alive.'

David nodded, guilty that it had been he, and not Mickey, who had walked away.

'What a terrifying piece of bad luck,' George went on. 'The odds against an accident like that happening must be several million to one. Let's hope they find the bastard who was driving the truck.'

David nodded again, thinking about the odds. Suddenly, and for no apparent reason, he remembered his brief encounter with a man called Emmot MacClancy at Newbury the Saturday before, and the little Irishman's damp, vindictive eyes. What if it hadn't been an accident? What, for God's sake, if MacClancy had really meant what he'd said? The man hadn't looked as if he had the resources, physical or material, to carry out the threat he'd made against David, not like this – and yet ... George was right, the odds against it happening accidentally were several million, probably several hundred million, to one.

But he couldn't tell the police – not about MacClancy; that would only open up a line of enquiry which would do nothing to help Mickey Thatcher now.

David stared at the road in front of him as George turned on to the motorway which had been the scene of the previous night's horror. He could hardly bring himself to look at the newly scarred concrete walls. He glanced up at the bridge and thought about a lorry dropping part of its load, just at that spot, just at that time...

* * *

George drove into the village of Barford a little before three. David asked him to stop in the village and wait for him for a few minutes. He climbed stiffly from the car. He knew roughly where Mickey Thatcher had lived, but asked in the post office for a precise address. The old postmistress shook her head forlornly as she gave it to him. She could remember Mickey coming into the post office when he was a week old. 'You'd have seen him too, Mr David. You was often down here then, wanting them sherbet lemons.'

David nodded. 'It's a terrible thing. He was a great little lad; eager as a ferret to be a jockey.'

'And him the only child they had.'

David walked the hundred yards along the village street to see Mickey's parents. Mrs Thatcher opened the door to him. Her eyes were wet and bleak. She was only in her mid-thirties, but the loss of a son had aged her ten years at a stroke. She didn't speak at first, wanting to blame someone for what had happened; seeing David as the culprit, knowing that wasn't fair.

'Could I come in?' he asked gently.

She nodded, opening the door wider, and led him into the small front room of the stone cottage.

Her husband, a mechanic at the village garage, sat on one of two worn easy chairs with his head in his hands. When David came in, he looked up, making no effort to hide the tears dribbling down his russet cheeks.

David took a couple of paces towards him, and placed a hand on his shoulder. 'I came straight here,' he said, 'to tell you how desperately sorry I am. I guess you wish he'd never come with me to the races.'

The father shook his head. 'Nothing weren't going to stop him going. It weren't your fault, no way,' he said generously. 'And he'd have been so happy to see Groats win; he was sure he would.' The man's shoulders shook as he lowered his head.

'He was more than happy about it, I promise you,' David said. 'If there's anything, anything I can do at all . . .' he went on, knowing that there was nothing he or anyone could do beyond recognising the depth of their grief. As he left the cottage he considered the grim irony that Sir Mark Tredington had found his son again and, as a result, the Thatchers had lost theirs.

As George drove him the last mile to the manor, David unconsciously braced himself to handle his family. They wouldn't blame him, of course, but he couldn't stop blaming himself.

If – and it was a small 'if' – someone, MacClancy maybe, *had* caused the accident, then David could blame no one but himself for Mickey's death.

George turned the car in through the main gates to the park which surrounded the manor and drove slowly along a four-hundred-yard drive beneath an avenue of robust old oaks in the final shedding of their gold-brown leaves.

The drive curved right to reveal the house in all its classic Queen Anne symmetry of dressed red sandstone. The simple beauty of the place gave David a tingle of pleasure every time he saw it, and he still hadn't adjusted himself to the idea that one day, with all the rolling acres around it, it would be his. At that moment, though, such thoughts were a long way from his mind. His reappearance at Barford was already causing problems, and the longer he was here, the worse they would become. He should have left well alone, stayed out of trouble in Ireland.

George pulled up among several other cars scattered at the back of the house. He didn't turn the motor off. He promised to come back later. 'You'll want to see the others without my being there, I'm sure.'

David was grateful for his sensitivity. He let himself out of the car to enter the house through a back door and a warren of flagstoned gunrooms and pantries. He looked into the kitchen. Lucy glanced up from the paper she was thumbing through while talking to a stout, aproned housekeeper.

Her expression, normally good-natured but slightly cynical, was warm with sympathy. She stood up in her paint-spattered smock and came to greet her brother with her arms outstretched.

'Poor David. What a horrific thing to happen. And poor little Mickey. I'm so sorry,' she said, wrapping an arm around his shoulder.

'I've just seen his parents.' He shrugged at the inadequacy of it. 'They'll not get over it, ever. Jesus, I feel terrible about it.'

'Don't be absurd. It wasn't your fault. How on earth did a railway sleeper fall over the side of a bridge, for God's sake?'

Inside his head, David registered a picture of Mac-Clancy pushing it.

'I don't know. But maybe I was driving too fast and

could have avoided it. Whatever, I can't help blaming myself.'

'I don't see as how you're to blame at all, Mr David,' Mrs Rogers, the housekeeper, said. 'It was an accident, pure and simple.'

David shook his head, unconvinced. 'If he hadn't come to the races with me, those people would still have a son; there's no escaping from that.'

'I think Dad's in his study,' Lucy said. 'He'll want to see you.'

'Sure. I'll go now.'

David gently removed Lucy's arm and, with his head bowed, walked through a faded green baize door into the hall and across the polished oak floor to his father's study.

Sir Mark Tredington's eyes showed a gladness to see him that made David burn with shame. The baronet rose slightly breathlessly from his chair to put an arm around his son's shoulder.

'Thank God you're back and nothing happened to you,' he said with an embarrassing intensity of feeling. 'You look a lot better than you did this morning. Is there any damage still?'

'A couple of bruises where my head hit the wheel, that's all. Less than I deserve. But Mickey's dead, and the car's a write-off.'

'It's terrible about the lad. He could have had quite a future. It couldn't matter less about the car, though. Look, sit down, have a drink.' He walked to a small cabinet and took out whisky and glasses. As he poured, a thought occurred to him. 'By the way, I didn't want to ask you in hospital. Did the police breathalyse you?'

David took his glass and sat down. He nodded. 'They did, and it scarcely registered. I'd only had a couple of glasses of champagne with George.'

'That's a great relief. When I spoke to George last night, I got the impression you'd had a fair bit – understandable after that win.' Sir Mark gave a short laugh. 'Well done, by the way. With all this drama, I haven't had a chance to congratulate you. I watched the race on SIS; the way you kept that old villain running was tremendous. I really thought he'd thrown in the towel at one point.'

'I expect he'll take a lot more coaxing next time. Still, he won this time, that's the main thing.'

David's younger sister, Victoria, had come into the room while they were talking.

'Groats was brilliant, wasn't he,' she said excitedly, unable to disguise her priorities. Her soft brown eyes shone from her round face. 'I wish I'd been there.' The choice of Groats's sire had been hers, and she had been making a fuss of the horse since the day she had watched it emerge from its mother in the foaling box.

'He was brilliant,' David agreed soberly.

'I'm sorry,' Victoria blurted. 'How awful of me, going on about a horse after what happened to Mickey. Poor Mickey. But are you all right?' she added quickly.

David briefly assured her he was. He was saved the torment of answering her next question by Sir Mark, who promised to explain to her later just what had happened. 'I must help the Thatchers with arrangements,' Sir Mark went on, thinking of his duties. 'I'd better pop in and see them. Perhaps you ought to do the same, David.'

'I already did.'

Sir Mark looked pleased and proud of his son. 'Good.'
He placed a firm hand on David's shoulder and gently
rocked it. 'Good. That was absolutely the right thing to
do.'

David thought about the 'right thing to do' as he walked
down to the village in the weak November sunshine that
pierced the clouds from the south-west.

The wind rustled crackling leaves, and gulls keened
and shrieked above him in competition with the raucous
calls of homing crows.

Glimpses of the stark, rolling contours of Exmoor
reminded him of his home in Mayo, where his soul still
lived.

When he reached the village, he headed for the old red
phone-box. He had already made up his mind what he
wanted to say to Johnny Henderson, but he was going to
have to do it face to face. He dialled a London number.
Twice he was answered by the frustrating long bleeps of
the engaged tone. When, finally, he heard Johnny's
voice at the other end of the line, he knew it was going to
be hard to persuade Johnny to accept his decision.

'I want a word with you,' David said.

'About what happened yesterday?'

'What d'you think?'

'Are there any other problems?'

'Not yet, but for sure there could well be.'

'There was always that possibility,' Johnny said,
allowing agitation to show through his normally seam-
less charm. 'But, OK. I'll meet you in Lynmouth
tomorrow evening. I wanted to come down and see Lucy

anyway. Seven o'clock, in the Anchor. We can have a drink there, then take a drive.'

Over twenty-four hours, David thought. He hoped he could keep resolved until then.

'Right. I'll see you there.'

'Well done yesterday, by the way. I won twelve hundred quid.'

'Well, Mickey Thatcher didn't,' David said angrily. 'Just make sure you're there tomorrow.'

David hung up and stood stiffly, still mentally continuing the conversation. After a moment he barged open the door of the smelly cubicle and set off for home.

Johnny Henderson sat on a stool in the saloon bar of the Anchor hotel. His long legs stretched lankily in front of him, clad in the first and, as it happened, last country tweed suit he'd had made in Savile Row ten years before. The well-worn, slightly shabby raffishness of his Jermyn Street shirt, tie and shoes indicated equally either considerable wealth or advanced penury.

Johnny was a classically good-looking type, sandy-haired and bright-blue-eyed. He was brimful of old-Etonian confidence, but he lacked the financial back-up needed to realise the potential of these attributes. At thirty, heavy drinking and minimal exercise were beginning to make their mark on his once flawless features. As the physical ravages increased, so the once easy, natural charm with which he had faced the world had developed a slightly desperate, overstated edge.

He was discovering that the looks, intelligence and charm which had made life so easy for his first thirty years had not prepared him for the job of making a serious living.

He had drifted into the field of bloodstock because he knew a little about race-horses and a lot about the people who owned them. His contacts had earned him his first clients; his lack of application had subsequently lost him most of them. He had come more and more to rely on an unreliable source of income from gambling. The occasional piece of high-quality information had saved him from going under completely, but life was lived on a knife-edge, and the women he pursued, no longer in the first flush of innocence, were beginning to expect more from a man than good looks, easy charm and reasonable – though inconsistent – performance in bed.

The smile which seldom left Johnny's public face was aimed now at the appreciative girl behind the bar. He flicked back his fringe as he took another drink from a pint glass, and she laughed at the story he had just told. He was Sir Mark Tredington's godson, well known at the Anchor and, generally, well liked.

He had stayed in the small hotel a few times in his ongoing pursuit of Lucy Tredington, usually on the pretext of seeing some local trainer or potential owner. In the old days, when he'd spent a lot of time at Barford Manor, he and George had sneaked in and had their first pint of bitter together, under-age and under the indulgent eye of a since-dead landlord.

When David walked in, Johnny was still flirting with the self-possessed but not immune barmaid.

Johnny turned on his stool. 'Hello, David. Let me get you a pint, then we'll go and have a look at this horse.' He greeted him with a heartiness he wasn't feeling.

'Sure, thanks Johnny, but I'll have a Murphy's. I've still not got used to your English bitter.'

'Yours too, David, now you've returned to the fold.'

When they got outside about twenty minutes later, Johnny didn't disguise his nervousness. 'We'll take my car and drive up to the moors.'

They got into his old BMW. They didn't speak as Johnny drove out of the small town via a narrow sunken lane that led up towards the looming contours of the moor. Johnny knew what was on David's mind. He'd lain awake most of the night searching for answers. They were playing a game that needed both of them, and Johnny had no intention of letting David throw in his hand now. He slowed to negotiate a hairpin bend round a dingle and glanced at David. 'Now, what the hell's the problem?'

'I'm pulling out of the deal,' David said bluntly. 'It's gone too far. Mickey was killed yesterday; I think it was meant to be me.'

'What the hell are you talking about?'

'I think it was set up. Someone was waiting for me at that bridge.'

'Don't be crazy. Who the hell would want to do that?'

'I don't know, but it could have been Emmot Mac-Clancy.'

'MacClancy? That chap who talked to you at Newbury last week?'

'That's right.'

'Why the hell should he try to kill you?'

29

'I don't know.'

'I mean, what does he know about what went on in Ireland?'

'That I don't know either, but he seemed pretty damned sure of himself. Of course, I bluffed it out, told him he was talking through his hat; but he knows something.'

'Well if he did, then surely he'd have tried to get some money out of you; and you can't get money out of a dead man. Who is he, anyway?'

'He says he's a Mayo man; I don't know who he is, but I'm not going to take a chance on his blowing this thing wide open.'

The north-westerly blowing off the Bristol Channel was carrying in a bank of black clouds, heavy with rain. Fat drops began to drum on the roof of Johnny's car where he had parked it at the entrance to a deserted barn on the northern slopes of the moor.

Johnny reached for his cigarettes and lit one, trying to keep the lid on his frustration. He couldn't blame David. There had always been the chance that someone, somewhere would appear out of the woodwork to point a finger.

He inhaled a deep drag.

'You told me that no one in London knew where you went when you left for Ireland. How the hell would this chap have connected you with the twelve-year-old boy you were then?'

'God knows. But from the way he spoke, he bloody well knew what was going on.'

'It's a real bastard, this happening now, when it's all going so well.'

'You're missing the point, Johnny! For Christ's sake, a kid, a perfectly innocent kid, has died!'

'That wasn't your fault.'

'Of course it was. If someone's trying to kill me, or warn me or whatever, it's because of what I've done; there's no getting away from that.'

Johnny didn't reply for a moment. He took several more long drags on his cigarette. 'Look,' he said at last, 'there's no point in your playing the white man now. For a start, it would shatter your father if you were carted off to jail. You must know that he's chuffed to bits to have you back. I haven't seen him so chirpy for years.'

David knew this, and it mattered to him. 'OK. We'll look into this MacClancy business first and find out what the score is. Maybe it won't cost a lot to shut him up, if he really does have a line.' He made a quick decision, and hoped he wouldn't change his mind. 'Look, you saw him at Newbury. Would you recognise him again?'

'Of course,' Henderson nodded with relief.

'You'll have to hang around until you spot him at the races. Somehow you've got to find out where he lives.'

'What am I supposed to do then?'

'Don't worry. Just find out where he lives. I'll do the rest.'

Chapter Two

Later, in the small stone farmhouse where he had lived since moving back to Barford, David lay awake, alone, torn apart by what had happened.

Darkness seemed to intensify the feelings of grief and guilt which daylight had made bearable. He couldn't divert his thoughts from the images which kept flashing into his mind – images of what he had been, of what he had chosen to do, of Mickey, large as death, impaled on the seat beside him.

Tired of the torment, David groped for the switch of his bedside light and clicked it on. He sat with his back against the wooden headboard, his knees tucked up.

Was he really the cause of Mickey's death? Maybe it was, as everyone said, an accident after all.

The warm glow from the lampshade began to calm him, and his thoughts became more rational. But still he couldn't be certain. It was only a few hours before dawn that doubt finally allowed him to slip into a crumpled heap and sleep.

He was woken by Victoria jangling his brass doorbell.

Bleary-eyed, he went down and let her in.

'God, you look rough. What were you up to last night?'

David ran his tongue around his teeth. It felt as if he'd been sucking cotton wool all night. His first attempt at speech was more of a croak. 'Nothing worth talking about.'

Victoria offered little sympathy and walked past him into the cottage. 'You've forgotten, haven't you, I'm coming over to Sam's with you this morning? And if we don't get a move on, you'll be too late for second lot. I was still in bed when Jason left to ride first lot.'

David groaned and pushed all the doubts and indecisions of the previous night to the back of his mind. That morning he was due to ride out on Deep Mischief, the Tredington entry for the Hennessy Gold Cup. He'd had his first race on the gelding at Newbury the previous Saturday, over the same course and distance as the Hennessy, and had ridden him into second place. He was fairly sure that, if he'd known the course, he would have won, easily. He was absolutely sure that Deep Mischief was the best horse he'd ever ridden.

'Thank God you came round,' he said to Victoria. 'I clean forgot to set my alarm. Would you ever make a pot of coffee for me while I get dressed and pull a razor across my face?'

'Sure.' Victoria smiled and went through to the tidy little farmhouse kitchen.

Later, driving his father's Mercedes the fifty miles to Sam Hunter's yard, David had to fight again to banish the images of the night before. At the same time, he did his best to keep up with Victoria's enthusiastic prattle. She noticed his reticence.

'You're a bit gloomy this morning,' she remarked. 'Sorry, am I going on a bit? It's just so great to have someone who'll talk to me about the horses, especially a brother who's turned out to be a star jockey.'

'I wouldn't say "star" was the word.'

'Well, you will be, if you win the Hennessy.'

That was more or less true, at least as far as an amateur rider was concerned, and it wasn't going to improve already strained relations with his brother-in-law. 'But I don't suppose Jason's too happy about it,' David said. 'He told me he was getting the ride, until I turned up.'

Victoria looked through her passenger window, across the misty Somerset levels. 'I don't know why he said that. I'm sure Dad didn't promise him the ride.' She turned and gave David a look of embarrassed anguish. 'I'm really sorry he's been so difficult with you.'

David shrugged. 'It's understandable. He's probably thinking of you. I guess he feels you've been sort of cheated out of what you were expecting by my coming back after you'd all given me up for good.'

'That's not true, David. I always knew you'd come back. And anyway, it isn't not getting the farm that makes Jason so tricky with you. I'm afraid he hates it when you win. I mean, if you *do* win the Hennessy, he'll be furious. I just wish he'd accept that he's part of the family now, and show a bit of loyalty.'

'Well, we've a long way to go before we win the Hennessy,' David said lightly. 'And if we do, it'll be the horse who's done it, not me.'

Victoria nodded glumly. When David didn't speak for a few miles, she said quietly, 'Sorry about my rabbiting on so much. I expect you're still upset about Mickey.'

'I am.'

She glanced at him, concerned by the tone of his voice. But it wasn't in her nature to press. 'OK. I'll shut up.'

The lads at Sam Hunter's yard liked having David out with them. He spoke their language and he'd earned their respect by showing them that he could ride the trickiest horses in the yard, as well as the best. Deep Mischief was notorious for dropping lads at the bottom of the gallops, but he'd never yet got the better of David.

That morning, the circumstances of Mickey's death dominated their conversation. The lads made it clear they considered David blameless, but all of them wanted to know exactly what had happened; how a railway sleeper could have fallen off a bridge accidentally.

A couple of them suggested it had been some stupid kids, fooling around. David wondered if they were right. He'd feel a lot less guilty if they were.

Deep Mischief strode out forcefully on the way up to Hunter's gallops on a low ridge above the River Parrett. Every so often, the horse would test David's resolve by jiggling, preparing for a buck or a plunge. David knew the signs, firmly admonished the horse, and sat hard into the saddle to show he was aware of what it had in mind.

Sam had paired him up with one of the stable's star chasers.

'Don't overdo him. If you feel him getting tired, keep hold of his head. This is his first piece of hard work since Newbury,' he shouted as the string left the yard.

Sam needn't have worried about the horse getting tired. He didn't have the speed of his workmate, but he was relentless in his stride. The four-length gap by which the other horse had pulled clear after seven furlongs had been reduced to half a length by the time they reached the end. A bit further, and David knew which one would win. If the ground remained soft for the Hennessy, the race would become a slog, and Deep Mischief would be in his element.

But as they clopped back into the yard, the nightmare of the crash seeped inexorably to the forefront of his consciousness. As soon as he had jumped off Deep Mischief and thrown the reins to a lad, he walked quickly to the Mercedes and got in. In the quiet insulation of the car, he picked up the phone and dialled Portsmouth police station.

After a frustrating few minutes, he was speaking to the constable who was handling what had evidently been logged as a fatal accident.

'No, there's nothing new to report, sir. We put out an appeal for witnesses who might have been on the bridge at the time, but so far no one's come forward.'

'But for Christ's sake, surely someone must have noticed a truck hurtling around with a stack of sleepers on board?'

'No need to worry about that, sir,' the policeman said frostily. 'Obviously, we're doing all we can to trace whoever was responsible; after all, they could face a prosecution for criminal negligence as there was a fatality involved. If we need to talk to you again, or we make any more progress, we'll let you know.'

Johnny Henderson stood on the platform at Ascot racecourse railway station, hands dug deep into the pockets of his long brown coat. When he had seen Emmot

MacClancy at Newbury, he had recognised all the characteristics of a regular race-goer; one of that band of men who travelled from course to course, subsisting mysteriously on unidentifiable sources of income in which winning bets could have played only a small part. Johnny had to go to Ascot that day to support a client, so he drove down early to give himself a chance to spot the Irishman arriving.

His guess that MacClancy would arrive by train – no great feat of detection – proved correct. He watched him step down from a stuffy, smoke-filled carriage, and shuffle along the platform with the rest of the punters towards the path up to the course. He was carrying an already very dog-eared copy of the *Sporting Life* tucked under his arm. Johnny checked the time-table for return trains to Waterloo and followed MacClancy.

Johnny spent the rest of the afternoon talking to friends and clients, avoiding his bookmaker, and went back down to the station in time for the first train to London. MacClancy, not much to his surprise, took the second, twenty minutes later. Johnny climbed into the same carriage, two doors down.

At Waterloo, he kept a good wedge of other gloomy punters between himself and the Irishman and followed him easily to the Angel, Islington. From there, MacClancy walked a few hundred yards to a huge cathedral of a pub, where he ordered a whiskey and settled on a bench, evidently to review his day's performance.

Johnny got himself a drink. He hoped he wouldn't be there too long; he had arranged to meet a girl who worked on the front desk at Christie's that evening – an odds-on certainty, if he was any judge. He glanced at his watch in frustration as MacClancy made his way to the bar for another drink.

Moving quickly, he went and sat close to where the Irishman had left his *Sporting Life*. He picked up the tattered paper and started to read it.

'Here, that's mine.' There was a slur in MacClancy's voice.

'Oh. I'm terribly sorry. I thought it had been discarded.'

'No,' MacClancy said, mollified by the warmth of Johnny's apology. 'I keep them till I've written all the results in my little book at home.'

Johnny folded the paper neatly and handed it to MacClancy as he sat down. 'Did you go to the races today?'

'I did.'

'How did you get on?'

'Not bad.'

'Did David Tredington ride a winner?'

MacClancy's shifty little eyes focused on him like a ferret on its prey. 'Why do you ask that?'

'It's just that I've been following him. He rides well.'

'He ought to, with his background, but he didn't have a ride today.'

'Oh. I didn't have a chance to look at the card. Did you have a winner or two?'

MacClancy nodded but didn't speak.

'I had a couple of bets yesterday, but . . .' Johnny made a face to show his lack of luck. 'Anything you fancy at Kempton tomorrow?'

MacClancy perked up. 'You get me a drink, and I'll give you a horse.'

'Sure!' Johnny said, as if he couldn't believe his luck. 'What do you want?'

'A large Jameson's.'

Johnny fetched the drink and one for himself. Philosophically, he wrote off his evening with the Sloane Ranger from Christie's and settled down to drink and talk horses with MacClancy. He also managed to extract a few details of the Irishman's personal history.

MacClancy had been born in Mayo, as he'd told David, but apart from one recent visit, he'd lived in London for the past thirty years.

He was reluctant to say more, so Johnny, with a good helping of his practised charm, switched to MacClancy's current circumstances. He was the caretaker in a small convent nearby, where he had a room, two square meals a day, and a couple of evenings off each week. He had worked with the same order of nuns for many years, at one time in another of their houses in Roehampton.

Later, when the conversation had reverted to racing, Johnny said, 'I've got to go now, but if this tip of yours comes up, I'll want to know where to deliver a bottle of whiskey; I'll have a good-sized punt.'

Johnny left the pub with the address of the convent in his wallet, and the information that MacClancy would be on duty the following evening. On his way to salvage what he could from his wrecked social arrangements for the evening, he rang David to report his progress.

David asked his father if he could take the next day off to go to Kempton races and afterwards to London to see a friend.

'Why not? There'll be a couple of good races. Take the Merc if you want; I shan't be needing it.'

'Are you sure?'

'Of course I am. And why not give Lucy a ring? She's gone back up to London for a couple of days until Mickey's funeral. I'm sure she'll put you up for the night.'

Johnny was driven back into London by David after the last race at Kempton. He was in better spirits. He had sensibly ignored MacClancy's tip and picked a ten-to-one winner of his own. He waited until they were in the car before he expanded on his meeting with the Irishman the evening before.

He told David how he'd sat and talked with the little Irishman for an hour or two. 'I got out of him that he used to work in a convent in Roehampton.'

'Good God! Now you say that, I think I remember him. Quiet little chap. Of course, he was a bit more sprightly then. I can't believe he's been with those nuns all that time. It's quite possible he put two and two together and worked out some fantasy about extracting enough money from me to get away from the convent once and for all.'

'I can tell you one thing,' Johnny said quickly, 'if your crash wasn't an accident, I think it's very unlikely he had anything to do with it. I'd say he hasn't got the nous to organise it. Besides, I had it from him during the course of our conversation that he'd never been to Fontwell. He only goes to courses he can get to easily by train.'

'He could have paid someone else to do it, though,'

David said. 'He'd have known from the papers where I was riding that day.'

'Maybe, but I doubt it very much.'

David glanced away from the road in front of him for a moment and tried to believe that it really had been an accident.

'If he didn't do it, someone had to.'

'But for God's sake,' Johnny said impatiently. 'Even the police think it was an accident.'

'They still haven't traced the lorry, though.'

'That doesn't mean it was deliberate, does it? These things do happen.'

'There's nothing I'd like more than to think that,' David said. 'But I can't. It'd be too much of a co-incidence.'

'When you go and see MacClancy, you'll see what I mean. But what the hell are you going to say to him?'

'I'll tell him that if I have so much as a sniff of a threat, I'm going straight to the police. I don't reckon he'll bother to work out how unlikely that is.'

David dropped Johnny in South Kensington and, with the help of an *A–Z*, found his way to Lucy's mews house in Chelsea.

It was exactly the sort of place he had imagined: primrose-yellow with a lovingly tended display of autumn flowers in the window-boxes. Inside it was light and bright with pictures, hanging tapestries and kilim rugs. David felt at home as soon as he walked in. Lucy treated him as if he were a brother who had never been away, without ceremony and with a lack of effort which he knew didn't signify indifference.

In fact, as they had got to know each other again, they had become closer than he and Victoria. It was only Lucy who had noticed the tension between him and Susan Butley; she had recently taken to teasing him about it.

'I think our Susan secretly fancies you, Davy, though she seems to be keeping her feelings at bay by being as hostile as possible.'

They were sitting over a bottle of Chablis that Lucy had found in her fridge. David sank back in the beige hessian-covered sofa, enjoying being her brother.

'D'you think so? I just thought she resented my coming back to Barford for some reason.'

'Yes, she does. I don't know why, either. She still fancies you though. You'd better be careful; she's very determined. That's how she ended up working for Dad. She knew he needed someone around with a thick skin and a head for figures.'

'Well, I'll do nothing to scare her away.'

Lucy looked at him, speculating. 'Did you have any girlfriends back in Ireland?'

David blushed and, knowing it, blushed harder. 'To tell you the truth, that was one of the things wrong with the place. Thousands of lonely farmers, and no women for them. All the girls get off to Dublin, or England or America, if they can. If it weren't for the television, of course they wouldn't think to go, but there it is...'

'You've set a few hearts fluttering here among the racing groupies, I can tell you. It must be that blushing modesty that does it. Anyway, who's this mysterious person you've come up to see?'

'He's just an old relation of... of Mary's. I promised I'd

look him up. But I'll not be all that long. He lives somewhere in Islington.'

Lucy nodded. David had told them about Mary Daly the day he arrived so unexpectedly at Barford Manor. 'I've got a girlfriend coming round later for dinner. You can have some, too, if you're back in time.'

'Thanks. I'll make sure I am.'

David stood irresolute outside the Convent of the Holy Infant, assailed by ancient memories.

He saw a small group of nuns arrive and go in; although they had abandoned the white wimples and black habits of twenty years before, there was a serene goodness about them that reminded him sharply of how sorry they would have been if they had known what he was up to.

Looking across the road at the painted sign of the Virgin Mary dandling the Baby Jesus on her knee, David didn't want to go in. But he had to see MacClancy.

He took a deep breath and crossed the busy road. When he reached the tall, neo-gothic front door of the convent, he pulled a worn brass handle and heard the clanging of an old bell, incongruous against the traffic noise of the street.

The door was opened by a small nun of fifty in a plain, knee-length grey dress. She smiled. 'Hello?'

'Hello, Sister,' David said. 'I wanted to see Emmot MacClancy.'

The nun scrutinised him more closely. She had certainly recognised the Irishness in his voice. 'I think I know you,' she said. 'Were you at Roehampton?'

This feat of recognition shocked David. Certainly, he

had absolutely no recollection of this particular nun. He nodded slowly.

'Well, come in then.' The nun opened the door wider to admit him. 'Emmot always said you'd gone to Ireland with Mary, but try as we might, we never found out. How is she?'

'I'm afraid she's not well.'

'I'm so sorry to hear that. Is it serious?'

David nodded. 'It is. I'm afraid she has multiple sclerosis.'

'Lord bless her, the poor woman. We'll pray for her. When you've seen Emmot, you must come and see the other sisters. They'll want to hear all about it.'

She led him along a musty corridor, past a number of large closed doors, to a smaller door at the back of the ground floor. From the other side of it came the sound of a television. The nun knocked. After a moment, it was opened by Emmot MacClancy. He was dressed only in a vest and a pair of ancient flannel trousers, and stood for a moment, blinking with disbelief at David.

'Look who's come to see you,' the little nun announced cheerily.

David attempted a smile. 'Hello, Emmot.'

'My God! What do you want?'

'Can I come in?'

MacClancy hesitated, unsure whether or not he should be frightened by David's visit. Eventually, he stepped back with a nod, and David walked into his hot, stuffy bed-sitter. David turned to the nun. 'I'll come and find you before I go, Sister.'

The nun smiled and went on her way. MacClancy closed the door nervously.

'Why have you come here? Did you know who I was when I saw you at Newbury?'

David didn't answer.

'I'm sorry,' MacClancy went on. 'I didn't mean no harm. I was a bit down on me luck that day, and you looked like a gift from heaven.'

'Was it worth an innocent young lad dying?' David asked quietly.

MacClancy's eyes opened wide with horror. 'What are you talking about?'

As he spoke, David tried desperately to detect signs of subterfuge in the man's manner. 'The lad who was killed when I was driving home from Fontwell on Monday.'

'I read about that. It was a terrible thing. They said it was an accident.'

'I know they said it was an accident. But you know it wasn't, don't you?'

MacClancy sat down with a thump on his iron-framed bed to show his indignation at the idea that he might be implicated. 'What in God's name are you saying?'

David looked at him. This would be his only real chance to assess from MacClancy's reactions if he was involved or not. There was a guilty shiftiness about the man's manner, but David had no way of telling if this was due to his half-hearted attempt to blackmail him at Newbury, or a full-blooded attempt to murder him on the M27. He was going to have to press harder.

He stared at MacClancy with hard, uncompromising eyes. 'You know damn well what I'm talking about. The thing was set up while I was riding. That sleeper didn't drop out of the sky by accident. Either you did it or you paid someone else to do it.'

'I don't know what you're talking about, I swear by Almighty God. I've never been to Fontwell. It's too far for me. I've no car and I don't drive. I've told you, I'm sorry about what I said to you at Newbury. I was only trying, like. I'll cause you no more trouble, I promise.'

David wanted to take MacClancy at his word; it would have been far more comfortable to believe that the crash was the accident everyone else seemed to think it was. He sighed. 'I hope to hell I don't have to come and see you again.'

He wanted to leave the convent without seeing anyone else, but the nun who had let him in appeared from the shadows before he reached the front door.

'Are you going so soon?' she asked.

'I'm sorry, Sister, I have to.'

'What did you want with old Emmot?'

'It was nothing,' David said, then a thought occurred to him. 'But tell me something, how does he get around? He says he's no car or driving licence?'

'He hasn't. He always takes the train. One of his brothers is a track-layer for British Rail. Whenever Emmot wants to go anywhere, I'm afraid to say he borrows his pass so he can go for nothing.'

'And where does he go?'

'Just to the races. It's his only real interest now,' she added defensively, 'so we turn a little blind eye to it.'

Driving back across London, David tried to persuade himself that unless the Hampshire police came up with anything that proved otherwise, MacClancy wasn't involved. But he knew that his mission to extract a clear-cut confession or denial from him had failed.

He arrived back at Lucy's house in time for dinner, and tried temporarily to put the crisis out of his mind.

The sight of the girl leaning back on Lucy's sofa helped. She had, David thought extravagantly, the legs and eyes of a Greek goddess. She was in her twenties and looked better than a model in a fashion plate in one of the glossies.

Lucy watched David as she introduced them. 'Emma, this is my brother, David. Emma works for *Harper's*.'

A few months before, David would have had no idea what *Harper's* was. They certainly didn't stock it in the paper shop in Louisburgh. But since he'd arrived at Great Barford, he'd been a quick learner.

He still wasn't prepared for girls like Emma, though. Beneath her exquisitely presented exterior he sensed there lurked a kind of anarchic hedonism which alarmed and excited him. At first, David assumed they wouldn't have much in common, but she seemed fascinated by the idea of an heir to a large English country estate taking more than fifteen years out on an Irish small-holding.

David found himself describing the farm and the Mayo hills where he had spent the greater part of his life with a lyricism that made him wonder why he had been prepared to leave it behind.

Emma was delighted by him and encouraged him. He guessed, though, that hers was a professional, journalistic interest. He had no way of knowing what a refreshing contrast he was to the smug, self-centred men with whom she spent most of her time in fashionable London.

Over the small round table, while they ate a simple but skilfully prepared meal of *moules,* monkfish and more Chablis, it became clear that Emma had more than a passing academic interest in David. Sitting next to her, he felt her bare foot on his leg and her hand on his thigh at the slightest excuse.

It was only with great self-control and an instinct that it would yield the best long-term results that he restricted his response to mild flirtation and a light glancing kiss on the cheek when she left.

As the door closed behind Emma, Lucy grinned. 'You've had it now,' she said. 'She's an absolute sucker for a brush-off.'

'She'd no brush-off from me,' David protested.

'She did, by the standards she's used to. It'll take a lot to turn her off now.'

David shrugged. 'Well, I'm never in London, am I? And I didn't have the impression she was much of a country girl.'

'We'll see,' Lucy laughed. 'Anyway, it was great to see you in action; you're obviously not half such an innocent as you pretend.'

'I don't pretend anything,' David said emphatically. 'What you see is what you get.'

'I've been meaning to talk to you about that. What I see is OK, but it could do with a bit of polishing. The Val Doonican cable-knit and cords are a bit homespun, don't you think? Would you like me to take you shopping tomorrow? And to a proper hairdresser?'

David laughed. 'I didn't think you cared.'

'Of course I do. It's not that I don't love having a brother again, but I wouldn't mind one who looked a tad less as if he'd just finished a gig with the Dubliners. And while we're at it, I could mark your card, as they say, on a few other English habits you seem to have forgotten.'

'You wouldn't want me to confuse my own identity, would you?' David asked.

'No more than it is already.'

'Earth to earth...'

The vicar's sober words of burial were plucked up and scattered by the blustering wet wind that drove across the graveyard outside St Kenelm's Church in Barford. And the wind, whining through the ancient yews, drowned the sound of Mickey's parents' sobbing at the graveside.

David stood on the edge of the small crowd huddled around the trench in the damp earth, and he mourned the young man's death with the rest of the village.

Sir Mark stood closer to the grave, sombre and silent with his daughters, leaning down when invited to drop a trowelful of reddish soil on to the coffin lid.

Afterwards, in the village hall, David drank tea among the murmuring villagers, feeling the eyes that were on him, aware that loyalty to the son of the big house was being severely tested. Across the hall, he saw Susan Butley looking at him and talking to Mickey's tearful mother.

Lucy found him. 'Don't look so guilty. No one's blaming you.'

'Aren't they? Most of them are looking at me as if I were a saboteur at the hunt ball.'

'It's natural enough to want to blame somebody, but they'll get over it.'

Driving back with the rest of the family, David was aware just how much it mattered to him that the people in the village should get over it, now that he was once more considered a part of the place and committed to it.

By the time they reached the gates of the park, though, Sir Mark and Victoria were discussing horses again. David was to ride a novice chaser at Newton Abbot the following day. The horse was keen, green and wilful; it wasn't going to be an easy race. Lucy and Jason were in the car too and, for their different reasons, didn't join in. David's own contribution was less than half-hearted. He had found that Mickey's funeral had forced him to review in sharp focus everything that had happened since he had arrived in Devon two months before.

Chapter Three

England: early September

It had been on a bright, late summer Sunday that David had set off from his home in Mayo to fly from Dublin to Bristol. He hadn't told the family he was coming. After fifteen years without a single communication, it was hard to know how best to make the initial contact. However it was done, it was going to come as a shock. There was bound to be some doubt that it was really him.

For the last few weeks, David had tried to guess what their reaction would be. Would there be resentment? Indifference, maybe? Sometime in the next twenty-four hours, he would find out.

Now that he had embarked on the journey, animated as he was at the prospect of seeing the family and Barford, his courage began to ebb. Like a nervous diver making his way to the top board, he was torn between a fear of what might lie ahead and the knowledge that there was still time to turn back.

But he knew he couldn't back out; there was too much to lose.

He tried to read during the short flight, but found

himself looking blankly at the pages of his paper as he fingered the small blemish on his neck. A stewardess offered him a drink. He asked for a Coke. He wasn't much of a drinker and, from now on, he'd want his wits about him.

The Aer Lingus plane landed at Bristol Airport just after midday. David hired a small car and set off south on the M5. An hour and a half later he was driving through the late afternoon sunshine between the brown rolling bulk of Exmoor and the craggy cliffs of north Somerset.

When he reached the steep hill that dropped down into Lynmouth, he pulled into the side of the road and stopped. This was the point of no return.

For five minutes he gazed down at the small port, recognising landmarks, wondering what had changed. He asked himself why he was doing this and then whether he had any right to be doing it. And he thought of Mary Daly and the never-ending struggle to survive amidst the craggy beauty of the Mayo hills.

He took a deep breath and made a sign of the cross. He started the car and moved off down the hill once more.

He had already booked a room for the night at the Anchor. The young woman who came from the back of the hotel to deal with him gave no sign of realising the momentousness of what he was doing. He grinned at her and relaxed. The real test wouldn't be until the next day.

He took his bags up to the small room he'd been allocated, and lay on the bed for a while. He reviewed the past few weeks of his life, the decisions and plans he'd made and the extraordinary activity which made arriving here now seem like a long-delayed case of *déjà vu.*

Feeling fit and suddenly confident that he could handle whatever happened over the days to come, he swung his legs off the bed, changed into a pair of jeans, and went downstairs to let himself out into the street. The town was quietly busy with strolling tourists and locals. David drew deep breaths of fresh, salty air and set off on a quick tour to find out what had changed in the past fifteen years.

Down near the front, he went into a paper shop to buy himself a packet of small cigars to help deflect the slight nausea he was feeling. As he walked in, a tall, dark, striking girl, a few years younger than himself, was coming out.

She glanced at him as she passed, then stopped for an abrupt moment to take a second, closer look. David nodded with a friendly smile which acknowledged her without admitting acquaintance. If he should have known her, it was perfectly excusable not to recognise her after at least fifteen years. He carried on towards the counter and asked for his cigars. When he turned to leave, the girl had gone.

The encounter gave him a sharp stab of excitement. He was sure she thought she knew him, even though she couldn't have been more than nine or ten at the time of his disappearance.

In an hour's walk around the town, he twice more saw people half recognise him; even though this had been predictable, his confidence grew. His temporary anonymity gave him a strange sense of power. Evidently, even after all this time, his face fitted. That was going to make it a great deal easier to deal with the family the next day.

He went back to the hotel and ate a steak and salad in the dining-room before walking through to the bar. There were under a dozen people there, none of whom showed more than a passing curiosity about him.

At a table in the far corner, two girls sat huddled in private conversation, one with her back to him. It was only when she stood and came over to fetch two more drinks that he recognised the girl he'd seen earlier leaving the tobacconist's. He looked at her with interest and a slight quickening of his pulse. Her build was a cross between a dancer's and an athlete's; she had long legs and neat, well-moulded breasts. Her gleaming dark hair was well-cut and cared for, and there was an impressive forthrightness to her manner.

She didn't notice him at first; he was sitting at a small table in a corner. As she waited for her drinks, she glanced across. She smiled at him this time, with a curious excitement in her eyes. The barmaid put the drinks on the bar, but the girl ignored them and walked over to him.

'Hello. Are you who I think you are?'

David smiled back. She really was a tremendous-looking girl, he thought; certainly as beautiful as any he had ever met. His eyes sparkled. 'That would depend, wouldn't it,' he said, 'on who you think I am.'

The look of certainty on the girl's face faltered. 'I ... I'm not sure now. You sound Irish,' she added doubtfully. 'Are you?'

'In a manner of speaking.'

'I'm sorry. I thought you were someone else, then;

someone completely different, from round here, but I haven't seen him for years.'

'Well, I'm sorry too. I'd like to have known you. Would you ever let me get you and your friend that drink, to make up for the disappointment?'

'Thanks very much,' the girl said in a soft Devon accent. Whoever he was, she thought, this man had lovely eyes and a nice wicked smile. 'Do you want to join us?' she ventured.

'Only if I'm not muscling in on some vital private discussion.'

'You won't be,' the girl laughed. 'I've been Marje Proops long enough for one evening.'

David carried his glass of stout to the corner table from which the other girl had been watching with interest, smiled at her and settled down for a chat.

The second girl had few of the obvious physical attractions of her friend, but she had a friendly, appreciative face. David's life in Ireland had scarcely brought him into contact with English girls, and his knowledge of them now was based on all the usual clichés. He was surprised and pleased by the response he seemed to be getting from these two.

They asked him what he was doing in Devon.

David, not wanting to lose this limbo period of anonymity, adopted a deliberate vagueness. 'Bit of horse business.'

'Are you in racing then?' the first girl asked with obvious interest.

David stretched a point, and nodded. He told them some of the more outrageous stories about his point-to-pointing in the west of Ireland, knowing that this aspect of his previous existence would probably soon be common knowledge around here, and the girls would learn who he was soon enough.

During their conversation, he gathered that the good-looking girl was called Susan, and her friend was Wendy. But he managed to avoid offering any clues to his own identity.

With a firm resolve not to let on the real reason he was in Devon – at least until after he had seen his family – David bought two more rounds of drinks while they talked and laughed, until Wendy announced it was time for her to go. 'But you stay, Sue,' she said. 'I'll be all right.' She had seen the clear signals of a strong rapport growing between her glamorous friend and the dramatically good-looking Irishman; she didn't want to be accused next day of deliberate gooseberrying.

Susan didn't protest. When Wendy had gone, she insisted on buying two more drinks.

An hour later, looking into her strong, black-coffee eyes, David found himself reluctantly pulling back from the brink. Unless he wanted to get himself into tricky explanations before he'd even arrived officially, he'd have to wait a few days, until everyone knew that David Tredington was back. Then he would have plenty of time to follow up this very promising relationship.

'Well,' he said reluctantly, 'I've to be up early tomorrow to be about my business. Maybe I'll see you around?'

'How long are you staying, then?'

'Who knows,' he answered enigmatically. 'If all the women round here look like you, I could be here for ever.'

The girl wasn't sure how to take this, but she smiled encouragingly. 'Well, if you're in the horse business, you ought to come up to where I work, at Barford Manor. They've got a big stud up there and they keep a lot of horses in training.'

David abruptly looked down and fiddled with his empty glass to hide his reaction. When he looked up, he managed a reckless grin. 'Well, there's a thought,' he said as he got to his feet. 'Now, can I take you home?'

'No, it's OK. I only live down the road, with my mum,' she added meaningfully and with a hint of regret.

Next morning, Monday, soon after ten, David parked his hired Ford Escort on a large circle of gravel in front of the handsome weathered stone bulk of Barford Manor. For a moment, before he climbed out of the car, he gazed at the place. Even though he could recall every nook and corner, he couldn't calm the convulsions in his guts.

He walked self-consciously, not with his usual easy stride, towards the great oak front door. Before he reached it, he stopped and stared at it. If he was going to change his mind, he had to do it now. If he didn't want to disrupt the lives of the people inside, and change the whole course of his own life, he would have to turn back before he rang the bell.

In the stillness, he heard a thrush fluting loudly in the bushes by the side of the house. He took a deep breath and stepped up to tug the worn, wrought-iron bell-pull.

A few moments later, the door was opened by Susan.

'Hello again,' David grinned. 'I didn't know you were the butler here.'

She laughed. 'You're not slow to get off the mark,' she said.

'I knew about this place. It was on my list. Meeting you just pushed it to the top.'

'Have you ever met any of the Tredingtons?' she asked in a voice which hinted at some uncomfortable doubt.

'As a matter of fact, I have,' David answered.

Susan opened the door wider to let him into the cool mustiness of the main hall. 'Did you want to see Sir Mark, then?'

'If that's possible,' David nodded.

'He's in,' she said, more guarded now. 'But you really need an appointment if it's stud business.'

'Would you mind asking him for me, though? And, er ... just tell him it's some Irish chap, OK?'

She looked at him, half wanting to return his smile to let him know she hadn't forgotten how well they'd got on the evening before, but already suspecting that he hadn't been entirely honest with her.

'I'll go and see if he's free,' she said.

She left him standing where he was and walked to a door at the back of the hall which she opened and closed behind her.

As David prepared to meet his father, he looked around, recognising the statues, the hangings, and the huge painting of his great-grandfather's Derby winner which adorned one wall.

The girl reappeared. 'Sir Mark says he'll see you,' she said with undisguised curiosity and suspicion.

David shrugged an apology for whatever he had done to sour her view of him, and walked towards the study door. He tried to quell his nervousness, and unconsciously wiped his sweaty palms on his trousers.

He knocked.

'Yes. Come in.' The instruction was issued in the crisp tone of a man used to giving orders.

David pushed the door open and stepped into the high-ceilinged, panelled room. One large window gave on to a fine westward view of the park. In front of it was a large desk and chair. Besides these there were a couple of big armchairs, a large, low table covered in sporting magazines, and a television.

The man sitting at the desk had his head down, reading some papers in a folder. 'Won't be a moment,' he said without looking up.

David didn't speak.

Receiving no reply, Sir Mark Tredington raised his eyes from what he was reading sooner than he would otherwise have done.

Looking at David was a man in his mid-sixties, whose face, once handsome, had faded, but still displayed features unmistakably the same as the younger man opposite him. His eyes, dimmer than they had once been, were honest but cautious beneath a thick crop of silver hair.

David remained silent. He took a couple of paces towards the desk.

Sir Mark was gazing at him, astonished and bewildered. He glanced back down at his papers in confusion, as if to clear his head, before he looked up again.

'Good Lord!' he whispered. 'David?'

David smiled, but he didn't speak.

Sir Mark stood up and walked around his desk towards David. 'David? David?' He came closer, glanced at David's neck and, motionless for a moment, faced him a few feet away. 'David! Good God! I can't believe it!'

He stood, almost rigid with shock and an apparent reluctance to believe, in case he was wrong.

'Hello, Father,' David said at last. He smiled with affection, and apology.

The man in front of him, up until that moment utterly self-possessed in his display of emotion, abruptly stepped forward and put both his arms around David, hugging him to himself while his chest heaved with the release of over fifteen years' pent-up feeling.

It was a full minute before he stepped back, unashamedly sniffing away his tears and wiping his eyes with the heel of his hand.

He smiled and shrugged. 'Forgive me; it's been a long time. I can hardly take it in.' He stepped forward and hugged David again.

This time David returned his embrace.

'I'm sorry. I should never have gone,' he said quietly, surprised at his own emotion. 'But somehow, the longer I was away, the harder it was to come back and face what I'd done.'

The older man moved away, looking at David proudly, taking in his son's handsome face, sturdy physique and black curly hair. He shook his head slowly, as if he still couldn't believe what was happening. 'Some time – not now,' he said, 'you must tell me why you went. All that matters for the moment is that you're back.' Sir Mark was gazing with unbounded affection at his only son. 'And, by God, you look very well, fit as a fiddle.' He laughed with a touch of hysteria. 'And you sound like an out-and-out Paddy. You've been living in Ireland?'

David nodded. 'I have.'

'What have you been doing there?'

'Messing around with horses mostly,' David grinned. 'Nothing very grand; didn't have the money for it, but I won a few modest point-to-points.'

'Did you, by God? You mean my son turns out to be an Irish jockey!' He chuckled. 'Could have been a lot worse.'

He stopped suddenly, and the laughter died on his lips as if he was suddenly overcome with the enormity of what had happened. He shook his head. 'God, this is going to take some getting used to. And we must be sensible about it.' David had the impression he was talking to himself, had suddenly realised that he should hold himself back, at least until he'd checked everything out.

But David had no doubt that all Sir Mark's instincts were to believe that his son had come home.

'I understand,' David said. 'I'd understand if you asked me to turn around and walk straight out, and I wouldn't blame you.'

Sir Mark looked startled, even at the thought. 'David, my dear David, there's absolutely no question of that. We all realised how bloody miserable you were at the time you left; I just hadn't appreciated how much you were missing your mother. In fact, I thought you'd got over it pretty well, but when we got your note...' He shrugged. 'I felt terrible about not talking to you as much as I should; I was away far too much of the time. I made sure the same thing didn't happen with your sisters, I can tell you.' He stopped abruptly as another thought occurred to him. He blew a breath through his teeth. 'I wonder how Lucy and Victoria are going to take this.'

So did David.

David thought that Victoria, the younger and less sophisticated of the two sisters, would welcome him back without reservation. Lucy, less trusting, would want him to be real, but wouldn't lose sight of other possibilities.

Sir Mark was making up his mind how to handle the extraordinary news. 'Look,' he said, embarrassed by the possibility of a negative reaction from the rest of the family and, more importantly, George, 'why not have a drink?' He waved at a table of bottles and glasses by the window. 'I think I'll get the girls and let them make up their own minds.' He had, it seemed, opted for the same tactic as David.

He left the room. David considered his father's offer of a drink. He went through the motions and poured himself a tiny measure of whisky which he drowned with soda.

While he waited, gazing at the landscaped grounds which dropped away from the window, David examined his conscience. The sense of guilt that had regularly plagued him since first he had decided to come to Great Barford was, for the moment, neutralised by the undoubted happiness he seemed to have provided so far.

He heard voices and footsteps approaching the study.

He had his back to them when the girls came into the room.

He turned slowly. He met two pairs of eyes and watched their mild curiosity turn to astonishment.

The plumper, darker of the two – David recognised Victoria – quickly showed signs of an ecstatic realisation of what had happened.

Hesitating at first, she took a few quick paces towards him, then stopped, unsure of how she should greet a brother she hadn't seen – guiltily assumed gone for good – for so many years. She glanced at her father. 'It is David, isn't it?'

Sir Mark said nothing, made no gesture. He wanted the girls to make up their own minds.

Victoria ran the last few paces that separated her from her brother and flung her arms around him. David's conscience was momentarily troubled by the strength of her affection; at the same time, this sense of belonging was an elixir to him.

After a while Victoria released him and stood back to look at him, shaking her head in wonderment. Behind her, Lucy stood staring in disbelief. Her brother was dead; she had been sure of it. And yet here he was, less than ten feet from her.

She glanced at his neck – looking for confirmation – searching for some sign of the discoloured blemish that had once been there. The sight of it threw her into confusion. It really was him.

David looked back at her with a rueful half-smile.

'Hello, Lucy. Here, I've got something for you.' David felt inside the pocket of his jacket and pulled out a small cardboard box which he handed to her.

Lucy took it suspiciously and opened it. Nestling in some tissue paper was a blue-green egg, a little smaller than a bantam hen's.

Lucy stared at it for a moment, then slowly a smile spread across her face. 'My guillemot's egg!' she laughed. 'You took your time.'

'Better late than never,' David grinned.

'What on earth are you talking about?' Sir Mark asked.

Lucy turned to him. 'The day Davy disappeared, he said he was going up to the cliffs. I asked him to see if he could get me a guillemot's egg for my collection. I've never forgotten; it was the last thing I ever said to him. And now he turns up with it fifteen years later. I hope you've got a good excuse,' she said to David with mock severity.

Sir Mark laughed. 'Don't start squabbling. I'm sure David'll tell us what happened when he's ready to.'

'I will, of course I will. God knows I owe you that. I'd almost rather get it off my chest right away.'

'Let's go into the kitchen and make some coffee,' Lucy suggested. 'Mrs Rogers isn't going to believe this.'

But Mrs Rogers had already been told by Susan Butley.

David met her disbelieving stare. 'Hello, Beryl,' he said to the stout middle-aged woman who had been nanny, then housekeeper at Barford for twenty-five years. 'You've lost a bit of weight. Have you still got that apron I gave you?'

Tears seeped into the corner of the housekeeper's eyes as she shot a reproachful glance at Susan Butley.

'Davy! It *is* you. Of course it is! I'd have known you even after all this time. And you're looking so well. Wherever you've been, they've been feeding you all right.'

'Not too much, mind,' David grinned. 'I can still do ten seven.'

As they talked, Lucy had filled a tall cafetière. 'Right,'

she said, 'come on, then. Sit down and tell us what happened.'

They drew up chairs around the lumbering elm table in the centre of the big bright kitchen; all except Susan Butley who stayed where she was, leaning against the Aga.

They sat silently, waiting for David to start. He took a mouthful from the cup Lucy had poured for him and shook his head.

'You've no idea what it feels like to be back here. Nothing seems to have changed, though I'm sure this kitchen used to be green.'

'It was,' Sir Mark nodded, 'but we gave it a face-lift a few years ago.'

'It all seems like I was another person then. I don't know what I was going through. I missed Mum, terribly, but it wasn't just that. I think it was when I realised that I was going to have to take this place over, the thought of it sort of terrified me; so much seemed to be expected of me. I don't know why. And you were away all the time.' He looked without accusation at his father. 'Anyway, I sort of felt I wanted to make my own life, away from memories of Mum. I took all the birthday money I'd saved over the years and went to look for Danny.'

'Danny Collins? The old groom?' Sir Mark asked.

David nodded and laughed. 'I used to love old Danny. I'd talk with him for hours, and I was sad when he went. I knew he'd gone to live somewhere near Dublin, but I didn't know exactly where. I had the address of his sister in London, so I found my way to Roehampton where she'd been living with some nuns. But she'd gone and no one knew where. Of course, the nuns wondered what on earth I was doing. I wouldn't tell them, so they pressed me to stay. They were very kind to me and I stopped there a month or so. I thought about coming back again, but I was quite enjoying not being me any more. I knew a lot of people round here didn't like me all that much; I think I must have been a terrible little prig then...

'Anyway, I made up my mind to go to Ireland to look for Danny. I knew the trains for Fishguard went from Paddington, so I walked all the way there, but there wasn't a train until the next day. I found out which would be the first to leave in the morning, and sneaked into an empty carriage and slept in it till dawn. No one caught me though and I got to the ferry all right. They didn't seem too worried when I got my ticket. I told them I was being met at the other end. But there was one woman on the boat who guessed something was up. Mary Daly, she was called. She was very kind, bought me some lunch, asked me what I was doing, and I told her. I needed to tell someone. In a way, I suppose I half hoped she'd send me back, but she didn't. She said she was going through Dublin and she'd help me look for Danny Collins – and she did.'

'But you never found him, I presume, or he would have told us,' Sir Mark said. 'Anyway, though he had a daughter in Dublin, he retired to somewhere down near Killarney, where he came from.'

'No, you're right. We didn't find him, but Mary Daly was on her way to Mayo; her uncle had left her a farm there. When we couldn't find any trace of Danny, she asked me if I wanted to go back to England. I wasn't sure, but I told her I didn't, and she said would I like to come and stay with her for a while. She told me it was very beautiful and there'd be lots of horses.'

David shrugged. 'I guess it avoided facing up to what I'd done. When I got there, I thought it was heaven – a bit like here, though the mountains are higher, and the coast more rugged, and all the lakes . . . I fell in love with the place, fell in with the rhythm of it, I guess. I helped Mary with the farm and she'd no trouble persuading me to stay. She sent me to the school in Louisburgh and told everyone I was her son. They'd no reason not to believe her; she'd not been there since she was a young girl herself, and none of them knew what she'd been doing in England.'

David's eyes became thoughtful as he looked back to those years. Lucy poured him another cup of coffee before he went on. 'I was quite content, quite happy; I was one of them. But, I suppose, underneath, I knew I wasn't. I began to feel a terrible guilt, as if I'd duped these people – not Mary, of course, but I began more and more to feel as if I was there under false pretences. But then again, I got on well enough with everybody and I was enjoying the horses.

'After I left school, I worked on the farm, but I found time to bring on a few poor-bred animals we had about the place, started to ride them in the local races, even caught the eye of one or two Englishmen that strayed to them, but I made damn sure to avoid them, especially when Mary got ill. She urged me to come back here, but I couldn't just leave her after all she'd done for me.'

They were all looking at him intently, needing to know what had finally persuaded him to come back now.

David knew he must break it gently.

'Poor old Mary's been told she has to go into hospital, or find a way of being cared for at home.' David shrugged. 'With the way the farming is over there, it's not much more than subsistence now. We got by while the subsidies were on, but there was no way we could afford what she needed. My only hope was to use the skills I'd learned with the horses. So, I've come to England to see if I can make my way here – riding, maybe, or training, whatever. I knew that I'd have to come and see you all first, though.'

'You mean, you haven't come back to stay?' Victoria said.

'No,' David said firmly, 'I've no right. I turned my back on you all of my own free will. There's no way I expect to be taken back. I wanted no more than to see you again, and to let you know I was alive and in England before you found out some other way. I knew my face would give me away soon enough otherwise.'

The father and the two sisters stared at him. His Tredington features were unmistakable now. Victoria looked like a child who had been offered a wonderful new toy only to have it snatched away from under her nose.

Sir Mark looked worried, and Lucy puzzled.

'What on earth was the point of coming back, if you're not going to stay?' she demanded. 'This is your home.'

David shook his head. 'It was once, of course, but now my home's in Mayo.'

'I understand that, of course,' Sir Mark said, 'after what you've told us; but there's no reason why you shouldn't look on this as home too.'

'It's not possible. I'm a stranger here. Of course, it

would be great to come and visit now and again, once I'm on my feet. But I plan to go to Lambourn or Newmarket. I've a couple of strings to pull there.'

'But what are you known as in Ireland?' Sir Mark asked.

'Aidan. Aidan Daly. It was Mary who suggested it – though you've got to understand, she never put any pressure on me.'

Sir Mark looked hard at him. 'Aidan Daly? An Irish jockey, for heaven's sake! Well, from now on, you can go back to being David Tredington.'

'Oh no. I forfeited all claims to being David Tredington when I left. Aidan Daly I've been for the last fifteen years, and Aidan Daly I stay.'

David spent the rest of the warm, early autumn day at Barford Manor. Sir Mark walked round the grounds with him, pointing out landmarks and changes that had taken place since David had left. As they walked, he tentatively tried to persuade him to stay, but David was adamant.

Sir Mark didn't refer again to David's plans to keep his adoptive name and identity. Nor, when David saw them later, did the girls. But they begged him to stay for dinner. The talk was all reminiscing about events in David's childhood – some remembered, most forgotten. He made no excuses for his forgetfulness; the family understood that the act of running away had been a watershed in his life, and what had gone before had become in his consciousness a misty period of pre-existence.

Quite early, before his father and sisters were ready

to let him go, David insisted that he was going back to his room at the Anchor. He drove off in his small hired car with the family's exhortations to collect his things and move back into the house the next day.

David had little sleep that night. He was regretting already that he wouldn't see Great Barford again for some time. But he knew he had made the right decision, and he was going to stick with it.

At six, giving up any hope of more sleep, he got out of bed, dressed, and let himself out into the empty streets to walk down to the harbour and organise his thoughts. Shortly after half-past seven, he arrived back at the hotel, planning to have some breakfast. He found Susan Butley waiting for him outside.

Chapter Four

'Hello, Susan. What a lovely sight on a beautiful morning,' David said, stopping outside the front door of the hotel.

'Hello ... David.' She stood, long legs apart, hands on hips, barring his entrance. 'I want to talk to you.' She nodded her head to suggest that they walk up the street, away from the comings and goings in the hotel entrance.

David gave a puzzled shrug and started to stroll with her along the narrow pavement.

'You're a crafty devil, aren't you?' Susan said with disdain. 'Playing hard to get with them.' All trace of their intimacy of Sunday evening had vanished.

David looked at her in amazement. 'What's come over you? What are you talking about? You heard what I said yesterday. I'm going to make my own way. I realise what I did to them by going when I did. I expect nothing from them, but I had to come back to put the record straight. It would have been cruel to let them find out by themselves.'

'Put the record crooked more like, you mean. I just wanted to warn you: they may believe you, but I don't; and you won't get away with it if I can help it. That family's been very good to me, and I'm not going to see them taken for a ride by some Irish con-man.'

David shook his head with a disarming smile. 'Look, I knew some people would find it hard to take my coming back, but I don't see how it makes any difference to you. OK, I'm sorry I didn't tell you everything when I saw you on Sunday evening, but I couldn't, could I – not till I'd seen my father. But you already knew who I was; you as good as said so in the bar.'

Susan looked back at him doubtfully. 'I admit, I did think you were David for a few minutes, but now I know I was wrong,' she said.

'I'm sorry you feel like that, especially after we were getting on so well the other night.' The corner of his mouth twitched into a mischievous smile. 'I thought we were to be friends. But then, I'm not staying around here, so I guess it's not the end of the world.'

'You can't fool me. There's one thing I know for certain about you: you'll be back.'

Annoyed by her stubbornness, David abandoned his attempt to charm her. 'If I do come back, it'll only be when there is not a shadow of a doubt about who I am. Do you think I didn't realise people would be sceptical? Do you think my father would accept me back without being utterly certain? Frankly, that's one of the reasons I'm not staying; I don't want to be the focus of everyone's gossip and speculation while there's still any question of who I am. So, when I next see you, you won't have anything to worry about, and maybe we can carry on where we left off.' He gave the girl a dazzling smile.

She shook her head. 'I don't think so,' she said, but

with enough doubt in her voice to leave David confident that the relationship which had started so well could yet be salvaged.

He watched her walk away, wishing he hadn't had to lie to her when they'd first met. He guessed it was the very fact that he was David Tredington – and not the Irish jockey he'd introduced himself as – that had so radically altered her attitude towards him.

When David didn't reappear at Barford Manor that morning, Sir Mark Tredington telephoned the Anchor. The Irishman had checked out at half-past eight, they told him.

The post arrived a little later. There was a letter for Sir Mark from a firm of Australian lawyers. Anxiously, with a slight trembling of his hands, he tore open the envelope. He quickly read down the two pages and relief flooded through him.

He had instructed the firm to check the identity of a young man, named as David Tredington, who was reported to have been a member of the crew of *White Fin*, a small yacht which had gone missing off Norfolk Island over a month before.

They could tell him no more than the fact that a man of approximately the right age had booked into a hotel in Sydney a few days before *White Fin* had set sail, and that his name appeared on the harbour register as a member of the crew.

But they could get no further back than that. They had found no record of his entry into Australia, nor of a previous address or domicile. It was possible that this man was their client's son, but they had exhausted every avenue trying to prove it and could offer no serious hope. They would keep their files open; in the meantime, they enclosed their account to date.

Sir Mark rang the senior partner at his London solicitors' and told them to expect him the following morning.

At about the time Sir Mark was telephoning his lawyers, David was booking into a small hotel in East Garston, three miles east of Lambourn, in the name of Aidan Daly.

Making no mention of his connection with Sir Mark Tredington, he set off in search of the one trainer who had advertised in the *Sporting Life*, offering employment with the chance of rides to the right applicant.

Ian Bradshaw was a young trainer in his third season. David knew a little about him from what he had read in the Irish racing papers. The horses he saw while he was waiting to see the trainer didn't inspire him. Neither did the scruffy, unscrubbed yard. Still, he couldn't afford to be choosy.

Neither could Ian Bradshaw. He came out of his house in a hurry, wearing dirty brown jodhpurs with broken zips where they met his filthy boots. He was a wiry individual with a sour look about him.

'You the lad who's come for the job?' He spoke quickly, eyeing David up and down as he carried on walking.

'Yes, sir.'

'Well, you look as though you can ride. Start tomorrow.'

David wanted to ask about the chance of rides, but before he could speak, a horse had been brought out and the trainer had disappeared from the yard.

David shook his head in disbelief. A lad walking across the yard saw, and grinned in sympathy.

'Ah, well,' David said to him. 'I suppose I have to start somewhere.'

By lunchtime, David had returned his hired car to a depot in Newbury and moved his bags into the run-down cottage where he had been billeted with half a dozen other lads.

Three days later, he sent a postcard to his father, letting him know that he was working in Lambourn and giving the address of the hotel where he had stayed the first night.

The following evening there was a telephone call for him at the cottage.

'Hello, David. I got your card.' Sir Mark didn't disguise the hurt he was feeling.

'I thought I should at least let you know what I was doing this time,' David said apologetically.

'I'm at the hotel where you stayed. The chap here told me you'd gone to work for Bradshaw. Look, let's talk. Let's have dinner, at least, and if you insist on following a career in racing, let me see if I can't get you in somewhere with rather better credentials.'

'There's no need for that. I know what I'm doing, Dad. I told you, I've no claims on your goodwill.'

'For God's sake, David, have a heart. I'm your father. I've forgiven you the hurt you caused us all. Why prolong it?'

'Because your forgiveness doesn't purge my guilt, I

suppose,' David said, reflecting the style of the old priest in Louisburgh.

'Well, it damn well should. Come on, old chap. At least let me buy you dinner and discuss the matter sensibly.'

'OK,' David said, giving in willingly. 'I could do with a decent meal. I think we get worse fed than the horses here, and that's saying something.'

They arranged to meet at seven-thirty in the hotel at East Garston. David changed into a clean pair of cords and shirt and scrounged a lift in another lad's battered old Capri.

Sir Mark was waiting for him in the bar, sitting at a table, flicking through the pages of the evening paper. He greeted David with no less warmth than when he had said goodbye four days before.

'You don't look as though you've been doing too badly on a lad's diet,' he said. 'What'll you have to drink?'

David asked for a glass of stout and the two men went to sit in a corner where they wouldn't be overheard.

'I'd far rather you came back to Barford,' Sir Mark sighed, after David had briefly described the slipshod manner in which Bradshaw ran his yard.

'How can I? I told you, I made my choice when I was twelve years old, and it's not fair to go back on it now.'

'But that's absurd,' Sir Mark said testily. 'You were young; you were obviously emotionally disturbed. I have to take some of the blame, going away so much after your mother died, leaving you to the grooms and Beryl Rogers. I should have been there for you and I wasn't. I was too busy pandering to my own grief.'

'The other thing is,' David went on as if he hadn't heard, 'I want to be sure I'll be happy back here in England. Whether you like it or not, I'm Irish at heart now – a simple Catholic, west coast boy.'

'Simple you are not, that's very evident, and I've no objection to your being Catholic, if that's what you want. The point is, you belong at Barford.'

'Are you sure about that?' David searched into the old man's eyes.

Sir Mark looked embarrassed, circling the top of his glass with his finger. He sucked a deep breath through his nostrils. 'I went to see my solicitors in London on Tuesday. Their preliminary investigations bear out everything you've told me.' He shuffled awkwardly in his chair. 'Not that I had any doubts that you were David, but for legal purposes, and to quell any rumours that might get about...'

'I understand,' David said. 'To tell you the truth, I was amazed you all accepted me so easily – well, all except Susan, and maybe Lucy. I mean, I thought there was bound to be some resentment, even doubts. But I've told you, I've not come to make any claims. That's why I've got to make my own way, earn my own living. As far as I'm concerned, you owe me nothing.'

'Fair enough. I realise that. That's why I've come to offer you a job. I haven't seen you ride yet, but I don't doubt you know what you're doing, and I need a stud manager.' He raised a hand to pre-empt David's protests. 'No special treatment. You'll get the going rate for the job and the cottage that goes with it – no more. For heaven's sake, that's got to be preferable to living in some scruffy lads' hostel.'

David couldn't keep a grin off his face. All other considerations of his current position apart, the prospect of running a stud like the Great Barford was in itself an overwhelming temptation.

'That's a hell of an offer,' he admitted.

Sir Mark beamed. 'And don't worry about the girls. They'll come round soon enough.'

When Sir Mark had told his daughters that he was going to find David and try to persuade him to come back and live at Barford, he had all their support. Lucy decided to stay on down in Devon so that she would be there when her brother returned. The sisters couldn't stop talking about this momentous event in their family: there was no question that it felt like the filling of a void in their lives which they had been unwilling to admit had been there for the fifteen years since David had run away.

When he came back five days after his first appearance at Barford, they helped him settle into the stone cottage, two hundred yards from the house, which had been the stud manager's house since before the war.

Afterwards, the sisters walked back to the manor together.

'What do you think of our prodigal son returned to the fold, then?' Victoria asked.

'At least Dad has had the sense not to kill any fatted calves.'

'I don't think David wanted that at all, anyway: he's very unassuming.'

'Yes,' Lucy said thoughtfully. 'He's changed a hell of a lot – not just physically, of course – but then I suppose we all change a lot between pre-pubescence and adult-hood. I know I was a ghastly arrogant little prig when I was twelve.'

'You still are,' Victoria laughed. 'No, you're not,' she added quickly, to be sure her sister knew she was joking. 'But I know what you mean. He really is a very nice man, now. I'm afraid Jason doesn't think so, though.'

'No, I don't suppose he does.'

'I wish you wouldn't use that tone when you're talking about him.'

'I'm sorry, Vicky, but you know he and I don't really get on.'

'Poor Jason, however much I tell him he's part of the family now, he can't seem to just accept and enjoy it. After all, Dad's been pretty fair with him.'

'Oh, I dare say he'll get over it,' Lucy said, unconvincingly. 'But what has he said about David?'

'When I told him it might mean we won't get Lower Barford, he was furious, said Dad was cheating me and God knows what. It was awful.'

'Poor Vicky. Frankly I couldn't care less about not getting any land; it would just be a lot of hassle.'

'And you're really pleased about having David back?'

They had reached the front steps of the big house. Lucy didn't answer for a moment. 'Yes, I think so.'

'What? Aren't you sure?'

Lucy opened the door and they walked into the hall. 'I suppose I've still got a lingering doubt that it's really him.'

'Don't be ridiculous, Luce. What about the guillemot's egg? Of course it's him. Dad started getting it all checked out right away. He's not in any doubt at all.'

81

'But he wanted his son back very badly.'

'Let's go and talk to him, see if he can convince you.'

Victoria led the way past the library to Sir Mark's study. Their father was sitting at his desk.

'Dad, we wanted a word, now that David's back for good.'

'Come in then. Shut the door. What's the trouble?'

'Lucy's still not sure he's David.'

Sir Mark looked at his elder daughter. 'I can understand that. Believe me, even though all my instincts were to accept him, I didn't want to make a disastrous mistake. Everything he's told me adds up. I've had his story checked in Ireland, and when I took him to London, he made no objections to giving a blood sample.'

'Oh no,' Victoria said, 'you didn't make him go through that, did you?'

Sir Mark raised an eyebrow. 'I had to, to be absolutely sure.'

Victoria turned to her sister. 'There you are, Luce, it really is him.'

Lucy nodded with a smile. 'I suppose so, but it's just such an extraordinary thing to happen. I couldn't help thinking of that chap who came back – when was it? some time in the 1860s – claiming he was Sir Roger Tichbourne, and even his mother believed him. He turned out to be a butcher from Wapping called Arthur Orton.'

Sir Mark smiled. 'Well, don't worry, I don't think David's going to turn out to be a butcher from Wapping.'

A week after he had first turned up at Great Barford, David Tredington was sitting in his small, chintzy sitting-room, on his own for once. It was a quiet, windless evening. He listened to the birds chirruping in the small grove of oaks outside, and thought about the wealth of high-grade bloodstock that he had been invited to oversee. So far, he had only glanced briefly through the stud book, but every pedigree had a top-class horse in it.

He unwrapped one of the small cigars that he liked occasionally, and lit it. As the blue smoke wafted towards the low ceiling, he thought that, even if he never inherited the huge house and estate – which anyway seemed a surreal, distant prospect – he'd be quite happy running the stud and living here for the rest of his life.

Then, with a twinge of guilt, he thought of Mary. It was her condition that had first made him decide to come to Barford. Her illness had prompted his leaving Mayo, and yet he hadn't thought of her all day. He got up from his squeaky armchair and sat down at a small bureau. He found a pad of writing paper and began a long letter to her. He was reaching the end when there was a light knock on the door followed by the sound of it being opened.

'Who is it?'

'It's Victoria. Can I come in?'

'Of course you can.' David got to his feet and walked through to the flagstoned hall to greet his sister.

Victoria, if she thought she had made a mistake by marrying Jason Dolton, was very loyal in not letting it show. But they lived in a cottage only a hundred yards from David's and she was obviously delighted to have her new brother so close at hand.

David saw that she had grown into the kind of woman he had learned to respect. Despite her dumpy looks, she had her attractions. She had a sharp sense of humour and was fond of saying exactly what she thought. David was impressed by her sincerity and gentleness, particularly with the horses. He recognised in her his own fondness for the animals, and this was fast forging a bond between them.

'I was just wondering what you thought about everything down at the stud, now you've had a really good look round.'

'Potentially, I think you must have one of the best studs in England.'

'*We* must have,' Victoria corrected. 'Yes, it could be. It's great to have an extra member of the family to help, especially as you seem to understand so much about breeding.'

Nothing triggered David's enthusiasm more than a discussion about the requirements for producing good race-horses, but there was something he was curious to know.

'Why did the last stud groom leave?'

'Because he never had a feel for horses. He knew pedigree well enough, but he didn't understand about temperament – and that's the most important aspect, don't you think?'

They happily discussed the stud until they got round to the subject of David's racing.

'Dad's been talking about you riding some of the horses in training,' Victoria said.

'Has he? Well, he hasn't talked to me about it yet. After all, he's not even seen me on a horse, and if

I'm to run this stud, I won't have time to be gallivanting around race-courses. To tell you the truth, though, I wouldn't mind a chance to ride some of the horses he has at Sam Hunter's. A couple of them look useful.'

'And he was talking to George, who's bought a horse from Ireland. It's a beautiful gelding, but apparently they can't get him to jump. Letter Lad, he's called. Maybe you should have a look – see if you can tell George what he should be doing.'

'I wonder what he'd think about that, taking advice from me after all these years.'

'I'm sure he wouldn't mind. He's no genius where horses are concerned. He's only decided to train a few because he thinks it's the right thing to do.'

'We'll see. I think, on the whole, it would be better to wait till he asks for my advice before I offer it, don't you? After all, I've not spoken to him for fifteen years. He may not take too well to my bursting on the scene and telling him what to do.'

David spent the next few days getting to know everything he could about the mares, the foals, yearlings and assorted young-stock on the stud. He relished the chance to use all the knowledge he had accumulated over the last dozen years of breeding horses in Ireland. Up in the Mayo hills, he had spent many hours pipe-dreaming as he pored over the stallion books, gazing at photos of animals which he would have given all he had to send his mares to. His knowledge of breeding was as good as that of people in the mainstream of the industry on both sides of the Irish Sea. Now – it seemed almost incredible – he found that he had the opportunity to deal at first hand with a quality of bloodstock which exceeded his most extravagant fantasies.

He quickly learned which mares were in foal to what stallions, when they were due, which colts were off to the sales, and which fillies Sir Mark intended to keep and run. He had fitted quite naturally into the place, and the other four members of the stud staff found no difficulty in accepting him – not just as Sir Mark's son, but also as an able boss in his own right.

David got into the habit of having all his meals in the house. Susan Butley was usually at lunch; even though she was no more friendly than she had been outside the Anchor, she had evidently decided to play down her own scepticism so as not to antagonise the family. But David, frustratingly, was hampered in his campaign to win her over by the physical thrill her presence always seemed to cause him.

Life quickly settled into a pattern. David had been working on the stud for a week. It was early evening, all the horses had been fed and bedded for the night. All but one of the staff had left for the day. Only Mickey Thatcher had stayed on to chat to his new boss.

Mickey was seventeen, in no doubt where his future lay. As soon as his parents would let him leave home, he was going off to become a jockey. And there was nothing he liked more now than to listen to David telling stories of racing in Ireland. He hung on to every word, savoured every snippet of David's experience.

David had already grown really to like Mickey. He

recognised the boy's utter commitment to horses and his own particular charges in the yard. Besides, he admitted to himself, it was gratifying to have such an eager listener.

They were still talking half an hour later when Sir Mark appeared.

'Evening, Mickey. Still here?'

'Yes, sir. Mr David's just telling me a bit about racing in Ireland.'

'You've probably heard more than I have, then. As a matter of fact, David, I thought it was about time we saw you up on a horse. Do you think that Nashwan filly's ready for you?'

'I'd say so,' David nodded.

'Well then, let's see you up on her tomorrow morning.'

Bred by a Derby winner out of a mare who had won a Group Two race, David had never sat on such a precocious youngster. She had only been ridden away three weeks earlier. but she carried him around as if she were an old hand. He worked her round the small indoor school and took her for a gentle canter on the sheep-cropped pastures that separated the stud buildings from the cliff-top.

His father watched him every yard of the way until he had brought the horse back to a walk on the track down to the stableyard.

The baronet greeted David with a broad smile. 'What do you think of her?'

'If confidence counts for anything, she'll be unbeatable.'

'It could be the man on board, of course. I'd say

you've got as fine a pair of hands as your Great-Uncle William.'

'The fella who won the Foxhunters in the twenties?'

'That's right. He was one of the best amateurs of his day. How would you like a few rides in England?'

'So long as it's on something bigger than this, I'd love it.'

Sir Mark nodded, pleased. 'Right. We must get straight on to Portman Square and get you an amateur licence. In the meantime, why not go over to Sam Hunter's and ride out a couple of days a week? I'll tell him you're going to have a few rides in some suitable races.'

David slipped his feet out of the irons and swung himself off the horse's back to lead her into the yard. 'If you don't mind messing up your horses' chances, then I don't,' he grinned.

George Tredington arrived for the weekend a day earlier than usual. Sir Mark had telephoned him to tell him the good news about David's return. He turned up at the manager's cottage on Thursday evening while David was in the bath, scrubbing off the day's accumulation of equine smells. He called up the stairs.

'Hello, David? George here – your cousin George.'

'I'll be right down.' David had been anxious about this first encounter with his cousin, knowing George had expected to inherit. He braced himself as he climbed out of the bath, dried himself down and pulled on some clean clothes.

He came down the stairs with a friendly smile on his

face, and the confidence that already belonging had given him.

'Hello, George. How are you?'

George's bright little eyes, buried in his chubby red cheeks, met David's directly. There was a moment's scrutiny and hesitation before, with a look of relief, a smile broke out on his thick lips.

'My God, David! It really is you! How bloody marvellous!' He held out a sweaty hand in greeting. 'I didn't believe it when your father told me you were back.'

David returned his firm shake. 'It's good to be back,' he said with a nod.

'I hear you're already stuck into the stud. Frankly, it could do with a bit of strong management.'

'It seems like a pretty tight set-up to me.'

'Yes, well, I suppose it's a bit different to Ireland. Your father tells me you're going to ride some of his horses under rules.'

'Maybe. I hope so.'

'I'm training some pointers myself. I've bought a few from Ireland. Or rather Johnny Henderson bought them for me. You remember Johnny?'

'Of course. How is he? What's he doing with horses?'

'He's a bloodstock agent; not a bad one, though he never seems to make any money at it. And he's not always reliable. One of the horses he got for me came from the part of Ireland where you've been living, as a matter of fact; lovely-looking animal, plenty of speed, but won't jump a straw bale.'

'That's the way it goes,' David said sympathetically.

'Come over and take a look some time.'

'Where do you live?'

'Didn't your father tell you? I took over Braycombe when my father died. I'm in London most of the week, scratching a living in corporate finance, but my heart's down here. Of course, the farm doesn't make much – wouldn't make anything at all if it weren't for the dear old CAP. But I've managed to buy myself an interest in a wholesale butcher's and an abattoir; vertical farming you could call it. I'm running the shoot on the estate now, too. I dare say you'll want to take a gun.'

'Maybe, though I've not shot a driven bird for a very long time.'

'You always had a good eye as a boy,' George said.

'It's probably deteriorated since then,' David said modestly. 'Anyway, I'd be glad to come and look at your horses and, of course, if there's anything I can do...'

'That would be marvellous,' George said heartily. 'Right!' he slapped his thigh. 'I must get on. There's a hell of a lot to do and I'm having dinner back up here this evening.'

'See you then, then,' David said blandly.

George beamed a smile and let himself out of the front door. With a palpable easing of tension, David watched him through the window as he walked to a big BMW parked outside the front gate.

For a man who faced having a substantial inheritance lifted from under his nose, George was behaving with admirable civility. David guessed that this was what was called being a gentleman; that he was prepared to accept without rancour this change in his own prospects.

When he was next alone with Victoria, David asked her about George's attitude.

'I suppose he's rather old fashioned, at least in some ways,' she said. 'I'd say he's got such respect for the rules of correct succession that he's quite happy to welcome you back as the natural heir. Besides, he's got quite a bit of money in his own right, and he seems to be making a pile in London.'

On Sunday, David went over to Braycombe, at George's urging, to look at Letter Lad.

Although he didn't tell George, David immediately recognised the horse. A big, powerful chestnut, almost roan, with a black stocking on its off-hind, it was in far better condition now and it was already half fit. Jan Harding, George's groom, had been preparing it to qualify with the Exmoor hounds. She rode it round the paddock to show its paces.

'He looks like a nice horse,' David said. 'And he moves well.'

'Yes, he does, or Johnny wouldn't have bought him. Trouble is, as I said, he won't even think about jumping a fence. I think I'll have to get rid of him.'

'I wouldn't be too hasty. Something could be made of him. He looks an honest sort of a horse. Could I just get on him for a moment?'

'Sure,' George gestured generously, beckoning Jan to bring the horse to the gate where they were standing.

David swung himself over the horse's back and geed it forward. He worked it round the field, trotting, cantering and finishing with a short burst of speed.

He jumped off and handed the reins to Jan.

'He feels the part. I'd persevere with him if I were you. You'd have to go a long way to see a better one.'

George showed David the four other horses which had recently arrived in his yard.

'Johnny Henderson bought all these in Ireland for me,' George said. 'And bloody cheap.'

They all looked capable of winning modest point-to-point races. Johnny Henderson had done a good job for George.

'Point-to-pointing's getting tremendously popular round here,' George went on. 'The cost of keeping a horse in training for National Hunt is so high now. I thought it might be fun to try and make a bit of a mark – and just as much fun as racing under rules for half the cost.'

Half the prize money, too, David thought; and it also depended on your idea of fun.

As George showed him round, David's first impression that his cousin was genuinely glad that the rightful heir had turned up at Great Barford was confirmed. He even deferred to David, as eventual owner, when talking about his plans for the shoot. As David drove away from Braycombe, he should have been grateful that George had accepted him without reservation, but, guiltily, he found himself already thinking of a plan to ease the big roan from George's yard. One thing he was sure of, on the evidence of his own eyes in Ireland, was that the horse had a colossal jump in him.

Since David had arrived at Barford, nearly everyone he had met had accepted him. Old estate workers, the villagers, local land-owners and farmers, the shop-keepers in Lynmouth who had known David the boy, all recognised him as David the man. Susan Butley, Jason Dolton, and possibly Lucy, remained the only people to show any scepticism. He knew what Jason's reasons were; he could understand Lucy's; he wished Susan would tell him hers.

As he settled in, David deliberately kept his own needs modest, settling for the use of one of the older Land Rovers on the farm as his personal conveyance. At the same time, he worked hard and was conscious that he was making a measurable difference to the running of the stud. He was able to send most of what he earned to Mary. He had plans to start making larger sums by buying, bringing on and selling horses on a scale he could not have attempted in Ireland. His father had already agreed that he would help with the modest funding this would need.

A fortnight on, his amateur licence was confirmed and he was booked to ride his first race in England under Jockey Club rules.

Sir Mark was determined to see his son succeed. He had told Sam Hunter, a small but effective trainer in neighbouring Somerset, to find some suitable races for David to ride in. The first was arranged at the end of September, at Wincanton, on a small mare from Hunter's yard.

Sam Hunter put down the telephone in his office wearing as close to a smile as he ever got. Thin, weather-beaten, he was a Devonian through and through. He was tough, honest and independent. He had only moved to Somerset reluctantly, and in the pragmatic hope that it would provide a bigger catchment area for owners.

Perhaps it had, but now, he recognised, he had reached a plateau in his training career beyond which he would never rise. At fifty-two, he had settled into a comfortable routine that produced an average of thirty-five winners a year. The burning ambition to be champion trainer with which he had set out had now cooled to a warm contentment in knowing that, given the right horse, his training skills were a match for anyone's.

He'd gone into racing as soon as he'd left school. His dreams of becoming a top-class jockey, however, had come to a painful end at Newton Abbot. Looking back, the fall had probably saved him a few wasted seasons coming to terms with the fact that his abilities in the saddle would always be limited.

Over the years, he'd watched dozens of youngsters start out with the same ambition. They had come and gone as regularly as the seasons, and always there had been something missing. Some rode well but wouldn't work for their chances. For most, it was the opposite, and all the hard work in the world couldn't produce natural talent.

In eighteen years as a trainer, he'd had only two lads in his yard who could have made it. Both rode well and grafted hard, but they'd missed reaching the very top because they lacked the confidence and the canniness to make an impression with owners; and owners paid the bills. 'No conversation – no rides,' is what Sam had emphasised to every budding jockey who had passed through his care.

Although he had never watched David race-ride, Sam could see that all the essential qualities were there and, of course, he had that Irish charm to go with it. He had found that David was guaranteed to improve whatever horses he put him on at home. They jumped better and worked harder for him. He relaxed the nervous ones and encouraged the moderate. All the man needed was luck and the right opportunities.

Only fate would decide if Lady Luck would turn out for his side, but it was within Sam's power to provide him with the chances.

He had promised Sir Mark that David's first ride in England would be a winner, and he was determined to do everything he could to deliver on that promise.

He had a small, narrow bay mare in his yard called Bideford. She was a shade over sixteen hands, with a big splash of white across her face. When David had first seen her, he hadn't been too impressed, but the moment he had schooled her over fences, he had changed his mind. She rode as if she were a hand higher with a long, easy stride. At the same time, she was as nimble as a pony and loved to jump. She could weigh up her fences and sort out her stride quicker than any other horse he'd ridden.

Bideford had been off the race-course for more than a year, since she got cast in her box and managed to pull a tendon over her near-side hock. Sam had slowly brought her back to fitness. She'd done fourteen weeks of roadwork before setting hoof on a gallop. After another six weeks' cantering, she'd begun working. Two race-course gallops had put her spot-on for her return.

Sam had entered her in a claiming race at a price ten thousand pounds below her value. She'd need to fall twice to get beaten.

* * *

It was a mild day at Wincanton. Big clouds billowed in from the south-west, but the sun shone through and the rain held off. The going at the windy race-course was on the soft side of good, and a big crowd of West-Countrymen turned out to watch large fields in all seven of the day's races.

Despite the hundreds of rides he'd had in Ireland, and even with all the self-assurance the last few weeks had given him, David couldn't calm his nervousness at his first English race. As he walked into the paddock with the other jockeys, he found himself needlessly fiddling with the strap on his helmet and tapping his whip on his boot. David knew, like Sam Hunter and his father, that his mount was running a few grades below her mark. He also knew that he would need a very good excuse not to beat Jason Dolton on a moderate animal from a small local yard.

Sir Mark, Victoria and George had come to support David in his first appearance. David found them with Sam Hunter, standing in a group close to the exit on the far side.

'Where's Lucy?' he smiled as he doffed his cap in the customary manner.

Victoria was standing, legs apart, wearing a brown fur hat and an unflattering overcoat. 'She's busy, but she wishes you the best of luck. Are you nervous?' she went on, twisting the strap of her binoculars tightly round her fingers. 'I am.'

'I'll be fine as soon as I'm in the saddle,' David answered honestly.

The bell rang for the jockeys to get mounted. David

and Sam walked across to Bideford, who was fidgeting, eager to get on.

'She'll stay longer than a tattoo, so make plenty of use of her,' Sam said as the mare's lad legged David on board. 'And good luck.'

The start of the two-mile five-furlong course was just around the bend from the stands, beyond the water jump. David eyed the jump apprehensively. This would be the first time he had jumped water in a race. In Ireland, they'd been banned as a result of the number of horses who had injured their backs jumping them.

Bideford was clearly excited by the prospect of racing again. Cantering across the middle of the course to the start, it was all David could do to stop her running away. When they had reached the start and were waiting to have their girths checked, she refused to walk quietly with the others. She jig-jogged and shook her head, rattling the rings of the bit. Sweat began to drip from her neck. David wished he'd worn gloves, but it was too late for that now.

Eventually, the starter called them in. Almost before he had released the tape, Bideford had set off for the first fence as if the devil were after her. David knew better than to fight her. He just kept a firm hold of the reins and sat as still as a mouse.

But her speed increased. If she failed to take off for some reason, David guessed his next ride would be in an ambulance. Almost subconsciously, he began counting the strides to the fence as they galloped towards it like an express train. With two full strides still to cover, Bideford did little more than bend her tiny knees and propelled herself towards the top of the fence. It was an action that frightened her almost as much as David. She was travelling so fast, she lost her footing as she landed, her nose banged into the turf and, for an instant, David thought he might be pulled over her head.

In the stands, Victoria gasped and fiercely grabbed her father's arm. She relaxed her hold a little as Bideford managed to find another leg from somewhere and galloped on, ears pricked, towards the next.

The shock of almost falling brought Bideford back to her senses. The fizz disappeared and she settled into her normal stride. David could barely hear her feet touching the grass as she bounded up to the next. This time she measured it perfectly. David gave her a pat on the neck but she was enjoying herself too much to notice. She galloped on, eating up the ground, springing over the fences as they came, leaving the other runners trailing in her wake.

The water jump came and went without incident. David let her get in close and she made nothing of it.

Hard as the others tried, they couldn't get within ten lengths of her, until, as they turned for home and all but two had given up, David felt the mare begin to tire. Her long stride shortened and her honest head began to bob wearily. She was like a car running out of petrol. David sat still and let her freewheel for a dozen strides, giving her time to suck some oxygen into her lungs. It was all downhill to the finish, which would help, but she couldn't freewheel for ever. The moment he felt her recover, David began to squeeze and push, holding the reins firmly to help her balance. With a gasp of relief, he felt her respond. Her stride didn't lengthen but it became stronger. She pinged the second last fence, but

David could sense another horse beginning to close on his outside. There was less than a furlong to run and one fence to jump when a grey head appeared at David's left leg. Bideford had seen it before he had. He felt her strain every sinew. She just didn't want to be passed, but her short legs were weary and her body was burning with exhaustion. David helped her all he could, galvanising her, urging her not to give up.

As they raced down to the last fence, the crowd were on their feet, roaring encouragement. What had started off looking like a formality had now turned into a fierce battle. It was all or nothing.

David drove the mare hard at the final obstacle, as if it weren't there. With one final effort, she put every last part of her energy into a leap that landed her a length clear of her rival. And there she stayed, until the winning post rushed by in a blur.

Lucy Tredington's decision to steal into David's cottage had taken all her courage. Snooping through somebody else's belongings, even her brother's, was completely alien to her nature. In some ways, the fact that it was David's cottage only made the act more reprehensible. But it was something she had to do; she had to be certain he was really the brother he claimed to be.

Using the spare keys from the manor, Lucy nervously let herself in through the back door. Her heart was racing as she stepped lightly across the stone floor, through the narrow hallway and up the staircase to a landing which led to two small bedrooms. Both doors were ajar. Hesitantly, she pushed the first, which creaked as it swung open.

Lucy leaped back at the sound. She waited a moment, scolding herself for being so jumpy, and then summoned the courage to walk into what was obviously David's room.

The bed was made, but his jodhpurs were lying in a heap beside an upright chair. Lucy wavered again before she began her search, then, resolved now, she started to feel inside every pocket and lining. She turned over mattresses and delved into every place where something could conceivably be hidden.

After an hour of scouring the cottage from top to bottom, all she had found of interest, in a small bureau in the sitting-room, was a neatly written list of the rides David had taken in Ireland – far more than she had realised. She also found a note-book containing a list of horses with prices beside them, presumably those at which he'd bought and sold. He appeared never to have lost any money, but then again, he hadn't made much either. Lucy was just putting the book back into the drawer of the desk where she'd found it when the phone rang.

The sudden break in the silence startled her, she'd been so engrossed in her task. She sat rigid while, after four rings, the answerphone cut in and began to rewind itself to play back a single message. The disembodied voice of a woman with an Irish accent wished David luck in his first English race. Lucy glanced at her watch. It was five to three. David would already be on his way down to the start at Wincanton. How could he be calling his home to pick up his messages?

Lucy was still puzzling over the mystery as she walked quickly back to the manor.

* * *

David's heart was pumping like a boxer's punch-bag as Bideford crossed the finishing line with two lengths to spare.

It was as if the win finally confirmed his identity. He was cheered into the winners' enclosure by a crowd who appreciated the significance of an amateur newcomer beating a dozen professionals, albeit on an obviously underrated horse.

Among the people waiting in the bar to celebrate his first win was Johnny Henderson.

Sir Mark introduced them.

'David, I'm sure you remember my godson, Johnny Henderson?'

David nodded. 'Of course I do. How are you?'

Johnny shook his head in disbelief. 'My God, David, of course I'd heard you were back, but somehow I couldn't really believe it. But there was nothing make-believe about that finish.'

David was impressed with Johnny's performance. David and he had been friends as children, and there was no reason why they shouldn't be again. The difficulty was going to be not letting it show just how well they knew each other now.

Beforehand, they had agreed not to talk too much to each other on this first meeting. But there seemed no harm in letting it be seen that they were going to get on.

After half an hour or so, when the party had settled down and another race had been watched, David was on the stand between Johnny and Sir Mark.

'George tells me you bought most of the horses he's going to send pointing this season,' he said to Johnny.

'All five of them, and all bloody cheap. Well, except one. They all ought to win a race somewhere. With any luck that'll confirm his taste for the game.'

'He asked me over to look at them a couple of weeks ago. He's not happy about the expensive one – Letter Lad – won't jump, he says.' David gave a hint of a smile.

'Just needs a bit of schooling, I should think,' Johnny said.

'That's what I reckoned. I tell you what, if he wants to sell him for what he gave, he'd be worth getting. If I could borrow the money to buy him, I think I could do something with him.'

Henderson grinned, also unable to resist the irony.

'Sure. I'll see what I can do. Maybe George will let the horse go for what he cost plus his expenses so far.'

Over the next few weeks, David rode in several races, chalking up a respectable number of wins and attracting some attention from the racing press. He took it all in his stride, working hard at the stud and enjoying every moment of his new life. When his father asked him if he'd like to ride Deep Mischief at the end of October in its warm-up race in preparation for the Hennessy, he was pleased and flattered, even though privately he didn't think he merited the ride. When Sir Mark hinted that he might even have the ride in the big race itself, he could barely contain his excitement. If the horse performed in the Hennessy, its next target would be the Cheltenham Gold Cup.

But he thought often of Ireland, and knew that soon he would have to set about seeing what he could do to ease Mary's circumstances. Knowing how the next relapse would hit her, he had tried to persuade her to undergo a five-day course of methylprednisolone injections to hold back the deterioration of her spinal cord, but Mary was adamant that she wouldn't go into hospital. At least, for the time being, her condition had got no worse, as she told him in their weekly phone-calls.

At the beginning of October, his father asked him to go to Newmarket, where they had two colts entered in Tattersall's yearling sale. To his surprise, he found that Susan was coming with him as groom.

'She loves going to the sales,' Sir Mark said. 'I hope you don't mind.'

David didn't mind at all, but he was surprised Susan wanted to make the journey, given her continued hostility towards him.

David volunteered to drive the lorry, so that he and Susan would be alone together for the six hours it took to get from Devon to Suffolk. At least it would give him a chance to find out what it was that still made Susan distrust him.

The two yearlings were due to be sold in Tuesday's morning session. That meant getting them to the sales complex for Sunday, in order to give prospective buyers time to view them.

Susan and David, with the help of one of the stud grooms, loaded the box first thing after breakfast on Sunday and set off east for Newmarket. Susan behaved in her usual businesslike manner and with apparent indifference towards David. It was only after they had passed Bristol that he noticed a change in her attitude. She had become polite, even friendly, but she spoke to him as if they had only just met. David wondered what had altered her disposition.

They had been travelling and talking for another hour or so before he realised. She had been so subtle about it that he hadn't noticed until then that she was quizzing him, sometimes in minute detail, about his knowledge of Barford and Tredington family history.

And it became clear from another slight shift in her manner that he was doing a lot better than she'd expected.

David smiled to himself. He wasn't seriously annoyed by her persistent scepticism, especially as it was now generally known that Sir Mark had had professional confirmation of his identity, but he still wondered what caused it. To amuse himself, he decided to pre-empt some of her questions.

'How's your father, by the way?' he asked after a short lull in the conversation as he turned on to the M25.

Susan gave him a quick look and didn't answer at once.

'I hardly ever see him,' she said eventually.

'I was sorry to find he'd gone. I used to really like old Ivor. He taught me how to ride.'

'And he told my mum you weren't much good,' Susan countered quickly.

David laughed at the ambivalence of her answer which seemed to create a temporary truce between them. But however hard he tried to recapture the buzz there had been between them the first time they'd met, Susan's aloofness persisted.

David found that he and Susan had hardly any time alone together once they'd arrived. There seemed to be a lot of people at the sales keen to look at the two lots Great Barford were offering. This kept Susan busy, while David was besieged by stallion owners eager to strike up a friendship with him in the hope of selling a nomination or two. Each of them was ready to reduce the fee for the chance of getting a good class mare on the books. David listened to them all politely, but he wouldn't let the prospect of cut-price deals blur his own views on breeding.

Although Newmarket, the sales, and the whole razzmatazz of the bloodstock sales were new to him, David didn't feel out of place. Back in Ireland, he'd been reading reports of the sales for years. But it was with a mixture of relief and anxiety that he watched their first colt enter the ring. He knew that each yearling had only one chance to sell well. If any mishap prevented it from keeping its allotted sale time, its value would be drastically reduced; buyers were always wary of any excuses for withdrawal, however valid.

As Susan led the young horse round the ring, David made a mental note never to allow her to do it again; she was much too attractive. He could tell from their faces that a lot of the bidders crowding the entrance and along the ringside were discussing her, not the yearling.

The sum which the auctioneer chanted increased slowly. Unconsciously, David tensed up. He knew that the colt had to make fifty thousand pounds simply to cover the cost of the stallion fee, its own keep and the depreciation of its dam. But the bids were coming sparsely now. It looked as though the colt was going to be knocked down for half its cost when an agent with close links to one of the large Japanese owners stepped in. The auctioneer quickly stepped up the bids to five thousand guineas a call as he sensed that the new bidder was there to buy.

It took less than two minutes for the price to soar to a hundred and twenty thousand guineas, at which point the underbidder – that most important but most neglected ingredient of any sale – called enough. The hammer fell, and Susan led the yearling away to embark on a career which might or might not prove that the new owner had bought wisely.

Although he'd had little to do with the preparation of the yearlings, David was elated by the sale. As manager of the stud, even as the owner's son, it was his responsibility to make sure that it ran at a profit. Their next lot could now sell only moderately and the kitty would still look healthy; though this animal was more of a race-horse in David's opinion. An hour later, his view was confirmed as their second offering topped the sale at three hundred and sixty thousand guineas. The bidder was the rich widow of a shipping magnate who had recently won a Classic with a grey colt with similar markings to the one she'd just bought. David made his way round the side of the ring to her seat beside the auctioneer. He shook her hand. 'Best of luck with him, and let's hope lightning strikes twice for you.'

She acknowledged his good wishes with an appreciative smile; David beamed back and went on his way to organise the smooth transfer of the young horses.

First he checked that both yearlings had passed the mandatory test for defects in their breathing, then he found the people who would now be responsible for their welfare and gave them a brief summary of the colts' characters. This done, he made his way to the stables and gave the horses a carrot each. He'd known them less than two months, but it felt like saying goodbye to a child.

Susan had tears in her eyes as they loaded their tack on to the lorry. The formalities were completed, and David climbed up into the cab to drive them back to Devon.

Susan didn't take long to recover. 'Congratulations,' she said sarcastically. 'Your first sale's been quite a success.'

'Come on, Susan. You know that I know I've been back far too short a time to have made any contribution to those yearlings.'

'I didn't mean that,' she said. 'I meant in convincing everyone in racing that you're David Tredington.'

David didn't rise. He glanced at her with a grin. 'Do you know, Susan, I've come to the conclusion that you're a bit of a snob. Just because I've the manners and the accent of a Mayo farmer, you think it's impossible for me to be a Tredington.'

Susan didn't reply.

'That's it, isn't it?' David said triumphantly. 'I've finally hit the nail on the head, haven't I? Well, I'll tell you one thing, I'm not going to suddenly change just to fit in with your idea of how an English land-owner should behave. If I was more like George, would that suit you better?'

Susan grinned, despite herself. 'No, it bloody wouldn't,' she said. But she wouldn't expand and, despite his encouragement, she wouldn't talk about anything but horses and the stud for the rest of the journey back to Devon.

After the conversation he and David had had at Wincanton, Johnny Henderson had been quick to get to work on George, persuading him to part with Letter Lad, though not, unfortunately, for 'a penny less than a monkey profit'.

David knew the gelding's arrival at Great Barford might create tension between him and George, but he was prepared for that. At the same time, there was considerable satisfaction to be earned in discovering why a horse which in Ireland he'd seen jump an iron gate as if it wasn't there, now found difficulty in getting from one side of a straw bale to the other.

The morning after Letter Lad arrived at Barford, David got to work on him. He started by popping him over a couple of cavalettis no more than a foot high. As he had suspected, there was no point in going on. The horse was obviously in pain each time it landed. It had only attempted the small jumps out of natural bravery. Its front feet barely left the ground before David felt it snatch them down again.

He took Letter Lad back to his stable and fetched a pair of metal calipers with flat ends. The horse had been jumping out to the right, favouring his off-fore to land on. David picked up his near-fore and held it between his legs with his back to the horse's shoulder. He began squeezing the wall and sole of the foot. He worked his way round, pressing gently, fairly sure of what he would find.

About an inch back from the point of the frog, he scraped away some dead sole with his finger and picked up the calipers again.

He had barely begun to ease them together when Letter Lad leapt backwards, snatching his foot from between David's legs and snorting with pain. He stood trembling, with his nostrils flared, looking fearfully at David and ready to run for his life.

Slowly, quietly, David held out a hand. 'Come on, old son. I didn't mean to hurt you.'

Letter Lad gave a sharp snort but, warily, allowed David to stroke his muzzle. After a couple of minutes of soft talking, the trust between them began to return. With a few gentle words of encouragement, David left the horse and went off in search of a blacksmith's paring knife and a small bucket of warm, disinfected water.

He also found Victoria and brought her back to the stable. She held Letter Lad's head while David picked up his near-fore again.

The semi-circular end of the wooden-handled knife was designed for cutting narrow grooves in horses' feet, as well as for trimming in preparation for a new shoe.

Being as careful as he could, David began to cut away the sole of Letter Lad's foot. The corn he had identified might have been festering slowly for some time, building up pressure like a bruise beneath a fingernail. The height of the shoe had given the corn some protection and it had taken time to come to a head. As David cut closer to the bottom of Letter Lad's sole, the big roan became anxious to get his foot away. David squeezed his knees tighter together to prevent the horse from snatching his hoof back. He could see a small vein of light-coloured flesh begin to appear. He gave one last short cut, and a fountain of blood burst out over the straw.

Victoria gasped softly. The relief of seeing an end to the pain was as welcome to her as it was to the horse. 'No wonder he didn't want to jump.'

David shoved the paring knife in his pocket and reached for the bucket. He began to swab the opening he'd made. 'I'm surprised he even *tried* to jump with this. I guess he must have trodden on a sharp stone or a nail or something soon after he arrived at George's. I'll put a poultice on it for a day, then get the blacksmith to put a leather pad across his foot to protect it for a while. He's got a really thin sole; if we're not careful he'll get a corn every week.'

When Letter Lad had had the pad on for five days, he began to regain his confidence. A couple of days later, he was jumping the way David knew he could, and loving every moment of it.

The following Sunday, George discovered where his horse had gone.

He found David in the tack-room. 'Is that Letter Lad two boxes down?'

David laughed. 'Sure. I thought you'd recognise him.'

George's red face showed signs of growing curiosity. 'How's he jumping?'

'Getting better. I was just thinking of selling him on,' David said, 'when I found a corn in his foot. He's jumping like a salmon in spring now his confidence is back.'

'Why didn't you tell me you were buying him?'

David grinned. 'Come on, George. If you'd known I was after it, you'd have asked double the price.'

With an effort, George forced himself to take it with good grace. 'Ah, well,' he said, 'I suppose all's fair in love and racing. I was rather pleased with myself for getting rid of him at a profit.'

David raised his eyebrows. 'You must have bought him damn well,' he conciliated.

'I gave Johnny a pretty precise brief,' George answered, pleased with himself. 'Still, I do think he might have told me who was buying it,' he added peevishly.

Once a week, David telephoned Mary Daly. She gave no signs of impatience at his absence, receiving the news of his progress and successes with audible pride. She assured him that she was able to cope for the moment with the bad spells when they came. There were two neighbours always ready to come and help when she needed them.

Johnny Henderson had once said of a fiancée who had gone away for six months, 'Absence makes a fond heart wander, and that's what mine did.' David hadn't found that his heart had wandered so much as his memory of Mayo and Mary. It troubled his conscience. He could forgive himself for losing his love of Ireland, but not Mary; she had been everything to him for so long.

It was six weeks after his first ride in England that David rode Deep Mischief in his pre-Hennessy run at Newbury.

'Whatever happens, I don't want this horse to have a hard race.' Sam Hunter's instructions to David as he stood with him in the paddock had an unusually stern edge to them. In the week leading up to the race, there had been a niggling doubt in his mind that the horse hadn't done enough work for his first run of the season.

Sam had considered missing the race altogether and going straight to the Hennessy, but Deep Mischief badly needed experience. He had only run five times over fences, and never in top-class company. It would be unfair to throw him into the deep end when he had barely learned to swim. What Sam did not want was the horse to come back exhausted, unable to recover in time for his main objective. Deep Mischief was an honest individual and always gave everything; Sam knew that if David didn't take care, he would run himself into the ground.

David knew it wasn't going to be easy to carry out Sam's instructions. Deep Mischief was always enthusiastic about everything he did. Whatever was asked of him, he did willingly, with ears pricked and a wish to please.

There were nine runners for the two-and-a-half-mile chase. The distance was on the short side for Deep Mischief. Under normal circumstances, David would have set him off in front, but there was a pair of other jockeys anxious to make the running. David didn't want to get into a battle in the early stages of the race. As they settled down and got under way, he deliberately primed the breach and let his horse tag along at the back.

The leaders set a modest gallop until they passed the stands and jumped the second fence down the far side. At this point the tempo suddenly increased, and Deep

Mischief was caught a little short of speed. Sam's instructions were still fresh in David's ears: he sat as still as a mouse while the horse tried to adjust to the change of pace in his own time.

Shortly after they reached the next, David found himself more than a dozen lengths adrift and going nowhere. Deep Mischief had misinterpreted David's lack of movement and, quite out of character, had begun to sulk at not being part of the action. Intuitively, David sensed the animal's mood, shortened his reins, and started to push.

It took another five fences to persuade Deep Mischief to start trying again. Slowly but surely, though, he pegged back some of the ground he'd given away, as his long, steady stride began to find its rhythm. He flew the downhill fence and hugged the rail tightly, his ears flat back as he raced on into the straight.

Three fences from home, David felt Deep Mischief increase his effort as he drew encouragement by passing another runner.

A couple more horses began to fade, enabling Deep Mischief to overtake. Despite this, it was obvious to David as the horse put in an enormous leap at the second last that victory was out of the question. He was making ground all the time, but the leaders were gone beyond recall.

When he had let Deep Mischief run on for another half-furlong to make sure he'd done enough work, David took a tight hold of his head, before they got so close that they would be involved in the race for the minor placings.

Deep Mischief passed the post in sixth place, twenty

lengths behind the winner. David grinned to himself. With this race under his belt, and the extra distance, he had no doubt that, provided all went well, Deep Mischief would have a great chance in the Hennessy. Sam Hunter and his father would be more than happy with his performance.

Later, when David had changed and was walking towards the members', he had been drawn up short by a voice behind him.

'Aidan!'

He had turned involuntarily, but not particularly perturbed. He had made no secret of his previous Irish existence.

He was caught in the gaze of the damp, melancholy blue eyes of a small man in a long, grimy raincoat. David guessed the man was in his late fifties, nicotine-grey hair, balding slightly, with a patch of missed stubble beneath his left nostril. David had recognised the type, but not the man.

'Hello?'

'Hello, my friend. Could we have a little talk?'

The man spoke with a Mayo accent. David nodded. 'I'm on my way to meet someone in the bar.'

'It'll not take long.'

David shrugged as the small man came alongside him, matching his stride. 'We should get out of the crowd where we won't be heard.'

'Look, what do you want?' David tried from natural politeness not to let his impatience show.

The man caught hold of his arm and gripped it with unexpected strength. 'My name's Emmot MacClancy.

I'm from Mayo, too, and I used to know Mary Daly when she was in London.' He charged the words with heavy significance.

Mary had always assured David that there was no one from those times who would be aware of her flight to Ireland and change of name. He believed her, but this man's words had his nerves tingling. He looked at him bemused.

'I don't know what you're talking about.'

'Oh yes you do.' He held up a battered hand. 'Don't deny it. But don't worry; I'll not tell a soul where they've to look to find out the truth, provided you show your appreciation of my discretion.'

David stared at him with amazement. 'I think you've got your wires crossed. It's someone else you're thinking of.' David was determined to go, to leave this confrontation before it developed but, before he could, he was assailed by a stare of such bleak, self-pitying resentment that he was almost hypnotised by it.

'My wires aren't crossed at all, and if you turn away now, I promise, you'll regret it. I know as well as you do, you're no more David Tredington than I am. And if you go on denying it, I won't answer for what will happen.'

Summoning up all his will-power, David spun abruptly on his heels and walked back towards the entrance to the members' enclosure. His heart was thumping as he cursed himself for his inadequate performance. The success of the last few weeks had almost made him forget his vulnerability; even Susan Butley had shown no signs of renewing her attack.

Now, this one assault from a watery-eyed, scruffy music-hall Irishman had rudely jerked him back to

where he had been five weeks before he had arrived in
Devon, to a time when he had never even heard of
Barford Manor.

Chapter Five

Ireland: August

The winds of fortune often blow when they're least expected, arriving to surprise, and scatter plans into the air. To Johnny Henderson their coming was sudden, but not unexpected. He had been sitting at a rusty black table outside Brady's Bar in Westport, County Mayo. The sleeves of a red and white striped shirt, once crisp, were rumpled up to his elbows. The creases he had pressed on to his fawn cotton trousers had long since disappeared, and his brown brogues were coated with dust. From beneath the rim of a high-crowned Panama, he surveyed the passing townspeople, tourists and visiting farmers with easy detachment and well-disguised frustration.

Johnny had been in Ireland for two weeks, flogging his weary old BMW along hot empty roads in the full discomfort of a rare Hibernian heat-wave. He had driven over a thousand miles, and had got nowhere.

He had orders – at least vague verbal instructions – to look for a dozen or so jumpers with potential as yet unrecognised by their breeders. He had never met an Irish breeder who had not recognised the potential of their horses, however slight or, indeed, non-existent it might have been. He didn't hold out much hope of ever finding one, but he was prepared to be as adventurous as he was eager to do some deals.

This was one of the reasons he had come to the midwest of Ireland, well off the beaten path normally travelled by English buyers of bloodstock. The breeders here, generally less exposed to those opportunities, he hoped, might be a little less complacent in their attitude towards a genuine buyer.

He had decided to sink his last few hundred pounds into a trawl round Ireland for cheap horses for the meaner or more impecunious of his clients. He would be lucky to make a thousand quid a horse, if he ever found anything suitable.

Looking at the farmers in Westport, in town to buy or sell or just to meet their friends and drink, he wondered if any of them harboured some sturdy youngstock in their wind-blown barns; some talented Pegasus looking for a real challenge across the Irish Sea. Surely some of them did.

As he mused and fantasised, ordering another Jameson's to help, his eye was caught by a man – a farmer, by the look of his clothes and the scarred muddy pick-up which had brought him to town. But it wasn't the man's occupation or the possibility that he might have an undervalued colt in his paddock that fired Johnny's excitement. It was the man's un-Irish, uncanny resemblance to the Tredington family of Barford in the English county of Devon that almost stopped his breathing for a moment or two.

Not too tall, with the same straight, dun-coloured

hair and grey eyes, this individual, now strolling across the street towards him, also had the same square chin, straight nose and well-proportioned face which had characterised Tredingtons for the last four or five generations. Other, not immediately specifiable features would have allowed him to step straight into a Tredington family photograph with no questions asked.

Johnny's heart thumped; his right hand, still grasping his glass, twitched and sloshed whiskey on to the table as he realised what he was looking at.

The farmer was only a few yards from him now.

'Good morning!' Johnny called. 'How are you?'

The man faltered a step, looking to see where this greeting had come from. He didn't identify Johnny at first, assuming, from the tone in which he'd been hailed, that it had come from someone he would recognise.

'Good morning,' Johnny said again, determined not to let this man by without accosting him.

The man glanced at Johnny and saw the friendly, knowing smile on the Englishman's face.

'Good mornin' to you,' he said, with habitual Irish affability and an accent that could not have been confused with a Tredington's.

Johnny looked surprised. 'Good Lord! You're not David Tredington, are you? I'm sorry, but you're an absolute dead ringer for him. I do believe you could have fooled his own mother. You must let me buy you a drink.'

A drink was just what Aidan Daly wanted in this un-accustomed heat. He wasn't in a hurry – nothing happened in a hurry on the thin-soiled, rocky farm which he worked under the shadow of Croagh Patrick. 'Sure,' he said, pulling out a chair opposite Johnny, 'I'll admit, I am a little dehydrated.'

Surprisingly, the exuberant, self-assured Englishman and the unassuming Irishman turned out to have a lot in common, led by their shared interest in bloodstock.

Johnny told Aidan why he was in Ireland.

Aidan, without much hope of interesting this obviously well-connected bloodstock dealer, did admit that there was quite a decent colt, going on four, still growing, though not what you might call classily bred, gobbling up a lot of his best hay at home, where there was scarcely a blade of grass to be seen in the fields.

'Sounds nice,' Johnny said, 'but probably too expensive for me. Fact of the matter is, I operate in the rather lower echelons of the business. Pointers for punters without a pot to piss in is really my line. Do you think you could help me there at all?'

Aidan heard this and recognised that he might well be able to help this sympathetic Englishman, and at the same time make a bit of money without taking too much advantage of him.

The Dalys' farm was not a profitable enterprise, even with the subsidies that still dribbled down from Brussels. Aidan's mother had told him only a few weeks ago that the hospital had confirmed that she was approaching the advanced stages of multiple sclerosis. Soon, Mary had lamented, she would be presented with the options of going more or less permanently into hospital, or somehow finding the money for a full-time, live-in carer at home, so that Aidan would still be free to run the farm.

As things stood at the moment, there was no prospect of finding that money. Perhaps, Aidan thought with excitement, if he could build up a relationship with this Johnny Henderson, he could supply a steady stream of horses to what he had always heard was an endless queue of aspiring English owners. He also had no doubt that Johnny was being falsely modest about his own importance in the market. It was obvious that a man like that would know all the right people.

'As it happens, John, I might. I've ridden a fair number of races out here – just little point-to-points, like – and I'd know where most of the horses are coming from and which could perform if they were ridden well. Some of them wouldn't be what you'd call extortionate prices.'

From the moment he had set eyes on Aidan, Johnny's interest in horse-dealing had taken a distant second place to a scheme of far greater importance.

For the time being, though, he knew that it would suit him to wear his bloodstock agent's hat.

'Aidan, that would be fantastic. To tell the truth I was beginning to despair of finding anything suitable. But with your local knowledge, I think we could get a hell of a deal going between us.' He grasped Aidan's hand across the table. 'I know what, why don't we start with what you've got at home, and then take a look at any others you know of – as soon as you can manage it?'

'Sure. But to get them at the right money, we'll have to employ what you might call a little subterfuge,' replied Aidan, warming to the idea. 'They'll have to think they're selling to me and you're just a friend along for the crack.'

'Of course,' Johnny agreed. 'Then we'll go halves on the profit I make back in England.'

'England's a long way for me. I'll be happy just to earn a couple of hundred a horse.'

Johnny laughed. 'You think a bird in the hand's worth a whole flock in the English bush? You needn't worry. I'm an honest man, but I'm also a businessman, so I'll be more than happy to go along with your terms.'

They had more drinks, until it was too late for Aidan to do what he had come into Westport to do; he had to get back home to his sick mother, he said, who was waiting for him. They arranged that Johnny would drive out to the farm next morning, and Aidan walked a little unsteadily back to his pick-up.

Johnny had observed that his own head was more accustomed than Aidan's to alcohol in warm weather and, still relatively sober, he set about his researches before Aidan was more than a mile along the road west towards Louisburgh.

In a bar where the clientele was notoriously committed to horse-racing, he made enquiries about Aidan Daly.

Aidan, he discovered, even in this backwood, was considered something of a backwoodsman by the few men who claimed to know anything about him.

'There's a man that should be wed and breeding children,' a small, toothless man who looked like Rumpelstiltskin said. 'But eight and twenty, he's still living on his mother's farm, fifteen miles up the road past Croagh Patrick. It's seldom he'll put in an appearance here in town.'

'But,' his other informant told Johnny, 'that is a man

who could have been a prince among jockeys if only he'd let himself be a little bit more adventurous. I've seen him win races on horses that didn't deserve to start. He can do everything bar talk to them.'

'Sure, he's some kind of a jockey,' Rumpelstiltskin agreed, calling for another three pints of Guinness. ''Tis a terrible waste to see. He could have been up with the best of them over in England, earning a king's ransom. And he's a mind like an encyclopaedia when it comes to breeding. He dreams of winning the lottery and sending his poor old mares down to Coolmore to be covered for fifty thousand pounds.'

'They say 'tis his mother is the stumbling block to him. She has a small, scrubby sort of a farm – not enough to graze a goat, but she won't leave, and she can't do without Aidan. There was a husband, but he died or deserted her, no one knows for sure, before she came back from England.'

After this, Johnny judged, the information became more speculative, but if what he had been told so far was true, it would fit very well with the plan taking shape in his head. But to start with, he would stick to being a bloodstock agent, even if it meant having to commit himself to one of the nags Aidan had in mind to show him.

The sun glittered off the blue, island-spotted water of Westport Bay as Johnny Henderson drove west next morning. On his left, the dark side of Croagh Patrick loomed. It was a stirring sight, but all Johnny's concentration was on the chase that lay ahead. Having been presented with a box of gold in the shape of Aidan

Daly, he was well aware of the problems that lay ahead in forging a key to its lock.

After ten miles, he stopped to look at his map. He identified the small hill to the south, beneath which Aidan had told him he would find his mother's farm. Johnny turned up a narrow lane and soon spotted the dirty white buildings half-way up the hillside.

Even on this sunny morning, no one could have described the surroundings as lush. Whatever homesteader had been responsible, centuries before, for settling here, could not have had many options open to him. But there was a craggy beauty to the place.

Johnny turned off the lane on to the deeply rutted track that led up to the farmhouse and a few crumbling barns that belonged to it.

As he approached the house, he saw a couple of incongruously well-kept young horses grazing in a scrubby field, and the dilapidation of the place became more apparent. Even his battered BMW looked out of place among the mess of the farmyard where he came to a halt.

He turned the engine off and got out into the still, silent sunshine. It was a moment or two before his arrival produced any reaction from the house that faced him. Then, hobbling painfully with the help of a pair of old hazel sticks, a woman appeared.

She smiled. 'Good morning to you. And you'd be the man my son met in Westport?'

'That's right,' Johnny beamed. 'Good morning, Mrs Daly.'

'You can call me Mary,' the woman said. 'Come on in out of this sun. Aidan'll not be a moment.'

Johnny followed her through the front door of the house, straight into a tidy farmhouse kitchen. Mary sat down.

'Excuse me,' she said. 'I've this creeping paralysis. It comes and goes; today, it's come. Help yourself to a glass of Paddy's.'

'Thanks. I will.' Johnny reached down the bottle she had indicated and filled a glass that was already on the table.

'So,' the woman went on, 'Aidan tells me you're from England, looking for horses.'

'That's right.' As he spoke, Johnny studied Aidan's mother. Grey-haired, with bright blue eyes, she was probably not yet fifty, but illness had aged her. It was obvious that she had once been a very good-looking woman. She also had the look of someone who had known a lot of pain in her life. 'Good, well-nurtured stock is what I'm looking for, not grand pedigrees.'

'You'll find nothing grand in our bloodlines, but Aidan knows what he's doing. I sometimes wish,' she said quietly, 'that he'd the chance to make use of his talents, but he's a good son and he'll not leave me here alone.'

Johnny identified the stumbling block in his path and mentally adjusted his approach. 'I saw two nice-looking colts in the field outside. Are those yours?'

'Yes, but I'll let Aidan tell you all about them ... here he is.'

Aidan tapped the dust from his boots as he came in through the front door. 'How are you?' he said to Johnny. 'You've not let my mother tell you the truth about the horses, have you?'

125

Johnny got to his feet and shook Aidan's hand. 'They look pretty good to me anyway.'

'We'll deal with them later. I've in mind to show you a few animals ready to race. When you've finished your drink, we'll head off down to Doo Lough where there's a few to look at.'

Aidan insisted that they drive in his pick-up, on the grounds that Johnny's car was too flashy.

'That's encouraging,' Johnny remarked. 'If anyone thinks my old banger's too flashy, their expectations are not going to be too high.'

Aidan nodded and grinned.

They covered a hundred miles that day, including a quick foray into Connemara, and inspected more than twenty animals. At each isolated farm, Johnny did as he was told and kept in the background, looking but saying little. He heard twenty different reasons for selling horses, and twenty more for buying them.

Back at the farm, Mary insisted that Johnny should stay the night, as he and Aidan planned to visit half a dozen more farms next day. The following evening, Johnny suggested they have a drink in the bar in the nearby village of Louisburgh.

'Well?' Aidan asked anxiously as they settled down with their drinks. 'What did you think of them?'

To his surprise, Johnny had been rather impressed by the horses Aidan had been able to show him over the last two days of driving around the craggy Mayo hills. Now, though, he was non-committal. 'I don't know, Aidan. I know I said my budget wasn't all that great, but frankly I was after individuals with a bit more class. That colt of yours will make a fine strong chaser, I'd say – certainly worth a thousand or two.'

Aidan's face fell. 'Is that all you think he'd be worth in England? I've had better offers here, but I was going to win a few races with him first. The truth is, there's so little to be made on the farm, we've really to look to the horses to keep us going. My mother's a brave woman – she wouldn't let you see how ill she is – but soon I've to find the money to pay for her treatment and a nurse in the house, and I just don't know where I'm going to look for it.'

Johnny shook his head sympathetically and sucked a mouthful of air through his teeth. 'I'll buy what I can through you, I promise, Aidan, after all the trouble you've gone to. But I can't really see it amounting to much.' He also disliked himself for the satisfaction that Aidan's disappointment gave him. 'But look,' he went on, 'surely it can't be that bad? Won't the health service pay for your mother's treatment?'

'Only if she goes into hospital, and she'd rather pass away than leave the farm; it would break her heart to do that. God knows, sometimes I wonder when I'll ever get the chance to go out looking for a woman and making a life of my own. But there it is, I never knew my father and there's only ever been her and me for as long as I can remember. Now she has only between five and ten years to live. You can see why her peace of mind has to take priority.'

'Of course I can,' Johnny spoke gently and nodded. 'So you really need a lot of money if she's to stay on the farm?'

Aidan nodded.

'Well, I'm terribly sorry if I built up your expectations about the prospects for some profitable horse-trading, but it very much looks as though I'm going to have to go back to my old tried-and-tested sources.'

He ordered more drinks for them. When two full glasses were on the table between them, he gave Aidan a long, speculative look. 'D'you know, I've been thinking of another way you could make some money, possibly a great deal.'

Aidan looked up. 'What? How? Out here in Mayo?'

'You've got one very valuable asset you could use.'

'And what might that be?'

'Your face.'

Aidan stared at him for a moment, then burst out laughing. 'You think I might have some future as fillum star, do you?'

Johnny smiled. 'You might, for all I know, but that's not what I had in mind.' He leaned forward to emphasise the confidentiality of what he was going to say. 'Do you remember when we first met, three days ago in Westport – it seems like months – I thought you were someone called David Tredington?'

'The fella you said I'm a dead ringer for?'

'That's right. What I should have said was that you'd be a dead ringer for him if he were still around. Nobody's seen him for more than fifteen years.'

Aidan, trying to see where this was leading, became suspicious. 'Why have they not seen him for so long, for God's sake?'

Johnny shrugged. 'He ran away from his home – one of the most beautiful houses in Devon – after his mother died, when he was twelve. He's never been seen since.'

'How did they know some accident hadn't happened, that he hadn't been killed somewhere and just couldn't be found?'

'The police searched every inch of Devon without a sniff or a sighting. They went over the estate with a fine-tooth comb, but he'd just vanished into thin air. Then, a note arrived, posted a couple of days later, saying how miserable he'd been at Barford. I used to be there a lot in those days. Sir Mark Tredington's my godfather. I was quite a friend of David's, and his cousin George. We were all at school together. My family lived in London, so I used to go down and stay there the whole time during the holidays. I was already interested in horses then, and they've a wonderful stud there. I was at Barford when it happened. It was a few weeks after his mother had been killed out hunting. He was a bit of a mummy's boy and he was devastated. He couldn't seem to come to terms with it, and Sir Mark was away a lot in those days. David just seemed to retreat into his shell.'

'Jesus! So this little fella was so miserable that he ran away and never came back? What age would he be now?'

'Twenty-seven, twenty-eight.'

Aidan started. 'That's my age, twenty-eight.'

'Is it really?' Johnny said with excitement. Then he asked earnestly, almost prepared to believe it. 'Look, you aren't really David, are you? You so easily could be.'

Aidan shook his head. 'I lived in England till I was twelve, too, but I'm not this David Tredington, no chance. My mother was housekeeper in a small hospital run by the sisters of the Holy Infant in Roehampton, near to London. We'd a couple of rooms there. D'you know, I scarcely remember a thing about it. I wasn't happy there. I went to the local Catholic school. I didn't like it at all. The only pleasure I ever had was helping out at the livery stables in Richmond Park. When my mother inherited the farm from her uncle, there was no stopping us getting over here. I'd never been before, but it was love at first sight. I mean, the old farm may not make much of a living, but it's the most beautiful place in the world, is it not?'

'It certainly is,' Johnny agreed, happy to become sentimental about it. 'And of course your mother shouldn't have to leave and be taken off into some anonymous place to die.' Lightly, he thumped the table with his fist. 'And she needn't, Aidan, she needn't!'

'What is it you have in mind?' Aidan asked doubtfully, less inclined than some of his countrymen to believe in miracles.

'You'll probably think this is a crazy scheme, but I think you could take David Tredington's place.' He leaned back in his chair with a slight smile.

Aidan looked at him without speaking for a moment. 'Why,' he asked, 'should I want to do that?'

Johnny took a swig of his stout and began to speak slowly to underline the significance of what he was saying. 'Because he was the only son of Sir Mark Tredington whose estate when he dies will be worth something in the order of ten million quid.'

'You mean, I should turn up and claim this fella David Tredington's inheritance?'

'That's exactly what I mean.'

Aidan stared at Johnny. 'But that's absolutely crazy! And downright crooked.'

'Not a hundred per cent ethical, I'll grant you, but not

crazy. I'll have to check out a few things before I can be sure it'll work but, as far as I can see, and I know most of the facts, it's perfectly feasible.'

'But for Jesus' sake, man, I could never carry it off! Who's going to believe I'm some kind of an English nob? I'm a Mayo farmer.'

'Fine. That's what you've chosen to be since you were twelve years old, but now you've decided to come home. Your Irish speech doesn't matter a damn. I once met a full-blown belted earl who spoke broad Australian. What you will need to do is learn everything I can tell you about the place and the family.'

'John,' Aidan said, shaking his head, 'it's not on. I can't do it. It'd be theft, or deception, or whatever criminal, that's for sure, and I'm no criminal.'

'I'm not so sure. If David doesn't turn up – and as far as I know he's missing presumed dead – the whole shooting match, estate and title will pass to his cousin George. I can tell you, you'd make a far better job of it than George. He's fat, smug and pompous: Barford would be wasted on him. You'd be doing the family and Devon a favour by squeezing him out.'

'Look, I don't care what this George is like; it's his in-heritance, legally, and I've no moral right to do him out of it, and that's that.' He moved in his chair as if to get up.

Johnny held up a hand to cover his irritation. 'I take your point, Aidan, but hold on. What I'm saying is true, and you'd have no more problems about what to do with your mother. There'd be enough income for you from Day One to pay for a houseful of carers.'

This time Aidan wasn't to be put off leaving. 'I'm

happy to do a bit of horse-trading with you, John, but there's no way I'm getting involved in this crazy deception. It wouldn't work, and I wouldn't do it even if I thought it would. Now, I've got to be getting back. If you'd like to take another look at the colt, and revise your offer a bit, you'll be very welcome.'

Johnny gave in with apparent good grace. 'OK,' he grinned, 'but do just think about it. You could be certain your mother would have no more worries, plus the best possible treatment and care there is to be had; and surely she'd be very grateful to you for that.'

Chapter Six

Johnny Henderson kept a smile on his face until Aidan had left the bar. Even then, it didn't disappear entirely.

As he had talked to Aidan, the impersonation he was proposing seemed increasingly plausible. Everything was in its favour, even down to the fact that Aidan himself hadn't arrived in Mayo until he was twelve. It was as if this Irish farmer had been tailor-made for the role of David Tredington.

Johnny realised now that he had sprung the idea on Aidan too abruptly, and that he had failed to take into account any moral objections Aidan might have. It was too late to remedy that but, even so, his instincts told him that these could be overcome if Mary Daly's comfort were presented as a worthy end to justify questionable means.

He had at least planted in Aidan's mind the idea that the financial problems of his mother's tragic illness could be solved. In the meantime, he'd have to be more subtle in promoting it.

'Morning!' Johnny Henderson put his head inside the front door of the Dalys' crumbling white farmhouse.

Mary Daly, sitting at her large pine table scarred and

133

stained with a hundred years' use, looked up and smiled with a serenity that gave no hint of the constant pain that afflicted her. 'Did you want to see Aidan?'

'I did,' Johnny answered; the Irish reluctance to say 'yes' was infectious.

'He'll be glad. He's out in the barn with the colt. Be sure and come back to the house for a little cup of something before you go.'

'I will,' Johnny said. 'Thank you.'

He nodded to her and turned to pick his way across a yard littered with archaic farm implements, discarded wagons, old horseshoes and empty feed bags. A tribe of countless scrawny cats lurking among the debris coexisted in truce with a flock of wary chickens.

A cockerel of incongruous magnificence stood haughtily on the pinnacle of a mountainous muck-heap outside the barn where Aidan had put up his stables.

The cock lifted his beak to the sky and yodelled to announce Johnny's approach. A moment late Aidan came out through the high double doors of the whitewashed stone building.

Johnny saw at once the look of relief in the Irishman's eyes.

'Hello, John. You came, then, in spite of my lofty moral tone in the bar yesterday?'

Johnny laughed. 'Don't worry about that. I've met loftier. Anyway, forget the suggestion I made. It wouldn't work if your heart wasn't in it; if you weren't convinced, no one else would be. No,' he dismissed the idea with a backward wave of his hand, 'I came because there was one horse I thought might be worth a second look.'

'Which would that be?'

'That big chestnut roan we saw; belongs to a tinker on the other side of the mountain, by the lake.'

Aidan grinned and nodded. 'You've a better eye than I gave you credit for. That horse has only ever been ridden by a man you wouldn't trust to walk your dog, and who sits a horse over a fence like a bag of corn.'

'You said he'd never won?'

'That's right, but he has a real turn of foot, some real talent there. If I had him, I'd get him winning in a matter of months.'

'The only trouble is, that chap was talking about seven grand.'

Aidan dismissed this with a shake of the head. 'That's only his way of letting me know the animal was for sale. He'll sell it to me for half that, and still feel happy he was cheating me.'

'If you can get him for three and a half thousand, we've got a deal. I've got a client back in England who'll give me a profit on him.' Johnny thought of George Tredington's ambition to send out winning horses from his own small farm, and boast afterwards how he'd paid next to nothing for them. George had charged him with the task of finding four or five that might help him to achieve this and, incidentally, show his Uncle Mark that he had all the skill and judgement needed to run a stud like Barford. At least – as George had put it – make the old buffer say 'Well done', for once.

They were walking back across the yard towards the house now. 'You leave it to me,' Aidan said. 'If you come with me again, he'll know it's you that wants it, and your English accent would double the price.'

'Fine,' Johnny agreed. 'If you say the animal can be

bought for three and a half thousand and then made to perform, that's good enough for me.'

'You'll not regret it,' Aidan said.

They walked into the kitchen where Mary Daly still sat. 'You'll forgive me for not bustling around,' she said with gentle apology, 'but I'm not so good on my pins today. Aidan, would you ever shove the kettle back on the ring?'

He did as she asked, while a worried look flashed across his nut-brown face.

When the three of them were sitting at the table with mugs of tea in front of them, Mary Daly asked Johnny about England.

'I've not been back these sixteen years,' she said, 'not since Aidan and I left the convent. It's strange, I never thought I was leaving for good, but once we came here, I didn't want to go back at all. I was always promising Aidan we'd go; now the poor boy has never been further than Dublin, with the farm to run and all.'

'Don't worry, Mother. I'll get my chances.'

'I just hope you do. Anyway, Mr Henderson, tell me how it is back in England now.'

Johnny aimed his answers at Aidan, and dwelt on the quality of equestrian life, the prospects and pleasures to be found in the still hugely popular English sports of National Hunt and point-to-point racing. Mary Daly didn't miss the responsive gleam in her son's eyes.

Later, when Aidan went out to deal with his cows, his mother confided in Johnny.

'I don't keep him here, you know. I've never said to him that he shouldn't go, and yet, though I know he wants to – to see more, to make more of the brilliant talent he has with the horses, he'd feel he was abandoning me, for I've no real family left here now – a couple of old uncles too petrified of the devil to move.' She shrugged. 'Maybe I should insist that I go to the hospital.'

Johnny shook his head. 'That wouldn't release him,' he said. 'He'd know you'd be missing this place too much. But look, it's just possible he might be able to help me with a couple of projects. As you say, he has a superb eye and, from what I've heard, great skill with a horse. It does seem an awful shame to leave it buried up here. And, of course, he'd make enough money to pay for all the care you need.'

Mary looked doubtful, torn between conflicting wishes. 'I wish to God there were an easy answer,' she sighed.

When Johnny left later in the afternoon for the small hotel in Westport where he was staying, Aidan set off to buy the horse from a scruffy little small-holding on the other side of Croagh Patrick.

He drove up to a rickety five-bar iron gate, and parked his pick-up. Stepping out on to a muddy track, he let himself into the yard beyond, closing the gate behind him. The only thing that moved was the big dark chestnut head of the animal he'd come to see, protruding from a makeshift window in what looked like a chicken shed. Aidan walked towards it, nodding with a smile.

Without a sound, as if he had materialised from the dung-scented air, a small dark man appeared at Aidan's side. His black eyes glinted. 'Now, that's a real hoss.'

'I didn't think it was a pig,' Aidan said. 'Though it's hard to tell with all that mud on him.'

The little man looked hurt. 'The mud is only on the surface. That animal is in beautiful condition within himself.'

'We'll see,' Aidan said, unimpressed by the sales pitch. 'I'll have another look at him.'

The horse's owner let himself into the shed, and knotted an ancient halter rope around its large head. As he led it out, the horse had to duck to pass through the low opening.

As Aidan looked on, trying not to let his appreciation of the animal's obvious qualities show, a frantic squawling erupted in a corner of the yard. A lean ginger cat shot out of a barn and streaked across the yard between Aidan and the horse, hotly pursued by a pair of yapping terriers.

The powerful chestnut took one look, spun round in terror and, tugging the grimy rope from its handler, took off across the yard towards the gate. Without missing a stride, it bunched up, stretched out and flew over the top rail as if it had been a twelve-inch cavaletti.

The sound of the cat's flight dwindled into the distance behind the shed; the wiry little farmer just stood proudly with his hands on his hips. 'As I said, that's what I call a real hoss.'

That evening, Johnny rang George Tredington to let him know that he'd found a horse of suitably unrealised potential, and at an appropriate price.

Aidan arrived triumphantly later that evening with the news that Letter Lad was theirs for three thousand five hundred and fifty pounds. The extra fifty, he said, was a necessary sop to the vendor's vanity.

Johnny phoned George Tredington again, asking him to transfer half the price of the horse – seventeen hundred and fifty pounds – to a bank in Ireland first thing next morning. George grumbled a bit, but then, he'd set a budget of four thousand pounds an animal, and whatever else he thought of Johnny Henderson, he trusted his judgement of a horse.

After some persuasion, to Johnny's great relief, George agreed. Certainly, Johnny couldn't get the money from anywhere else. Aidan had agreed with the gelding's distrustful owner that the deal would be done in cash, and cash it had to be. Then there was Aidan's two hundred, and the cost of shipping the horse to Devon.

Aidan and Johnny sat at a table in the bar with a bottle of Paddy's, celebrating their first deal, until Aidan announced that he would have to get home soon.

'Hang on a minute.' Johnny didn't want to waste this chance to work on Aidan. He leaned back in his chair and looked at the lean, handsome, guileless man who looked to him more like a Tredington than ever. 'I was talking to your mother this afternoon while you were out feeding the cows. I think she'd understand completely if you were to go out and really try to make something of your breeding and training skills.'

Aidan shrugged. 'Maybe. But like I said, who'd look after her? And anyway, where would I get the money to set up a decent yard?'

'If you really wanted it, I've told you how you could get the money. There's no question about it, believe me.

Why not sound her out on it? I mean, for God's sake, you're wasting yourself flogging a few old knackers round these local tracks, and trying to rear cattle on ground that a goat would sniff at.'

Aidan sighed. 'Sure, I'd like to get my hands on some real good horses, and I'd know what to do with them.'

Johnny decided to take a punt. He drew a deep breath. 'Look, talk to her about it. Tell her that I can set you up in a yard in England, with the chance to make far more money than you could ever scratch out of the farm.'

'She's not one to put much store by money.'

'I think you'll find she's just a realist. She doesn't complain, because there's no point – it wouldn't achieve anything. But if there was the real chance of your getting somewhere, I think you'd be surprised by her reaction. And if it meant her definitely being able to stay on the farm, with someone to look after her besides you, she'd love to see you make something of yourself. I think she feels very bad about your being tied down the way you are.'

Letter Lad was to be delivered to Aidan's farm the following afternoon. In the morning, Johnny drove into Westport to collect the cash. With the notes tucked in his wallet, he headed back to the Dalys' farm. When he arrived, Aidan was out mending a fence in one of the outlying fields. His mother, more active than the day before, was looking for eggs among the hay-bales in the barn. She greeted Johnny with no less warmth than the last time. He couldn't yet tell if Aidan had talked to her about the possibility of his going away.

She ushered him inside. As soon as he had sat down,

she said, 'Aidan's been telling me about a possible opening you may have for him in Devon.'

Johnny's head jerked up. He hadn't expected Aidan to go quite so far. He wondered just how much he had told his mother. Nothing in her attitude gave him a clue as to her approval or disapproval, pleasure or sadness at the prospect.

Still, at least Aidan had talked to her. She didn't mention the subject again. It was only when Aidan came back in that Johnny had an inkling of the way things had gone. There was a new look of determination and expectation about Aidan that made him somehow taller, more confident. He winked at Johnny. 'Come on out to get the stable ready,' he said.

When they were in the barn, he asked, 'Have you got the money? Yer man'll be here with the horse soon.'

'Sure. And I've got yours.' He pulled the notes from his wallet and passed them over.

'I like to deal with a man who's as good as his word,' Aidan said as he stuffed the money in the pocket of his threadbare cords.

'Your mother said you spoke to her about going to England,' Johnny said.

Aidan nodded.

'Well?' Johnny asked quickly.

'I told her the whole scam.'

Johnny couldn't believe Aidan had been so naïve. 'What? Everything? About the Tredingtons and Barford?'

'Sure. She's all for it.'

'Good God. I hadn't meant you to discuss the whole thing with her, but ... she didn't disapprove?'

'It is a little surprising,' Aidan agreed, 'but when I told her about the opportunities with horses I would have, and that the whole lot otherwise would go to this pompous cousin...'

'The same pompous cousin who's just provided you with your two hundred quid finder's fee.'

Aidan laughed. 'Well, there's what you might call a sort of poetic injustice to that.'

'So,' Johnny asked, 'are you going to do it?'

'D'you mean become Mr David Tredington?' Aidan pretended to prevaricate but his eyes gave him away. They were sparkling in a way Johnny hadn't seen since he'd met him. 'What the hell?' He shrugged with a laugh, then became more serious. 'It's the only way I can see to be sure that my mother can stay here. And she's desperate to, though she'd never say as much to me. To answer your question, I am going to do it. I just hope I don't have to wait years before I can get something back to her.'

'I've told you, it shouldn't be hard to swing it so that you're getting enough to make a difference very early on. You'll be the son and heir, after all.'

Three days later, Johnny Henderson and a handful of Irish point-to-pointers arrived in Devon at more or less the same time. As Johnny was urging his car up Porlock Hill, a horse transporter drove through the gates of George Tredington's farm.

Braycombe Farm consisted of a cluster of white-washed buildings – long-house, barns, cattle-sheds and stables – which lay in a small valley in the middle of four hundred low-grade, upland acres. Ten miles from the great estate at Barford, it had once been an outlying part of it. George's grandfather had given it to George's father, Peregrine, in a moment of paternal guilt.

As a gift, it was of questionable generosity. It had a value, but its income never matched the effort needed to run it. Nevertheless, when George had inherited it, he had insisted on keeping it. George now had all the bluff, hearty mannerisms of a countryman, and liked to joke that he was merely serving time in the City – where he was said to be making a substantial amount of money – to allow him to come and live full-time at Braycombe when finally he had found a wife to live in it with him.

On the hot August day on which the horses arrived, George was at Braycombe. He had taken a few days off from the bank in London to oversee arrangements for the Barford shoot, a task with which his uncle had recently entrusted him, and which he took seriously.

He was in his small study, on the cool side of the house, when Mike Harding tapped on the half-open door.

Mike was a red-haired, stocky Devonian in his forties, who ran the farm for George almost single-handed.

'Those horses have come from Ireland, Mr Tredington.'

'Great!' George got to his feet eagerly. There was a gleam on his podgy, russet face – inherited from his mother's family – as he lifted his bulky frame from the leather desk chair which almost entrapped it. 'I can't wait to see this Letter Lad. Johnny Henderson found it on some farm in the back of beyond in County Mayo. It's run in a few point-to-points over there, but never won because it's always had a rotten jockey. Johnny thinks we could do really well with it. I'm going to train it myself, though I might need a bit of help from Jan.'

Jan was Mike's wife.

'You'll have to ask her,' Mike said, reluctant to commit anyone to anything until terms had been agreed.

George walked with a busy, short-legged stride through low doorways, out into the clean cobbled yard where a driver was lowering the lorry's ramp.

'Last of the load,' the driver said with satisfaction.

'Did you have any others for Henderson?'

'Nope. Just these.' He clattered up the ramp to swing a partition back to reveal Letter Lad. A moment later he was leading the dark chestnut roan down to its new home.

'Blimey,' he said. 'I've never seen a race-horse this colour.'

Mike Harding eyed it critically. 'He could do with a bit of grass, but he's got the frame of a proper horse.'

George nodded. He would need to hear a few more people's views before he formed his own. 'Moves well,' he ventured as Mike led the horse away to a row of cage boxes in one of the long barns. 'Anyway, get him in and settled down, then we'll put him down in the river meadow. There's still a bit of grass there.'

The telephone rang in the house. George hurried back inside.

'Hello, George. Johnny Henderson. Have those horses got to you yet?'

'Yes. They've just arrived.'

'What do you think of Letter Lad?'

'Looks a bit scrawny, but otherwise all right.'

'If I'd bought him from someone who knew how to get a good bit of condition on him, he'd have been a couple of grand more. Don't worry about it. Chuck him in a field and give him plenty to eat for a few weeks. Try and get a lot of flesh on him before you start exercising him.'

'That's just what I planned to do. Where are you now?'

'In a call-box, coming down into Lynmouth. I'll be with you in half an hour for the rest of the money.'

George laughed. 'I thought you might be. I might even give you a drink as well.'

Johnny blinked through the grimy glass panes of the phone-box at the sun gleaming off a pale blue sea and thought about George. Specifically, he wondered how he would take the reappearance of David Tredington. It was hard to guess.

After fifteen years, and many thousands of pounds spent on searching and advertising for the missing heir to Barford, it was now generally accepted that George was heir to his uncle's baronetcy. The family had not actually applied to the court for presumption of David's death, but the possibility had been raised several times. Whether or not the great estate would come with the title was a source of constant local speculation. Johnny had never heard Sir Mark or George say anything about it, but he was less intimate with the family now than he had been fifteen years before. Nevertheless, he was still in fairly regular contact with Sir Mark and, with no pretensions to innocent motives, Lucy.

'Lucy! Phone!'

Irritation flickered across Lucy Tredington's deceptively soft features as she glanced up from the canvas propped on an easel in front of her. She was sitting in the shade of a mulberry tree, trying for the hundredth time to capture the subtleties of Barford's walled garden. She had attacked the project in almost every month of the year. It seemed constantly to change, and there was a wonderful incongruity about the old stone walls, the espaliered peach trees, the elegant decaying Victorian greenhouses, and the rows of domestic vegetables in their midst which she wanted to reproduce but which always seemed to elude her.

Shaking a curtain of fine brown hair from her face, she got up and walked towards the house.

Inside, she flopped down on a hummocky old sofa in the sitting-room where the family spent most of their time, and picked up the phone.

Her sister, Victoria, who had called her in, watched her face for reaction, but Lucy gave nothing away. She spoke with neither animation nor boredom as she fingered the buttons of her paint-spattered, embroidered Indian blouse.

When she put the phone down, Victoria asked, 'That was Johnny, wasn't it?'

Lucy nodded.

'What did he want?'

'Invited himself to stay for a few days.'

Victoria's eyes lit up. 'Great. It's ages since we've seen him.'

'Yes. I wonder what he wants.'

As it happened, Johnny had seen Sir Mark Tredington,

though not his daughters, only a few weeks before. They had been staying in the same house-party for Goodwood. Johnny had extracted from Sir Mark some idea of the kind of horses he was looking for over the coming year. He had asked if he might have the opportunity of looking for some for him.

Sir Mark, shrewd, and familiar enough with Johnny Henderson's strengths and weaknesses, had agreed to consider anything that Johnny came up with. He still had an affection for Johnny anyway: as one of his own missing son's few close friends at the time of his disappearance, he enjoyed the occasional references to David which their conversation produced.

When Johnny arrived in the middle of that warm afternoon, he found Sir Mark in his study with Victoria, watching the racing from Newmarket. Sir Mark waited until the race in progress was finished before he spoke.

'Hello, Johnny. I didn't know you were back.'

'I phoned earlier; spoke to Luce. She said I could stay for a few nights. I hope that's all right.'

'Fine by me.' Sir Mark turned down the volume on the television. 'Well, how did you get on in Ireland?'

Johnny glanced at Victoria. 'I think I might have found something for you.'

Sir Mark gave him a quick glance. 'Good, you must tell me all about it later. Now, it's a bit early for a drink, I suppose. I'll ask Susan to get us some tea.'

He stood up, and Johnny followed him through the welcome cool of the dark hall into the back of the house. Beside the kitchen was a more utilitarian sort of an office which housed Sir Mark's secretary.

Johnny met Susan Butley's eyes with difficulty. Although Susan was a local girl, she had the kind of looks and presence that would have excited the producer of a Hollywood soap. Johnny knew that she guarded the family she worked for with fierce devotion. Once, without thinking, he'd made a play for her. She had summarily rejected him out of loyalty to Lucy, who she thought was still interested in him.

'Here's Johnny,' Sir Mark said, 'come to stay for a few days. You might tell Mrs Rogers if Lucy hasn't already. You wouldn't be kind enough to bring us a pot of tea, would you?'

'Of course, Sir Mark.' The girl swung her long legs from beneath her desk and rose to her feet. She was wearing a pair of saffron leggings that showed every curve of her well-shaped haunches. Johnny couldn't help grinning with approval as she strode from the room.

When she had brought tea into the study and Victoria had poured them all a cup, Sir Mark seemed prepared to spend a while chatting.

'So, what horses did you find for me in Ireland?'

'Not a lot. I bought a nice pointer for George, though.'

'Did you indeed? And what's he planning to do with it?'

'He says he's going to train it himself.'

'Oh dear.' Sir Mark raised his eyebrows. 'I hope he didn't pay too much for it.'

Johnny laughed. 'He did not,' he said with an Irish brogue. 'But,' he probed, 'why do you say, "Oh dear"?'

'You know as well as I do that George doesn't know the first thing about horses.'

'Maybe not,' Victoria said, 'but there's no harm in him learning. After all, if he's ending up with the stud here...' She left the implication trailing.

Sir Mark nodded in answer to Johnny's quick glance. 'It does rather look as though George will end up with the stud. I don't know; it seems unfair on the girls, though I'll make sure they'll always have enough, but the estate should really go with the title.'

'You haven't heard anything new about David, have you?' Victoria asked with a tremor in her voice.

The older man nodded again. 'Yes. I haven't given up hope, of course, and it's all being checked out now, but I was contacted by the Australian High Commission last week. They've had a report of someone called David Tredington going missing in a small yacht somewhere off Norfolk Island. There was a crew of three, all lost, sailing from Sydney to Fiji.'

Johnny couldn't speak for a moment. The unfairness of the timing was too hard to swallow.

Sir Mark saw the disappointment in his eyes. 'I know; it's hard to take – even after all this time. But as I say, it's by no means certain yet. I've got a firm of lawyers dealing with it. I shouldn't really have told you, not before they're a hundred per cent certain of the identity. I just pray it's not him.'

'God, I hope not,' Victoria said fervently. 'I still feel sure he'll come back one day.'

'Well, you never know,' Johnny humoured her, 'there could easily be some mistake, so keep praying.'

'You're quite right, Johnny; never say die. Come on,' Sir Mark said, achieving an abrupt change of mood, 'let's go out and look at the horses.'

'I'd love to. Would you mind if I just fetch my video camera from the car? I'd rather like to get a few shots of what you've got in the yard, just for my records.'

'Why not?' said Sir Mark. 'Good idea.'

Later, Johnny found Lucy up in the small attic room which she used as a studio when she was at Barford.

'Hello, Luce.'

She was squinting at the canvas she had brought in from the garden. She looked up when he came in, smiling despite herself. 'Hello, Johnny. You're looking nice and tanned; whose villa have you been squatting in?'

'No one's. I've been working. For once the sun was shining in Ireland.'

'It's been amazing, hasn't it? I was supposed to be down in Aix, but it's so beautiful here.' She waved through the mansard window behind her at the green hills rolling down towards a distant view of the sea.

'What are you working on?' Johnny asked, walking around behind her to look at the canvas.

'Don't say anything,' Lucy said. 'I'm not interested in your opinion.'

'But it's wonderful. I love the way you've handled those vegetables.' He put a hand on her shoulder and kneaded it gently.

'Don't start getting all smarmy with me, Johnny. And if you think you can come down here just for a quick leg-over, forget it.'

'Oh no! Don't tell me there's a new man in your life?'

'No there bloody isn't, and I'm not interested in a re-run of our last scene.'

Johnny straightened up. 'Oh, all right,' he said with an exaggerated pique which wasn't entirely false. Now he was close to her and could smell her warmth and the sun in her hair, he felt the old familiar churning in his guts and a twitching in his loins.

Lucy laughed. 'I wouldn't mind if you weren't such a spoilt shit. You're too used to getting your own way.'

'Only with women,' Johnny protested.

'Anyway, what have you come here for?'

'To see you, of course.'

'Balls! I presume it's because you want to try and sell Dad a few horses.'

'There is that, too. But to be honest, I had to come and see George, and I felt like a few days loafing, and,' he waved out of the window as Lucy had done, 'where could be better?'

Johnny decided that any serious attempts to get Lucy back into bed with him could easily backfire and curtail his visit. His vanity, though not his sexual urges, was amply served by Victoria's admiring attention. He responded to her with kindly charm; there was always the chance that this would arouse Lucy, and it would make it harder for them to kick him out before he was ready.

With an effort, he made himself useful about the place, helping with the horses in the stud, pottering around the pheasant pens with George, and poring over the stallion books with Sir Mark.

And all the time he slipped in questions, references to the changes that had been made to the place over the years, trying to establish what had been the status quo at the time David had disappeared. He took photographs and videos on the slightest excuse, and buried himself in old family albums in the library. He achieved all this with a naturalness and subtlety that evoked no questions from his hosts.

Only Susan Butley, ever vigilant for the family, showed any suspicion about his motives. He kept his contact with her to an inoffensive minimum. When he once found himself alone with her for a while, he reminded her that when he had stayed in the house as a boy, her father, Ivor, had been a groom on the stud. Innocently, he asked after him.

'Never see him,' she said curtly. 'Hardly have done since he left Mum.'

But with a little encouragement, she was prepared to reminisce about her childhood in one of the grooms' cottages, and Johnny was able to establish exactly what had been the personnel on the estate when David had last been seen there.

As he compiled his dossier on the Tredington household, a history of the family and their friends, Johnny managed to push to the back of his mind the possibility that the real David Tredington might yet be proved to have drowned in the South Pacific. That would have been a terrible waste of Aidan Daly's remarkable likeness to the Tredingtons.

Two weeks after George had taken charge of his point-to-pointers in Devon, Aidan Daly climbed into his old pick-up to drive to Westport. As he drove along the empty road between the mountains and the sea, he was experiencing the same kind of nervous tingle he had before his first few races. He felt more vibrant and purposeful than he had ever done, now that he was presented with a real alternative to the impasse that his mother's illness had created.

Johnny perked up when he saw Aidan's handsome face enhanced by a new, confident smile and bright, eager eyes.

'You look as though you've just won the lottery.'

'To tell you the truth, now I'm committed to this ruse, I'm looking forward to it.'

'Great. I've got more than enough to kit you out with David Tredington's boyhood memories.'

They were in the dark, empty bar of the small hotel on the outskirts of town where Johnny had established his HQ for the purposes of turning Aidan Daly into David Tredington.

They spent the first afternoon in his cramped bedroom, looking at the videos Johnny had taken and the maps, plans, and photographs of the house, the grounds, the other farms on the estate.

Johnny had also produced a family tree, and lists of names of all the neighbours, the doctor, stud staff, maids and housekeepers young David would have known. He also drew on his memories of their time at school together. From the stud records, he had drawn up a list of the horses which had been there at the time. As an additional stimulus, he played the video of the thirty or so horses currently in occupation.

Now that he was committed, Aidan was quick and keen to learn.

Johnny himself became more animated after a few days, as the Irishman reeled off the names of the cousins and connections of the entire Tredington family, and demonstrated his familiarity with every aspect of the estate. Johnny could see no point in mentioning the small yacht missing with its crew off Norfolk Island. He also decided that it was time to broach one of the trickier obstacles.

'You're doing fantastically. The more you know, the more convincing you become.'

'I've been thinking,' Aidan said. 'I'll have to have a fool-proof story of what I've been doing for the last fifteen years. The simplest thing would be to stick more or less to the truth. The problem is how to deal with my mother. She's agreed to say that she and I met on the boat when I came from England, and that she sort of adopted me as I had absolutely no wish to go back to Barford then. That way, everything will tally.'

'Great!' Johnny nodded. 'I can't see much difficulty there. The only thing that could stump us is if they do a blood test on you. But I'm convinced that, if you handle it right, Sir Mark won't think it's necessary. After all, if you're a convincing enough David, it would be very insulting. But even if he does ask for a sample, I'm pretty sure if you've offered it willingly, he won't use it; we'll cross that one when we come to it. Obviously there are going to be things that I simply haven't been able to find out about – small incidents within the family, but my guess is that after so many years, you won't be expected to remember everything.' He paused and nodded encouragingly. 'There's one problem which we are going to have to deal with, though. David had a small birthmark, just here.' Johnny pointed to a point half-way down the left side of his neck.

Aidan's face fell. 'How the hell am I going to deal with that?'

'It's OK. It won't hurt, at least, not much. I've arranged for a tattooist here in town to make it look as though you've had the thing removed, some time ago. Then, if the family ask about it, you say that you'd been told it might become malignant in some way.'

Johnny held his breath as he waited for Aidan's reaction.

Unexpectedly, Aidan grinned. 'Ah well, I don't suppose I've got any choice. In for a penny, in for a pound.'

'That's what I like to hear. The chap'll do it tomorrow.'

By the following weekend, Aidan agreed with Johnny that he was ready to go. The uncanny experience of seeing photographs of David and himself at the same age, looking almost interchangeable, had removed most of his last doubts. Besides that, he'd immersed himself so completely in the life and surroundings of the young David Tredington that he sometimes found himself thinking he really had become the missing boy.

With a guillemot's egg in his pocket, which Johnny knew Lucy had asked her brother for over fifteen years ago, Aidan said goodbye to his mother, promised her that he would do everything he could to make sure she spent her remaining years in comfort, and set off for Dublin, fully prepared to step into another world and another man's shoes.

Chapter Seven

Devon: November

The morning after Mickey Thatcher was buried in the graveyard of Saint Kenelm's Church, Ivor Butley stirred two heaped spoons of sugar and a slug of whisky into his tea. He sat at a chipped formica-topped table in the grimy kitchen of a council flat on the outskirts of a small Devon town twenty miles from Great Barford. There was a smile on his face. It was dole day, and he was going racing.

He heard a rustle and thump at his front door and shuffled in his slippers into the hall to pick up the *Sun* and the *Sporting Life* which a paper-boy had just pushed through the letterbox. He turned to page three of the *Sun*, gave a quick, lewd chuckle and pushed it away. He opened the racing paper and leafed through to that day's card for Newton Abbot.

He ran his finger down the columns of jockeys' names until his eyes reached the words 'David Tredington', where they lingered as his mind travelled back through fifteen years.

It seemed to him that every second of the day Sir Mark's son had gone missing remained clear in his head. Every tiny detail was etched on his memory as if it had only just happened. There was good reason for this, for the boy's disappearance had been the fundamental cause of all his troubles since. It was the reason he had started to drink; almost before he realised what was going on, he'd lost his job and then his family. The bottle that had been his downfall had become his comfort.

He closed the paper with a groan and a shake of his head. He was very curious to meet David Tredington; Newton Abbot would be as good a place as any, and watching him ride would prove that his mind hadn't been playing tricks on him.

Aidan Daly let himself into the back seat of Jason Dolton's Subaru. Victoria, sitting in the front with her husband, had offered him a lift to Newton Abbot.

Jason had four rides, including the one in which Just William, owned by Sir Mark and to be ridden by his son, was running.

As Jason drove too fast along the sinuous back road to South Molton, Aidan avoided any awkward conversation and thought about David Tredington.

In the nine weeks that had passed since he'd first appeared at Barford, Aidan had thought almost continuously about the man whose identity he had assumed. He had tried, like any good actor, to get inside the mind of the character he was playing. He had succeeded to such an extent that sometimes he almost convinced himself that he *was* David Tredington.

He felt somehow that he had a lot in common with the boy who had disappeared, though he had soon realised from other people's reactions to him that the David they remembered as a twelve-year-old boy had not been universally liked and that, over fifteen years later, the new David was in most ways a great improvement. Aidan had the impression that they thought the self-imposed exile in Ireland had done nothing but good. He was helped by the fact that, with very few exceptions, no one showed any sign of doubting his identity. Word had gone round very soon after his arrival that Sir Mark was completely satisfied that this man was David. He had even told Aidan to his face, looked him straight in the eye as he'd said it. It had been Aidan's greatest challenge so far. He'd almost come clean, so strong were the feelings of guilt at his deception. If the old man hadn't sounded quite so convincing and looked so happy, Aidan was sure he would have confessed.

The biggest potential problem that he and Johnny had feared had not materialised. There wasn't so much as a lock of David's hair or a nail clipping that could be used to establish a DNA match. When Aidan had been asked to give a sample of blood for comparison with Sir Mark's, he had shown no sign of the great trepidation he felt. Presumably, though, Sir Mark had taken his apparent composure as confirmation that he was genuine, and had pursued the test no further, because no mention had ever been made of it again.

After that hurdle had been side-stepped, Aidan had felt completely confident in his role, and determined to do everything he could to justify the trust of his new 'father'. At the same time, he didn't lose sight of the whole purpose of the exercise. He planned to go back to Ireland as soon as he plausibly could to start making arrangements for his mother's care. He saved all the salary he received from the estate, and had started to earn supplementary and legitimate income from some skilful horse-dealing.

The biggest difficulty he had was containing Johnny's impatience. Aidan had agreed that Johnny would get five per cent of whatever assets found their way to Aidan as a result of his impersonation.

So far, Aidan had taken and received nothing tangible that he hadn't earned. He didn't deny that he'd received other great advantages by being David Tredington, but he also felt he was giving something back. He had been enjoying himself enormously, and had managed most of the time to quell his conscience – until Emmot MacClancy had shuffled into his life, and Mickey Thatcher had been killed.

Although the police had been unable to establish any real evidence that the falling sleeper had been anything other than a horrible accident, Aidan was still convinced that it wasn't – and that he was responsible for Mickey's death. He didn't have the impression that the police were doing much more to investigate the circumstances. Somehow, he was going to have to find out the truth himself – he owed that to Mickey – but for the time being he was going to have to do it without official help.

For two or three days after Fontwell, though, all his instincts told him to drop the deception and own up, before anything else happened. So far, to Johnny's immense relief, he had delayed the decision, but life as David Tredington had suddenly become a lot less comfortable for him.

* * *

Aidan, Victoria and Jason arrived at Newton Abbot shortly after Sam Hunter's lorry. Jason went off to change for his ride in the first race. Victoria and Aidan walked to the lorry park and watched apprehensively as one of Sam's lads started to lead Just William down the ramp.

The chestnut gelding was in an agitated state. It was looking around wildly with its ears back and a lot of white in its eyes. It made a fuss about negotiating the ramp, then leapt down the last few feet, almost dragging the lad over.

Victoria was standing beside Aidan. 'Crikey!' she said. 'He's in a filthy mood today. Are you sure you still want to ride him?'

'Why? Do you think Jason'd like the ride?'

'He's already got one.'

'I know, but it's even nappier than this one. Anyway, of course I'm going to ride him. If I can stop him pulling himself up as he passes the stables, he could win. Mind you, that's a big "if".'

Their race was the fourth on the day's card. Fifteen maiden chasers ranging from five to nine years of age, most of whom were likely to remain without a win until they retired to the point-to-point field. Aidan was the only amateur, Jason the only full professional in the race. All the others were conditional jockeys at various stages of their claiming allowance.

Walking round at the start, it wasn't difficult to spot the riders to steer clear of. They had their goggles pulled down long before the starter had finished checking their girths. Their mounts were sweating and edgy from the tension transmitted by their riders' hands and legs.

'Anyone want to make the running?' Aidan called out as the starter walked across to mount his rostrum. Nobody answered. Aidan moved Just William across to the inside; two young jockeys pushed in front of him, stirring up their horses for a quick start. Neither looked at all safe. Aidan quickly weighed up the possibility of going round the outside to avoid them, but that would have given Just William too much of a chance to duck out. If he were going to get this horse round the course at all, it would only be by keeping it well and truly boxed in until they were heading for home. He didn't have a choice. He would have to follow the two spacemen and hope to God that the horses they were riding knew how to jump.

It was Aidan's first ride at Newton Abbot. He had walked the course and guessed the race would be run at a fast pace on such a sharp circuit. Jumping would be important. He could see that if he lost his position, it would be hard to make up the ground again. And that was how it turned out.

The fifteen runners set off towards the first fence as if they were sprinters. It still surprised Aidan just how fast even bad horses could gallop. He followed the first two, who were racing far enough apart for Just William to see something of the fence between them. If Aidan could keep him on their quarters, Just William wouldn't be able to run out, unless he took one of them with him.

As they thundered forward, Aidan felt his horse cock his jaw and look for the right-hand wing. Before he had travelled three more strides, Aidan had lifted his whip and leathered him hard down his right shoulder, welting his skin. Just William rushed up between the two leaders. Two strides from the birch, he dug his toes in. He was travelling too quickly to stop altogether but, as he took off, in what appeared from the stands to be slow motion, another horse cannoned into him from behind and knocked him over. Aidan shot from the saddle like a rag doll, right in the path of the horses to his left. He had curled instinctively into a ball, knees tucked tightly to his chest, even before he had touched the ground.

Watching from the stands, Victoria froze as she saw her brother tumbling and bouncing across the grass, with horses galloping past on either side of him. Miraculously, it seemed, he escaped any real injury, until one of the last horses trampled right over the top of him and its flailing hooves prised open his defensive curl.

Victoria cursed the jockey who had made no attempt to avoid him. When she recognised the colours, she gasped. It was Jason.

By the time Aidan had been driven the short distance back to the ambulance room, Victoria was waiting for him. The back doors of the ambulance swung open and Aidan was standing inside, smiling. He was plastered with mud and a bruise was blooming on his left cheek. Apart from that, he looked fine.

'Are you OK?' she asked anxiously, not really believing what she was seeing.

'Sure. Slightly battered by your husband, that's all.'

Victoria didn't miss the sarcasm in his voice. She

thought about trying to make an excuse, but her loyalty to Jason didn't stretch that far. She said nothing.

'Give me a few minutes and I'll see you back in the weighing-room,' Aidan said lightly, guilty now at having embarrassed her.

Victoria nodded, tight-lipped, as a couple of St John's ambulance-men insisted on helping Aidan inside.

Five minutes later, after the doctor had checked him over, he picked up his helmet and whip and walked outside. He was heading for the changing-room when a short, red-faced man in an old waxed jacket and grimy cloth cap shambled up to him.

'David!' the man hailed him in broad Devonian. 'Young David Tredington! I'm glad you got up after that fall.'

Aidan looked at the small, rustic individual and wondered who the hell he was.

'Hello. How are you?'

'Still pickin' a few winners, but out of work. Have been for a few years now with all these yards closing down.'

Aidan nodded sympathetically, while his mind raced through the mountain of information with which Johnny had supplied him back in Ireland. This chap was evidently involved in horses in some way. Perhaps he was one of the grooms who had been at Barford at the time of David's disappearance. Aidan racked his brains for a name. Meanwhile, the other man was looking at him with an indulgent, shifty grin.

'You don't know who I am, do you? Not s'prisin', after fifteen year, and o' course, I heard tell you was back.'

Triumphantly, Aidan lighted on a name and took a gamble.

'Of course I know who you are, Ivor. The number of times you legged me up on to those moody ponies.'

Ivor Butley stared at Aidan in startled amazement for a moment before he recovered himself. 'So you remember me, do you?'

Aidan looked at him carefully. He heard a hint of sarcasm in the man's voice. Maybe, he thought, he hadn't got it right, and this wasn't Ivor. But he didn't panic; it would have been perfectly excusable to have confused the man after all this time. He didn't let his relief show when the man went on. 'But I bet you never heard what happened to me after you'd gone from Barford?'

'I'm afraid not.'

'Sir Mark got rid of me. Said I was drinking too much. Bloody rubbish it was. I never let the horses down. O' course, Sue's there now, but she won't even talk to me, nor do her mum.'

So, Aidan thought; this was Ivor Butley – Susan's father, who had been sacked, abandoned his wife and daughter, and wandered from job to job in livery yards and riding stables around the West Country until there was no one left who would tolerate him, even at the negligible wages he demanded. Aidan inspected him with greater interest. It was just possible to see, through the broken veins and damp drinker's eyes, something of Susan, though they had nothing obvious in common as far as personality was concerned, except, perhaps, for a streak of stubbornness.

'Well, will you have a drink,' Aidan offered, 'as soon as I've dumped this stuff?'

'No. I won't embarrass you. But I'm glad you recognised me – must have taken a bit of doin', after all that time, like.'

On the way home with Victoria and Jason, Aidan mentioned his meeting with Ivor.

She nodded. 'He's often around the local courses, poor old chap. It's rather pathetic. Sue says he's ended up living in some grim little flat in Tiverton, drawing the dole and studying form all day. Still, he manages to keep himself in whisky somehow.'

'What happened to him, after I left?'

'I don't really know. I mean, he'd been with us for years, hadn't he, certainly as long as I could remember. It must have been very odd your seeing him. He was your great chum in the yard, wasn't he? Didn't he teach you to ride?'

Johnny had told Aidan this. He nodded. 'He did. But what happened to him?'

'Well, after you left, he went to pieces. I don't know why. But he started really hitting the booze, and I think Dad just got fed up with having to get him out of bed to do the horses. Shirley, Sue's mother, tried to cover up for him, but I think they started rowing the whole time, and Shirley and Sue moved out, down to Lynmouth. Shirley got a job in one of the hotels, and I'm afraid Ivor got the boot.'

Aidan nodded. 'He seemed a bit of a sad case. Frankly, I'd not have recognised him if he hadn't come up to me. I offered him a drink, but he turned me down, said he didn't want to embarrass me.'

'Would it have embarrassed you?'

'Not a bit, though he is a pretty scruffy-looking little individual now. It's hard to see how he sired someone like Susan.'

'Yes, isn't it? She's turned out to be rather a star. Her mother worked like hell to make sure she went to the sixth-form college in Ilfracombe. We all thought she'd go up to London and get some high-powered secretarial job when she passed all her exams and with her rather glamorous looks, but she was determined to come and work for us. Very lucky, really.'

'I don't think she's taken to me all that much, though,' Aidan remarked lightly.

'Just the opposite, if you ask me; but anyway, you wouldn't want an efficient busybody like that, would you?'

'That I wouldn't know,' Aidan answered thoughtfully.

Jan Harding came in from doing evening stables at Braycombe Farm. Mike, her husband, who was George Tredington's farm manager, was already sitting in the kitchen of their cottage reading the local paper.

'How are they all?' he asked routinely.

'In bloody good shape. His nibs shouldn't have anything to complain about. Though I'm bloody annoyed with him.'

'Why's that?'

'I've just heard from Sam Hunter's yard that Letter Lad's there now. Apparently he had a corn. They said that David schooled him at home for a couple of weeks and he's jumping beautiful now. He's going really well and they're running him at Sandown tomorrow – and it was me as got him fit,' she added sourly.

'Who's riding him, then?'

'David, of course. I *told* George if he gave it time we'd get him right ourselves, but the silly bugger thought he'd be smart and take a quick profit on it when Johnny Henderson said he had a buyer. Mind you, I don't think he was too happy when he found out it had gone to Barford.'

'Serves him right. But you've got to hand it to David. He only rode him the once here. He must have known what was wrong with him then. Which reminds me, your blasted brother Ivor was on the phone, pissed as usual, saying something about seeing David at the races. He wanted to talk to you.'

Jan didn't answer for a moment; her husband didn't miss a worried look that flashed across her wind-worn face. 'Did he? Well, I suppose he was bound to bump into him sooner or later.'

'Why? What's the problem?'

'I don't know, but I've always thought it was David going missing that started all poor Ivor's troubles.'

'Poor Ivor, my arse!' Mike expostulated. 'He was always his own worst enemy, you know that. Everyone bent over backwards to help him after that, and they all ended up with mud on their faces.'

'What did he say?'

'He wanted you to go down and see him as soon as you could, this evening. I told him no way. Like I say, he was already half-cut. You wouldn't have been able to have much of a conversation with him anyway.'

'I'm going.'

'What! Just because your useless elder brother summons you, you'll drive thirty miles to listen to his moaning?'

'It's not often that he asks me to, is it? It must be important. Sorry, Mike. I'll try not to be back too late.'

Mike sighed. 'Do you want me to come too, then?'

'No. I'll be all right.'

Ivor hadn't really expected Jan to come, even after she'd telephoned to say she would. But when she rang the bell on his battered front door, he opened it to her gleefully.

'Hello, Jan. I'm bloody glad you've come. I had to talk to someone. Come on in. Do you want a drop of scotch?'

'No, I don't, and you sound as though you've had enough already.'

'Hardly had a drop.'

'Well, what's so important I had to drive down here?'

'It's important all right. After what I saw today. I can get my own back on those bloody Tredingtons, after they wrecked my life and stole my daughter.'

'Stole your daughter?' Jan exclaimed, incredulous. 'Susan worked like hell to get taken on there, you know that. It was her own choice.'

'All right, but she was sort of seduced, like, by their money and all that. And she's turned into a right little snob now.'

'I don't know how you know that. You haven't seen her for two years.'

'Maybe not, but I've heard.'

'Look, I don't know why you should think the Tredingtons owe you anything after the way you behaved, but how the hell do you think you're going to get even with them?'

'Not just get even with them, but make myself a tidy sum too. No more living in this bloody hovel.'

'Wherever you lived would be a hovel ... but go on; how are you going to do it?'

Ivor took a sip from a dirty glass of whisky and looked mysteriously at his sister. 'I know something Sir Mark Tredington doesn't; he can't do, or he wouldn't have had that bloke back in the house.'

'What bloke? You mean his son, David?'

'No. I don't mean his son David. I mean that bloke that's turned up calling himself David.'

'What on earth are you on about, Ivor? Everyone knows it's David. They had it checked out. I heard George telling someone over the phone, and you can still see where the birthmark was and all.'

'You don't want to be fooled by that birthmark. Whatever he's done to convince them he's the long-lost David, I can tell you, he bloody well isn't.'

Mike Harding was still up when his wife got back from Tiverton. He looked up from an old form-book he was reading.

'Well, what did the old bugger want, then?'

'He wanted to tell me that he's going to get even with the Tredingtons for sacking him and for stealing his daughter.'

Mike laughed out loud. 'That's a good one, stealing his daughter. Anyway, how's he going to do it?'

'He didn't tell me exactly. I suppose he thinks he's going to try and blackmail David.'

'Blackmail David? That's ridiculous. David hasn't been back long enough to have done anything, has he? Or does Ivor think he knows about something David got up to in Ireland? I suppose he might. After all, why did David suddenly decide to leave Ireland?'

'No. It's nothing like that. He says there's absolutely no way that David is David.'

'What the hell does he mean?'

'He says this David is an impostor; and he couldn't be anything else.'

'In that case, his mind must be completely pickled. Everyone knows Sir Mark checked it out when he turned up. I mean, there weren't just a few people who thought he must be a fake, after all. But no one's in any doubt about it now. Your brother's gone off his rocker; if he tries anything, he'll end up in bloody jail, which will probably be a relief for us all.'

'Don't say that about him. He is family, when all's said and done.'

'What's he ever done for you, besides letting you down every time you recommended him for a job?'

'Whatever, he's certain it's not David, and it wasn't just because he was drunk. He's obviously been excited about it all day since he saw him ride.'

'Did he say why he was so certain?'

'No. I tried to get that out of him, but he clammed up; just said this bloke doesn't even ride like David.'

'What's he talking about? How could he tell the difference after fifteen years?'

'I don't bloody know, Mike, but he just kept on repeating that it couldn't possibly be David, and he was going to make the Tredingtons pay for what they did to him.'

'It's all bollocks, isn't it? It's got to be. He's always been sore as a fox in a wire about what happened to him, and he thinks he can get his own back by stirring up a few nasty rumours to embarrass them.' Mike considered his own involvement. 'I'll have to talk to George about it. I mean, we work for the family, and George may be an arrogant so-and-so, but he pays well, and I don't want to be connected to anything your brother does. It could cost us our jobs.'

Mike's eyes flashed with angry concern that his wife's loyalty to her waster of a brother might threaten the cosy life he and Jan had secured for themselves on George's farm.

Jan found herself panicking slightly at Mike's reaction. She was regretting, too late, that she'd told him what Ivor had said. Disguising her own doubts, though, she laughed off her husband's suggestion. 'Of course it won't,' she said. 'No one's ever going to blame us for anything he does. Besides, like you say, it's probably all bull anyway.'

November the fifth dawned bright, clear blue. The sun, rising above the bulk of Exmoor, illuminated a faint, glittering coat of frost on the ground as Aidan walked from his cottage to the stableyard.

Out exercising a newly broken colt, Aidan's sheer pleasure at the sight and smells of the autumn morning vied with other feelings of excitement and, just below the surface of his consciousness, doubts that this life could go on for ever.

He was excited, above all, because that afternoon he was riding Letter Lad in its first race under rules. Since he'd had the gelding at Barford to school it, he had become more and more impressed with it and, though he didn't admit it to anyone, he had great hopes for the animal. A tingle of pleased anticipation ran through him as he urged the beautifully conformed colt beneath him into a bouncy, ground-covering trot.

For a while, with an unfamiliar churning in his guts, he thought about the rest of the weekend that lay ahead. Lucy was arriving for lunch with a group of friends from London. They were going to organise a great firework display on the lawns in front of the house. Among the guests would be the lovely, long-legged Emma, Lucy's journalist friend.

Since he had met her, Aidan didn't pretend to himself that her blatant interest in him had turned him on. He knew that she wasn't his type, but then Sue Butley, who was, wasn't having anything to do with him, and he had found that Emma kept sneaking uninvited into his thoughts.

Aidan's charm and strong good looks disguised his lack of experience with women. Since his late teens, there had been several covert flirtations with local girls, which from time to time had led to love-making of variable passion and quality. He was self-consciously aware of how little he knew, especially for a man of his age, about how to deal intimately with a woman. Perversely, and without his knowing it, there were a lot of women for whom this diffidence only increased his attractiveness.

He didn't know why Emma should have made it so clear that she fancied him, but he was a fit man with all the normal appetites and he didn't feel like questioning it. Now he knew he was looking forward to seeing her almost as much as riding Letter Lad, and with almost as much confidence.

Aidan was well on his way to Sandown by the time Lucy and Emma arrived at Barford with four friends, Johnny Henderson among them. When it was time for the race to be shown on television, they all settled down with Sir Mark to watch.

Aidan wasn't disappointed with his first novice hurdle race on Letter Lad, who was now so pleased at his own performance in finishing fourth that he jig-jogged all the way back to the unsaddling enclosure, eager for people to notice him.

'What a show-off,' Aidan remarked to the lad as they came back. If he hadn't over-jumped at the downhill hurdle, where he'd pecked badly on landing, he'd have been even closer.

Aidan weighed in, feeling pleased with himself and the horse. Next time out, he'd press the throttle and see what he could really do.

Walking back to the changing-room, he felt a moment's *déjà vu* as a scruffy little figure in an old Barbour and flat hat shuffled into his line of vision.

There was the same shifty, cocky smile on Ivor Butley's face as there had been the day before at Newton Abbot.

Aidan gave him a friendly nod. 'Hello there, Ivor. It's a long way you've come. I hope you didn't come to back me.'

'No, though I reckon you could have won. I wanted another word with you.'

'Fine. I'll get you the drink you wouldn't have yesterday.'

'Nope. We'll want to talk private.'

Aidan shrugged. 'OK. I won't be long.'

Fifteen minutes later he found Ivor where he had left him.

They walked out of the race-course together, towards the car-park, an incongruous couple. Once they had left the crowds behind, Aidan asked Ivor what he wanted.

'Well, let me see now,' Ivor answered with a puckered forehead. 'A decent living wage for not too much work; one of them nice little cottages in Barford. That'll do for starters.'

'You mean, from the estate?'

'That's right.'

'Look here, Ivor, you'll have to talk to my father about that. I just run the stud, and we've all the grooms we need at the moment. I heard that you fell out with Dad after I left, and I was sorry to hear it, but there's not a lot I can do.'

'There'll be plenty you can do when Sir Mark goes and you get the whole lot. And don't try to tell me there isn't something you could do now, if you wanted to.'

Aidan heard the confidence in the little man's voice, and the hard edge that was making demands, not asking favours.

'I'd like to do something for old time's sake, of course,' Aidan said tentatively, 'but I can't yet. I told my father when I came back that I wanted no special treatment, just the same pay as an outside stud manager would have got, and that's what I get, besides turning a few horses.'

'You're a crafty bugger aren't you?'

Aidan suddenly thought of Susan Butley using much the same words when he'd bumped into her outside the Anchor in Lynmouth when he'd first arrived in Devon. He looked more sharply at Ivor. 'And what makes you say that?' he asked with a laugh.

'Because you made the old boy fight to get you back. My daughter told me. I spoke to her last night on the phone, first time in nigh on two year.'

'It wasn't a matter of being crafty,' Aidan said uneasily. 'It was just that I knew how much grief I'd caused, and I didn't really feel I had an automatic right to come back and demand a place to live.'

'I should think you bloody didn't, being as you haven't got no right at all. Being as you're no more David Tredington than I'm the Duke of Edinburgh.'

Although Aidan was half-prepared for this accusation, he faltered for a couple of strides. From Ivor Butley's tone, there could be no doubt that he knew he wasn't David.

Aidan stopped walking, drew himself up and gazed at Ivor with puzzled indignation. 'And what on earth makes you think that?'

'I knows,' Ivor said firmly. 'No matter Sir Mark is supposed to have checked you out and that, and that job you've done on your neck to look as though you had that birthmark taken off.'

'I see,' Aidan said, not letting his nervousness show. 'Do you mind telling me why you're so sure?'

'There's a few things, which anyone could have seen who knows what to look for. For a start, I taught David to ride, remember, and I taught him to run his reins inside his little finger. He'd have never changed that. But I've been watching you ride these last two days, and you wraps your reins right round the outside.'

Aidan laughed. 'Good Lord, Ivor, I don't think that proves much. I changed my style completely when I got to Ireland.'

Ivor shook his head confidently. 'Oh no. Once you've learned to ride one way, you won't ever change. Besides,' he added, wiping a drop from the end of his nose, 'that's only one of the reasons I knows you're not David. There's others, much bigger, you'll find out. I don't know who the hell you are, but I knows, sure as I'm standing here, there's no way you can be David Tredington.'

Aidan looked long and hard into Ivor's aggressive little eyes. Then he smiled, and shrugged. 'OK. So what are you going to do about it?'

Ivor cackled triumphantly. 'Nothing – so long as you agree to give me what I want. It ain't a lot, not to someone who'll have the money you will.' He challenged Aidan with a confident flash of his normally shifty eyes. 'But then, if you don't, I'll tell everyone you're not who you say you are. And I can prove it – no trouble. Then George Tredington will get the bloody lot and you'll end up in jail, if I don't get to you first,' he added with menacing bravado.

Aidan watched Ivor Butley shamble away across the car-park. He was feeling sick. This new threat from Ivor had far more potency about it than MacClancy's. It wasn't just a matter of the birthmark or the way he rode; Ivor's delivery had left him in no doubt that the little drunk knew as an absolute certainty that he was a fake, and could demonstrate it if he had to.

Aidan couldn't face going back into the stands. He walked round to the jockeys' car-park, climbed into the Mercedes that Sir Mark had lent him for the day, and headed back for Devon, for home.

Back at Great Barford, there was a houseful of people determined to have fun, mostly Aidan's age, confident and urbane. He was greeted with some interest by those of Lucy's friends who hadn't met him but had heard about him. Sir Mark, more privately, congratulated him on his ride and showed that he fully appreciated what he had been doing. 'Very wise to get the measure of him first time out. It looks as though you've got yourself a good horse there.'

Aidan couldn't rise to the spirit of merriment in the house-party. Most were sitting around in the drawing-room with drinks before the firework display. He saw Emma looking at him with undiminished interest as he slipped from the room. He wanted to talk to Johnny Henderson.

Johnny was playing snooker in the billiard-room at the back of the house. He was taking a shot as Aidan walked in. He glanced at Aidan and carried on lining up his cue. 'Why the hell didn't you win that race?' he asked peevishly.

'You didn't back me to win, did you?'

'Yes, I bloody did.'

Aidan shrugged. 'You should have asked me first. I'd have told you he wasn't going to win today. Next time, mind...'

'Anyone could see you were taking him for a walk. I'm surprised the stewards didn't ask you in for a chat. He'll never be that price again.' Johnny sent a long ball the full length of the spotless green baize and potted the pink. Only the black remained on the table. His opponent, an untidy, long-haired man in his late twenties, raised his eyebrows and peered with resigned disgust down his aquiline nose.

'If you pot this,' he drawled, 'I suppose I'm going to owe you a hundred.'

'Yah,' Johnny said as he walked around the table, choosing the right shot. 'Start getting your chequebook out. I'm not interested in IOUs.'

He took the shot and potted the last ball on the table. He wasn't smiling as he put his cue back in the rack.

The loser grudgingly wrote out a cheque and handed it to Johnny. 'I think I need a large drink now,' he said as he wandered out of the room. Johnny waited until his footsteps had faded down the corridor before he spoke.

'What an arsehole! Still, another four games at that price and I'll get back the money I lost on you.'

This was the first time Johnny had shown any animosity towards Aidan. He was obviously fairly drunk, and Aidan sensed that something else had upset him.

'Your betting doesn't have a thing to do with me.'

'Doesn't it? Well I'm not too happy about you muscling in on Emma, either. Anyway, she's only interested in you because she thinks you're David.'

'I wouldn't know,' Aidan said. 'I've only met her once before. But am I going to tell her I'm not David, or are you? The way things are going, she'll find out soon enough anyway.'

Johnny looked startled. 'Why? What's happened? I thought you'd dealt with MacClancy.'

'I have. I don't think he'll cause any more trouble.' Aidan heard more of the party coming towards the billiard-room. 'Come on, we'll take a walk, go and check on the fireworks or something.'

Johnny came reluctantly.

Outside, in the crisp, clear, early night-time, they walked away from the house towards the vast bonfire which had been prepared beside the old kitchen garden. In a dim light from the windows of the house and a newly risen moon, a guy was visible, perched on top of the heap of brushwood and logs. Its face was made from a turnip with a carrot for a nose. There was a sly grin on its face. Instinctively, Aidan and Johnny moved away, as if it would hear what they were going to say.

'Well?' Johnny asked. 'What's the problem now?'

'Ivor Butley. He saw me yesterday, at Newton Abbot. Came up to me and challenged me to recognise him. I was flummoxed for a moment, but I thought back over all the people you'd told me about and took a punt on it being him. He was surprised, but not for long. Then he grumbled a bit, about the way he'd been thrown out of the stud here. I offered him a drink, but he wouldn't take one.'

'So, what's the problem?'

'I haven't finished. He turned up again today at Sandown, cornered me and told me he knew I wasn't David and he could prove it. From the way he said it, I'm bloody sure he can.'

Johnny didn't reply at once. Aidan couldn't see the expression on his face, but he could tell that he was prepared to accept Aidan's judgement.

'Shit! I wonder how the hell he's so certain?'

'He said I held my reins differently from David, but he only noticed that because he has some other, much better reason for being sure. Obviously, he didn't tell me that one. Maybe he's still in touch with David. Maybe David told him where he was going; you said they were good friends in those days.'

'They were. David used to spend a hell of a lot of time down at the stables with Ivor. Ivor wasn't a bad little jockey then, and he knew his horses. It was only after David disappeared that he went to pieces and took up piss-artistry in a big way.' Johnny took a deep breath. 'What a bugger! When we've been doing so well. What the hell are you going to do about him?'

'If he's got the kind of proof he says he has, there's not a lot I can do.'

'For God's sake, Aidan!' The thought of his cut of the Tredington inheritance slipping away evidently sobered Johnny up. 'You can't give up now. What did he say he wanted to keep quiet?'

'A pension and a cottage, for starters.'

'Well, that wouldn't be the end of the world.'

'Don't be crazy, Johnny. The man's a boozer and a gambler. Once he knew he could touch me for that, he'd be after me the whole time, and there wouldn't be a thing I could do. You know, this time we're really going to have to call it a day. I mean, for God's sake, if it wasn't Ivor, it'd be somebody else. I'm never going to be able to lie in bed nights. My conscience is shot to ribbons as it is.'

Johnny struggled with his frustration. 'Just hold on, Aidan,' he said quickly. 'I know damn well you don't want to give up all this. You're loving it, being the dashing, blue-blooded amateur jockey, with all the girls looking googly-eyed at you. I just don't believe you want to go back to being an Irish peasant. And anyway, what about your mother? She's depending on you to sort out some kind of a life for her. Are you going to let her down now?' He gripped Aidan's arm. 'Listen, you've got to find a way of dealing with Ivor. I did last time – at least, I tracked MacClancy down so that you could deal with him. But please, don't do anything now, on the spur of the moment.'

Aidan grunted and kicked a mole-hill that had freshly risen in the smooth green turf. 'I don't know. Of course I like it here, and of course I don't want to let my mother down, but that Mickey being killed – it shook me . . . And I like these people, for God's sake; I hate lying to them.'

'You're not doing them any harm,' Johnny said desperately. 'Far from it. And that lad's death wasn't your fault. It wasn't MacClancy – it was an accident; these things happen.'

'I'm damn sure it wasn't an accident, and something tells me the police think so too.'

'They're just going through the motions; but as there's no possible motive, they're not going to get anywhere, are they? Stop worrying about it,' Johnny begged.

From the house, fifty yards away, floated the sounds of the rest of the party coming out into the night to light the bonfire and launch the fireworks.

'We'll talk about it tomorrow,' Aidan said quietly, then shouted across to the approaching figures, 'Lucy, who's the guy meant to be? It looks like Jeffrey Archer.'

Chapter Eight

Tom Stocker, the Barford gardener, put a blazing torch to the fire. A flame licked ten feet up into the still, cool air. Within minutes a crowd had gathered around it, glowing in the heat and dancing light.

The party had swelled to thirty or so. A dozen were staying in the house, the rest were local family friends, some of whom had known David and were taking the opportunity of seeing what he was like after his long absence.

Aidan, despite the tension caused by his encounter with Ivor Butley, took them in his stride, helped by it being common knowledge that he was fully accepted by the family. Some were struck by his apparent Irishness, at least in his speech; most seemed happy enough that this was the man who would one day be taking over Barford, an important focal point in the social life of that part of Devon.

Two of Lucy's friends brought out a gleaming copper basin full of a rum punch which they had concocted. They put it on a garden table near the fire and ladled it into beer mugs. After Aidan had had a couple of glasses of the deceptively innocuous-tasting drink, he was beginning to enjoy himself. Johnny Henderson, in an effort to appear helpful, had taken on the job of setting off the fireworks.

Rockets flared fiery-tailed up towards the stars and burst into umbrellas of twinkling multi-coloured light. Roman candles fizzed and popped, and Catherine wheels squealed. The audience, loosened by the punch, gasped and giggled as they were expected to.

Aidan found Emma beside him, and felt her hand grasp his arm as a series of rockets exploded deafeningly right above them. It seemed quite natural that he should put his arm around her.

'Are you going to keep me from the chilly, chilly dew?' she asked.

He looked at her face in the light of the fire, and grinned. 'What do you think?'

She laughed and wriggled slightly in his arm.

Beyond her, Aidan saw George Tredington watching him. George grinned and turned to the punchbowl to refill his mug. And across the fire which had soon collapsed into a pile of glowing red logs, Susan Butley was looking directly at him. Aidan gave her a smile and took his arm from Emma's shoulder.

When the fireworks were over, the punchbowl empty and the fire a pile of embers, the party drifted back to the house. There was supper and music, billiards and cards. Victoria tried to organise some games, but the London contingent weren't having it. They were more concerned about keeping the booze flowing and consolidating any promising relationships.

Over all this, Sir Mark beamed bravely, holding court in the drawing-room with those who shared his interest in racing. Aidan was brought in and introduced to the people he hadn't met before, and asked to recount his successes so far on English turf.

He lost sight of Emma until much later, when she drifted into the room with a fixed, contented smile on her lips, and curled up on the floor beside Aidan.

Later she shook his arm. 'Come on, Davy, you've talked horses for too long.'

Aidan was glad enough to get away from the racing buffs. 'I'll take this girl out and give her a bit of air. I think she needs it, and I can show her that great Irish giant in the sky.'

'What Irish giant?' someone asked.

'O'Ryan.'

He stood and held out a hand to draw Emma to her feet. As they were leaving the room, they passed Susan Butley coming in.

The sight of Emma naked came as no disappointment to Aidan; nor did the first real physical contact between them. He hadn't made love to a woman for months, since he had been in England, and making love with Emma was an entirely new experience for him.

The constant, frustrating nearness of Susan, and her *de facto* rejection of him, had built up a head of sexual energy in him which was bursting for an outlet. There was nothing about Emma's matter-of-fact, earthy attitude to induce any feelings of guilt in him, and he guessed her motives were not much different from his own.

It was some time after their first mutual and explosive climax that Aidan wondered if Emma had meant the things she had said, though he didn't much mind if her words owed most of their inspiration to the amount of punch she had drunk.

He lay beside her, serene and spent for a while, still tingling in the aftermath of orgasm.

'All right?' he asked softly.

'Mmm. Couldn't be better. I've never fucked a jockey before.'

'Ah, well, I'm only an amateur.'

'It doesn't show,' Emma murmured. She rolled half over, stretched a long leg over his, and felt for his briefly limp genitals.

Later, when they had been coupled so long that it was hard to tell whose body belonged to whom, moist with each other's sweat, they came again and she collapsed on top of him with a throaty, contented gurgle.

'That was *good*,' she whispered.

'Wasn't it just,' Aidan agreed.

Emma propped herself on her elbows so that her nipples caressed his chest. She looked into his shining blue eyes. 'You're a bit of an enigma, aren't you? For some reason or other, I didn't really expect a nice, wholesome man like you to let go the animal in him; but I had to find out.'

Aidan laughed. 'And I thought you'd be so drunk you wouldn't know if you were going or coming.'

'Tell me,' she said with a mischievous grin, 'are you really a Tredington?'

Aidan blinked. 'So far as I know,' he recovered himself enough to say lightly.

'I don't think your sister's so sure,' Emma said, not showing that she knew the effect this would have on him.

'Which sister?'

'Lucy, of course.'

'Why? Did she tell you that?'

'Not in so many words, but there's just something about the way she talks about you.'

'Good God,' Aidan said, 'I'd never have known. I wonder why?'

'Well, are you David?'

Aidan laughed. 'No, of course not. I'm just a fella breezed in from the West of Ireland and saw the chance of a comfortable living here. It was just lucky the blood tests and everything checked out . . .'

Emma looked at him uncertainly. 'Lucy never told me you'd had to take a blood test.'

'I don't suppose Dad told her.'

'So you really are David?'

'You look disappointed.'

'I am, in a way. I really fancied the idea of you being a complete con-man.'

'Well, don't tell Lucy what I said. I'll enjoy watching her over the next few days.'

'All right.' Emma grinned, and stroked his chin. 'By the way, I feel something stirring. Anything to do with you?'

Aidan looked at Susan's flushed cheeks and found himself blushing.

It was Sunday morning, but horses still had to be fed and mucked out. Susan always came in to help in the yard every other Sunday so that the regular grooms could have a lie-in.

Aidan wondered if she'd seen Emma leaving his

cottage half an hour earlier to get back to the house before it awoke. She looked annoyed about something, but at first Aidan kept up the affable politeness with which he had treated her since he'd arrived back at Barford after his short stay in Lambourn.

He got on with feeding the mares and foals, while Susan dealt with the yearlings. After ten minutes or so, he went into the feed house and found her leaning over a corn bin with a scoop in her hand. He walked up quietly behind her, until she turned and saw him, taken by surprise.

There was an uncharacteristic vulnerability in her eyes.

'What's up?' Aidan asked, before she could hide her feelings.

Susan hardened herself. 'What do you mean "What's up"? Nothing's up.'

'But you looked upset about something.'

Susan emptied the scoop of barley into the rubber bucket at her feet.

'I am upset,' she said without looking at him, 'because you're such a bloody fraud.'

Aidan looked blank. 'In what way?' he asked.

'In loads of ways, by the look of things. For a start, what the hell have you got in common with that tart, Emma?'

'Not a lot.'

Susan met his steady gaze. For the moment his answer seemed to satisfy her. 'OK, but however much everyone may be taken in by you here, I'm still as sure as I've ever been that you're not David.'

'That's what your father told me yesterday. Was it him who told you?'

'Sort of. When David disappeared, Dad was very upset, and when people were saying that David would come back, after they got the note from him, he kept on saying that they'd never see him again. He never told us why, just said there was no hope of him coming back.'

'Did you speak to him recently?'

'Yes, the day before yesterday, for the first time in ages. He told me he'd seen you at the races, and what the hell was going on here?' She shrugged. 'I said that you were back living here, and as far as the family and all the neighbours were concerned, you're David. He laughed and said you were no more David than the Pope.'

As she talked, Aidan was trying to decide on the right approach. There was a part of him that really wanted to tell her the truth, to remove the blockage to the relationship he knew they could have had. His feelings for her certainly hadn't diminished as a result of his night with Emma.

But he couldn't risk her reaction: she might be prepared to accept his reasons for what he'd done and go along with it, or she might not.

'I'm afraid your father's not in too good shape these days. If you've not seen him recently, you maybe don't know how far gone he is. I'm afraid he's probably a complete alcoholic now and, like most alcoholics, living in a fantasy world of his own.' Aidan sat down on a table next to the feed bin. 'Listen, he still resents what happened to him after I went.' He shrugged. Susan was looking less certain than she had a few minutes before.

Aidan went on. 'I don't know what happened. I was very fond of him. I spent a lot of time with him, you know that. He sometimes used to bring you up to the yard; you were maybe nine or ten then, do you remember?'

'Yes, I remember,' Susan faltered.

'Well then. What are you talking about? You and I were getting on so well before you knew who I was.'

'Do you think I don't know that? And even if you are David, what'd be the point of us having a relationship anyway? I'm just the secretary round here; and after what happened last night, I'm not so sure I'd be that interested.'

'What happened last night?'

'I saw that skinny tart leaving your cottage, stumbling about.'

'If it's a saint you want, I'd not be the man for the job anyway.'

The sound of footsteps across the yard reached them through the open door of the barn. A moment later, Victoria walked into the feed-store. Aidan and Susan just managed to put on a businesslike appearance as she came in.

'Hi, David. I didn't think you'd be up so early this morning, after Hugo's bloody rum punch.'

'I'm glad I'm not riding a three-mile chase today, but I'm just about up to heaving a few feed buckets, and of course Sue turned up to help.'

Victoria smiled at Susan. 'You are brilliant. I don't know how you do it.'

'Well,' Aidan said, 'I've done mine. I'm heading up to the house for a bit of breakfast.'

'Mrs Rogers will be pleased; she's been there an hour waiting for takers and no one's appeared yet – though,' Victoria added suspiciously, 'I did see Emma, that weird friend of Lucy's, wandering about. But I don't suppose she eats a lot of breakfast.'

Ten miles away, at Braycombe, George Tredington heaved himself out of his large oak bed and into a silk dressing-gown.

He creaked down the stairs and filled a percolator with strong Brazilian coffee, and poured himself a tumbler full of water and dropped three Alka-Seltzers into it.

He was just draining the fizzing dregs, when Mike Harding knocked on the kitchen door and walked in.

'Morning, Mr Tredington. Good party?'

'I'm not sure. I don't think so.'

'You should have stuck to orange juice.'

'With the benefit of hindsight, I should. What brings you in so early on a Sunday?'

'Early? It's after ten.'

'Well, what do you want?' George asked irritably.

'There was something I thought I should tell you about, to do with the family.'

'You'd better sit down, then. The coffee'll be ready in a minute.'

Mike Harding dropped into a kitchen chair and tried to decide how to start.

'It's about Jan's brother, Ivor,' he said.

'I thought you said it was about my family.'

'It is ... about David.'

George looked at him more keenly. 'David? My cousin?'

'Yes. You know before he disappeared, when Ivor was at Barford, they used to be thick as thieves.'

'Yes, of course. Ivor taught him how to ride, though I must say, no one thought he would turn out to be as good a jockey as he is. Anyway, what's the old drunk been up to now?'

Mike took a deep breath. 'I think he might be going to cause some trouble.'

George didn't say anything.

'He's told Jan that he thinks David's not David.'

George looked flabbergasted. 'What on earth are you talking about?'

'It's not me, Mr Tredington. It's Ivor who's said it. He says he knows David isn't really David; says he's an impostor, like.'

'What? That's absurd,' George said dismissively. 'I wouldn't take any notice of the bloody fool; I mean to say, he's drunk most of the time, wouldn't know if it was Christmas or Tuesday.'

'Of course, that's what I said to Jan, but she went to see him Friday night. She said he was pretty sober, but very excited. He'd seen David at the races at Newton Abbot, and he said there was no way it was him.'

'How the hell would he remember? And for God's sake, of course David's changed a bit since he was twelve; most people do.'

'Ah, but he says he can prove beyond any doubt that it's not David.'

Slowly, George poured coffee into two cups. 'How can he possibly prove it?'

'I don't know. He didn't tell Jan, just said he could, and he was going to use the information to get his own back on the Tredingtons.'

'Get his own back? What for?'

'For sacking him, I suppose, and he says for stealing his daughter.'

George let out a burst of laughter. 'Now that really is absurd. Susan Butley was always determined to worm her way into Barford. Frankly, it's probably a jolly good thing she did; she's made the world of difference to the way Uncle Mark runs things.'

'Well, that's what Ivor says, and it looks as though he means it.'

'But he wouldn't get anywhere. My uncle had David's story thoroughly checked out. He hasn't told David, of course, though if you ask me it was perfectly reasonable. After all, he's now been officially reinstated as heir,' he added ruefully.

'I had heard that, Mr Tredington, but I'm only telling you what Ivor said, and him being Jan's sister, if he did do anything, I didn't want it reflecting on us, like – you being part of the family and everything.'

'Good God, I'd never hold it against you or Jan for anything Ivor did.'

'Well, I just wanted to be sure. Besides, I thought it was my duty to tell you.'

'Quite right. Thank you very much, Mike. And I shall certainly see what I can do about it.'

Mike looked relieved. 'Thanks, Mr Tredington. Maybe if you was to go and see Ivor ...'

George put his hand to his mouth, tapping his upper lip with his index finger while he considered the idea.

'That's a very good notion. Give me his address and I'll try and get down there soon.'

After breakfast at Barford, when Emma didn't appear, Johnny Henderson and Aidan went out to the stud to look at the yearlings.

Susan had gone and there was no one else in the yard. Johnny didn't waste any time getting to the point.

'Right, Aidan, I've been thinking about Ivor bloody Butley. Why don't I go and see him, find out how much he knows? Maybe I could tell him I can help him do a deal with you. If he really does know anything, and can prove it, we'll just have to buy him off.'

'I've told you, Johnny, there's no way of buying him off. If we give anything, he'll just keep coming back for more.'

'Let's talk about that when we've discovered how much he really knows. My guess is he's got a hunch, for some reason or other, and he's blown it out of proportion, got himself excited about the possibilities. Maybe he's just trying it on; he's got nothing to lose.'

'OK, but I can tell you, he's doing more than playing a hunch. He knows all right. It's a matter of whether or not he can prove it.'

'Right, I'll get on to it. Trouble is, I've got to get back to London tomorrow – I've got a meeting with a punter who's keen to buy a couple of expensive yearlings. Then I'm shooting here on Tuesday. I won't be able to get down to see him before Wednesday. Look, Aidan,' he pleaded, 'please don't do anything until I've seen him. I bet I can sort it out.'

Aidan regarded him, resolved. 'Listen, Johnny, if he

really can let the cat out of the bag, I'm through with this. There's no way I'm having that hanging over me as long as I'm David Tredington.'

Johnny let out an exasperated breath. 'Don't worry about it; I'm sure he's trying it on. You'll see.'

The house-party at Barford Manor broke up on Sunday afternoon. Aidan watched the cars pull away with a lot of shouted 'goodbyes' and promises to keep in touch.

Johnny Henderson's was the last car to leave. There was a pleasing calm about the place when it had rolled off down the drive with Emma curled up sleepily in the back seat.

Aidan smiled to himself and walked back into the house with Sir Mark.

'Come and have a drink in the library,' the baronet suggested.

'As long as it's not that rum punch we had last night.'

Sir Mark laughed. 'There wasn't a drop of that left by midnight, thank God.'

In the library, the older man's manner became more serious and self-conscious. He poured a drink and sat with it in a favourite armchair. 'Help yourself,' he invited Aidan gruffly.

Aidan sat down opposite him, on the other side of an unlit fire. A horizontal shaft from the last of the afternoon's autumn sunshine pierced the tall window, glittering on a silver statue of Saint George, and on the bookshelves beyond.

Aidan glanced at his adopted father. 'You look tired.'

Sir Mark nodded. 'I can't take these weekends like I used to. Not that I don't like having the house full of the next generation; I still wish Victoria had met someone she liked before that jockey came on the scene. Not,' he added, 'that I've anything against jockeys as a breed.' He sighed. 'Still, I suppose I shouldn't complain. She's been a model daughter, considering she was brought up by an old blimp like me.'

'I don't think anyone would call you an old blimp.'

Sir Mark smiled, but the smile quickly faded and his face seemed to collapse into a mask of overwhelming sadness. He looked at Aidan. 'David, there's something I ought to tell you. I should have told you before, but even the girls don't know yet, though maybe they suspect.'

Aidan held his breath.

'I'm afraid I've never been a great man for quacks, and when I first started getting a pain in my guts, I ignored it. One can put up with quite a lot of pain if one feels inclined to.' He paused and looked thoughtfully at Saint George about to plunge his sword into a small, hapless dragon. 'A few months ago, just before you reappeared, it became intense enough for me to take it seriously. I'm afraid by the time it was diagnosed, it was too late to stop.'

Aidan felt himself close to tears at the bleak bluntness of Sir Mark's delivery. 'What is it?' he asked almost in a whisper.

'I'm afraid the spleen and now the intestine. They could hack a lot of it out, and subject me to monster doses of radiation, but there's small guarantee that it would work and, frankly, if I've got to go, I'd rather do it with a bit of dignity.'

'But surely,' Aidan said, panicking, hating the idea that the whole purpose of Johnny's plan was so much more imminent than they had imagined. 'Surely it's worth a try? I mean, you're only sixty; you could have another twenty or more years in front of you, and you've a lot to offer.'

'Have I? To whom? I'm just a man who was born lucky enough to be handed this place.' He waved his arm to take in the house and grounds. 'I've bred a few good horses. Hardly mould-breaking stuff. Most people would call me an anachronism.'

'You've a lot to offer the people close to you. Lucy, Victoria ... and me.'

Sir Mark nodded. There was a faint smile on his lips. 'And you. That's made me very happy. It makes the whole thing a lot easier to bear.'

'Have they given you something to deal with the pain, at least?'

'Oh yes. I'm taking a jar full of pills a day – rattling like a tin can.' He forced a smile, trying to make light of his condition. 'They take the edge off it, but they seem to make me more depressed. Or perhaps I'm just getting more depressed anyway.'

Aidan stared at the man who had trusted him, who had shown him a paternal affection he had never known. And he knew he didn't want him to die. All his instincts wanted there to be no secrets between them. If admitting to his own deception would have prolonged the man's life, even for a few years, he'd have done it. As it was, his conscience told him, it would probably have the opposite effect.

'Jesus, Dad, I'd no idea. You've not shown it at all. I wish to God there was something I could do.'

'There is. You're helping me just being here. Having a

son again.' He grinned. 'There is one other thing you could do, and that's win the Hennessy with Deep Mischief for me. And you never know, he could be a Gold Cup horse after that; I've never won a Gold Cup.'

Aidan laughed. 'We'll win the bloody race for you, just you wait. And make sure you win yours, too,' he added gently.

'Thanks,' Sir Mark nodded with no hint of self-pity. 'I'm aware that I'm not the only one with problems, though. I've been meaning to ask you how Mary is? It must be a worry for you – after all, she was virtually a mother to you for fifteen years.'

'Yes, it's a worry,' Aidan said. 'Things don't seem to be getting much better, and she has the odd bout of almost total immobility. As soon as I've made a bit of money turning a few horses, I'm planning to organise things for her so she'll have the care she needs at home.'

'I could probably help out with that.'

Aidan looked at Sir Mark, more grateful than he could express for the generousness of the offer, but he shook his head. 'No, Dad. She's not your responsibility and, I told you from the start, I want to make my own way here – and I can.'

'Yes, I believe you, but it will take a while before you can build up much of a base to start dealing in the kind of horses that will really earn you some money.'

'I should do well out of Letter Lad.'

'You're planning on selling him?'

'As soon as he's given a hint of what he can do.'

'I hope you don't do *too* well out of him; that would really upset poor old George.'

'He doesn't seem to have taken it too badly so far.'

'No,' Sir Mark agreed. 'I'm rather impressed . . . Getting back to Mary, though: don't you think you ought to pop over and see her? We can manage without you for a few days here. You're riding on Saturday, aren't you?'

'No, I'm not as a matter of fact.'

'But you told me Letter Lad was running at Chepstow. Has Sam decided to withdraw him?'

'No, but he's only to carry ten stone. I can't do that, so I'm going to ask Jason.'

Sir Mark nodded. 'Good idea. I wonder if he will? Still, I expect you'll want to be back in time to watch it. Why not fly over to Ireland after shooting on Tuesday, or on Wednesday morning, and spend a couple of days there?'

Aidan smiled. 'You're very perceptive. I'd been thinking exactly that myself.'

'I tell you what, that Taunton builder – what's his name? Bruce Trevor, the chap you won that race for – he's got a plane and a pilot. He'd always get you over there. He keeps it at Weston. I'll give him a ring. I'm sure he'll do it, if I ask him,' Sir Mark added.

After a night of patchy sleep, tussling with his conscience, Aidan woke wanting more than ever to throw himself into his work to repay Sir Mark for his generosity.

He and Johnny had agreed not to do anything about Ivor Butley until Johnny had seen him. Aidan wasn't riding out at Sam Hunter's that day, so he spent the morning working on two well-bred fillies he was breaking before they were sent to a Newmarket yard to see how they would perform on the flat.

The Tredingtons stuck to a policy of hanging on to all

promising-looking fillies, and selling the colts. Normally, the fillies would have been sent to their trainer for breaking at the end of their yearling year, but Aidan had persuaded Sir Mark that he could do it just as well, and save a few months' training fees.

He loved dealing with the young horses, and knew how crucial it was to their later performance that they were handled correctly now. He had the capacity to be utterly single-minded while he was doing the job, and several satisfying hours passed before he went to the house to face Sir Mark and his conscience over lunch.

They didn't refer to their conversation of the previous evening, and spent most of the meal discussing possible stallions for mares who were due to be covered the following spring. There was no doubt that Sir Mark derived a lot of pleasure from a task which had occupied him for over thirty years, despite the fact – of which they were both tacitly conscious – that it was probable that he would never see the progeny of the unions they were discussing.

After lunch, Aidan wanted to get out on his own, away from the house and the yard, to try to come to terms with the dilemma which faced him. The wind that had been threatening to blow up a storm all morning had relented, and there were even a few patches of blue showing through the wispy winter clouds.

He tacked up one of the older mares who had failed to get in foal that season, and walked her out of the yard towards the pasture that swept up to the cliff-top. To reach these big open fields, he had to make his way for half a mile along a track through a wood of sycamore and twisted oaks. At the end of the track, a five-bar gate gave on to the first of the fields. On any of the chasers, he'd have popped over the four-foot obstacle without a second thought; on an unfit old mare, it was too risky.

He dismounted and led her towards the big metal catch. As he reached it, he stopped. His eye had caught a movement on the far side of the field. There was a straggling, wind-swept hedgerow which led up towards the cliff before petering out.

A man dressed in a khaki jacket and leggings was walking along below the hedge; something about the cautious, uneven way he was moving suggested he didn't want to be seen.

Aidan's natural curiosity made him stop and watch as the furtive figure reached the end of the hedge and darted across the open grassland towards the cliff-top, where he disappeared.

Aidan had ridden these top pastures a few times. It was the traditional exercising ground, despite the lack of fences along the cliff-edge. Water drained fast through the thin soil, leaving a consistent surface of sheep-grazed sward.

He was about to open the gate when a second figure appeared below the hedge, moving stealthily, almost certainly following the first. Aidan strained his eyes to try to identify them, but the distance was too great. He could be sure only that this person, probably a man, was dressed in a long brown coat. He watched, fascinated, until the pursuer also crossed the open field and disappeared.

He wondered what on earth they were doing: possibly it was a game of cat-and-mouse between a poacher and a keeper. He opened the gate quietly, led the mare through, closed it and remounted, then trotted gently over to the hedge and followed it up to the top. Tethering his horse to the last sturdy blackthorn trunk, he walked the thirty yards to the top of the cliff.

There was a slight dip into a shallow, grass-lined gully where the two men must have dropped out of sight. There was no one there now. Aidan walked down to where the cliff fell away sharply. At this, the lowest point, a rough and under-used track started a switch-back course down the cliff-face.

The man in the long brown coat was just reaching the bottom of the track. Aidan flung himself down so that he wouldn't be seen against the skyline. He eased his head through the damp grass to get a clear view of the small, isolated beach below.

The brown-clad individual was now moving quickly but cautiously along the back of the beach in the direction of a naked rock headland that projected into the sea. It was clear that he was only concerned about his quarry spotting him; he didn't once look back up the cliff to where Aidan lay watching. Before he reached the end of the beach, he clambered up on to a low outcrop of rock and tucked himself into a shallow indentation scooped in the bottom of the cliff, and there he waited.

Twenty minutes later, Aidan was concerned about the old mare he had left tethered. The damp was beginning to seep through his long waxed riding coat, too, and the tide had turned and was creeping back in towards the foot of the cliff. The man in brown hadn't moved, and Aidan had given up trying to identify him from that distance.

Aidan thought it was time to go; whatever was

happening down there was probably none of his business. But his curiosity kept him hanging on. A moment later he was rewarded.

The first man emerged from what must have been a cave-mouth invisible from Aidan's viewpoint. His pursuer had also spotted him and sank deeper into the shadow of his hiding place.

The khaki man seemed confident now that he hadn't been followed. He set off back across the shrinking beach without looking back. He had almost reached the bottom of the track that led back up, when the brown-coated man, instead of following, darted down and round to the point where the other had come out of the cliff.

Aidan watched, fascinated, but quickly switched his attention to the man who was now clambering up the cliff below him. Half-way up, he was close enough for Aidan to see who he was, if only he would look up. It wasn't until he reached a tricky stretch of track, fifty feet below Aidan, where it was crossed by a stream trickling down the cliff, that the man raised his face.

It took Aidan a fraction of a second to take in who it was; quickly he pulled his head back among the cover of the damp grass tuffets. Keeping doubled up, he scrambled to his feet, sprinting back to where he had left the mare. Within seconds he was on her back and urging her into a reluctant canter, back towards the gate into the woods.

This time, Aidan had to risk the mare's rusty limbs. He put her squarely at the gate, helped her with her stride, and kicked her up and over it. She flew into the gloomy opening without any hesitation. Aidan grinned and slapped her neck. He pulled her up as quickly as he could and wheeled round to see if Ivor Butley had reached the top of the cliff.

To Aidan's intense relief, it was a few seconds before a silhouette appeared on the skyline. He heaved a sigh of relief and watched Ivor head for the cover of the hedgerow and start back down towards the woods.

Aidan walked the horse back through the trees, guilty that he had pushed the old mare harder than he should have done, but she seemed none the worse for it and was still sound when he arrived back at the yard.

He handed her to Billy, one of the stud-grooms, and asked him to give her a good dressing over. 'Any messages?' he added.

'No, Mr David, except Jason was here looking for you earlier.'

Aidan stopped walking. 'How long ago?'

'Dunno. Half an hour?'

'What did he want?'

'Didn't say.'

'If he comes back, tell him I'm up at the house.'

Aidan checked some of the horses before jumping into his Land Rover and driving the few hundred yards to Jason and Victoria's cottage. Victoria opened the door to him.

'Hi, Davy,' she beamed, 'you look rather damp. Do you want a cup of tea or something?'

'No thanks. I just wanted a word with Jason.'

'He's not in. I'm not sure where he is. He was out when I got back.'

'When was that?' Aidan asked, more sharply than he'd intended.

'Is it important?' Victoria asked, worried.

'No. It's just that he was looking for me. I thought it might have been about him riding Letter Lad.'

'He was wondering why you wanted him to.'

'He can do the weight; I can't,' Aidan said simply. 'Anyway, tell him I'm up at the house.'

Mrs Rogers made Aidan some tea. She told him that Sir Mark wasn't feeling well and had gone up to his room. Susan had driven down to Lynmouth to pick up some stationery. Aidan tried to chat to the kind old housekeeper, but his mind was full of Ivor Butley, coming clandestinely to Barford, clambering down a slithery cliff-face to spend half an hour in a cave in what he had been told was one of the most inaccessible beaches on the North Devon coast.

Not wanting to let his impatience show, Aidan left Mrs Rogers in the kitchen when he finished his tea, and walked through the silent house towards the library. As he passed the office, he heard the fax machine in action. They were expecting details of race entries. He went in to see what had arrived.

He picked up the piece of paper that the machine had spewed out. It was a message to Sir Mark from a firm of lawyers in Sydney, Australia.

'We have a report that three members of the crew of White Fin, lost off Norfolk Island, were picked up and arrived in Fiji on 2 November. We have no confirmation that David Tredington is among them, and no further information relating to the identity of this person. We will inform you as soon as possible of any further development.'

207

As he read, Aidan grew numb with shock, until he could scarcely feel the sheet of paper between his fingers. There was turmoil in his guts as all the conflicting possibilities paraded themselves in front of him.

After what he had seen that afternoon, he had been in no doubt that Ivor Butley's visit to the cave had been prompted by his need for proof that Aidan wasn't David. And that someone else – the brown-coated man – was presumably on a similar quest. But who the hell was this David Tredington in the South Pacific? And what did Sir Mark know about him?

He listened for a moment for sounds of anyone else in the house, heard none, folded up the sheet of paper and tucked it in his pocket just as he heard a man's voice from the back of the house. A moment later, footsteps echoed along the corridor and George Tredington walked past the office door.

Aidan went out to meet him. 'Afternoon, George.'

'Oh, hello, David. Mrs R said you were in the library.'

'Just on my way there. Are you having a drink?' They carried on together across the hall towards the library.

'Thanks. I wanted to see you; I really need to know if you've decided to take the spare house gun tomorrow. I've a couple of eager paying stand-ins if not.'

Aidan nodded as he poured two whiskies. 'I thought I might, though I don't suppose I'll worry the birds much.'

'It'll be interesting to see how you shoot now. I used to be very envious of you as a boy.'

'Well,' Aidan said cautiously, 'I've had no practice at all since.'

'Never mind. Should be a good day.' The sound of

someone else walking across the hall reached them. George turned expectantly towards the door. 'I hope this is your father. I just wanted to check he's happy with my instructions to Jim Wheeler.'

Jason Dolton walked in. He was wearing muddy jodhpur boots, and a long brown waxed coat, similar to the one Aidan had hung in the back hall half an hour earlier.

He gave Aidan a surly nod. 'Vicky said you were back 'ere. What's this about me riding Letter Lad Saturday?'

'You can do ten stone without any trouble, can't you?' Aidan asked.

'Yeah, 'course I can.'

'Well, I can't get near it. He's right down the handicap, and I thought you might like the chance of an easy win.'

'That's very generous of you,' Jason grunted sarcastically. 'I'll take the ride, if I don't get offered a better one.'

'Great!' Aidan said with an enthusiasm he didn't feel. 'You won't get a better offer. Letter Lad should just about win, after his last showing.'

'We'll see,' Jason said, turning to go.

'Hang on, Jason,' George said, finding it difficult to talk to him as a member of the family. 'You still haven't told me if you're shooting tomorrow. You know you really should; it makes it very tricky to organise properly otherwise.'

Jason looked at Aidan. 'Is he shooting?'

'Yes,' George said impatiently.

'Then so am I.' Jason left the room this time without another word.

Aidan didn't speak either as he listened to the footsteps fade across the hall and through the green baize door. He was trying to relate Jason to the figure he had seen following Ivor down to the beach. George interrupted his thoughts.

'Chippy bugger. I can't think what possessed Vicky to marry him.'

'I doubt he's like that all the time,' Aidan said. 'It was probably a pretty daunting prospect for him marrying into this family. And,' Aidan added, 'maybe he's just beginning to realise that he's never going to make it to the top.'

'You think so?'

'I'm afraid I do.'

'Hmm,' George grunted. 'That reminds me,' he said, 'I was meaning to talk to you about Letter Lad. How did he go on Saturday?'

Aidan shrugged. 'Did you not see the race?'

'Yes, I did. He didn't really seem that interested.' George found it hard to keep a touch of irony from his voice.

'Ah well,' Aidan said with a grin, 'I can't expect to win them all. Maybe I was a bit too optimistic, and you did the right thing by selling him.'

'I think you'll find I did,' George said with a laugh. 'Still, best of luck with him.'

'Thanks,' Aidan said, relieved that George had misread the race at Sandown. 'Now, I'm still half-soaked. I'm going home to wallow in a bath for a while.'

'Fine,' George said. 'I'll hang on until your father gets down.'

Chapter Nine

Tuesday, the day of the shoot, dawned dry and still beneath a blanket of thick grey cloud.

Sir Mark had suggested that Aidan walk up and have breakfast at the house. Johnny Henderson had invited himself to stay the night before, and had turned up from London at three in the morning. He and George were already at the table when Aidan walked into the dining-room.

Mrs Rogers waddled in and out with dishes of scrambled egg and bacon, while George talked about the quality of sport they were going to have.

'I've given my gun to Johnny for the day as a tip for finding me some decent horses,' he said heartily, 'despite the fact he sold you Letter Lad. Also, I'll be able to keep my eye on Jim Wheeler's beaters. I want to make sure they do the job properly. With no wind, we should get some good high birds on the coomb drives, and there are plenty in the oak coppice woods. It would be marvellous if old Lord Barnstaple hit a few for a change.'

'Listen,' Johnny said, chewing hard on a piece of bacon, 'when those horses I bought you start winning, I shall want a few more days' shooting here.' He kept his eyes fixed on George, knowing that just the thought of training a couple of winners, seeing his name in print, was enough to have him promising the earth.

'Of course, dear boy, of course. I'll make damn sure there are plenty of birds next season, just for you.'

Aidan listened apprehensively. Apart from a few surreptitious outings with one of the keepers, a clay-pigeon trap and a borrowed twelve-bore, he had scarcely fired a gun in his life. It wasn't an activity in which he had ever participated in Ireland. And David the boy was supposed to have been something of an infant prodigy with a four-ten.

Lord Barnstaple, the owner of a neighbouring estate, and two local farmers of considerable substance, all of whom contributed to the costs of the shoot, appeared during the course of breakfast. There were to be eight guns in all. Mike Harding and Victoria, with a sixteenbore, were coming to make up the numbers.

As the table filled, Aidan was able to catch Johnny's eye and indicate that they had to talk, somewhere else.

No one took much notice of them leaving together – to sort out their guns, they said. In the gun-room they made certain they couldn't be heard.

'Look, Johnny,' Aidan said, 'things have been happening down here.'

'Like what?' Johnny asked nervously.

'I saw Ivor Butley yesterday, and someone else following him down to the beach.'

'To the beach? What beach?'

'Down below the gallops, near a point called Stanner Head on the map.'

'Why the hell was Ivor going down there?'

'I don't know, do I?' Aidan said testily. 'But I'd say it

was pretty likely to have something to do with his proving I'm not David.'

'But why down there?' Johnny shook his head.

'God knows! Maybe David left something there which Ivor's kept hidden for years. He went into a cave and came out about half an hour later. Then this other fella slipped in after he'd gone.'

'Who was that, then?'

'It was too far away for me to tell.'

Johnny looked at him keenly. 'But you've got an idea, haven't you?'

Aidan sighed and nodded. 'I can't be sure, and I can't make the connection, but I think it was Jason.'

'Oh my God. That's all we need,' Johnny moaned. 'I wonder what the hell he knows about it. Of course, he's totally pissed off about you turning up; he's made that pretty clear all over the place, because he thinks Vicky won't get her farm now.'

'Sure, I know that. But I'd like to know how he got on to Ivor.'

'I'll find out what I can from Ivor tomorrow when I go down and see him.'

'That may not be soon enough.'

'It'll have to be. It'd look very odd if I suddenly ducked out of a free day's shooting.'

'Yes, I suppose that would be a little out of character. Mark's arranged for me to fly to Shannon tomorrow, so I can see Mary but, for God's sake, you must get down there tomorrow. I don't trust that Ivor. And there's something else I've got to show you.' Aidan pulled out the fax he had pocketed the evening before and handed it to Johnny.

Johnny's mouth twitched into a grimace as he read. He handed it back to Aidan with a shrug. 'Don't worry about it.'

'What do you mean – don't worry? If the real David has turned up in Fiji, that's the end of it.'

'I don't know who the hell he is, but I'm pretty damn sure it isn't the real David and, more to the point, so is Mark.'

'You knew something about this, then?'

'As a matter of fact I did, yes. Mark told me when he first got the report that a David Tredington was one of the crew who had gone missing on *White Fin*.'

'When was that, for God's sake?'

'When I was over here in August, gathering up material for you.'

'Why the hell didn't you tell me then?'

'I didn't want to put you off your stride unnecessarily. And anyway, not long before you arrived here, Mark got a report from these lawyers saying they couldn't find a trace of any David Tredington who'd been in Australia. And since then, he's accepted you without reservation, so he obviously doesn't think this chap is his son.'

'God, you might have told me.'

'But at that stage I still wasn't sure you were going to do it anyway. I took a punt.' Johnny grinned. 'Lucky I did, or we'd never have got as far as we have.'

'I wish to God we hadn't,' Aidan said. 'I was leading a peaceful life out in Mayo until you turned up, and now Mickey's been killed, and I'm being threatened by a drunken old groom, and Jason too, if it was him I saw yesterday.'

214

'Look, don't worry about Ivor. I'm sure he can be sorted out, whatever he knows.'

'I hope to God you're right. Anyway, we'd better get a move on and join the others, or George will start fussing.'

As they were walking back to the dining-room, Mrs Rogers intercepted Aidan to tell him he was wanted on the phone. Johnny went on; Aidan made his way to Sir Mark's study.

'Hello?'

'Mr Tredington?'

'Yes.'

'Sergeant King here, Hampshire CID. A couple of things have cropped up on this accident in which Mickey Thatcher was killed. I'd like to come out and interview you as soon as possible.'

Aidan's heart pounded. 'What sort of things?'

'I'll tell you when I see you. When would be convenient? I'd like to come today, if possible.'

'I'm tied up most of the day,' Aidan apologised, 'but I could be free by six.'

'That'd be fine, if you could just give me directions.'

Aidan gave them as calmly as he could and put the phone down, itching with frustration. It would be hell having to wait until the evening to hear what this policeman had to say. But he was sure that, whatever it was, it would confirm his suspicion that the crash had been no accident, and that he had been the intended victim.

George had concocted a new ritual for drawing peg numbers. After breakfast, when Jason had arrived, each gun was given a small silver tumbler filled with port, which they all drained at the same time, to find their number etched into the bottom of the tumbler.

'I've reorganised all the drives and the numbering,' George declared, 'so you won't know what you're in for until you get there.'

The party set off south in a convoy of Land Rovers which left the metalled drive and lurched down a farm track to the river. There, a crowd of twenty or so beaters, keepers and pickers-up waited. They were gossiping, stamping their feet to keep out the seeping damp, yelling at their dogs, nodding to the guns they knew.

Johnny Henderson was in Aidan's Land Rover. As they pulled up beside the other vehicles, he grabbed Aidan's arm. 'Christ! Have you seen who's beating?'

Aidan looked more closely at the group of thickly wrapped men, some with dogs, most carrying stout sticks with which to beat the woodland undergrowth. Among them, hunched over his stick, Ivor Butley was blowing on his hands.

'Jesus!' Aidan hissed. 'Does he usually beat?'

'I haven't seen him out for years.'

'Can you try and find out why he's come?' Aidan asked. 'See what reason he gives?'

'Sure. I knew him well enough when he was working here.'

They climbed out and joined in the general banter between the other guns. Only Jason stood apart from the group, not feeling part of it and resenting it.

'I'll be with the beaters and the pickers-up,' George announced in the manner of a general before a battle. 'Any queries, refer them to me.'

Johnny strolled across to the beaters and said hello to those he knew, until he reached Ivor.

'Good heavens! It's Ivor, isn't it? Haven't seen you for years. What brings you back here?'

Ivor was on the defensive. 'Mr George came round my place Sunday. Said he was short of beaters. Says he wants to raise the standard now he's taken over the shoot.'

'Great to see you back. No dog, though?'

'Haven't kept a dog in years.'

'I expect you'd rather be carrying a gun, eh? You used to be a bit of a crack-shot in the old days. Anyway, I'll get you a drink afterwards if you make sure to flush a few my way.' Johnny gave a hearty laugh and carried on to talk to a couple more of the regular beaters he knew.

George was directing the guns to their pegs now. Aidan was already walking to a peg at the far end of the valley. George pointed Johnny in the opposite direction.

To get the day off to a good start, George had arranged to drive a conifer wood on the steep valley side both ways and, as he had predicted, a thick flock of pheasants screamed out of the top of the trees and across to the cover on the far side of the deep coomb.

Trying to remember everything that had been told him, Aidan aimed well in front of the racing birds and, to his amazement and mild disgust, downed a couple at each of the first drives.

Afterwards, George appeared by his side and made a point of coming over to congratulate him. 'Not bad for a man who hasn't shot for fifteen years. I'm afraid you won't get much of a crack on your next peg, but things will improve after that.'

Jason, who had hit everything he'd aimed at from the next peg, was less complimentary and more disgruntled than ever.

'I've had enough of this,' he said to George. 'I've got better things to do than stand around shooting these easy driven birds with a bunch of snobs.' He pointedly started putting his gun back in its sleeve.

'That's a shame,' George said, not disguising his relief. 'Still, it'll leave more for the rest of us to shoot at.'

'If you can hit them,' Jason said, striding off towards his battered pick-up without saying goodbye to any of the other guns.

Twenty minutes later, Aidan found himself completely alone on the next drive, out of sight and hearing of the rest of the shoot. He was supposed to be covering the flank of the oak coppice wood, where the birds would tend to leave by the other end. A few might fly back over the beaters, if he was lucky, George had promised.

He heard the head-keeper blow a whistle to start the beaters. This was followed by the sound of wood hitting wood. Shrieks and whoops echoed back to him from the close cover. A few minutes later, the sound of multiple gunshots reached him from the far side, where the pheasants were evidently emerging in some numbers. None came back towards him. He wasn't sure that he wanted to shoot them if they did, but he kept his gun cocked and ready.

Behind him was a swathe of thick mixed woodland

where the Exmoor deer sometimes came and sheltered. He heard a distant movement from inside the wood and wondered if there were any there now. He turned to have a look, but his gaze didn't penetrate more than a few feet into the dense woodland. As he was turning back, he heard the sound of a shot from the woods behind him. Almost at the same instant, there was a vicious burning sensation in his arm.

He had been hit, and not by a shotgun.

For a moment, he couldn't take in what had happened.

He glanced at his stinging arm where a little blood had seeped through and stained the ragged edges of a tear in his Barbour. He flexed his arm and winced, but the arm functioned. He dropped his cocked twelve-bore and leapt as the trigger caught on the branch of a small gorse bush beside him and exploded at his feet; the shot scattered harmlessly across the tussocky ground in front of him.

He pulled off his waxed coat and the tweed jacket he was wearing under it. His shirt was bloody but he was able to examine the wound. It had already stopped hurting so badly, and after gingerly prodding round it, he concluded that the damage was only on the surface. Whatever had hit him had skimmed past and carried on.

Thinking fast now, Aidan pulled his jacket back on and snatched up his gun. He rejected the empty cartridge, replaced it and ran towards the wood behind his peg. There was no obvious way in there. He ran twenty yards along the edge until he reached a narrow fire-break. The grass was long and wet between the ruts made by timber-hauling tractors. After ten yards, there was a crossing of ways and, along the track to his left, above a small clearing, he spotted a wooden platform about fifteen feet high; it was a 'high seat', used occasionally for the culling of the Exmoor deer. He ran to it, stopped below it, and listened.

He could hear nothing besides the melancholy autumn calls of small woodland birds, obliterated now and then by the alarmed honking of pheasants and the blast of guns on the far side of the big oak coppice.

Aidan scrambled up the ladder to the sturdy timber platform. As his eye came level with the floor, his heart thumped harder. There was a discarded brass cartridge case lying a few feet in front of his face. He clambered the last few steps and reached across for it. It was still warm. Whoever had fired it couldn't have gone far. He listened again, more intently, for ten or fifteen seconds. But there was no sound of human movement.

He stood up on the platform and looked through the trees towards the point where he had been standing at his peg. Though partially obscured by scantily leafed branches, there was a viable view of the spot, especially with a telescopic sight.

His mind raced. After what had happened to Mickey, he'd promised himself that, whatever it cost, there'd be no more deaths – his own or anyone else's. But then, there didn't seem any reason to kill him, not for anyone who knew and could prove that he wasn't David.

Shaking with uncertainty and anger, he climbed down to the ground and looked for signs of a departing human. But he had no tracking skills, and there was no obvious disturbance among the woodland that bordered the fire-break.

In the distance, the shots were becoming more sporadic.
The drive would be over soon, and he would be expected
to join the rest of the party to move on to the next. He
was running back towards his peg when he heard the
plaintive whistle of the head-keeper bringing the drive
to an end.

He looked around to see if there was anyone else
nearby who might have seen what had happened. There
didn't appear to be. He rubbed some earth on to the tear
in his Barbour to obscure the bloodstains, unloaded his
gun and walked back round the wood to the Land
Rovers.

George was fussing around, overseeing the beaters
and pickers-up who were gathering up the twenty or so
brace of pheasant which had just been shot. He glanced
at Aidan.

'Any joy your end? I heard a couple of shots.'

Aidan shook his head with a self-effacing grin.
'Missed 'em both,' he said.

'Bad luck. Never mind, they had a good haul here.'

'Aren't you sorry you're not carrying a gun yourself?'

'I'm quite enjoying myself overseeing things, though I
might take Jason's peg for the next drive.'

'He's gone, then?'

'Yes, missed the last drive, silly bugger.'

There were two more drives before they stopped for
lunch in a small abandoned woodman's cottage. Mrs
Rogers and a couple of women from the village had
arrived before them with a large stockpot of casseroled
venison, a case of claret and port. They had managed to
squeeze a splendidly laid table, with silver candelabra,

in what had once been the parlour of the small timber-framed house.

Johnny and Aidan walked in together. Johnny appreciatively sniffed the aroma of the venison. 'That smells fantastic, Mrs Rogers. Did you make it?'

'No. Victoria did.'

'Did she? I wondered what had happened to her. She was supposed to be beside me on the last drive. I suppose she came back to help you.'

'No. I haven't seen her. Look, here she comes now.'

Victoria walked in looking flustered.

'Hello, Vicky. What happened to you?'

'Sorry,' she said. 'Jason was having one of his moods and wanted to talk to me,' she said uncomfortably.

Aidan glanced at her sharply. He had already gathered that Jason hadn't been seen since the second drive. Looking away from Victoria, he was abruptly assailed by a series of crazy possibilities. But Johnny didn't give him the chance to ponder them now.

'Do you remember lunches in here when we were kids?' he asked.

Aidan nodded absently.

'Don't you remember, David,' Johnny prompted across the room, 'when we were about ten, trying to snaffle a bit of port?'

Aidan laughed at his non-existent memory of the event.

The party in the old cottage became rowdier as it filled up and people took their seats around the table. The claret started to flow, and carried on flowing until all the food had been eaten and the port was being passed round. It was traditional to have this lunch late, and leave only two short drives for the afternoon when the light would fade fast.

As he tried to join in, Aidan couldn't tear his mind from the fact that someone had attempted to kill him. Every so often he fingered the empty cartridge case in his pocket to remind himself it hadn't been some kind of horrible daydream.

None of the party seemed to notice his discomfort: they were past such subtleties by then. But when one of his neighbours went out to relieve the pressure on his bladder, Johnny Henderson came over and sat down beside him.

'What the hell's wrong with you? You look as though you've seen a ghost,' he said out of the side of his mouth.

'Sorry.' Aidan made an effort to brighten up. 'I'll tell you later.'

Johnny raised his eyebrows and turned to the conversation on his other side.

When lunch was over and the guns walked out of the cottage, the beaters started to climb out of the back of a Land Rover where they had been eating their sandwiches. Aidan, watching them, caught Johnny's eye. Johnny nodded slightly and walked over to talk to them.

Aidan turned to George who was beside him.

'Wasn't old Ivor Butley beating this morning?' he asked.

'Yes, he was as a matter of fact. I went down to see him on Sunday evening.' George glanced around to make sure that they weren't being overheard. 'The fact is, he's got some funny ideas about you.'

With an effort, Aidan restricted his reaction to a slightly raised eyebrow while George went on.

'His sister Jan's my groom, and he told her he'd seen you at the races and...' George paused awkwardly. 'Well, to be quite frank, he said he was sure you weren't David.'

Aidan laughed. 'Well, he's not the first to have thought that since I came back, and I dare say he won't be the last. Silly old fool; I recognised him the minute I saw him.'

'Of course,' George said. 'Anyway, I thought I'd better see what his idiotic theory was all about, you know, just in case. I told him that the family had made absolutely certain that you are David, and there was not a scintilla of doubt about it. I think I managed to convince him. Anyway, when he asked if he could come up and beat, I thought that might put an end to his story.' George looked anxiously at Aidan. 'I do hope you think I did the right thing?'

'Sure, you did, George. Thanks very much. I dare say the old fella's still bitter about what happened after I left. Maybe if he feels he's been summoned back into the fold a bit, he'll get over it.'

'Just what I thought,' George said with relief at Aidan's evident approval. 'He used to be pretty useful in the old days, so I agreed. But he must have brought a hell of a big flask with him because he was fairly pissed after the first couple of drives, and unfortunately I had to send him home.'

Aidan couldn't hit anything after lunch, but nobody took much notice. Though George, now on Jason's peg next to him, was watching him with interest, he made no comment. After what seemed to Aidan like several hours, the party finally loaded their twelve-bores back into the vehicles and wound their way across the estate towards the house. Johnny Henderson went in Aidan's Land Rover.

'What's happened?' he asked as soon as Aidan had started the motor and joined the convoy.

'Someone tried to shoot me this morning.'

'Shit!'

'Yeah, and they'd have killed me if I hadn't just been turning round. As it was, I've got a small chunk of flesh out of my upper arm.'

'Is it OK?'

'I'm fine; it's not serious. But this thing is getting out of hand. Maybe whoever dropped that sleeper on the car was trying to kill me, not just warn me; maybe it was MacClancy.'

'Why the hell should MacClancy still want to kill you? You said he wouldn't cause any more harm. And anyway, how would he have been able to get anyone to have a go at you down here?'

'God knows. I don't know what the hell to think. Maybe I should have reported it to the police at once, but I've left it too late now.'

'No. You can't go to the police, not without telling them who you are.'

'Of course I can. The only reason I didn't was for Sir Mark's sake. You were right this morning when you said he's accepted me totally. And there's no doubt it's done him a lot of good. I'm beginning to feel guilty as hell about it, but I know damn well how much it would harm him if he found out now.'

Johnny looked at him cynically. 'That's a pretty

speech, Aidan, but I don't think you want to do a few years' porridge, either. And what about your mother and the money you're going to need to take care of her?'

'If there's one thing I've learned since I got to England, it's that I'd have no trouble making a decent living out of horses here.'

'There's a difference between making a living and coming into ten million quid – less my half-million,' Johnny said.

Aidan pulled up the Land Rover in the courtyard behind the house where the rest of the party's vehicles were parked.

'Well,' he said as he switched off the motor, 'I'd not hold my breath over that, if I were you.'

All the guns were invited to stay for drinks before heading home after tea. Although Jason hadn't come back, Victoria was there, trying to disguise her mortification over her husband's ill-humour. The guests were gathered in the big drawing-room to talk contentedly about the day's sport before moving on to wider topics.

Most of them had an interest in racing and took advantage of Aidan's presence to glean a few inside tips. But all the time he talked, his mind was a maelstrom of conjecture about who had shot at him.

It had to be someone connected with the shoot, or the house; at least someone who was aware that he would be shooting that morning, and which peg he would be on.

Jason hadn't reappeared since he had left after the first valley drives, and Aidan was still fairly sure that it was Jason he had seen following Ivor down to the beach.

He had no doubt at all that he'd seen Ivor on the beach, and then Ivor had turned up to beat that morning for the first time in years. But he could see no good reason why Jason, or Ivor or, for that matter, MacClancy or anyone else would want to kill him. Whilst it was true that the jockey held a grudge, and he had been at Fontwell on the day Mickey had died, Aidan just didn't think Jason had it in him to attempt murder.

Maybe it was Ivor; perhaps he had concluded from Aidan's attitude at Sandown that he wasn't going to get anywhere, and was motivated by pure bitter frustration...

These thoughts and the conversation he was holding simultaneously were interrupted by Mrs Rogers coming in to tell him he was wanted on the phone.

He excused himself and went to take the call in the office.

'Hello, Davy?' Emma's voice purred down the telephone line. 'How did the slaughtering go, then?'

'OK, provided you weren't a pheasant.'

'Were you all right?'

'How do you mean?'

'It's just that Lucy said on the way back to London that you seemed a bit nervous about shooting again.'

'Nervous, me?'

'Well, maybe she didn't say nervous, just apprehensive.'

'It was all fine. I hit a few and everybody was very happy.'

'Nothing else happened?'

Aidan hesitated. 'Like what?'

'It's just that you sound a bit odd.'

Aidan managed a laugh. 'That's fifteen years of living in Ireland for you.'

'Anyway, are you coming to London again soon?'

'God knows,' Aidan answered, then added quickly, 'Things are quite busy with the horses just at the moment. And I'm off to Ireland tomorrow morning until the end of the week.'

'Maybe I'd better come and see you racing one of these days.'

Aidan felt a stirring between his legs as an image of Emma, naked, lying on his bed sprang into his mind.

'Make sure you don't tell me you're there till after the race, then. Otherwise I might have trouble getting my breeches zipped up.'

Emma laughed. 'Just thinking about you squeezing into them turns me on.'

'You're a wicked woman. I'll be in touch,' Aidan said, 'but I'm needed back at the party now.'

Aidan winced guiltily at the edge in Emma's voice as she said goodbye. When he had put the phone down, he reminded himself that she was a girl who was quite capable of looking after herself. Besides, he was a lot more interested in Ivor Butley's altogether more substantial daughter.

He left the office but didn't go straight back to the drawing-room. Instead, he made his way through echoing corridors at the back of the house to the courtyard where the cars were parked.

He let himself out of the back door and stood silently for a moment, making sure there was no one else around. A steady drizzle had set in and the worn cobbles gleamed in the light of a single naked bulb. When he was confident that he was on his own, he selected two vehicles and walked across to them.

Both were unlocked and he was able to make a thorough search of each. He had been nursing a hope that he might find a rifle that fitted the cartridge he still had in his pocket. But he found nothing suspicious in either car, or in the other three that he searched. Jason's pick-up, which he guessed Victoria must have driven up, only contained a brace of pheasant.

He was just closing it when he heard someone open the back door of the house. He ducked down by the passenger door of the Subaru and hoped it wasn't Victoria.

He listened carefully. The footsteps, a heavy clip on the cobbles, suggested someone heavier. He peered over the car bonnet. It was George, who walked across the courtyard to a green door on the far side of the yard. This opened into an all-purpose store-room. He went in and, after some clattering around inside, came out again carrying a bulky object which he took over to his Range Rover and placed in the back. He banged the tail-gate down without locking it and walked quickly back to the house.

Once he was inside, Aidan got up from where he was crouching and made straight for George's car. Holding his breath, he lifted the tail-gate. It turned out to be nothing more than the clay-pigeon trap which he had been using himself over the last week to improve his own shooting. He guessed that George had decided after his performance that day that he also needed a bit of practice, but didn't want to publicise the fact.

Frustrated that he hadn't discovered anything to help

him, Aidan went back to the drawing-room. No one in the party seemed to have missed him particularly, now that some of them had gone into the billiard-room. He joined in the conversations going on around him as naturally as he could, while his mind raced, selecting and rejecting a dozen different courses of action.

Within half an hour, the guns began to leave, until only Sir Mark, George, Johnny and Aidan remained.

George was as affable as ever, congratulating Aidan again on his moderate performance on the shoot and chaffing him light-heartedly about Letter Lad, until he too announced that he was going home. As he drove out of the gates, an anonymous Vauxhall drove in. A few minutes later, Mrs Rogers was opening the door to a tall, shambling figure who identified himself as Detective Sergeant King. Mrs Rogers showed him into the library and went to fetch Aidan.

Aidan walked in a few moments later. 'Good evening.'

'You're Mr David Tredington?'

'That's me. Have a seat.' They sat in chairs either side of an unlit fire. 'How can I help?'

'As I told you on the phone, a couple of things have cropped up. We think we may have traced the truck which was carrying the sleepers, and forensic have established that some kind of fluorescent marker paint was sprayed on your vehicle, possibly very recently.'

'Fluorescent paint? Where? How? I certainly didn't see any.'

'Well you wouldn't have done, from the ground. Even though you're quite tall, you're probably not tall enough to see over the roof of a Range Rover.'

'There was paint on the roof?'

'Yes. A small "X". Do you recall seeing it there before?'

'God, no. And I'm sure I'd have seen it some time or other. Why do you think anyone did that?'

'To identify your vehicle as you drove along the motorway. No problem from the bridge with the sodium lights reflecting on it.'

'You think someone was waiting for me?'

'Why else would anyone go to the trouble of marking your car?'

Aidan didn't answer at once. 'Jesus! You're saying you think someone was trying to kill us?'

'I'd say someone was definitely trying to kill you.'

Official confirmation of what Aidan had felt in his guts since the incident eight days before produced another rush of guilt about Mickey. He got up and walked across the room, unable to look the policeman in the eyes. 'You're saying you now think someone tried to ... murder me?'

'That's right.'

Aidan turned to face him. 'But who the hell would want to do that?'

'I'd have thought you were in a better position to answer that than we are. That's why I'm here. Who do you think might want to kill you?'

Aidan's head was crowded with all the possibilities that had been running through it since the crash had happened. He shook it to clear it. 'No one,' he muttered. 'There's absolutely no reason anyone should want to kill me – no reason at all that I can think of. I mean, I'm a new boy over here. I've not been in England over two months.'

'So we gather. But you could still have put a few noses

out of joint since you got here. Or was it something you got up to back in Ireland?'

Aidan shook his head. 'No. There's nothing like that.'

'What were you doing in Ireland, then?'

'Farming a small place in Mayo. I'd no enemies over there. There was no reason why I should have.'

'What about someone trying to stop you ride here?'

'Why should they? If I couldn't ride one of my father's horses, there'd always be a few pros ready to do it, and probably make a better job of it than I would. Anyway, it's not as though anyone's had a big gamble on any of our horses.'

'Yet.'

'I have to tell you, I think that's a pretty unlikely scenario. Are you really sure about this mark on the car?'

'Yes, we're sure. Only found it by chance, when the security lights at the compound lit it up. You rolled the car and slid it on the roof for about twenty yards.'

'Yes, I remember.'

'And also, we've had a sighting of someone clambering on to the vehicle, in the car-park. The witness thought he was just playing a prank with a bit of graffiti. It's not a lot, but it's a start. And you're telling me definitely that you can't come up with any names for us to follow up?'

'I'm afraid not, though of course I'll do everything I can to help.'

'I'm sure you will, sir.'

'You said you may have traced the truck with the sleepers?'

'Maybe. We know where the sleepers were stolen

from.' The detective stood up and took a few paces towards the door. 'Not all that far from here, as a matter of fact. Travellers probably. The local force think they might have a line. We'll see.' He took out a note-book, scribbled his name and telephone number in it, tore out the sheet and handed it to Aidan. 'Get in touch if you've got anything to tell me, won't you? I'll probably need to see you again, so see if you can come up with any names for us, all right? Don't worry. I know the way out.'

Aidan watched the policeman stroll from the room. As the footsteps faded across the hall, he dropped back into the chair he had been sitting in and stared at the empty fireplace.

Later he went upstairs and found Johnny Henderson coming out of a bathroom. They went to Johnny's bedroom, where Aidan told him what he had heard from the Hampshire policeman.

'Look,' Aidan said, 'you'd better be bloody careful with Ivor. I mean, all these things may be connected.'

'I don't see how.'

'Nor do I. If I did, I'd know what I was dealing with. I'm being picked up at half-six tomorrow morning, so I won't see you. I'll ring you from Ireland in the evening.'

Johnny nodded. 'Sure. I'll have to go back to London after I've seen Ivor. You can reach me there.'

Chapter Ten

Bruce Trevor had not only agreed to Sir Mark's suggestion that he put his plane at Aidan's disposal, he had also offered to send a driver to collect Aidan from Barford.

When Sir Mark had described him as 'that Taunton builder,' he had been understating the property king's commercial standing. Bruce Trevor had been responsible for developing shopping malls all over the southwest of England, and had sold out the previous year for a rumoured sixty million. These days he spent most of his energy and some of his enormous resources trying to capture the major trophies of English jump racing. Aidan had twice ridden for him, and won, and Trevor was anxious for him to do so again in the more prestigious big amateur chases: he would have done almost anything to curry favour with Sir Mark.

By eight o'clock, Aidan was installed in one of the six seats of a Cessna Citation, while a taciturn pair of pilots ran their checks and prepared to take off on the short flight to Shannon.

Driving up through Galway to his old home produced an irreconcilable blend of emotions in Aidan. He felt that he was, after his two months as David Tredington, an altogether new person. At the same time, the sight of the hills and coast tugged at him, making him almost sick with nostalgia.

Mary's greeting confused him further.

She was, as he had expected, overjoyed to see him. There had been no deterioration in her health in the two months he had been away, and she had lost none of her cheerful courage.

As they sat at the old farmhouse table eating the stew she had made for their lunch, she pumped him with questions about his new life, the family and his racing ambitions; she seemed delighted with his answers.

Reluctantly, and only under pressure from Aidan, she revealed the most recent medical report on her condition. It was hard to tell exactly what the doctor who had compiled it really meant. Reading between the lines, Aidan inferred that Mary's illness was entering a new phase and was likely to take a turn for the worse soon. She might be looking at no more than a few years of uncomfortable, increasingly immobile existence. Aidan made a note of the specialist who was handling her case so that he could contact him directly and extract a more precise prognosis.

Besides this, Mary told him, the farm finances were in a dire state. The odd bits of money he had sent her had helped to stave off an immediate crisis, but the bottom of the barrel was in sight.

As he talked, Aidan did everything he could to prevent his mother seeing the strain he was under. The last thing he wanted her to know was that a lad had been killed as a result of his deception, and that just the day before, someone had tried to shoot him. As he smiled and talked about his hopes for Deep Mischief in the Hennessy and, God willing, the Cheltenham Gold Cup, he couldn't keep his thoughts off Ivor Butley, and Jason and MacClancy. Every few minutes he found himself wondering what Johnny had found out, counting the hours till he could phone him in London.

A wet north-westerly followed Johnny Henderson from the North Devon coast to Tiverton.

Cursing the puddles in the rough ground that served as a car-park for the block of council flats in which Ivor Butley lived, Johnny picked his way to the shabby building and up the open staircase to Ivor's front door.

He pressed a little-used button and heard a buzzing inside the flat. Five minutes later, he had supplemented his buzzing with hammering and yelling through the letter-box. He still hadn't succeeded in arousing Ivor, when an old woman in slippers and a frayed apron appeared at the neighbouring door.

'If you're looking for Mr Butley, he's gone out.'

'But it's not nine yet.'

'I know. But sometimes he goes out to a farm for a few days to look after some horses when they goes away.'

'But I thought he didn't have a job?'

'Are you from the social, then?' the woman asked with interest.

'Lord, no. I ... I'm a friend.'

The old woman wasn't convinced, but saw no reason not to help. 'He don't work much but, like I say, there's a farmer, sort of a friend of his, he helps him now and again. They come and pick him up, to make sure he turns up, I s'pose.'

'Do you know where the farm is?'

'Not far, just out at Washfield. Bacon, the farmer's called; suits him, too. He looks a bit porky.'

Johnny nodded. He didn't imagine any friend of Ivor's could be anything other than repellent. 'Bacon, in Washfield?'

'That's it.'

'And you're sure that's where he's gone?'

'Yes, I saw them go off together not half an hour ago.'

'I'm most grateful to you. I do need to see him rather urgently.'

'I shan't complain if you locks him up.'

Johnny didn't stay to explain that this wasn't his aim. He turned and went back down the concrete stairs, ignoring the mud which splashed his trousers as he ran through the rain to his car.

Once in, he pulled out a map, found Washfield, a few miles outside the town, and skidded off on to the road.

An enquiry at the first cottage in the village told him that Mr Bacon had a small-holding called Withy Farm a mile further on, not far off the road. He got the impression from his informant that Mr Bacon wasn't held in great esteem locally.

When he saw Withy Farm, he wasn't surprised. The fields and dilapidated buildings which it comprised showed all the signs of slack farming, apart from the quality of two well-rugged mares in a paddock beside the road.

Johnny gingerly drove his BMW along the pot-holed

track that led to the house and a range of stone-built barns with corrugated iron roofs. He drove through an open gateway and parked his car among the discarded trailers and muck-heap in the weed-infested yard.

He got out and tucked a bottle of Scotch into a pocket of his Burberry. The rain had eased to a misty drizzle. He walked carefully to the front porch which sheltered a worn and flaking grey door.

There was a rusty knocker and no bell. He hammered hard.

This time Ivor appeared promptly, shabbier than ever and chewing something. The old groom took a second or two to register who he was looking at.

He grinned, revealing a few bad teeth and a mouthful of toast. 'Hello, Mr Henderson. You come to buy a horse off Bert?'

'No. I've come to see you. I was told you were looking after the horses here for the day.'

''Sright. Bert's taken a couple to the Ascot sales. What d'you want with me?'

'OK if I come in?' Johnny asked, walking into a cluttered, dirty hall where a strong smell of frying prevailed.

Ivor let him through and pushed the door shut behind him. 'What do you want?' he asked with growing suspicion.

Johnny turned and looked at him. 'It's about David Tredington.'

'What about him?' Ivor stiffened.

'Relax, Ivor. We're on the same side. Is there any-where remotely civilised in this house where we can sit?'

Ivor quickly picked up the way the conversation was

going. He gave another grin, less uncertain now, and pushed open a door into a front room – an old-fashioned parlour furnished two generations before.

Johnny pulled the bottle of whisky from his pocket, put it on a table and took off his raincoat.

'Any chance of a couple of clean glasses?'

Ivor nodded and went out. He reappeared a moment later with two grimy tumblers. Johnny pulled a handkerchief from his pocket and carefully wiped one before filling them both with whisky. The two men sat down in ancient chintz armchairs either side of the table.

'I gather you have some doubts about David being who he says he is,' Johnny said.

Ivor took a large gulp of whisky and exhaled deeply. 'Did he tell you that?'

Johnny ignored this. 'Why don't you think David is who he says he is?'

'It's not I don't think he's David; I know bloody well he isn't.'

'But Sir Mark had him checked out. An investigator was sent to Ireland and David's story was confirmed, and the family have formally accepted him.'

'Maybe, but it's not him, sure as you're sitting in that chair,' Ivor said firmly.

'Why are you so sure?' Johnny pressed.

'Don't you worry about that. You tell me why you says we're on the same side?'

Johnny took a sip of whisky – his first – while he watched Ivor take another big slug.

'David asked me to come and see you, to work out a deal.'

'You mean the bloke as says he's David.'

'We'll call him David, OK? If you know something that might be embarrassing to him and you can back it up with hard evidence, he's prepared to come to reasonable terms with you.'

Ivor grinned again. 'That's more like it. So, I keeps quiet, and your friend gets the estate. Serves the fuckin' Tredingtons right if they lost the lot to a con-man.'

'I also have an interest in a satisfactory outcome,' Johnny said quietly.

'You're in for a cut too, are you?' Ivor cackled. 'I always thought you was a bit of a chancer. It was you put him up to it, was it? Well, you didn't do a bad job. He looks the part, all right, and he knows what's what. Give me a real turn, he did, when he knew who I was. If it hadn't been for me knowing he can't no way be David, I reckon he'd have got away with it.'

'And now he is going to get away with it.' Johnny filled Ivor's glass with whisky again.

'It'd be worth a tidy bit, then, for me to keep quiet, wouldn't it?'

'That depends on what proof you can provide.'

'That'd be tellin', wouldn't it?'

'If you want anything out of it, you're going to have to tell me – or there's no deal.'

'I'll tell you what happened, but I won't tell you where the proof is, otherwise you might try and get rid of it, if you could ever get at it. And then where'd I be?'

Johnny sighed. 'We'll see.'

'First, what's in it for me?'

'No chance. When you've told me as much as you're prepared to, I'll tell you what it's worth.'

A smile spread over Ivor's face. He was feeling in control of the situation now.

'I know where David Tredington is, right now.'

Johnny didn't move a muscle. He stared back at the little man.

'At least,' Ivor said, 'what's left of him.'

'You mean – he's dead?'

Ivor nodded. 'Oh yes.'

Johnny gulped. 'How ... how do you know?'

Now he was talking about it, Ivor became nervous. He clutched his whisky glass for support. 'I found him, dead, on the beach, the day he disappeared.'

'Good God!' Johnny whispered at the final revelation of the truth behind the puzzle that had mystified David's family for fifteen years. 'What happened?'

Ivor's eyes misted over. He let out a long groan as he nodded. 'It was all my fault.'

Tears filled his eyes at the memory and his own guilt. 'I felt terrible. I really liked the boy; he always treated me like a real friend. But I couldn't bring him back to life, and I knew I'd get the blame.' He stopped again, looking down into his glass.

Johnny waited silently for him to go on, but Ivor would say no more.

Johnny gazed at him without speaking. The rain and the wind outside seemed louder. For the first time, he noticed a dog barking out in a barn. 'Have you ever told anyone about this?' he asked at last.

Ivor shook his head. ''Course not. I went to pieces after, knowing I was sort of to blame. I couldn't ever tell anyone why, could I? But I got the sack anyway, and Shirley and Susan had moved out. No one wanted to know after that.'

Johnny nodded sympathetically. 'Of course, you'd have done much better to tell them what happened in the first place, but you couldn't, I suppose.'

'I wish it never happened. It weren't my fault, but it ruined my life. Whatever I did wasn't going to bring him back, and I knows they'd have all blamed me.' He nodded his head slowly, relieved, it seemed, to have unburdened himself of fifteen years of guilt.

It occurred to Johnny that he'd overlooked something. 'But what about the note? Did you send it?'

Ivor looked puzzled. Johnny pressed him. 'You know, the letter David was supposed to have sent, saying how unhappy he was?'

'Oh that,' Ivor nodded. 'No. That's a mystery, that is. I put it down to someone playing a sick joke.'

'You could be right,' Johnny said. Abruptly, he changed the subject. 'What suddenly brought you back to Barford, beating for the shoot the other day?'

Ivor's eyes slid sideways as he answered. 'I told you, Tuesday. Mr George asked me, when he came down to see me. I thought I could keep my eye on this so-called David.'

'But you went after the second drive.'

'I had a couple of other things to do.'

'Like what?'

'None of your business.'

'It is, if it had anything to do with David.'

'Well, I ain't tellin' you, nor nothing else till I has something in writin' from your con-man friend.'

Johnny stood up. 'OK. It'll take a few days, so don't do anything to rock the boat. I'll be back at the end of the week to talk terms.'

At Barford that afternoon, as Aidan was away, Sir Mark went down to the stud to do the rounds with Victoria and the head-groom. They were half-way through the horses when Susan Butley arrived in the yard, breathless from running and with tears streaming down her face.

'Sir Mark. I'm sorry, but I'm going to have to leave early,' she tried to say calmly.

'Whatever's the matter, Susan?' He could see that she was struggling not to break down completely.

'They've just found my father. He's been kicked in the head by one of the stallions at Bert Bacon's.'

'Good Lord! Is he badly hurt?'

'Yes. They've taken him to hospital in Exeter. He's in intensive care, but they say he may not last more than a few hours. He'd been unconscious in the box for several hours at least, but there was no one there to find him.'

Sir Mark put a comforting hand on her shoulder. 'Why don't you let Victoria drive you?'

'No!' The refusal sounded sharper than Susan had intended. 'No, thank you. I'll be better on my own.'

Sir Mark glanced at Victoria over her shoulder and shrugged. 'All right, but ring me later and tell me what news.'

'Of course. Thanks.'

Susan turned and ran back to the house to get her car.

'Poor old Ivor,' Sir Mark said, watching her. 'Though God knows, he shouldn't have been allowed to deal with horses any more.'

He and Victoria followed Susan back to the house. In his study, Sir Mark picked up the phone and dialled Mary Daly's farm in Mayo.

Aidan answered, and involuntarily flushed with guilt when he recognised Sir Mark's voice.

'Hello, David. How's it going over there?'

'Not too bad, thanks. I'm glad I came.'

'Well, I'm sorry to disturb you, but I felt I ought to ring you. There's been a rather nasty accident. Susan's father has been kicked in the head, apparently very badly. They think he may not live, and she's had to rush off down to the hospital in Exeter.'

Aidan blanched. That Ivor Butley should have had an accident like that, on the day Johnny had gone to see him, was more of a coincidence than he could accept. And yet, and yet, he admitted reluctantly to himself, if Ivor did die, it would solve a problem. Unless, that was, he talked before he died.

He turned his head so his mother couldn't see his face. 'Poor old Ivor,' he muttered. 'I remember him well.'

'Do you?' Sir Mark sounded surprised. 'I'm afraid he became very unreliable and I had to let him go. I suppose, in a way, that's why I took Susan on; though frankly I don't think she had much to do with him for the last dozen years. It was a great shame. Ivor was as good a groom as you could have found, honest and conscientious, and he had a natural empathy with most horses. But the fact is, he'd become a more or less complete drunk. I can't think why Bert Bacon would have left him in charge, poor old chap. If he dies, I suppose we'd better let them bury him in the church at Barford, if that's what they want,' he added.

Aidan thought of the burial he had already witnessed there – Mickey Thatcher's. Maybe, indirectly, he was to blame for this second one, too.

'I think I'd better come back right away,' Aidan said, regretting it almost at once. 'With Susan away,' he went on hurriedly, 'and all the arrangements, there'll be no one to do my work.'

'Well, that's up to you. Can you get in touch with Bruce Trevor's pilot?'

'Sure. He gave me a number; said he'd come back and get me whenever I wanted, if he wasn't on another trip. Otherwise I'll get a flight to Bristol.'

'Let us know if you want collecting, then.'

An hour later, Aidan drove down to Louisburgh to phone Johnny Henderson in London.

Johnny answered after two rings. 'Aidan? I've been waiting here an hour for you to call.'

'Did you see Ivor?'

'Yes, I did. I had a very interesting chat with him. I can't tell you the details over the phone but, for the time being, the situation's under control.'

'Don't you know what's happened to him?'

'What?' Johnny picked up the urgency in Aidan's voice. 'What is it?'

'He's had some kind of accident. They found him unconscious in the stallion's box, and they don't think he'll survive.'

'Jesus Christ! When did this happen?'

'Earlier today. What time did you leave him?'

'About eleven. He'd had a skinful of whisky by then; I'm surprised he even made it out to the yard.'

Aidan couldn't tell whether or not he was lying. He didn't speak and waited to see what Johnny would say next.

'Aidan? Are you there?'

'Sure I'm here, Johnny,' he said quietly.

'Look, it wasn't me, I swear! It must have been a bloody accident; of course it was. I couldn't have asked the bloody horse to kick him, could I?'

'How do you know it was a kick?'

'Well, what else could it have been? And anyway, what did they tell Susan?'

'They told her it was a kick.'

'See!' Johnny sounded relieved. 'It couldn't have happened at a better time.'

'That's what worries me.'

'For Christ's sake, Aidan, I wouldn't do a thing like that.'

'You were mad enough when I told you.'

'Sure I was annoyed, bloody pissed off in fact, but I squared him, no trouble.'

'He may pull through; he may talk. We've got to be prepared for that.'

'Shit!'

'Well, if he does, he does,' Aidan said. And maybe, he thought, that would at least bring this episode of the nightmare to an end. 'Look, there's nothing we can do. We'll just have to wait. If I get more news, I'll let you know. I've got to get back now.'

'I'll ring the hospital and tell them I'm a relation.'

'I wouldn't. I don't think they'll believe you, and they may trace back the call. Ring me tomorrow and we'll arrange to meet.'

Aidan put the phone down. He stared through the grimy panes of the phone-box at the lights from the bar across the street glowing in the dark night, and wondered, not for the first time, what the hell he'd got himself into.

George Tredington was waiting early next morning to meet Aidan at Bristol Airport. Aidan sank gratefully into the leather upholstery of the big BMW.

'Morning, David,' George said sombrely. 'Have you heard about Ivor?'

'I heard he was in hospital.'

'I'm afraid to say he didn't pull through. He's dead. Poor old bugger. I wonder what the hell he was doing in that stallion box.'

Aidan couldn't help the relief he felt. 'Did . . . didn't he come round before he died?'

'No, he didn't. It's a bit of a mystery how he was kicked, but that horse had a bad name apparently and, frankly, Ivor probably wasn't sober.'

Aidan looked out at the grey morning, trying to gather his thoughts. 'He looked bloody rough out beating on Tuesday, and when I saw him at the races.'

'I told you, didn't I, he had this bee in his bonnet about you?'

Aidan nodded. 'Yes, you did.'

'I expect the police will want to talk to you about that.'

'The police? What have they to do with it?'

George grinned. 'Don't worry. I was joking. There's

no question of foul play, though I suppose there'll have to be a coroner's hearing, given the rather bizarre circumstances.'

'Who found him, then?'

'Bert Bacon.'

'Who's he?'

'He's a rather disreputable breeder and dealer. Oddly enough, he's bred a few good horses in his time, despite the fact his farm looks like a pig-sty. But then, he's always had a good eye for a mare. He was about the only person who'd still give Ivor a few days' work, and that wasn't often. He got back from Ascot mid-afternoon, found Ivor laid out in the box, stinking of whisky with the hell of a dent in his head.'

'Is Susan down there?' Aidan asked.

'Yes. So's his sister, Jan, my groom.'

'She's Ivor's sister, is she? I'd forgotten that. Is she upset?'

'She is rather. God knows why. Ivor caused her nothing but trouble for the last fifteen years. Still, she'll get over it.'

They talked inconsequentially for the rest of the journey. Aidan had to be alert not to show what he was thinking. To his relief, George dropped him at his cottage and said he had to be getting back to Braycombe.

It was still only half-past ten. Aidan should have gone straight up to the house to see Sir Mark, or down to the stables. Instead he went upstairs to change. When he got to his bedroom, he succumbed to the temptation to be alone for a while and lay on his bed, staring at the ceiling.

His head was reeling from the events of the past week.

Two threats to expose him.

Two accidents?

Two deaths.

Two attempts on his own life.

Even if he'd wanted to, he couldn't back out of the position he'd got himself into; not now he knew about Sir Mark's condition. Aidan was suddenly determined to get at the truth, for the sake of Sir Mark and the missing boy, as well as himself. Feeling calmer with this decision made, he went up to the big house. Sir Mark greeted him with another bombshell.

'Rather alarming news about poor old Ivor. Susan rang from the hospital. The pathologist who carried out an autopsy on him last night has declared that in no normal circumstances could the stallion have kicked him the way it did.'

'What? How do you mean?'

'I'm not too sure exactly, but apparently the angle at which the shoe hit his head was wrong. And also, the indentation is from a rear hoof, and the animal was only shod in front. I'm afraid they suspect there may have been foul play.'

'Jesus! Why'd anybody want to kill someone like Ivor?'

'God knows. Maybe he owed money or something.'

Aidan was beginning to feel as if a rope were tightening about his throat. He poured himself some coffee and took a gulp. 'You know I had a visit from the police Tuesday evening.'

'So I gather. Something to do with your crash. But that's got nothing to do with Ivor.'

'No, I was just mentioning it.'

'What did they want?'

Aidan sighed. 'They say there was some kind of mark painted on the roof of the car; they think it was to make identification easier, for someone who was waiting on the bridge to drop the sleeper on us. The fella who came asked me who I thought might have done anything like that. Of course, I told them there was no one.'

Sir Mark gave him a long worried look. 'And is there?'

Aidan shook his head. 'Of course not. Why would there be?'

Aidan spent the rest of the morning frustrated at having no word from Johnny. He wanted to see him face to face, to be sure he wasn't in some way responsible for the kick on Ivor Butley's skull. And he was desperate to hear what Ivor had said. But when he phoned, there was no reply from Johnny's London number. He wrote a card to his mother, feeling guilty about his abrupt departure, and went to the village to post it. When he got back to his cottage, Victoria was waiting there for him.

Although the grounds for his suspicions about Jason were skimpy – his possession of a brown raincoat and his disappearance after the second drive of Tuesday's shoot – in the absence of more plausible ones, Aidan still had him up among the prime suspects, especially now that Ivor was dead. But he knew that whatever the case, Victoria wasn't involved, and he found himself over-compensating and greeted her with more effusiveness than he'd intended.

She looked pleased. 'Hi, David. Where have you been?'

'Just posting a card.'

'Oh? Who are you writing to? Not Emma?'

Aidan laughed at Victoria's look of disapproval, and

the fact that Emma hadn't entered his head for two days.

'No. Only to Mary. I felt bad about cutting the visit short, though, to tell the truth, she wasn't too upset. I had to promise I'll go back again soon.'

'It must be odd for her, having treated you as a son for so long, and now you're a young English blade. Anyway, I only popped in for a chat and to ask you if you're going to Sam's tomorrow.'

'Sure,' he said airily, 'I might as well. I wouldn't mind seeing how Letter's going before Saturday.'

'Are you all right, David? You seem sort of flustered.'

'No, no. I'm fine. I was just wondering how Deep Mischief will run too. I really want him to win the Hennessy. Dad would love it.' He looked at his watch. 'I told him I'd pop back up and see him before lunch, so I'd better go. I'll see you tomorrow, if not before.'

Aidan's discomfort increased when Susan Butley arrived at the house at the same time as him. She wasn't expected. When she had rung early that morning, she had said she would be in Exeter for a few more days, until her father was buried.

She nodded at Aidan. 'I'm glad you're here; I want to speak to you.' She seemed a lot less self-assured than normal, and said no more than this as they walked through to find Sir Mark sitting in the library.

'Hello, Susan,' Sir Mark greeted her warmly. 'There was no need for you to come back so soon.'

'I've got to go back tomorrow. Jan's still there and Mum wanted me to come back with her anyway and, er' – she hesitated – 'I wanted to speak to David.'

Aidan took his cue. 'Why don't we have our discussion at lunch, Dad? The vet's down at the yard now and there's a couple of things I want to sort out with him. You come with me if you want, Sue.'

Susan looked relieved.

Outside, they walked across the spongy lawns towards the stables.

'I'm very sorry about your father,' Aidan said.

'Are you?'

'Of course. He may not have been the man he was, but he was a good man before things went wrong for him.'

'You mean before David was killed?'

Aidan stopped dead in his tracks with his heart thumping.

He forced himself to speak lightly. 'What are you saying now? I thought we'd had all this out on Sunday?'

'So did I,' said Susan calmly enough. 'But when the autopsy showed that Dad's death was no accident, my mother nearly broke down while we were driving back and told me something she'd never let out before.'

Aidan cleared his throat. 'And what was that?'

'She said that Dad had made her swear never to tell anyone, not even me, and she'd stuck to it, even though it got so bad she had to leave him.' She paused. Aidan didn't speak although his thoughts were racing. There was only the sound of their footsteps crunching on the gravel path which led across the lawns to the yard. 'I suppose,' Susan went on, 'she understood why Dad felt so bad, and perhaps she didn't blame him.'

'Blame him for what?' Aidan asked hesitantly.

'He thinks it was all his fault. David had been

pestering him for weeks to ride one of the colts that had just been backed. He was a beautiful horse, apparently, but he broke his leg a few months later and had to be put down – I don't really remember him.'

'That doesn't matter,' Aidan said, trying to conceal his impatience to hear Susan's story. 'What happened?'

Susan sighed. 'Anyway, Dad let David take the colt out. David said he was going up to the cliff gallops. He was a good rider, and strong for his age, but Dad should never have let him go on his own.' She stopped, then blurted out, 'The colt came back without David, an hour later. Dad realised he must have dumped the boy somewhere and went out to look for him, petrified that something awful had happened and he'd be blamed – Sir Mark had specifically forbidden David to ride any young horses.'

Aidan heard Susan gulp with the telling of the story. 'Poor old Dad, he must have been wild with worry. He hunted everywhere, but he couldn't find a sign of David in the fields. He went down to the beach, really panicking now. At first he couldn't see him there either, but he found him in the end, lying below some rocks by Stanner Head . . .' Susan's voice faltered. 'He must have fallen right down the cliff. You know what it's like there – he'd smashed his head on the rocks on the way down. The tide must have carried him round and washed him up by the cave. He was dead.'

'Jesus,' Aidan hissed, letting out a long breath. 'Fifteen years of mystery, and all the time your father knew what happened.'

'He thought it was his fault; he'd be blamed, sacked, lose his job, the cottage . . . And he loved working here,

Mum said, up till then. He hid the body, he told Mum. No one ever found it. They looked, of course, but when they got the letter, everyone thought he'd just run away.'

'But who sent the letter? Was it your father?'

'I don't know.'

'Does ... does your mother have any idea where he took the body?'

'None at all. He wouldn't tell her; said he didn't want her involved. I suppose he must have buried it somewhere.'

Aidan thought there had to be a connection with Ivor's visit to the beach. He considered coming clean and telling Susan right there what he'd seen the day before the shoot. But other options raced through his mind.

He could bluff it out, say that he, David, hadn't died, but had come round and walked away. There was only Ivor's word against his, and that couldn't be heard now.

But Susan *knew*. Whatever he said, however he said it, she wouldn't believe him.

They were approaching the yard now, where there were a dozen pairs of ears to hear them. He stopped. 'Let's walk on past. We can take a look at the mares in the paddocks.'

Susan nodded. She looked helplessly distressed, vulnerable in a way he had never seen before. He smiled, sincerely, affectionately.

'What are you going to do about it?' he said quietly.

Susan looked back at him with an uncertain expression that showed none of the hostility of the past few months. Inwardly, Aidan heaved a sigh of relief. He knew at last that he and Susan had reached a turning point in their relationship. Tentatively, he reached out a hand and took her forearm, squeezed it with gentle encouragement.

'I've thought about that. There's not a lot I can do, is there? Without knowing where Dad put the body, and without a body, who's going to believe me? But if Dad was *murdered*, I've got to know why. And I'm sure you want to know why, too.'

'Do you think I had something to do with it then? Since he'd told me he knew I wasn't David?'

A faint smile spread across Susan's lips, surprisingly generous lips in a woman so self-reliant. 'I considered that, of course. It seemed obvious. But I thought back and reckoned I could say where you were getting on for twenty-four hours before he died.'

'Maybe I paid someone else to do it?'

'No. You're no killer, though I don't know how the hell you ended up here, doing what you're doing. Actually, if you really want to know, now everybody assumes you are David and will inherit, there's been a lot less tension about the place. And it's made Sir Mark happy.' She gave a weak smile. 'Look, I don't think you had anything to do with my father's death, but it may have had something to do with you.'

'I hope to God it didn't.'

'You think it might?'

Aidan shrugged. 'I wish I knew.'

'Johnny Henderson went to see him,' Susan said.

'They know that, do they?'

'He was seen in the village quite early, and someone else saw him again later. I think the police want him in for questioning.'

'He never told me.'

'Why should he?' Susan asked drily.

Aidan realised he'd tripped. Maybe it didn't matter now.

'Anyway,' Susan went on, 'I'd already guessed that Johnny might be involved, especially when he told me where that horse Letter Lad had come from – a few miles from where you lived in Mayo. It seemed a bit too much of a coincidence.'

'OK,' Aidan nodded. 'But he swore blind to me that Ivor was still very much alive when he left him. He did say he was very drunk, though. We'll see what the police say, but I very much doubt Johnny did him any harm.'

'Who else do you think it might have been, then?'

'It's too early to say.'

Susan looked at him, imploring now, ready to trust him. 'Look, I don't know why you turned up here, or how you managed it, and you know I've never believed you were David, but right now I think you can help me find out what happened to Dad, because it's got to involve you somewhere along the line.' She looked at him with sudden warmth. 'And whatever you are, I know you're not a criminal, not at heart.'

Aidan looked back at her, drawing strength from her trust. 'You're right, I'm not, and I need to know as much as you do what happened to David. If we knew that, we'd probably know who killed your father.'

'You've got an idea?'

'I have a suspicion, but there's no way I'm going to tell you or anyone else about it until I'm damned sure, and then, even if it means me giving up my life as David

Tredington, I will. It's only right that the family should know if David really was killed. First, it would help if we could find anything that's left of David's body.'

'But Dad could have put it anywhere. He could have rowed out and dumped him at sea.'

'Maybe, but I've a hunch he didn't.'

'Why's that?'

'It's only a hunch,' Aidan said firmly.

In the afternoon, the wind picked up, and for the first time Aidan had a taste of the full force of the north-westerly blasting off the Bristol Channel. A gale howled through the trees around the yard, rattling the doors and the roof tiles.

But, after hearing what Susan had told him, nothing was going to put him off his search for David's body.

He wrapped a full-length Dryzabone round him, pulled the hood over his head, and set off for the cliff-top.

He reached the place where David Tredington must have come off all those years before. The wind whipped his eyes to tears as he gazed out at an angry, growling sky over a grey, white-flecked sea.

The gale buffeted him and whined in his ears. Way below him, he could see great waves rolling in to smash themselves savagely against the rocks at the back of the narrow beach. There was no point going down there now.

It wasn't on a day like this that David had gone missing, he knew, but even on the quietest of summer days, it was a hell of a fall down the near vertical cliff. He turned his gaze eastwards towards Stanner Head, the sheer, jagged promontory that jutted into the sea at the end of the bay. Slowly, unconcerned about the weather, he followed the cliff-top towards the naked stone crag.

When he reached it, he stood looking down, thinking about the small boy who had perished there, whose identity he had assumed as a result. He felt a new affection for the boy, an affinity with him, now that he was beginning to know what had happened to him. He owed it to David to uncover the truth, even if that meant exposing his own deception.

Making up his mind, Aidan carried on along the edge of the cliff for another mile until he was approaching the small, sporadically manned coastguard building. There was a van parked outside it, and lights glowed from the windows of the squat concrete building beneath a flat roof bristling with aerials. He walked on up and opened the door into a warm, smoky fug.

The broad back in front of him turned to reveal a man in his mid-forties, red-cheeked and blue-eyed above a mass of auburn whiskers.

'Mr David,' the man said, by way of welcome. 'Not much of a morning for a walk. I've been watching you come this last mile.'

Aidan grinned. 'I don't mind the weather, I'm used to a bit of rain, as long as I'm dry inside.'

'Cup of tea?'

'Thanks. Any trouble out there?'

'No. Not yet. Funny thing is, we usually gets more problems on a beautiful sunny day when the people who don't know what they're doing go out. Only the people who've got to be are out in this sort of shit. Still, even the pros come unstuck from time to time.'

As he talked, he organised a boiling kettle, big tin mugs and tea-bags.

'Has anyone ever come to grief from the cliff-tops here?' Aidan asked.

'Not for many a year. There was a girl, out on a hike in weather not unlike this, maybe ten years ago. She fell down the cliff by those gallops of yours.'

'What happened to her?'

'I should think she was dead before she touched the beach.'

'I mean what happened to the body? I suppose it got washed along this way, got caught up on Stanner Head, or on the rocks before it.'

'Oh no. There's no tide'd wash anything this way. It'd always take anything on towards Lynton.'

'Always?' Aidan asked casually.

'That's the way the tides run along this side of the Channel.'

The kettle boiled and the coastguard filled the two mugs. Aidan took his and drank gratefully while he absorbed the implications of what he'd just been told.

He encouraged the man to yarn on for a while, glad of the warmth. He left the hut with the dramatic details of some of the more famous wrecks along the coast, and the knowledge that either David had crawled from where he had landed at the foot of the cliff, or someone had carried him, to hide him below the rocks where Ivor had found him.

Chapter Eleven

It was nearly dark by the time Aidan walked back into the yard. He joined the grooms giving the horses their final feed, but his mind was still back on the cliffs. From what Susan had told him, and from what he had seen of the coast that day, Aidan had in his head a clear picture of the dying boy. He tried to concentrate on his jobs around the stud, and make arrangements for Letter Lad's outing on Saturday. But the vision of the boy, so like himself, lying dead on the beach, stubbornly remained.

Susan had supper with the family that night. So did Victoria and Jason. When they were all sitting round the kitchen table, Sir Mark asked Aidan where he had been that afternoon.

'I love to see the sea in a rage,' Aidan said, not entirely untruthfully and keeping an eye on Jason for his reaction. 'I walked up to the coastguard post and back.'

'Good Lord! Sounds positively masochistic.'

Aidan laughed. 'It was great, honest. And not a drop of rain seeped through my coat.'

He met Susan's eyes for a moment, and saw a glimmer of approval. He relaxed a little. If, in the end, he was to own up to what he'd done, he wanted it to be in his own time and voluntarily. For one thing, it would have to be broken very gently to Sir Mark. Deliberately, he steered the conversation away to talk about Deep Mischief's preparation for the Hennessy, and Jason's ride on Letter Lad the following Saturday.

Victoria was pressing for decisions on stallions for several of the mares who had not yet been booked in and, despite the drama of Ivor's death, the rest of dinner took its normal course. Just before ten, Aidan announced that he was going to bed as he had to be up early to ride out next morning.

The wind howled most of the night, but eased off by the time Aidan got out of bed at six next morning. Victoria, reliable as ever, was knocking on his door at six-thirty, ready to come with him to Sam Hunter's.

Aidan was riding Deep Mischief back from the gallops when Johnny turned up at Sam Hunter's yard. The gelding had shown all his usual form, striding out effortlessly alongside two of his struggling stable-mates.

Aidan spotted Johnny's well-worn car as he walked his horse into the stableyard with the rest of the string. While he had been riding, he had concentrated exclusively on the animal beneath him. Now his problems came back to him with a rush.

He slid from Deep Mischief's back. Johnny was chatting earnestly to Sam Hunter.

'Morning, Johnny,' Aidan called.

Johnny looked up, pretending to be surprised. 'I didn't know you were riding out here today.'

'Just keeping Sam up to the mark.' Aidan managed a quick grin. 'As a matter of fact, I wouldn't mind a word with you back at Barford. We've a couple of colts we may not want to send to the sales. We'd like you to look at them. I'd stay and have a chat now, but I brought Victoria over with me this morning.'

Johnny nodded, acknowledging that they couldn't speak now. 'Fine,' he said. 'I was coming over anyway.'

'I'll see you back at Barford then.'

As Aidan drove home, he listened to Victoria enthusing about Deep Mischief's progress.

'Did you have to put him under any pressure to pull past those other two on the gallops?' she asked.

'No. I gave him no more than a squeeze. He's a very classy animal, but he'll not need to miss any work between now and the Hennessy. He puts on weight just looking at food. But don't worry, Sam doesn't need to be told what to do. He's probably forgotten more about training horses than most people ever know.'

Victoria beamed excitedly as she let her hopes for Deep Mischief have some rein. 'It'd be great if we could start winning some big races with him. I always said from the day he was born that he was going to be a star.'

Aidan laughed. 'There must be ten thousand girls every year who say the same thing each time they watch their mares foaling.'

'That's not fair,' Victoria protested. 'I don't think every foal we produce is perfect.'

'I know you don't. I'm just teasing. He's one of the best horses I've ever sat on.'

'Did you ever ride anything really good when you were in Ireland?'

'I did not, not in that class anyway. Where I lived, we were trying to make silk purses out of sows' ears.'

'Isn't it funny that you should have become so good with horses, even though you've been away for all that time.'

'Not really. I always did enjoy the horses from when I was a small lad, before you could even walk. I was straight into it when I got to Ireland. I've always felt happier riding a horse than doing anything else.'

'Anything?' Victoria said with a grin.

'I don't know what you mean, you coarse-minded little sister.'

'Not half so coarse as Lucy.'

'That wouldn't surprise me.'

'I heard her having a very graphic conversation about you with Emma on Sunday.'

'I don't want to hear about it, and I think it's a sin to earwig,' Aidan laughed but within himself, he felt a long way from laughter.

At half-past ten, Aidan drove back through the park gates, followed closely by Johnny. He dropped Victoria at her cottage and drove on down to the yard. Twenty minutes later, out in a paddock beneath a grey sky, and a long way from any prying ears, Aidan looked Johnny straight in the eyes and tried to read the truth.

'OK, what exactly happened when you went to Ivor's?'

'Basically, he told me that David was dead.'

This didn't produce the dramatic effect that Johnny had been expecting.

'Yes,' Aidan said. 'I know.'

'What? Who the hell told you?'

'Susan, yesterday. When they heard that the pathologist thought there was something fishy about the way Ivor was kicked, her mother broke down and said that Ivor had told her years ago that he'd found David's body at the bottom of the cliff after he'd taken a tumble on some young horse.'

'That's right,' Johnny said. 'That's just what he told me, and he thought he'd be blamed so he hid the body – Sue's mother didn't tell her where, I suppose?'

'No chance. He never let on – didn't want her to know.'

'Well, at least that means the chap in Fiji isn't anything to worry about, and with Ivor out of the way, our problems are over.'

'That's what's worrying me,' Aidan said coldly. 'It's a little too convenient; and who the hell else would want to kill Ivor?'

'For God's sake,' Johnny pleaded. 'I *swear* it wasn't anything to do with me. I didn't even touch the smelly little bugger.'

Aidan didn't say anything. He almost believed Johnny but, knowing him, his word wasn't enough to convince him entirely. He sighed. 'If only you weren't such a slippery devil. I wish to God I'd never got involved in this thing. You seem to have forgotten, someone tried to shoot me on Tuesday, and I don't think it was Ivor – why should he? He was relying on me to feather his nest for him. And if you didn't kill Ivor, someone else did.'

'Look,' Johnny said, 'the pathologist could have got it wrong, or Ivor might have been done in for some reason completely unconnected with you.'

'And what about the fella who dropped a sleeper on me?'

'That's just a possibility, for God's sake. Last week the police were happy to believe it was a genuine accident.'

'Well, they're not now. They think someone marked the roof of my car with fluorescent paint to identify it. This Sergeant King rang to say he's coming up to see me again.'

'He probably just wants a day off, a chance to look at the Devon countryside.'

'Who are you kidding, Johnny? Listen, we're in a mess here and we've got to sort it out – I don't mean just for me, but for my mother's sake, and for Sir Mark. I owe him that – he's been incredible to me. You've no idea what it's like to have a father when you've never had one before. It would really upset him if I'm found out and end up in jail. And the man's not well.'

Aidan immediately regretted telling Johnny that, especially when Sir Mark had told him in confidence. He tried to play it down.

'It's not much, but he's been suffering a bit from his back.'

'Oh, is that all?'

'That's not the point. I'm beginning to feel a real shit about taking them in, all of them. They've been so good to me; made me feel as if I've belonged here all my life.'

'Brilliant. That's just what we wanted. I told you you could do it.'

'Shut up, for Christ's sake. You may not have a conscience—'

'Yes, well it's a bit late for you to start developing one now.'

'Look,' Aidan went on more quietly, 'maybe they won't find this fella who dropped the sleepers, and maybe the

Ivor business will blow over. But I wouldn't count on it. I tell you, I couldn't stand it if anything else like this happens, or anyone else gets killed or hurt. Nothing could justify that. I don't have any choice. I can't go to the police, but I can't let go of this until I know what happened to that boy and where Ivor put his body. And, believe it or not, I would rather like to know who's trying to kill me,' he added.

Aidan didn't see any point in telling Johnny his plans in detail. He hadn't decided, anyway, exactly what his next move would be, but he was sure he wasn't the only person with an interest in finding David Tredington's last resting place.

Susan had gone home when he arrived back at the manor. He wanted to ring her, to let her know what he was planning in case anything went wrong, but he didn't want to risk using the phone in the house. He got into his Land Rover to drive down to the village to use the phone-box there.

He changed his mind before he reached the main gates. He wouldn't ring from the village. He might be seen, and he well knew country people's propensity for storing up instances of unusual or unlikely activity.

He turned left at the top of the drive and headed up the lane; he knew there was a public telephone two miles along the Porlock road. The phone-box was set on a muddy layby on the edge of a small wooded coomb. Aidan parked his car and went into the scarlet cubicle. He dialled Susan's number in Lynmouth and let it ring a dozen times before he accepted that it wasn't going to be answered.

Through the narrow belt of trees that lined the road, he could see the beginnings of the pasture fields that eventually joined up with the Barford cliff gallops. As he put the phone down, staring absently up towards the coast about a quarter of a mile away, he saw a brown-coated figure striding up towards the cliffs.

With adrenaline pumping through him as if he were at the start of a big race, he darted out of the phone-box back to his car. He pulled his OS map from the shelf under the dash and spread it on his lap. He soon found what he was looking for. A few yards from the phone-box, on the other side of the road, a red dotted line showed that there was a path which followed the edge of a field up towards the coast, where it joined the South-West Coast Path, just above Stanner Head.

The rain had stopped, and the wind was half the strength it had been in the early morning. Aidan pulled on his wellies and his long waxed coat and set off through the belt of trees to find the path.

He guessed that whoever he was following had a good fifteen-minute lead on him and had probably reached the cliff by now. But he kept close to the hedgerows where he could, well camouflaged in his khaki clothing.

At the east end of the bay, before Stanner Head jutted out into the sea, a small brook plunged over the cliff-edge and trickled messily down the almost sheer drop. At this point, the cliff dipped and a steep, crumbling path had been created to provide the only way down to the beach. Locals had used it for years, as well as the more adventurous walkers along the coast path. It wasn't for the faint-hearted or the clumsy.

Aidan stopped at the top of the cliff where he had watched Ivor on the previous Monday. Again he crouched, so as not to break the skyline visible from the beach below.

The tide was out, revealing a steep, sandy beach no more than seventy yards deep. From his viewpoint Aidan couldn't see anyone on it, but he waited, judging that the man he was following wouldn't have reached the bottom of the cliff path.

A few minutes later, the brown figure appeared on the sand below him and hurried across to the east end of the beach which was enclosed by the promontory. He went round some flat rocks which projected into the sand, and disappeared from sight.

Aidan got quickly to his feet and arrived at the top of the track down the cliff. A chamois would have found the going tricky. The surface was wet bracken, mud, and jagged, slippery rock. Though the drop from the top of the cliff was little more than three hundred feet, the track covered a third of a mile as it traversed the cliff-face, zig-zagging across the plunging brook.

Aidan was crossing the stream for the second time, below a waterfall where the rocks were worn smooth and coated with green slime. He slipped so smoothly and painlessly that it took him a moment to realise he had. He tumbled down a sixty-degree incline, bouncing from ledges of marram grass on to patches of bracken and bramble that clung to the cliff-face between naked rock and shale.

He had fallen fifty feet before he was caught by a wider ledge, a tussocky mattress half-way down the cliff. He heard the clatter of loose rocks that had accompanied him carrying on down to the beach below.

He glanced over the ledge towards the jutting rocks. While he waited to see if the noise of his fall had alerted his quarry, he checked himself for damage.

The whole thing had taken no more than ten seconds, but he felt as if he'd been put through a mangle. The scab on his arm from the gunshot graze had opened up. He could feel the warm seepage of blood into his shirt. There were scratches and cuts on his face and a painful throbbing in his hip. He groaned to release some of the pent-up pain, and stretched. At least nothing was broken.

He waited until he was certain that his fall hadn't alerted the man he was following, before he set off down the last leg of the track, taking more notice now of the tumbling brook.

When he reached the beach, Aidan could see the clear prints of a pair of Wellington boots on the damp brown sand. He followed the trail across the beach, and round the protruding flat rocks where they led straight to a cave which couldn't be seen from the cliff-top.

Beneath a narrow cleft, the mouth of the cave widened out to a width of twenty feet. Aidan kept close in to the cliff-face so that he couldn't be seen by anyone inside the cave. When he reached the edge of the entrance, he stopped and listened. But, against the whine of the wind and the surf breaking down at the low-tide mark, he couldn't be certain of what he heard from inside. He sidled round the edge, trying to avoid being silhouetted against the light. Further in, there was a secondary cleft into which he could tuck himself.

The sandy floor sloped steeply up towards the back of the cavernous tunnel, and there was a steady deluge of rainwater draining through cracks in the rocky ceiling.

He glanced out towards the sea which had lost most of the fury of the early morning, and wondered how long, once it had turned, it would take the tide to come back.

Slowly, he craned his neck round the buttress of rock that obscured his view, and peered into the depths of the cave. The sound of small stones clattering down to the sandy floor reached him, but it was too dark for him to see where they were coming from. He slipped out of his crack. Keeping his back to the wall, and his ears pricked for any sign that he'd been seen, he edged his way up the steeply sloping floor of the cave, along the creases of the rocky wall.

After twenty feet, the noise of the wind and surf were more muted and the trickle of escaping springs sounded more clearly. Above this he heard irregular movements, metal grinding on stone, and the occasional heavy thud of a larger rock bouncing down on to the sand.

Whatever the man was doing, Aidan guessed it was taking most of his concentration. He risked a moment's exposure to the direct light from the cave-mouth by stepping round a protruding buttress. As he darted back into the protective shadow beyond it, he heard a distinct grunt and a gasp of pain. With his eyes now attuned to the gloom, Aidan caught sight of a familiar brown coat and green Wellingtons.

The man wearing them was leaning face forward on a wall of rock which sloped back from the ground at an angle of about seventy degrees, and was worn smooth by a few million years' action of the incoming sea.

Standing on tiptoes, he was stretching to the end of his fingertips to grapple with some smaller boulders which had become lodged in a gap of no more than ten inches between the top of the rock slab and the roof of the cave. He had brought some kind of lever with him; it looked like an iron crowbar to Aidan. Evidently he had managed to dislodge a few of the stones which were scattered on the sand behind him, but he was having problems with the larger ones which were lodged fast beneath the roof of the cave.

Aidan held his breath. Abruptly, the distant sounds of the sea and dripping springs were shattered by a great, echoing shout.

Aidan looked sharply back towards the cave-mouth. Two people had come in and were experimenting with the resonant qualities of the rocky tube, laughing at the echoes they produced. Hastily the man at the back of the cave pushed himself away from the rock and spun round. Aware of the movement, Aidan turned his attention towards the cave's rear again. And in the fraction of a second before Aidan sank back to bury himself in the shadows, he saw a familiar, angry face.

George Tredington.

Aidan stifled a gasp, trembling with the relief of knowing at last who his enemy was.

The two visitors, coming further up the cave, saw George.

'Morning,' one said cheerily.

'Morning,' George answered uneasily. He had evidently realised that he was dealing with a couple of walkers who had strayed down from the coast path. 'Pretty bloody day for caving,' he said. 'But a friend of mine thought he'd got a surfboard washed up into the back here. I said I'd have a look for him.'

The walkers apparently accepted the explanation.

'Does much get washed up in here?' the other, a woman, asked.

'Can do,' George answered cagily, 'but not this time. Anyway, no luck with this chap's board.' He had walked down to join them, to lead them out of the cave with him. 'How far have you walked this morning?'

The walkers were glad to talk about their progress and turned with him. 'Not much so far, only about six miles from Lynmouth, aiming to be in Porlock for lunch.'

Their voices faded as they left the cave. Aidan stepped out of the cleft to watch them. He gave them a few moments, then ran down to the entrance. Keeping in the shadows, he glanced out. George and the walkers were heading for the foot of the cliff path which Aidan had come down earlier. He waited until they were well on their way up before he went up to the back of the cave where George had been scrabbling.

Aidan looked back down the steep gradient to the cave-mouth, sixty feet away, ten feet below the level at which he now stood. He turned and faced the rock and peered at the tantalising gap at the top. He was taller than George, and able to get a better look at what had to be moved if the gap was to be opened up. He also established that it was going to take more than his bare hands to clear it. He remembered that he hadn't seen George carrying the crowbar as he went to talk to the walkers. Aidan glanced down. It lay where it had been dropped, a little to his right

Rolling a couple of big stones up to the foot of the wall

to give himself more height, Aidan swung the heavy iron bar above his head to plunge it down the side of one of the larger boulders. He gritted his teeth and called up all his strength.

He had been straining for a few minutes before he felt any movement. With a grinding of rock on rock, the boulder moved a few millimetres and then stuck fast again.

After this small taste of success, Aidan renewed his attack. This time he went the other way and tried to deal with the large hunk of granite above his left shoulder.

He had no idea how long he had been heaving at the immovable objects that George was so desperate to shift. But he was sure that whatever he found behind there would answer some of the questions that had been taunting him for the past two weeks.

Determined to go on, first he went back down to the cave-mouth to make sure that George, or anyone else, wasn't coming back. Only the sea had approached, but not enough to worry him yet.

He returned to the rock wall and the first boulder he had tried to shift. After another session of straining, Aidan suddenly loosened it. Triumphantly, he prepared for one last enormous heave. He positioned himself so that when it came down it would pass by him. He inserted the crowbar once more to give himself maximum leverage, then pulled back on it with every fibre in his body. He could feel it move infinitesimally, then, abruptly, it was past the point of no return. It almost sprang from its lodging between the roof and the upright wall, and seemed to leap out and land with a great thud on the damp, sandy floor.

Aidan could hardly believe he'd done it. He had opened up a gap like a child's missing front tooth. He used the fallen rock as a step and heaved himself up to the lip. He stared into black nothingness. Hardly a glimmer of light penetrated past him into whatever space lay beyond. He heaved his shoulders a little higher, wanting to go straight in. He guessed that there was enough of a gap for his long slim body to go through. But there was no point without any light. He wouldn't see anything of what was beyond. Reluctantly, seething with frustration, he slid back down to the ground.

The sound of the wind outside had risen in pitch, disguising the crashing progress of the incoming tide. A leading wave hit the cliff either side of the entrance with a thundering slap; a huge wet tongue was sent hissing up the sandy floor, to swirl for a moment around Aidan's legs, sloshing over the tops of his rubber boots. He turned, alarmed.

The wave ran back, and the sea settled for the next onslaught. The mouth of the cave was already full of water. With horror, Aidan judged it was already several feet deep.

Though it was obvious from the absence of marine animals and plants that the sea didn't reach the top of the wall he was leaning against, it clearly settled at a point around his feet – which would mean that the mouth itself became completely submerged at high tide.

He cursed himself for not checking the speed of the turning tide, though he'd had no plan to come to the cave when he'd left Barford that morning. He realised he must have been heaving away at the rocks for maybe several hours and, if he didn't move fast, he was going to be stuck there.

He glanced back at the gap he had made, hoping that by opening it up he hadn't given the sea a way to get in and disturb whatever lay behind the wall. Another resounding crash and the blocking out of the grey daylight announced the entrance of another mass of angry, hissing water into the cave. This time it soaked up to his thighs.

When it subsided, the sea level was within a few feet of the top of the cave-mouth.

If he was going to get out, he was going to have to do it now.

He waded back down the sandy floor, keeping pace with the retreating wave until, still twenty feet from the opening, he found he was out of his depth. Another wave surged more gently towards him. Barely hesitating, he pulled off his Wellington boots and mackintosh, filled his lungs, and plunged beneath its turbulence.

His open, stinging eyes could make out nothing through the sand-filled, churning water which gripped him with an icy clamminess. Desperately, he headed down to make contact with the safe, sandy bottom. He touched it with his fingers, found it with his feet and, fighting the extra buoyancy his clothes gave him, struggled to propel himself forward through the murky, heaving water. He didn't dare come up until he was through the arch. On the surface, the sea would crack his head like a ping-pong ball against the rocky roof.

He felt another surge push him back, but he dug his feet into the sand and faced the current as horizontally as he could, until finally he felt the water run back out. He pushed off and took the current, thrashing his legs and heaving through the water with his arms, going ever deeper to avoid the turbulence of the surface.

Another wave came to push him backwards, and then run out seawards with him. He couldn't guess how long it was since he'd taken a breath. His lungs were screaming and he hardly cared any more that they would fill with water if he opened his mouth.

Suddenly, the sea became lighter, a grey glitter appearing at the surface above him. With a last supreme effort, Aidan drove himself on, knowing that it wouldn't take much to drive him back towards the cliff.

Then he couldn't stand any more. Help me, God, he pleaded, and his head broke the foaming skin of the water above him.

He opened his mouth at last, emptied his lungs of spent air, and gasped to fill them again. Through his stinging eyes, he could just see a heaving mass of grey-white water – a wall of it six feet high surging towards him. Gasping again, he plunged into the midst of it, praying that it would pass him before it broke.

He felt nothing more than a slight tug as the crest passed over him. He bobbed up again, breathed again, and turned to see how far from danger he was.

The top of the cave-mouth gaped just fifteen feet away. He tried to remember the shape of the rocks around the foot of the cliff, turned and swam out as strongly as he could. All he could think about was getting away from the cliff.

It was five minutes before he dared turn back and look again. He had managed to put another thirty yards between himself and the visible rock-face. Gratefully, he turned parallel to the shore and swam westwards, until he reckoned he had cleared the bed of flat rock that protruded into the sand at the east end of the bay.

He turned landward and, exhausted, let the waves help him in towards the beach.

Ten minutes later, he lay on the sand; bruised, bleeding, completely spent, but safe. He crawled away from the sea until he was above the high-water line, where he lay shivering, trying to recover his strength.

It took Aidan twenty minutes to scramble barefoot back up the rocky cliff track to the soft pasture at the top. He looked both ways along the path that followed the coast. There was no one in sight. Sore, aching, but ultimately sound, he hurried as fast as his battered feet allowed back along the path to the road where he had left the Land Rover. There was no sign of George, or a car. He guessed that George must have hidden his BMW further up the road before he'd set off up the path.

Aidan's watch had stopped, but it showed half-past two. He guessed it was nearer three now. He had missed lunch, and people would be beginning to wonder where he was.

He drove to his cottage where he pulled off his sodden garments. He stood under a blissfully hot shower for five minutes, then did his best to patch up the more visible scratches he had received from the rocks and brambles. He rubbed liniment into his bruised feet, and winced as he inserted them into a pair of tight brogues. He was coming down the stairs when the telephone in his kitchen rang. It was Victoria from the house.

'Where have you been? We were expecting you for lunch,' she said, but didn't wait for an answer. 'Are you coming up for tea?'

'I'm just going down to the yard. I'll be up in half an hour.'

There had been no dramas or problems at the stables. Aidan checked each of his charges and gave the grooms a few last instructions. Feeling more able now to deal with the scrutiny of the family, he hobbled painfully up to the manor.

As he walked into the kitchen, he gritted his teeth and tried to smile.

Victoria looked at him with concern.

'What's happened to you? You look as though you've gone ten rounds with Tyson.'

Aidan tried to smile. 'The Land Rover ran out of diesel; I had to bleed the engine. I slipped into some brambles.'

'What a bore,' Sir Mark said sympathetically. 'Was there anything in the spare can?'

'There was, thank God, or I'd have had a long walk.'

'Anyway, I'm glad you're back. Sam Hunter just phoned. He's declared Letter Lad for tomorrow.'

'Great!' Aidan made himself sound enthusiastic.

'Sam's pretty confident this time,' Victoria grinned. 'And, though he won't admit it, so's Jason. George will be livid if he wins.'

'Do you think so?' Aidan asked, disguising his true state of mind. 'He seemed pretty relaxed about it all to me.'

'He may have been to you, but Jan told me he's

furious; he feels you've made a real fool of him. She says George thinks you did it deliberately.'

'Well, in a sense, he's right. When I rode that horse at Braycombe, I knew something was hurting him, but George wouldn't hear of it. Anyway, Johnny made sure George earned a bit of a profit on the animal so he'd not lose too much face.'

'You may have underestimated dear old George's sense of his own dignity. And after all, he hasn't got much to thank you for since you came back.'

Sir Mark intervened. 'That's not entirely true. Though he expected the court to grant him the right to inherit the title, on the presumption of David's death, I'd never given any firm indication about the future of this place.'

'Maybe not, Dad, but he and everyone else assumed most of it would go to him, didn't they?'

'I suppose so, but that's no justification for resenting David's success with this horse.'

This was the first time Aidan had been present at anything like a family discussion about George's attitude, although the substance of what was said had been implicit in other conversations about George. What came as more of a surprise to Aidan was the report of George's ill-feeling over the horse. The man was obviously a skilled actor when it suited him. But, though the Letter Lad incident had clearly added in a small way to George's dislike of him, this could have no bearing on his frantic scrabbling above the wall in Stanner Cave that morning.

Aidan was determined to get back down there as soon as possible, as soon as the tide would allow him back into the cave with lamps and climbing ropes. He told Sir

Mark and Victoria that he wanted to catch up on some paperwork, and went back to his cottage.

The first thing he did there was to ring George to establish where he was.

George was at home in Braycombe. He sounded exceptionally irritated when he answered the phone.

'What's the problem?' Aidan asked.

'It's nothing important.' He spoke as if Aidan were not his only audience. 'The police are here. They've come to talk about Ivor Butley.'

'But surely that's all cut and dried? He was kicked by a horse; he died. What's the mystery?'

'God knows, but someone saw Mike Harding's car at Bert Bacon's farm that morning. As it happened, I'd borrowed it, but I didn't go near the place.'

'Well, I hope you sort it out.'

'So do I. I must get back to them. What did you want?'

'It doesn't matter. I'll ring later. Will you be in?'

There was a pause. 'Yes, I should be. The vet's due round at six and I want to see him myself.'

'Fine. I'll call before then.'

Aidan judged that George couldn't be planning to have another go at the cave himself that day, not within the time he had, and especially not if the police were stuck into him. The likelihood that George had been down to see Ivor on Wednesday morning opened up a whole new set of possibilities.

Aidan put the phone down and went to gather up what he needed for his return visit to the cave. This time he made sure that he was fully waterproof, and properly equipped for scrambling over the rock wall into the unknown on the far side.

He parked his Land Rover where he had that morning, and retraced his steps back up to the coast path. It was nearly dark now, and he had to use his torch to negotiate the cliff path. He just had to hope that there was no one around to see him. On this remote stretch of coast at this time of day, it was unlikely. Wearing studded boots, he made better progress down the track, and arrived on the beach as the last wave lapped up to the mouth of the cave. That would give him all the time he needed to get in and search.

He entered the cave and walked up the steep slope of wet sand towards the wall of rock at the back.

The great boulder which he had loosened that afternoon hadn't been shifted by the waves which had swept in to block his exit. Aidan shone his torch at the smooth, six-foot wall. The upper lip showed no signs of dampness. It looked as though it was out of reach of the tongues of seawater which penetrated the cave at high tide.

He unwound the rope he was carrying round his waist, and tied one end of it firmly to the last boulder he had dislodged. He flung the other end up towards the gap and scrambled up after it, until he was able to put his head through the gap.

He played the beam of his torch into the space beyond.

On the face of it, it was a continuation of the cave, though how it had been hollowed out with this great bar of rock across it wasn't obvious. The floor of the cave beyond the bar was higher than on his side and, as far as he could see, consisted of fine, dusty, dry sand.

He pulled through a lamp he had tied to his waist,

fastened it to the end of the rope and lowered it to the floor.

Beside the lamp, clear in the light that it cast, lay a small but complete skeleton.

On its side, with legs crossed as if in deep, relaxed sleep, the bones were those of an immature human. Still clinging to the bones were a few tatters of clothing, and on the feet were a pair of shoes.

Aidan's heart almost stopped.

It was the picture that had haunted him since first he had found George desperately trying to get into this undisturbed resting place. He had no doubt at all that he was looking at the remains of the real David Tredington, and that the body had not been seen since the day the boy had disappeared.

He found himself trembling at this final meeting with the person whose life he had hijacked, and at the thought of whatever horrifying events had laid an innocent twelve-year-old boy to rest in this bizarre tomb.

Chapter Twelve

Aidan gazed at the skeleton. He felt that he'd always known the boy; now he was trying to cope with the finality that the bones represented. Not just the termination of David's existence, but also the end of Aidan's impersonation of him.

He wanted to touch the bones, to be sure they were real. He began to squeeze himself forward through the gap, which was no more than eighteen inches wide. He pushed his head and neck through and managed to insert one shoulder, but the other was blocked by the bulk of the rock which he had failed to budge. He had been sure he would be able to get through, and now he was desperate to, but, however he contorted himself, he couldn't get both shoulders into the gap. He yelled his frustration into the cavern beyond and winced as it echoed back at him.

Temporarily beaten, he slid back out and dropped down to the ground. He found the crowbar which he'd abandoned earlier, and thrust it in a crack between the stubborn boulder and the wall of the cave. He heaved and struggled until his hands were raw, growing more certain every minute that he wasn't going to do it.

Beginning to accept that he would never be able to break through into David Tredington's tomb on his own, he obstinately carried on while he tried to think about who to go to for help. And he had to make sure that George didn't get in first.

After an hour and several more attempts to squeeze himself over the ledge, he acknowledged defeat.

He pulled the lamp back from the inner cavern, and stowed it with the rope and crowbar on a shelf of rock beyond the reach of the waves.

Aidan saw no one on his way back to his car. He drove to Barford with a plan taking shape.

It was after seven. From his cottage, he dialled Susan's number at her mother's. Mrs Butley seemed strangely distraught at the death of a man she had rejected many years before, but managed to tell Aidan that Susan had gone back up to the manor to finish some work.

Aidan guessed that Susan was finding Shirley Butley's grief over Ivor hard to take; in fourteen years she'd never heard her mother say a good word about her estranged husband. He went to look for her in the house. She was still in the office, staring at the screen of her PC. Aidan had already checked that Sir Mark was safely out of the way in his own study.

'Susan.'

She turned and looked up at him. Her eyes widened. 'You look as though you've seen a ghost.'

Aidan nodded. 'I feel as if I have.'

She stood up. 'What? What is it?'

'I need to talk to you – not here. Could you tell

Sir Mark you're popping down to my cottage for something?'

'Sure.'

'Could you be there in ten minutes?'

She nodded.

Susan came in without knocking. Aidan was pacing up and down his small kitchen. He waved her into a chair and poured a cup of coffee without speaking.

'What the hell have you seen?' she asked.

'I've found David.'

Susan leapt to her feet and clutched Aidan's arm. 'What! Where?'

Aidan took a deep breath. 'In Stanner Cave.'

'But how did you find him?'

'When you told me about your father hiding the body, I was sure then there was some connection with the cave. I didn't tell you, but I saw your dad going there on Monday. There was someone else following him; I didn't know who – I didn't get near enough – but I saw Ivor clearly, climbing back up the cliff path. I spotted someone on their way there today, and followed him right into the cave. It was George.'

'George?' Susan gasped.

'Yes, George. And he went to see your father on Wednesday morning.'

'How do you know?'

'I phoned him this afternoon – I had to know where he was before I went back down to the cave. He was in a filthy mood; he said the police were there because Mike's car had been seen near Bert Bacon's farm – and George had borrowed it that morning.'

'But what's it got to do with George?'

'I'm not sure yet, but I've got a pretty good idea. I followed him up to the coast path this morning, then down to the beach by Stanner Head. He went into that big cave below it and I went in after him and saw him scrabbling about above the rocks at the back. He didn't see me, and after he'd gone I went back and had a look myself, then I got caught by the tide coming back in and had to swim for it.'

'Christ!' Susan said. 'No wonder you looked so rough when you got back here.'

Aidan nodded. 'But there was no real damage done, thank God. I've just been back down there with a couple of torches. I managed to lower a lamp the other side of the rock bar.' He paused, looking at Susan.

'What was there, for God's sake?' she asked, not wanting to hear it.

'Bones. A full human skeleton, lying just as it must have fallen, fifteen years ago.'

'David?' she whispered.

'I'm sure of it.'

'But how could he have got there?'

'He must have been put there.'

'But who by?'

Aidan looked at her horrified face. She already knew, but he spelt it out for her.

'Your father.'

Susan winced, closed her eyes and shook her head.

'He'd told your mother, hadn't he, that he'd hidden the body?' Aidan went on.

She nodded. 'He must have told George, too, when

George went to see him,' she blurted. 'Do you think George killed him?'

'I don't know. It makes no sense. With David's body finally found, George would be more certain of inheriting his share of Barford – and the title – but that's what it looks like. Listen, I'm going to need some help. As soon as I've found out exactly what happened to David, I'll tell Sir Mark.'

'It'll really break him up,' Susan said quickly. 'It'll be like losing two sons at once. And ... he's not well, you know.'

'I already knew that.'

'Maybe you should leave it until ... for a while,' Susan said quietly.

'I couldn't do that. I couldn't live with myself. And besides, I'm not sure that I'm safe until the whole mess is cleared up. I've opened a whole can of evil worms since I arrived here.'

'What do you want me to do?'

'Somehow, I want you to stick to George, keep tabs on him for every moment over the next couple of days. The chances are he'll come to the races tomorrow. It would look odd if he didn't. It'd look even stranger if I didn't. So we'll go out and win that race. Then we'll see what happens. There's another thing I want you to do for me. George borrowed the clay-trap from the house on Tuesday night. Could you get Jan to have a look around for it and bring it back up. Ask her to leave it in the store-room where it usually lives. And tell her to be sure George doesn't know she's done it.'

'What do you want it for?'

'I'm not sure, until I've had a look at it. But I saw George taking it, and there was something very shifty about the way he did it.'

Trying to behave as normally as possible, Aidan talked with Sir Mark that evening. He asked about his health – on which subject Sir Mark was non-committal – and, more animatedly, they discussed Letter Lad's chances the following day. All the time they were talking, Aidan was wondering how the man sitting opposite him would react when he learned the truth about his identity. Aidan knew that he had duped a man who, out of a longing for the return of his son, had fallen willingly into the trap he and Johnny had conceived.

Sir Mark had given him the father's love he had never had. And how had he repaid him?

Aidan doubted that, when the inevitable moment came to own up, he would have the courage to do it face to face. It would be easier simply to disappear and leave a note. But that, he reflected, would be the harshest blow of all.

He thought of the note David had sent. There was something about it that nagged at him for a few moments, until finally it came to him. Of course, David couldn't have sent the note. That was impossible; it had been posted three days after he had died. But Johnny had told Aidan that the handwriting was definitely David's; there had never been any question of that.

'What do you think?' Sir Mark was asking him, jerking him back into the present. He managed to bluff his way back into the conversation, but soon found an excuse to leave and go back to his cottage.

Aidan's night was disturbed by constant playbacks of the terrifying minutes he had spent fighting the thundering sea that morning. He was mentally and physically drained, but he scarcely slept.

At seven the next morning, he didn't feel much better, but he was determined to go out and make the most of the horse he had worked so hard on. He felt he wanted to justify George's resentment, increase it, perhaps, to provoke the maximum reaction.

But first he walked up to the house. He went round to the courtyard at the back and into the store-room with the green door.

The clay-trap had been left there as he had asked. Aidan knelt beside it, this time to examine it thoroughly. He didn't know what he was looking for, until, from the iron cup which held the clays to be ejected, he picked out three or four white hairs. He rolled them between his fingers to feel their texture, and nodded to himself. Satisfied, he put them carefully into an envelope which he tucked into a pocket in his Barbour, got up and went back to the stud.

Sam Hunter had been quietly concerned that Letter Lad might boil over before his second race-course appearance. The horse was so eager to race again that he had barely walked a stride since returning from Sandown – and that was despite being ridden by a lad specially chosen for his patience.

Over the years, Sam had trained dozens of horses who had behaved in a similar way after their first run.

Usually, a few days spent walking on their own away from the string settled them down, but in Letter Lad's case, it hadn't worked. The boy who looked after him was convinced that his next race at Chepstow would relax him, and had persuaded Sam that it wasn't a real problem. It turned out that he was right.

When Sam walked across from the weighing-room to saddle him, Letter Lad was walking around the parade ring as quietly as a child's first pony.

Rain was beginning to spit from a low, grey sky as Aidan legged Jason into the saddle and wished him luck. To his surprise, Jason looked back and thanked him. A pang of envy passed quickly as he watched his favourite horse leave the paddock ridden by someone else; Aidan knew he had no choice.

The soil at Chepstow was clay. When it was wet, it clung to the horses' feet as at no other course in Britain, hampering their natural action. Horses that could normally handle soft going were often completely lost. For Letter Lad, it was like coming home. He'd been raised on the clay in Connemara, played and galloped through it with the other youngsters in all kinds of foul weather. Now he was cantering happily to the start in what had become a heavy shower.

Aidan, watching through his binoculars, felt proud as his horse moved sure-footedly down the track while the horses around him slithered and slipped. Letter Lad looked as if his strength had doubled since his previous race; he seemed totally in control of every muscle in his body.

As Aidan surveyed the other runners, he had seldom felt so confident of winning. Even from a distance, he sensed Letter Lad's arrogance. The horse seemed to be looking at his rivals with disdain. It wasn't just that he was much bigger than them, he also knew he was much better.

All that was needed now was for Jason to do his bit.

Aidan had told his brother-in-law to sit in about fourth or fifth to make certain that the horse settled properly, but the big roan was having none of it. Jason held him until the first flight, but that was it. Letter Lad put in a leap that took him straight to the front, and there he stayed.

From then on, he jumped and galloped his rivals into the ground. He didn't put a foot wrong, barely broke into a sweat, and came home in a common canter with his ears pricked.

When the initial excitement of Letter Lad's first win had died down and people were starting to think about the next race, Aidan slipped out to the car-park to use his mobile phone.

He keyed the number at Barford Manor. Sir Mark answered himself.

'Hello. It's David.'

'Well done! The horse ran a brilliant race. Jason did a perfect job. A wise decision. Congratulations!'

Aidan winced at the depth of feeling in the baronet's voice. 'Thanks. He'd a bit of luck, but it went more or less as we planned. The horse jumped really great.'

'Thanks to your schooling. I imagine George is pretty fed up?'

Aidan sighed. 'He doesn't look too happy.'

Sir Mark chuckled. 'Serve him right.'

'Look ... I wanted to talk to you this evening. I've something important to tell you and I wanted to sort of ... prepare you.'

There was a moment's silence before Sir Mark answered. 'I hope it's something I'd like to hear. It would be a pity to spoil your win.'

'It's something we have to talk about, and I can't put it off any longer. That's why I'm ringing, to give myself no excuses.'

'All right,' Sir Mark said with reluctance. 'We'll talk when you get back. There'll only be the family here anyway.'

Back in the bar, there was still a large group of celebrators. Sam Hunter had joined the party. He made his way over to Aidan as soon as he came back in.

Over Sam's shoulder, Aidan spotted George looking at him. For an unguarded moment, a look of undiluted hatred flashed from George's deceptively placid eyes.

'David,' Sam was saying, 'I've got to congratulate you again. To tell the truth, I wasn't half as confident as you, but that horse has definitely got some ability.'

'Listen, Sam, it was you who trained him. I don't know what you think, but it's my guess he'd probably get a longer trip if we wanted him to, and jump a fence.'

Sam looked at Aidan with a hint of doubt. 'A few more runs over hurdles first, though.'

Aidan nodded with a smile. Sam didn't like to be hurried. It had been hard enough to persuade him to run Letter Lad as early as he had. 'I hope we get the same breaks in the Hennessy.'

'You've ridden the course a few times now, and you

know most of the other runners. Provided Mischief gets there in one piece, he should give a good account of himself.'

'The only thing is, there may be an upset in my training,' Aidan said slowly. 'But I'll let you know in good time if I can't ride him.'

Sam looked shocked. 'Why the hell shouldn't you? You're all right, aren't you? You look fine – a bit peaky maybe.'

'There could be something coming on, let's say. But you'll find someone to give him a good ride.'

'I don't like saying this to an amateur, but I'm not so sure I'd find anyone to give him as good a ride as you.'

'Flattery helps, of course,' Aidan grinned. 'But I'll let you know, probably tomorrow.'

Sam shrugged. 'Leave it till the day, if you like.'

'We'll see.'

Victoria drove Aidan back across the Severn Bridge and down the M5 to Devon. She was still bubbling over at the day's success, not least at the part her husband had played. Aidan reflected what a great sister she'd been to him; he was hating the idea of losing her. But he was committed now.

He hoped he'd be able to put his mother's mind at rest about finding the funds elsewhere to pay for the care she needed. While he'd been in England, Aidan had become far more confident of his own skills. He was sure that even without the backing of the Tredington family, he'd already made enough of a name for himself to go out and earn a good living on the open market. Whatever was discovered about David Tredington's death, and the inevitable change that would make to his own circumstances, he was determined to do everything he could to make his mother's life bearable as the disease took its final hold on her. The proceeds from selling Letter Lad would see them both over the first few months.

Aidan and Sir Mark found an excuse to be on their own in the library when they'd finished dinner with Victoria and Jason.

Somehow, Sir Mark seemed reluctant to let the conversation begin. He fussed about, pouring whisky for them both, and carried on talking about Letter Lad's race.

Eventually, when they were sitting in front of the fire as they so often had, he seemed to accept the inevitable. 'Well, what's this burning topic you have to discuss with me?'

Aidan took a big gulp of whisky, and stood up. He didn't want to look at Sir Mark.

He walked across the room and gazed at the silver Saint George. He took a deep breath. 'It's very hard for me to tell you this...' he began. He turned round. Sir Mark was sitting quite still, with his glass in his hand, watching him. Aidan closed his eyes. 'I am not your son,' he said, slowly and deliberately. 'I am not David Tredington. My name is Aidan Daly.' He let out a long breath and opened his eyes.

Sir Mark didn't move, nor did the expression on his face alter. He looked back at Aidan. Slowly, he put his glass down and leaned back in his chair. 'Why have you decided to tell me this now?'

'Because ... I've found David.' Aidan put his head in

his hands. Then he peered over them at Sir Mark. 'What's left of him. He must have been dead since the day he disappeared.'

This time Sir Mark reacted. He sat up and his face suddenly showed a strange combination of great sadness and relief. 'Thank God!' he muttered to himself. 'How do you know it's him? Where is he?'

'In Stanner Cave, beyond a rock bar across the back. Believe me,' he said emphatically, 'it is David. He must have been pushed over, and then someone blocked up the gap with some boulders: they've stayed fast in place ever since. Yesterday I prised one out and saw inside. The skeleton's lying there; I'd say it was untouched since the day it was put there.'

Sir Mark sighed. 'All this time ... We even searched the far end of that cave, under the pot-hole.'

'What pot-hole?'

'It's not a true pot-hole; it's a kind of chimney fault in the rock, about a hundred yards back from the cliff. The top of it's all covered with brambles now, has been for years, it's so dangerous. And we've never talked about it – don't want to encourage any intrepid oafs to kill themselves down it. I sent two men down, thinking David might have fallen into it, but, as I say, they only searched the area immediately below the chimney. There wasn't any question of his being nearer the front, because of the bar. No one's ever got over it, as far as I know.' Sir Mark thought back over the events around his son's death. 'What made you look there?'

'George. I followed him there yesterday morning. Something happened to me that made me think he knew more about David than he's ever let on.'

'What happened to you?'

'Someone tried to kill me when we were shooting on Tuesday.'

'Good God!' Sir Mark stood up, shocked, and walked across to where Aidan still stood by the inlaid round table. 'Who? Do you know?'

'Not for certain, but ... I don't know why exactly – just from a change in his attitude – I had a sort of hunch that George was involved. I had thought it might be Jason, or Ivor, especially when he turned up out of the blue on Tuesday to beat. I'm sure George had something to do with that. Later that evening, I saw him go into that store-room and take out the clay-pigeon trap. I asked Jan to see if she could find it at his place, and she brought it back here last night. It was in the store-room this morning.'

'But what's that got to do with it?'

'I'm not sure yet, but I'm working on it. Anyway, I'm certain now it wasn't Jason who shot me and if it was Ivor, it was because George put him up to it. Or it was George himself.'

'But where were you when this happened, for God's sake? And why didn't you say anything about it then?'

'How could I? I hadn't made up my mind to tell you the truth about myself. It was while I was on that solitary peg on the third drive. People just thought I'd had a crack at a couple of birds myself.'

'But ... why did George go to the cave?'

Aidan lifted his shoulders. 'I imagine to see if David was still there.'

'Do you think George put him there, then?'

'No. I don't. I think Ivor Butley did.'

Sir Mark shook his head in astonishment. 'But Ivor didn't kill him?'

'No, no. Ivor thought he'd fallen from a horse and come down the cliff, near the path, and smashed his head on the rocks at the bottom. He thought it was all his fault because he'd let your son out on a young horse you'd forbidden him to ride. I guess he panicked.'

Sir Mark shook his head slowly. 'Yes, he would have done, but why should George be interested?'

'Maybe he wants to prove I'm a ringer?'

'Maybe,' Sir Mark said thoughtfully, 'but we'll have to make certain.'

Although the news of David's discovery had taken a lot out of Sir Mark, he stiffened up, determined to make some clear decisions about how to deal with what he'd just heard.

'How did you know about Ivor hiding David's body?'

'Susan told me.'

'She knows about this, then?'

'Some of it. Her mother told her after her father was killed what had happened. But they didn't know what he'd done with the body, just that he'd got rid of it.'

'Right. We'll have to let George tell us how he knew.'

'I don't think he'll tell you. He might tell me, if I set it up right, but we'll need some independent witnesses. How about the police who've been investigating Ivor's death?'

Sir Mark looked at Aidan and nodded. 'You're right . . .' He paused. 'Aidan,' he added with a faint smile. 'But just for the moment, I think you'd better continue to be David, don't you?'

Aidan could hardly believe the calmness with which

Sir Mark had taken the news. He looked at the man who had been his father for the past two months; his affection for him had not diminished at all. 'I'm truly sorry about that, about deceiving you, and all the others. I couldn't go on doing it, knowing that the real David was lying down there under the cliff.'

'I understand that. And I'm grateful – more than grateful – for your honesty.'

'I'll accept whatever happens once we've got at the truth about your son.'

'I've no doubt of that. Are you prepared to tell me who put you up to the whole thing?'

'I'd rather not say. There'd be no point involving other people unnecessarily. I'll take the rap on my own.'

'Very noble of you, but there's only one person, besides George and my daughters, who could have prepared you so well, and that's Johnny.'

Aidan said nothing.

Sir Mark shrugged with a faint smile. 'I understand.'

The telephone beside him chirruped. He answered it, then passed it to Aidan.

It was Susan. 'I thought you might still be there,' she said to Aidan when Sir Mark had handed him the phone. 'I'm at Jan and Mike's cottage at Braycombe. George seems to have settled in for the night. I don't think he's going to go out again now.'

Aidan glanced at Sir Mark before he replied. 'And he hasn't been anywhere near the cliffs today?'

'No. He came straight back here after the races and hasn't gone out since.'

'OK. Will Jan let you stay the night?'

'Yes, of course.'

'Then stay there so you can keep your eye on him tomorrow. I'm not going to take any chances, though; I'm going to keep a watch on the cave tonight. Tell Jan to give him a message from me in the morning. He's to meet me at the Anchor in Lynmouth at midday. Tell her to stress that it's vital I see him. I'll ring just before to check that he's coming.'

Aidan shivered and huddled himself more tightly into his sleeping bag. He had found a dry niche, a draughtless cleft inside the cave.

He didn't think that George would come back down here in the middle of the night, but it was possible, and if the boy's skeleton were destroyed, the truth about his death would be lost for ever.

He dozed but didn't completely fall asleep. As a dull light gradually lit the silver-grey sea, he shook himself and looked at his watch. It was just after seven. Aching and exhausted after two nights without real sleep, he heaved himself back up the cliff track and across the fields to the phone-box by the layby. He dialled the Hardings' number. Jan answered sleepily.

'Sorry to wake you so early on a Sunday morning,' Aidan said cheerfully, 'but I need to speak to Sue.'

'Hang on.'

A moment later he heard Susan's voice. 'Hello?'

'Is he still there?'

'Yes. Unless he's walked. No cars have gone.'

'Good. Make sure he doesn't go anywhere before you've got my message to him. I'll ring back every half-hour or so to check.'

Aidan walked down the coomb to where he had

hidden the Land Rover, climbed in and sleepily drove home.

In his cottage he lay on his bed, trying to prepare himself for the confrontation that would take place that day. It was going to take all his wits to get the right result, unequivocally and in front of witnesses. In his exhaustion, his mind wandered to Sir Mark and the lack of animosity he had shown on being told that the man he had accepted wholeheartedly as his son was not; to Susan and the strength in her passionate eyes. Whatever happened over the next few hours, even if it meant he had to spend months in jail, he had one aim he was now confident he would achieve.

Chapter Thirteen

At eleven-thirty, Aidan telephoned Jan's house to speak to Susan again.

'What's going on?'

'It seems to have worked. Jan delivered your message, and he's just left in the BMW, looking really pissed off. I'm sure he's gone to meet you.'

'Let's hope you're right. Come up later this afternoon. We may have got somewhere by then.'

'Best of luck.'

Aidan nervously fingered his beer glass. He wondered what all these people in the pub were going to think when they heard the truth about him. They would despise him, probably, for taking advantage of the Tredingtons and making fools of everyone else.

George walked into the bar.

He saw Aidan. For the benefit of anyone watching, he managed to produce a friendly grin.

'Morning, David. I got your message.'

'Have a drink, George,' Aidan said.

'I thought you wanted to talk,' George muttered impatiently.

'I do, but not here.'

George nodded. 'I don't think I'll have a drink, then.'

Aidan drained his glass. 'I'll walk back to your car with you.'

George didn't speak until they were outside and there was no one within hearing.

'Well,' he said, with no pretence at friendliness. 'What the hell's so urgent?' There was a barely controlled nervousness in his voice.

'What I have to say has to be said very privately, just between the two of us. Go back to Braycombe and I'll ring you in an hour or so and tell you where to meet me.'

George glanced at him. Guilt and fear flashed in his eyes. 'What the hell is all this cloak-and-dagger stuff about?' he said, not making any attempt to disguise his anger now. 'I've only just come from there.'

'I know,' Aidan said patiently. 'But I wanted to be sure you understood the importance of what we have to discuss.'

'Look, whatever it is, I haven't got time to hang about all day. Anyway, what's so important and what's it got to do with me?'

'Things that happened, fifteen years ago,' Aidan said quietly.

George opened his mouth to speak, but stopped himself.

They had reached his car. George, uncertain and surly, let himself into it. Aidan had parked his Land Rover a few yards further along the road. He walked to it and climbed in. He waited before he turned the ignition key; he heard George's starter whine for a few moments without any response from the motor. Aidan grinned to himself. He had estimated that it would take a good twenty minutes for George to identify the trouble and get it put right on a Sunday morning.

Sir Mark met Aidan by a clump of brambles that covered the top of the deep shaft in the granite, a few hundred yards from the edge of the cliff behind Stanner Head. There were two men with him, in jeans and anoraks – a sergeant and a constable from Devon CID.

The sergeant seemed irritated. 'Sir Mark's told me what you're trying to do,' he said to Aidan. 'I'm not too happy about it. Do you think it'll work?'

'He'll come. He'd have been up here before if he'd had the chance. Now he thinks he's got an hour, he won't be able to keep himself away.'

'How long till he gets here?'

'Fifteen minutes, no more.'

'I have to tell you, sir, we shouldn't be doing it like this.' The sergeant appealed to Sir Mark. 'If there are human remains down there, the place should be sealed off and left to forensic.'

'For God's sake,' Aidan said, 'the man's on his way. If he sees you lot, he'll run a mile. This will be the only chance you'll have of getting a confession out of him. I've the measure of the man now, believe me.'

The detective believed him only reluctantly, but he nodded. 'Right. Let's get on with it then.'

The policemen had already cut back the vegetation to reveal the little-known crevice. They efficiently secured a rope around Aidan's waist. He gave them a nervous grin, pulled on a helmet lamp, and eased himself into the damp black hole. The two detectives took the strain and lowered him down a two-hundred-foot shaft. He only knew he was at the bottom when his feet touched a soft, sandy floor.

He knew from the maps that Sir Mark had shown him that he was about a hundred yards from the rock bar across the back of Stanner Cave. He gave the rope a tug to tell the men above him that he was safely down, and untied the rope from his waist.

With the light from his helmet and a hand torch, he looked around the cavern into which he had descended. He shivered in the cold, damp air and at the knowledge that no other human had been down here for the past fifteen years. And he knew that now no obstacles lay between him and the remains of the twelve-year-old David Tredington.

He set off along the narrow cleft in the rock, sometimes having to drop to his hands and knees to get through. After a few minutes, he saw a needle-point of light from the opening he had made above the bar two days before.

The policemen helped Sir Mark Tredington down the cliff path. They would rather not have had him with them, but then, it was the murder of his son they were investigating now. Besides, Sir Mark could be a difficult man to say 'No' to.

At the bottom of the path, one of the policemen glanced at his watch.

'If George does decide to come straight here, we haven't got more than a five-minute lead on him. It took longer than we thought to lower Aidan down the hole.'

'I'm sorry,' Sir Mark said. 'Let's run for it.'

'We'll have to stick to the bottom of the cliff, or he'll see our footprints.'

They set off, scrambling along the rocks and dry sand at the top of the beach, checking every few yards that they hadn't left any tracks.

As they entered the cave itself, where the sand was still wet, the younger policeman went last, brushing over their prints behind him.

They quickly identified the dark cleft in the western wall of the cave. Aidan had been right. It was comfortably deep enough for the three of them to sink right back out of sight, and wait.

The sergeant carried on up to the rock wall that barred the way to the cavern beyond. It took him only a moment to find a secure hiding place for a sensitive radio-mike he had brought with him. He switched it on and ran back to join his colleague and Sir Mark.

They didn't hear George coming until he was inside the cave. He was panting heavily. He ran straight past them towards the bar, waving a lighted torch.

A moment later, they heard him exclaim, 'Oh, shit!'

The sergeant activated the tape-recorder in his pocket and gingerly leaned forward around the buttress of rock to watch George.

Aidan was standing beside the skeleton, looking through the gap down the long tunnel of rock that ran up from the beach, when he heard George coming into the cave. Every nerve in his body came alive and he ducked back into deep shadow as George's torch flashed nearer and picked out the spot where Aidan had removed the boulder.

He heard the other man swear.

'Hello, George,' he said.

George spun round to look behind him, sweeping the rocky walls with his light. At the same time, he pulled a nine-millimetre Browning from his jacket pocket.

Even where he was, hidden and protected by the wall of rock, Aidan felt a sudden surge of fear crawl up his spine and tighten his bowels.

'You got here a bit sooner than I planned,' Aidan said.

This time George worked out where the voice was coming from.

He pointed the beam of his torch directly into the cavern, where Aidan stood, out of reach of the probing beam.

'What the hell are you doing here?' George hissed nervously.

'What do you think? A bit of archaeology, you might say.'

'Where are you? How did you get in there?'

'I think you should come and have a look what's behind here.'

'Why should I?' George blustered. 'I don't give a damn what's behind there.'

'You were anxious enough to get at it on Friday morning,' Aidan said with a hint of surprise.

'Look, you fucking Irish con-man. Whatever's there, you can't do anything about it – not without landing yourself in jail.'

'And you with me. It could be worth it.'

'Nobody can pin anything on me,' George was shouting now.

'Ah, that's where you're wrong. You haven't seen

what's here yet. D'you want a look? If you chuck that gun back down towards the front of the cave, and pass me through your crowbar which I left on the ledge there, I'm pretty sure I can get this last boulder out from behind, then you can pop your head through and take a look.'

'Will you stop fucking about. What is it?'

'You know damn well what it is. Ivor told you he'd put it there, didn't he? And you just couldn't be sure he hadn't told someone else as well...'

George was leaning against the rock now. The torch beam filled the aperture. Aidan pressed his back hard against the wall, so that George wouldn't be able to see him unless he got his shoulders through the gap.

'You'll not get through,' Aidan said. 'I didn't, and I'm not carrying half as much fatty tissue as yourself. If you want, do as I say, chuck away the gun and pass me the bar.'

'Where the hell are you, you bastard?'

'Now stop getting excitable. Just calm down and let's talk about this like grown men. We're both after the same thing. You know about me, and I know about you. I'd say there was scope for a little horse-trading.'

'That's something you should know about, you bloody tinker. I know damn well that you set me up with that Letter Lad – you and Henderson. Is he in on your scam? I'll bet he put you up to the whole thing. I know – he was in Ireland during the summer, and he was seen with you. It was obvious. I don't know why my uncle was such a fool as to be taken in.'

'You had the advantage of knowing I couldn't possibly be David though, didn't you?'

George didn't answer.

'Didn't you?' Aidan insisted more harshly.

Still George didn't answer.

'Because you killed him, didn't you? And then you lost the body and you never knew what happened to it, until Ivor told you he'd found it. Poor old Ivor, he thought the boy had fallen from his horse and come down the cliff, and that it was all his fault. But that's not what happened, is it? I can see that from in here. If Ivor had looked a bit closer at the body, he'd have realised there was more to it than that.'

'What the fuck are you talking about?' George shouted nervously.

'I've told you, I can open up the gap enough for you to have a look for yourself – see what David was clutching in his hand when he died.'

Aidan heard his quiet words echo away towards the mouth of the cave, and George breathing heavily.

'Oh God,' George sighed, subdued suddenly. 'He is there.'

'Why did you kill him, George?'

'He was an arrogant little prick. He thought he had it all, and he was going to get it all. He was just a spoilt brat. And he pretended to be all cut up about his mother, just to get his father to pay a bit more attention to him. He'd have been unbearable if he'd ever inherited Barford.'

'You felt you were a more worthy candidate, did you, even then, at the age of sixteen?'

'Yes, I bloody did.' George's voice was rising again. 'And I still do, and I'm not having it taken away from me by some fucking ignorant Irish gypsy.'

'I've already told you, you needn't lose it all. I'll keep quiet about you, and you keep quiet about me. We put the rock back in the hole I made, and poor little David can stay in here for ever. Now Ivor's dead, there's no one besides you and me knows he's here.'

'I'll see you rot in hell before I do any deals with you. Do you think I'd let the title go to a bloody nobody who's got no right to it?'

'Well, we seem to have reached a bit of a stand-off. You can't kill me in here, and you missed when you tried on the shoot. And when I get out of here, I may just have to talk to a few interested parties – about David, lying here, about Ivor, and about the clay-pigeon trap you forgot to clean off – how did you use it exactly? I couldn't quite work it out.'

'You're a fucking idiot if you think I'll let you out of there alive,' George snarled.

'The only problem there is that, if I go missing, or I'm found dead, Mr Edwards, that nice lawyer in Lynmouth, will open up the little package I've left with him in case of such an event, and that'll tell him where to tell the police to look for David's body. And you're never going to get in here to get rid of it. And,' Aidan went on as he heard George starting to speak again, 'they shouldn't have too much trouble tracking down the fella you got to spray the roof of my car that day at Fontwell. And maybe you'll get done for pinching those sleepers, too. You could be charged with the manslaughter of poor little Mickey Thatcher, maybe even murder, who knows?'

There was a pause before George spoke again. 'How long have you known?'

'Not long, only since I saw you coming here on Friday morning. Up till then you had me completely fooled. It's funny, now I realise why you looked so relieved when you first saw me. Maybe you had an idea David had somehow survived, and really had run away. But you knew I wasn't him.' Aidan paused a moment before he went on thoughtfully. 'I've been wondering how. Maybe there should have been some kind of a scar on him which only you knew about; from something you did to him the day you killed him. Of course, it doesn't show on these bones in here.'

There was a moment's silence.

'How the hell do you know all this?' George almost whispered.

'I didn't know that last bit. I was busking. But you couldn't blow the whistle on me, could you, so you tried to kill me?'

George laughed. 'This time I'll do it. I'll starve you out in there if I have to.'

'We'll see, but in the meantime, just tell me how you killed David.'

'I didn't. The cliff did. I just helped him over. I'm an opportunist, always have been, that's how I've made money. The precocious little prick did most of the damage himself, thinking he could handle that colt. It threw him off – Ivor was right about that – but he was fifty yards from the cliff-top. It was just chance I was up there shooting seagulls with my four-ten. There was no one around and we were out of sight of the coastguard station. I ran across to him; he thought I was going to help him up.' George gave a short grunt of laughter. 'But I smacked him on the head with the butt of my gun. He struggled a bit but it didn't take much to drag him across to the cliff-top, and he bounced all the way down to the beach. I went down after him and carried him up this end, tucked him under the rocks to deal with him later.'

'And when you came back, he'd gone.'

'I thought the sea had got him. I hoped it had; a corpse then would have suited me much better.'

'But now it's a bit of an embarrassment, isn't it?' Aidan laughed. 'Do you know what'll make it a bit more of an embarrassment? When he was struggling with you, he must have grabbed a handful of your hair. He's still got it, as a matter of fact, clutched in his bony little hand. Pity you can't get in here to retrieve it, really. They'd have no trouble making a DNA match these days.'

There was a scrabbling sound as George tried to climb the rock-face again. This time, with a grunt, the top of his head appeared. He pointed the torch through the gap, followed by the gun.

Aidan, still pressed hard against the rock, waited until both were a little further in, as far as he judged they were ever going to get. He raised his hand, holding his own heavy-duty torch, and smashed it down on the dull metal snout of the automatic.

The Browning rattled down the rock and thudded on to the sandy floor beside the undisturbed skeleton.

'Fuck you!' George hissed as his head and the torch abruptly retreated.

Aidan stepped round to give himself a view through the opening. George stood glowering back.

Behind him, three figures had detached themselves

from the shadows and were advancing up the steep sloping floor.

George suddenly heard them and spun round.

'George Tredington, I am a police officer and I'm arresting you for the murder of David Tredington, and others. Anything you say will be taken down and may be used in evidence against you. Do you understand?'

Aidan was in the bedroom of his cottage, packing his sparse collection of belongings into the suitcase and rucksack with which he had arrived ten weeks before. He was trying to get used to the idea that he was no longer going to live and work at Barford; that all his actions and motives would be scrutinised by the courts and the press; that all the fame he had earned in the last two months would backfire, splattering the story of his deception across the front pages of every tabloid newspaper.

He had agreed that he would present himself for questioning at Exeter police station the following morning. He hadn't rung Johnny; there was no point now. Anyway, he hadn't the heart.

Every so often, he paused in his packing to glance out of the window at the ancient trees and green pasture that surrounded the house. Despite the gloomy sky, there was a gentle warmth to the scene. He was surprised how much he felt as if he were leaving home. And he was dreading breaking the news to his mother. She would understand – after all, she hadn't objected to the plan in the first place. But he had wanted to be able to assure her that he could still make a good living in English racing, even without the Tredingtons.

Now that he was faced with the likely consequences of what he had done, he wasn't so sure.

He heard someone let themselves into the small hall below. He dropped the pile of clothes he was holding and went down. Sir Mark was standing at the bottom of the stairs.

'What are you doing, Aidan?'

'I'm packing. I've booked a room at the Anchor for tonight.'

'There's no need for that just yet. Come on over to the house. The girls and I would like to talk to you.'

In all the commotion since George had been arrested, Aidan hadn't been alone with Sir Mark. In fact he hadn't seen anyone since a police-car had driven off carrying George – limp, sweating and grey-faced – in the back.

Now that he had to face the family on their own, he dreaded it.

Sir Mark said nothing more as they walked the few hundred yards to the manor house. He led Aidan into the library, where a fire of large logs blazed, glitteringly reflected in the brass fire-irons.

Lucy was sitting in an armchair, lounging back with a leg over one arm. Victoria sat more awkwardly on the front edge of a sofa.

'I've told Lucy and Victoria what happened today.'

Aidan nodded and looked, first at Victoria, then at Lucy. 'I'm sorry,' he said simply. 'I know that's not enough, after all you've done for me.'

Lucy met his gaze with a blank stare. 'I can hardly believe it, though, God knows, I was never utterly convinced you were genuine. I even went to your cottage and had a snoop round. I didn't find anything much, but something odd happened while I was there. Someone rang in to get your messages. It couldn't have been you. It was the day of your first race at Wincanton, and you should have been on your way down to the start.'

Aidan nodded. 'It must have been George. He lent me that phone. He must have been monitoring all my messages.'

Lucy was looking at him sceptically. 'I still think the whole thing's incredible – George killing David, and you pretending to be him. It's like something out of a Gothic novel. How could you do it?'

'Do you think I'm proud of myself? Accepting your trust, then betraying it? There were lots of times when I wanted to own up, but the longer I was here, the harder it was.'

'But what made you do it?'

'Believe me, I didn't want to at all at first, but,' he sighed, 'it seemed like a way of helping my mother. She's dying; she's not got more than a few years. There was no way I could have given her any comfort from what we were making on the farm.' Aidan drew a deep breath and tried to grin. 'And then there was the chance to be with the kind of horses I'd only ever dreamt about at home. I didn't really believe I could do it, but Johnny was so sure...'

'Johnny Henderson?' Lucy said sharply.

Aidan glanced at Sir Mark, who shook his head ruefully. 'I hadn't told her that bit yet.'

'The rat!' Lucy was fuming. 'After all the friendship we've shown him! I suppose he told you to pull that stunt with the guillemot's egg when you turned up here. I remember, he was here the day Davy went.'

316

'Oh, Lucy,' Victoria protested, 'you've always known what Johnny's like. I've often heard you say you wouldn't trust him further than you could spit.'

'And you don't know what his motives were either,' Sir Mark added.

'No, but I can guess.' Lucy made a face.

'Well,' Aidan said, 'I let him talk me into it, and when I got here, hardly anyone seemed to doubt my story. To tell you the truth, I was amazed, but it made me bolder, and after I'd been here a while, I loved it – having a family, a father even ... I can't tell you how grateful I've been for that, and how much I'm going to miss it.'

Victoria was listening to Aidan with wide, glistening eyes. She stood up now and crossed to where he stood. 'It's been great for us, too. For me, anyway, having a brother,' she said. 'I can hardly believe you're not. I mean, you're so like the family – except for being Irish, of course.'

Aidan looked at her affectionate face with embarrassment. 'Well, you'll be able to come and visit me in jail when it all comes out.'

Victoria stared at him with amazement. 'What do you mean, jail? For God's sake, they can't send you to jail. Who would ride Mischief in the Hennessy?'

Aidan couldn't help laughing. 'I've already told Sam he'll have to get a substitute.'

'But no one will give him as good a ride as you.'

'Well, there it is. What I did was wrong, and I can't claim the purest of motives. Frankly, I'm relieved to be able to look you all in the face and know I'm not lying to you.'

'Aidan,' Sir Mark said, 'sit down. Let me get you a drink. Black Bush all right?'

Aidan nodded and sat on a sofa opposite Lucy. He was confused and disorientated. This conversation wasn't going at all as he had expected.

Sir Mark handed him a glassful of Irish whiskey. 'I can't claim this is the happiest day of my life but, thanks to you, I now know the truth about David's death, and he can be properly laid to rest at last. Whatever your motives may have been, you showed your true colours when you found out what had really happened to David and didn't try to hide it from me. Obviously George's part in it all makes it particularly unpleasant, but if it hadn't been for your ... deception, we'd never have known the truth. So you see, I'm rather grateful to you. And there's no question of your going to jail. The police can't proceed against you without my cooperation and, so far, you've taken nothing from me. Your pay and conditions have been exactly those of any stud manager – if anything, you've been somewhat underpaid. It would be very difficult for the prosecution to prove a specific fraud without my cooperation.'

Aidan could hardly believe what he was hearing. He didn't want to speak, in case he found he was dreaming.

'And, as Victoria says, who would we get to ride Deep Mischief?' Sir Mark was still standing in front of the fire. He looked at Aidan for a moment. There was the ghost of a smile on his face. 'I think we'd better leave things as they are, just for the moment. Quite honestly, I'm not sure that I could cope with two scandals at once. I've told those policemen that I won't be pressing any charges against you. You won't have to go down to

Exeter tomorrow; they're coming here, and so is that chap from the Hampshire police.'

'What have they done with George?' Lucy asked.

'They've taken him into custody. He'll be formally charged, and appear before the magistrates tomorrow.'

'Will he get bail?'

'Facing a charge of violent murder? I doubt it. In any event, I certainly won't be standing it.'

Lucy was looking at Aidan. She laughed. 'I suppose Dad's right. It's wonderfully ironic. If you hadn't turned up to con us, George would have got away with it himself. And at least you weren't a complete bastard; you could have kept quiet about it and done a deal with George, or bumped him off.'

Aidan couldn't help smiling at her capitulation. 'Maybe I would have done, if I'd thought I could get away with it.'

'No,' Lucy said thoughtfully, 'you wouldn't.' She turned to her father. 'When are we going to announce to the world that David Tredington isn't David Tredington?'

'I suppose it will have to come out when George comes up for trial. But that gives us plenty of time to think about the best way of dealing with it.'

Aidan was unpacking again, a few hours later, when he heard a knock on his cottage door. He stiffened. He still couldn't reconcile his conscience with the way the Tredingtons were treating him, and he was expecting something to reverse it all.

He went down and opened the door to Susan.

She was wet from the rain which had been pouring

steadily for the last two hours. Aidan had been hoping to see her all afternoon, but she hadn't come up to the house. 'Jesus, you look like an otter coming up for air,' he said, opening the door wider for her. The wet did nothing to diminish her attractions. Her eyes gleamed from her dripping face and her hair hung in shiny strands.

'I ran out of petrol at the gates, would you believe it, and I didn't have a mac or anything.' She walked in. 'I've been to the house. Vicky told me roughly what's been going on; I had to come straight here to see you myself.'

Aidan took her hand and led her into his tiny sitting-room, where the woodburning stove he had lit half an hour earlier was drawing well and blasting out heat. He filled a glass with whiskey for her. She took it, gulped and spluttered. Aidan laughed. 'Sip it. I'll get you a towel – a couple of towels – and some dry clothes.'

He went upstairs and collected two bath towels and a long-tailed white cotton shirt of his own. Back downstairs in the sitting-room, he drew all the curtains and closed the door. 'We'll try and keep the heat in until you're a bit drier.' He sat down in one of his two armchairs, poured himself a drink and looked at her with a grin.

'You're in a very subtle mood tonight,' Susan said, undoing her blouse, turning her back on Aidan a little to undo her bra, dropping them in a damp pile in front of the fire. She wrapped one of the towels around her, just below her armpits, unzipped her jeans and wriggled out of them.

'Jesus, I don't know about you, but I'm getting very warm,' Aidan said huskily.

'Yes, well ... keep cool. You're still here, which is something, but what the hell else has happened? Jan told me George has been arrested, but Sir Mark told me to come and ask you what happened; he said it was all down to you.'

'I don't think he realised that you were convinced I was a ringer, right from the start.'

'How's he taken it, you not being David?'

'He's been amazing. I can hardly believe it. He's told me I can stay here: he's not pressing charges.' Aidan shrugged. 'I don't know what I've done to deserve it, but I'm still going to ride Deep Mischief next week.'

'It's that irresistible charm of yours,' Susan laughed.

Aidan's eyes lit up. 'Irresistible, is it?'

Susan shook her head and wrapped the towel more tightly around her. 'Not that irresistible. Can I go upstairs and change?'

'Sure.'

'I'll put all my stuff to dry in front of the Rayburn in the kitchen.'

She gathered up her wet clothes. Aidan watched her as she left the room.

When she came back down, wearing his shirt like a model on a cat-walk, she was looking more serious.

'Right. Tell me exactly what happened.'

Aidan relived all his experiences of the last three days, stumbling over the naked terror he had felt being trapped in the cave, and then, that morning, being confronted with George's Browning. As accurately as he could, he related the admissions he had extracted from George.

Susan hung on to every word until he had finished.

'When you first told me,' she said, 'I could hardly believe that George might have killed Dad, but I suppose he must have done, knowing he was the one person who could say where David's body was. But how did George kill him?'

'I told the police, I think the weapon was a horse's hoof.'

'But the Home Office pathologist has already said he couldn't have been kicked by the horse – the angle was wrong, and it was the wrong hoof.'

'But I didn't say he was kicked by a horse.'

Susan looked puzzled.

'Look,' Aidan went on, 'I'm not going to tell you what I think until the police come up with something firm, but I'd take odds of ten-to-one-on that George killed him. I'm sorry. It looks as though your Dad suffered years of guilt about David; and it was never his fault.'

'Poor old Dad.' There were tears in the girl's eyes. 'We all gave him such a hard time. If only we'd known.'

'At least you know now,' Aidan said softly.

Chapter Fourteen

Detective Sergeant King arrived soon after nine, looking pleased with himself. It had, he said, been a beautiful drive across the country. He had set off at six and watched the sun come up through the mist over Sedgemoor.

'We've got a result,' he said cheerfully. He produced a police photograph of a thin, wiry face and hostile eyes. 'Recognise this bloke?'

Aidan stared at the angry individual and shook his head.

'Didn't really think you would, but Dennis Knight's his name. He was the villain who sprayed your car. He finally admitted that George paid him to do it.' The detective laughed. 'We'd told him he'd told us – he hadn't, of course, but I'm going down to interview George in Exeter, and I'll be able to tell him what this bloke Dennis told us.' He tapped the photo with his forefinger. 'But first I want to run through your statement again, from start to finish, so's we haven't missed anything. I mean, we'll probably get a confession out of him, but the court likes to see a bit of corroboration after all these recent cock-ups. And the local nick wants to tie it in with the two murders they've got up here. Of course, they've got George on tape, admitting to the whole thing. That should do the trick, even though it wasn't double taped. Ours isn't so easy.'

'But what about the sleepers?' Aidan asked. 'When you came up here last week you said you had a line on where they'd come from.'

'We do, sir, but we can't tie them in to George yet. I can tell you what probably happened, though. He bought half a dozen of them and a small trailer. He drove it over and left it just outside Boarhunt – a small village near Fareham. When he left the races, he picked it up and drove to the roundabout above the motorway and sat there until he saw you coming, with the fluorescent marker to identify you. He heaved one of the sleepers over, just missed, but almost did enough damage, dumped the rest, scarpered, and dumped the trailer back in Boarhunt. That's where it was found. Forensic confirmed that it carried the sleepers, but they can't prove George handled it or towed it with his car. We've got one unsatisfactory witness so far. But you never know, we could get lucky. In the meantime, at least we've got Dennis. Now, if you don't mind, we'll run through your version again, just in case you missed something last time.'

When Sergeant King had left, Aidan went down to the yard to see the horses. As long as he was at Barford, he had a job to do. But he hadn't been at the stables long when the sergeant who had arrested George turned up.

'I've left the forensic lads down at the cave. They've gone down the way you did. They'll photograph the remains of the victim, then bag him up and take him back to the lab. They may find something else to nail

Cousin George. Not, of course, that he is your cousin,' the policeman added with an ambivalent grin. 'But you're a lucky man. Sir Mark says you haven't nicked anything off him, so we can't do much about you. That's up to him, I suppose. But we'll still need you as a witness.'

'OK.' Aidan shrugged. He would have to deal with the publicity this would generate when the time came, but if Sir Mark stayed on his side, he should get through it. 'What do you want now?'

'Just to check a few more things, like what made you first suspect George.'

'Let me show you something. I didn't tell you about it before, because I couldn't see how it was relevant. It's up in the back courtyard.'

Aidan led the policeman to the house and through the arch that led to the back door. But they didn't go into the house. Instead, Aidan opened the battered green door to the store-room. They both went into the unlit gloom. Aidan pulled the tarpaulin off the clay-trap.

The detective looked at it. 'Well? What about it?'

'I think George killed Ivor with it.'

The policeman looked at it sceptically. 'How?'

'Take a look at the end, where the clays are released.'

The detective leaned down and played his torch on the arm of the trap. He pulled a pair of tweezers from his pocket and carefully lifted something from it. He stood up and walked out into the daylight.

'A white hair.'

Aidan nodded.

'But Ivor was killed by a blow with a horse's hoof, or at least something shaped like it.'

'That's not one of Ivor's hairs; and a horse's hoof fixed on the end of the launch aim would pack a hell of a punch.'

The policeman looked more closely. 'A horse hair?' He smiled. 'Right, I'll take this for forensic. We'll get the trap dusted. I'll need your fingerprints to eliminate them. And I suppose we'd better look out for a horse with one hoof missing.'

'I reckon you'll find it's already been processed in George's abattoir.'

The detective looked at him sharply, annoyed he hadn't been aware of that possibility. 'We'll check that out. By the way, talking of hair, when you were down in the cave with George, you told him there was some hair clutched in David's, er, hand. Our boys haven't found a trace of it and, anyway, they say there's no way it could have lasted that long.'

Aidan grinned. 'I was just trying it on. I didn't know if it was possible or not, and I didn't reckon George did either. Lucky really, wasn't it, because it was after that that he confessed.'

The sun was setting in a haze of bright orange mist by the time the local police left Barford Manor that afternoon. David's skeleton had been examined minutely and photographed where it lay, before it was carefully dismantled for removal to the police laboratories. The clay-trap had been bagged up and taken, too, along with the tapes of a two-hour interview with Aidan Daly.

Aidan went back to the stables to see the horses bedded down for the night. Conflicting rumours of the events of the past seventy-two hours were being aired among the staff on the estate. Aidan wanted to tell the grooms in the stud the truth, too, but Sir Mark had been adamant that they maintain the status quo for the time being. Nevertheless, everyone seemed to know that Aidan had been responsible for trapping George, and that was cause for general approval.

And though he wanted above all to tell them that a culprit had been found for Mickey Thatcher's death, he knew he had to wait until the police were able to confirm their case.

He tried to act as if everything were normal, as if he hadn't been packing his bags to leave the night before, and as if he were still Sir Mark Tredington's son.

He was about to leave and go back to his cottage when Victoria appeared.

'Hi. Dad wants to see you,' she said. 'Come and have dinner up at the house later.'

Aidan nodded.

As he showered and changed, he found that he was still nervous about his reception. Although even Lucy seemed to have overcome her scepticism about his motives, the fact remained that he was a stranger, an attempted usurper in the family, and there was no good reason why they should tolerate his presence longer than it would take Sir Mark to decide how to avert another unpleasant scandal.

When he arrived at the house, he found that Lucy had gone back to London. Victoria wasn't around. Sir Mark was, as usual at this time of the evening, in the library.

He stood up when Aidan came in, offering him a drink as he had done most evenings over the months since Aidan had arrived at Barford.

Aidan detected a nervousness in the baronet's manner, and his heart sank. It looked as though Sir Mark had decided he was going to have to give him some bad news.

First, though, Sir Mark asked a question. 'Tell me, Aidan, how are you feeling about what's happened over the last few days?'

'Relief, mostly. Of course, I realise it must be terribly hard on you, having to face up to what happened to your son.'

'In one way that's been a source of relief to me too,' Sir Mark said. 'Though I was always pretty sure he'd been killed.'

Aidan gulped on his whiskey. 'But . . . but surely, you thought he'd run away. Johnny told me about a letter he'd sent a few days after he disappeared, saying how unhappy he was.'

'It wasn't exactly a letter. I've got it here, as a matter of fact.'

He picked up a school exercise book of lined paper, opened it and took out a single sheet that was loose. It looked like a leaf from the book, but the top of it had been torn off, neatly, with a ruler. He passed it to Aidan.

Aidan took it and saw a few lines of tidy, boyish writing.

'*I'm still missing Mum, as much as ever. I wish Dad hadn't been away so much. I feel I've got no one to talk to. The girls are too little, and just cry. I'll just have to cope with it without anyone.*'

Aidan read it again and glanced at Sir Mark. 'That was the letter he sent?'

'That's what arrived in the post two days after he'd disappeared, post-marked Bristol.'

'And it was definitely from him?'

'There's no doubt that he wrote those words. This book was a sort of diary he kept. Some builders found it when we were having all the fireplaces taken out of the bedrooms. It was stuffed a few feet up the flue. That page was taken from this book.' Sir Mark opened the book at a point where a page had been carefully torn out. He handed it to Aidan. At the top of the pages on either side of the missing one, was written the day of the week and a date. Aidan stared at it, leafed some pages further on. 'This was written a few weeks before he disappeared.'

Sir Mark nodded.

'So you knew someone else had torn out the page and sent it?'

'I couldn't be sure. David was a curious, rather devious boy. It was always possible that he'd done it himself to confuse us, except for the fact that the book was so well hidden it was unlikely we'd ever find it. All my instincts told me David wouldn't have run away, though. I also had a lot of searches made, but they came up with absolutely nothing, not a trace, so I became even more convinced that he was dead.'

'Until I turned up, fifteen years later, claiming to be him.'

'No,' Sir Mark said with a faint, apologetic smile. 'I knew you weren't David, but I also knew that, if David had been killed by the person I had begun to suspect most, your appearance would very likely flush him out.'

Aidan stared at him. 'Jesus!' he burst out with a

laugh. 'You mean all the time I thought I was taking you in, you were using me ... to trap George?'

'Once I'd met you, I formed the opinion that someone as resourceful as you would stand as good a chance as anyone of dealing with it. Yes, reluctantly, I admit that I used you.'

'So, all along you knew I wasn't your son?'

Sir Mark looked into his glass for a moment. 'I didn't say that. I said I knew you weren't David.'

Aidan leaned forward in his chair, staring at Sir Mark, trying to take in what he was saying. 'I don't understand. What do you mean?'

Sir Mark stood up and walked across the room to one of the library shelves. He pulled out a book and opened it. From between its pages, he plucked a photograph. He glanced at it for a moment, then looked at Aidan.

Slowly, with an air of submission, he walked back towards Aidan and held out the photo.

Aidan took it. It was a grainy shot, taken with an old-fashioned, cheap camera. It showed a young woman, standing in front of a neo-gothic, monastic sort of a building, holding a child of two or three.

Aidan stared at it for a long time before he looked up at Sir Mark.

'How long have you had this?'

'Since shortly after it was taken.'

Aidan's heart almost stopped for a moment. He tried to speak but his throat was suddenly dry. 'Why?' he croaked.

Sir Mark sat down opposite Aidan and leaned back in his chair, gazing at his whisky as he swilled it around his glass.

'I met your mother just before I was married, in 1965. My brother, Perry, had organised a rather extravagant sort of stag party for me. He took a fishing lodge up on the Dee and asked the ten friends he thought I'd most like to see for four days' fishing and drinking. And when I say drinking, that's putting it mildly.'

Aidan gazed intently at the old man.

Sir Mark glanced at him, then looked away at the fire.

'There was an old Scots woman at the lodge, who did the cooking and so on. And there was a young Irish maid.'

'My mother?' Aidan whispered.

Sir Mark closed his eyes and nodded his head. 'She was a very pretty girl. My friends bet me.' He shrugged. 'I'd probably had a little too much to drink, but if she'd made it clear she didn't want me, I wouldn't have touched her, I can promise you that, on my word of honour.' He sighed. 'It was a wonderful night, but she knew, and I knew, I was getting married at the weekend; I was never going to see her again. But I never forgot her.'

He looked up at Aidan. 'It's extraordinary, isn't it, the huge ripples in our lives the smallest pebble can make. I often thought about Mary after that, though I loved Henrietta and respected her enormously. After a couple of years – I don't know why, on some whim, a rough patch in my marriage, a sense of guilt or something – I hired an agency to track her down. They brought me back this photo; they'd bought it from one of the other domestic staff there. I knew at once the child was mine.'

Now the words were out, Aidan got to his feet, almost trembling with excitement. He wanted to show Sir Mark what he felt in some dramatic way, but he couldn't yet. He walked around the room, shaking his head in amazement. 'Jesus! You mean ... God, I can hardly take it in.' He took a deep breath to force the words out. 'You're my natural father?'

Sir Mark nodded slowly, and a smile spread across his face. 'I knew it the moment I saw you. And, of course, I was expecting you.'

Aidan was mystified. 'Why?' he asked.

'Johnny had told me he'd found you.'

'Good God! You mean he told you about me, when he first saw me in Westport?'

'I mean, I told him about you when I asked him to try and track you down in Mayo.'

'I can't believe it. There I've been, racked with guilt about what I was doing to you, and all the time, you'd set the whole thing up, right from the start.'

Sir Mark nodded with a grin. 'Don't feel too guilty about it. I may as well tell you that you'd never have got away with it. Though I admit Johnny prepared you very well, and of course my acceptance of you removed most of the doubts anyone else round here might have had.'

'Jesus!' Aidan was laughing now at the bizarre irony of what had happened, and out of sheer happiness at knowing that this man really was his father. 'It's just incredible.'

His father was laughing, too. He stood and walked towards Aidan. When he reached him, he put his arms around him and hugged him tightly. After a moment he asked, 'Did you tell your mother where you were going when you came here?'

Aidan nodded. 'Now I know why she didn't mind. She knew.'

'I thought she might.' Sir Mark took his arm from around his son and stood back to look at him with pride and affection.

'But, Dad – thank God, I can say it without lying now – what about this fella who was supposed to have been shipwrecked somewhere in the South Pacific?'

'Johnny told me you'd found out about that. When I first heard about it, it worried me for a bit, but I was pretty confident there was nothing in it, and there's no doubt the chap had assumed the name deliberately before the yacht went missing. I think we'll find that George was behind all that. It just so happened he was getting impatient that we hadn't applied to the court for presumption of David's death, clearing the way to his inheriting the title, at least.'

'You think he set up the fella and rigged the boat being lost?'

'Yes, probably. I don't know for sure. By the way,' he said, looking oddly contrite, 'before we tell the girls about all this, I owe you an apology – not least for the fact that you nearly lost your life twice. I almost had to put a stop to it all after that crash, but at that stage the police seemed fairly sure it was an accident. When you told me George had shot you, I realised it had gone far enough, but we were nearly there, and you seemed determined to see it through. I also admit that I had set out to test you, in a way. And I couldn't be more proud of the result. Now,' he went on before Aidan could answer, 'go and find Victoria. We must tell her right away, she'll be absolutely delighted to hear you really are her brother. And pick up a bottle of champagne on your way back.'

The day the Hennessy Gold Cup was due to be run dawned grey and overcast. Aidan woke an hour before the light began to seep through the windows of his cottage. Since riding Deep Mischief on the gallops the day before, he had found it hard to control his excitement; the horse had been at the top of his considerable form. Aidan and his father had studied every performance of every other runner in the race. There were three who might have improved beyond Deep Mischief's rating, but Aidan's faith was undiminished. He had spent hours watching videos of steeplechases round the Newbury course to make up for his relative lack of experience of it. He felt he knew every yard of the running now, and he would ride as if his life depended on it.

The traffic making its way to Newbury race-course tailed back in long, trickling streams which converged on the large iron gates at the entrance. The first major steeplechase of the season always attracted a large, enthusiastic crowd.

Almost two inches of rain had fallen on the Berkshire course in the preceding week. The going on the chase course was distinctly soft. Aidan wanted to be absolutely certain he knew where to find the good ground. As he left the car-park, he turned up his coat-collar against the fierce wind which buffeted the marquees by the entrance, tugging the guy-ropes tight on their metal stakes. Whatever route Aidan planned for Deep Mischief, it would be as well to keep him protected from the gale. Three-and-a-quarter miles of racing into the wind could waste a lot of vital energy. He looked up at the sponsor's flag flying horizontally at the far end of the course. The wind would be blowing directly into the runners' faces as they headed up the straight. He would have to be sure that whichever horse he used as a shield was a safe jumper.

The Hennessy would be Aidan's first ride in a Grade One race. As he pushed his way through the crowd to the changing-room an hour before the first race, he was surprised by all the excitement around him.

Up until then, he had managed to keep fairly relaxed, not letting himself think about what the race meant or the sense of occasion with which it was held. But people he had never seen before reached out to wish him well as he approached the new weighing-room, and the adrenaline began to seep into his veins and his muscles began to tingle. His stomach felt empty. The pressure on him to succeed was almost all his own. As far as the punters were concerned, Deep Mischief had a good each-way chance at best; they wouldn't be looking for blood if he didn't win. But for his father's sake, he wanted to succeed as never before. He knew, too, that Sam Hunter would be very disappointed if he didn't do well, and Aidan didn't want to disappoint Sam: he had developed a great respect for him. The trainer had an aura about him that brought out the best in people, made them raise their game.

He dropped off his kit-bag and went to walk the

course. By the time he had completed the whole circuit, he had come to the conclusion that the faster ground was close to the inside. With no running rails on the far side, except on the bends, it would be possible to jump a fence and then pull slightly to the left so that Deep Mischief would be racing marginally off the course until he came back in for the next. That meant that he would only be sheltered from the wind on one side of the course, but Aidan calculated it was worth risking that for the sake of the better ground.

Sam's instructions were simple enough. 'You go out and enjoy yourselves.'

Aidan told him about his plans for dealing with the wind, but Sam didn't seem unduly worried about keeping the horse covered up.

'He's got no weight, so don't be afraid to let him bowl along in front if he's happy. It's harder to make ground in the wind than it is to gallop in it.'

Of the twenty other runners, Sam was concerned about only one, a strongly built mare called Kirsten who had finished third in the previous season's Gold Cup. She was big and only seven years old, so entitled to some improvement. On the strength of that, and despite carrying top weight, she had emerged as four-to-one favourite. Jason Dolton was riding a hardened old campaigner who had been made an each-way chance more out of nostalgia than form-book logic.

With three committed front runners in the race, the pace was bound to be furious, and as they set off from the start at the beginning of the back straight, Aidan found Deep Mischief struggling to hold a position. Aidan didn't want a repeat of the uncharacteristic sulking of his last race. He niggled away quietly at the horse, just doing enough to keep him in the running, but not letting him race so fast that it affected his jumping.

They had covered more than two miles before the murderous gallop of the leaders began to ease, and Aidan at last had a moment to catch a breather. Deep Mischief seemed to sense that he was getting on top of the others, and the boost this gave him renewed his enthusiasm.

The early pace had already wiped out any chances of winning for half the field. Three had fallen at the first ditch on the straight; another two had gone at the second fence on the final circuit. Others just couldn't keep up.

Aidan had stuck with his plan to use the good ground on the margin whenever he could. He had just moved off the course after jumping the penultimate fence on the far side when Jason moved up quickly to take his position. For a moment, Aidan was sure his brother-in-law wasn't going to let him back inside the next wing. Jason looked across at him like a chess-player holding a checkmate position. After a few strides, to Aidan's relief, he gave a half-smile and moved fractionally to his right to let Deep Mischief squeeze in.

Four more leaps put Deep Mischief where he wanted to be, without another horse in sight. His backers in the crowd may have been in the minority, but they were a very vocal minority. Deep Mischief heard them through pricked ears, and seemed to sense they were on his side. Aidan took a quick glance behind and grinned. He wouldn't even have to raise his stick.

It wasn't only the speed of Deep Mischief's finish that

blurred Aidan's sight of the winning post as it flashed by.

Once the first euphoria of victory had diminished, and Aidan's back was sore from the congratulations, he found a chance to walk down to the rails with Johnny, partly to watch the runners in the second last race take the water jump in front of the stands, but mainly because they wanted some privacy.

It was the first opportunity they had had of talking alone together since George had been arrested, and since all the revelations that had followed.

'Christ, you had me fooled,' Aidan grinned. 'I was beginning to hate you. It didn't occur to me once that you weren't a genuine chancer. It was a brilliant performance.'

'You didn't do such a bad job yourself.'

'That's rubbish. Dad said I'd never have got away with it if he hadn't accepted me.'

'Your sisters did. All the locals did.'

Aidan shrugged. 'I'm not so sure. Still, I'm bloody glad it's over. I hope I never have to live through another two weeks like the last two. But Dad's been brilliant about it.'

'So I hear. I hope I can continue to count on your custom.'

'I dare say I'll need the odd old knacker from the west of Ireland,' Aidan laughed. 'By the way, he never told me what kind of arrangement he had with you.'

'I only really did it for the crack,' Johnny grinned. 'I had a long talk with Mark over Goodwood. We were staying in the same house-party. When he told me he was worried about his health and he wanted to sort things out in case he got worse, he also told me about your existence. Actually, bringing you over was partly my idea. He gave me all the back-up I needed and, as it happens, he's shown his appreciation in a way that could only be described as generous. And Lucy's promised to help in my pursuit of Emma, now I gather your interests lie elsewhere.'

Aiden's face rippled into a grin. 'That's for sure.'

Aidan drove straight from Newbury to Heathrow, to catch an Aer Lingus flight to Shannon.

When he had landed in Ireland, he hired a car and took the road through Ennis towards Galway. As he drove through the soft misty drizzle that drifted in off the Atlantic, he contemplated the extraordinary changes that had taken place in his life in ten short weeks.

He was the same man, in the same body, but he had undergone a complete metamorphosis, as if he had finally burst out of a chrysalis shell.

And though he was happy to see the soft brown-green hills and lush, lake-strewn pastures of his homeland, he knew that his future belonged to England.

His mother had almost sounded relieved when he had told her, somewhat obtusely over the phone, what had happened. He had thought that in some way she would feel betrayed, but she had protested little, only asking him to come and see her as often as he could manage it. He had arranged at once to fly back to Ireland.

When he saw her, he was worried by the decline in her since he'd last seen her ten days before. It was clear that every movement she took caused her pain. But mentally, spiritually, she was as strong as ever.

Her neighbour's daughter had moved in full-time to help her, until a more professional arrangement could be made. The girl, Maeve O'Keane, in her twenties, was gentle and kind, and censorious of a son who could have gone off and left his mother like this. But when they were eventually left on their own in the house, Mary made it clear to Aidan that she didn't support this view.

'Aidan, if you knew how I've enjoyed reading about you in the papers,' she said, 'even though I couldn't tell anyone around here that it was you.'

For a moment, Aidan didn't answer.

'You knew,' he said, 'as soon as you heard the name Tredington.'

'Of course. And I trusted in God that the truth would be revealed to you, if it was . Iis will.'

'It's funny really,' Aidan mused, 'I made a complete fool of myself, thinking I'd taken Dad in. He's a canny old fella.'

'He was a fine young man. I stayed in love with him for years. Somehow, I found the strength to cope with the shame, and the hardship, at first for him, then for you.'

'I understand why you couldn't ever tell me. You weren't to know that he would want to find me again.'

'I always thought he might, though.'

'He's an honourable man,' Aidan nodded. 'He told me he'd never forgotten you. I think when he realised that he might not have too long to live himself, he wanted to put the record straight, before it was too late. You know, he offered a house for you, back in Devon, but I told him you wouldn't want to leave here.'

'I would not, and besides, there'd be no purpose in trying to put the clock back that far. It's better that we never see each other again. Both of us on the way out – it would be too miserable. No, I shall be happy staying here, just so long as you come and see me every now and then.'

Aidan looked into her brave eyes. Now that he knew the secret she'd been keeping for so long, his regard for her was limitless.

'Well, your trust paid off,' he admitted. 'The result of my mission couldn't have been more different than I planned with Johnny Henderson. I feel terrible, though, that it led to the death of a young lad – a real keen young horseman – and poor old Ivor Butley.'

'Was he something to do with this Susan you've been telling me about?'

Aidan nodded. 'You'll like her. She's a real strong girl, no side to her, and the loveliest thing you ever set eyes on.'

His mother smiled. She'd almost lost hope of her son setting his eyes on a girl long enough to become committed.

'You bring her out here to see me now.'

Aidan accepted that his mother could never move far from home again. 'I will,' he said, then, more briskly, 'I'm into Galway tomorrow to sort out the nurse and everything for you. We'll let the ground to Eamon O'Keane. You'll not want the bother of the animals. And everything else you need will be taken care of by the lawyer in Galway. You're not to worry about a thing, now.'

Mary smiled. 'That's all fine, but the best thing is

knowing you've found yourself at last. You're a changed man, Aidan Daly.'

'David Aidan Tredington, I'll be, at the end of the month.'

'And so you should. That'll keep the wagging tongues busy around here. Old Sean MacClancy from Westport was telling some tale he'd heard from his brother Emmot. You remember Emmot? He was the odd-job man at the convent. It seems he realised who you were from something he'd read in the papers.'

'Yes,' Aidan nodded with a rueful smile. 'I remember Emmot MacClancy.'

Over the following week, Aidan made arrangements for his mother's care. He and his father had agreed that she would know nothing of the trust that was to be settled on her, of which Aidan was sole trustee.

But all the time he was there, among the soft hills he had known most of his life, part of him longed to be back in England.

Mary showed no signs of trying to keep him as he said goodbye to her and promised to be back soon. He flew to England the next Saturday with an easy conscience, and drove back to Barford feeling that he was finally entering his new world, rightfully and for good.

He parked his car outside the front door and let himself in. In the hall, all he could hear was the deep ticking of an ancient long-case clock that had stood there for two hundred years.

A slit of light showed beneath the library door. His heels clicked across the oak boards as he walked towards it.

He pushed the door open.

'Welcome home!'

Lucy, Victoria and Sir Mark were standing expectantly as they shouted their greeting. Susan and Jason stood in the background. Even Jason was smiling.

Aidan stopped and grinned. 'Hello, Dad, sisters.'

Later, after a celebration dinner that had left his face aching with too much laughter, he let himself into his cottage and went upstairs to change. He had removed his final sock when he heard a rapid knock at the door. Tired but cheerful, he wrapped a towel robe around his naked body and went down to see who it was.

Susan was standing outside, soaked again.

'D'you know,' Aidan said. 'I think it's about time you bought yourself a brolly.'

Susan grinned and slipped past him into the hall.

'I'm afraid there's no fire going this time for you to dry your clothes,' Aidan said.

'You get that Rayburn going. They'll be dry in the morning.'

'You're a wicked temptress.'

Susan reached forward and took hold of the tie around his robe. Slowly she unknotted it. The robe fell open. She slipped her arms inside it, wrapped them around him, and squeezed herself to him.

'Now it's my turn to welcome you home,' she whispered.

Dead Weight

John Francome

'Thrills to the final furlong . . . Francome knows how to write a good racing thriller' *Daily Express*

There's no hiding place for a jump jockey when his courage deserts him. After a crashing fall, champion rider Phil Nicholas returns to racing, but though his body has healed his mind has not. Flashbacks of his accident invade his dreams, rob him of his sleep and freeze him in the saddle. The tough guy of jump racing has lost his bottle.

But when one of Phil's colleagues is viciously attacked after losing a race he should have won, the jockey can't sit on the sidelines any longer. If he wants to save the sport – and the woman he loves – it's time for Phil to recover his nerve . . .

Ex-National Hunt Champion Jockey John Francome has been voted TV's most popular racing commentator for his broadcasting for Channel 4, and he has established himself as one of the front runners in the racing thriller stakes. Don't miss his previous bestsellers from Headline:

'Francome provides a vivid panorama of the racing world . . . and handles the story's twist deftly' *The Times*

'Francome brings authenticity to tales of the horse-racing circuit and, like Dick Francis, goes beyond the thunder of the turf to the skulduggery of the trading ring' *Mail on Sunday*

'The racing feel is authentic and it's a pacy, entertaining read' *Evening Standard*

'An action-packed storyline that gallops to a thrilling end' *Racing Post*

0 7472 6608 5

headline

Lifeline

John Francome

'Francome provides a vivid panorama of the racing world'
The Times

Unlike some of his fellow jockeys, Tony Byrne has never taken a bung and never ridden a dishonest race. All the same, his career is heading for the rocks, dragged down by weight problems and woman trouble – and too many slow horses.

In comparison, star rider Freddy Montague has never been fussy about sticking to the rules, either on the racetrack or in bed with another man's wife. And if there's money on offer to fix races, Freddy's guaranteed to be first on the gravy train.

Unfortunately for both men, the guarantees run out once Freddy's train comes off the rails. That's when the gravy turns to blood . . .

Ex-National Hunt Champion Jockey John Francome is a broadcaster on racing for Channel 4, and has established himself as one of the front runners in the racing thriller stakes. Don't miss his previous bestsellers from Headline:

'Francome brings authenticity to tales of the horse-racing circuit and, like Dick Francis, goes beyond the thunder of the turf to the skulduggery of the trading ring' *Mail on Sunday*

'The racing feel is authentic and it's a pacy, entertaining read' *Evening Standard*

'Thrills to the final furlong . . . Francome knows how to write a good racing thriller' *Daily Express*

0 7472 6607 7

headline

Tip Off

John Francome

It's every punter's dream to beat the bookmakers and Toby Brown is doing it regularly. The son of a top trainer, Toby has a telephone tipping service that is slowly bringing the old enemy to its knees.

A plea from the bookmakers prompts a Jockey Club investigation which uncovers a plot of jealousy and deceit where the stakes being played for mean more than just money – and where one horse, Better By Far, lives up to its name.

Tip Off is a compelling racing thriller sure to be a winner with John Francome's multitude of fans.

One of the greatest jockeys of our time, John Francome has been voted TV's most popular racing commentator for his broadcasting for Channel 4. Don't miss his previous bestsellers from Headline.

'Francome provides a vivid panorama of the racing world . . . and handles the story's twist deftly' *The Times*

'Francome bring authenticity to tales of the horse-racing circuit and, like Dick Francis, goes beyond the thunder of the turf to the skulduggery of the trading ring' *Mail on Sunday*

'The racing feel is authentic and it's a pacy, entertaining read' *Evening Standard*

'Thrills to the final furlong . . . Francome knows how to write a good racing thriller' *Daily Express*

0 7472 5927 5

headline

Now you can buy any of these other bestselling books by **John Francome** from your bookshop or *direct from his publisher*.

FREE P&P AND UK DELIVERY
(Overseas and Ireland £3.50 per book)

Inside Track	£5.99
Dead Weight	£6.99
Lifeline	£6.99
Tip Off	£6.99
Safe Bet	£6.99
High Flyer	£6.99
False Start	£6.99
Dead Ringer	£6.99
Break Neck	£6.99
Outsider	£6.99
Rough Ride	£6.99
Stud Poker	£6.99
Stone Cold	£6.99
Riding High (with James MacGregor)	£6.99
Eavesdropper (with James MacGregor)	£6.99
Blood Stock (with James MacGregor)	£6.99
Declared Dead (with James MacGregor)	£6.99

TO ORDER SIMPLY CALL THIS NUMBER

01235 400 414

or visit our website: www.madaboutbooks.com

Prices and availability subject to change without notice.